I0763458

THE SEBORGA TRILOGY

BY
JAMES VASEY

THE SEBORGA TRILOGY

Cooking Up A Country

Unlikely Pairings

Recipe For A Nation

by

JAMES VASEY

The Seborga Trilogy:
Cooking Up A Country
Unlikely Pairings
Recipe For A Nation

ISBN-978-1-3999-0051-5

This book is dedicated to the people of Seborga
for whom family, food and friendship
transcend all else.

Questo libro è dedicato alla gente di Seborga
per la quale la famiglia, il cibo e l'amicizia
trascendono ogni cosa.

Contents

Cuneo
ITALY
FRANCE
CUNEO OR BUST
Rossese
di
Dolceacqua
VENTIMIGLIA
NICE AIRPORT
Eze
Menton
Monaco
Nice

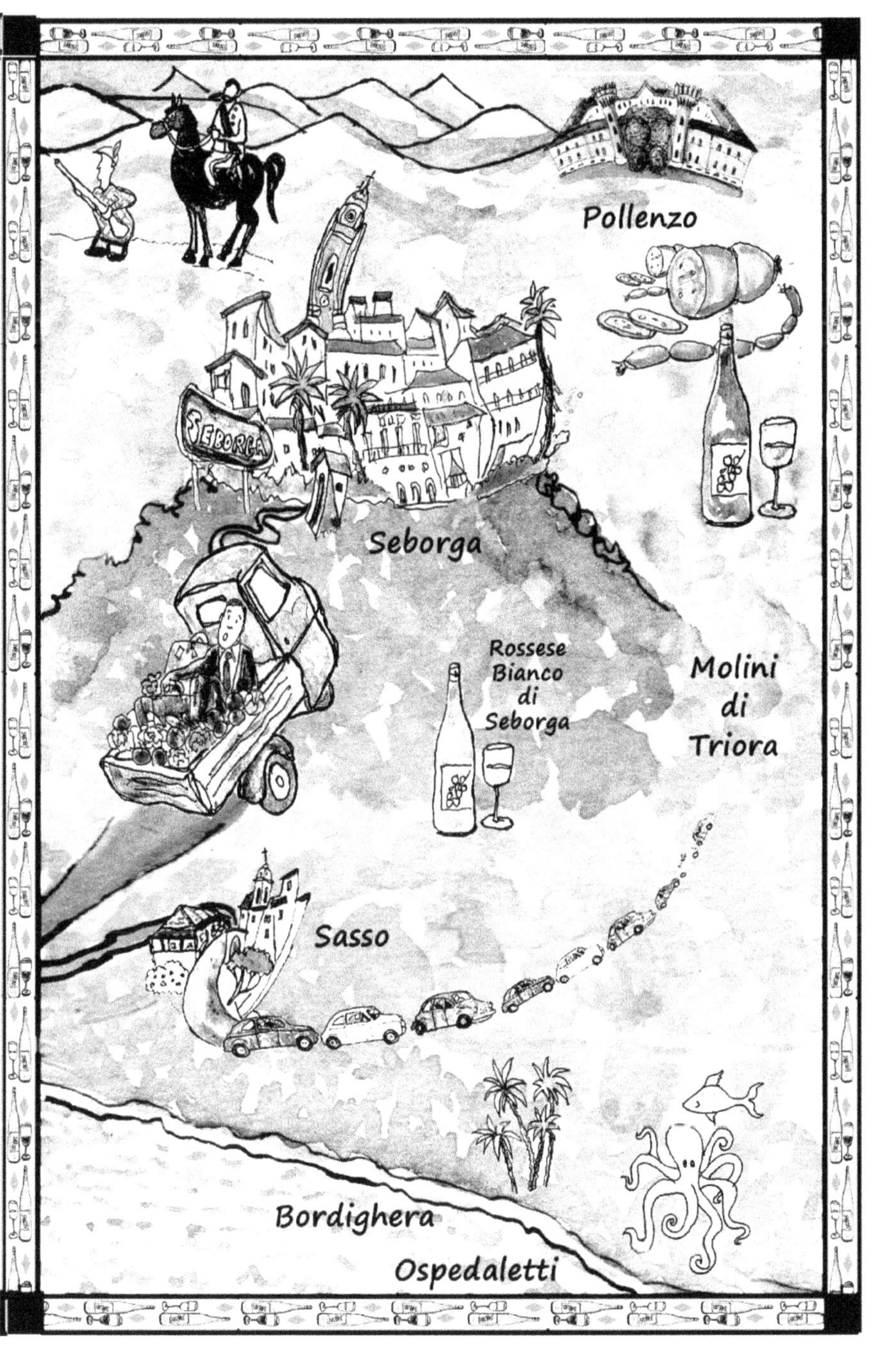
Pollenzo
SEBORGA
Seborga
Rossese
Bianco
di
Seborga
Molini
di
Triora
Sasso
Bordighera
Ospedaletti

Foreword

These three novels were inspired by my discovery of the real, but also slightly surreal, Principality of Seborga. It is a place suspended somewhere between its fantastical past and an uncertain future. In sight of both the Riviera and the Alps, it combines contrasting climates and two very different ways of life. My neighbours quickly taught me that their lifestyle and cuisine are tightly bound to this unique environment. I decided to use the local dishes to help describe how Seborgans have eked-out a living from this land for over a thousand years. To tell my story, I needed a cook to act as teacher and a ravenous outsider to serve as a pupil. Alessandra and Ben take you on an Italian foodie adventure over the Maritime Alps to the plains of Piedmonte and back to Monaco on the glittering Mediterranean coast.

BOOK 1

COOKING UP A COUNTRY

1. COQUILLE ST JACQUES

What to eat for lunch, and the wine which would accompany it, dominated Ben's thoughts. All worries about career, family and finances had evaporated as soon as the ferry left Portsmouth harbour. He had escaped.

The next morning, disembarking the ship at St Malo—his choices—had been to turn east towards Burgundy and Champagne or south into the Loire Valley and then on to Bordeaux. After a long winter in the north of England, he was feeling the need to hasten the journey towards warmer climes and so pointed the car directly south. Tempting as it was to take the shorter journey south-west to Saint-Nazaire for, perhaps, some fresh Atlantic crab with an icy-cold Pouilly Fumé, Ben directed the Audi's satelite-navigation further down the coast to La Rochelle.

La Rochelle held many fond memories for Ben; early summer sunshine, coquilles St. Jacques and mouclade de moules, washed down with a crisp Cotes de Bordeaux. That was worth another hour's driving, he had quickly decided. France's geography may have made it the battleground of Europe, but it also gifted the nation a coastline on three entirely different seas, a moderate climate and a landscape capable of growing or grazing almost anything. The resulting bountiful larder made available to French cooks has created a rich and varied cuisine, often with the liberal use of dairy produce. Cream and butter are staple recipe ingredients. Cheese is a religion practised with fanaticism in France.

Ben had no idea how to prepare the seafood delicacies from Brittany, which had become his own and international foodie favourites. Although he did know they served a version here containing several of the things he loved: shellfish, butter, cream and cheese. He also knew the legend of St James (St. Jacques), who was said to have saved the life of a drowning Knight and emerged from the sea covered with scallop shells. Ben was not, however, aware that a consequence of the story was that the scallop shell later became the symbol of the crusaders of the Order of the Knights of St James; something which a year from now he might have thought to be prophetic.

A progressively brightening morning of stress-free driving along roads, thankfully absent of heavy traffic, brought the increasingly cheerful Englishman to the Bay of Aiguillon National Park. From here he knew that succour was within his grasp and he could almost taste it. As he approached the Atlantic coast, the sky was already several shades bluer and clearer than it had been over the Channel and broken only by the white dots of seabirds swirling above. A brisk warm breeze was bringing salty air from the sea in through the part-open window of the car, with it, that unmistakable iodine odour.

He would head straight for the beautifully restored Old Town and a harbour-side restaurant he knew quite well. There would be no need to book this early in the year. By now the Breton fishermen would have unloaded their haul of shellfish and be enjoying a well-earned coffee and perhaps a pastis in one of the few remaining working men's cafés. Chefs and cooks would have scrubbed and rinsed these precious fruits of the ocean, menu blackboards would have been chalked-up with the plat de jour, and Ben would arrive in time to ensure all their skilled work was not in vain.

However, in reality, none of this was actually happening to Ben on this particular day; although it was a memory as crisp and clear to him as a Cotes de Bordeaux. He was merely playing a mind game he had learned many years ago and which he found worked without fail. When faced with pain or unpleasantness of any kind, imagining himself in agreeable situations—almost always related to food and wine—acted as a highly effective distraction; an anaesthetic for the mind. It worked for him at dentists where he couldn't face injections of painkillers or when his ex-wife was berating him for investing in collectable Burgundy instead of a new kitchen, and it was working again today as he waited to hear his fate.

The Dean of the University was pacing his office deep in conversation on his mobile phone. From time to time he glanced sideways at Ben through the glass walls of his office. He was expressionless and Ben could not hear anything of what was being discussed, although intuitively he knew that his alleged indiscretion was the topic of the call. He also guessed that any discussion was almost certainly an autopsy on his all-too-short academic career. The cause of his final demise would doubtless be recorded as terminal stupidity.

Cowering in the corner of the open-plan reception, Ben had rehearsed his plea for clemency from the sacking that he was sure was coming his way. For a week now, he had been trying to envisage any conceivably positive outcome from the meeting he was about to have. His first and, almost certainly, last encounter with the man holding the key to his future. The most optimistic scenario he had been able to imagine was a redundancy package, although, with less than five years' service as a lecturer, even that did not look very attractive. If his actions were judged to be a breach of his professional contract, dismissal seemed the much more likely verdict, probably without a severance package, and his reputation, such as it was, in tatters. He would be cast adrift without significant savings and unemployable whilst still nearly fifteen years away from state retirement age. What a total mess, he thought.

His twenty five year career at the bank had ended in alarmingly similar circumstances, and what had been a nicely maturing pension pot was brought to an abrupt full stop. What remained of it was decimated in his subsequent divorce settlement. With two children, then still in education, a wife holding the moral high ground and Ben just too embattled to offer any meaningful resistance, she kept the house, their savings and mostly everything else. Several years later and still without property or significant assets of any kind but with liabilities up to his elbows, how would he survive, he wondered?

The lucky break, which saw him begin a new career as a lecturer at nearly fifty years old, was a lifeline thrown to him by the University from which he had graduated twenty-plus years previously. A chance sighting of an advertisement in an alumni newsletter and a reference from one of his old lecturers who had remembered him as a keen undergraduate, saw him back in Newcastle upon Tyne making a fresh start. The job's adequate salary allowed him to run a ten year old Audi and lease an acceptable two bedroomed apartment in a leafy street in an up-and-coming suburb. He could eat out once or twice a week and still afford his month-long summer tours of French vineyards. All that was about to come to a very sudden end he imagined.

Before the Dean could say anything, Ben began to blurt out the explanation he had rehearsed, "I'd just like to say in my defence–," but he was immediately interrupted by his employer.

"I really do have better things to do than deal with this sleaze and coercion."

The senior academic wandered the room seeming distracted and disengaged, like a man struggling to deal with too many issues at once. Although speaking out loud, it was as though he were delivering a lecture to a theatre full of students rather than addressing Ben in person.

Ben was now even more frightened, but also slightly confused, by his boss's last statement. Even though he could see that his behaviour had perhaps been foolish, he failed to understand how it could be considered as coercive. But having already had his clemency plea cut short once, he just listened in dumbfounded silence. The Dean was reading from a file which was apparently Ben's personnel record. His employer's monologue began along the predictable path of character assassination.

"You have had a few ups and downs since you joined us, haven't you Ben? A couple of late arrivals at early morning lectures; the complaint of alcohol breath during an afternoon dissertation support session; and now this ignominy."

As he had no wish to listen to any more of this, especially when his accuser wouldn't even look him in the eye, Ben's mind began to wander back to the Bistro André in La Rochelle. Should he choose the crème brûlée or their—speciality, 'La petite fromagerie'—a quandary that would occupy his thoughts for some valuable minutes.

In his view, Ben reasoned that he had led a mostly blameless, if unremarkable, existence. Once again, he felt circumstances had conspired against him. However, he also recognised that, by some standards, his life so far had been mostly meritless. He had achieved little of note. His head had been kept firmly below the parapet except, some would accuse, where women were concerned. He had never captained a sports team, won a trophy, fronted a rock band or rescued a cat from a tree. A hero he was not. He suddenly felt painfully unfulfilled and somewhat spineless.

However, now cornered and with his back firmly against the wall, there was a part of him that wanted to be fearless and make his mark: to make a difference and be remembered and to stand up for the underdog. A big part of him wanted to start right now by telling this academic bureaucrat to stick his job where no sun would ever shine on it. Just as his sap was rising the Dean broke this train of thought.

"That was our retained law firm on the phone, and earlier, I spoke with our public relations officer. They have both been considering the University's exposure here and it's not good news."

All thoughts of heroism evaporated and Ben sank further down into the soft leather chair as he realised that lawyers were already involved. There was no way this was not going to hurt him badly. He steeled himself for the worst. There was a long pause while the Dean returned to his desk to collect a different file. He carried on talking, still reading and rarely making any eye contact,

"Anyway, we have decided to draw a line in the sand and tackle this sort of behaviour head on."

This pronouncement finally confirmed Ben's worst fear: this was it, dismissal. His life was about to get even shittier than it already was.

In his mind he was already running through all the consequences; explaining his change in employment status to his children, giving notice on the apartment, selling the car, and so on, while the Dean continued to outline the case for the prosecution. Then, in a brief moment of clarity, he thought he heard the word 'sabbatical.' Surely, he must have said, 'sackable'? Ben reasoned.

During this conversation, Ben's demeanour had graduated slowly from abject despair to benign acceptance and finally, to complete incredulity. The Dean, who now had Ben's full attention, was suddenly also fully engaged and looking directly at him.

"I have a proposal I'd like to put to you."

The Dean explained that another member of the University's academic staff owned a second home in a tiny principality in north-west Italy; a would-be Kingdom headed by an old man as its 'de facto' prince. The academic had recently lobbied a University's board requesting someone to assist this tiny rural community in producing an economic development strategy. He had explained the region had excellent tourist potential but that its ancient rural economy, based mainly on olive farming, was failing. Although the community was weak and had no funding of its own, there was a substantial EU grant available to cover the costs of producing the strategy.

Ben was trying to take all this in but, because of his confused state of mind, his comprehension was slower than his boss's delivery of the information. Finally, he began to understand that the Dean saw this as the way to get him out of the way, avoiding conflict with Ben's trade union and at little or no cost to the University. He now listened very carefully while his boss filled in some of the details. After a short pause, Ben tried to mentally summarise what he understood the Dean to have just told him. "For the avoidance of any possible doubt; to avoid my saying or doing anything further to complicate this unfortunate situation, you are suggesting that I walk away from my nine-to-five job in cold grey Newcastle? You want me to abandon my hapless and unmotivated students to take a fully paid summer sabbatical on the Riviera, as the house guest of Italian aristocracy?"

Now smirking like a judge handing down an acquittal to a man expecting execution, the Dean responded, "As I don't know how long it will take to make this nightmare go away, you might need to stay out of sight for up to nine months. We will require a twenty thousand word report at the end of it to appease the EU, but otherwise, that is the essence of the offer on the table."

"When would you like me to start?" was all Ben could think of to say.

2. KIPPERS

The unmistakable odour of cooking kipper arrived well before the dish in which it was the key ingredient. The familiar smell stirred Ben from the maelstrom of thought going around in his head and caused the young couple on the table next to him to sniff the air and then grimace in unison. The golden kipper shards were just visible under wedges of griddled lemon. The fish had been pulled from its skeleton and mixed with finely chopped capers, red onion, olive oil and mint. The dish sat atop a slice of toasted Stottie bread and was finished with a knob of smoked paprika butter, which was by now melting slowing into the fish. A little sprig of mint on the top was the final unnecessary embellishment, thought Ben.

He deemed this tabbouleh interpretation of his favourite food a gentrified version of the original; a twenty-first century makeover of the working-class treat it was when Ben had first discovered and fallen in love with it. Back then, it was the perfect hangover cure after a night in the student bars of Newcastle upon Tyne, drinking cheap beer and smoking endless fags. In those days, the town's quayside was not the destination for party-goers and fine-diners that it is today. The area was peppered with dark, narrow boozers with strange and exotic names—The Baltic, The Crown Posada, and The Free Trade – frequented by shipyard workers, merchant seamen and dockers. Back then tattoos were almost obligatory, although their subject matter was less grandiloquent. The pub regulars tolerated students during the day but most of them found these places just too intimidating when darkness fell. As the effects of the after-work Newcastle Brown Ale kicked in, the riverside pubs became unpredictable and dangerous places for the unwary.

Amid the frenetic quayside activity, Kenny's Café was, in those days, a greasy spoon café with a fishy difference. Situated opposite the gloriously flamboyant Victorian architecture of the old fish market (now a nightclub, sardonically named 'Ocean'), the café had survived. Originally its location had meant easy access to a ready supply of cheap fresh produce and a steady stream of fish-loving, budget-conscious customers. The original version of the dish was merely a whole warm kipper placed between half a Stottie loaf, which had been split in two, generously spread with salted butter and scattered with plenty of white pepper. It was cheap, hearty and tasty.

The unattractive kipper is a product of pragmatism rather than design; it is function over form. No one ever named a yacht 'The Kipper' as it has none of the caché or élan of the Swordfish, Stingray or Barracuda. But, when protein was in short supply and expensive, herring, from which they make kippers, were landed in titanic volumes by fishing boats along the Northeast coast. However, this natural bounty only lasted for short periods of the year. Before freezers became commonplace, preserving the surplus herring to last through twelve months required either pickling, salting, or smoking. Smoking was easy and cheap. It required only a hardwood fire and a shed and was, therefore, the poor man's choice and resulted in what became known as the kipper. While killing bacteria and drying out the fish for extended storage, the smoking process also imbues the kipper with its synthetic-looking yellow hue and a dry intensely smoky flavour which people either love or hate: Ben called it, 'the Marmite of the fish world'.

Kippers were found wherever herring were landed, and that was many of the wilder parts of the UK coast. The Stottie, however, is a uniquely Geordie phenomenon. It is a twelve-inch circle of heavy dough-like bread and has a very firm consistency and a robust, almost rubbery crust. When halved or quartered and split in two it became the workingman's sandwich bread. It would be filled with ham, bacon, cheese, pease pudding or, if there was no money left in the housekeeping jar, just beef dripping. The Stottie never really caught on in any other part of the country, and it is not difficult to see why. Their bread is like the Geordies themselves: tough, thick-skinned and sometimes hard to swallow; but it was also robust, capable, and reliable. It was not designed for taste or aesthetics but to survive, being stuffed into a jacket pocket for a rickety bicycle journey over cobbled streets to a shipyard or mine shaft. It might be eaten a mile underground in a smoky, dark boiler room in the bowels of a mighty ship, or high up the side of a steel hull while balancing on a plank suspended from ropes. It would be washed down with pint mugs of strong tea, or even weak beer in the days before health and safety.

When Ben graduated from university and returned south to begin his career in banking, of all the many fond memories he had of Newcastle, this simple meal was the most vivid. He would salivate just thinking about it. As he waited, he contemplated whether it could even have been one of the subconscious factors in him deciding to return more than twenty-five years later. Needing to escape the fall-out from losing his job, his wife, his friends and his home, Newcastle seemed far enough away, yet familiar and, importantly, affordable. Fortuitously, the University was expanding to accommodate a sudden increase in overseas students and so was also eager to recruit someone with his practical experience who would work for less than a full professor's salary.

With much of the Newcastle's inner-city listed 'of architectural interest'; the streetscape had been little changed by development in the intervening thirty years. Only the names of shops, bars and clubs had changed. It immediately seemed very familiar to Ben. During the industrial revolution, the engineering, shipping and coal industries, which created the city's wealth, had crept right up to the edge of the shops and offices in the city centre. Industry almost merged with commerce because the River Tyne carves through the very heart of the city: a pulsing artery of transport, trade and construction dominating both banks.

In these areas today, warehouses and goods yards have been replaced by, or re-developed as, modern offices, hotels and apartment blocks. Ben wondered if the architects of these uninspired commercial edifices felt humbled by Sir Norman Foster's spectacular Sage performing arts building, now dominating the south bank of the river. The vast glass and shining steel armadillo-like structure which, Ben thought, from any viewpoint, inside or out, was a sculptural triumph. It was opposite here that Ben went in search of Kenny's, fully expecting it to have disappeared along with the coal staves and towering shipyard cranes of his youth.

To his surprise, in more or less the same location under the iconic Tyne Bridge, he spotted a neon sign proclaiming, 'Jamie's Fish Shack.' It turned out that about ten years ago an enterprising business student, who had been working at the café part-time, had taken over the firm when his graduation coincided with Kenny's retirement. The entrepreneurial home-cook had seen the changing face of Newcastle and spotted an opportunity. He re-named and re-invented the café for the twenty-first century: ironically re-introducing some of the features and furnishings that had been around when Ben first frequented it. Although the originals had long since been thrown out, replacement vinyl-clad booth seating, a blackboard menu and half-pint builders tea mugs were a few of the features reinstated as 'retro-cool.'

What had changed dramatically were the prices, the portions, service and the presentation. What had once been cheap, substantial and plain, was now expensive, barely adequate and over-fussy; or at least in Ben's somewhat cynical view.

Where food was concerned Ben was a traditionalist. He therefore failed to understand the rationale for preparing a kipper in the style of the cuisine of Syria, a country and culture which could not be further removed from that of the northeast of England. Nevertheless, the kipper Stottie had once again become Ben's comfort food of choice when hung-over, worried, or depressed. He had started the day of his meeting with the Dean suffering from all three but was now unsure exactly how he felt then decided one of his favourite dishes might help anyway.

Knife and fork in hand, he pushed the lemon and parsley to one side and paused to savour the smell, anticipating the flavours to come. As he ate, he read the colourful music event posters covering an entire wall opposite him but recognised none of the names of the bands on them. Still a favourite of students, this was a great place to promote a gig and the artwork added to the grungy post-industrial look the owners were apparently trying to cultivate. The whole atmosphere was making him nostalgic for those carefree days of his youth when all he had to worry about was how he could keep himself in beer, fags and kippers until his next student grant cheque arrived.

Ben, or Benjamin Millar Morton BA, as his name appeared on the University list of staff, was fifty-something, tall, slim—bordering on skinny. He carried his years lightly, considering the stressful consequences of a life of poor judgement calls. Nevertheless, his once fair hair was now mostly silvery-white. It was worn slightly too long for a man of his age and his current calling. His legs, fingers and his nose also seemed elongated relative to his mass. His body angles were unusually asymmetric, making him look slightly different depending on the aspect from which viewed. A few women thought him handsome; others odd looking. Most at least agreed that he was striking and that he had kind eyes. He stood out in a crowd and so people remembered him. He much preferred the company of women, which was as well because many men often thought him smug. He was unwilling to engage in football or rugby banter and share bawdy jokes. He was a person on whom everyone had an opinion but few of those views coincided. He was an enigma even unto himself.

Some of his clothes had the obviously superior cut of prestige labels, but these few garments were now well worn and supplemented by cheaper high-street brands, some slightly too fashionable for a man of his vintage. He wore a quality Swiss watch: a simple understated gold one with a crocodile strap. A gift from his wife on their wedding and, ironically, the only thing of any real value he had left after his divorce. But he was well aware that this was only because she had forgotten about the expensive timepiece. He owned several pairs of costly hand-made shoes, but these were also now shabby with heels worn and badly needing the attention of a good cobbler. The less costly items of clothing were more recent purchases. These were made with little consideration, no female advice and with a budget in mind. Some of the prestige items of clothing were the legacy of a wealthy former lover who he'd met a year after his divorce.

With emotions still raw from her own divorce but flush with half of her ex-husband's considerable fortune, she had initially showered Ben with gifts. These were mainly of clothing and shoes but also expensive aftershaves, moisturisers and other male grooming products. He sometimes felt as though she had taken him on as a kind of property refurbishment; something with potential but in need of remodelling to her taste. Her upgrading of Ben lasted until about three years ago when he had been abandoned, an unfinished project.

His abrupt relegation to single status came about when he left his phone on her kitchen table while he had popped out to the shop to get a bottle of white Burgundy.

Whilst cooking their supper, his then partner had seen an incoming text appear on his phone's screen. It was from a woman she had never heard of using over-friendly and overly familiar language. On his return, she confronted him but was not convinced by his bumbling explanation. So she tipped a full tub of cumin powder over him followed by the contents of a vase of lilies and then stood back to approvingly admire the outcome of her handiwork.

"How appropriate: yellow is the colour of cowards," she said.

Ben just stood silently dripping for a moment before turning for the door, still clutching the green bottle of Waitrose St Veran.

It took weeks to wash the smell entirely off his skin and the colour out of his hair. For the first week, he looked like a jaundiced punk rocker. Fortunately, it was summer recess and he could just wait until it eventually faded out of his hair and skin. Ben swore that the woman's messages were unsolicited, advances from someone he had met briefly at an academic conference. She had evidently mistaken his congeniality for something more amorous. But the damage was already done and another unfortunate chapter of his personal life was behind him.

In the intervening years since his divorce, his general appearance had gradually reduced from smart city banker to one of faded grandeur: like a once-elegant hotel denied investment and care. Beneath the peeling paint, it was still possible to glimpse the shadow of its former greatness. Nevertheless, he retained a confident presence when he entered a room that made him difficult to ignore. Often people said that he looked like an actor from TV or film but no one had yet pinned down exactly who he was a look-alike of.

On the face of it, he was a serial Lothario: the survivor of several other failed relationships. In truth, he had never actively pursued other women whilst in long-term relationships. Rather, he had often unknowingly encouraged the interest of the opposite sex and had then been too naive to see that he had got it. Often, by that time, it was too late and flirtation, or a full-blown sexual lunge, was the almost inevitable outcome. If sober and not in company, these were usually not too dangerous. If they were drunk and, or, in public, the result had been at times catastrophic. Abstention was not something which came naturally to him, and so these types of events had punctuated his adult life.

It was one such encounter with a younger married colleague, seven years ago, which had ended his cushy career in banking. It turned out this was not just any colleague but also the daughter of the Chairman. The penalty was becoming a somewhat reluctant lecturer in economics and marketing. But he had quickly become bored with teaching and would have liked to quit if he had a choice.

Initially, designing and drafting his lectures had been stimulating enough, but then delivering them to mostly disinterested and disengaged students had become frustrating. After a couple of years of delivering the same material term after term, he had stopped caring if anyone was listening and was now merely going through the motions. He thought a computer could do his job and it would be more punctual and make fewer mistakes. But he still had maintenance to pay and somehow bridge that period of time until either his pension kicked in, he was made generously redundant, or both his children finished their education; whichever came first.

Baptised plain Ben Morton, he had elongated his Christian forename to Benjamin and added Millar as a middle name (a subtle nod to his then infatuation with the writer Ernest Millar Hemingway) while in his first year at university. He did this to emulate many of his posher public school friends who had double-barreled or hyphenated names. He thought it gave him more gravitas on job applications and, as a bonus, would help him meet a better class of women. It turned out that it did both, and so it stuck.

His need for this personal re-branding and a deliberate vagueness about his age, pointed to a pretentiousness and vanity that were the least attractive aspects of his personality. Otherwise, he was a loyal friend, engaging social company and a responsible parent—albeit in a hands-off kind of way. A lack of confidence in his parenting skills meant that he was reactive, as opposed to proactive, when it came to his own children. This mirrored his upbringing. He and his elder brother were packed off to boarding school as soon as they could write their names in the front of an exercise book. His brother had thrived in the all-male environment but being wrenched from his mother was a trauma from which Ben would never fully recover.

Poignantly, since he had been unattached, he had become a more popular dinner party guest. The prevalence of marital separation meant that there were always odd numbers that needed balancing up amongst his peers. He was also popular because he brought good wine for the host and elegantly wrapped flowers for the hostess. Although reasonably well-read and educated, he was not widely-travelled. An aversion (but not a full-blown phobia) to flying meant that he had preferred driving holidays, visiting the vineyards and bistros of France.

Food and wine were his chief pleasures now, although he saw cooking as a chore. Since his divorce, he ate out whenever he could afford it and bought Marks & Spencer or Waitrose ready-meals when money was tighter. No one could understand how he remained so slim considering his indulgent lifestyle. Although he could be frugal when required, he refused to compromise on wine; buying the best he could afford after having first researched every detail of its provenance. This obsession had endowed him an encyclopedic knowledge, not just of the wines, but of the soil, climate and viniculture which produced them. He justified his over consumption merely as conscientious research.

As he savoured his kipper, Ben once again went over the events leading up to his astounding meeting earlier that morning. He was aware of the economic belt-tightening that had been going on in further education since the Government removed direct support for universities. Shrinking budgets had brought about a swathe of voluntary redundancies amongst older colleagues, as institutions tried to shed long serving staff with old contracts at high salaries and with generous pensions. These long serving staff were quickly replaced by recent graduates, often with superficially more impressive 'paper' qualifications, but no actual commercial or teaching experience. These were usually recruited from overseas and would agree to lesser terms to secure a visa and a job at an English university. In summary, he had been expendable, and, because of this allegation, a prime candidate to go.

Against this background, all of this had added up to only one thing as far as Ben could see. He had been staring in the face of Armageddon. Quite how things had turned so completely around and morphed into his current extremely rosy outlook, he could barely comprehend. Later, he would rationalise, it was almost certainly his employers fear of the teachers' union and the possibility of civil litigation for unfair dismissal that had kept him in employment. That, and the publicity, which would inevitably accompany such a sensational case.

Whatever the reason, instead of the letter of dismissal and P45 he had been expecting, he had a minimum six-month paid leave of absence and a one-way ticket to Nice Côte d'Azur airport.

3. CITRONS CONFIT

Turmeric, ginger and chili were not ingredients that Ben had expected to read could be found in dishes from the Riviera. His only previous experience of Mediterranean climate and culture had been of the famous wine regions of south-west France. To brush up on his knowledge, he had picked up a book 'The Riviera Traveller' at the airport. He was already learning many new things about France's sunnier and racier region.

The region's multiracial population are a consequence of its proximity to the African continent and earlier French colonisations in those lands. This is one of the factors making the cuisine of the Côte d'Azur quite different from other parts of mainland France. According to the book, in Nice, one could find menus containing couscous, tagine-like aromatic stews and spicy kebabs alongside well-known French dishes. Although in classic French recipes prepared here, butter was replaced by olive oil and cream was hardly used at all.

Also, until as recently as the unification of Italy in the nineteenth century, Nice belonged to the Kingdom of Piedmont-Sardinia and so also retains many Italian-influenced foods, including rice and pasta. Indeed, Garibaldi, the man who finally brought Italians together, under one flag, and who has a statue, road, or public building dedicated to him in almost every town and village in Italy, was a son of Nice. In the old part of the city, which includes Nice's famous flower market, many of the street names are still in a form of Old Italian language.

The dish Ben had been reading about and was now looking forward to trying was chicken with preserved lemons (citrons confit) and olives. The recipe fused these ingredients with the also very un-European saffron, ginger, paprika, cumin and turmeric. Ben imagined that after ninety minutes in an oven these would smell and taste divine when served with a nicely chilled Côtes de Provence.

Preserved lemons impart a unique flavour to almost any dish, he read. The bittersweetness of the fruit is magnified by being pickled in a brine for several months: it is both sweet and tart but still intensely lemony. Ben reasoned people would presumably only bother to preserve lemons if there were in short supply part of the year or they needed to transport them on long sea journeys. He read on about the unique melting pot of cultures that is the modern-day French Riviera and how those people have influenced the cuisine there.

Although usually he would have much preferred to have driven or to have taken the train to Italy, so desperate was he to get away before they retracted the offer of the sabbatical that Ben took a travel sickness pill and got on the plane at Stanstead Airport. An attractive female passenger, about his age, was seated next to him on the flight. On seeing what he was reading, she asked if he were going on holiday to the Côte d'Azur.

Such was Ben's astonishment at the situation that he found himself in, he could not help but keep repeating the story of his good fortune to anyone who would listen. It was as if he felt the need to test if anyone else found it plausible, to perhaps reassure himself that it was not some kind of impossible dream. So Ben told her that he was, in fact, heading for the small Italian principality of Seborga, just over the French border from Nice.

"Have you heard of it?"

Before his fellow passenger could answer the question, Ben went on to add that he was to become the houseguest of the prince of this little-known but beautiful area of Italy.

"Indeed, I have heard of it, and I have also met the Prince of Seborga," she was eventually allowed to respond. "A lovely man. He delivered a case of his wonderful olive oil to my boat in Menton."

Perplexed by the strange image which this statement conjured up, Ben tried to interject seeking clarification, but the lady quickly continued, "Do not expect to find any of that French or African food that you are reading about once you cross the border into Italy. The Italians don't import foreign ideas or influences, especially where food is concerned. You're unlikely to find a tagine or some couscous any further east than Menton on the French border. In the Italian psyche, their food is the best in the world so why import anyone else's? And I must say that this is a position that it is hard to argue against. Anyway, please excuse me, but I always try to catch up on much-needed sleep during these flights."

As if she was regretting instigating the conversation, she pulled her straw hat down over her pale blue eyes, closed her eyelids and turned her head away. The encounter ended abruptly and with a business-like finality.

Ben was left pondering the revelation that the French and Italian Riviera may be geographically twinned and share a name, but they were culturally worlds apart.

When Ben collected his bags from the carousel at Nice airport, he was still grinning like a man who had just learned that his recent diagnosis of a terminal disease had been later found to be a terrible misdiagnosis. Pushing his trolley through the automatic doors into the airport arrivals lounge, he was still contemplating the curious remarks of the woman who had sat next to him on the plane.

Despite two or three scans around the arrivals lounge, there was no waiting driver as had been promised. There was a small open-fronted café bar between the arrivals lounge and the main doors. Ben parked his luggage trolley there and took a barstool. From here he could see anyone arriving who might be looking for him. He ordered a glass of Côtes de Provence and some mixed charcuterie with olives.

Maybe it was the warm climate, the wine, or the cured meat, but he was suddenly transported back to a holiday he had spent in southern Rhone, near where it merges into Provence – not so very far north from here. It was not long after his divorce had become final and he met a willowy Norwegian schoolteacher, also escaping a recently failed relationship. He recalled the salty taste of the charcuterie, and that of her tanned skin after a long day in the sun, when a loud-speaker announcement broke his train of thought. The next moment he heard, "Ciao. Ciao" as his glamorous fellow passenger strode toward him at pace pushing a baggage trolley with one hand and waving her straw hat with the other.

Ben thought that she was hailing him and waved back, but she went straight past him heading for a smartly dressed young man wearing a blue polo shirt, pressed white cotton shorts and deck shoes. Ben called after her, "I did not get your name or number."

She turned, and with a knowing look, answered "Cecily," but ignored the phone number request.

Before he could argue, a booming voice with a strong Italian accent shouted, "Signore Bin."

The words were more of an accusation than a greeting. The source of the voice was carrying a sign; the roughly torn-off lid of a cardboard box advertising soap powder. On the sign was scrawled, 'Dott. Morton', in what looked like a school crayon. He was a grim-faced, profoundly tanned man. It later transpired that Vincenzo was his name—although he did not introduce himself. His demeanour was in stark contrast to the still cheerful new arrival from England.

With nothing by way of a greeting or any formality, the big man turned and gestured for Ben to follow outside. Ben was wheeling his luggage as fast as he could to keep up. From behind Ben could see Vincenzo was tall and powerfully built. He walked with the confident stride of a man comfortable in his own skin. He still had most of his mousey brown hair, only the front half of which had gone to grey but was all lubricious and unkempt. A thinning patch on his crown, through which nut-brown skin was visible, was perhaps the signs of further regression to come. His worn working clothes were at odds with every other person in the Côte d'Azur terminal, and yet he was either oblivious or uncaring of this incongruity.

Once outside, they walked past a line of dark luxury cars lined up at the kerb. Ben's expectations rose in line with the air temperature. His smile quickly disappeared when Vincenzo passed all the limousines before indicating that he should climb into the back of an ancient Ape (ah-pay) three-wheeler pick-up truck.

He would later learn that Ape means 'bee' in Italian and refers to its small size and the buzzing noise that insect makes. The design was born when a roof, an additional wheel, and a carrying platform was added to the ubiquitous Italian motor scooter. After the Second World War, when metal and petrol were both in short supply, this cheap, easily constructed, and economical vehicle became the workhorse of the Italian economy. Its small size and surprising cross-country agility meant that, to this day, it is the vehicle of choice for farmers. It is equally at home squeezing through narrow urban streets or weaving between olive trees.

Ben reluctantly clambered into the rusty and dirty vehicle bed unsure where to place himself to be comfortable. Eventually, he used his suitcase as a backrest and wedged his feet against the tailgate. As he did so, he heard a toot of a passing car horn. He turned to see his former fellow traveller smiling out from the passenger seat of a navy-blue Bentley Corniche with its roof down. She had donned dark glasses, a headscarf, and sardonic half-smile. She also raised a hand of recognition, as if to let him know she had seen him and his embarrassing transport.

Vincenzo pulled straight out into the lane of cars, narrowly avoiding a speeding bright orange Lamborghini, and they left the airport in a pall of blue exhaust smoke accompanied by a rattly engine noise. After a humiliating and terrifying ride on the coastal road, they skirted around Monaco and crossed the border into Italy at Menton. After just a few more kilometres, Vincenzo turned the Ape off the coast road and began a slow climb north into the foothills of the Maritime Alps. The journey took just over an hour but felt like half a day to Ben.

Until now he had not dared look up to enjoy the view, but now the steep climb had slowed progress to a steady crawl and Ben was able to take in the breath-taking band of azure blue Mediterranean stretching along the coast back into France. The land, sloping at first steeply and then more gently down to the sea, appeared dotted with terracotta, yellow and white buildings. Surrounding them, floral patches of the most vibrant purples, reds and blues. Indeed, the more he looked around, the more he realised that every fence, hedge and wall was a riot of coloured flowers and every garden green with vegetables. Spring blossom on the trees had now transformed into small young oranges, plums, figs and apricots. The only areas not brightly coloured were the olive groves. These narrow, terraced strips contained severely cropped trees looking like diminutive weeping willows. They were olive trees covered in slender, silvery-grey/green leaves but they were not yet showing any signs of fruit. It would be a long wait until December, or even January, before they could be harvested.

As they climbed relentlessly upwards the houses became scarcer and the roads got thinner, the buildings became noticeably shabbier but remained pretty, at least from a distance. Up close many of the properties looked poorly constructed and poorly maintained. The bright blue dots in the landscape, which lower down the hill had been swimming pools, were now replaced by round rough concrete water tanks. From these tanks, ingenious irrigation channels trickled water to neatly hoed furrows at the lifting of a wooden dam gate.

Every so often, Vincenzo stopped the Ape and disappeared over a wall only to return with an armful of vegetables or fruit, which he placed unceremoniously in the back along with Ben, his suitcase and hand luggage. These, it turned out, were the home-grown ingredients for the small family restaurant he helped his uncle and a distant cousin run to supplement their meagre income from olive growing. Strangely these patches of land were spread over a couple of kilometres, not apparently physically connected in any way, and varying in scale from the size of a small yard to that of a football pitch. It transpired that these Ortos, as they are known, were the legacy of many generations of inheritance remaining within the extended family and shared by several connected branches of the original owners.

The workload of maintaining these various plots and hierarchical distribution of their output is one of many mysterious workings of Italian rural culture. Their wide geographic distribution also has another less obvious benefit; they all had a different altitude, slope and angle to the sun and soil, meaning that each plot is better for growing specific things at certain times of the year. Much more sophisticated than mere crop rotation, this ensured there was a good supply of a wide variety of produce nearly all year round. Also, even if pests ravage a crop at one site, another likely remains untouched further down the valley. It was a kind of horticultural insurance policy on which a family's very survival may have once relied. Even today, and despite its location on the Riviera, these gardens were still very much in use, suggesting that twenty-first century global consumerism had not quite reached here. Every family fortunate to own these small parcels of land could, and still do, grow most of what they need to survive.

Both historically, and to this day, olives are the only substantial cash crop of which there was a surplus that could be sold. This annual bounty had always been a commodity that could be turned into cash or traded for goods they could not grow themselves—salt, rice, flour, etc. Astonishingly, here, less than an hour from Nice and thirty minutes from Monte Carlo, there were still older people living pretty much like generations of their forefathers, albeit now with some back up from meagre state and EU hand-outs.

Gradually, as older generations pass and many of the young fail to return, empty properties are deteriorating and parcels of land are increasingly being left to return to nature or sold to outsiders as building plots. This unused land was snapped up by wealthy folk escaping the cramped apartments, crime and clogged roads of the French Riviera. So, there is from time to time bizarre scenes when these two very different worlds collide; rusty old scooters, battered Apes or rusting Fiat 500s, often over-burdened with vegetables, smoking slowly up the hillsides. These slow-moving convoys created frustration amongst the drivers of the luxury cars with blacked-out windows rushing to get to their weekend retreats.

It was into this cultural, political and economic anomaly that Ben unknowingly blundered one bright day in May.

If he was expecting a red carpet, trooping of the guard, and a ten-gun salute, he was to be disappointed. What greeted him was a deserted piazza, two of the mangiest feral cats he had ever seen and an old man of about eighty sipping a small glass of wine under a wide-branched plain tree. To Ben, it looked like a scene from a Clint Eastwood spaghetti western and was only missing the Ennio Morricone theme tune. The Ape rattled into the piazza, scattered the cats and jerked to a halt beside the tree causing the tomatoes, aubergines and green bean cargo to almost drown Ben in a tsunami of vegetables. The old man was more athletic than he looked and was on his feet and offering an outstretched hand into the bed of the pick-up before the last tomato had come to rest.

"Dottore Bin. Benvenuto a Seborga. Welcome. Welcome."

Taking what he thought was a hand-shake, the old man gripped his hand with the power of a vice and tugged Ben out of the Ape embracing him like a long-lost relative.

"Buongiorno. And you are?" Was all Ben could think of to say.

Vincenzo interjected, "Let me introduce you to his Supreme Tremendousness Prince Claudio Biancheri the Third of Seborga, servant only to God, The Pope and his loyal subjects," in an apparently well-practised speech without any hint of irony whatsoever.

Ben struggled to find the words that would allow him to respond appropriately to all that he was taking in and so he just said, "Blimey" and then "good heavens," words which, fortunately, meant nothing to his hosts.

He was later to discover that formal court introductions were one of Vincenzo's many and varied roles in this community. He already knew this included chauffeur and gardener, but he was later to learn the role also extended to guard of honour, border control and royal decree enforcer: in fact, he, along with his retired father and two cousins, also constituted the entire force of the Seborgan military.

The prince had the look of a man who was once powerfully built but the ravages of time had reduced his stature; his shoulders had sagged slightly, his waistline expanded, his legs had thinned and bowed slightly. His hair and beard, however, were still thick and unusually dark for someone his age. He had kind eyes, Ben thought, but they also had the steely quality of a man not to be messed with. Above his left eyebrow was a deep indented scar about the size of a thumbnail. The scar tissue was pale compared to the deep tan of the remainder of his skin. The powerful hands that had grasped his own were calloused and rough; the working tools of a man of the land. As unlikely an image of a prince as it was possible to imagine, was Ben's conclusion.

When Ben finally gathered his thoughts and adjusted his expectations, he managed to thank the prince for his kind invitation and ask how he should address him.

"Claudio, Claudio. Non formale."

While Vincenzo began unloading the pick-up, Claudio led Ben into one of the narrow alleys leading from the Piazza, taking them from bright sunshine to dark shadow. These passageways were at most two metres wide and varied along its length in some places, getting down to a point where he could see gouges in the stone walls from the many scooters and Ape handlebars squeezing past. Ben pulled his sizeable rolling suitcase into an ever-deeper warren of alleys until one opened into another smaller bright piazza of such beauty that it took his breath away.

A beautiful ornate stone fountain stood at its centre trickling water into a large pool at its base in which children played with floating paper boats. Painted iron balconies on all sides had been festooned with terracotta pots filled with trailing flowers of the most vivid colours. The houses were all the hues of a Monet painting, plus a few shades even he had not thought of. Old wooden doors were leaning at odd angles. Some of the wood was splitting with age and too much sun but all with ornate handles and knockers in the shapes of unfamiliar animals. When his eyes readjusted to the light, Ben could see a church bell tower reaching into the blue sky above. Its dome had evident Moorish influences, being covered in leaf-like ceramic tiles of many different colours. Somehow all the irregularities of the architecture and the imperfections in the paintwork made it even more fantastic. Just perfect, was how it seemed to Ben at this moment.

It was the ideal place at this painful time in his life and so far removed from his job, his debts, his children and his woman trouble. He still really could not believe his good fortune. Claudio's neighbours all shouted ciaos, salves and buon pomeriggios. Ben noted that there was no one bowing, scraping or forelock-tugging to the prince. He was apparently not only an informal ruler but, apparently, also a universally liked one. Even the parish priest, it seemed, was expecting Ben. The smiling young man in an immaculately pressed white cassock waved a greeting from the steps of the church.

The plastic wheels on Ben's suitcase bounced and scuttled over the stone paving in the maze of narrow alleys until they reached an impressive old wooden door, bearing what he took to be the prince's coat of arms. Claudio held open the solid old door and Ben stepped into the cool and dark hallway with well-worn, off-white marble steps rising immediately into the gloom. Before he could pick up his weighty case, it had been tugged from his grip by Vincenzo who hoisted it over his shoulders like it was a mere sack of feathers and bounded up the stairs two at a time. Ben set off to follow but was soon sweating and out of breath.

His eyes were struggling to adjust to the sudden changes from light to dark but he followed as best he could to the first-floor landing, where the others were now both waiting. As soon as he caught up, off they set up another flight of white marble stairs. There were landings with narrow windows, shuttered tight against the heat of the sun. Just when he thought he had reached the top, his host and his nephew started up a third flight of, this time, wooden stairs—but so steep as to be considered ladders in his eyes. Now having to stop every few treads to get some air into his lungs and let his aching legs recover, Ben's shirt had sweat-soaked patches front and back.

Finally, Vincenzo, showing no signs of breathlessness or discomfort, dropped the case onto its wheels and, with a shove, nudged it through an open door into a dark room. Ben saw an old wooden chair into which he slumped fearing for his heart. Claudio undid the catches on the window and swung them inwards revealing the iron rails of a Juliet balcony. With his eyes only just having got used to the gloom, Ben almost recoiled from the intense sunshine bursting in through the full height double windows when the shutters were thrown outwards.

"Ecco—hai visto che bella vista?" exclaimed Claudio beaming like a proud parent presenting a newborn child for the first time.

With oxygen now restored to his lungs and flowing back through his blood, Ben raised himself from the chair and walked to the now open window. Several things were gradually becoming clear. As he had approached the village on the winding road, what had looked to be a single fortress-like building perched on the hill were, in fact, the collective outer walls into which were interwoven the various homes of most of the villagers. Few windows were at the same height, and many sections of the outer wall were painted different colours showing that individual family boundaries were a haphazard affair. One neighbour's bathroom might be above another's living room, while their kitchen was below that of the bedroom of someone living on the other side. Part of the explanation for these different levels was more apparent from the inside than from the alleys and piazzas through which he had entered this labyrinth. The mountaintop was just that—a pinnacle of rock. It was both impossible and unnecessary to dig foundations into it. Everything was built straight onto the cliff following the natural contours of the hilltop, rising and falling through the village in line with the natural strata. The architecture was organic, rather than planned, and all the more pleasing to the eye for that lack of conformity, thought Ben.

The village's extreme elevation meant that the original inhabitants would have seen any enemies approaching hours before they arrived and be able to secure the fortress by closing a single narrow entrance. This high up, unfettered by coastal mists, the sun is often fierce. This construction layout meant that the centre of the village, piazzas, front doors and balconies all had some shade from the intense sun for a good part of the day. It also meant that those highest up on the outer walls, like the room Ben found himself in, had an awe-inspiring vista.

On either side of the valley, ancient green forests funnelled the view down to the sea, some two thousand feet below and seven kilometres distant. On the fringes of the land, a thin line of hotels and apartment blocks could be made out stretching along the coast. From here, these were the only faint signs of twenty-first century development before the bluer-than-blue Mediterranean took over and blurred into the horizon.

Surrounding the village on three sides was a patchwork of stone terraces, olive groves, rows of grapevines, and small houses, painted in a palette of pinks, browns and yellows. All these buildings boasted terracotta pan-tile roofs in the most wonderful shades of browns and pinks. Smoke rose from several fires amongst the groves, where farmers were pruning and tidying. Dogs barked in a sequence around the valley as if passing on messages from one to another. Distant church bells rang out, perhaps celebrating a marriage or christening. It was a bucolic idyll—an Italian Nirvana, and here he was for the summer: an expenses-paid guest on full pay. Could this really have happened, he wondered yet again? Vincenzo and Claudio left Ben staring at the yachts cutting white swathes across the distant Mediterranean, with a call from Prince Claudio of, "Mangiare at otto—dinner at eight pm—in the Piazza."

After eventually finding the bathroom and figuring out the quirks of ancient Italian plumbing, Ben enjoyed a refreshing (if not too powerful) shower and changed into a plain white cotton shirt, beige chinos and tan suede loafers but no socks. Thinking he wanted to make a good impression and underline his status as the English Professor, at the last minute he grabbed his straw Panama hat but carried, rather than wore it. A sideways glance in the wardrobe mirror as he exited confirmed he had achieved the look he wanted.

4. BRUSCHETTA

For a nation obsessed with their digestive systems, Italians seem to have remarkably little understanding of basic human physiology. They believe that to maintain the equilibrium of the stomach, they must carefully observe dietary rituals. While all Italians agree with this fundamental principle, they often disagree widely on the actual methods. Each region, valley, village, or family may have their rituals of eating and drinking the right things, in the correct order, at clearly defined times. Most of these theories would not bear scrutiny by any doctor: unless he was Italian of course.

An alcoholic drink before dinner is a feature of many cultures, but the Italians collectively agree that alcohol on an empty stomach is potentially ruinous to the gut without something to nibble on. Aperitivo is therefore essential in preparing the stomach for what is to come. In theory, aperitivo should be small light bite-sized morsels of food but in practice are often what the British would call lunch. Sandwiches, pizza, quiche and small pies can all constitute aperitivo and, remember, this is all just a precursor to the four or five (or even six) course eating marathon that makes up the average Italian dinner.

Often the ingredients of aperitivo are not sourced specially for the purpose. It might be whatever is in season or left over from previous meals. That day's bread, which is starting to go stale, when toasted and rubbed with a garlic clove, forms the base for many aperitivo.

Unlike tapas, no choice is on offer; it's a take-it-or-leave-it offer. The snacks could be vegetarian, meat or fish and vary from the familiar to the mysterious. Vegans, allergics, dieters or fussy eaters of any kind are a mystery to most Italians. They eat everything: bones, skin, scales, smoked, dried, cooked, raw and sometimes even alive.

Aperitivo is usually presented free, and unordered, with any drink purchased after about 5 pm. They are a gastronomic fait accompli. Italian customers compare and measure establishments by the quality and generosity of their aperitivo. After all, Campari and sodas are the same everywhere, but these freshly made snacks will vary from the modest to the extraordinary.

Ben's introduction to the art of aperitivo could not have been less grandiose. The bruschetta were two slices of toasted ciabatta liberally spread with chopped fresh tomatoes. Although not an obvious accompaniment to beer, these were tomatoes the like of which he had never seen; small with almost plum-black skins and dark purple flesh. They were drizzled with rich dark green olive oil, with the consistency of single cream, and scattered with vivid green basil. Initially, they were more appealing to his eye than to his appetite.

Ready too early for his meeting with the prince, Ben had decided that he needed a drink to steel his nerves and stopped at the tiny café just a few paces from the front door. He took a seat on the bench outside in the sun and waited. There were no other customers, and after waiting a few minutes, still, no one had come to take his order. So Ben entered the darkness of the bar. It was empty but he could hear chopping in the adjoining kitchen. He shouted aloud, "Hello".

"Buonasera," answered a distant voice.

Emerging from the gloom a handsome smiling young man added, "You say 'buonasera' at this time of day."

"Thank you," Ben said apologetically, "I just wanted a beer."

"Birra? You want una birra." came the next Italian lesson. "Peroni OK? You must be the English professore who has come to bring the tourists up from the coast and save our businesses?"

This seemed more a statement of fact than a question.

"Sit down. I bring you your drink."

Taking a long swig of the glacier-cold beer, Ben at first ignored the bruschetta on the plate delivered with the beer. Until, that is, his curiosity got the better of him. They certainly looked like tomatoes but he had never seen black ones, and so took a bite off the crispy end of the toasted slice. The tomato flavour was more intense than anything he had ever tasted before. It was simultaneously sharp and acidic but with a sweetness accentuated by the olive oil and basil. Although crisp at the edges, the bread at the centre was moist and chewy. There was also the pungent flavour of garlic. The combination of the aromatic olive oil and herbs made the dish irresistible, and the slices were reduced to crumbs in three or four bites.

The cheerful young man reappeared with another plate and another beer, neither of which Ben had asked for. Depositing the repeat order on the table, he offered his hand,

"I am Valerio. Was that good? The tomatoes are from the agriturismo outside the village and are a speciality of these valleys. They are small and often misshapen but taste like no other. It's a combination of the hot sun by day and the mists which come off the mountains and the sea by night which give them their unique flavour."

Ben shook his hand and said that he agreed that he had never tasted their equal.

"So, you are aware of why I am here?" said Ben.

"Everyone in the village knows about your work and are praying that you will be successful. This village, and the few others remaining like it, are dying a slow death. Neither our own government or the EU are doing anything to help us. We were struggling to make a living before the banking crisis, but since then things have got worse. The only thing we can grow here are olives, but the slopes are so steep everything must be done by hand. It's almost impossible to harvest enough for our own use and also a surplus to sell to make a living. The supermarkets on the coast sell cheap oil imported in tankers from Tunisia for less per litre than it costs us to mill it. It's been getting worse for decades. Tourism is the only answer. All the young people have left. Of my school friends, I am the only one left living here. My father died, I am the youngest, and so I must stay to look after my mother. All the others have gone to Milan, London, or New York. We need to get the rich people from the coast to come up here and spend money."

Ben pondered the younger man's comments while he was buzzing about wiping tables and placing napkin holders. He then asked him, "And what do you think will bring tourists here?"

Valerio put down his tray and joined Ben, taking a chair at the table.

"Many of my friends think Claudio is crazy clinging onto this idea that Seborga is still a Principality with him as our prince. But I believe that this and our history with the Templar Knights, are the only things we have going for us. Sure, our village is pretty but so are a hundred others around here. Our olive oil, wine and food are also excellent, but every valley within a hundred kilometres could claim theirs are good too. But we are the only village with our Templar history and Principality heritage. Claudio is a living remnant of all that. That is why we already receive a small number of visitors here but not enough to make a real difference. We need to make it much better known and capitalise on it."

Ben's confusion must have been apparent to the young bar owner.

"From your expression, it would appear you do not know about the history of this place Professore? I imagined that you had been briefed before accepting this role?" Valerio said, now looking slightly doubtful of Ben's credibility.

Ben confessed to him that he had no idea why this tiny community had its own prince, or what the connection was with the Knights Templar. This was merely a trial exercise in microeconomics for failing agricultural communities, as far as he had been told.

Valerio explained, "The Knights Templar were an immensely powerful Christian force – mainly French nobleman but also English and some other northern Europeans. They had money, the latest war-making technology and, most of all, religious zeal. The Pope encouraged them to unite and travel to Palestine to fight a common enemy, in what became known as the Holy Wars. Their task was to protect pilgrims travelling to the Holy Land as well as the religious sites themselves from the control and influence of the increasingly powerful Arab powers."

Pausing to wave and offer a cheery 'buonasera' to a passing neighbour, Valerio continued, "In those days, anyone travelling on horseback from northern France or England towards the eastern Mediterranean—to avoid crossing the high Alps—was forced to head south until they reached the Mediterranean Sea. This route brings you to approximately where Seborga lies, here on what is today the coast of Italy. But back then, it was just one of a number of small independent feudal states. This journey of up to a thousand miles would take several weeks. From this point, some of those who became known as the Crusaders, would continue the journey by ship while others travelled overland. So this very spot on the Mediterranean became a terminus for the journeys of pilgrims and the Crusader Knights to and from the Holy Land."

Over the course of thirty minutes, the young man completed the abridged history of the extraordinary place in which Ben had accidentally found himself.

Before the Templars, Seborga was little more than a fortified monastery-run community, controlled from Rome. The Benedictine Monks living here cultivated the surrounding terraces producing oil, wine and fruit; as well as the things needed to sustain a long journey. Its elevated position made it easy to defend and a nearby sheltered harbour gave it access to the Mediterranean. It therefore became a strategic staging post for those Knights setting out for Palestine. For returning Crusaders, particularly the sick or injured, it also became a hospital and place for recuperation on reaching European soil after their long sea voyage. It was a place where the Knights brought the spoils of war, refreshed horses, collected supplies, trained and exchanged intelligence on the enemy.

Although he thought he had a reasonable grasp of history, Ben was surprised by the revelation that Italy had not become a single state until as recently as the mid-nineteenth century. Up until this point, it had been a collection of independent feudal states. Many of these were small kingdoms, some of which were owned by, or effectively controlled from, Rome. Seborga was a monastic community under the immediate rule of a type of 'prince bishop' but ultimately under the jurisdiction of the Pope.

However, such became the strategic importance of Seborga to the fighters embroiled in the Holy Wars that the Pope withdrew governance from the local monks and handed total control to the Knights Templar. In recognition of their crucial role in the war, and keen to support their efforts any way, his Holiness declared it to be the Templars' own independent state. He also awarded them the right to collect taxes, elect a prince from amongst their ranks and bestowed upon him all the power of a sovereign; a Principality of Knights Templar.

When the wars were over, the Templars were no longer needed. Indeed, The King of France and the Pope feared they had also grown too powerful and independent and believed they now posed a threat to their absolute rule. They told them firmly to leave Seborga or be driven from the Church. They went in haste, reluctantly abandoning the Principality to its fate. In later research Ben found that recorded history became a little hazy after this point, as fact blurred into myth, rumour and speculation. However, it was known that the Templars' motives were not always altruistic and their exploits sometimes less than chivalrous. They departed taking with them anything of value that could be carried and destroyed anything they could not. The only tangible legacy of the Knights remaining in Seborga today being the small stone church, which they built, and some strange rock carvings in the surrounding hills. They were also a highly secretive society and virtually no documentation about their time survives. However, the scope of their influence can still be found in iconography from Cyprus through Corsica, across France, Spain, Portugal, the UK and Ireland.

So politically and commercially insignificant was this tiny patch of rocky land, running from a mountaintop almost to the sea, that for the next six hundred years it was largely forgotten. When Italy became unified as a single country in the mid-nineteenth century, all its other independent states were brought together to form a single nation. Seborga was, notably, left out of all the documentation. Its independent status had been ignored for so long that it had faded from the memories of administrators in Rome. It was, therefore, not named at all in the unification treaty and it was blindly enveloped in a map covering its neighbouring states.

Consequently, Rome claimed it was included in the unification by default. Some argue that, legally, this is a dubious assertion. After that, the ancient Seborgan Principality continued to be mentioned only in the stories of the older people who lived there. Although there is no evidence of its existence, Claudio and his citizens still believe that written proof of Seborgan independence still lay in the Vatican's vaults in Rome and it was just not in the Church's interest to reveal it.

Ben thanked the knowledgeable barman for this history lesson and his invaluable insights into the local politics. He went to put his hand in his pocket to pay, but Valerio waved him away saying:

"Tonight, you are my guest. If you succeed in bringing the tourists, you can drink Rossese wine on the house from morning until night."

With a lot to think about, including finding out why Rossese wine was so prized here, Ben left to keep his appointment with the prince. Armed with a much greater understanding of the situation, he felt better prepared for whatever was ahead.

In the main square, Piazza Santa Maria, Claudio was waiting surrounded by what appeared to be his inner circle of Seborgan courtiers. These were mainly old, exclusively male and were all the colour of polished briar. Ben assumed, wrongly it turned out, that the remainder of the substantial crowd must be the good citizens of Seborga. Upwards of fifty middle-aged couples sat under the broad canopy of a bar. There were as many again spilling out onto the well-worn stone steps around the fountain. Younger single people were using their scooters and parked Apes as temporary seating. Hundreds more sat at trestle tables and benches which had been set up in lines across the piazza since he had walked through it just a few hours ago. The whole place was buzzing with people.

A few of the men were still in working clothes and looked like they had come straight from their olive groves or their Ortos. The remainder were in the Riviera equivalent of their Sunday best: men mainly in shorts or chinos in an extraordinary selection of rainbow colours. Younger men wore jeans and t-shirts with slogans, oddly, mostly written in English. Branded sunglasses, or at least fake copies, seemed obligatory. Young girls wore the same only with tighter jeans cut-off at a barely decent length. One or two exhibited tattoos that must have been the cause of many a blazing row in their traditional Catholic families.

It was the affluent-looking mature couples, now arriving in the piazza in a steady stream, which took Ben by surprise. These, it transpired, were mainly French citizens who had made the short journey over the border. Women's bosoms were bulging out of revealing tops and buttocks were squeezed into skin-tight skirts. Several teetered on heels so tall and thin, that in profile they looked like ten-pin bowling pins balanced on golf tees. The fabrics they wore were of the type rarely seen outside of Abba reunions, Pride marches, or ballroom dancing competitions. Both men and women sported a lot of overly coiffured hair with barely a strand out of place. Everyone had tried very hard to look what they thought was their best. Individually, any one of them would have stood out like a beacon in a provincial English town. Collectively the effect was a bit overwhelming to Ben: a kind of human kaleidoscope. It would have been a surreal spectacle in most places but here in Seborga, Ben thought, it seemed somehow strangely in keeping with a place which somehow seemed other-worldly.

Everyone had a drink of some type but, Ben noted, nobody looked drunk or even remotely tipsy. Just happy. The smell of meat cooking on an open fire wafted through the air and mingled with the designer perfumes and aftershave. Closer examination of the scene revealed a row of smoking BBQs. These had been set up at the very outer edge of the piazza, where it ended in a wall that appeared to drop vertically into the valley below. Smoke rose from them steadily while attendants rushed about with various knives, skewers and tongs. Flames flared-up periodically as melting fat dripped into the hot coals.

Despite the assembled crowd's bold attire, Claudio, Vincenzo and his father, Gianni, still managed to stand out, even from this colourful bunch. Prince Claudio sported a blue serge collarless jacket with gold buttons and a bright red silk sash, sweeping from his shoulder to his waist, from which hung a glistening short sword in a sheath. It had a gold hilt with a white tassel hanging from it. He had combed his hair, which was now slicked back on his head, and his beard was neatly trimmed. He suddenly cut quite the dashing figure, despite the battered working boots poking out from his white trousers with their cavalry-style side stripes. His gold-braided white military cap lay on the table in front him with his white gloves and what looked like the same half-empty wine glass from earlier in the day.

Vincenzo and Gianni flanked him in matching white berets, blue overall-style uniforms with white leather belts and shoulder straps with gun holsters. Ben was later relieved to discover that the holsters contained nothing more dangerous than a Zippo lighter and some roll-your-own cigarettes.

As strange as this scene was, Ben could not help thinking they looked impressive sitting there looking deadly serious. As he approached, all three arose while Vincenzo and Gianni stood to attention, clicked their heels and saluted with a flamboyant flick of the wrist. The men's uniforms were of Savoy blue; the distinctive colour of the Italian national football and rugby teams. This choice linked them back to the Dukes of Savoy who owned much of Northern Italy, Nice, and the islands of Sardinia and Corsica in the period after the Templars.

Savoys also annexed Menton from Monaco, 'forgot' to give it back and then later handed it over to the French in a deal. Had they not annexed this land, Monaco would now be almost ten times larger than it is today.

Silence descended on the piazza and Claudio began, "We, the proud peoples of Seborga, welcome you Professore Bi-en," began Claudio's speech in well-rehearsed English.

After which, he continued in Italian to the effect that Ben was the foremost expert in his field and had come from one of England's oldest and most respected universities. He was going to restore good fortune to the Principality by bringing wealthy tourists flooding into the shops, bars and restaurants. As he listened, Ben had a growing realisation that he was going to be expected to respond to this introduction and welcome with some type of speech.

So far, few of the citizens he had met spoke anything more than a few words of English and so this was a daunting prospect. He did, however, have a schoolboy grasp of Latin, from which he believed many Italian words must originate. He reasoned that a couple of short quotes might be well enough understood to make the right impression and underline his academic standing. However, it had been thirty five years since his last Latin lesson and to say he was rusty, was an understatement. Claudio wound up his welcome with a few 'benvenutos' to a big cheer from the crowd and all eyes then fixed on Ben.

From teaching, Ben knew that it was essential to get the audience engaged at the outset and there was nothing like a short silence while making direct eye contact with all present to achieve this. As he scanned the crowd smiling, he saw a striking female face staring straight back at him, unsmiling. She was leaning against the wall of one of the alleys leading out of the piazza wearing what looked like a smirk. He held her gaze because this was a look of such disdain that he thought at any moment she might spit on the ground in contempt. She did not, but turned her back on him with an upwards flick of her head.

With her hair tied back under a bandanna, no make-up and skin reddening from the heat of the grill, it was impossible to judge her age. There was no doubting that expression though, it was not a look of welcome.

With restless feet in the piazza starting to shuffle and people starting to look quizzically at their neighbours, Ben had to say something soon and so opened with, "Vir sapit qui pauca loquitur," (That man is wise who talks little). After a pause to let that sink in, he followed with, "Alea iacta est Ad praesens ova cras pullis sunt meliora." (Eggs today are better than chickens tomorrow) finally raising his voice to finish with, "Amicitiae nostrae memoriam spero sempiternam fore." (I hope that the memory of our friendship will be everlasting).

In reality, none of these words was remotely similar to the Italian translation of what he was trying to communicate. Even if the audience did not understand a single word, many of the older ones at least recognised it as Latin. As the language of the Church, that at least had some gravitas. The others at least knew it was not English and so looked mildly impressed that he had any second language, which most of them did not. After a slightly awkward moment, Claudio applauded vigorously and everyone joined in, some even throwing hats in the air. Ben needed a drink badly—a big one.

Claudio lifted his nearly empty glass in a timely gesture that Ben took to be the question he had been hoping was coming next.

"Si. Vino rosso," which used up about ten per cent of Ben's Italian vocabulary.

The order was communicated, apparently telepathically, to the bar. After what seemed like an eternity, but was probably only minutes, a drink arrived. It was a small glass by his usual standards but full to the brim with a slightly pale red wine, which Ben raised to his hosts and then drank with relish.

The flavour was, at first, like the colour, soft and subdued like a Pinot Noir. On second tasting, it had more complexity and something quite earthy in the background. It turned out to be Rossese di Dolceacqua, Rossese being a grape almost unique to this region and Dolceacqua being a village in the next valley, where the best wine made with the grape originates.

This wine variety is much prized in the north and is known for its quality throughout Italy but almost unheard of outside of the country. He was told that centuries ago the monks used to make a white Rossese for their own consumption. This practice died out when they left. The main thing for Ben was that it was alcohol, and, after his speech, he felt he needed its stimulus. It did not, however, seem particularly strong. It was nevertheless very welcome. The first small glass disappeared in no time and a second duly arrived without asking. His conversation was limited to 'grazie' for more small plates of aperitivo that kept appearing in front of him and greeting those being introduced to him with a 'ciao.' All enquiries about the quality of the food he answered with 'bellissimo,' which seemed to be the correct response.

After the third glass of wine, Ben was feeling much more composed but was desperate for meaningful communication in English. He turned to Claudio, gestured to the crowd around, and asked,

"Does anyone here speak English?"

Claudio rose with a cheerful, "Si, si," and then disappeared across the piazza now thronged with people eating and drinking.

While he was away, the fourth plate of food arrived on their table. They had already been through half a dozen small sandwiches, the filling of which was unclear to Ben but, nevertheless, were delicious. Then slices of what he took to be a Parma ham but later learned that, although it was produced using the same technique, had its origin much closer geographically. It was darker in colour with a broad band of slightly yellow fat. Served with this was a plate of dark pink chewy salami containing highly piquant grains, which he took to be pepper of some type.

Then came slices of a kind of vegetable pie made with a soft, thin pastry. Ben's favourite was another, even thinner, pie served hot and containing a melted mild cheese filling. Valerio would later instruct him that it was known locally as Focaccia di Recco al Formaggio. The appearance of the thin pastry was more like filo than the bread suggested in the name. Several pieces of this had slipped down nicely and gone some way to soak up the wine. Claudio re-appeared, making his way back through the crowd, holding the hand of a woman who appeared to be being pulled along reluctantly, like a naughty child about to be scolded. This was the strange woman he had seen staring back at him so intently earlier.

As she drew closer, Ben could see that her face was very flushed. Her skin had also been splattered with oil and something even red. Blood? She also now looked even more furious, presumably at being interrupted from her task and hauled in front of this stranger. Several strands had loosened from her tied-back hair and these hung limply in her eyes. She tried to brush them away with her spare hand, but they immediately fell back again. She wore an off-white apron, so splattered with blood that she could have worked in an abattoir. On her feet were those slip-on plastic shoes so favoured by twenty-first century hippies and Champagne-socialists: Crocs or some such thing. He hated them and usually also the people who wore them.

Penetrating ink-dark eyes peered out from below luxurious eyebrows set high on her forehead. But what eyes! There was something quite intoxicating about them. Ben thought she was the polar opposite of all the other women in the piazza. No attempt had been made to impress or attract anyone: this 'lily' remained entirely un-gilded. She looked simultaneously terrifying and strangely attractive to Ben, although he could not put his finger on exactly why.

Claudio almost dragged the woman before Ben and, with a flourish of his arm, let go of her hand in what seemed like a well-practised action from her childhood. Looking at her sternly, he announced,

"Dottore Bi-en lasciami presentarti Principessa di Seborga."

"Princess Alessandra Margherita Maria Biancheri of Seborga," Vincenzo quickly translated but also adding her full name for even greater effect.

Ben was on his feet quickly but was unsure whether to proffer his hand, lean in for French-style air kisses, or bow. Instead, he just blurted out,

"Princess?" involuntarily half laughing, as though that was such a preposterous statement.

He looked at Vincenzo, seeking a second opinion or an explanation that this was some type of joke. But the big quiet Italian was just nodding sagely as if to say, 'Yes. It's true. Although she may not look like it, she really is a princess.'

Before he could collect his thoughts, she spoke in perfect English but with a strange New York/Italian accent,

"If we are questioning credentials, I am more of a princess than you are a doctor." Her response came with a venom he was not expecting. "I checked out your CV online, and you have not yet finished your professional doctorate and so are not entitled to call yourself a doctor."

Ben was later to learn that Italy remains a hierarchical society where titles are important and highly respected. He was also to learn that, unlike the UK the title doctor, or 'dottore' as they say in Italy, is in fact used for any professional person with a university degree such as an architect or lawyer. Even schoolteachers without a degree are usually referred to as professore, and so it would be quite reasonable for an Italian lecturer to be referred to as 'dottore'. She already knew this but guessed, correctly, that he did not and so used it as a weapon. The inference that he was both a liar and a boaster struck home and stung, as it was surely meant to.

Ben was not expecting this highly confrontational encounter and was reeling from what he saw as an unprovoked put-down. Claudio looked puzzled, as he apparently did not entirely understand what was going on between his daughter and his guest but sensed something was wrong. Vincenzo, however, wore a knowing smile. Alessandra deftly snatched a beer from the tray of a passing waiter, seated herself in his chair and downed half of the bottle. Swallowing hard and catching her breath she looked up at Ben, who was still standing, and then continued her verbal assault.

"Let us get a few things straight here. I'm a New Yorker, and I really do not like the outdated English old-school system that you represent. You look like a character out of a Somerset Maugham novel and doubtless have about as much depth. I did not choose my title, and my father is really the only one who ever uses it. What is more, although I don't flaunt my title, I am at least entitled to it. You absolutely should not call yourself a doctor because it is at best misleading and at worst a downright lie."

Barely pausing for breath, she continued the attack, "I can see you are so conceited you also believe that these people have all turned out to see the grand English professor and hear your pathetic speech in public-schoolboy Latin. Well, you are wrong. Tonight is a festival to celebrate the arrival of summer. Most of these people have come up from the coast for the food and don't have a clue who you are or what you are saying. Many even drive here from France as we serve the best traditional food in Liguria.

So, Mr Ben, better a fresh, organic, Ligurian egg today than any of your plastic, factory-farmed English chickens at any time in my lifetime, you pompous English fool. I would advise that you go home before you start getting withdrawal symptoms from a lack of tea and processed food which has been fried in animal fat."

The adrenaline that automatically kicks in when anyone is attacked was now surging through Ben and, mixed with the alcohol, was generating anger he had not felt in a long time. Now seething and red-faced himself, he responded:

"Listen, Princess—as unsuitable a title as that is for someone who looks like a roadside café cook—I have never referred to myself as doctor in word or in writing."

He gestured to Claudio with his hand and added, "Your father and his friends have been calling me that since I arrived and I have an insufficient grasp of Italian to correct them. You will doubtless be happy to correct that for me?"

He went on:

"I have no idea why you think you are entitled to be rude, aggressive and arrogant with one of your father's guests. A spoiled and over-indulged princess behaving like a prima donna is a bit of a cliché, and yet here you are large as life? Living in America will have provided the final nail in the coffin of your good manners."

At this point, Alessandra decided she had heard enough. She had made her point, and so drained the remainder of the bottle of beer. Rising from her chair, she strode back across the piazza towards the braziers where she and her neighbours were still cooking meat.

As she made her way, Ben was not the only man who noticed a certain confident sway in her walk. Even beneath the formless chef's trousers and apron, it was clear to Ben there lay a very trim but womanly profile. Some of the groups of men stood around chatting were nodding towards her, smiling and appearing to comment amongst themselves. With another flick of her hair back over her head, she took up a long, two-pronged fork and stabbed a large chunk of raw meat. She tossed this onto the brazier with such force that the metal grill bounced up from the base, causing a huge flare of flame to rise up into the night sky. Smaller flames continued to spurt upwards, and sweet, meaty smells wafted around the assembled party-goers.

Although few of the citizens had understood the heated dialogue that had passed between the Englishman and their Princess, none were left in any doubt about the animosity it contained.

The flimsy paper plate suddenly thrust in front of Ben was barely able to support the chunks of chargrilled meat that had been piled upon it. Ben thought that it smelled divine and his thoughts turned to more pleasant things. Another plate arrived filled with skinny golden potato chips.

"Bistecca di manzo Piedmontese—il meglio," said Prince Claudio.

Ben turned toward Vincenzo looking blank.

"The best beef steak brought from Piedmont," he translated, pointing vaguely over his shoulder towards the mountains.

Ben was not at all sure how much English Vincenzo understood. Increasingly, he thought, more than he let on. A third plate arrived with some chunks of soft chewy bread, and the unpretentious dinner was served. Everyone else was already eating and Ben joined them, taking the knife and fork from the rolled-up paper napkin he had been given. He noted that most of the older men used their personal pocket-knives to cut off chunks of the beef, wiping them clean on a paper napkin afterwards and returning them to their trousers.

He had been ushered to one of the dozens of trestle tables in the centre of the piazza and given a space on a bench between the prince and Vincenzo. The tables had been spread with paper tablecloths and scattered with sachets of ketchup and mayonnaise. Around them sat what looked like the same men who had been under the canopy, as if they were a group of the prince's courtiers perhaps with some special status. But there was no distinction between the prince's table and all the others. No linen tablecloth. No candelabra, or silver cutlery. This barbecue was not the royal banquet he had imagined to be his first meal in the Principality. This was apparently an egalitarian monarch; Claudio was literally a man of his people.

Every other seat at all the other benches were taken. Couples and entire families were laughing, eating and drinking. Ben looked up at the balconies above where the washing had been taken down: sheets and underwear replaced with the blue and white flags of Seborga. He had noticed nearly every house had a Seborgan flag, but he had yet to see a single Italian one. The temperature was still in the mid-twenties at 10pm. There was not much wind and so the flags hung straight down. Smoke from the cooking spiralled up through the flags and the purple bougainvillaea growing around the houses. The black night sky was now scattered with bright stars, clearer than any other he had ever seen, and the moon cast a silver swathe across the sea down below. The light of the moon silhouetted the ridges of the higher mountains further up the valley, which appeared to be shades of blue and purple. Ben thought the place was possibly even more beautiful by night than it had been during the day.

"This is the best steak I have ever tasted," Ben directed at Prince Claudio, but loud enough so Vincenzo could also hear.

He thought he detected a smile from Vincenzo who, it seemed, understood him perfectly. Speaking with his mouth full, Vincenzo answered,

"Si. Of course, it is. You are English. This is Italian beef," he said dismissively as if he was the only person in the world not to know the difference.

He then said something in Italian to the remainder of the table which had them raising glasses towards Ben with a chorus of, 'Si. Si's and molto bene's.'

Feeling that he was now saying the right things to please his audience, Ben pushed on by asking,

"Vincenzo, why exactly is this steak so delicious?"

Vincenzo smiled, only for the second time since they'd met.

"It's meat from a woman," was the response.

Now laughing out loud, he half-stood, first clutching one cheek of his bottom and then his left rib cage in his enormous spare hand.

"The steaks are only from the asses and chests of female animals. No bulls. That is why they are more... tender. That is why they taste good too."

Understanding from the gesture what he was telling Ben, the remainder of the table now joined in with the laughter. Finally getting the joke, Ben joined in and it felt as though an invisible barrier of formality had been dismantled. Ben started making mental notes of the things he was learning about the food and culture of the area, which he would write up later in his log. If he were at least to try and come up with an economic plan, he had better look like he had done some actual research, he rationalised.

While Vincenzo was in such a good mood and spoke sufficient English, this seemed as though it was a good time to ask him, "What is the problem with the princess? Why is she so angry?"

The previously surly Italian continued chewing on his steak and washing it down with swigs of wine, apparently considering his response carefully. Characteristically economical with words he answered,

"She thinks your work will change everything."

Ben looked surprised.

"I thought change was what everyone wanted?"

After a little more chewing, Vincenzo said, "Almost everyone but her. She has had enough change in her life. Now she wants things as they used to be."

At which Vincenzo rose swiftly from the table, squishing his paper plate into a ball and tossing it into the nearby bin, before striding away and disappearing into the crowd around the fountain. That short conversation was over, but Ben was not much wiser for it.

Vincenzo's parting comment about Alessandra wanting things to remain the same brought to Ben's mind a quote he used in 'Change Management' lectures. Over a century ago, the philosopher G.K. Chesterton said, 'If you leave a thing alone you leave it in a torrent of change.' That would certainly be the case with Seborga, he concluded. Although it had so far remained largely untouched by the pressures of the twenty-first century, that could not continue. The 'enemy' was already at the gate, and the Seborgans simply had nothing to fight with. As capable as they may be, Vincenzo and his cousins could not defend against the overwhelming economic forces of globalisation raged against them.

Still Prince Claudio kept topping up Ben's glass with the Rossese, which he realised he was now starting to like very much. It was a quaffing wine, he thought to himself. The steak had been amazing but, after what must have been four servings of aperitivo, he was now completely and utterly full to bursting. He also felt completely relaxed for the first time since the fateful night at the pub in Newcastle that nearly ended his career.

A horribly out-of-tune band had struck-up somewhere out of sight, consisting mainly of brass instruments but with an electric rhythm section. What they lacked in musical talent, they more than made up for with enthusiasm. Dancing had spontaneously broken out in several parts of the piazza and what dancing it was. There was a mixture of formal ballroom and a kind of western line dancing. The most flamboyantly dressed couples were, inevitably, also the most exuberant dancers.

Valerio suddenly appeared at his shoulder and thrust his hand at him again.

"Professore, I would like you meet my girlfriend, Abelie. She is studying economics in Milan and she wanted to meet you."

Standing, Ben took her extended hand and, instead of shaking it, brought it to his lips and kissed it gently.

"The pleasure is mine, signorina. Abelie, what a beautiful name."

Although it was the wine talking, it seemed to do the trick because she smiled demurely and blushed. Valerio laughed, and apparently assuming no threat from the ageing academic, suggested that Abelie take Ben to dance. Although any movement was uncomfortable with such a full stomach, he could not resist the beautiful young student tugging his hand towards the centre of the piazza.

She was rhythmic, stylish and fluid. Ben was animated and theatrical but shambolic. He thought himself rakish and dashing. No one else apparently noticed or cared. As he swivelled around in a flourish of rhythmic enthusiasm, his eyes met those of his nemesis from earlier. The princess now wore her hair down and had at least wiped her face clean. She was dancing with a group of people of mixed ages and genders—her fellow cooks. The apron and the headband had gone, but she had not applied any make-up or combed her hair. Nevertheless, Ben could see that she was a beautiful woman from any angle, whose age, he felt, was difficult to determine.

Children of all ages ran in and out of the swaying dancers, sometimes followed by dogs and an occasional mother or grandmother trying to keep an eye on the tiny ones. Ben was struck by how the different generations all seemed happy to mingle and how relaxed the parents were about their children wandering freely while they joined in the dancing. Stranger after stranger greeted him with a smile and a "Buonasera", to which he had now learned to respond in kind. Another word added to his still limited Italian vocabulary.

The music changed to a strange Germanic oompah band tune, and Abelie was joined by one of her friends plus Valerio. Ben's dancing was becoming more extravagant as the wine entirely removed any remaining inhibitions. Suddenly he felt a shove in his lower back and the next thing, he was prostrate on the stone floor. Struggling to regain his feet and his composure and wondering what exactly had happened, he realised that Princess Alessandra was standing above him looking distressed.

"I am sorry," she was repeatedly saying. And then added, "Are you OK? Did you bang your head?"

Ben sat up on the stone slabs, feeling his head with his right hand. He had bumped his temple on the stone floor. It was grazed and a small trickle of blood had appeared.

"I'm fine. What happened?"

Trying to stand up, several hands, including those of the princess, reached down to offer support. The band played on and only those in the immediate vicinity had stopped dancing. Back on his feet but slightly wobbly, he was led to a nearby bench where he sat down. The Princess was still alternately asking if he was okay and then saying she was sorry. She looked genuinely concerned, he thought, with all the earlier animosity apparently having disappeared.

"I bumped into you dancing," she said, "it was only a slight nudge, but you just toppled over."

Beginning to realise what he thought might have happened, Ben grasped the opportunity, he touched the graze on his head and winced at the contact. The Princess grimaced in sympathy, as though she was also feeling the pain.

"I am feeling a little dizzy. Perhaps a seat inside and a brandy would help me recover," he said nodding towards the Osteria door.

She placed her arm under his elbow and steered him inside, still apologising.

"I doubt we will have any Cognac but would a Gappa help?" she said over her shoulder, leaving him seated while she headed for the bar.

The Princess was now feeling a great deal of remorse at the gentle shove which she had given Ben when she thought he had danced too close to her. She knew several people had seen her do it and so was also feeling childish and more than a bit embarrassed. When she returned with a glass of Gappa, full to the brim, Ben said,

"I am sorry, I caught your grand title but not your actual name. How should I address you?"

"Alessandra. I am plain Alessandra."

Ben smiled.

"I doubt anyone has ever referred to you as plain," he said, "but Alessandra is certainly a lot easier to remember than your full title."

Although uncertain whether he was flirting or teasing, she smiled, giving him the benefit of the doubt for now. She had helped herself to a Gappa and now offered a "Salute".

After the initial shock of the strong alcohol, the warmth hit home. Now that she could see he was not severely hurt and he was not going to make an issue out of it, they both relaxed somewhat.

"After you have finished that, I should walk you home."

He almost choked on his drink, then laughed out loud.

"Surely that is supposed to be my line. You are certainly the most forward princess I have ever met."

Now laughing at the realisation of how that sounded, she said,

“Please drop the princess thing. OK? You can see that no one here uses it. It’s a meaningless title. You have had a bang on the head and you are our guest, so we live in the same house. We will walk home together. No arguments.”

Ben realised what a relief it was to speak to someone in English. Alessandra smiled again as if she had just rediscovered the sensation after a long abstention. ‘What was it about this woman?’ he pondered. When he studied her carefully, he recognised that she was a melange of all the women he had ever admired or desired. She had the figure of his wife when they first met, the nose and cheekbones of his favourite ballet dancer, the luxurious hair of his first teenage love, and finally, that smile; the Julia Roberts-like smile, spreading out gradually until the corners of her mouth almost met her earlobes. The only thing that jarred slightly was that strange Italian/New York accent. But, like a good Bordeaux, she combined many different facets into something that was much greater than the sum of its constituent parts.

Valerio and Abelie popped into the bar to check that Ben was okay and, when it was clear that he was, said their goodnights. Alessandra again looked embarrassed, knowing that they both saw the shove. They made small talk while finishing their drinks, agreeing what a charming young couple Valerio and Abelie were.

“Young people like them, who have lived here all their lives, are still largely untouched by the cynicism and greed of the world we both know. They’d be eaten alive in New York,” suggested Alessandra.

“So, they’re a bit like Adam and Eve–” Ben interrupted, “–and this is the Garden of Eden?”

“I guess,” she laughed.

“It certainly seems like it to me,” he concluded.

He raised his glass containing the last sip of Gappa and offered a toast.

"Here's to keeping the serpents out of Eden."

As they left the Osteria, the festa was still going strong in the piazza and the band was still playing slightly out of tune. Prince Claudio had retired an hour ago and thankfully, before seeing Ben's fall. Only one person noticed them leave. Vincenzo was on the opposite side of the piazza, some one hundred metres away, but he still saw Alessandra's arm under Ben's and the faint smile that she was now wearing.

Approach to Seborga

Drawing by Linda McCluskey

5. FOCACCIA

At around eight in the morning, the delicious smell of freshly baked bread creeping through the shutters finally encouraged Ben to throw off the thin cotton sheet, get showered and dressed. Baking bread has the draw of a powerful magnet in most cultures, but this was different to any English, or even French, bakery smell because of the herbs and spices that he detected in the air. Rosemary and cinnamon were just two he could identify, but there was also something else. Sweet onion?

He was a light sleeper and so had been roused first by the cockerel at about five thirty, again by raised Italian voices below at six thirty, and then the church bells started at seven in the morning. He later learned that he was lucky to be discovering this place in the twenty-first century because, up until about thirty years ago, the bells chimed throughout the night every fifteen minutes. Only in recent years had an eight-hour amnesty been negotiated between 11pm and 7am. These were not just ordinary church bells, chiming one for each hour. This was merely the precursor to the cacophony to follow. After the 7am and 11pm chimes, there was a demonstration of the bell automaton's art which consisted of an unfamiliar tune chimed at an impossibly rapid tempo using several smaller bells.

The church bells of towns and villages in Italy were more than just an ancient way to tell the time and call the devout to prayer. Their loudness and the sophistication of their chimes was a statement of the community's wealth and prestige, as well as its devotion. Villages tried to out-do each other in the length and complexity of the tunes. Seborga's were modest compared to some nearer the sea. In valleys where several could often be heard at once from any one point, the chaotic music competition can last for up to five minutes every hour. Some villages even deliberately ignored the actual time to make their bells chime before those of their neighbours.

After dressing, Ben opened the windows and threw back the outer shutters letting the morning sun rush in. Not sure if the temporary blindness was last night's wine, the knock on the head, or the astonishing brightness, he half closed his eyes again to reduce the glare. Everything in this place seemed visually so much more intense. Colours were bolder, skies bluer, mountain-sides greener—he rationalised that it was at least partly the result of the altitude – that, and the lack of air pollution. Whatever it was, the scene that greeted him captivated the Englishman's heart and held him there for several minutes just staring out at the valley before a familiar voice below snapped him back to reality. That strange slightly Italian but very American accent speaking near-perfect English was unmistakable.

"Breakfast is at the Osteria in the piazza."

Focaccia is prepared on large flat trays and dimpled with deft fingers by the bakers to create the familiar cratered surface. The dough is then liberally smeared with olive oil and scattered with sea salt then optionally: rosemary, olives, onions or even anchovies. The craters hold the oils and flavouring and allow them to soak slowly into the bread. Shortly after arriving and taking a seat outside, Ben was presented with a plate containing nothing more than a slice of the classic version of focaccia and a tiny cup of espresso. Alessandra offered a brief "Buon giorno" but nothing more and Ben thought that some of the hostility from earlier last night had apparently returned with the dawn.

"Could I?" Ben tried to ask for more hot water with which to transform his espresso into a more palatable Americano but was either just too slow to catch her, or she was deliberately ignoring him.

The pale-yellow crust of the focaccia looked unappetising, especially since it was speckled with large crystals of what looked like sea salt. On his regular summer trips to France, one of Ben's many treats to himself was to start the day with a pain au raisin and a café allonge. A childhood abhorrence of school porridge had fuelled an indulgence in sweet things in the mornings.

Neither Alessandra nor anyone else came to ask if he wanted anything more to accompany the bread and no one could be seen moving about inside. The Osteria appeared deserted but for him. Taking a sip of the coffee, he winced at the strength and bitterness. He tore off a piece of the bread to counter the strong coffee and was firstly surprised at just how elastic it was. The olive oil in the dough, finger-thickness, and dimpled surface, gave it a different consistency. The initial saltiness of the yellow outer skin was subdued by the light sweetness of the white inner. Like popcorn, it was a sweet/sour combination that worked. He took another large bite and tried sipping a bit more coffee. If the bread was improving with tasting, then the espresso was not.

Rising and taking the cup with him, he made his way into the darkened interior. Inside there was still no one to be found. At that moment, he was startled by the door bursting open behind him, as though it had been kicked hard by a large boot. The glass rattled inside the old wooden frame as the door was caught by the heel that opened it and flicked deftly closed again.

"Professore. Buongiorno," Claudio said with a huge smile.

"Café Alessandra" was his next utterance but much louder this time.

"Si Papa" came a reply from somewhere in the distant shadows.

Gone was the elegant blue uniform, white sash and peaked hat. Claudio was now dressed in the same indigo work-wear he had been wearing when Ben arrived from the airport. He was struggling to come to terms with this dual persona. It was almost as though the prince and Claudio were two different people. The old man gestured towards a table to the right of the door, inviting Ben to join him there. The ageing prince continued for some time speaking to Ben in Italian until Alessandra appeared with his espresso. He turned to Ben,

"Un altro café, Professore. Another coffee?" he translated as an afterthought.

Ben nodded vigorously, and asked Alessandra for a 'big' coffee.

"A weak English coffee with milk, I'm guessing?" she said contemptuously.

"Just black, but yes, much bigger, like a large French café allonge," recognising the frost had returned to her voice and trying to demonstrate that he was not completely untravelled. Adding at the last minute, "And, if there's another slice of that delicious bread?"

She turned and looked over her shoulder, as though she were looking for signs of sarcasm about her focaccia. There were none that she could determine, only Ben's lightly grazed face with a hopeful expression staring back at her. Her guilt feelings returned but she also appeared puzzled, as though she was experiencing another sensation concerning the Englishman that she could not quite put her finger on: A fondness for his vulnerability and English correctness?

After a few minutes, Alessandra returned with coffee and another plate of focaccia. Three pieces this time, the same plain version, one covered in sweet white onion baked with the bread and another with small Taggiasca olives embedded in it.

These almost-exclusively-Ligurian olives are noticeably different from those usually found in France, Italy or most of the areas of the Mediterranean. They enjoy the sparse calcareous soil of the Riviera and thrive in the variable climate of the foothills of the Maritime Alps, which imbues them with low acidity. Much smaller than most varieties: the fruit of a single tree will often be irregular in colour; ranging from traditional olive green, through a spectrum of browns, to almost black. They have a mild but distinctive flavour quite unlike their larger cousins and are consistently sweeter and less bitter than others. These olives are a key constituent of so many Ligurian dishes, it is easily possible to find yourself eating them at breakfast, lunch and dinner.

It is widely believed that it was the St. Columban monks from nearby Lerins Island who first brought these olives to the monastery of nearby Taggia on the mainland—hence the name Taggiasca in Italian. However, the introduction of this new variety of olive also coincided with the Templars arrival in Seborga, leading some to claim it was they who brought them from the Holy Land. Others believe the plants were first carried from Tuscany, from where the Benedictine monks originated. Whatever the truth, they have been an integral part of Ligurian life for a thousand years, being used for medicine, washing (still today, as olive oil soap), beautification, heating fuel, light, cooking, preserving food and just eating.

Claudio held back another chair and gestured for Alessandra to join them. Ben was to be there for at least six months and yet, less than twenty-four hours since his arrival, he was about to have his induction tour. It appeared that they intend to get their pound of flesh for their bed, food and wine. Alessandra translated while Claudio told his version of the story of Seborga. He barely paused for breath while he gave a condensed history of the Principality, its current perilous economic situation, as well as justifying his claims for statehood. He argued that the only hope for them was the recognition of independence, which would bring cash streaming into the Principality from foreign investors.

Ben thought Claudio's assumptions about investors were flawed but said nothing. He listened carefully while eating his way through all three types of focaccia. Occasional nodding and making 'mmm' noises with his mouth full to acknowledge his understanding of key points. Some of what he was being told seemed contradictory, and he had the impression that Alessandra was not merely translating what her father was telling her. It sounded as if she was adding her own analysis and conclusions of the situation, which were sometimes at odds with his. He was not at all sure what was going on here. It was all fascinating but also somewhat baffling, he concluded.

Ben's summary of what he understood the prince was expecting him to do was to find some way of attracting inward investment now, based on the gamble or expectation that independence would eventually come. It was clear that Claudio did not understand how investors work. They are not gamblers, Ben thought to himself, at least not the high-risk type found at the casinos down on the coast. Without some hard evidence that there existed a clearly mapped-out, short-term, high-rate return and a medium-term exit plan, Claudio would have more luck throwing coins in the village fountain and making a wish. His concerns about the economy were undoubtedly justified though, Ben reasoned, an alternative strategy was badly needed.

Although the citizens of Seborga had survived for hundreds of years as subsistence farmers, this was not a sustainable economic model in Europe at the dawn of the twenty-first century. Something needed to change radically or their lifestyle, and the unique culture created by it, would be lost. The village would be abandoned to its fate: most likely as holiday homes for wealthy foreigners with the surrounding agricultural land being returned to nature. After all, this had been the fate of so many other rural communities in Italy. Parts of rural Tuscany have been bought up by so many British that it is often, only half-jokingly, referred to as 'Chiantishire'.

Ben did not share his thoughts but merely nodded sagely. Now determined to stretch out his stay here as long as possible, he told them he would need at least a month to assess the scope of the task at hand. Then he would devise an outline plan with which to progress. The meeting lasted about an hour and ended with the offer of a glass of wine from Claudio. It was 9.30am—too early even for Ben. Claudio said something to his daughter in Italian and then she stated that he should return here in the morning if he wanted a guided tour of the village.

Returning to his room, Ben spent the morning setting up his laptop with the mobile Wi-Fi dongle he had brought with him. There was, as yet, no broadband Wi-Fi in the Principality. This took longer than it should but eventually worked after a re-boot of his laptop. When Google's geolocation system pinpointed where he was logging on-line from, a helpful message popped up saying 'Traffic in your area is slower than usual.' Ben looked out of the window and the only traffic in sight was an old Lambretta scooter struggling up the hill, burdened not only by its overweight rider, but also the two bags of cement carried at his feet. He realised the only major roads on which Google could base its assessment of traffic were those down on the coast and so this was its broad generalisation. Nevertheless, he could not help but laugh out loud at this scene, considering the message.

After a brief walk and leisurely lunch of toasted panini and beer in one of the little bars, Ben slept through the afternoon church bells without a problem. Despite his siesta, he was still tired after the stresses of recent weeks, the journey, and the long first night partying. He purposely avoided the Osteria that night. He had a few quiet glasses of wine at Valerio's with the inevitable aperitivo. He was planning an early night to do some research into the mysterious Knights Templar, when he asked the owner, "How did the princess end up back here in Seborga running the Osteria?"

Valerio smiled.

"You don't know that Alessandra was a Michelin-starred chef before she returned to Seborga?"

"What? Her own Michelin Star? Do you mean that she worked for a chef who had one?" said Ben, sounding incredulous.

Valerio confirmed, "Alessandra and her husband had two of the best restaurants in New York for many years before their break-up. She was one of the most famous chefs in America."

"So how has she ended up cooking ten-euro pasta dishes for olive growers in Seborga?"

Valerio started collecting glasses from tables and said, "You must excuse me. I have to clear up because we are closing early tonight."

Ben was left with this extraordinary revelation but with no further explanation. He tried to get to sleep, but a dozen unanswered questions about the perplexing Alessandra were consuming his thoughts. Some on-line research into the mysterious Knights Templar provided the distraction he needed to eventually doze off.

6. PANSOTTI

The name pansotti comes from the Ligurian dialect for a fat belly. No one is sure if that is because that is what this bulging pasta parcel resembles, or if a fat belly is a consequence of eating too many pansotti. As most find they are so irresistible, it could be either. These vaguely triangular pasta parcels have rounded corners and, unusually, in Alessandra's version, the egg-less pasta dough is made with a mixture of water with a dash of Vermentino white wine. These are then stuffed with something she called Preboggion, a name which locals say links back to a Genoese crusader knight. The filling is a mixture of ricotta cheese with various vegetables and herbs, the exact recipe for which varies depending on the geographical location and time of year. Ideally, these should be bitter greens to counter the sweetness of the cheese and pasta.

Ben was about to discover the delights of pansotti, as this was the piatto giorno written on the blackboard propped up outside the Osteria. Under it was written 'alla salsa di nocci'. He guessed that was the sauce but could not translate it to understand the ingredients.

It had been explained to him now that his lodging arrangements included breakfast and dinner, plus a picnic lunch. Wine was included, but his menu choices were not a la carte. It was whatever the dish of the day was at the Osteria, or what Alessandra chose to give him. As his Italian was virtually non-existent and the menu was never in English, this lack of options was a somewhat academic luxury. So keen was he to accept the sabbatical offer that he had, not for an instant, thought of discussing the details of the arrangement. However, even if he had known and considered them less than ideal, it would not have prevented him getting on that plane. He was here: far away from the unpredictable weather, lazy students, a complaining ex-wife and needy children. As it turned out the food was delicious and the wine remarkable as well as, apparently, unlimited. 'What a bonus,' he acknowledged. One of the locals later told him of a popular local expression which translated to 'don't count the years or the glasses of wine', which Ben interpreted as drink more, live longer.

The short stroll to the piazza took him past a shop which had previously been closed when he had passed it. Today its bewildering array of wares were haphazardly spilling out onto the pavement, as was its equally curious proprietor. He greeted Ben with a "Buongiorno" and swept his cigarette-free hand towards the open door in a clear invitation to browse around.

As he passed the proprietor, Ben noted that the smoke from the small stub in his hand smelt like a Glastonbury air freshener; as a marijuana joint had become known when he was at university. The pale-skinned, middle-aged man sported shoulder-length blonde hair and wore a faded cotton paisley pattern shirt and unbuttoned tartan waistcoat with a small bow tie. The eccentric shopkeeper looked Ben up and down like a marine surveyor assessing a yacht for barnacles or leaks. Eventually, he enquired, "English?" and Ben acknowledged that he was with a nod.

The shopkeeper told him that he was Dutch as though this was somehow empathetic both being foreigners in a strange land.

"Call me Rikki," said the Dutchman offering his hand.

Ben shook it and responded simply with "Ben".

Outside the shop were hung large copper pans with the scars and dents of a century or more of cooking. There were piles of crockery and bundles of bone-handled cutlery. Glass demijohns, stone oil jars and a tatty rolled-up rug were propped against the window frame, and a host of wooden-handled implements for the kitchen and garden were strewn around. Inside the window was a couple of tall chests of drawers and, on top of these, various jugs, vases and urns. Commenting that he had not previously seen the shop open, the Dutchman said that a coach party of tourists were due today. I buy from the locals in the villages around here and sell to the tourists, so no point in opening the shop when only the villagers are around.

Wandering inside the gloomy interior was like entering the lair of an ancient culinary kleptomaniac. The contents of Italian kitchens, workshops, and Ortos, going back several generations were crammed into the tiny single room. Following him inside and seeing Ben's surprise, he explained, "Kitchen stuff is what sells best. People from Stockholm to Milan spend tens of thousands of euros on a state-of-the-art kitchen. Then they want a three-hundred-year-old granite sink, an old brass tap and a couple of copper pans to get that Tuscan farmhouse feel. Crazy if you ask me but what can I tell you? I can get five hundred euros for a good stone sink and battered old tap."

Ben picked up a gnarled twist of polished wood inset with a metal corkscrew.

"Grapevine," offered the shopkeeper without being asked, "it's made from a cutting from of grapevine. These corkscrews are from over the border in France, circa 1920s—1930s. Forty euros."

When he put it back down, the shopkeeper offered, "Thirty to you."

Ben did not respond. Seeing an old wine crate in the corner, he was drawn to the inscription on the side of it. 'Rossese di Dolceacqua Superiore' it read. In the spaces where the wine bottles would go were old, rolled-up paper scrolls. He carefully withdrew one. It appeared to be an old property deed in Italian with a plan attached relating to a small piece of land. Another looked like a last will with a list of chattels to be bequeathed. The last one had a crest the same as that on the door to Claudio's house. This was written in Latin script and had been decorated with elaborate coloured scrolls of fleur-di-lis and had a red Templar cross at its centre.

"Ah... yes. Templar Knight stuff sells well of course, but It's all fake. There is an American artist working in the valley who turns them out. She has a stock of old parchment and clever ways of ageing it, using Earl Grey tea and a pizza oven. People then take them home and pass them off as genuine to their friends. Just sixty euros for that one."

It was a fascinating place and he decided to come back another time and explore further. As he made to leave, the Dutchman said,

"OK, fifty euros cash and I'll throw in the corkscrew. But you also owe me a glass of wine if I see you in the Osteria?"

Pleased with his silent non-negotiation Ben peeled off three banknotes, thanked him and arranged to collect the items later. Looking at his wristwatch, it was 9.15am and so he quickly walked the final hundred metres to the piazza.

He had come to meet Alessandra for a tour of the village arranged by her father and to be given some points of reference for exploring on his own later. Tomorrow, Vincenzo would take him on his first tour outside the village. He had been told that he would be shown the olive groves, Ortos and vineyards surrounding the village. These tour instructions were 'decrees' handed down by Claudio, but neither recipient looked thrilled at the prospect.

Well used to exploring the wine-growing areas of France on foot, Ben had arrived suitably equipped with stout boots, shorts, a wide-brimmed hat and a small backpack. At the Osteria, there was no one in sight, and so he went straight inside. The contrast between the white light of the morning sunshine and the back shuttered interior was stark. His eyes took a few seconds of squinting to adjust. He could hear a voice singing quietly in the kitchen behind. It was a contemporary song that he vaguely recognised but could not name. Leaving his pack, hat and sunglasses on a nearby table, he went in search of the singer. In front of a huge old stone sink, he could see Alessandra standing with her back to him.

Her hair was up again but with no bandanna this time. Light streamed in from the windows in front of her, which had a view down the verdant green valley to the impossibly blue sea. She was selecting leaves from several bunches of a green plant that Ben could not identify. These were being rinsed vigorously in a zinc basin and then tossed into a plastic colander to drain.

Music came from a radio somewhere out of sight, and she was sometimes singing and occasionally humming along with the tune. The DJ cut into the closing strains of the song to announce, 'It is going to be another cloudless day with temperatures reaching mid-thirties and so my last tune here on Riviera FM just has to be Bill Withers with Lovely day. This is Mark Michaels signing-off until the usual time tomorrow morning.'

When Ben shouted "Ciao," loud enough to be heard over the blaring radio, she shrieked like an injured spaniel.

"Holy mother—what are you doing creeping up on people like that?"

Ben apologised but sounded unconvincing about the sentiment. He did not believe it was so unusual for anyone to just wander into the kitchen like that. He thought that she was making more of it than was necessary just because it was him.

Turning off the tap and keeping her back to him, she then quickly rolled down the sleeves of her blouse without drying her hands. She was flustered by something which was causing her to panic. The white cotton shirt soon displayed damp patches from the water remaining on her arms. She fumbled with the buttons, making hard work of an otherwise simple task. Finally, turning off the radio, she pointed back to the bar as the direction she wanted them to go in.

"You've come for your induction into Ligurian peasant life?" she said, somewhat sarcastically.

It seemed that whatever it was that had caused their initial confrontation was unresolved. Ben decided it was time to clear the air. He held out a chair for her at the table where he had left his belongings.

"I think we need to talk like grown-ups."

Sensing she did not welcome his presence here, although not entirely sure why, he began with an abridged version of the truth. He told her that he had not wanted to be sent here. The University had pressed him into it because they wanted to claim the not-insubstantial EU research grant that came with the task and he was the only one sufficiently qualified to do it. The prince's offer of free accommodation had sealed it because the University did not even have to pay to rent him a house, or for his daily expenses. As far as his employers were concerned, the outcome of his work was irrelevant so long as he fulfilled the terms of the contract. He had to stay a minimum six months and then produce a report, which probably no one would ever read.

Alessandra listened intently, somewhat surprised by his frankness. On the one hand, she was relieved that he was not especially motivated to fulfil his task with much consciousness. On the other, she was angry at the cynicism of the corrupt European system that had paid to bring him here on the pretence of helping them. Also, because she had to feed him for free when her profit margins were already under pressure.

Sensing he was now saying what she wanted to hear, Ben pressed on to add that he thought their village was beautiful and the people warm and welcoming.

"Well, most of them," he joked.

He would be delighted to spend some time here and help the village in any way he could. If the task for which he had been assigned was unsuitable for the real needs of the citizens, he saw no reason why the scope of the research should not be unofficially widened.

"Provided you don't tell anyone at the European Parliament."

Alessandra looked as though she needed to think about this unexpected development before deciding how to respond.

Looking for signs of deception in his manner or body language, she scrutinised him long and hard, but saw none so said nothing. He, however, thought he detected a chink of light in her demeanour. Alessandra then stood up and took two small plastic bottles of water from the glass-fronted fridge behind her.

"Let's go before it gets too hot."

With that she headed for the door, undoing her apron and dropping it on the bar as they passed by. Ben scrambled to collect his belongings and follow her. Back in the piazza, the temperature was indeed rising, and dogs were seeking shade in the shadows.

"We'll walk and talk," she said.

Striding off into the shade of one of the narrow streets radiating from the piazza, Alessandra began her version of the condensed history of the Principality of Seborga. She explained how the community came to be here on this rocky hilltop, when the best land, the sea, and a kinder climate were all down on the coast. The agricultural bounty of the Riviera's temperate climate was too tempting for all manner of foreign peoples who had mastered the sea. Raided for their olive oil, wine and women by Ostrogoths, Moors and Byzantines, the people eventually moved to higher ground that was easier to defend.

Seborga was, in effect, a large stone fortress inside of which the villagers had created their homes. Perhaps more importantly, it is where they kept their oil, wine, and other provisions in cantinas dug into the rock. These were then safe and cool all year round.

Sometimes the men worked parcels of land too far from the village to walk there and back in one day. On these occasions they would sleep in their Rusticas; the tiny buildings, little bigger than a garden shed, that were dotted all around the hillsides. Here they also kept their tools; shovels, hoes, and nets for collecting the olives.

"They would often have secreted a demijohn of wine in there to help them through the long nights," Alessandra explained. "Some of these shacks have now been extended – usually illegally – and converted into holiday homes."

Ben realised that this explained the hundreds of what looked like tiny stone houses without windows, scattered around the hillsides nowhere near any roads or any other apparent reason for them being there.

Alessandra's first stop was the house where they were both living: her home and his temporary lodgings. Such a labyrinth of corridors was it that he had yet to cross paths with her. The prince's palace was once the heart of the castle, she explained, but gradually it was incorporated into the village by additional building.

"Medieval urban sprawl, you might say."

She described some of the events that had taken place here; coronations, visits by Cardinals from Rome, and princes from France.

* * *

"Prince Rainier brought Grace Kelly here to meet my father before they were married. There's a photograph of them there on the wall."

He was told that legend had it, it had also been the safe house for the precious relics brought back from the Holy Land. But as soon as Ben began to question the specifics of this claim, she turned and walked on without responding.

Ben thought about this for a while and reasoned if this was the point of departure and arrival of knights fighting in the Holy Land, it made perfect sense that this was where they would store and guard anything valuable. Had the Turin Shroud been kept in his bedroom? He speculated only half-jokingly. Although Turin, once the capital of Italy, was just a couple of hours due north of here, this is more or less the nearest point to it on the coast where the Knights ships would have landed. So why not, he concluded?

Ben finally found himself seduced by the notion that there might be something in all the claims made by the people of Seborga. On first hearing these, he had dismissed them as just so much romantic fantasy dreamt up for the tourist business. But the more he learned, the more plausible some of it sounded. They were an enigmatic bunch, he had decided. Sometimes Ben was never sure how seriously the citizens treated the stories themselves.

Although the others all paid lip-service to the Templar tales, only Claudio ever sounded passionate enough to give them any real credence. The other villagers all seemed indifferent, or perhaps they were just weary after a lifetime of the disbelieving looks and the jokes of sceptical outsiders. Ben would later understand that their Italian neighbours on the coast adopted a similar wavering stance on the merits of the independence claims of Seborga. The inclination was to dismiss them as imperious buffoonery, but a lingering doubt prevented them ever articulating such thoughts.

Claudio was treated with due deference by all, but this was at least partly because everyone also liked and respected him. Alessandra had told him that on rare trips into Monaco or Nice, some of the older police officers who recognised Prince Claudio's car, would stand to attention and salute as he passed. Ben pondered the fantastic image of traffic being stopped to allow a care-worn old man riding an antiquated Ape to enter Casino Square in Monte Carlo, lined with white-capped saluting policemen.

Alessandra continued to walk, pointing to other old buildings clearly now converted into homes or shops, but explaining their former role in the nation state—the armoury, blacksmith, mill, Royal Mint.

"The principality had its own currency?" Ben managed to interject this time.

"We still do," came the reply, "it's just that only we recognise it now and so we are forced to use the euro."

The signs of the Knights were everywhere. Their distinctive emblem was carved into pillars displayed on gables and mosaic pavements had been laid with patterns of the Templar cross. How many of these were original and how many were added much later, no one could tell, she cautioned. During the tour, Ben had tried to instigate conversation other than about the history of the village but she steered him away from anything about her personal life. Always she returned to the task at hand, as if she could not wait to get it over with. After an hour and a half, she looked at her watch and said, "I have to get back to the Osteria and prepare pasta." She then turned, waved over her shoulder, and strode off with a brief "Ciao, Ciao".

In the relative cool of the narrow alleys, Ben continued his stroll having lost all sense of direction some time ago. He marvelled at the ostensibly ad-hoc architecture. Occasionally stone arches bridged the gap between the high buildings above them, as though either holding them apart or pulling them together. It was impossible to tell. Sometimes the floor of a house would span the entire divide forming a tunnel underneath – perhaps two families joined by matrimony and needing an extra room he reflected? Alessandra had explained earlier that a lack of access to straight timber joists but the abundance of rock resulted in the almost exclusive use of vaulted stone ceilings. This building technique required strong thick walls and created small low rooms, but at least these remained cool even in the heat of high summer.

The local method of stone walling used larger blocks of random sizes, laid touching where their irregular shapes allowed. Smaller shards of rock were then wedged tightly into the gaps, a method requiring little or no mortar to create a stable structure. The colours of the blocks varied from dark grey to pale sandy browns. A roughly applied lime plaster bonds the stones and provides an internal finish, regularly lime-washed to prevent insect infestation. Although this method is probably thousands of years old, substantially the same technique is still used to this day, although now it is often only a façade to a more substantial inner building conforming to modern regulations.

All the windows were firmly shuttered. These elaborate inventions seemed at first over-complicated with flaps upwards as well as outward. Ben would later learn that this design was the consequence of generations trying to keep out the sun and draw in the breeze, both of which they had achieved very well.

All the houses had copper guttering to catch and carry away rainwater. This seemed to Ben an unnecessarily expensive metal for such a simple, practical task. He would later learn that, once installed, copper would last indefinitely. As an aesthetic bonus, the metal also tarnished to a lovely burnt ochre colour blending perfectly with the stonework.

Eventually Ben emerged into yet another tiny piazza, which was open on one side falling away steeply to the valley below. Here there was a well-worn stone shrine containing a small painted Virgin Mary looking down serenely on some recently picked wild flowers. In this area, shaded by a large tree, Ben paused for lunch on a marble bench next to a trickling fountain. The bench bore a plaque commemorating the role of the partisans in the Second World War and listing names of those who had given their lives in the struggle against the Nazis. Biancheri, Claudio's name, featured on it twice.

Ben opened the neatly wrapped greaseproof paper parcel Alessandra had left him. A small bread loaf with a crusty outer, a small salami sausage, a wedge of hard cheese and a small plastic Tupperware tub containing rich dark tapenade. It could not possibly have been plainer, or more delicious. The quality of the produce and the vista from this makeshift restaurant required no further embellishment. Another hour after lunch exploring churches, shops, and finally, a glass of wine at Valerio's café bar, left him tired and much in need of a nap.

That night the pansotti was preceded by the inevitable aperitivo—black tomatoes, slices of cured ham, and a vegetarian pie of some type (still unidentified). Eventually the bulging pale pasta parcels arrived, which did indeed look like the potbelly of a man who'd enjoyed a lifetime of excess. The sauce was light and creamy with flecks of pale brown. Ben was at this point wondering if he could do full justice to this meal after all that had gone before it. He need not have worried. Ben cut into the pansotti and revealed the pale moist interior, speckled with green. Dipping the forkful in the sauce, he took his first bite. It was the lightest pasta he had ever tasted. The filling was similarly feather-light with all the subtle bitter flavours of the herbs and mild cheese. He could identify perhaps, a hint of fennel, certainly parsley, but there were others he could not. Walnut was the prominent flavour dominating the sauce. It tasted like creamed walnuts into which crunchier bits of nut had been scattered. The entire dish was gone in a blink of an eye, and he was seriously considering an Oliver Twist-like appeal for more.

Alessandra arrived to clear his empty dish, but he prevented her from whisking it away by holding solidly onto one edge.

"Did you make this pasta?" he asked almost accusingly.

"Si," she answered aggressively.

"It is lighter than any pasta I have ever eaten," he offered, "and delicious."

Pausing to absorb the compliment she answered quietly, "Thank you. The pasta dough is my mother's own recipe made with a splash of Vermentino white wine, as well as some water."

Ben went on, "The filling and sauce are also a marriage made in heaven."

Somewhat taken aback by this charm offensive she responded, "Pansotti Ligure con salsa di nocci is a typical dish here. It is cheap and tasty, and all the ingredients come from all around you." She swept her right arm in a gesture to encompass the green hills surrounding them. "We serve it probably once a week. That is why I had to get back before lunch to make pansotti for twenty people by hand."

"Then I will spend the next six days in anticipation of the taste of your pansotti," Ben rounded off the praise.

For a moment, he thought he saw the beginnings of a smile on the edges of her mouth. But she caught herself, spun around with the dish and headed back to the kitchen expertly collecting several other plates and glasses as she went.

Ben managed the panna cotta but could not face the cheese and fruit. He had already drained two small carafes of Rossese when she appeared with limoncello in an ice-frosted bottle with no label.

"Digestivo?" seemed like a directive, especially as she was already pouring it into two glasses.

When full, she took a seat at the table and offered her glass with a "Salute".

The first sip was bittersweet with an after-burn like a fighter jet.

"Phewww," he exhaled.

"This is also my mother's recipe, made with organic lemons from our terraces."

"Well, thank her from me. It's truly sensational."

"My mother died when I was a child," she said, taking a swig of the drink to hide the pain that clearly still lingered in those words; even after all these years.

To try and establish a subject where there was some empathy between them, Ben revealed that his parents also had both been dead for over twenty years.

"Any other family?" she probed.

Not spotting the significance of her question, he answered, "A brother who I rarely see."

Undeterred, Alessandra continued the interrogation by being more specific, "Any children?"

Still missing the point, he added, "He has two girls—my nieces—the kids from hell."

Now getting impatient she pressed further, "Any children of your own?"

The penny finally dropped, and Ben gave her a summary of his marital status leaving out the affair that sparked it. He told her about his two children; a son still at university and a girl who had graduated, leaving out the fact that he rarely sees or hears from either of them. Unless that is, they wanted something badly which their mother would not pay for. Then he revealed that he took some satisfaction in giving it to them if he could afford it, which in recent years had not been that often.

Refilling his now empty glass, she finally had him regurgitating some insightful personal background. At no point did he try to probe into her history. Fuelled by sixty-percent proof limoncello, he was becoming carelessly candid and was content to divulge more of his somewhat chequered past. Ben thought that the yellow dye incident with his former partner now made for an amusing and colourful anecdote. Having heard it though, Alessandra jokingly said she believed that the woman should have used something more permanent.

He continued to talk and she kept topping up his drink, although Alessandra was still on her first glass—and that was still three-quarters full. After an hour, Alessandra appeared to have decided that she had extracted enough background from him and suggested he head home. She said that she still had some clearing up to do in the kitchen and headed off in that direction, taking the bottle with her.

Back in her private domain Alessandra fussed about tidying and wiping kitchen surfaces while pondering all that she had learned. She decided that Ben, like so many men she had met, had never properly grown up. He had a child-like irresponsibility and a slightly romantic view of the world. However, although he may be naive, thoughtless, selfish, and vain, he appeared to be an inherently good person: or at least, not entirely a bad one. There was also something she could not help finding attractive about his English politeness and old-world charm. He appeared a hopeless romantic in a world of grasping cynics.

7. CINGHIALE

The narrow strip of flat land between the Mediterranean Sea and the Alps, which constitutes most of the populated area of the Italian Riviera, was unsuitable for grazing domestic animals. The sloping, sandy, rock-strewn band of the coastal plain drained too quickly when it rained and had the full force of the sun during most of the hours of daylight.

The coast had been almost exclusively populated with people eking a living from being next to the sea; either by fishing, or more latterly, tourism. The only expanses of cultivated green grass to be seen along the Riviera are man-made, pock-marked with sand bunkers and have little holes with triangular pennants stuck in them. These golf greens would soon wither and die were they not watered continuously and periodically shaded by fat golfers riding electric carts.

A consequence of the lack of grazing land has meant the only meat widely, cheaply, and consistently available to the people of Liguria has been that found wild in the hills above them. Travelling inland just a few kilometres from the coastal strip, the land rises quite rapidly into the Maritime Alps. This mountain range connects Liguria to the French and Swiss Alps and, from there, forms a natural sparsely populated corridor stretching across most of northern Europe: Ideal territory for wild boar, goats, rabbits, and deer, but not cattle. Therefore, the meat dishes found in traditional Ligurian cuisine are from wild and rarely domesticated animals.

The wild boar, or cinghiale, are by far the most common mammal and so have been hunted by man for as long as there have been records. They are also a pest to farmers and gardeners and thus were pursued relentlessly. However, their ability to procreate, hide and survive in this terrain, means that hunting has had little impact on their numbers. They remain both a severe problem and a staple food source to this day.

The challenge of cooking any genuinely wild meat is that it is usually very lean. The well-used muscle is often almost fat-free. Such meat requires maturing, marinating, and then slow cooking. It is not fast food. To allow Alessandra the time to prepare that night's cinghiale con polenta, it was Vincenzo who met Ben at the Osteria after breakfast. Today Claudio's faithful retainer would be his guide for a tour of the nearby countryside. Although he had seen it at a distance during his Ape ride to the village, he was looking forward to getting down close to the soil and the plants, to see how the land compared to the wine growing regions of France he was more familiar with. He knew that the Calcareous soil here was similar to that found in the Rhône Valley, where it produces their famous Côtes du Rhône blend of Grenache, Syrah, and Mourvèdre wines.

Looking around him, Ben could see that the cultivated terraces rose no further up the hillsides than the village itself, although the mountains encircling it continued for another three hundred metres or more. It was as though there was an invisible barrier preventing cultivation higher than five hundred metres above sea level. He was to learn that, above this height, in the clear air and without shade, the sun was fiercely bright by day but at night temperatures plummeted so rapidly that only the hardiest species of plants could survive. As a result, all the tended agricultural land was below this line, falling away quite steeply from the village into the valleys below. As a broad rule, the lower the land, the more productive it was, but other factors such as drainage, aspect, and shade also played a part.

Seemingly endless terraces formed flat steps of just a few metres wide and followed the topography of the landscape downwards until it eventually flattened out on the distant coastal plain. Vincenzo explained that the hard-won level areas were just broad enough to tend an olive tree and harvest its fruits. Anything wider was unnecessary and too high a price to pay in labour for the construction and maintenance. Most terraces were, therefore, only as extensive as the branches of the trees they supported. The farmers spread nets under these branches and then shake or claw the olives to the ground where they can be rolled up in the net before tipping into large plastic tubs. The groves are also just wide enough for Ape or tractor-barrow to gain access to extract the heavy haul of olives.

Vincenzo was unusually talkative today. He too was asking Ben questions about his family. He also asked precisely what Ben hoped to achieve during his time in Seborga.

"What will you give us for your board and lodging?" was his blunt enquiry.

Ben started to explain that it would be a document.

"A strategic plan for... " he began to say and then realised that this would mean little to Vincenzo or his compatriots.

If Vincenzo returned to the village and told the residents that all they would get was a lengthy paper report, they would despair. He changed tack, telling him that he would come up with practical ideas to get the economy going again. Effective plans to revitalise the business and agriculture. He was bluffing of course, to buy breathing space, but calculated that by the time his report came out, he would be back in Britain anyway.

After a thankfully short Ape ride, they bumped to a halt and parked in what looked like a long-abandoned private road. Vincenzo was out of the car and striding away up a path, opposite where he had left the vehicle. A wooden footpath sign read 'Passo del Bandito', and even Ben's poor Italian could roughly translate this as 'bandit pass.' He smiled broadly at the image which the sign conjured up and called ahead to Vincenzo.

When he turned to look back, Ben pointed to the sign.

"Si, long ago it was the road used by the bandits going up into the mountains and during the last two wars by the partisan fighters."

Ben chuckled at the unambiguous clarity of the name. Then he pictured Nazi troopers in pursuit of fleeing partisans, pausing here to wonder if it was wise to venture up the path in pursuit of a handful of peasant farmers armed only with ancient weapons. One thing was sure, they would have to have abandoned their vehicles to do so. If the Ape could not scale the incline, it was beyond anything heavier.

His guide was now climbing like an antelope. Ben was struggling to keep up when they reached a turning to another path on the right. This time the direction was across the hillside and so reasonably level. This next wooden sign read 'Ospedaletti 5km', and Vincenzo volunteered the explanation,

"The place of the Knights 'hospital."

Ben had, of course, heard of the Knight's Hospitaller, which much later became the St John of God first-aid organisation and wondered if this was to what he was referring. He made a mental note to do some more research into this. They marched for almost an hour. The path occasionally turned into the natural folds in the hillside down which ran glass-clear narrow mountain streams. These waterways cut deep furrows into the rock, sometimes disappearing entirely underground before emerging again to traverse another facet of the hillside. The path was narrow; just wide enough for one walker along most of its length and was mostly shaded by overhanging trees. Every now and again Vincenzo muttered "Cinghiale," as though he was daydreaming about dinner tonight.

This had happened several times before Ben asked, "Why do you keep saying Cinghiale?"

The sun-browned face turned to him with a withering look, pointing to the disturbed earth at the side of the path. It looked as though someone had dug up sods of grass and then replaced them but roughly and haphazardly scattering soil around. The earth was still dark and moist and so clearly freshly dug.

"Cinghiale," he said again.

It seemed that the wild pigs routed up the earth looking for roots, buried nuts and insects. The evidence of their visits became easy to spot once he knew what he was looking for. Along the route this seemed to be every few hundred metres, and so they were evidently endemic in these hills.

The sun was now clear of all the ridges and the temperature was rising. Suddenly they were in a clearing created by a large slab of rock. The stone had formed a small cliff on one side of the path and on which nothing grew. Several smaller rocks were scattered about, creating a natural picnic area complete with boulders suitable for tables and chairs. The result of a significant landslide Ben assumed.

"It's like a scene from a Flintstones cartoon," he joked.

Vincenzo apparently did not get the joke but simply added that such landslides caused by minor earth tremors were frequent in the area.

Vincenzo sat on one of the rocks, removed his pack, and produced two still reasonably cold beers plus a paper packet containing lunch identical to Ben's. He deftly knocked the tops off the two bottles on the sharp edge of a rock and handed one to Ben. It was only now that he was seated that the stunning view afforded them of the village became apparent. Their route had taken them to a slightly elevated position on the opposite side of the valley. From here you could see the whole layout of the buildings and walls, as well as the surrounding Ortos and olive groves. It was spectacularly beautiful in the morning sunshine, the sun's rays glinting on the tiled dome of the church tower.

It was now clear why Vincenzo had brought Ben here. Over lunch he pointed out the various parcels of land, explained who owned them, and what it was best to grow on them. He estimated their output in terms of litres of oil, demijohns of wine, or crates of fruit. From what Ben learned, it seemed that a single olive tree only produced about three litres of oil per year.

Vincenzo pointed towards the land immediately below the village saying, “From that concrete water tower beside the big oak tree, along to that abandoned grey Fiat, and then down to the seventh terrace from the village, the land belongs to Claudio.”

The highest terrace next to the treeline was still partly in the shade and he could see a large black horse grazing there. Although no equine expert, Ben could tell it was a large male with a long mane and big feet. These hooves were covered in the same long black hair as its mane. It looked old, like its master, and yet still very capable. The remaining hillside was scattered with olive trees and Ben quickly estimated about one hundred and fifty in total.

He tried to recall the average UK supermarket price of olive oil and thought that it was about three pounds for a 330 cl bottle. A quick mental calculation, therefore, gave him a retail value of about thirty pounds sterling, per tree, per annum. That was the retail price with sales tax, and so the producer’s income must surely be somewhere less than half of that, he calculated. An income, therefore, of about two thousand five hundred euros per year, before production costs, was his final estimate. Hardly even a subsistence income. Ben wondered who in their right minds would care for and harvest such a crop to end up with a return of only about fifteen hundred pounds a year. The economics of olive farming on this scale just did not add up.

This time the thick tanned arm pointed further down the terraces.

“From Claudio’s land, for five terraces further east, but also out as far as the gully running down from the mountain, is Valerio’s family land. They face south-west, have water from the stream, and so grow the best wine grapes. That is why they have a café in the village to sell their vino.” And so, he went on naming and estimating plot after plot, working his way around and down the hillside.

Occasionally Vincenzo also added some interesting local gossip about family feuds, usually over disputed boundaries.

"Somebody moved a rusty old Fiat and thereby changed the boundary?" Ben quipped.

But land and property were apparently not a laughing matter and so he received no response at all, just a disdainful look. Vincenzo had begun his land inventory at the edge of the village, worked around it and then downwards until he had detailed the purpose, approximate economic value, and agricultural heritage of practically the whole valley. His knowledge of the area was encyclopaedic.

Vincenzo had been right to bring him here. In an hour he had learned an astonishing amount about how this subsistence agricultural economy worked, or more accurately, did not work. It might have been fine when each family only had to produce enough for themselves to survive plus a bit extra to trade. Indeed, it had done this job admirably for at least three millennia. But this was a model unsuitable for the twenty-first century and everyone could see that. It was only a matter of time until it ceased and was replaced, but with what? Ben wondered.

After they had eaten their lunch and Ben had received his geography and economics lessons, it was time for history. Vincenzo pointed to a feature in the huge rock behind them which he had so far overlooked, an unmistakable Templar cross splaying out slightly at the four ends. The symbol was about two to three feet square. Plants had seeded in the cavity and helped disguise the feature, but it was evident enough when pointed out. It had been cut deep into the solid stone, wide enough for him to insert his fingers not quite to the wrist.

Vincenzo took a small machete from his bag and gestured for Ben to watch him. With the blunt back of the knife, he struck the corner of the rock with a glancing blow. It sparked, but not a fragment of the stone was removed.

"Molto difficile—this type of rock is very hard".

Although by about 1100 AD the technology for producing metal tools was relatively advanced, carving into this granite-like rock was still some considerable feat of engineering. The time alone required to cut such an emblem so deep into this granite-hard rock must have been substantial. This seemed to be clear evidence of the Templars having spent a lot of time in the very spot where they were now sitting. It was suddenly a genuine link to the past, and this was somehow also quite eerie. Turning back to look at the view, Ben wondered, apart from the rusty Fiat, water towers, and telegraph poles, how much of this scene had changed since the Knights looked down on it. Very little, he quickly concluded.

Vincenzo rose from where he had been sitting and started to climb up around the side of the immense boulder. He beckoned for Ben to follow. It was a steep climb on the loose rubble surface, and there was no path to speak of. Brambles, bushes, and other smaller boulders had to be circumnavigated. They did not go far before the ground levelled slightly, which had encouraged larger shrubs and small trees to take root. Where the cliff started to rise again, almost vertically this time, was a natural crevice in the rock. It was about a metre and a half tall and less than half a metre wide. Vincenzo was nearly two metres tall, but by putting his feet in first, then bending his knees, he could slide through the gap. Ben applied the same technique and followed him.

Inside, his guide produced a new LED torch, which he deployed, lighting up the darkness they had entered. The passage was now a little wider but not much. After just a dozen steps, the rock opened into an extensive cave, not quite tall enough to stand full height but almost. Vincenzo turned his torch to the walls where Ben was amazed at what he saw. Elaborate but primitive paintings of knights and horses in battle. The mounted Knights had flags flying on tall lances and swords flailing at hordes of dark-skinned warriors surrounding them who were brandishing curved swords. Another scene showed lines of knights in convoy carrying a wooden litter piled with something—presumably the spoils of war, thought Ben. Further scenes were truly gruesome, with all manner of executions and tortures. Vincenzo broke the silence.

"Holy warriors. Defenders of the Faith."

"Who in the village knows about this place?"

"Claudio's cerchio interno—the old families: those still known as The Templari. The prince wanted you to see it so that you understand the significance of our history."

Ben was quiet for a while, taking in the extraordinary site which he had been confronted with. He then asked, "Who painted these and why?"

The lofty Italian suddenly looked menacing; the torchlight was creating shadows on his features. He answered slowly and thoughtfully, as was his way,

"No one is sure, but most think it was the sick. Knights who had been injured or were diseased had come here to recover before the long journey home, or to die."

Those knights that did survive the battles did not always fare well on the long sea voyage back. In those days, people did not understand the need for fresh fruit and vegetables to avoid the effects of scurvy. Although some believe that it was the Templars, bringing back citrus trees to grow at home, who accidentally discovered that fruit was an effective treatment for scurvy. Other diseases contracted in strange lands also took their toll on the Europeans.

"Myself, I think the sick were posted here as look-outs. This task would have kept them away from the other healthy men and made them feel useful. From here they could spot any enemy approaching as much as a day before they could reach the fortress. Stuck up here with nothing much to do, they painted or carved away at that rock while they either recovered or died. The old men in the village said that there used to be many human bones and other artefacts in here, but these have long since been taken and given a Catholic burial elsewhere."

Vincenzo also told him that the way they had entered was not the original entrance. Another popular theory is that the original opening had been buried by the big boulder, possibly trapping some inside and hence the carved cross outside. Subsequent minor earthquakes and landslides had later opened up the void higher up. He also told Ben that this was just one of many such caves scattered around these hillsides, mainly at higher altitudes than this one.

Looking at these scenes, it was not too difficult to imagine being back in that time; over a thousand years ago. Those knights must surely have thought that after the horrors of war in that hostile foreign land, with enemies who played by different rules, that Seborga was a peaceful, safe place to hold up and let mind and body recuperate.

On the walk back to the village, Ben quizzed Vincenzo on why, if the claims of independence were based on fact, why had Claudio not been able to prove it?

"Il Papa" came the reply without hesitation this time. "If they chose to, the Vatican could prove the claim tomorrow by opening their archives and revealing Pope Gregory's charter which gifted Seborga to the Knights Templar. But they do not choose—partly because it serves no purpose to them but mainly because of the political pressure from Rome. No Italian politician wants to lose an inch of territory for any reason. Also, the Church does not want to remind anybody of its cosy relationship with the Templars."

Ben summarised, "So, without the copy of the charter that was presumably given to the Knights, the claim is nothing but that; an unsubstantiated assertion."

"Si," confirmed Vincenzo.

Although much of this explanation was supposition, because no one in either of Rome's centres of power could ever admit it, Ben had to admit that there was logic in what Vincenzo had told him.

Seborga had mostly, but not entirely, been abandoned by the time of the unification of Italy in the mid-nineteenth century. The monks had gone and the native population had been ravaged by years of wars, disease and famine. There was no access to news from outside and so it is hardly surprising that it was left out of the 1861 treaty, which brought together similar states under the Italian flag. No one noticed or cared until after the First World War. By then people had started to repopulate the area, and the victorious allies were also redrawing the map of Europe once again.

In the Second World War, Ligurian Partisans had played an important strategic role in the battle to free Europe, and many had fought and died courageously; some alongside British Special Forces who had been dropped into the mountains by parachute. Vincenzo told him that Claudio's father had been the leader of a local band of cut-throats who had caused mayhem amongst the many Nazi columns traversing their way along the coast road, which connected Italy to France.

His contribution was later recognised by the Allies and he gained the ear of a high-ranking British general; one whose campaigns he had greatly assisted by distracting Nazi forces with guerrilla attacks in strategic locations. This officer saw to it that Claudio's claim of independence, as well as his considerable help in winning the war in Italy, reached the ear of Winston Churchill. The British Prime Minister then wrote to the Pope, and, although it took nearly a year, a meeting was finally arranged between Claudio and a College of Cardinals in Rome. It was at this meeting that the old man claimed to have seen the original ancient charter, which had been brought up from the Vatican's archives. The Cardinals had examined it and acknowledged that independence had indeed been granted and subsequent authority was indeed vested in the then prince and his successors. Although they confirmed that position, their view was that it was not their responsibility to enforce it. When it became a Templar protectorate the Vatican gave up all rights, and so the Cardinals effectively washed their hands of the matter. Anything further was up to the Italian Courts. Not long after the War, Churchill's conservative government had been replaced by the Labour Party and the great man's influence had been much diluted by the effects of peace.

The Italian government, having been on the wrong side for most of the war, were faced with conceding territory to the victors in the peace treaties that followed. They had no appetite for losing any more territory and, at the same time, creating a potentially troublesome enclave within their remaining borders; especially one in a position so close to the French border. Also at that time, many other more critical negotiations were already taking place between the Vatican and the new government on the future of an Italy without Mussolini. Seborgan independence was a distraction no one wanted except one old partisan from Liguria, and so a deal was struck to make it go away.

Claudio had already admitted to the Cardinals that he did not have the other copy of the charter and that no one else had seen it in living memory. From that moment on, the Vatican suffered amnesia and said they could not now find their copy either. They also denied ever displaying it at the meeting with the representative from Seborga. Without it, or any evidence it ever existed, he was advised a legal challenge was futile even if Claudio had been able to afford it.

Despite petitioning every subsequent change of government since the War, not one of them had progressed the independence claim any further. A couple of the more principled local politicians had written to the Vatican, who again denied all knowledge of the document. Claudio had a file full of polite letters on official stationery, suggesting that he first find some hard evidence before bothering them again.

"Impasse. Stallo. Or check, as you say in chess." said Vincenzo, struggling to find the words to summarise the situation from his limited English vocabulary.

They did not talk much on the way back to the village. Vincenzo stopped from time to time and left the path to collect bunches of plants growing alongside or near the trail. He deftly swung these bunches over his shoulder and tucked them neatly into his backpack without even breaking stride. The sun was high in the sky by then, and Ben was sweating with the exertion of keeping up with Vincenzo. He would typically walk at a more leisurely pace, taking in the views and savouring flora and fauna. His walking partner today was not a sightseer and probably had more important things to do.

The pair arrived back at the Osteria, which was currently in the shade, and Ben flopped into a chair outside.

"Beer?" offered Ben.

Vincenzo extracted the bundles of plants from his bag and took them inside. He quickly returned with two bottles of Moretti, still frosty-cold from the fridge.

"Salute" he said, draining the bottle, placing the empty on the table and departing with a brief, "Ciao".

It took Ben just a few gulps to finish his beer, after which he fancied a second. Resisting the temptation, he headed back to his room to do some research into the Templars presence in this area and the role of the Partisans.

Deciding to take aperitivo at Valerio's bar that night, Ben arrived freshly showered about 7pm. Without asking, the smiling proprietor brought him a beer and a small plate.

"What do we have tonight, Valerio?"

"Farinata. A chickpea tart. My mother makes them. Anyway, how is your head, Professore?"

Touching his forehead where it had been grazed Ben replied, "It's fine, but the princess has decreed that you can't call me professore."

The young waiter raised his hands in a gesture of exasperation.

"Take no notice of Alessandra. She wants everything to remain as it is and thinks that your work here will spoil this place."

Valerio went on to outline what he saw as Alessandra's agenda and how her desires differed from most of the population, including himself and the other business owners. Listening and digesting what the young man said over two beers, one tart and a salami bruschetta, Ben thought he then had a grasp of the situation.

As far as he could see, both groups acknowledged the need for visitors to create a new economy but differed on the type of tourist they wanted. Most envisaged coaches of day-trippers but others thought that they somehow cheapened the place, spent little money, and left only litter. Although Valerio agreed they were sometimes annoying, they at least bought ice creams, coffees and Cokes, and that was better than nothing. Valerio excused himself saying he had work to do and Ben was left to ponder these insights.

At the Osteria, the aromatic Cinghiale was already being consumed with apparent enthusiasm by several local diners. The almost coal-black sauce contrasted starkly with the creamy white polenta. Unusually there was no other colour on the plate, making it look more like an English casserole served with mashed potatoes.

Ben was, by now, being acknowledged by one or two of the regulars in the bar and received a few 'buonaseras' as he took his seat. At the bar Alessandra was holding up a frosted beer bottle, but he shook his head and mouthed 'vino rosso' to which she nodded acknowledgement.

Tonight, instead of wearing her hair all tied back, she had formed a thick ponytail which bounced from side to side as she walked towards his table with his wine and more aperitivo. With just a brief 'buonasera' she headed back into the kitchen. He watched her, analysing everything he could to try and establish her age. It was not easy.

Was she wearing some make-up tonight? He suddenly wondered. There was definitely something different about her. Something softer, he speculated. Then something else struck him. She was wearing a long-sleeved white cotton blouse, fastened at the cuffs. Not that there would have been anything unusual about that in the UK, but in this heat, long sleeves were reserved for nuns and lawyers. Everyone else was dressed down in t-shirts and polo shirts exposing as much skin as possible to the cooling breeze.

He then recalled that each time he had seen her, her arms had been covered and it had just struck him how odd this was. Pondering the possible explanations for a moment, he finally concluded she must be tattooed. He guessed that her youthful escape to New York must have given her the freedom to rebel against her strict Catholic upbringing, and she had decided to celebrate it in pen and ink. What could she have there that she is so keen to keep covered—a declaration of love; her favourite band; or perhaps something more esoteric? Whatever it was, back here in conservative Seborga, she was very embarrassed and apparently profoundly regretting it now, he concluded. A tattooed princess – how amusing, he thought.

Sipping his wine, he noticed that the aperitivo being served was his favourite thin cheese and ham pie. Having already had two plates at Valerio's, he had planned to skip it here but now could not resist this delicacy. Fortunately, his Cinghiale arrived before any more pie. A lot of red wine and olive oil provided the base of the sauce for this dish, but it also had a sharper edge. He would later learn that this was a consequence of Alessandra's addition of Gappa to the recipe. The meat had been diced into small pieces to help it absorb the marinade and cook more easily. He could see that bacon (it was pancetta) had also been added. The flavour was as intense as the colour suggested. The bay leaves and juniper berries were providing the spicy edge to the dish. It was also quite salty from the pancetta.

He had tried it only a couple of times, but polenta was an ingredient Ben had never really come to terms with. It had the colour and consistency of too many school dinner dishes. The maize flour is a product of Piedmont, the neighbouring region of the Ligurians on the other side of the mountains. Their flat fertile plains were suitable for cereal crops and it is the source of much of Italy's polenta, pasta and of risotto rice. Sea salt had long been traded by the Ligurians to obtain these staples. Donkey and mule trails crossing over the mountains were created for this trade. These formed the networks that he had learned from Vincenzo were later also exploited by bandits, partisan fighters, and now today's hikers and mountain bikers.

The day's walk had given him a healthy appetite, but even though he had left much of the polenta on his dish, the meal left him full to bursting. So, when Alessandra came out of the kitchen heading towards him carrying a panna cotta drizzled with raspberry juice, he wondered how he was going to resist. When it came to it, he could not. Instead, he left it in front of him for a while contemplating its cool, light, creamy consistency until he could resist no longer. It was lighter than air and yet so silky with subtle dairy flavours. Replete, he pushed his chair away from the table and leant back, taking in the scene laid out before him.

The Osteria was three-quarters full of noisy animated diners. A few French tourists were amongst the customers having crossed the nearby border for some great value Italian cooking. Another large group of ten were German visitors, who had come up from the hotels on the coast to taste authentic Alpine cuisine. Judging by their loud, jovial behaviour they had not been disappointed. The remainder were locals, and interestingly, Ben was beginning to feel more empathetic with them than with the other foreigners. All the customers had by now been fed and were either leaving for home or savouring a digestive. Only some of the foreigners were drinking coffee. No

Italian in his right mind would be ingesting coffee at this time of the day.

Alessandra emerged from the kitchen looking remarkably fresh considering the hectic night of cooking and serving she must have had. Gone was the blue apron protecting the front of her white blouse, but her cuffs remained firmly buttoned. She carried a bottle of limoncello and two glasses and took a seat opposite Ben. Now sensing a certain familiarity with her, and with the reckless daring only a combination of beer and wine can produce, he welcomed her with,

"I have finally worked out your little secret," he said gesturing to her covered wrists, "you have tattoos on your arms. Is it an old boyfriend's name? I know. It's an embarrassing band from the eighties."

Taken aback by this assertion, Alessandra continued to pour one small digestivo into a glass, which she drank down in one. She then paused and looked at him, as if waiting for further explanation. Ben merely pointed to her cuffs and nodded, as though waiting for confirmation. As none was forthcoming, he continued to justify his theory.

"Since I arrived, you have been wearing long sleeves when everyone else is dressed in t-shirts or vests. Even that first night at the festa when you were working on an open brazier and now in a kitchen in what must be thirty-plus degree heat. I think I have just worked out what it must be. Tattoos! You got yourself 'inked' when you were in New York, and now back here in conformist Seborga, you regret it. It must be something that you now find embarrassing."

Alessandra rose slowly and walked around to Ben's side of the table, lowering her head to the height of his, as though she were going to whisper in his ear, or possibly even kiss him. Ben was leaning back on the rear two legs of his chair. As she put her mouth near to his earlobe, a lock of her hair fell onto his face. Her scent was not perfume or shampoo but that of the kitchen; garlic, basil and rosemary. Nevertheless, it was as intoxicating as Chanel to him. Then she whispered huskily, "Professore, you are too smart. You have found me out. I should have known that a man of your education would see through my thin deception."

At which point she poured the remainder of the bottle of limoncello down the front of his open shirt until it ran out above his belt, soaking the area around his fly zipper. When he jumped to his feet, it looked like he had peed himself. Looking around, Ben realised to his embarrassment that most of the locals had witnessed this encounter. They were nudging their neighbours and laughing amongst themselves none too discretely.

Alessandra was back in the sanctuary of her kitchen when Ben moved toward the door, hoping to make as discrete an exit as possible under the circumstances. Just outside into the piazza where the chairs and tables spilled onto the pavement, Vincenzo stood barring his way. He had been sitting just outside the door presumably listening in to the encounter. He greeted Ben with "Buonanotte," but not before looking him up and down and asking, "A little accident, Professore?"

Unsure, as usual, how much Vincenzo knew, or of any inference attached to his words, he answered, "You could say that Vincenzo."

It occurred to Ben afterwards, that when anything of significance happened in Seborga, Vincenzo was never very far away.

"I was waiting to ask if you wanted to join me for a car rally in the morning. I am a member of the Fiat Cinquecento Owners Club. Once a month we take a trip together and tomorrow is a drive to Molini di Triora. It is a beautiful drive and a wonderful lunch at the end."

At that very moment, a whole day away from the village and from Alessandra sounded very attractive and so Ben agreed.

8. CAPPON MAGRO

Ben had struggled to get off to sleep following the debacle with Alessandra, not helped by the cacophony of tree frogs croaking outside his window. To Ben, it sounded as though there were at least twenty of them sitting on his window ledge, each with a megaphone. Yet, in a room situated ten metres above ground level, this was obviously not possible: even if amphibians had access to that sort of sound technology, Ben joked to himself. This nightly chorus was something he would eventually find soothing. But for now, it was so very different from the emergency vehicle sirens and other night sounds of a city. As was the distant braying of a donkey and the strange, irregular, short 'hoot' from a Little owl hunting somewhere close by.

It was in this restless state that Ben emerged from Claudio's house into the sparkling bright morning. He decided to avoid breakfast at the Osteria and another potentially embarrassing confrontation with Alessandra. Instead, he stuck to the shaded east side of the piazza where it transpired Vincenzo was already waiting in his splendid classic car. The engine was running. The car's note at idle was a subdued rumble but suggested a potential volume greater even than a valley full of courting amphibians.

The six-foot driver had shoe-horned his sturdy frame into yet another micro-vehicle. At least today's transport had four wheels, Ben thought, remembering the hair-raising Ape ride from the airport. The car radio was playing, and the Italian was tapping his fingers on the white Bakelite steering wheel in time to the Latin disco-pop, unaware that Ben had arrived behind him. All this was very evident because the car's canvas sunroof was peeled back revealing the pristine interior and Vincenzo's thinning scalp. The cherry-red bodywork gleamed in the morning sun, wax polished to showroom condition, despite what Ben estimated to be its fifty-plus year heritage.

The Fiat Cinquecento (500), launched in 1957, preceded the first Austin Mini by two years and followed on a theme of micro-cars from its predecessor, the Topolino. The Cinquecento was, if anything, even more ubiquitous in Italy than the Mini was in Britain. Both cars were often the first drive of the Baby-Boomer generation, and so they are now each held in the same nostalgic veneration in their respective countries. Neither cars nor drivers of that vintage have enjoyed uneventful lives. Those that have survived, often find themselves reunited in celebration of sheer endurance. Both now re-live their youthful glories in events such as today's Cinquecento rally.

Vincenzo's pride and joy aspired to greater things than its original ex-factory specification. It gave off all the appearance of being its sportier hybrid; the rare and expensive Cinquecento Abarth conversion. It was, in fact, merely a conventional Fiat 500 with a facelift and some mechanical tweaks. The wheel arches had been professionally flared to accommodate wider tyres, the suspension stiffened, and exhaust flow improved. Basic modifications of the original 479cc engine gave it slightly more than the standard 20-brake horsepower and an increased potential top speed approaching 70mph. These seemingly inadequate statistics by today's standards, are at odds with the driving sensation which Ben was soon to experience. A lightweight body, a rear engine and rear-wheel drive gave this car challenging handling characteristics. Road holding was good in normal circumstances but when pushed, even slightly beyond its limits, the car very suddenly became unpredictable. Keeping it just the right side of this fine line was an art form mastered by few.

When Ben eventually found a way of getting both his torso and his long legs into the car at the same time, he found it was impossible for his shoulders not to touch the driver's. Most Englishmen would have been uncomfortable with this level of intimacy even with people they knew well, and Ben would not have included Vincenzo in that group. So it was, in these less than satisfactory circumstances, with the two men squeezed into the Cinquecento, they set off on their road trip, tyres screeching on the cobbles.

On the very first right-hand bend, Ben was forced into even closer contact with Vincenzo and then almost immediately thrust the other way against the side window at the next left-hander. Through the open sunroof, the tyres could be heard grasping at the poorly maintained tarmac for grip; like a dog scrabbling on a polished wooden floor. Vincenzo seemed to have set out to test Ben's nerve by pushing the car to its limit right from the off. Perhaps he was hoping the Englishman would ask him to slow down, or even to stop and let him out. Any such request would be a clear admission that he was somehow less of a man. He had underestimated Ben.

It was not that Ben was particularly brave, careless, or foolhardy, just that he appeared unaware of the danger. It was a kind of naivety born out of inexperience of hazard—an inability to recognise when a threat presented itself. And, because he did not see any danger and did not feel the need to react to it, the danger often just evaporated. In the same way that some top predators will often leave prey that just lies still and does not run away, adopting a passive stance sometimes defuses potential perils.

Often walking home from bars and restaurants late at night, he had been accosted by rowdy young people loud and aggressive with too much to drink. But Ben, unlike most, never saw them as potentially dangerous. Neither did he pretend he had not seen them. He merely smiled, greeted them cheerfully, and walked on, often with a farewell wave over his shoulder.

This attitude had worked all his life to date and he saw no need to change it now.

After just ten minutes they arrived at the starting point rendezvous; a café bar in the tiny hamlet of Sasso, half-way down the mountain. Parked outside already were another half dozen of the tiny cars with big personalities. These were mainly in primary colours; yellows, powder blues, reds, but also one in a dazzling metallic bronze. Most displayed badges and bright coloured stickers showing allegiance to the owners' clubs: Touring Club Italiano or proclaiming events they had participated in; San Remo Rally, Monte Carlo Classic, Retro Turin and so on.

Like the cars, their owners did not appear to possess the same level of power and agility as their modern-day contemporaries, although some of them apparently still believed that they did. There was much shouting, macho back-slapping and arm punching as the ageing men jostled to order espresso at the small bar. Vincenzo looked as though he might be the youngest of the drivers gathered. He was indeed the tallest. The remainder looked far better matched in stature to their vehicles, although their waistlines looked as if they would be detrimental to the vehicle's power-to-weight ratio. Ben was not introduced and yet everyone seemed to know who he was and offered warm verbal greetings but, thankfully, no physical ones.

Eventually fuelled with thick espresso and unleaded petrol the convoy, now made up of a dozen Cinquecentos, set off with Vincenzo and Ben at the head. Taking the narrowest of side streets out of the village, the road suddenly plunged down towards the valley bottom at a seemingly impossible gradient. Such was the angle of the car on the road, Ben felt that if his less-than-toned pelvic muscles failed to hold him back in his seat, he would end up with his face pressed against the windscreen.

The route also seemed impossibly narrow as it clung to the side of the hill, switching back and forth to reduce the ferocity of the descent. Vincenzo occasionally deployed the handbrake to make the tighter bends possible at the speed they were travelling. Still Ben did not flinch. Instead, he started to ask more questions about the small-holdings they were passing through. Now on the valley floor, they crossed a river and then turned upstream following its twisting course.

"What is that plastic pipe for that follows along the side of that stream?"

"Irrigation," came the irritated one-word reply.

"What are all these green tubs stacked up for?"

"Collecting olives, of course," as though that were the stupidest question in the entire world.

After twenty minutes Vincenzo gave up trying to scare Ben out of his wits and settled down to a brisk but less dangerous pace so he could engage him in conversation. Ben had continued questioning without a break until the Italian interrupted him with,

"You know that Alessandra is still married?"

Ben glanced at him and, unsure of the significance of this announcement, decided to say nothing.

"Her husband is a convicted drug dealer with Mafia connections. He's in jail in America, but I hear he is due out soon."

Again, Ben was unsure how to respond to this revelation and so he did not.

"He came from around here and still has many family along the coast near Imperia. It's a messy business."

Finally, Ben began to realise he was being warned off Alessandra. But why? What was Vincenzo's interest?

When the Italian added, "Alessandra and I were at school together," Ben finally joined up the dots of the puzzle that he had so far been unable to unravel. Unmarried Vincenzo was still besotted with the teenage princess who had run off to America all those years ago. Running away from Vincenzo and all he represented? Ben further speculated. Whatever the reasons, the message was clear enough. 'Stay away. She's mine.'

Ironically, after last night's encounter with the highly volatile princess, Ben should have needed no persuasion to stay away. However, the Englishman enjoyed a challenge and certainly did not like being told what company he should keep. So, with the same sense of invulnerability that made Ben appear immune to amateur rally drivers, he decided if Alessandra apologised for last night, he would ignore Vincenzo's warnings.

For almost ninety minutes they had wound their way slowly and gently up a valley. For most of that time, they followed the Fora di Taggia river. Lower down the valley it was a broad flow but gradually narrowed into a stream, except where it was dammed by large boulders creating inviting pools of clear, emerald green water. These pools often occurred along its route. Houses and signs of agriculture had become scarcer, and much of the valley was now densely forested with a mix of naturally-seeded pines and hardwoods. Finally, up ahead, a small car park appeared and then a tall stone building with a waterwheel.

"We arrive," announced Vincenzo, who then turned suddenly and skidded to a halt in the gravelled car park, empty but for an ancient Ape and a rusty Japanese 4x4 pick-up.

The remainder of the cars arrived over the next ten minutes and all lined up with fronts facing the road. Smokers, of which Ben realised there were still plenty in Liguria, lit up and puffed away. The drivers gathered in small groups, apparently discussing the performance of their vehicles. There was lots of body language suggesting steering, swerving, and horn honking.

The olive mill, it turned out, was a highly regarded local restaurant and Ben would soon realise why. Even before they had gone inside, other cars and motorcyclists started arriving. As the Cinquecento owners mustered in the doorway, a dusty yellow truck containing five forestry workers, wearing high-visibility waistcoats and hard hats, pulled into the car park. This restaurant certainly had an eclectic clientele, Ben thought.

Inside were small tables and upright wooden chairs crammed into a small dining room. About fifty covers in a space where usually only thirty could dine. There were no table clothes, just a paper napkin, one knife, fork, and spoon, plus a small glass tumbler. Six dishes – two starters, two mains, and two desserts—were chalked on a blackboard of which only 'semi-freddo' Ben could interpret. There was no wine list: simply "Vino Rosso e Bianco Organico".

As the party took their seats at four small tables pushed together into one, jugs of water and baskets of bread appeared. These were swiftly followed by some of the same pitchers containing wine. The red was relatively pale and translucent, while the white had more colour than most. Ben was poured some of the white by a fellow diner, without being asked, and sniffed it discretely. It was highly aromatic as it colour had suggested but was lighter on flavour than he'd expected and packed with unfamiliar notes. The aroma of woodland flowers came to Ben's mind, and then he narrowed it down to Elderflower. It was like nothing he had tried before. He liked it very much.

A single staff member appeared to be serving the entire room, which now contained almost thirty diners. The middle-aged woman buzzed from table to table, notepad and pencil in hand, with a shortness of tone which made her appear grumpy. Ben came to realise that it was, in fact, a necessary economy of dialogue and movement that allowed her to serve fifty covers per sitting—single-handed efficiently.

The foresters were seated at one table, still in their high-vis waistcoats. Two separate groups of bikers—one younger group of off-roaders and an older group of Moto Guzzi tarmac cruisers—were struggling to find space for all their helmets and gloves. They were waved outside to dispose of their gear by the expressionless and unsympathetic waitress. A few young professionals in business attire and some older couples made up the remainder of the diners.

Ben puzzled at how all these people knew about such a remote place, let alone took the time to drive here on a mid-week lunch break. And yet, here they all were, and more were arriving all the time. He thought about asking the waitress about the wine but doubted that she would speak English, or that she had time to answer. Looking around he saw a small desk near the entrance on which were a credit card machine, receipt pad, and two unopened bottles—one red and one white—both with hand-written price tickets. Rising from his chair and taking his glass with him, Ben made a bee-line for the desk. As he did so, the waitress caught his eye and gave him a wary look. He pointed to the bottles, held up his glass and managed a questioning look, which must have worked.

"Si," was all she said.

The label read 'E Bunde vino Bianco 2017'. The address of the grower showed that it was made at almost the same location as the restaurant where it was now being drunk. One of Ben's party had also left his seat and came over to offer in excellent English, "You are interested in the wine?"

"Very much so," replied Ben.

He explained that the name on the white wine was a house brand name rather than a type. It was a rare blend of two ancient native vines, Massarda and Moscatello di Taggia. The red was almost certainly from the Rossese grape but, because the location is not designated for that grape, they cannot refer to it as such on the label. The stranger thought it might also be blended with some Ormeasco grapes but could not be sure of that.

"A shame for them because they could charge twice the price for a Rossese but good for us," added his new acquaintance.

They both returned to the table where the man poured Ben some of the red wine and offered first the glass and then a handshake.

"I am Danilo. I worked in London for many years, but my English is a bit rustic."

"Rusty," Ben offered by way of correction.

"Si, rusty," the man agreed laughing out loud.

Tasting the red Ben recognised the soft, light fruit of the Rossese that he'd tried so far, but this one had another dimension; a dry, caramel note. The Ormeasco? Ben wondered.

The waitress appeared at their table, pad in hand, and still blank of expression. Vincenzo ordered

"Agnolotti del plin e braciola di maiale con fagioli."

Not recognising anything on the menu, Ben quickly added "Due," and the waitress duly added another line to her order without even making eye contact with Ben.

With only a couple of exceptions, the men ordered the same meat dish as though it were the speciality of the house.

"You are experiencing the Cucina Bianca?" observed Danilo.

Seeing Ben's puzzlement, he explained, "Literally, white food. Cucina Bianco is typical Ligurian mountain food." He went on to explain, "Being so far from the coast or any flat arable land, in days gone by the people relied on pasta, pulses, nuts, and white meat – pork, chicken, or rabbit – often leaving their food lacking in colour but not in flavour."

Danilo pointed out that their journey today had taken them ninety minutes by car on tarmac roads. Until probably the 1960s that journey would have taken a full day by horse or mule. A journey too long and, therefore, too costly for trade in fish, vegetables, or imported goods that would have given their food colour and variety.

"In times gone by, in a mountain house like this, if they could not see it or hear it from their kitchen window they could not eat it. Simple as that. They had to be inventive to make their few staple foods taste different and thereby make a hard life tolerable."

The clatter of china plates on hard wooden tables silenced the men's chattering. The steaming hot pasta had arrived.

Plump parcels of almost transparent pasta parcels crimped around the edge to hold in the filling. Today it was ricotta, breadcrumbs, and forest herbs. The thin sauce was light but indistinguishable. Perhaps a little pasta water, white wine and some butter? Ben wondered. Indeed, this was Cucina Bianca, he mused. The men grabbed chunks of white bread from a bowl and began eating without ceremony. The chattering resumed between mouthfuls.

Ben thought that the portion looked daunting but the pasta was so light and delicious it disappeared in minutes. Also, in no time at all, Ben's fellow diners had cleared their plates. Ben asked Danilo about the origins of the dish.

Danilo continued, "Plin translates roughly as 'pinch' because that is how they seal the folded pasta parcels by hand and what gives the edges that rough appearance." He demonstrated the technique with his napkin. "The filling can be anything. If it's meat, then it's usually what's left over from making another dish."

Considering at least half of the men were driving, a considerable amount of wine was being consumed. Although Ben noticed Vincenzo was being relatively parsimonious. The big man had been quiet since they had arrived. Possibly pondering his lack of any apparent success in scaring Ben with either his driving or warning of irate husbands with Mafia links. Ben would later discover that the scheming Italian was, in fact, hatching a plan B to keep him away from Alessandra.

With what seemed like Swiss Railway timing, no sooner had the pasta plates been cleared than the air filled with the intoxicating smell of roasted meat. Pork chops bigger than a man's splayed hand almost filled the plates on which they arrived. This domination of the crockery proved not to be a problem as the only other thing on the plate was a portion of white beans and a wedge of gnarled lemon atop the chop. The girth of the pork chop was in proportion to its width; it being a good inch thick. The ends of the bone and the outer surface bore the seared lines of a brazier. It smelled delicious, Ben thought.

On cutting into the white meat, Ben found its cooking to have been perfectly judged. It was soft and moist inside and just lightly pink near the bone. Ben found the combination of the burnt outer fibres, juicy inner flesh, and lemon juice dressing just sublime. The best pork chop he had ever eaten, without a doubt. The unappealing look of the beans was discovered to be false upon tasting. Cooked in garlic, lemon, and white wine, they were the perfect accompaniment.

The thing that struck Ben was the simplicity of this dish.

"How can something as apparently modest as pork and beans be so good that people will drive for an hour and a half up a mountain to eat it?" He had directed the question at Danilo, but Vincenzo broke his silence to answer.

"It's all natural. No animal feed and no antibiotics. The pigs eat what falls off the trees or come out of the earth. What is more, the soil is pure. No fertilisers have ever touched it."

"That's not entirely true," interrupted Danilo, "the pigs plough and fertilise as they go."

"True," agreed Vincenzo, "they do." he said laughing.

Lunch was a leisurely affair stretching well into the early afternoon, ending with a big plate of fruit and cheese plus more wine and short, strong coffees.

The men said their 'adios' and 'ciaos' in the car park and set off in colourful convey back down the valley. As they approached the coast, individual cars peeled-off towards their respective home villages. Vincenzo, however, sped past the junction where they had first joined the valley road and continued towards the coast. Seeing Ben's questioning look, he explained, "I will take you to see something at the beach which you might find interesting".

Ben was in no rush to return to Seborga where he would have to face Alessandra and so said nothing by way of protest. When the land became flat enough, the leafy green of the valley's olive groves and Ortos gave way to vast glass greenhouses.

"This is known as the Riviera dei Fiori—Riviera of Flowers," Vincenzo offered as an explanation for all the glass houses. "We once grew most of Europe's flowers before the Dutch took over with their artificial cultivation and mechanical automation. But certain specialist flower and herb production is still an important industry on which some families still rely."

As the land softened into the coastal plain, Ben could now see acres of glass houses stretching as far as the eye could see. Many of the ones they passed, however, looked abandoned with broken glass and long grasses growing out of the gaps. These seemed clear signs of a once great industry in decline. The floriculture finally gave way to the urban sprawl of houses and small apartment blocks spreading back from the coastal towns of the Riviera.

Nearly two hours after departing Molini di Triora they screeched to a halt outside Bagni Regina, where every available surface had been freshly painted in what Ben called 'Greek taverna blue'. It was that pale sky blue that is just so evocative of Mediterranean culture, sunshine and sand. Since leaving the restaurant up in the shade of the valley, the temperature had climbed steadily during their descent and was now mid-twenties centigrade. Ben had brought his straw hat and was now glad of it.

"My sister, Sofia, runs this place helped by her mother, her daughter and, in the busy summer weeks, also a couple of cousins."

Sofia was tall, not as tall as her older brother, but you could see the genetic lineage. Also, her hair and skin were paler than most Italians. Ben thought she could have been German or Scandinavian. He guessed her age at forty but was not sure about that. Although not conventionally pretty, she certainly had an air of sexuality that was not easy to explain by her physicality. She did not dress in a revealing way, although it was still easy to see that she had a great, if slightly generous, figure. There was no exaggerated hip swaying in her walk, tossing of hair, or pouting of lips that would broadcast signs of overt availability. Her smile on greeting was warm but not overly so. Yet there was definitely something unusual in the magnetism that Ben felt radiating from her presence.

"Welcome," was all she said but in doing so maintained eye contact for longer than was usual.

Vincenzo then took over the conversation, jabbering away to her without pausing for breath for three or four minutes. She looked at first puzzled, then annoyed, and finally resigned. Ben had discerned all of this without understanding a word of what was said, but by merely reading her typically-observable Italian body language. During this walk-and-talk dialogue, Ben had followed them through into the cool, shaded restaurant, across a wooden decked area, and finally down some steps into the sand. Here he was offered a seat at a table under a canvas canopy. Behind the tables was a bar, open on one side to the restaurant and on the other to the beach. As Ben's eyes adjusted to the brightness of the late afternoon sun, the full beauty of the view along the beach became apparent. The bay arced away into the distance for a good kilometre before a promontory blocked the view of the shore beyond it. A larger landmass further on was clearly the distinctive outline of the rock of Monaco, its tall glass towers now gleaming in the sunshine. The sea was pure azure to match the name given to its nearby coastline by the French. When a tall, frosted glass full of cold beer arrived in front of him, unordered, that completed a vision to match any Ben had ever witnessed.

Vincenzo had ordered himself a Coke and settled with it in his canvas chair.

"Beautiful setting, no?"

Without averting his eyes from the view, Ben agreed.

"It certainly is".

They both sipped from their glasses while Ben also drank in the view. A slight breeze off the sea took the edge off the heat but was barely enough to ripple the cloth on their table. Probably an hour passed without much being said. Ben people-watched and sank into a kind of comatose state, perhaps finally believing what he had so far found so hard to; he had escaped his accuser, his indifferent students, the grey British weather, and all his financial responsibilities—at least for the foreseeable future. In a couple of weeks, he would have a sizable surplus in his account for the first time in years. His flat had been rented for more than he was paying on his lease, his car had been sold for him by a local garage, and his monthly salary would arrive with no food or bills to pay out from it. He was unusually solvent.

Ben's eyes barely glanced in the direction of the bar when he caught Sofia's looking straight back at him. She was holding up another frosted beer glass which she had just extracted from the freezer, as if anticipating his wish for a second. Wow. That's what I call service, Ben thought. 'What is it with that woman?' he started wondering again. Maybe it was the eyes he decided. They seemed to maintain contact wherever she was or whatever she was doing or saying – like the Mona Lisa, he remembered. Here at ten metres distant, they still managed to hint at an unspoken invitation.

Another extended period of quiet reflection passed before Vincenzo was up out of his seat, suddenly animated and rubbing his tummy.

"Apperitivo time I think," he announced.

Ben began to protest that he was still not remotely hungry after the enormous lunch, but the big man waved away his protest and shouted to his sister.

"Cappon magro?"

"Si. Due?" came the instant reply to an almost rhetorical question.

"Cappon magro?" repeated Ben questioningly, wondering what huge meal might arrive at any moment.

"A fisherman's Christmas lunch," explained Vincenzo. "On Christmas Eve rich Ligurian people would have a cappon for dinner. The poor fisherman could never afford such luxury, and so their wives created a dish using the best seafood they could land. The luxury seafood was what they would normally sell, but which people weren't buying that day because they would be eating a capon. Depending on their luck this would be white fish, red prawns, or even lobster. Because it was Christmas, they also went to a lot of trouble to make it look special. Not just another dinner. Even if they were poor, they felt they were entitled to a little luxury once a year."

Two large round glasses of prosecco arrived with a basket of fresh bread and a small bowl of brown and black olives that Ben now recognised as Taggiasca.

"What do you think of my sister's place? She used to run it with her husband, but she is now a widow."

"I think it's way beyond wonderful," Ben answered. "Beach, sea, view, warm sunshine, cold beer. What else do you need?"

"And women," Vincenzo indicted towards the bar where Sofia had now been joined by what Ben presumed to be her daughter.

"I can't fault the view or the service," he agreed cryptically.

"You could have all this and for much less than you'd think."

"What do you mean?" asked the intrigued Englishman.

"We have a small studio above the restaurant, which the visiting summer staff sometimes use. It is not an official residence and so Sofia is not supposed to rent it to tourists. If she could, with this view and closeness to the beach, it would be full all the time."

As they chatted, Sofia's daughter arrived bearing two plates and a broad smile.

"Uncle Vincenzo, you old rascal," was her welcome in near-perfect English.

“Ciao, Kesia,” was Vincenzo’s warm reply before air kisses were exchanged.

“Please explain to our English guest what is in your famous cappon magro,” he instructed.

“OK, we start with thin toasted bread. Like used for bruschetta but bigger slices from a round bun like a bagel. Then you build upwards layers of vegetables—whatever is in season. Usually sliced boiled potatoes, green beans, carrots, and celery. Sometimes in spring and early summer, asparagus, which still grows wild here if you know where to look. Then some flaked white fish—often sea bass but any good fish without too many bones. Some more vegetables and then a layer of shelled red prawns. San Remo if we can get them, but otherwise pink prawns will do.”

“It’s a kind of American open sandwich made with fish?” offered Ben.

“Si. Si, exactly so. You would not eat it like a sandwich, but yes, it is similar. On display on the top go the luxury seafood. Some lobster chunks and a couple of langoustine in their shells. You drizzle on olive oil, lemon and a little vinegar.”

“And the green sauce?” quizzed Ben. “What is in that?”

“Ah, now that I can’t tell you because my grandmother is watching. Although she is deaf, she can read lips at fifty metres and will kill me if I reveal anything about her recipe.”

Appetites now miraculously restored, both men exchanged a ‘chin’, drank from their prosecco and started on their cold fish salad. It was the perfect dish for a warm evening by the sea, Ben thought. Cool, light and sea fresh and the crispy bread at the base adding another crunchy texture to the soft topping. The sauce indeed contained anchovy, Ben decided, but there were several ingredients he could not identify.

Now even more captivated by this place by the sea, Ben was prompted to ask,

“You were saying about this studio apartment?”

"Si. Officially, only staff can use it to rest between shifts. But as you are working for the prince that is close enough to grant you, and us, immunity from any complaints from anyone. For two hundred euros a week you can have bed and breakfast right here on the beach. The piatto del giorno including wine would be ten euros to you. Cheap rent to live on the Riviera, eat well, and be well looked after." As he added this final remark, he gestured over his shoulders to the two women behind the bar.

Ben had to admit it was possibly even more appealing than his current arrangement. This was partly because of the proximity to the beach but also because of his growing unease with his current hostess, the far too readily combustible Alessandra. The alluring Sofia was far easier to deal with, and there would appear to be at least the prospect of something more interesting here.

The rent was less than he was receiving in rent for his Newcastle apartment and, he rationalised, he would be no worse off than if he were at home but with apparent fringe benefits. From where he sat, both the view and the prospects looked rosy.

"I'm definitely going to give it some thought," he told Vincenzo.

To which he replied, "And, you would be far from all the villages' political infighting and its gossiping women. Oh, and Alessandra's crazy husband, if he should turn up."

"Let me sleep on it, Vincenzo. You've certainly tempted me."

The pace on the drive home was thankfully leisurely. Climbing uphill steeply, the Cinquecento containing the two large men just did not have the power for anything else. Ben was relieved but only because he was so full of food, wine, and beer, that he feared being sick on Vincenzo's beautiful interior.

When he thought about it, he was amused by just how much trouble Vincenzo had gone to, to try and get him out of the village. His rival clearly saw him as a serious threat, which was flattering in a way. As far as he had been aware, Ben had never had such an obvious challenger for the affections of a woman. This was a game that was unfamiliar but which he was also somewhat enjoying. Especially now that he understood the rules of engagement.

By the time they reached Seborga, Ben had made up his mind to remain in Seborga. As appealing as the beach, Sofia, and her cappon magro were, they were simply no match for the challenge of taming Alessandra and the allure of her pansotti. He also realised that Claudio would be deeply offended if he were to spurn his hospitality and that might put his whole position here in jeopardy. The thought of returning to work at the University was just too horrible to entertain.

9. BOURSOTOU

Already, Ben's old life in Newcastle—cold damp walks to campus, Groundhog Day lectures, nights in alone, marking, laundry, and the occasional kipper—were becoming a distant memory. His long warm days were now filled with his passions, walking through vineyards and farmland before consuming their marvellous bounty. His thoughts were largely occupied with finding a way to save the village's dwindling economy and, if possible, also to find a way he could prolong his stay.

The princess was continuing to be something of a challenge to Ben but the more she threw at him, the more he wanted to tame her. When his children were small, he had bought a Labrador puppy. At dog training classes, he had learned that this friendly breed needed, and expected, to be loved by all. Indeed, in public his Labrador would quickly single-out and make the most fuss of those people who really didn't like dogs and were avoiding them. All of Alessandra's signals were saying 'stay away' and yet all he wanted to do was win her over. He was like a Labrador; tail wagging, tongue out, and big eyes wide open saying, 'You will like me if only you would take the time get to know me'.

She must have got to hear about Ben's visit to Sofia's because one day when he asked what was in a cappon magro sauce, she answered with, "Probably arsenic, if you eat it at Sofia's."

Seeing Ben's mystified expression, she continued, "Vincenzo's sister has already killed-off two husbands and I'd heard she was looking for a third."

Ben frowned at her very obvious loathing of this woman and challenged her with, "Vincenzo told me that her first husband had a heart attack and the second a motorcycle accident. How could they have been poisoned?"

"Slowly, one cappon magro at a time. A heart complaint brought on by feeding him poisoned fish. The second one had mysterious stomach cramps while riding his motorbike and crashed into a truck."

Realising that Alessandra was now teasing him, Ben joined in the game.

"There would be worse ways to die than eating seafood by the beach, cosseted in the ample charms of Sophia."

"Well, I am sure that door is firmly open Professore and I'd be glad to have rid of your food and wine overhead. Shall I ask Vincenzo to arrange a transfer to the beach?"

"I have already made it clear to Vincenzo that the cooking and the view is better here and, anyway, I would not wish to offend your gracious father."

If the way to a man's heart is through his stomach, then understanding the skill that goes into cooking must surely be the way into the affections of a female chef, Ben reasoned. He had finally broken the coolness which had inevitably followed the 'limoncello incident' by continually asking Alessandra direct questions about the meals that she presented him with each day.

"What was that herb in that sauce? Is that ricotta cheese in this ravioli? Where are those chestnuts from?"

At first these questions were ignored, then, as days went by, answered very briefly and abruptly before the explanations finally lengthened and softened in tone. Alessandra's passion for food and a desire to share that with anyone showing genuine interest finally got the better of her irritation. Her sleeves were however still firmly buttoned, and no alternative explanation was volunteered or requested.

Ben had read on a tourist website that there was a library in the nearby coastal town of Bordighera which had thousands of books in English. The collection was a remnant of the wealthy

Victorians who had flocked here in their thousands around the turn of the century. Other surviving clues to winter occupation of the English gentry were Anglican churches, formal parks, a tennis club, and many hotels named after famous London establishments: The Carlton, The Bristol, The Ritz, etc. Back then the town had boasted the surgeries of two Harley Street doctors, a branch of a London bank, and an English language newspaper.

The Clarence Bicknell Library was stocked with the English academic's impressive collection of British classics, plus many textbooks on Italian history, culture, geography, and flora & fauna. A ten euro temporary membership and day spent in its dusty reading room, supplied Ben with both a good selection of research material on Western Ligurian cuisine, as well as the Knights Templar and their role here.

He spent the next week walking and reading. He retraced the routes both Alessandra and Vincenzo had showed him on their tours but was now better informed as to what to look out for. Armed with his new knowledge on these walks into the untamed hillside, he began seeking out and collecting wild greens and herbs such as borage, chard, and flat-leaf parsley. There were also less familiar plants such as cicerbita, plus two members of the dandelion family called talegna and dente di cane. Some combination of these plants was often contained in the filling of his now favourite pansotti. Indeed, various members of the dandelion family, the curse of British gardeners, were a staple of the wild larder used in any number of old Ligurian recipes.

When he first started delivering these green bundles to Alessandra at the Osteria, she was sceptical about their authenticity, looking sniffily, examining them much too carefully, then pulling out any odd strand of grass or foreign plant that had been included. As she came to acknowledge that Ben knew exactly what they were, she warmed slightly, sometimes exchanging information with him on what they might be used for.

"This is good for gattafin, or that is great in boursotou."

Sometimes Alessandra would even decide to prepare one of these ancient Ligurian pasta dishes for him to demonstrate the effect of what he had collected on the flavour. He had worked hard on his research, and his rewards were two-fold; she was clearly warming to this approach, and he got to eat the results.

It turned out that boursotou was another local variation of ravioli; usually crescent-shaped with turned-up ends and with a filling like pansotti. But again, countless adaptions of the basic recipe depending on family or village tradition, height above sea-level, time of year, and so on.

"Sometimes, as a treat for my father, my mother used to make bread or pasta with chestnut flour, like his mother had made when he was a child. When I was young, my mother rarely bought produce from the shop in the village, other than coffee, wheat flour and tobacco. These were the only things that my father could not grow or forage from the land. Shopping trips away from Seborga – down to Bordighera or San Remo – were even rarer and usually only for agricultural supplies. Olive nets and glass demijohns were about the only thing they bought with cash they earned from olive oil. My father could make virtually everything else himself: wheelbarrows, hoes, rakes, etc. My mother told me that my grandmother was even less reliant on imported goods because she made her own chestnut flour. They didn't smoke and drank wine at all meals instead of coffee. The wild chestnuts were gathered in the hills around us, dried, and ground into flour. From this, she produced pasta, bread, cakes and biscuits. They lived a truly self-sufficient life, never needing to leave the village or rely on outside help. Had the Nazi's not executed them, they would probably have both lived past one hundred years old like many of their neighbours."

In parallel to Ben's botanical and culinary education, Valerio was becoming his local wine mentor. He was the font of all knowledge on matters of Italian viniculture. Seeing his enthusiasm for discovering and tasting new varieties, the bar owner had set about acquiring examples for him to try. Some of these were from local farmers who only grew enough for their family's consumption and so had simple hand-written labels or, more often, no identification whatsoever. Valerio also revealed that, until quite recently, this local production would usually have been sealed with nothing more than a tablespoon of olive oil in the neck of the bottle.

"The oil floats above the wine but does not mix with it."

His explanation for this strange practice was that cork would have had to be imported and paid for with cash, while olive oil was almost free and made an effective air-tight seal which would last a year—the maximum that these wines would last before being drunk. The liquid stopper could easily be 'un-corked' with a deft flick of the wrist, which Valerio demonstrated with the empty beer bottle he was carrying.

"You will still sometimes see Ligurian waiters practising this flick to remove bits of cork floating on top of an opened bottle. Foreigners think this is a very strange custom."

Ben was encouraging and paying for these informal wine tastings and so it made good business sense to Valerio, who also welcomed practising his English. He also enjoyed Ben's conversations and did not restrict his teachings to the fruit of the vine; he even strayed into Alessandra's culinary territory

It was Valerio who introduced Ben to pisciadela, the Ligurian version of pizza. The single common topping of this north-western Italian flatbread is the anchovy, either whole or ground into a paste, known locally as machetto. To this, can be added sliced white onion, whole olives, occasionally tomatoes, but never ever cheese, and certainly not mozzarella. There are no buffalos anywhere close to Liguria.

Ben also used these chats to extract snippets of information about Alessandra, but his young friend was guarded about saying too much. Ben sensed that her title, unrecognised though it was outside the village, still granted her certain deference within its walls. The one thing he did learn about her was that Alessandra had been a childhood sweetheart of Vincenzo and that he still harboured strong feeling for her. The brusque Italian seemed to spend nearly as much time hanging around the Osteria as Ben did, even if Vincenzo was mainly in the company of other men.

Ben also often found himself at the Osteria, and not just at mealtimes, although dinner was the highlight of his day. Each new dish from Alessandra's kitchen now came with its own lesson in social history, horticulture, foraging, or cookery. She was a knowledgeable teacher and he was a willing student. He joked. She laughed. She increasingly used her extraordinary smile; now so broadly that her cheeks crinkled pleasingly, framing her naturally white teeth. It was a smile that perhaps she had not practised for some considerable time. It appeared as though she was rediscovering the sensation. Whatever scars she bore, were they finally healing? Ben wondered.

While sampling Alessandra's latest wine offering, a Barbera d'Asti from the Dogliotti family vineyards in Piedmont, Ben asked her,

"Why is it that only a few varieties of bland, mass-produced Italian wine were widely available outside of Italy?"

Alessandra shrugged her shoulders admitting that she had no clue to offer, except that, "It's the same in the USA. Apart from those restaurants with a private supply from back home, Italian wine there is inferior quality compared with what we find here. Why do you think that is?"

"Marketing?" he answered without hesitation.

He went on to argue that the French had spent years investing in brand-building for their wines. Not just marketing private brands, but also regional generic types like Burgundy and Bordeaux. These government initiatives had marketing budgets like those to promote regional tourism. The French had also invested in modern production technology and could produce quality in volume, which still commanded premium prices.

"Now I understand a little bit about Italian culture; I think I am also beginning to understand why I've never come across some of these great wines before. They are good, but all from relatively small productions and so you Italians drink them all here in Italy!"

Alessandra smiled and quoted an Old Italian proverb:

"Nella botte piccola c'è il vino buono" (In small barrels, there's good wine).

Ben laughed.

"I like it. The Italian equivalent of: Nice things come in small packages."

10. POLPETTE

Pacing the arrivals hall at Nice Airport, Ben had mixed feelings about the impending rendezvous. He had not seen or spoken to his daughter for two months, and then her photo-image appeared on his ringing phone screen two days ago. Their last encounter had been bruising and ended in harsh words on both sides. She wanted to borrow a fairly large sum of money to set up her own business. Her mother had apparently already turned her down, and he simply did not have anything like that amount to give her. She accused him of being mean and selfish. He was hurt and called her childish and irresponsible. He therefore felt sure it would not be good news that had prompted today's call.

He was correct. His daughter's long-term boyfriend had moved all her stuff out of their shared flat, dumped it at her mother's house, and then unceremoniously dumped her by text.

"How bloody dare he?" she had wept angrily into the phone.

To say that she was distraught would be an understatement. She was simultaneously crying, screaming and cursing. For five minutes he could hardly get any sense out of her. Conscious that she was calling him abroad on her mobile phone, he told her he would call back to save her bill but not for ten minutes, to allow her time to compose herself.

In the meantime, he put in a call to her mother. Although they had not spoken in nearly a year, she was not too surprised to receive the call. But she was less than delighted to hear from him. Feeling the antagonism in her voice, he asked, "Simply give me a synopsis of the facts and spare me your opinions."

His ex-wife briefly explained what had happened, as far as she could tell, but could not resist adding, "She could not blame Dale. It was all Selene's fault, she was a selfish little bitch."

Ben took this all in and finally said, “I take it she called you first and you offered her the same opinion that you just gave me. Hence my reappearance on her radar?”

“Good luck,” came her reply, just before the phone went dead.

She didn’t sound as though she meant that though. Now remarried, his ex-wife had ‘moved-on’ as they say. When both children left for university within a year of each other, their teenage posters were removed and their rooms were redecorated. She made a new start.

Selene came through the glass doors looking as affluent and confident as all the other Côte d Azur regulars, only much paler. Her big sunglasses hid any visible sadness or delight in her eyes, but the spare arm not attached to her roller-case was outstretched for a hug, which he stepped into. It felt good to hold her and smell her mane of hair again. Memories flooded back of happier times together in childhood. She hooked her arm into his and they headed to the exit, her still pushing her enormous pink plastic case.

“Buon giorno. Have you come in your Ape?” came an English voice which he did not at first recognise.

When he turned Ben saw that it was Cecily who he had met on the flight when he arrived in Nice.

“Not this time,” replied Ben, “but you are also something of a regular here?”

“You’ll discover that many people routinely commute from London to Nice and so the faces soon become familiar. Anyway, ciao, ciao. Maybe we’ll meet here again.” With that she disappeared into the crowd heading in the direction of Departures.

Taking off her sunglasses to watch the woman walk away, his daughter joked, “You don’t waste any time getting to know the locals,” adding a wry smile.

This light-hearted remark and the manner of her greeting bore none of the despair he heard in her voice just a couple of days ago. How quickly women's moods changed, he thought.

Selene added, "And wealthy locals judging by those trousers and shoes."

He thought about trying to explain that he barely knew this woman; that her conversations were, like that one, usually brief and often conducted over her shoulder as she walked quickly away from him. But he decided not to bother. As they exited the doors to the drop-off parking area, Cecily's blue Bentley was just cruising away with only the sound of its tyres on the tarmac to be heard.

"Cool," commented Selene as the big car purred by.

"Wait until you see our transport," Ben said.

The Dutchman owned a Kübelwagen which he had let the Englishman borrow to collect his daughter. Inevitably the deal included dinner and drinks, but that was fair enough Ben calculated. Volkswagen first made these Ferdinand Porsche-designed utilitarian versions of their legendary Beetle in the nineteen-forties. They were a cheap military all-terrain vehicle: the equivalent of the Allies' Willis Jeep. They continued in small numbers of production on-and-off right up until the seventies.

"They are now mostly owned by militaria collectors or strange Dutchmen," explained Ben, "they remind me of a sixties beach-buggy, only with corrugated sides. Only the Dutch could love something that looks like this."

Selene stopped to take in the strange looking vehicle, leaving her suitcase and walking all around it.

"No. I absolutely love it. It's even cooler than a VW camper van."

With no doors or windows to worry about, it was easy to lift the suitcase into the back and then step in over the sides.

"You would not think it was entirely cool if we drove back on the auto-route because you would get buffeted by passing traffic, so we will go the slower scenic route around the coast."

The car had no keys as such and starting it required finding two loose wires under the dash, temporarily removing the insulating tape, and sparking them together until the unmistakable sound of the air-cooled Beetle engine spluttered into life. There was a small knob that turned on the power and a metal tap to twist for the fuel; rather like a petrol lawnmower but without the pull cord. Despite all the exotic cars around at the airport, the washed-out yellow Kübelwagen still turned a few heads as it exited the terminal and turned onto Nice's famous Promenade des Anglais.

The talk on the drive home was all just catching up.

"How is your mother?" To which her response was silence.

"What is your brother up to?"

This required a slightly longer answer of, "Rugby, beer, curry and tarts. Just the usual."

Ben quickly ran out of questions so it became her turn to learn his news.

"How on earth did you manage to get suspended from your job? Mum says someone's suing you."

Turning to look at her sternly he said, "I am on paid sabbatical, and no one is suing me," he corrected. "If you ever want to be a serious journalist you need to find more reliable sources and to learn to check your facts."

He went on to tell her his version of the story adding that the University was expecting him back at work the following academic year. Selene seemed not entirely convinced by his version of events, demonstrating a cynicism she had unquestionably inherited from her mother.

"I suppose the fact that they gave you this gig must mean that they have some faith in you, otherwise you would just have been fired," she speculated. Looking around at the Nice seafront and the grand hotels she said, "You certainly fell on your feet this time, Dad. A paid sabbatical on the Riviera for... how long was it?"

He paused before answering, suddenly being reminded that this wonderful adventure would someday come to an end.

"At least six months. Maybe nine," he answered.

It was not easy to hold a conversation when exposed to the buffeting wind and traffic noise in an open-sided vehicle, so the journey settled into a comfortable silence, punctuated only by occasional pointing and exclamations such as 'wow' and 'cool'. Selene was enjoying the scenery and noting the glamorous, immaculately dressed women. She was also occasionally pointing out some 'gorgeous' men driving 'very smart' cars. Ben smiled broadly as he realised that she now assumed this was the Riviera life she had come to share with him for a little while.

"Make the most of this excess," he said cryptically.

When they turned off to begin the journey up to Seborga, Ben pulled in at the side of the road where there was a clear view both up the valley and back to the coast they had just travelled along. He pointed up towards the far ridge of the mountains.

"Can you see the highest village, the last one before the mountain becomes all trees? It has a pink church bell tower spouting high out of the centre."

She followed the line of his arm, squinting through her sunglasses, until she agreed that she could see it.

"That is Seborga?" There was a pause while she took in the scene. "It's very high. And very small." Then deciding she should add something which sounded more positive, added, "Like Florida's Magic Kingdom."

He laughed. "Truly, that is a fair comparison. It is more like a magic kingdom than you could possibly imagine. Except that this is Prince Claudio's magic kingdom."

He turned around and pointed back to the road they had travelled along, showing how close they were to Nice, Monaco, and Menton, all now shimmering below them in the afternoon heat. They agreed it was spectacular.

As they started to make a few hairpin turns and climb higher, he found his daughter leaning further and further in towards him. The road became quite narrow at points, leaving the car wheels perilously close to the edge. With the open sides of the Kübelwagen, Selene was suddenly aware that the terraces, which had been cut out of the hillside to accommodate the road, were often too narrow for two vehicles to pass. She also noticed as they climbed that the painted buildings down below were, by now, appearing to be only the size of sugar cubes. She calculated they were already several hundred feet above sea level.

Ben kept trying to add colour to the journey by pointing out places and things of interest. There was the ancient salt trail up from the coast and the Co-operative olive mill, where everyone took their harvested olives to be pressed. She marvelled at the tiny stone Rusticas clinging impossibly-precariously to the sides of the mountain across the valley. Yet it was all she could do to force open her eyes to catch a glimpse of these attractions before closing them again to avoid looking over the edge of the next bend with an even more perilous drop.

The lack of vision accentuated her other senses. She could smell the fruit trees in blossom and begin to 'hear' the silence. Or, at least, she became aware of the lack of noise, other than from the car in which they were travelling. The cicadas were the only discernible sound until she heard a high-pitched piercing call causing her to open her eyes and look up. An enormous eagle soared high above them, its wings motionless, cruising on the hot air sweeping up from the coast. Its head was tilted down, its eyes panning back and forth across the hillside seeking a rabbit, snake or mouse. It was apparently oblivious to human presence. She was starting to become conscious that each kilometre they travelled also seemed like stepping back a century in time. Maybe the Kübelwagen was, in fact, a time machine, like the DeLorean in Back to the Future.

Along with the car, the Dutchman had offered Ben a small room above his shop for Selene to use while she was there. He had lived there himself at first but now had a converted Rustica outside of the village. Selene would also have use of the small bathroom and kitchen at the back of the shop, with a single gas ring for a coffee pot and a microwave oven. All this for one hundred euros a week plus, of course, another free dinner with the two of them and their conversation, during which he could practice his English. The room had a little window at the front looking out into the small piazza and a slightly larger one at the rear looking over the tiled rooftops towards the mountains. It was, like the Dutchman, quirky and a bit shabby but somehow charming none-the-less. The Dutchman had no sooner left her in the bedroom when his interior design talents and the view from his spare room were being broadcast around the world on Instagram and Pinterest, attracting lots of positive comments, questions, and 'Likes'.

Ben had warned Claudio and Alessandra of his daughter's impending arrival and they had invited them both to a dinner at the Osteria. Alessandra would not be able to sit down with them at first because she was working, but was to join them when she could. Alessandra explained to Ben that her teenage son, Cristiano, who was also in the village that weekend, would be joining them, along with Vincenzo.

Unbeknown to Ben, Claudio had decided that his guest's daughter warranted the full state visit treatment, so both he and Vincenzo had dressed in their official uniforms. Ben and Selene were already seated at the table when the royal party came striding across the square, Cristiano lagging behind them and looking slightly embarrassed. Selene spotted them and turned to her father, mouth ajar and eyes wide, but strangely for her, now speechless.

Ben had not seen the prince in his regalia since the day he arrived and had forgotten just how imposing he looked. Claudio stopped in front of Selene looking very serious and regal.

Vincenzo drew-up to the prince's right shoulder, clicked his heels together, and saluted, holding his hand to his blue beret for some time, emphasising the action. His usual stubble had finally succumbed to the razor and, Ben thought, he caught a waft of aftershave in the evening air.

The guard of honour then gave his now familiar introduction,

"His Supreme Tremendousness Prince Claudio Biancheri the Third of Seborga, servant only to God, the Pope, and his loyal subjects."

Claudio bowed slightly and reached for Selene's hand and kissed it gently on the back. She rose from her chair as he did so and Ben thought he saw a hint of an involuntary curtsey. He was smiling broadly at her mixture of wonder, embarrassment, and sheer delight at the scene which confronted her.

"Senorina, welcome to Seborga. It is a great honour for us to have the daughter of the professore here."

Selene looked at her father briefly, as if to check that was who the prince was referring to. Claudio then introduced his grandson and Vincenzo, adding that his aide would be available to act as her 'guida e aiutante' while she was here.

"Kind of bodyguard," Cristiano offered her as a translation in his strongly American-accented English.

"I have my own bodyguard?" she exclaimed with the absolute glee of a six-year-old been given a new puppy. "How cool is that? Does anyone mind if I take photos of us all?"

Claudio waved his hand dismissively as though she did not even need to ask, and she snapped away with her mobile phone. Within seconds the images and messages, 'Me with the prince of Seborga' and 'Me with my own personal royal bodyguard' were beaming around the world, or at least her personally-networked version of it, via Instagram and Facebook.

He could see Alessandra hovering outside the kitchen with plates ready to serve. And so, Ben suggested that they all dispense with the formalities and take their seats. No sooner had they done so then texted replies of disbelief, amazement, and envy came pinging back to Selene's phone. So much so that she had to turn it to silent to avoid embarrassment in the restaurant.

Claudio held court dispensing wine and essential information about its quality and provenance, mainly in Italian. Cristiano was polite and smiled when spoken to but suffered from the perpetual discomfort of teenagers in the company of their elders. Nevertheless, they enjoyed a spectacular dinner, including most of Ben's now favourite dishes: pansotti, coniglio alla Ligure, and finally panna cotta.

Alessandra joined them for the panna cotta, sitting down between Claudio and Cristiano, who moved around the table next to Ben to accommodate his mother. Ben noticed again that Alessandra wore long sleeves and buttoned cuffs on this very warm evening. Selene leant closer to her father and whispered, "What's with you and the cook? You have not taken your eyes off her all night. Every time she comes out of that kitchen you track her across the floor."

Ben stood slowly and deliberately to get everyone's attention and then announced loudly, "Selene, please allow me to introduce Her Sereness the Princess Alessandra Biancheri of Seborga. Oh, and also our Michelin Star chef," he added with a little solo applause, "and, I hope, my new friend?"

If she had been astounded at Claudio's introduction, Selene was even more so by this one. Alessandra grimaced at Ben using her title to introduce her to his daughter. She said, "Take no notice of your father, my name is Alessandra, but you can call me Alex."

Selene was bursting with questions and desperate to seek further explanation of these remarkable revelations but she realised she could not grill her father in front of the very subject of her curiosity.

She turned her attention to Cristiano, who although much too young for her she thought, was a spectacularly beautiful boy. Those azure blue eyes, set in his deeply tanned skin and framed by a great mop of black curly hair, were a heart-breaking combination. Another selfie of her and the reluctant Cristiano went winging off around the Internet. This post also solicited almost immediate responses. Some of those from her closest friends made even her blush. The number of Facebook 'Likes' and people sharing these posts quickly went spiralling upwards as the news of a new celebrity 'royal family' spread throughout the on-line community. Secretly, she also hoped that her ex-boyfriend was seeing these photos and that her new circle of friends was making him jealous. The signal for the night to draw to a close was when Claudio downed the last of his limoncello, rose to his feet, and bid everyone, "Bene notte."

It was not late when Ben walked his daughter back to her apartment but they were both tired. Conscious of this, Seline tried to prioritise her questions.

"If they are really royalty, why do they sit and eat in a public restaurant? Don't they have a palace? And what the hell was the deal with you and the one star chef, or should I say Princess?" managing to sound simultaneously sceptical about both her royal title and Michelin Star provenance.

He walked a couple more steps, stopped and turned to her saying, "Look. A lot has happened in the past few weeks. It's a long story to explain and I am exhausted from the drive to the airport in that weird car. Will you settle for knowing that everything you have seen and heard since you arrived is real and true? And I assure you that Alessandra and I are nothing more than friends. We will go for a long walk tomorrow in the hills and I will fill you in on all the details then."

She thought for a moment and suggested a compromise, "One more question and I'll leave it for tonight. If Claudio is the prince and his daughter Alessandra is a princess, then if Cristiano is her son, he must also be a prince?"

Although the thought had never before entered his head, Ben agreed that he must. She shrieked and hopped up and down like a small child.

"I've been kissed by two princes in one night. Unreal. Totally unreal!"

She could not wait to get inside and start telling everyone on-line. Selene pecked her father on the cheek, bid him goodnight, and rushed up to her room, already furiously tapping on her phone screen.

11. POMODORO NERO

It was one of the rare days when clouds blowing over from the mountains above interrupted the sunshine and gave some respite from the otherwise punishing heat. A good day for a walk, Ben thought. Father and daughter strode out of the village just after nine thirty.

Selene had dressed surprisingly sensibly for a young woman of her generation, although Ben was unsure who all the make-up was meant to impress. He calculated that with the temperature more moderate today that they should make it up the ridge in good time to enjoy the picnic lunch Alessandra had provided.

Before they had even left the village, his daughter's questions came like gunfire. Ben did his best to précis the story of the events since his arrival. He glossed over the ups and downs in his turbulent relationship with Alessandra, but otherwise brought her up to date. Selene listened carefully and took it all in, occasionally making faces apparently indicating pleasure, distaste, and sometimes incredulity. He went on to tell her what he had learned about the Knights Templar and the extraordinary evidence Vincenzo had shown him of their presence here.

Selene could tell from the affection with which he described places, people, and their way of life, that her father was smitten with this place and its inhabitants—perhaps one in particular. She had never heard him talk so passionately about anything except French wine. Ben then outlined the task he had undertaken, to try and come up with a viable and sustainable economic master plan to revive the economic fortunes of Seborga.

"The place may look beautiful, but its economy is dying," he said, "farmers can't make a profit from their crops and the olive groves are being left to return to nature. The village's businesses can barely scrape a living, and nearly all the young people have already left. The only inward investment is in holiday homes, but they do not help the local economy very much because the people only use them a few months each year."

Ben went on to share his thoughts so far. He told her that the region had an almost unique terroir and climate; particularly the Maritime Alps environment, where warm sea mists mingle with cool clouds of the mountains. These highly skilled farmers can make almost anything grow in the most unlikely places. He was sure there was a ready, lucrative market for artisan food products which could claim this kind of provenance.

"The problem is, there is now a great deal of such produce entering the market. What I cannot figure out is how to square the circle: how to create a sustainable point of difference; a USP, to use the popular vernacular. Anyway, enough of me, what's been going on in your life? What's-his-name, the boyfriend's gone for good, has he?"

His daughter winced both at her father's inability to recall her long-term boyfriend's name and at being reminded of the whole sorry affair.

"Dale is history and good riddance," she confirmed.

Ben pointed out that this was something of a turn-around from their phone conversation of a week or so back when all she wanted was him back in her arms.

"I've moved on," she said, "Dale was a loser who's been holding me back."

Her father was tempted to ask what he was holding her back from but thought better of it. The last he could recall was, for a year and a half, she had been living off her boyfriend's earnings as an IT project manager. Having graduated in journalism from Southampton, only scraping a mediocre pass, she had not yet managed to find a job in the media. All Ben knew was that with only a lack-lustre degree and unrealistic expectations, she was still hell-bent on working in an industry in terminal decline. Not even freelance agencies were likely to be interested in her, he guessed. She was not alone, however, from her cohort of fifteen students. Only one friend had secured a job on a recognised newspaper and another in regional TV. The remainder were either in some on-line content blogging role or were would-be freelancers who had to subsidise their meagre earnings from writing by working in bars, cafés, or shops.

In an era where information from the Internet was free, so long as you were not too picky about the quality, there were decreasing opportunities for the remaining professional agencies selling quality news. She had talked about writing a book but had never got past the first few pages before throwing them in the bin.

"Maybe there is a novel in the story of this place?" Selene suggested.

Ben agreed that it was certainly a unique and fascinating setting for a story, "But you would still need a storyline. Without a plot, it's just another pretty backdrop."

As they walked, Ben repeated some of the social history that Vincenzo had shared with him and pointed out the flora and fauna Alessandra used in her cooking. Above them, they were aware that the sky was darkening significantly, but Ben had seen this happen many times, only for it to blow over in minutes and sunshine return. Anyway, they were only fifteen minutes from the ridge. The last hundred metres were less steep and allowed Selene to get her breath back before they crested the ridge and the view took it away again.

"Wowwwwww," she exclaimed as she looked out from the edge.

The folds of further tree-covered mountains, each layer higher than the last, retreated towards the horizon until tree-less, snow-capped versions took over. While she absorbed the amazing vista, Ben added,

"Wild boar, antelope and wolves still roam Italy's mountains – there are even bears further east of here."

She peered incredulously trying to focus on the highest peak.

"This is nature in the raw," she said, "like a place lost in time and yet within an hours' hiking distance of the twenty-first century. Truly incredible!"

Cumulous clouds rolled over, and sometimes around, the high peaks in the distance apparently heading towards them but still some way off.

"Snow in June?" she asked.

"There is snow all year on the Alps if you get high enough," he explained.

It was not only spectacular, it was beautiful, she thought. Ben placed his hands on her shoulders and turned her around. Seborga was below them rising like a pink terracotta wedding cake from the green landscape around it. The ceramic tiles of its church dome were glinting, even in the reduced light.

"I can see why you love this place, Daddy," she said.

They sat on a bench under a shelter built for the hikers and bikers who now used the old trails over the mountains. Scattered around were the detritus of the less responsible ones, some of whom appeared to have spent the night up here. There were signs of fires and throw-away barbeques.

Where salt traders, bandits, and partisans once passed with laden donkeys, now lycra-clad Milanese on five thousand euro mountain bikes peddle by. Alessandra had packed some rustic bread and a string of small Cacciatorini (hunter's sausages). There was also a small plastic box containing black tomatoes (pomodoro nero) stuffed with Brös cheese, breadcrumbs, and herbs. This is a pungent, creamy cheese from Piedmont made with Gappa. On top of the tomato was a crust of tapenade, the juices of which has seeped down into the cheese filling during cooking.

Selene agreed it was a feast. Looking for a reaction from her father as she added, "She knows her food that woman. She is also very pretty."

Ben just concentrated on serving their lunch and ignored the probing comment.

"Daddy, look!" Selene said, pointing to the sky above the ridge.

Ben disliked her calling him that. It was another of her mother's pretentious traits, inherited from her parents but which he had thought sounded affected when the children were three years old, and at twenty-three, even more ridiculous.

"The sky looks like it's falling on us. It's like an avalanche of cloud."

The rain-laden grey cloud was rolling off the mountains high above them and, being heavier than air, was taking the route of least resistant towards the coast. Before they had finished their picnic, heavy raindrops were pinging off the metal roof of the shelter, slowly at first, but quickly becoming more constant. The wind had picked up, and some of the rain was blowing in the sides of the shelter, but they were mostly dry inside. The rain was now pounding on the flat roof and thunder raised the noise level further. Lightning bolts flashed across the sky, briefly lighting the darkness. Ben placed his arm around his daughter and they huddled under the shelter, just about keeping dry. The thunder lasted only fifteen minutes but as quickly as it came, the wind dropped off, and then the rain just came down in what seemed like a relentless vertical torrent. They filled in the time chatting about past holidays in the rain, her hopes for the future, his hopes for Seborga, and eventually the rain began to ease. It seemed longer, but it was all over in about an hour and, not long after that, the rays of the sun were peeking through the gaps that had opened up in the cloud. Collecting their belongings and repacking the knapsack, they took one last look at the stunning views across a wild landscape with patches of blue now opening up all over the sky.

"This vista will not have changed since Napoleon marched his rag-tag army over here two hundred years ago and before that, probably not for another two thousand when the Romans came this way on their way to conquer France."

His daughter took in the enormity of that thought and agreed, "It is timeless. Thank you for bringing me here to see this. I've had a lovely day."

The path back down was slippery in parts and small streams of water sprung out of rocks and trickled down the mountain. Nevertheless, they made good progress downhill. Ben pointed to an eagle soaring on the thermals high above them. Selene asked if he thought it was the same one but Ben said there were many of them and several different species. Even from this distance, it seemed a huge bird to stay aloft without flapping its wings. They watched in awe for several minutes; not once did the eagle resort to using anything but the energy of the wind and the sun.

After about an hour and a half, they made it back to the fold in the valley where two facets of the mountain came together and the path turned east. They paused to look back at the ridge where they had picnicked and the path they had taken down from it. As they did so, Selene suddenly aimed her forefinger at a point about half-way down and asked, hesitantly,

"Are those trees moving?"

Ben focused on where she was looking. He shook his head in disbelief but sure enough, a patch of woodland appeared to be moving downhill in slow motion while the trees on it were still perfectly vertical. Below the first clump of trees others started to move, and then more even further away, until a slab of the mountain the size of a football field was creeping inexorably downwards. The enormous slab was not moving quickly, but soon some of the trees started to fall as their roots had little left to cling to. Ahead of the moving mass, large rocks were being excavated and these were rolling down the slope ahead of it. Some of these rocks were huge boulders the size of cars. They both felt the earth beneath their feet tremble slightly and heard a rumble like thunder now echoing around the valley.

After the initial disbelief, they now realised they could be in danger. Ben looked up, and the dense trees above them were all still. He also looked around them but there was simply nowhere to hide. Pulling Selene with him he fell to the ground into a hollow alongside a previously-fallen tree, feeling it might offer some protection. He was trying desperately to think of a better plan of action when the tremor stopped, the noise died down, and only an occasional falling tree or tumbling rock broke the silence. The slice of mountain had somehow arrested itself in its descent but had left a deep brown scar of exposed earth several hundred metres wide, and nearly as long, behind it. Remarkably, many of the trees remained upright or leaning only slightly.

Down below them, swathes had been cut in the trees and undergrowth by tumbling boulders and sliding trees stretching most of the way to the bottom of the valley. While Ben had been panicking about what to do to protect them, his daughter had been filming the whole thing on her phone. Ben thought her reaction of "Oh my God" was such an overused and predictable one that it hardly fitted the circumstances in which they found themselves.

"Was that an earthquake?" she asked, not really expecting her father to know any more about it than she did.

"It was certainly a landslide," he replied, "but I am not sure if the landslide made the ground tremble or an earthquake caused the landslide. Or maybe it was just all that water coming down so quickly after a long drought that triggered it?"

Ben was trying to work out what their next move should be. If only Vincenzo were here, he would know. Ben was amazed at just how composed his daughter was considering the events which had just unfolded. He had imagined she would have been hysterical and panicky. The contrary was true; she had the self-composure to record the event on her phone and was discussing options with him quite rationally. This newly found self-control was a revelation to Ben who had only seen her at her worst in recent years. He felt unusually proud of her.

What he did not know was she also felt proud of him. She too thought of her father as a city boy. And yet, here he was hiking in wild mountains, and competently making snap decisions in a real life-threatening emergency.

Ben now reasoned that if everything heavy was heading downwards, it would be wise not to continue their descent into the valley at this point. He recalled that a little further along they had earlier seen a fork in the path heading around the hillside. This route would hopefully take them both away from the unstable area and keep them on a level until they could find another safer way down. They had the great advantage of being able to see their ultimate destination below them, albeit still some way off.

Both somewhat stunned by what had just happened, and conscious that they were not yet out of danger, they walked on without talking and taking great care where they put their feet.

12. CONIGLIO

Ben immediately recognised the enormous stone now obstructing the path. Unless there was more than one massive slab of rock with a cross carved deeply into it around here, this was the place where Vincenzo had brought him but which he had subsequently been unable to find. The rock that had been to the side of the path had tilted outwards from the hillside by about a metre and now totally blocked their route. It was leaning slightly past vertical and below it was a steep fall. Ben looked all around and everything else seemed stable. There were no signs of earth movements or fallen trees.

"This is the cave of the Templar Knights that Vincenzo showed me when I first arrived."

His daughter looked slightly unconvinced but said only, "Really?"

Scrambling behind the boulder, he could see that the crack by which he and Vincenzo had first entered the cave was now a gaping chasm over two metres wide. The drawings on the walls, which he had previously seen with only a torch, were now illuminated by daylight and were even more impressive. Ben pointed to them and his daughter gasped.

"Please don't say, oh my God," Ben suggested, "it is not appropriate."

One of the drawings, which he recalled as being intact, now had a huge chunk missing from it leaving bare rock where previously there had been images. The missing piece, about the size of a large dinner plate, lay on the floor, face down. Ben picked it up and turned it over. It showed a sick-looking Knight lying prostrate against his shield; sword by his side and with an angel, apparently hovering over his left shoulder. In both his hands, he appeared to be clasping a large-stemmed cup, from which he was drinking something.

Ben placed it to one side, face up and his daughter snapped the object several times with her phone camera. She also recorded the remainder of the image still on the wall from which it had fallen. Further inside, Ben could see that the cave seemed more expansive than he remembered. There was also lots of loose rubble on the floor becoming deeper the further back into the cave they went.

Natural light became sparser as he stepped gingerly deeper inside, but he could pick out the shape of something man-made under a pile of loose rock. It was a box or chest, with the dimensions of a small suitcase. Another stone fragment, similar in size to the chest itself had crashed from the ceiling, crushed its lid and pierced the wood and metal construction mid-length. Ben could not lift it but managed to tilt it to a point where it rolled from the box, which had been holding it upright, and crashed to the floor in a cloud of dust. The falling stone brought a yell from his daughter, fearful of more landslides, but all was still again.

Ben could just about see inside the box, but everything was covered with a layer of dust. He tried blowing it away, revealing what appeared to be a book or a substantial document. The fabric of the cover was already disintegrating.

"Wait, Dad," Selene said urgently, "let me photograph it first."

She stepped forward and took several shots of the box but also put the lens in the opening and snapped the contents. The automatic flashes illuminated the cave for a split-second. They were both well aware they were looking at something extraordinary and probably very significant.

"What the hell...?" was all she could say but, once again, she was not expecting her father to have an answer.

They both froze as somewhere distant they heard a rumbling which quickly grew louder. Within seconds the noise peaked nearby but then started to fade into the distance.

"I fear that was another boulder rolling down from above us," warned Ben, "we need to get away from here now."

Realising the chest was too heavy to carry down the mountain, and its contents probably too fragile to remove, they retreated carefully from the back of the cave towards the entrance. Ben picked up the fragment of the wall painting that had broken off and slid it carefully into his backpack. Back in the glaring daylight, they scanned the hillside for signs of danger. All they could see was a track of broken branches and trampled undergrowth, where something large had recently careered past. This must have been the rumbling sound they had heard earlier. A boulder appeared to have bounced high into the air when it struck the path they were walking along, because below it, there was a gap of fifteen metres before the wreckage of its trajectory could be seen to start again.

The remainder of the trek back was thankfully uneventful, with the weather improving all the time. Eventually Selene had to ask, "Do you think that painting shows a Templar Knight drinking from the Holy Grail?"

Her father considered his answer carefully.

"There are so many stories, legends, and myths surrounding what people refer to as 'The Holy Grail' and no one is entirely certain what it was, or indeed, if it ever existed at all."

Ben revealed what he learned from his research about the connections between the Templars and this now iconic object.

"According to legend, it was variously a stone cauldron of some sort, the cup from which Christ drank wine at the last supper, the vessel in which his blood had been collected from the crucifixion, and then there is Dan Brown's Da Vinci Code theory."

He acknowledged, however, that if it existed at all, in whatever form, it was entirely possible the Templars brought it back from the Holy Land. If that were so, there was a better than good chance it at least passed through Seborga on its way to wherever it ended up. Ben even speculated that it was remotely possible it had got no further than here when the Knights fell out of favour with the Pope and they either took it with them or, fearing being caught in possession of it, hid it somewhere before they left. Selene's incredulity at this revelation was palpable. Ben pointed out that her mouth appeared to be frozen open and she closed it.

"You mean that..."

Her father merely nodded and added, "It's only infinitesimally, theoretically, possible."

She smiled. "From an academic, I'll take that as a maybe."

After forty-five minutes of traversing along the mountain, a path emerged heading down the hillside and they took it. The route met a stream and followed that for a while until they reached what passes for a road in these parts: a flat track two metres wide scraped out of the hillside. There were signs of car tyres, discarded plastic bottles, and signs saying, 'La caccia è vietata' – hunting forbidden. They were almost back in the twenty-first century, relieved and grateful they were both safe after their ordeal. Two very different trains of thought had been going on between father and daughter during the couple of hours it had taken them to make it back to the village.

Selene had been only too aware that her failure to get the kind of job she had talked about for so long in the industry she had chosen had damaged her self-confidence. Her best friend from university, who she considered to be nowhere near as smart as herself, had a job with one of the national broadsheet newspapers. This especially bothered her as, although they were friends of sorts, there was also a fierce rivalry between them. Now, although her friend might be reporting the news from the safety of her desk in London, she was here right in the middle of news being made—rather like the BBC's Kate Adie, on the front line of the latest Middle East conflict. Selene was sure the images on her phone were the key to her future career. She just needed to decide how, where, and when, to turn that key.

Ben, meanwhile, also thought this might be a turning point in his quest for a sustainable future for the village, as well as a permanent place for him in it. Like his daughter, he was not at all certain just how it would all pan out. Although uncertain just how, Ben had a strange feeling that ultimate victory could spring from this near disaster, and the contents of his backpack would be somehow significant in that. He asked his daughter not to tell anyone about what they had found until he had spoken to Claudio. She nodded vaguely and said, "Sure, whatever," but without much conviction that her father could detect.

"Seriously, Selene. People's livelihoods might depend on how we handle this."

His daughter agreed but was really thinking more about her own livelihood.

Oblivious of the excitement in the mountains, late afternoon village life continued as normal in Seborga. The storm in the mountains had diluted into a three-minute shower at the lower level of the village. Any rainwater had evaporated from the pavements fifteen minutes after it fell. The scraggy stray cats soaked up the sun on doorsteps, and recently hung-out washing fluttered in the breeze. The Osteria was closed. The lady who ran the grocery shop was leaning against the wall outside in the shade, smoking, but most people were indoors behind tightly closed shutters trying to keep out the late afternoon heat.

Ben and Selene agreed they both badly needed a shower and a rest and so after a hug, longer and firmer than usual, they parted at the small piazza and went up different alleys.

As tired as he was, Ben could not sleep. He was holding the fragment from the cave painting. Exactly what had they stumbled upon? What could it mean for the village? Then there was whatever was in the box they had left behind.

He decided he needed to do some research and rang a colleague, Rob Appleton, back at the University in Newcastle. They were not close friends, nor did they work together directly, but the Head of History and himself shared a passion for a good Burgundy. That was currently about as close to a friend as Ben had in the north. Although surprised to hear from him, Professor Appleton took the call from Ben.

After exchanging pleasantries, Ben got to the point of the long-distance conversation. He asked Rob how rare Templar artefacts were, who had what, and where? His colleague confessed to only little direct knowledge of that period or subject, but conjectured that after over a thousand years it would be mainly metal objects which would have survived. He went on to qualify this by adding that although they merited a significant place in history, there were not that many of the Knights, and their era did not last for more than a couple of hundred years. Furthermore, because they were wealthy Knights, their metal objects would be high-value and so likely to have been melted down and recycled into other things later. In recent years metal-detectorists would doubtless have boosted the haul of items, but his overall conclusion was that he would be surprised if much by way of genuine Templar artefacts had survived.

But then there is the Church, he added as an afterthought. The Knights initially operated at the behest of the Pope and so the Vatican will doubtless have material. Indeed, they might have all manner of things but were unlikely to be advertising the fact, as they are now a bit touchy about their links with the Templars. Ben asked specifically about documents and he gave the same answer,

"Only anything stored carefully away from light and moisture would be likely to have survived a millennium; anything in archives like the Church's or, less likely, private collections."

Then his colleague recalled that about a year before, a Leeds antique dealer had spotted something unusual about a colourfully painted wooden plaque he saw at a car boot sale. His instinct was good, because it turned out to be the lid from a genuine Templar tabernacle.

"He paid a tenner for the piece, about the size of an A4 sheet, and he thought it was going to make his fortune. I doubt that was the case. There was speculation about its value in the papers for a few days because the guy said he was going to send it to auction. Valuation figures around fifty thousand pounds were mentioned. As far as I know, it never got to an auction house and no mention of it has been heard of since. My guess is that some Masonic Lodge or Da Vinci Code conspiracy theorist will have snapped it up for about ten grand cash and it will now be in a private collection."

He expressed his extreme envy at Ben's extended sabbatical in Italy then the pair said their farewells and hung up.

Ben decided he needed more time to think before telling Claudio about what they had found, and so sent a text message to Selene urging her to continue to keep quiet about what had happened, 'For a while, at least, while I decide the best course of action.'

Over in her room, Selene was already drafting a text message to her old university friend now working at the Tribune newspaper. Nikki had been one of the students who did everything by the book and consequently always got acceptable, if not brilliant, results. She never exhibited any great flair or imagination and seldom articulated any original thought, but her prose was faultless. She habitually ticked all the boxes on the journalist check-list: who, what, where, when, etc. Her sources were always attributed, and their names sure to be spelt correctly. Superlatives were rarely, if ever, used and then only when they could be independently verified. It was this precision which won her the internship with a national newspaper. However, Selene thought that she would have reported the break-in at Watergate with unerring accuracy as a minor crime, but completely missed the political significance of the story.

Ben used to say that in coffee terms, Selene was cappuccino to Nikki's espresso. One was blonde and frothy, the other dark and serious. Both were smart but Selene was impulsive and Nikki cautious.

They were opposites in so many ways and yet had gravitated towards each other at university. Their slightly unusual relationship had survived the inevitable trials of their differing viewpoints. They also attracted different men, yet their rivalry often saw them flirting with each other's boyfriends.

With her trial year soon coming to an end at the newspaper, Nikki was increasingly being asked to start digging up some more original material and not just reporting on things which fell on her desk. Her editor was of the 'old school' of journalism and had warned her she had any number of people who could report news that had already broken. What she needed was someone who could put themselves in situations where they could find breaking news. 'Give me a minor royal, smoking a joint with a naked footballer, i.e. sex, drugs, and royalty, and I'll give you a front page by-line,' was her recent definition of 'breaking news'.

Selene spent a long time drafting and editing the text message she was going to send to Nikki and finally settled on the text: 'Theoretically, if I had an exclusive story which involved a minor natural disaster which had unearthed an ancient artefact directly linked to the birth of Christianity – possibly even to the Holy Grail—and this was verified by an English university professor, who I am sure is shagging the princess of the land where it was found, what would that be worth to you?'

She hit send.

Nikki had already seen her friend's Instagram posts with one photo of what she said was, 'The Prince', but assumed, like everyone else it seemed, it was just some wag in fancy dress.

Now she was curious. Nikki responded, “What the fu– are you serious?”

“Totally,” came the instant reply.

“Can we talk?” asked the journalist.

“Don’t want to talk detail until I have the basis of a deal,” offered Selene, knowing that any conversation could too easily reveal vital clues.

“I am not going to my editor with what you’ve sent. She would have me carted off in a straitjacket. Can you give me something concrete?”

Anticipating this question, Selene had prepared a short, edited video clip of the landslide showing the date and time, plus a photo of the fragment from the painting. She sent these digital files. On receipt, the careful correspondent then checked to see if her friend’s location had been activated on Facebook, and it had. Selene had ‘checked-in’ at Nice Airport a few days ago and was now somewhere on the Italian Riviera. She then searched for seismic reports from that area and quickly uncovered a long history of instability caused by minor earth tremors.

Google was also quick to offer up a number of images of the Prince of Seborga, which she checked with the image on Facebook posted by Selene. They matched. A bit more digging around found that the prince indeed had a daughter and that the family had links back to the Knights Templar and the Crusades. She also now recalled that her friend’s father had been a university lecturer.

“Bloody hell,” she exclaimed out loud in the office, causing most of her colleagues to look away from what they were doing. However, they knew better than to ask her the source of her outburst and returned to their tasks.

Try as she might, Nikki could not remember which university Selene had said her father taught at. She sent a message to a mutual friend from their university and he had replied, ‘Newcastle. Why do you ask?’ Ignoring the question, she phoned the switchboard in Newcastle. She was given the usual options to choose from and, after a moment's hesitation, chose the Department of History. When someone answered, she told them she was a reporter doing research. The receptionist put her through to the Head of Department.

"Professor Robert Appleton," he answered.

She made her introduction and then had her questions ready.

"Is Ben Morton a colleague of yours?"

As that was public information, he confirmed that he was.

"Could you confirm that he was currently in Seborga, Italy?"

He told her that he could not answer that question unless he knew why she was asking. Nikki said she was an old friend of Ben's daughter and she had seen in a Facebook post that she was currently out there visiting him.

"My newspaper had also received a report of an earthquake in the area." So far, so true, she thought.

"But now I cannot contact her to check if she is Ok." Not strictly true. The academic relaxed his tone and became cheerier.

"By coincidence, I heard from Ben on the phone not an hour ago," he said, "there was no mention of an earthquake. He was asking about artefacts from the Knights Templar era. Must be something to do with his research project."

The reporter said she was relieved to hear this and told him that it was just a minor tremor and, perhaps, it was not too close or even out at sea. She thanked him for his time. When she hung up the phone, she said, "Bloody hell" again, out loud.

It was approaching 5pm in the UK, but no one would be leaving the office until after seven; her boss possibly not until after 9pm. She decided to go and have a coffee and think this over before approaching the editor. She sent another text to Selene before leaving her desk, 'My editor's in a meeting. Give me an hour. Also, I assume this is not a freebie and so tell me what you want – give me some idea – money, a credit?' This answer had already been prepared, 'I want a by-line on the story, plus one year's paid internship with the newspaper on a £30k salary'.

Selene had reasoned this was the maximum amount she might get for the story somewhere else but they would also get a year's work out of her, and so it represented a deal which she believed they could probably agree to. The by-line was just a bonus and some negotiating currency, but the job opportunity was her real goal. She was sure that within a year she could make a name for herself.

Over her coffee, Nikki made herself one of the checklists she was so fond of:

What? Seismic activity verified by BBC and Met Office. There was also a digital image of an artefact and enquiries about such an item had been made at the university only hours ago by one of the significant players.

Where? Location supplied by Selene, verified by Facebook and cross-checked with university.

When? Timeline confirmed by video-clip timestamp, BBC and university.

Who? The existence of Prince and Princess confirmed by numerous references in newspapers and other media. The professor and his role were confirmed by Head of the History Department at the University.

The only uncertainty, therefore, seemed to be the significance of the item which had been found, and that was her friend's ace card. Oh, and whether the professor was having an affair with the princess.

She knew her editor would especially love that little tit-bit.

She decided upon her strategy and went back to the office to see her editor. Her door was open as usual but she tapped on the frame anyway and was beckoned inside. Unusually, she closed the door behind her.

"This looks serious," the older woman quipped.

"I am not at all sure about this and so wanted to run it by you before I waste any more time on it."

Nikki outlined the messages she had from her friend and the subsequent research she had done, being careful always never to add or subtract any facts or include any supposition. She did not want to say anything her boss could pick on if this all went pear-shaped. The decision would be hers and based only on facts. All her boss asked was, "How much is a flight out there?"

Nikki said she had already checked and that it was, "Just seventy quid each way, and there is one at 7am in the morning."

"You have got a three hundred quid budget. Get there ASAP and call me immediately you get sight of something tangible."

No mention was made of Selene's price.

When she got back to her desk, she drafted a text in word and carefully edited it a couple of times and finally sent, 'We are interested. Your deal was not rejected. My editor wants me to see something tangible with my own eyes. I can be on a flight and in Nice tomorrow at nine. Can you meet me?'

Selene could hear the Dutchman playing his Tom Petty albums loudly downstairs and so ran down to speak to him. He was standing in his usual mist of dodgy tobacco smoke.

"Could I borrow your car to pick up a friend from the airport in the morning?"

He looked at her thoughtfully, "Male or female friend?"

Although puzzled at what difference it made, she answered, "Female".

He smiled.

"The pair of you buy me dinner and let me practice my English?"

She held out her hand, "It's a deal, if she can also stay in my room for a night or two?"

He took her hand, "You English are such cheapskates. You know how to squeeze the wine out of a stone."

Selene laughed and said, "That's blood out of a stone if you want to perfect your English. Wine is what you are squeezing out of me."

She dashed back up and texted her friend. 'I'll be there at nine outside Arrivals. P.S. you can share my little apartment here for two nights.' She decided that having to talk to the crazy Dutchman and buy him dinner was a detail she did not need for now.

Remembering that Selene had never been able to keep a secret from her mother or brother about surprise gifts or parties, Ben had decided he could not put off telling Claudio any longer. He also needed the photos from her phone to show him what they had found. He texted his daughter and arranged for them all to meet downstairs at what was now the formal dining room at Claudio's.

This was a remarkable space which had previously been used as a throne room. It was filled with, heaven knows, how many years of history of his family. The narrow-shuttered windows allowed in just enough light to see. There were large ceremonial swords in cases next to official photographs of them being presented by someone wearing an elaborately braided sash. Old oil paintings were hung high up on the panelled walls, presumably of ancestors, some wearing armour and sat astride fine horses. The furniture was all dark wood and inlays. There must have been some money in the Principality's coffers at some point, thought Ben.

Claudio was waiting for them when they arrived in his off-duty attire of blue overalls, white vest, and leather sandals. He had three glasses in front of him and a bottle of chilled Pigato from which he offered them a drink. Inevitably, there was also salami and focaccia, just in case anyone could not stave off hunger until dinner. Ben accepted the wine, thinking he might need the stimulus.

He got straight to the point and told Claudio the story of their walk, the landslide, finding the cave, and then discovering the box. At each stage, Selene was retrieving the appropriate photographs or video and showing this to Claudio. He was impassive until he saw the video of the landslide.

"Holy Mother! Are you OK?" he asked, looking them both up and down.

Seeing that they both appeared no worse for the experience he added, "Si unfortunately this happens around here. It is not unusual. You must be more careful."

When Ben reached the part of the story about the cave, Claudio's interest appeared to peak but he said nothing. Ben removed the painted stone fragment from his knapsack and placed it in Claudio's lap. The old man gasped and went slightly pale. Selene then began to show him the images from her phone of the chest and its contents and the old man suddenly started to weep. Quietly at first, but then more loudly, finally carefully placing the fragment on the table beside him, he rose to his feet and crossed himself.

"Alessandra!" he hollered in a voice so loud that it took them both by surprise.

He repeated, "Alessandra, scendi qui."

Tears were now running down his face as he stared at the mobile phone in his large brown gnarled hands. Selene took it from him and showed him how to scroll through the images. Alessandra burst through the door looking shaken and concerned by the volume and urgency of her father's call. She saw he was crying and asked, "What is it Papa? Are you OK?"

Claudio could hardly speak but managed to whisper, "Il professore ha trovato la carta."

"Found what charter?" she queried.

Remembering he had English guests, Claudio wiped his face and finally spoke in a more controlled manner, "The professore has found the lost copy of the Seborga independence charter."

Claudio turned to Ben, crossed himself and said, "Blessed was the fortune that brought you to our door."

He then hugged him long and hard before doing the same to Selene but with not so much force.

"But how do you know that is the document in the chest?" asked Ben, "We never took it out and could only see one corner of the cover."

Claudio smiled broadly.

"I am the only man living, outside of the Vatican, who has seen their copy of that charter and I would recognise its cover anywhere."

He went to tell them how it had occupied his thoughts for the fifty years since he first set eyes on it. How it was the only piece of evidence in existence that proved his claim of independence and Alessandra and Cristiano's birthright. He conjectured that when the Templars were being driven from Seborga by the Pope, they would think this document was, in effect, rendered worthless. They simply left it where it lay in the cave. In the intervening eight hundred years, one of the regular landslides must have cut off the access to it.

"Until the one which nearly killed us opened it up again." added Selene, filling the last part of the puzzle.

"I am the happiest man alive," said Claudio, "I was beginning to think that I would die never seeing this day."

Everyone's thoughts were racing trying to weigh-up the enormity of what they had just heard. Selene was trying to work out whether this was a bigger news story than the yet unproven, but implied, link to the Holy Grail. Try as she might, she could not work out the implications of the revelation but all her instincts told her that it was big.

Ben needed another drink and poured himself one.

Alessandra still looked stunned. Ben believed that although she would be excited for her father at having his dream fulfilled, he also knew she would be concerned about the uncertainty this could mean for the village.

Claudio, in contrast, was almost dancing around in circles talking partly in English and then, when the excitement got too much, reverting to Italian. Eventually, when he had settled down, he said,

"I need Vincenzo. Will you fetch him, Alessandra?"

After she had left, Ben explained the precarious position in which the box was last seen and that rocks had still been falling when they departed.

"Could you find this place again?" asked Claudio.

Ben said that Vincenzo already knew the cave but that it was now much deeper. Ben had begun to think through some of the possible scenarios which might unfold, and they worried him. He respectfully suggested to Claudio he think long and hard about what this meant before making any announcements.

"I am not in any position to offer advice to someone like yourself," he said to Claudio, "but I have to caution you that this could have far-reaching implications for everyone here and they might not all be good ones."

Claudio looked serious and replied, "Professore Ben, there is no one I would rather have advice from than you, but I have waited a long time for this moment and had begun to think it would never come."

The prince explained how he had had four decades to ponder the consequences and knew what he had to do. He asked to be alone with Vincenzo and promised to meet the following day. Selene saw an opportunity and asked, "I have an old friend arriving in the morning, and she would love to meet you."

"Si, Si," said Claudio slightly dismissively, as though he was unable to concentrate on what she was asking.

Ben and his daughter sat down at a table outside the Osteria where the more pressing matter of dinner was going on as usual. Today's piatto giorno was coniglio alla Ligure (rabbit with olives), which was evidently a favourite because the Osteria was full to bursting with both locals and visitors. Ben had the impression that if another earthquake occurred in the village, no one would leave their places until they had eaten their dolce and had a digestivo. They were both quiet, each trying to work out what all this meant to them.

Hardly containing her glee, Selene opened with, "This is going to be massive news. A proper new Italian royal family and new micro-state in the middle of Europe. A handsome teenage prince and his glamorous mother, who is also a Michelin Star chef. The media will eat it up."

Ben was about to caution her about the dangers of such thinking when she added, "All it needs is a secret affair between the married Princess and a commoner, who's also a foreigner, and it would be the perfect storm of news stories."

"Now just hold on young lady, you are going too far too fast with all of this."

Ben thought he had been discouraging his daughter when he warned of the political and economic implications for Seborga but, in fact, he was pouring fuel on the flames. Ben had pointed out that if Seborga was indeed independent, then it was no longer part of Italy and, therefore by default, no longer a member of the European Economic Community.

In that instant, Selene invented the term 'Seb-exit' as her own variation of Brexit and in her mind, saw the first headline 'First Brexit now Seb-exit', picturing the by-line 'by Selene Miller.' She was thinking this could not get much better.

For the remainder of the evening, they discussed all the 'what-if' possibilities. She put forward increasingly wild ideas such as, "It could become a tax haven like Monaco and attract the rich and famous."

Ben jokingly countered, "They would not actually want to live here. There would be nowhere to moor their yachts, and a Hummer would be too wide for all the narrow streets, plus there is no nail bar!"

She thought for a while and said, "They would knock it down and rebuild."

A horrible recognition struck Ben like a bolt. Demolish is precisely what they would do. There was just no space left in

Monaco. Forty years ago, half a nearby mountain had been blown-up and the rock dumped into the sea to reclaim more land for apartments, a marina, and football stadium at Fontvieille.

"More Monaco simply grew out of the sea," was how he had heard it described.

More recently, at vast expense, the Monegasques had even tunnelled all the surface railway tracks, and the entire train station underground, to claim back additional buildings land. There was nowhere left to build and, therefore, no room for any more tax exiles or oligarchs.

Seborga was more or less in the same location, had a similar climate, but was more than twice the size of Monaco. All it needed was to declare a tax regime based on spending instead of income, like Monaco's, and their billionaire overflow would migrate here. It would be remodelled by developers and sold off to oligarchs before the ink was dry on the declaration of independence.

Ben suddenly felt the need to be on his own and left the Osteria before Alessandra finished service. Selene remained behind speculating and making notes on her phone. Before he left, Ben reminded her,

"We keep this between us until Claudio decides what he wants to do. I am already out on a limb with my job and another embarrassment for the University would be just too much."

**View of Seborga from Passo del Bandito,
looking over Monaco and along the French Riviera.**

Drawing by Linda McCluskey

13. CANESTRELLI

The next day, on the drive back to Seborga from the airport, Selene filled in her friend on some of the details of events but, significantly, not all of them. She did reveal that this was a much more significant story that she had initially led her to believe, with a powerful political dimension. She implied she knew all this yesterday but had only told her enough to get her here. Selene said the story was too important and needed Nikki to see it for herself. Plus, her old friend would be here as it unfolded and, vitally, before any other media arrived.

Selene also pointed out that her father's position was a bit delicate, and therefore she insisted on her obtaining his explicit approval before his name or that of the University was mentioned in print. Being employed by the University but working with the co-operation of the prince, she explained, the legal position was a bit murky.

"You will have to do this undercover for now. I have told him that you are an old friend and you are visiting Nice for work. Looking on Facebook, you realised we were both here and got in touch. It's sort of true."

Nikki thought the story would not pass her editor's strict fact-test but decided not to point that out. Selene stopped the car by the side of the road not long after turning off the Autostrada, as her father had done a couple of days earlier. As he had, she pointed out Seborga basking in the Mediterranean sunshine nearly two thousand feet above them. One of the fluffy white clouds that were commonly rolling off the mountain was sitting immediately behind the church's bell tower, looking like a halo.

"What, that's it?" was all her friend could say.

"Seborga," answered Selene pointing upwards.

"That is the supposed independent country. It's tiny! It looks about the size of the Cotswold village that my parents have retired to."

Selene pointed out, "The whole of Monaco does not even cover one square mile, which is less than half of the area of Seborga, and yet no one questions its validity as an independent state."

Before they drove on, Selene wanted to be sure they had a deal and told Nikki that she wanted to speak to her editor on the phone.

"Right now?"

"Yes. You have been deliberately evasive about her response to my proposal. I want to hear the answer from her."

Nikki was taken off-guard and stammered,

"I don't think that would be..."

Before she could finish her friend added, "And in private. Or I turn around and drive you back to the airport now."

The young journalist knew if she went back without this story that would probably mean losing her job; that her internship would not be converted into a permanent contract. She weighed up the possibility of calling Selene's bluff and trying to find the story herself but she knew her old friend was too savvy for that. She would be able to do a deal with a rival media company within the hour and she had the inside track, doubtless more photo evidence, and direct access to the people at the heart of it. The call was placed, Nikki introduced her friend and passed over the phone. Selene walked away from the car far enough so that she knew she could not be heard. The conversation lasted just a few minutes and, before it ended, Nikki could see her typing something into her own phone. When she returned all she said was, "Now we have a deal".

Selene had left very early that morning to meet the flight and it was still only ten thirty when they arrived back at the village. In the big piazza, there was an unusual number of people milling about. Two separate groups were huddled near the two notice boards where the brightly coloured festa posters were glued and where notices from The Commune were pinned.

Nikki was out of the Kübelwagen and snapping away at the scenery with her camera. Usually, two pretty young foreign girls would have merited a bit more attention from the male inhabitants, but today they received nothing but a cursory glance. Selene saw her father had just joined one of the groups and was talking animatedly to a young man. The pair joined them and asked what all the fuss was about. The young man pointed to a poster bearing an elaborate heraldic crest and with a handwritten signature at the bottom which had been pinned over all the other notices.

"Claudio has announced that the Papal independence charter, which had been lost for centuries, has been discovered and he has named a date for a referendum to decide the fate of Seborga."

Nikki was already snapping the poster and shots of the men reading it. Ben apologised to Valerio and introduced him to his daughter. Selene beckoned Nikki and introduced her. Selene looked Valerio up and down as though she was measuring him for a suit and then gave him her biggest and brightest smile and asked, "Are you able to translate for us, Valerio?"

Her father interrupted and explained that he already had done so for him. "Let's go and have a coffee and some canestrelli. I will bring you up to date."

The two girls followed Ben and Valerio to the shaded side of the piazza and then along the alley to the bar. As they crossed the piazza, Vincenzo roared past in his Ape, looking very hot and sweaty, as though he had been working outside since dawn. In the bed of the pick-up were a pile of tools and an old tarp. Claudio's right-hand-man was obviously very preoccupied, as he did not even acknowledge anyone as he whizzed by in a cloud of smoke and fumes.

Selene said to her friend, as if by a warning, "That Valerio's mine. Hands off."

Nikki was more interested in getting the story and saving her job. She was also aware she was in uncharted territory in not declaring to these men that she was a reporter if she was later to quote anyone. This made her uncomfortable, and she was already concerned about what Selene had said to her boss. Nikki didn't like not being in control.

Valerio organised coffees and a plate of his sister's homemade canestrelli; a round biscuit with a hole in the middle which can take many forms, both sweet and savoury. This version was similar to shortbread biscuits in consistency and scattered with lots of sugar. The young man explained that the hole in them was used to thread the newly baked canestrelli onto a pole or rope so that mobile vendors could sell them as a hot, fresh snack to people on the streets.

Selene thought that today her father looked like a different man than when she had first arrived in Seborga. When he met her at Nice airport less than a week ago, he looked younger, fitter, and more vibrant than she could remember in a long time. Ben also seemed happy and genuinely pleased with her, which had not always been the case. This morning he looked like his old depressed and downtrodden self; as if someone had scratched his favourite old car and then let the tyres down for good measure. This apparent sadness, however, was somewhat at odds with what he was now to relate to them.

"The prince's decree says our discovery has ended sixty years of his personal struggle and seven hundred years of injustice by rediscovering the charter of Seborgan independence."

Selene shrieked: "Dad, you should be proud and happy. It makes you sound like a cross between Indiana Jones and James Bond." She nudged her father playfully to try and cheer him up.

He went on to quote, "Although the prince recognises that this will mean enormous upheaval for the Principality, in the long run, it would be for the better. He has called for a referendum to let the people decide the kind of future they want for themselves and their children. There will be two debates over the next weeks, where any citizen who has a view can express it, and then a poll will be held a month from today."

Ben was puzzled by the haste with which Claudio had made this initial decision. He wanted to talk to Alessandra and found her at home.

"Want to walk?" he asked.

She also looked melancholy and was distracted but nodded in agreement and followed him outside. They strolled out to the edge of the village where there was an uninterrupted view down the valley to the sea. They found a bench under an ancient olive tree and sat on it, close together. The distant Mediterranean sparkled in the afternoon sunshine while a mixture of boats from cruise ships to tiny fishing boats cut white swathes across it.

"Well?' said Ben.

The way she looked at him made him believe she was now unsure whether he was her hero or the villain.

"I just knew that daughter of yours would bring trouble."

Ben was shocked.

"Just wait a minute. You can't say that. This discovery is not Selene's doing. We just happened to be there when it happened."

Alessandra realised there was no real substance to her accusation. She was just looking for someone to blame.

"It would have been far better if you both just kept quiet about what you found the other day. I bet she's told the whole bloody world on that smartphone she can't let go of."

"What, and no one else would have walked or ridden their mountain bike along that well-trodden trail and found the gaping cave as we did?" he countered. "Frankly, that's ridiculous, and you know it."

It seemed as if, although she knew that he was right, she could not help being cross with him for what he had uncovered. Ben tried to turn the conversation to where they went from here.

"Why do you think Claudio has acted so quickly with this announcement and the referendum? Why did he not just wait a while? Have you spoken to him?"

Alessandra looked him straight in the eyes, with what looked like a combination of sadness and anger and said, "Don't underestimate my father, or what he means to this village. He may be old, poor, and appear stupid as a result, but the latter he most definitely is not."

She went to explain that although he had no actual power, he had been the de-facto ruler of Seborga since he was seventeen years old and, many would say, still is. Claudio joined the local partisan group age just fifteen and, within two years, was its leader. His father and mother were executed by the Nazis—this was their punishment for Claudio's actions because they could not catch their son to execute him.

"Later, Claudio was very nearly killed himself during a daring raid on a convoy travelling along the coast. A large calibre machine bullet clipped his forehead beneath the rim of his hat, leaving the scar you see above his eye.

"There had been many other partisan groups all along the coast and further into the mountains. Local legend has it that Claudio's unit was the bravest and most effective. They were highly respected and supported by all the others. So, he effectively became a general without a formal commission and coordinated the Partisans into a powerful force. By the end of the period of Nazi occupation, the guerrilla fighters effectively controlled all of Liguria from France to beyond Genoa. Claudio and his men caused havoc and helped the allies in many ways. Few other Europeans are aware that fifty thousand Italian men, women, and boys, died fighting the Nazis as partisans, including three hundred and fifty two executed near here by the Nazis in one day.

"Claudio proved a natural leader who was as evasive as he was fearless, knowing when to hide and when to fight. This meant his group's successes were numerous but crucially, their losses were less than most; as a result, he was trusted by his men and admired by all the others. That will also help you understand why he is held in as high-esteem outside of Seborga, as here. He paid the ultimate price in losing both his parents and we Italians have long memories for things like that."

She explained that it had always been so isolated here, that even when the war ended people looked to Claudio for leadership.

"No one else bothered with us, including you British who he helped so much, but Claudio has never let the people down and they love him like a father as a result."

Alessandra told Ben that she believed Claudio knew this news would leak out before too long. He would also be aware of the uncertainty that this would cause, and the consequence of that would be fear, speculation, and panic.

"People like certainty because it brings stability and Claudio has always represented that."

Alessandra said she also guessed that he was seeking to drive the agenda and not be driven by it. He knew when to pick a fight and had decided that time was now."

Ben realised that he had almost certainly underestimated Claudio, but he also could not help wondering if the old man did not also relish a final battle: one last hoorah for himself. The Englishman could see the appeal of sticking two fingers up at the establishment after the way they had treated Claudio over the years. Ben could certainly empathise with that.

"Anyway, for better or worse you and the Facebook generation have opened Pandora's Box," observed Alessandra, "there are no secrets anymore."

They sat in silence for quite a while watching as the wispy clouds rolling off the mountain floated over their heads and then evaporated as they merged with the warm wind coming up from the sea. Ben was thinking about what Alessandra had said and a lot of things now made more sense. He concluded that

Claudio was right in taking the initiative because if he were correct, very soon there would be plenty of others wishing to do so.

Ben was also watching the reflection from the aluminium roofs of the trucks moving along the Autostrada. From this height and distance, they were tiny silver boxes in small convoys east to west and west to east. He had seen all the assortment of different foreign number plates when he had been driving to and from Nice airport. He now speculated about where these were all going: France, Spain, Portugal, or even England in one direction; Greece, Germany, Austria, The Balkans, and all the eastern European states in the other. What a variety and value of goods must be flowing back and forth.

"Does the main Autostrada pass through the land which is included in the Commune of Seborga?"

Alessandra confirmed that it did and said that there was much opposition to it when the highway was built because it spoiled so many beautiful vistas all along the coast and Seborga received little compensation because the land had a low agricultural value.

"Now everyone is used to the road and it does make life easier on their rare trips to the city."

He rose suddenly and said, "I need to talk to Claudio. I'll see you tonight at dinner," and set off, leaving Alessandra bemused.

As he walked away, Alessandra watched him leave, walking with purpose, his white hair now a bit too long and slightly straggly on his brown neck. Feeling that she was watching him, he waved his hand but without turning around. 'This is the beginning of the end', she thought to herself. Another dream shattered.

Claudio was holding court in the big dark dining room at home. The painted stone fragment Ben had brought had been placed in a padded box and was at the centre of the table. It looked somehow more significant like this than when it had lain on the ground in the cave covered in dust. A room full of people were all talking: some to Claudio, others amongst themselves. When Ben entered the prince said,

"Ah, Ben, welcome. Come and join us."

The Englishman explained he had an idea but that they needed to talk in private and it might take a while. Claudio ushered everyone except Vincenzo out of the room. Ben looked at the younger Italian and then questioningly at Claudio.

"I have no secrets from Vincenzo. It is better that he knows everything."

Accepting the finality of that statement, the academic began telling them about the research he had been doing studying the economy, and some of his initial findings and conclusions. And, although he had by no means completed his work to his satisfaction, circumstances meant that he felt he needed to speak out now. He also added that Alessandra had helped him a great deal in his research and, although he had not told her about his ideas, he firmly believed she would support them when she could. It was just over an hour later before Ben left Claudio's, already having second thoughts about the responsibility he had taken on.

Nikki had meanwhile already drafted her first report and was fact-checking it. She was elated that her hunch in being open to Selene's wild claims seemed to be paying off and she already had a story that might save her job. Selene had pointed out that now the poster was up, the clock was ticking. It was only a matter of time before someone from the village went on to social media to tell their friends or family of the discovery before someone in the mainstream news media picked it up. When she was happy with her work, she gave it a draft headline, knowing full well that a sub-editor would change it before it went to press. It read, 'New royals mean more chaos for Italian politics', her sub-head read, 'Earthquake unearths evidence to shake Italy and the EU to the core'. She hit send and sat back pleased with herself.

14. PANINI

When the story appeared on the newspaper's website the next day, it was indeed the lead story, but the first thing Nikki noted was that she had no by-line. She thought it was maybe just an oversight in the online version but that it would be in the printed copy. Then she spotted a quote from, 'The new young Prince Cristiano', saying, 'while he thought England's Prince Harry was very cool, he had no plans to give him a call to ask for advice in dealing with fame and the media.' This quote was not in her report.

"Where the bloody hell did that little gem come from?" she said out loud.

She called her editor who answered with an abrupt, "I can't talk long as I am about to go into a meeting with the MD to get the budget extended so you can stay on this. This thing is going ballistic. Keep sending the reports but try and get some more reaction from the locals. Get me some video for on-line of human beings who have got opinions but do not talk like they are reading from press releases. Must go. Talk later." Then she hung up.

The story made BBC Breakfast TV, and a frenzy of speculation and chatter was building on the Internet. Selene was nowhere to be seen and there was no time to spend looking for her, so she decided to get out and get some interviews before the mass media vultures descended.

Ben had messaged Selene and asked her to meet him at Claudio's at nine and, if he was not already downstairs, to wait in the dining room on the left. Everyone else was already out and the door would be open, so she could just walk in. She arrived at nine-twenty, but there was still no sign of her father, so she entered the gloomy dining room whose door had been left ajar.

Suitably impressed by the great room with its memorabilia, she browsed around while reading labels on photographs and feeling the weave of the tapestry. On the big table were some books and files, one of which was open at a page. It was a collection of press cuttings neatly pasted into a binder. Judging by the colour of the paper and monochrome images, they were quite old. The main picture showed a young man dressed in a uniform, similar, or even the same as the one Claudio had worn when she had been introduced to him. He was on one knee; his head bowed in front of a row of Catholic priests in long robes and tall hats. She could only read the words Prince, Seborga, and Rome in the headline but guessed the remainder. This was Claudio in the photographs, she realised. Carefully snapping the images with her phone camera so that the text could be read and translated later, she flicked over a few more pages of clippings doing the same. When she heard heavy footsteps on the stairs, she stopped and put her phone away.

Her father greeted her with a "Buongiorno," looking more like the cheerful man who had greeted her at the airport a few days ago. "I thought we should have a quick local history lesson this morning."

Selene thought some background history would be useful and so was happy to go along.

"OK. But I need to meet Nikki for lunch."

Retracing the tour, which Alessandra had given Ben when he had first arrived, he showed his daughter the key sights around the village. He explained how the Templars came to be here at the invitation of Pope Gregory, what they did, and why they finally left. These facts had now taken on an entirely new significance. Approaching lunchtime, Selene started checking her watch, but by then her abridged education of Seborga was almost complete in any event.

She left him at midday and sneaked back to her room to use her PC. When Google Translate had converted the copy from the press clippings into English, another piece of the jigsaw was complete. In response to Claudio's claims, the Catholic Church in Rome had denied that they held a copy of an independence charter for Seborga. Furthermore, despite recorded history suggesting otherwise, they also cast serious doubts that one ever existed. Her father had already given her a motive for this denial. He had said, "After the Knights had done the Pope's dirty work, the Templars had become so rich and influential, they were a threat to his own power and he wanted to be rid of them."

This was dynamite; she realised a religious dimension to the story, with a Vatican that was already mired in many scandals. Here, in front of her, was written evidence of them denying something that had now proved to be true.

Nikki spent the morning interviewing anyone who spoke English who would talk to her, but that was only a handful of people. There was an artisan baker, a lady walking her dog, the man who ran the grocery shop, and finally, the postman; who turned out to live down on the coast but gave her an independent outsider's perspective, she argued. They were all bemused by the whole affair, but the consensus seemed to be one of general delight that Seborga's unique status was finally being recognised, balanced with a significant fear of what it would all mean. She roughly edited what she believed were the best interviews and sent them back to London. She also spent the day researching the history of Seborga and reading anything she could find on-line about the prince and his daughter. Afterwards, she wrote a five hundred word synopsis of the facts she had amassed and emailed that to her editor as background material.

By late morning, the phones had been ringing at every publicly-listed business in the village as the world's media tried to speak to anyone 'on the ground' who might fill in missing bits of the story. Meanwhile, better-funded foreign reporters were at airports trying to get on flights to Nice, while other media tried to locate local freelancers who could get to the village quicker. Selene, meanwhile, had retraced her steps from the morning with her father, photographing all the religious elements of paintings, which included the Templars, and videoing the church bell chiming. That done, she met her friend as planned at Valerio's bar for a panini.

Panini is one of the many Italian dishes which has now been embraced around the world and yet, unlike others, it remains mostly unadulterated from the recipe of its roots; a thin, hot toasted sandwich. It was cheap, tasty, and could be eaten on the move. Although not a Ligurian speciality, it is thought to have first been popularised by the Milanese, and so at least is northern Italian in origin. In the eighties, its popularity amongst the young, who hung around the café bars where they were sold, coined the term 'paninaro' to describe these trendy teenagers. These highly fashion-conscious children of the new middle-classes spurned Italian traditions for the British and American styles popularised in movies and the new phenomena of pop videos. The panini remains the failsafe snack choice of the young from Soho to Seborga. While Valerio was happy to serve them, Alessandra considered them 'Fast food – the work of the Devil.'

"Did you get that quote from Cristiano?" was Nikki's less-than-friendly greeting. "What the hell do you think you are doing messing with my career? My job is at risk here. This is not student pranks."

Selene looked suitably offended by the remark but avoided directly answering the question,

"I know where it could have come from," she said evasively, while at the same time trying to look self-righteous.

Selene explained she was now Cristiano's 'Friend' on Facebook and saw that the question was asked of him by one of his new local friends.

"Anyone could have got hold of that information."

Nikki was only partly pacified by her friend's explanation, but as she also needed to ask a favour of her, she let it go. She needed to extend her stay in Seborga and so asked if she could continue to share the apartment. Selene told her that the Dutchman had already said that she could not stay any longer than tonight because he had no license for letting the room and the two of them were drawing too much attention.

"He is worried the Guardia Finanzia will be giving him a call with a tax bill. He says he can always argue that one woman is a girlfriend but he believed that two was pushing his luck, even with the Italian police."

This was not in fact true. Selene had not asked the Dutchman. Knowing that alternative rental accommodation was virtually impossible to find in Seborga, she just did not want to make it easy for Nikki to stick around any longer than necessary. She had served her purpose.

That night the two girls had agreed to meet Ben at Valerio's for aperitivo. All three of them were looking quite pleased with themselves when they arrived, but for very different reasons. Nikki decided she had better come clean and tell Ben that she was now working as a reporter with The Tribune. She did not change the story of how she had happened to be in Seborga, and so her story was that it was just a lucky coincidence this major news story had broken while she was here. Ben appeared to accept her explanation at face value. She told him that because of the turn of events, she was going to stay around for a few days to cover things as they developed.

"That is fine, but you understand that I cannot say anything that can be quoted. I am here carrying out research on behalf of the University, which is unrelated to any of this."

Nikki agreed that, as Selene's father, he would remain 'uncontactable' as far as she was concerned. Ben also warned them that Alessandra was extremely unhappy about Cristiano's name getting dragged into this.

"But that is just naïve," said Selene, "he is part of a royal family, therefore public property and fair game."

Ben pointed out that, unlike our royal family, Claudio, Alessandra, and Cristiano, received nothing from the public purse, had no power, and so were not 'public property' in any sense. He added sternly, "And, if you ignore this warning, you will find life very uncomfortable around here and all other sources of information, including mine, will suddenly dry up."

His point made, the girls said they had to go and pay their agreed debt to the Dutchman by treating him to dinner. Ben warned them to watch his wine drinking, "Or he will run up a hundred euro bill."

Neither admitted that, as one of the few English-speaking residents, they were both really planning on extracting as much information from him as they could about the extraordinary turn of events. This would be the first of several such free meals that the Dutchman would enjoy in coming weeks from journalists with the same idea. What none of his hosts realised was that after his pre-dinner joint and a couple of drinks, the only discernible information anyone could get out of the Dutchman was who played the drums on some failed album by some obscure band three decades ago. The only relevant quote Nikki got was, 'Big shit is going to hit the fan' but thought that was a bit too colourful for their middle-class readership.

During an early dinner, Ben had become increasingly aware of some unfamiliar faces in the Osteria and the new cars with Rome, Bologna, Milan, and Turin plates parked around the piazza. The new visitors were smartly dressed men and stylish women, many of whom seemed to know one another. There was also a lot of technology hardware in evidence: iPads, cameras, etc., resting on tables amongst wine glasses and pasta dishes. The Italian media had arrived, he realised. Typically, he thought, they had decided to have dinner first and ask questions later. It was time for him to leave before they finished and one of them spoke to him.

"Have you seen the quote from Cristiano in the media?" was the first thing Alessandra asked Ben when she appeared at his table. "That bitch reporter friend of Selene's. I'll kill her when I see her."

Ben took the bottle of Limoncello and two glasses that she had been carrying. He poured two drinks and said,

"Take a seat and a deep breath. You may well be right, but you do not know for sure that it was her. According to Selene, it was apparently on his Facebook page, and so in theory, any number of people could have leaked it."

She took a sip. "But it was printed only in her bloody newspaper. That's a hell of a coincidence."

Ben sighed and conceded, "You are probably right, but we need the media on our side if we want to get the best result for everyone out of this. Do not go making unnecessary enemies when allies are what we need."

Alessandra was looking for an outlet for her frustration and Ben was it.

"WE! Who the hell is WE?" she snarled, "You've arrived here for your summer holidays and suddenly you're a local, is that it? Listen, the real WE have survived invasion by Moors, Romans, Templars, and Nazis. We can certainly deal with this latest crisis without the help of an English academic, Bridgette Jones, and the British press."

Ben realised that in her current frame of mind, it was hopeless trying to reason with Alessandra and so said good night. As he left, she added a parting shot, "And tell your two cub-journos to find somewhere else to interrogate the locals. I don't want them coming in here and bothering my customers when they're eating."

The next morning, Ben had been awake for some time wondering just when the emotional roller-coaster that he was on would stop. The constant shifting from highs to lows was deeply unsettling to a man who preferred calm routine. He had worked out some time ago that it was usually a woman who was the catalyst for any upheaval in his life. And that change was almost always change for the worse. Yet, try as he might, he seemed unable to steer clear of either. Here he was again with a woman, or three women if he counted his daughter and her friend, getting in the way of what should have been a blissful summer and a simple job. In his gloomy mood, Ben resolved to give up on any thoughts of wooing Alessandra. She was a princess after all. A Michelin-star chef. Out of his league. What was he thinking?

His miserable contemplation was interrupted by his mobile ringing. He pressed the green button without looking at the number calling him.

"The Dean here. Is that you, Morton?"

'Shit', Ben thought and almost said out loud.

"Or should I call you the fire-starter?" There was a pause while he let that sink in before the Dean continued, "I have just extinguished one inferno started by you and now I read in my morning newspaper that you have got another blaze on your hands. How on earth did you manage to get into trouble again stuck in a sleepy village in a remote part of Italy?"

Ben did not have any defence planned. He blurted out something about being a victim of circumstance once again and emphasised he had done nothing whatsoever wrong. It was merely a case of wrong time wrong place.

"You seem to have a knack of finding the wrong bloody place," his boss observed.

Not wishing to dwell on the negative, Ben swiftly moved to what he saw as the good news,

"This could be more of an opportunity for the University than a threat."

Intrigued, the Dean bid him continue and explain how that could possibly be. Five minutes later the Dean said, "OK. You might well be on to something. I'll give you some more rope with which to hang yourself. But remember, do not quote the University on anything and, if it goes wrong, we did not have this conversation. I'll come back to you when I have spoken to the powers that be." He then bid him good luck and hung up.

There was a gentle tap on Ben's bedroom door.

"Are you awake?" came Alessandra's voice through the door.

"Yes, come in," was his uncharacteristically curt reply. Alessandra entered but stood just inside the door looking contrite.

"I'm sorry to disturb you but I wanted to apologise before I went to work. What I said last night was unfair and I am sorry. I had no right to dump all of this on you."

Ben replied without much thought with, "You are correct it was unfair but, heh, I'm used to it."

Wincing slightly at Ben's reply, she continued, "I came with a peace offering. Tomorrow I am going to drop off some olive oil for my father in Menton. Would you like a trip to the coast – maybe have some lunch?"

There was a silence before Ben replied, "Can I let you know?"

Alessandra departed, feeling suitably chided by Ben's deferral, but was ultimately confident that her plan would work. She knew he was interested in her.

The Italian Prime Minister had had a similar unexpected phone conversation early that morning. It was with his Minister for Home Affairs, and the theme of putting out fires before they got out of control was tantamount to that of the Dean's. An election was on the horizon and yet his party had the narrowest of margins in the polls and was already embroiled in a political crisis. The Prime Minister was personally the subject of a financial investigation. The press could smell blood and they were out to get him.

"I do not want to be remembered as the man who made Italy smaller. Even if it is only four square kilometres. The press will hang me out to dry; they are already comparing it to Britain's Gibraltar. Get down there and do whatever you have to do to fix this and, if you cannot, don't bother coming back because neither of us will have a job left."

While croissants were still warm in Paris boulangeries, a long black Citroen was leaving the Elysee Palace heading for Gare Lyon, where the single passenger would board the TGV for Nice. He was carrying with him a personal verbal message from the President of France for Prince Claudio which went something along the lines of, "Monaco is an independent state but also a French Protectorate. If Seborga were to find itself in need of a similar friendship, my door is very much open."

Also, with an election coming up, the messenger was left under no illusion about how much importance the French President put on this story.

"At least try and get a photo shaking hands with the prince and we can make up our own press release about a 'special relationship' to piss off the Italians, the Germans, and the British," were his parting words between bouts of laughter.

Nikki's day also started badly. When she opened her email, there was one from her boss recalling her to London on the next available flight. No explanation but merely a terse, 'and do not call me. I'll see you in my office back in London.'

When the shock subsided, she looked at the newspaper's online pages. The front-page story read 'Vatican hushed-up Seborgan independence'. This was accompanied by a video-clip of the village church bells ringing and stills of paintings of Templar Knights with monks carrying out religious ceremonies. The sub-head read 'Prince says unearthed independence charter is the duplicate of one held in the Vatican but denied for decades'. There were lots of background detail and a potted history in the form of a time-line leading up to date. It referred to articles published in Italian newspapers going back fifty years and appeared to be a clear chain of evidence pointing to a cover-up.

"Where the bloody hell did all this come from?" she said out loud. Then hissed, "Selene!"

About the same time as the Italian Home Affairs Minister was receiving his first morning call, a minor cardinal in Rome was taking one along very similar lines from 'upstairs'. It ended with a similar stern warning.

"We have already got investigations into our finances and countless sex scandals. Do whatever you need to do to make this one go away, or you'll find yourself a missionary in Mogadishu. And get someone to dig this charter out of the archives in case we also need to make that go away, permanently this time."

There was also a second unattributed story which was headed, 'Princess also Queen of US cooking; new royal had Michelin Star in New York's top restaurant but now cooks for Italian locals.' None of Nikki's own material had been published, and she now realised why. They had an alternative source and one with an apparent inside track on the stories. The Tribune was the only one with new material and any insight as to where this story was going. All other papers and on-line channels had merely re-worked yesterday's news by adding their own baseless speculation, poorly informed assumptions, and what-if scenarios. Some of the tabloid coverage was frankly ridiculous, but it was all fuelling interest which was spiralling upwards. CNN and NBC in America had both covered the story on their main news programmes last night, but neither had yet spotted the New York connection. They would today, however, Nikki assumed.

Selene was still nowhere to be found this morning and was not answering her messages. Resigned to her fate, Nikki found the Dutchman having a coffee in the bar in the square. For fifty euros and lunch on expenses in Nice on the way, he agreed to drive her to the airport, although she did wonder if he should be driving at all after last night's excesses in the Osteria.

In nearby Monaco, the MD of the most significant American bank based in the tax haven was disturbed during his gym workout by a call on his mobile from New York. That conversation was terse. It went something like,

"Round up a posse of lawyers and ride up that hill behind you. If there is already a bank there, buy it. If there isn't one, buy a property and make one. Any time today would be good. Oh, and whatever the hell that place is called, make sure that is in the name. The Bank of Seborjia… where-ever-in-hell-it-is. Get a brass plaque on the door with a website address and call me when it's done. Don't screw this up."

In Seborga's main piazza, the pace of life was a little slower. Vincenzo was nailing another notice bearing Claudio's crest and signature to all the notice boards. The essential gist of the message was that the first public debate would take place tonight in the church at 6pm and the subject was 'Independence or remain part of Italy?' a footnote read, 'Citizens of Seborga only. Strictly no media'

Along with the TV satellite vans arriving in the village that morning, were several large expensive cars bearing more men in suits. Ben watched these arrivals from the shade of the doorway next to the Osteria. He had deliberately dressed in his scruffiest walking outfit and had donned his straw hat in the hope of passing for a local. He was tanned enough now to at least not look too English.

'It's going to be a very interesting day', he thought to himself as he headed off into the back alleys to avoid the new arrivals. The village had no signposting system to speak off, nor did any of the main buildings have names. Everyone who lived there knew where everything was and so signs were an expensive luxury. This fact, however, made it very difficult for strangers to find anything or anyone, even in a place so small. Strange men, unsuitably dressed for the heat, were wandering aimlessly down alleys desperate to find anyone or any building that looked like a seat of authority. Eventually, they were finding their way to Claudio's once-impressive front door where a small queue was forming outside and Vincenzo was keeping order; taking requests for appointments and writing them on a notepad. He had dressed in his military attire and was showing little by way of deference to either diplomats, ministers, or bishops.

5. ARANCIA SANGUIGNA

Despite his earlier decision to avoid her, Ben had justified his agreement to go on the trip with Alessandra with the rationale that it would help him understand the economies of other communities in the area. With the recent revelation that independence was now a very real possibility, there was even more pressure to resolve the challenge that he had taken on. Although now, the options were wider and much more complex, it would also give him a chance to quiz Alessandra about her hopes and aspirations for the principality. He had a lot of questions and only a few answers.

Ten minutes into the journey, he began with, "Why do you think so few foreign tourists visit this region of Italy?"

On his two visits to Nice, not an hour away, Ben had noticed that there were hordes of visitors from all the great tourist-exporters on the planet. Here, it was the same climate; the beaches were less crowded, the food better, the service friendlier, and prices of almost everything were considerably lower, he proposed.

"We don't want that type of tourist," came the disparaging reply from Alessandra.

"Who is WE?" he asked repeating the jibe she had made at him the night before. "Some of your fellow business owners and citizens would disagree vehemently with you."

She started to explain her strong views on the issue of tourism and then, realising that it would be easier to show him, said, "When we have finished in Menton, I will take you to see for yourself what mass tourism has done for a French village similar to Seborga."

Like many national borders, that between France and Italy has moved backwards and forwards with the ebbing and flowing tides of fortune and misfortune. As recently as the end of the last world war, it changed slightly again as the victors extracted advantage. Like Nice, Menton is one of the border towns which are coloured by the resulting identity crisis; although now French, it looks Ligurian, is still populated by many Italians, and the food is more Italian than Provencal.

Its harbour is bustling and full of boats unable to find, or afford, a mooring in neighbouring Monaco. Its well-heeled residents and superior French bureaucracy, means that its infrastructure is better maintained than the equivalent Italian town. There are well-tended floral displays at every junction. Pavements are all even, roads perfectly smooth, and the streets swept clean. It's like a sanitised version of Italy.

As they drove into the marina, they had to stop at a barrier. They were expected, it seemed. The uniformed man raised the bar and waved them through at the mention of Alessandra's name; he then noted their registration number in his log. Alessandra pulled into a vacant parking space against the harbour wall where a line of large yachts was moored, stern-on, to the quay. Most of the boats were modern, white with black glass, and towered two or three stories above the quay. Many of their uniformed crews were out polishing chrome and brass or washing salt water from their glistening hulls. At the end of the line, and therefore open on its starboard side to the water and a view of the mountains, was a much older-style sailing boat. Its polished teak decks in stark contrast to the white plastic of its neighbours. Although the shortest boat in the row of super-yachts, Ben guessed that this was still substantial; estimating its length at twenty-five metres. It was, in his view, certainly the classiest boat in the harbour.

As they approached – Ben carrying two 5-litre cans of best Taggiasca virgin olive oil – he could see someone dressed head-to-toe in white linen, sporting a straw hat and sunglasses. She was sitting at a table under a blue canvas Bimini cover. The figure rose from her seat and waved them aboard. Ben thought she looked familiar.

"Alessandra welcome. And I see you have one of my compatriots – your house guest – with you?"

Alessandra looked puzzled for a moment at how Ben knew Cecily but then he explained, "We've met at Nice airport, twice now."

Formal introductions were made and they were offered coffee by their host. Sitting at the large dining table, Ben became aware of the volume of highly varnished hardwood on every surface. Although he knew little of boats, this seemed like an expensive, well-cared-for thoroughbred. Everything that was not varnished wood was chrome or brass, and all gleaming in the sunlight which was reflecting off every surface. White ropes were either neatly coiled in decorative spirals on the deck or tied in elaborate knots on deck rails. A red ensign fluttered proudly on a stern flagpole, establishing this as a floating island of Her Majesty's territory. Many of the other boats had Panama or Bahamas ports of convenience, suggesting their owners were more reluctant to declare their nationality or allegiance.

"How is Claudio these days?" enquired Cecily.

While Alessandra brought her up to date on Seborga news, their host poured them all coffee from a silver coffee pot. Relaxed by the congeniality and the generosity of their host, Ben enquired what occupation provided Cecily with such a beautiful and desirable office. Seeing that she was reluctant to explain herself, Alessandra offered, "Cecily runs one of the largest fair-trade cosmetic and health product companies in Europe. Her products are used by the rich and famous."

"And royalty," added Cecily, "because the beautiful Alessandra here also uses them but refuses to let me put her in any of our PR."

Alessandra waved her hand as though dismissing the compliment and the suggested publicity as a ridiculous idea.

"I did try that blood orange body lotion you kindly sent me. It is amazing. My skin had been terrible. So much time in the heat of the kitchen and then my time off spent in the bright sunshine. Ten days after starting to use that product and the effect was nothing short of miraculous."

Cecily smiled a knowing smile.

"That product is rapidly becoming one of our best sellers. The science behind the benefits of blood oranges is fascinating and more is being revealed all the time. Our only problem is supply. The oranges only grow well in a few places and so supply is limited."

"Hence the exorbitant price?" challenged Ben.

He had been listening with interest. He had never ceased to be amazed at the women's beauty products market. From a business marketing perspective, there were so many incredible case studies. Profit margins were some of the highest in retail. Cecily sensed the cynicism in Ben's question and countered, "As you will probably know very well, most of our costs are marketing and packaging, although ingredients obviously do still have a bearing."

Alessandra ended this debate by saying, "The main thing is it worked for me."

Cecily laughed and asked, "Can I use that quote in an advertising campaign?"

At that moment the yacht's chef appeared behind Ben to collect his precious olive oil. He greeted Alessandra cordially and called her 'chef', a clear sign of peer-to-peer respect. He shook Ben's hand only after wiping his own on his apron.

"Just in time with the oil, Chef, or there would be no salad for lunch. I cannot use that awful supermarket crap or Cecily says she will sack me."

While they were all standing, it seemed like a good time to say their farewells. Lots of air kisses were exchanged and the couple made their way carefully back down the passerelle; their passage easier without the burden of oil cans. Alessandra, however, was now carrying a bag containing several new beauty product samples including a new, and as yet unreleased, blood orange hand-lotion.

Their little old Fiat climbed slowly back out of the town toward the Autostrada. At some points on the route they could look down on the harbour below and see Yacht Cecily, her teak decks easily recognisable amongst the palette of white and blue fibreglass.

In the hills behind Monaco was Eze Village, formed by the same violent forces of nature that created Seborga. It had also been a fortress village, built on a high hilltop to protect it from marauding pirates, or whoever was looking for easy pickings at the time. They have the same basic architectural style, use the same building materials and techniques, plus they have evolved rather than being designed or planned. Being cut into, and clinging precariously from, the edges of a mountaintop, any growth must be upwards. Like Manhattan, Monaco, or London, where land is scarce, people build skywards. It is not unusual for such medieval communities to be stacked six or seven stories high with terrifying drops and thigh-aching stone staircases to reach the higher ones.

The first thing Ben noticed when they left the Autostrada to climb to Eze was the volume of traffic. When leaving the main highway at the Seborga exit other cars quickly disappear. On the road to Eze traffic was slowly ascending and descending the winding road in a steady stream. The tarmac was also broader and smoother to accommodate the long, luxury tourist coaches straining up and around its hairpin bends. Approaching Eze itself, the traffic slowed to walking pace as drivers sought parking places where no cars were ever planned to go. Any parking provision created since the invention of the automobile was still woefully inadequate for the number of visitors. There were also yellow lines and parking meters, a concept as yet unknown to the folk of Seborga.

Alessandra wedged the ageing Fiat Panda into a seemingly impossible gap between two cars, and they set off to explore. Temporary stalls selling water, ice cream and hot dogs were set up on the edges of car parks and street corners. Leaving these open spaces, they entered the labyrinth of narrow streets that were a feature of all such mountain villages but these were immediately different. Instead of scrubbed slate doorsteps with colourful plant pots and the ancient wooden entrance doors to private houses, which are everywhere in Seborga, plain, plate-glass shop fronts had been created. These retail spaces sold all the usual things that people bought as souvenirs of a trip, as well as more practical consumables such as sunglasses, hats and flip-flops. There were also fashion shops selling all the designer brands that were readily available in Nice but somehow merited an even higher price up here. Lots of jewellery: bangles and necklaces. Also, eye-wateringly expensive Swiss watches; presumably, Ben thought, in case anyone had left theirs on the cruise-liner and couldn't possibly be seen in public without a Rolex on their wrist. One or two shops were selling what passed for local produce; lavender honey, olive oil, salami and cheese.

Alessandra picked up a couple of items, examined the small print of the labels and announced in an unimpressed tone, "Produce of France. Generic produce which could be from a factory anywhere between here and Spain. Mass produced, bland crap at absolute rip-off prices."

It turned out not all the cuisine was of the fast-food variety though. There were discrete gates into courtyards and gardens, where the sounds of cutlery clinking on china plates and corks popping could be heard. This was all taking place out of sight of the great sweating masses funnelling past in the alleys. In a small piazza, or 'Place', as they were now in France, Alessandra pulled Ben into a shady doorway and said, "Just stand here and watch for a moment."

Within a few minutes, the sound of fat car tyres on cobbles and whirring air conditioning could be heard; then a long black Mercedes drew up outside a pair of iron gates. The inside of the gates had been covered in green fabric, up to a height of two metres, so no one could see through them to what lay within. Immediately the car stopped, a smartly uniformed young man opened one of the gates, exchanged greetings with the occupants, and changed places with the driver. A folded euro note was pressed into the young man's hand and the car sped away; the people entered and the gate clanked shut. This discrete exchange took all but thirty-seconds.

"Two Michelin Stars," was all Alessandra had to say.

When the young man returned from parking the car five minutes later; walking into the piazza, swirling the fat Mercedes key around his finger, Alessandra hailed him, "Dites à Eugene Alessandra Biancheri qu'il veut lui parler."

He tapped a code into a pad next to the gate, held it open and gestured for them to enter. Detecting that Alessandra was not French, he said in perfect English, "Please wait here while I check if Chef is here."

After only a couple of minutes, a short, skinny man in full chef's whites appeared; he had long grey hair and powder blue spectacles which balanced precariously halfway down his nose. He was smiling and wiping his hands on his stained apron as he called out across the courtyard, "Alessandra, you gorgeous Italian totty. How the hell are you?"

Ben found it difficult to discern his nationality from his appearance or accent. He was later to learn that he was, in fact, Irish by birth but had lived and worked in many places including England and America (including a few years in New York). Hence his strange accent and the very familiar way he had with Alessandra.

"What are you doing here? Why did you not call to say that you were coming? I heard about what happened in New York and I am very sorry. Bad business. A nasty business. But you look fabulous as always."

Alessandra introduced Ben using the 'professore' word again. She explained that he was doing some research and she was showing him around. He used both hands to shake Ben's. He had a powerful grip for a slight man and Ben noticed that his hands were covered in stains, cuts, and burns.

"You must stop for lunch."

Seeing that she began to protest, he forcefully but gently placed his arm around her waist and guided her along the path down the garden. The valet parking man was dismissed by the chef with a wave and Ben followed them. From the outside of the gate there was little clue that this large hotel, standing in its own very private grounds, even existed. They had turned a corner, and suddenly they were reminded that Eze sits at almost two and half thousand feet above sea level. Even higher than Seborga and much closer to the sea.

From where they were standing, it appeared that below this terrace there was a sheer drop to the water below. That was not, in fact, the case, but that was the illusion created, and a hugely powerful one it was. Ben gasped, almost audibly.

"Pretty impressive?" prompted Alessandra.

"I'll say," was all he could think of.

The chef explained that Monday was the quiet day, but they kept the restaurant open mainly for the residents.

"I could give you a table here on the terrace, but then I can't talk to you properly, and you'll have all those poseurs staring at you wondering if you are richer than them."

The evidently-famous chef led them through the dozen or so diners, nodding and waving to some and being pointed out, ever so discretely, by others. Through the kitchen doors, past all the stainless-steel prep areas, and out again onto another small wooden platform. As he passed through the steaming, pan-clashing mayhem, he barked orders in French at no one in particular and yet, each seemed to know what he wanted them to do.

"This is my private space where I get out of the madness and have a cigarette. Any staff who do not cut the mustard get invited out here and tipped over the edge. Gone for good and no P45, or whatever they get in their crazy French bureaucracy."

For a moment Ben thought that he wasn't joking.

A small white plastic table and two moulded chairs of the type you would find in any suburban garden were the only furniture. These were the same as used outside Alessandra's Osteria.

"Just like home," Ben quipped looking at Alessandra.

She just gave him one of her beguiling smiles.

Eugene gestured for his guests to take a seat and said, "Now we can talk through the open window while I make you some lunch."

They sat and marvelled at the view, which was if anything better than that afforded the guests who were now completely out of site around the corner. From this angle, it was possible to see for miles along the coast past Antibes and as far as St Tropez. It occurred to Ben that this was essentially the same view as that from Seborga, but this was just further west and a bit higher up.

They enjoyed a lunch which was as spectacular as the view. The dish was a delicate seafood crepe stuffed with sea bass, scallops, and shelled San Remo red prawns, served with a creamy sauce made from the stock of the shellfish. This was accompanied by white burgundy by Olivier Lamy of Domaine Hubert Lamy, which Ben had read about somewhere but never tried. Food and wine were perfectly matched.

Two-star food, eaten off a plastic table placed on DIY wooden decking. Ben thought this would be the material of many dinner party stories to come. The famous chef was cook, sommelier, and waiter for them. Eugene and Alessandra chatted about old friends and former colleagues in common from New York; who was doing what, where, and how well. Ben recognised only the odd name and occasional restaurant but was happy to be passive in the conversation, greatly enjoying the excellent food, wine, and view.

Chef joined them for a glass of wine at the end of service, said he would come and see her at the Osteria on one of his days off, and they said their farewells. After they had walked away, but only made it halfway across the restaurant, Eugene shouted after them, "Even for an Italian princess, that's still a great ass," so that the whole restaurant heard.

She kept on walking and did not look back, but Ben could see that she was blushing while trying, although not entirely succeeding, to subdue a grin. The other diners appeared astounded at this outburst from the famous chef and seemed to be speculating about who this handsome couple were.

On the way back to the car, they passed more coaches unloading their cargos of ice-cream lickers, lavender buyers, and Instagram snappers. The coaches with the cruise-liner name in the windscreen, which had been parked near them earlier, had already departed for historic sites anew.

"So, what do you think of Eze?" asked Alessandra with a hint of irony.

"It's certainly a place of contrasts," replied Ben non-committally, needing more time to absorb what he had seen and experienced.

As Alessandra drove them back down the hill Ben was doing some basic maths, based on little more than reasonably informed assumptions. The cruise passengers, like them, had not been there more than two hours, and so based on the approximate cost of an ice-cream, baguette, and drink, plus maybe a small souvenir, their average spend, he estimated, would be about twenty-five euros per person. Ben then thought many of them would wait and eat for free when back on board the ship and rounded that number back to an average of fifteen euros. Even with a parking charge, the whole coachload was, therefore, bringing about seven hundred euros into the local economy.

If what Alessandra told him was correct, a good proportion of that was going straight out of the village again for the produce, which was being bought in. They had not seen a bill or a menu for their lunch, and so Ben asked,

"What would you expect the average spend to be where we have just eaten?"

Alessandra thought before she answered, "There will be big variations; partly because residents will have some meals included with their accommodation, which will be discounted, but mainly because of the wine element. Some bottles in there will be three to five hundred euros, and they will sell more of those than you might think."

Ben needed no convincing of this. Although out of his league, he had seen people consume similar bottles on his own trips to France.

"I would say an average bill would be three hundred and fifty, and so a hundred and seventy-five euro per head."

After a little more mental arithmetic Ben announced, "So, one table of four diners brings in more money than forty-plus day-trippers on a bus."

How astonishing, he thought.

"Much more of that money probably stays in the area as well, in wages and local produce," continued Alessandra.

Ben had already also worked out that the impact on the infrastructure was much less; parking, waste disposal, and toilet facilities. He had to admit that the public spaces looked tacky compared to Seborga, but the most significant thing was that few people he saw appeared to be living there. There were few private houses, as such, and no signs of people who were going about their ordinary business. The village was, in effect, like the out-of-town shopping and fast food centres now so prevalent in the UK, with a little bit of culture thrown in.

"OK. I get it. So, there is tourism, and then there are sub-groups of tourists."

Alessandra could not resist a smug smile. She had graphically demonstrated both the ugly and lucrative side of tourism. She drove home her point by adding, "Would you like to see Seborga becoming like Eze?"

He confessed that he would not but then argued, "But surely, by the same token, you don't see yourself in Eugene's place; your Osteria behind security gates, with valet parking?"

She grimaced at this thought and replied, "I did that for twenty years in New York and I now have left it firmly behind me. But there is a better way that does not require selling our souls to the devil."

Ben debated that the valet parking, uniforms, fancy cutlery and silver service were the added-value which allowed them to charge those prices.

"Surely, you cannot have one without the other?"

He then went on to try and explain the academic theory of 'place' in the marketing mix he had explained so often to his students, but Alessandra was dismissive.

"Added-value is not always in the packaging or presentation. Surely, if you make a good product you do not need all the other stuff?"

Ben smiled. "You mean, the build it and they will come theory? History is littered with the ruins of businesses that used that flawed notion as their business plans."

Ben thought for a while about what she had said. Although the meal they had just eaten was superb, it was not, in his eyes, as enjoyable as dinner at the Osteria. He would have gladly paid more for Alessandra's pansotti and was beginning to realise why.

"What I am enjoying in Seborga is not only the food, but I am savouring the knowledge of where the ingredients came from, that no chemicals were used in their production, and, in some cases, that I have met the man who grows the product. I am also drinking in the atmosphere created by a thousand years of people doing pretty much the same thing that I am doing, in a place that has probably not changed that much. That is all added-value to me. But I have had to learn that for myself; you did not put it on the menu or write it on a sign outside."

He went on to say that, "A tin of pasta with tomato sauce can be bought in the UK for as little as fifty pence, whereas virtually the same ingredients, marketed correctly by someone like Marks & Spencer or Waitrose, can make five pounds. In a central London restaurant you could quadruple that price. Currently you are describing the Heinz version on your menu and charging their prices but delivering the designer version of the product. Any marketer would tell you that is crazy!"

Alessandra was also beginning to understand some of what Ben was arguing. In her previous life her partner, Franco, had done all the marketing and pricing. He was good at it. She was happy to stay in the background and concentrate on cooking. She was enjoying the simplicity of cooking with what few ingredients were available and making less into more without worrying too much about what it looked like.

"I just don't want to do all that again and end up being a slave to the whims of rich ladies who lunch and their ridiculous diets, allergies, and food prejudices. Take Eugene; he could make you a simple spaghetti with local San Remo red prawns that would taste so good it would make you cry with joy. His problem is that his customers would not order it because there is not enough bling-value in prawns so small. Size is important when you're rich. So he has to buy huge prawns from Argentina, which taste of nothing, and out of season vegetables from Africa and create a pretentious dish which has no connection whatsoever with Eze but sells all day for sixty euros per portion."

Pragmatic as ever, Ben pointed out if that is what his market demands then that sounded like good business.

"No." she exclaimed in exasperation. "It's wrong on so many levels. The local prawns and other ingredients are harvested sustainably, are fresher, travel fewer miles, require less packaging, and put money back into the local economy. The imported prawns are often farmed unsustainably, damage the environment, exploit the foreign workers, and have to be flown half way around the world, with the profits often going to global conglomerates who only pay minimal, or sometimes, no tax. It's also diluting our individual culture. Ancient ingredients and recipes are being forgotten and our food is at risk of becoming homogenised like it has so many places in the world."

They were now back on the Autostrada which hugs the coast back into Italy. Ben told her that he had an idea and that they should turn off and go down to Monaco. Arriving in Casino Square, Alessandra parked the rusty old Panda next to the Ferraris and Lamborghini's lined-up outside the Hotel de Paris. Ben questioned the wisdom of her choice of parking, but she waved her hand dismissively saying, "It will be fine."

They had not even crossed the road towards the Casino when a voice called after them, "Madame, vogues ne peeves pas vogues garter lay-bas" (you cannot park there, madam). Meanwhile, his smartly-uniformed colleague was now tugging at his arm and pointing to the registration number of the old Panda. He then corrected himself in Italian,

"Mi dispiace. Non ho riconosciuto il numero della tua auto. Lascialo lì. Ci prenderemo cura di esso."

The two Monegasque policemen stood to full attention and brought their hands smartly up to their white caps in full salute. Alessandra merely smiled demurely and walked away without commenting.

"What the hell was that all about?" asked Ben.

"It's Claudio's car. It has his own Seborgan number plate. The rest of the world might not recognise him as a prince, but the Monaco royal family have essentially the same background and similar lineage. Although things have worked out a little better for them, they still see him as an equal in many ways and so offer due respect to him and his family."

"Bloody astonishing!" was all Ben could think of to say.

As they walked, Ben got to his reason for being here. "You said that it's just the product that is important? Well, what about this product? A ticket to the Monaco Grand Prix is at least fifteen hundred euros. At the Hungarian Grand Prix, you see the identical cars, with the same drivers, doing the equivalent thing for the same length of time. Ticket price? Two hundred and fifty euros. The product is the same. If it is only about the product, why do people pay so much to come to Monaco?"

Alessandra was quiet, as though she could see that he had a fair point. Although she could accept that these were valid arguments, she was unsure what Ben's point was or how it related to the village or the Osteria.

"What's this got to do with our problem?" she quizzed.

Ben summarised, "It is possible to get people to travel to a destination to consume a product if there is some added value in the location itself: the place is a brand."

Alessandra concluded, "Like Monaco?

Ben continued, "It is also possible to ask a huge premium for a product if it is perceived to have unique values – tangible or imagined – represents a lifestyle or has some cache in its history. No better example than Cecily's beauty products. Few of her more exotic assertions would withstand scientific scrutiny. But you must understand the value that people are seeking and have a way in which to communicate these benefits to the buyer. Cecily's brilliant at that and that's why she's a success."

She squinted as though she was thinking hard.

Ben expanded that there was not necessarily just one single value, but probably several with differing levels of importance to the buyer.

"Any combination of these complex motivators might push the buy button for them."

He argued that, for some, it was the high price itself that was the added value. The fact that people know this is an expensive product is the most significant value. Indeed, if it were much cheaper than say, Chanel, they would probably not buy it. He went on to say that, for a man, there were not too many bragging-rights at the local golf club in tickets to the Hungarian Grand Prix, but massive prestige in the Monaco version of the same thing.

"Based on the difference in the ticket price; five hundred per cent more, in fact!"

Seeing that Alessandra was still struggling to grasp the added-value concept, Ben tried what was perhaps a better example.

"Take the computer company, Apple. They innovate, design, produce, market, and even present their products in their own carefully controlled stores. They manage the entire process and add value at every stage of it, maximising quality, profit, and customer experience. The cables, the packaging, and the shops, are all unique. This business model has created the most successful brand in history by any measure, with the most loyal customer base ever."

When he had finished, she teased him, "It would appear, Professore, that you really do know something and don't just read lines off PowerPoint slides during your lectures."

He laughed, and she smiled broadly. He told her "I am very pleased to tell you that you have passed your first module in marketing. Have a gold star."

She curtseyed, he bowed, and they walked on.

Later, Alessandra told him that she believed an entirely new market had been developing around the world, which was entirely different to her previous super-rich customers. Real food tourists, she argued, were a rapidly growing group all around the world. Ben took a deep breath.

"Really?" he answered, pausing to consider this concept. "But who are they and exactly where can we target them? If you have identified a developing sub-market which has a different set of needs, then you might be onto something."

He tried to explore the hypothesis by asking her more questions: if they were not wealthy, were they middle-class and if not interested in style, what was it they needed?

"It's you," she suddenly yelled, "you are the wine version of a food tourist."

Ben thought about this and started ticking boxes in his mind: middle-class professional, educated, environmentally aware, disposable income, a little more concerned about quality than ostentation. He agreed that he would indeed spend a tidy sum each year travelling, staying, and eating and drinking his way around France. He had to agree he was, indeed, a sub-market.

“Are there enough Bens and Alessandra’s to save Seborga?“ she asked.

“Ten years ago, who would have thought that there were enough people who would spend up to a thousand euros on the latest phone every two years and create the most profitable company in the world?”

Although this discussion was all interesting and enlightening, Ben was unsure where the debate left them, other than that they both now agreed that they needed a marketing strategy for the village and its produce. How exactly to apply the Apple business model to Seborga, was another matter.

“Let me take you to Cuneo on my day off next Monday?” Alessandra asked.

“Where? Is it a restaurant?” said Ben, looking puzzled.

She explained that the city was one of the gastronomic centres of neighbouring Piedmont and that this region itself was, arguably, the food capital of Italy. Struggling for an analogy, Alessandra suggested, “The region is like God’s poly-tunnel; you can grow anything at virtually any time of the year. It is a flat and fertile bowl sheltered on three sides by mountains, the sun shines most of the time except when it’s raining; which it does a lot. The rainwater drains into the huge River Po which snakes through the region ensuring it is well irrigated even in dry spells. You can produce anything in Piedmont, and even if you left the land alone, nature would grow its own stuff anyway. The region has become a destination for Italian gastronomes and wine lovers but now also all kinds of foreign visitors as well. Restaurants and vineyards are becoming the Trevi Fountains or Colosseums of the twenty-first century where Barolo and truffles are taking the place of Cokes and McDonald’s.”

Beginning the drive back to Seborga, they agreed to meet the following Monday because the Osteria was closed on that evening and so she would not have to rush back for service.

16. LARDO

The five days leading up to their trip was spent in a frenzy of meetings at Claudio's house, punctuated by the comings and goings of suited strangers. Ben and Claudio seemed to have spent countless hours locked in discussion: sometimes on their own; often with one or more of the visitors.

Vincenzo was characteristically tight-lipped, and so nothing was known in the village about the nature of these talks. Both Ben and Claudio had refused to be drawn when Alessandra enquired, quickly changing the subject into questions directed at her about her thoughts for the future of the community.

"What are the people saying they want?" asked Claudio.

"What are their fears for the future?" Ben wanted to know.

"Do you think they understand what independence will mean to them?" they were both desperate to know.

The sun dawned brightly on the designated Monday. Ben and Alessandra were up early to catch the eight o'clock train from Ventimiglia direct to Cuneo, where it terminated. Ben welcomed being away from the village, where the pressure of expectation was building, and his sense of responsibility was beginning to get to him.

Grabbing a quick coffee and brioche at the station, they boarded with the other passengers. Some of these looked like day-trippers like themselves, with small backpacks, but others wheeled suitcases suggesting a longer stay. The modern diesel-electric train turned almost immediately away from the coast and headed inland, up the valley of the River Roja which meets the sea at Ventimiglia. Climbing steadily, they were soon into the foothills of the mountains, which could be seen looming in the distance. The housing developments of the suburbs of the border town quickly became sparser and then disappeared altogether. Occasional public utility buildings, and the sporadic aggregate processing factory, were the only signs of human activity along the next part of their route.

The train slowed noticeably, and the engine noise grew louder in response to the increased gradient of the climb. The track crossed deep ravines in which clear, blue-green rivers flowed. In places, the water appeared in a rush to get to the sea, in others it was not so hurried and checked its journey, forming inviting pools between solid rock slabs.

They sat opposite each other, both wearing sunglasses, perhaps each wondering what the other's eyes were doing behind them. Their relationship, if one ever really existed, had unquestionably warmed again, Ben judged, but only by degrees.

This interim stage was more familiar to Ben. He had been down this track before; several times since his divorce, and he understood things could easily go either way from here. In his experience, the more baggage each person had – kids, ex-partners, dependent parents, lack of money, too much money – the more reasons there were for a potential relationship to fail. They both had more than their fair share of complications, he thought, and the more parts made up the jigsaw, the less likely you can get them all to fit. Add the responsibility of the future of an entire nation into the mix, and any long-term future for this relationship looked hopeless.

Having had only one serious relationship in her life, which had ended in marriage, Alessandra was also profoundly uncertain where she was going with this. Did they have a relationship, or at what point did it become one? Did she want another one, after the last disaster? She had many more questions than answers. Unlike Ben, who was learning to spot the danger areas in these post-marital relationships and avoid them, she was still naively treating it as if they were both unencumbered by their pasts.

"Remind me exactly why you want me to see Cuneo," Ben said to change the subject that he was sure was occupying both of their minds.

Alessandra removed her sunglasses to answer. "You and my father have been asking what I would like to see become of Seborga. I have shown you Eze and explained why that is not what I want for our community. You also told me about your principal of added-value throughout the supply chain."

Ben was impressed by her recall, or more likely, it seemed, some self-assigned homework.

"Well, Piedmonte, as a region, practices what you preach, and Cuneo is the easiest town to get to," gesturing around the railway carriage with her hands to emphasise her point.

She went on to explain how nearly everything grown there is of the highest quality, partly because of the accident of their geography but also because growers place great value on traditional methods, which, as it happens, are also sustainable and largely organic. They then process their produce locally into products bearing well-known local family brands and can market these at a premium price because of this provenance.

"Such is the region's reputation. People who are interested in food are now travelling there specifically to seek out the products they cannot find anywhere else."

As the journey continued deeper into the foothills, Ben kept pointing out things of interest to him in the landscape and asking questions about them. She started to relax and to take pleasure in filling in these gaps in his knowledge of Italian history, architecture, culture, and rural life. They stopped at a couple of small stations, but virtually no one got on or off.

The track wound around increasingly tight bends, along ever steeper cliff faces, and crossed viaducts and bridges which spanned huge drops. It was undoubtedly spectacular, Ben thought. At one point a small town appeared as though the buildings had been glued to a high mountainside, like a cluster of house martin's nests clinging to a structure. How did they get up there and why, were just two of the questions which sprang to Ben's mind. Alessandra had answers to neither. She just shrugged.

An hour and a half into the journey, the train must have crested the mountain, although this must have happened in one of the countless tunnels because, visually, they were unaware of it. The tell-tale sign was that the engine noise had dropped and yet the train was moving faster and more quietly downhill. After only ten minutes descending the train entered the pretty skiing resort of Limone, where a few passengers disembarked, and a smaller number got on. The chalet-style houses and hotels looked more like Switzerland than Italy, thought Ben. It was the height of summer, but there were still hikers and other visitors about and many of the hotels looked open.

After leaving Limone, the countryside started to level out, and fields capable of cultivating crops appeared; sporadically at first but then more often. This looked like fertile land to Ben, and there were visible signs of economic prosperity. Newish cars stood in driveways and expensive agricultural machinery sat in wooden barns. As they approached Cuneo, there were also signs of industry: cement works, quarries, and timber processing; all things tied to the landscape in which they were set. From what he could see, Cuneo was a large and relatively prosperous place.

From the station, they walked towards the old city, which apart from the odd exception was a geometric grid of straight streets and alleyways. The alleys were mostly little more than a car width, leaving them in the shade most of the day. Via Roma was the only main thoroughfare and cut straight through the middle with only one opening into a small piazza on one side. The shops and cafés, lining both sides of this main street, were set under vaulted walkways stretching its full length. These created both shade from the sun and shelter from the regular showers. Underneath, the archways were paved in huge granite slabs of irregular sizes and interminable age. Each one must have weighed more than a car and taken several men to manoeuvre into place.

The hundreds of stone arches spanning the half-kilometre walkway turned out to be only one of the many triumphs of medieval architecture, which the City could boast. Entering this shady, cool, world, they wandered past shops, which, it seemed to Ben, were nearly all food-related. There were specialists selling cheeses, hams, salamis, uncooked meat, fish, olive oil products, and so on. These were interspersed with shops offering coffee making equipment, kitchen utensil of infinite variety, chefs' knives, cutlery, crockery, glassware, and even one specialising in condiments and pots to put them in. True, there were a few cafés, clothes and shoe shops, a bank and a pharmacy, but mainly it was food, things to go with it, eat it with, or off.

They browsed, tasted, enquired, and occasionally bought small things. As it was still only mid-morning and the temperature had yet to climb, coffee was taken in one of the few sunny open spots. A pleasing breeze blew down the length of the street, taking the edge off the sunshine. Ben realised that from the openness of the piazza, he could see mountains on three sides but no land or buildings in between. He, therefore, calculated that this part of the town stood at an elevated level; almost some kind of plateaux. Although they were in bright sunshine, large cumulous clouds were gathering over the distant mountains offering the prospect of rain at little notice.

Alessandra had not said too much since they arrived but appeared to be letting Ben arrive at his own conclusions about this place. After coffee, she offered, "There is a place I have heard about here which specialises in baked ham and salamis and is supposed to be very special. I thought we could have lunch there if we can get a table?"

Ben had no objections and they set off to look for the address. Off Via Roma, about midway along, was an alley, not much different from all the others they passed, except that this one had many clusters of tables along its length, revealing that it was lined with small eating places. Small discrete metal or wooden signs hung from chains or were hand-painted on windows; there was no plastic or neon clutter. The street sign read 'Via Dronero', but Alessandra told him, "the locals" call this restaurant street."

"Oh really? Why is that?" Ben joked rhetorically.

She found the place she was looking for after just twenty-five metres. A young man stood outside, arms crossed and eyes scanning up and down the street as though he was either weighing up his competitors or expecting a delivery. He was expressionless at first but as they approached his smile turned on like a light.

"Buongiorno," he beamed but then checked his watch to see if it was yet midday.

They returned the greeting, asking if there was a table free for lunch. Detecting the English characteristics of their accents, he replied, "Two high chairs at the bar are all I have remaining if that would be okay for you?"

He gestured through the open door to the light, airy bar, which could be seen clearly from the street. Without referring to Ben, Alessandra agreed and with one of her big smiles, promised to come back at 12.30. Ben realised that she was keener to try this place than her initial mention had revealed. He also found himself suddenly jealous of her handing out smiles to handsome young men who she did not know. Italian men feel unrestrained in complimenting women of any age, strangers or not, and 'ciao bella' (hello beautiful) is one of their most beloved phrases. They see no insult in recognising beauty and celebrating it and this young man had made his appreciation of Alessandra's plain.

Bove's was like the others in the street, not very large, dark and cool inside and unpretentious out. The graphics of its signage were modern and minimal. It would not have looked out of place in Clerkenwell or Chiswick. It made no grand claims or boasts but somehow communicated a seriousness about its business. Its business was meat. The strapline under its meat cleaver logo was quixotically ‘Meat and Coffee’—two things that Italians especially, but also most other cultures, would not usually consume together. The owner later explained they wanted to convey that you could come in for either at any time of the day, but not necessarily together.

The couple filled in the next hour exploring more of the alleys and looked in a few of the smaller local churches, which were usually plain and uninspiring without, but breath-taking within. The City’s architecture was incredible and apparently completely untouched for several centuries. It was like walking through a film set for a very high-budget movie, Ben suggested.

“It’s another of Italy’s well-kept secrets,” she replied.

In another open square, there was a large area covered with a metal roof and surrounded by parked cars. In the centre, a small market, of sorts, was going on. Battered old cars were backed into the covered area so that they could readily be unloaded and used as storage to access carrier bags, or for weighing things on the portable scales concealed within. Closer inspection revealed what appeared to be private individuals selling fruit and vegetables, presumably from their gardens. None of them had sufficient quantity to have been a business enterprise: just a few boxes of tomatoes, beans, plums, or whatever grew best on their land. Most vendors had a small collapsible table, or some old wooden crates covered in newspaper, on which to display their wares. There were no prices, no labels, no credit card machines, and, judging by their rag-tag mixture of small rusty cars, none of them was making a fortune from this activity.

The atmosphere, however, was more like a social club than a strictly commercial arena. There was a lot of banter between the sellers and with their customers. They laughed, they bartered, and they sometimes argued, but most acted like old friends. The simple purchase of a handful of tomatoes seemed to take twenty minutes. Ben judged the average age of the nut-brown gardeners to be the mid-sixties, but each looked as though they had at least another forty years left in them. He joked with Alessandra that they would undoubtedly outlive their vehicles.

Their fruit and vegetables were unequal in size, uneven in shape, and often had blemishes on the skins; the type of produce UK supermarkets would never display. Alessandra said she was sure that they would be the best-tasting ones it was possible to buy.

"That is why there are so many locals here, sniffing and tasting," she explained.

Their ensuing lunch was enjoyed sitting at a counter-top made of Carrara marble and perched on smart tan leather bar stools, which it turned out were more comfortable than they appeared they might be. The young man from earlier was now behind his counter and directing operations like a conductor, while smart, white-aproned young girls and boys rushed around with plates, glasses, and bottles.

The proprietor, curious about his foreign guests, asked where they were from. Alessandra gave him a highly edited synopsis but included the fact that she too was a restauranteur from Seborga.

"Bella. I've heard it is wonderful and ancient. Older, perhaps, than Cuneo."

He left them while retrieving a bottle of wine from a high shelf and then returned saying, "So, this is your English knight in armour?" having just remembered the Templar history of Seborga.

Until this very moment, neither of them had made this connection with the stereotype image of St George with the red cross on his shield; the English dragon slayer of legend. And yet, that was the image that was most often used around the village in association with the Knights Templar.

"Yes," she said without thinking. "A few weeks ago, he rode into our village on his white horse to save us from the inexorable onslaught of globalisation."

The young man laughed but did not understand what she was talking about it.

Ben was sure she was being sarcastic and was slightly hurt by the remark.

Chatting with some of the other customers, it was soon apparent that they too were here on trips to sample the food of Piedmont. They had come from all over Northern Italy, a couple from Spain, several from Germany or Austria, and two, seemingly gay, men from San Francisco. The Californians were real food and wine aficionados and claimed they had even heard of Alessandra and her restaurant in New York. They had not heard it had closed, however, and so when they promised to visit, rather than explain, she said, "Great, but book ahead; don't just turn up."

Ben assessed the customers and summarised them as over thirty, educated, professionals with disposable income, like himself. He noted there were no Prada handbags, flashy gold and diamond wrist-watches, or black Mercedes parked outside. These were conservative, middle-class people who understood food and wine and placed a high value on its provenance, not its label. The new market Alessandra had described.

The young owner now introduced himself as Fabio and asked what they would like to eat and drink. Alessandra ordered the selection of cold meats with a side dish of Cervere leeks, a local delicacy, and two glasses of a local Favorita wine to begin. At first glance the prosciutto, salamis and bresaola all seemed familiar to Ben, but the thin white slices were not.

"Lardo," explained Alessandra. "Pork fat flavoured with herbs. It tastes much better than it sounds. Put it on your tongue and let it melt."

Ben tore off a piece and did as instructed, savouring the subtle bitter-sweet taste as the solid turned slowly to liquid in his warm mouth. It did not have the cloying effect on his palette that he had expected. It was light and delicious. He had another slice. The other cured meats also had distinct flavours imbued in them by smoking, or the addition of tiny amounts of herbs, truffle, or alcohol.

Fabio recommended the steak to continue with because, not only was Piedmontese beef the best, but this was from his family's own butchery, "So, the best of the best."

With that he recommended Pelaverga, saying it was a rare red wine, produced only in the Province of Cuneo. When it came, the colour was an intense ruby red. Ben told Alessandra that he detected hints of violet, black currant, and rose, in its aroma. Ben said it put him in mind of, "A very good Fleurie but with something slightly earthy in the background."

Dessert was a chocolate and amaretto pudding known as Bônét in the local dialect, which means 'hat'. Fabio told them that the name came from old folklore; it was the thing that signalled the end of a meal, just as, in the old days, a hat is the last thing you put on when you get up from the table to leave a restaurant. With this, they had a refreshing glass of Moscato d'Asti, a sweet and aromatic wine popular in Piedmont. Ben said he detected flavours of nectarine, honey, and peach.

"It was very aromatic and a perfect way to finish a delicious meal."

They were both feeling very contented, if not a bit tipsy.

"How long are you here?" asked Fabio.

They explained that they would return on the train later in the evening.

"That is sad because tonight, later, we are hosting a restaurateur's club."

He explained that is was a monthly event where restaurant owners come together at one of the member's venues to sample food and wine from guest suppliers and chat about the industry.

"You would be welcome to be our guests. It starts around 9.30 after dinner service is cleared away."

Ben could see how appealing this was to Alessandra and so was slightly surprised that she said, "Thank you but no," quite so quickly.

That's a shame. This evening we have a special guest from Alba, who has brought some rare cheeses. These varieties had all but disappeared from the market but have been revived by receiving the Slow Food Presidia." Ben could see Alessandra was fascinated by this. He added, "We have a couple of letting rooms just down the street which are free tonight. You could stay there and get the train in the morning."

Ben could see that she was warming to the idea, so he took the initiative.

"Can we see them?" he asked. Alessandra looked at him slightly alarmed but did not argue.

After coffee and a complimentary digestivo, they walked, slightly unsteadily, following Fabio two blocks to a corner where an antique wooden door had no signage, house number, or identification of any kind. Once open, a solid staircase made from ancient granite slabs, spiralled upwards. The stairway had small slit windows in the landings, which allowed in just enough light to see where you were stepping.

After climbing two floors, they reached another, extremely old, hardwood-plank door with a very modern high-tech lock. It opened into what was a communal kitchen dining area from which two separate bedrooms could be accessed. It was all tastefully designed and decorated, with all its original medieval features restored and highlighted. Contemporary furniture and fittings had been added, and the whole effect was 'cool' they agreed.

"We'll take both the rooms," said Alessandra, "and also join you and your colleagues tonight if that is OK?"

Buoyed by the excess of wine at lunch, neither had given any thought to the path that they were heading down; they were going to spend the night alone together under the same roof, with all the suggestions that implied. They had not planned this, or thought through the implications, but now seemed to have past the point of no return. Or, were they?

Alessandra rationalised that having two rooms was perfect. It gave her time to think through the entanglements and weigh-up the pros and cons. She told herself that she was a grown woman and a mother, capable of taking control of her destiny. That is what she would do, she decided. She would take the remainder of the day to get back in control of this situation and regain some equilibrium. She was not a teenager anymore. She was sensible and had never been prone to irrational and spontaneous acts of self-indulgence. Satisfied that she had reclaimed command of her senses, she inhaled and then exhaled loudly.

After their early morning start and a boozy lunch, they were both tired and agreed to have an hour's nap before exploring the city some more. Alessandra said,

"Now that we are staying over, I need to find a shop to buy a few things."

Ben agreed to set his phone for four thirty, and they went to their rooms. Ben heard the other bedroom door lock solidly, and the handle click as Alessandra checked it.

Despite their epic lunch, the afternoon nap and later walk around the city had revived their appetites. They found a place that Fabio had recommended for supper at about seven thirty. Marco's was renowned for its Brasato al Pelaverga con patate arrosto—Veal braised with Pelaverga wine and oven potatoes.

As soon as they walked in they were greeted by two couples from lunchtime, apparently on the same culinary circuit.

"Buonasera Templari Inglese," was the amiable greeting. "Try the Plin Agnolotti with wild boar ragout; it's amazing," was their unsolicited, but nevertheless welcome, advice.

Alessandra explained to Marco that Fabio had recommended they visit, and that Ben was on a whistle-stop Piedmontese food tour.

"So, you have been to Bra, or are you going next?" he directed at Ben.

Alessandra answered for him. "Unfortunately, we have not yet been to Bra and don't have time on this trip. I need to be back by early evening tomorrow to open up my own restaurant."

Marco left them with the menus and started to walk away but then turned around and offered, "If you get up early, I can drive you there in plenty of time for lunch. I must collect some sausage and wine in Bra. You would get the train back to Ventimiglia from there by four or five."

Without even referring to Alessandra, Ben said, "OK. What time?"

He did not want this wonderful escapade to stop. Their relationship had found a new impetus during this trip and Ben was determined to keep it going as long as possible. With the food, the wine, and this woman; he was in his kind of Nirvana. Alessandra started to say something, which Ben knew was going to be a protest, so he interjected, "We will be back in the same time. Why not?"

Alessandra had to concede that she could not find any good reason why they should not go, and Bra was another must-do on any serious foodies must-see check-list. So it was agreed, and Marco was thanked for his kind offer. They got on with the serious business of dinner.

Ben gestured around the room, "Is this how the Osteria could look in a couple of years? Full of middle-class food tourists drinking thirty euro bottles of wine."

Alessandra also looked around the room to assess the clientele.

"Why not? These are not all foreigners. They look like a nice mix of locals and visitors. Everything on the menu comes from the region and, therefore, is supporting the local economy. The visitors will, like us, be staying in hotels or guest houses, and will doubtless go home with some salami, cheese, and some wine – just like us."

Ben had to concede that it was a compelling vision of a sustainable micro-economy, if only they could make it a reality. Alessandra continued, "There is a new breed of tourist who is no longer content to lie on a sun-lounger all day, or tour ancient ruins and dusty old churches. They want to immerse themselves in the culture of the places they visit, and much of that is encapsulated in the local food and wine. Italy, perhaps more than any other western European country, has clung fiercely to its culinary traditions and so it's hardly surprising it is becoming a place of pilgrimage for foodies in search of authenticity."

Ben spotted a Piedmont Rossese Bianco on the wine list; the white version of the red he now loved so much and suggested, "This has to be tried."

This was the rare white wine which Ben had read used to be produced by the monks of Seborga but had long been forgotten. It could no longer be found in Ligurian shops or restaurants and existed only as cheap home-produced wine in the private cantinas of a handful of local farmers. This Piedmont version was a rare find.

They were both now topping up on their wine consumption from lunchtime. Ben quickly lost his inhibitions. Alessandra seemed to hold her liquor better but was, nevertheless, on the same carefree path. When they arrived back at Bove for the cheese tasting, any reticence from earlier had evaporated. They were both giddy with wine and euphoric in their temporary freedom from responsibility.

Later, as they strolled the couple of hundred metres back to their rooms, Alessandra could recall only the wonderful Robiola di Roccaverano goat cheese from Asti, but their memories of the later part of the evening failed them after that.

They had linked arms to offer each other support and Alessandra's head occasionally lolled onto his shoulder. Ben could smell her perfume and feel her hair brushing his cheek. Ben found the key to the outer door and let them in.

The spiral staircase was easier to navigate then, he thought, as it was wide enough to climb two abreast and each step was a small rise. At the door, he struggled to get the other key into the lock. The task made more difficult as he was also holding onto Alessandra with one hand, in case she tumbled back down the stairs they had just come up. Just as he got the correct key in the right way up, she kissed him; experimentally at first as though testing the response, but then with more enthusiasm. Ben's fervour was less reserved.

As they shuffled into the central galley room without losing the embrace the intensity of it increased. Ben's hands, which had been on her shoulders, slid to her elbows and then to her wrists, which he held gently. He felt for the buttons on her cuffs to start undoing her shirt. Suddenly, without warning, Alessandra violently threw up both her arms, catapulting his away from her.

"Stop. Stop. Don't touch me. I'm sorry. It's my fault. Just stop."

Ben's ardour had already been cooled, very rapidly, by the violent breaking of their embrace. He tried to work out what exactly he had done to merit such an extreme reaction. Without further explanation, Alessandra turned, bid him good night, and closed her bedroom door behind her. Ben heard the latch lock. He stood there for a moment trying to work out what had just happened. He could still taste her and smell her perfume, it was definitely not a dream.

'Bloody women', he said quietly to himself before retiring to his own room, where but for all the wine he had drunk, he would have had a fitful night's sleep.

When Ben woke the next morning, he could smell coffee and hear a radio in the kitchen area. He showered quickly and managed as best he could to smooth down his wet hair without a brush or a comb. Dressing in the same clothes from last night he opened the door to the shared space. Alessandra was sitting with her back to him, hair similarly damp but more cared for than his.

"Coffee?" she said, without turning around.

"Please," replied Ben, although she was already pouring a long coffee into a large cup, as she knew he liked it. Ben moved around the table and sat opposite. He started to say,

"Look..." but he was interrupted by Alessandra.

"We need to drink up and get going if we are going to meet Marco."

Last night's events were apparently not going to be discussed, Ben realised. Not on this morning, at least.

17. GRAGNANO

It never occurred to either of them to have enquired about Marco's mode of transport for the hour-plus drive to Bra. The original Fiat Pandas were first introduced in the eighties, and Ben seemed to remember them self-destructing in a pile of rust within ten years in Britain's climate. They are, however, still ubiquitous in Italy nearly forty years after they were introduced. They are everywhere and used by everyone from nuns to mums and teenagers to pensioners. Marco's was of the same vintage as Claudio's, added to which its day job was restaurant delivery van and so smelled of not-so-fresh cheese, meat, and fish. When they set off, Ben still felt like they were on a reckless adventure. They had both run away from their respective responsibilities: if only for twenty-four hours but it still felt exciting and liberating. Most of the drive was with both front windows open to let the heat and food smell escape.

Marco told them that he had studied at the University of Gastronomic Science at Pollenzo. Alessandra explained that this institution had been established by the Slow Food Movement, which was founded in the neighbouring town of Bra.

"The organisation whose support revived the production of the cheeses that we tasted last night," Alessandra reminded Ben.

Marco continued, "In 1986, local journalist Carlo Petrini was so incensed by the rise of 'fast food', and what he saw as the industrialisation and globalisation of what we eat, that he started a movement to fight back. Its key aims were to promote indigenous local produce, preserve traditional gastronomy, and encourage sustainable food production. The idea struck a chord with people, and now, thirty years later, it has one hundred and fifty thousand members in one hundred and fifty countries. The

University is small—less than 100 students per year – but they come from all over the world to study there. They learn everything about food from production to consumption; or 'field to fork' as they say."

Ben was enthralled. "How bloody marvellous. A university degree in good food and wine. What a bold idea. Only in Italy could this happen. Does the course include the marketing of food and wine?"

Marco confirmed, "Marketing and brand management were very important modules. I especially enjoyed learning about those aspects. They have been vital to our success in business."

Seeing Ben's palpable enthusiasm for the concept, Marco said, "Would you like to go there for lunch?"

To a former Michelin-star chef and an academic, an invitation to lunch at the University of Gastronomic Science was too good to turn down, and in unison, they agreed. Marco explained that the campus includes the Banca del Vino (wine bank), and the Albergo dell'Agenzia – a hotel with a fine restaurant. When the young restauranteur stopped at a filling station, he phoned ahead to make a reservation and Ben heard him also mention to whoever answered, "Chef Americano e Professore Inglese."

Originally a Roman town, Pollenzo is really more of a village in size and almost the entire centre was designed and constructed by the ruling Savoy family in the late eighteenth century. They once ruled most of Northern Italy from Switzerland south to the Mediterranean, including Nice and Menton. The architecture looks immediately different from most Italian villages because it is laid out in a geometric pattern and constructed entirely of exposed red brick. Even the church of San Vittore is made in red brick and in the same strange romantic revival style. Although aspects of the Roman and medieval town remain, there is clear evidence of much later town planning and the creation of a uniform architectural template. This was the work of the Savoys.

What was the private royal summer palace is now the University's main building, which boasts a wonderful central courtyard, from which can also be accessed the Banco del Vino. The original family wine cellar, stretching the full width of the building, now contains one hundred thousand bottles of wine from three hundred producers across Italy – the bank's 'deposits.'

Another initiative of the Slow Food organisation and one of the Bank of Wine's remits, is to curate Italy's indigenous wines and make them available, when in their prime, for sampling by students and visitors. Italy has a huge variety of wines, mainly from small artisan producers, and many of these are almost unique to this country. The problem is that they are also appreciated and sought after by Italians, and their small outputs quickly disappear. This demand also often leads to their being consumed younger than would be ideal. By taking them into stock and storing these rare wines, the Banco del Vino, with no commercial agenda, can release them slowly by arranging tastings and events to celebrate their diversity and unique qualities. These tastings will also often be accompanied by similarly rare artisan foods, or old local recipes in danger of disappearing from our menus.

There was also a shop and tasting area where small surpluses of wine were sampled and sold to visitors. The stock was categorised by region, and each offering came with a card containing a detailed provenance in Italian and English. Ben was like a small child in a sweet shop, but this delight was mixed with frustration at the lack of time he had to browse and learn about these fascinating wines, most of which he had never heard of, let alone tasted.

He was surprised to find amongst these rarities a Viognier, a grape until quite recently almost exclusively grown in France but now found grown in small quantities around the world. On reading more, Ben learned that a winemaker based in nearby Bra, was one of only a couple of Italian vineyards growing this grape. Indeed, it was they who had pioneered its introduction into this country twenty years ago. With time short, and no way of transporting any more, he chose a bottle of this Viognier, as well as a 2009 Barolo by the same maker to take back with him. As he left the cellars, he vowed to return again.

The party were met in reception by the Dean of the University, and once his staff introductions were made, together they enjoyed, what was for Ben, a very memorable lunch. They were not the only visiting diners though it turned out. The Dean pointed to tables of English, Norwegian, American, and Spanish students, all here on visits arranged by their respective universities.

"Slow food and slow wine are the new hip subjects," said the Dean in near-perfect English. "For many around the world, it is an antidote to the inexorable march of technology and globalisation."

Today there was a special set lunch, with each course a traditional regional Italian dish considered to be at risk of disappearing from the nation's tables, either because of social change, the rarity of ingredients, or disappearing skills of production. Such products were awarded the status of Presidia, and with this, they were promoted via the organisation. The students were recreating dishes using these almost-lost products, recipes, and techniques. The set menu that day, made up of such dishes, was as follows:

Starter

Flan of hunchback cardoon from Nizza Monferrato (Piedmonte) with Castelmagno d'Alpeggio cheese sauce (Piedmonte) and mullet bottarga from Rebello (Toscana)

Main Courses

Gragnano Pasta (Campania) with San Gavino Monreale Saffron (Sardinia) and Carmagnola Gray Rabbit ragù (Piedmonte)

Roasted Mora Romagnola pig (Emilia Romagna) cooked with Dolcetto wine from Bormida Valley Terrace (Piedmonte) and San Michele Salentino almond-stuffed fig (Puglia) mustard.

Dessert

Almond cake with Noto Almonds (Sicilia) served with a Cocomerima pear sauce (Emilia Romagna)

Wines

With the Starter: Monotonic IGT Colli Aprutini (Abruzzo)

With the main courses: Dolcetto d'Alba DOC from Bormida Valley Terrace (Piedmonte) and Carema Classico DOC (Piedmonte)

With the dessert: Moscato Passito from Bagnario di Strevi Valley (Piedmonte)

Alessandra revelled in the detail of the dishes and ingredients, some of which were so rare or geographically-specific, that even she had never heard of them.

Ben asked what was special about Gragnano pasta, a question that she could answer easily.

"Gragnono is the area inland from the Amalfi Coast, famed for its air-dried pasta. It is made with durum wheat and the local water from Monti Lattari, which is low in calcium. The unique manufacturing process has been awarded Protected Geographical Status (PGI). We used to use their spaghetti in our restaurants in New York; unless we were making our own fresh, of course."

Ben told the Dean that he was utterly amazed by what they had created in Pollenzo, in a relatively short time.

"The University, The Wine Bank and this restaurant must be almost unique in the world. I have certainly never heard of anything like it. Your staff are also so passionate about what they do and, perhaps more importantly, appear extremely happy in their work."

And why would they not be, he thought? This was in stark contrast to Ben's experience in higher education in the UK. In his short academic career, the emphasis had shifted markedly from quality to quantity, to the detriment of both staff and students.

While Alessandra and the staff were chatting, and he was savouring the fine wine, it suddenly dawned on Ben that the principles of the Slow Food movement were what Alessandra was practising every day in the Osteria. But she was doing it without conscious planning or marketing. Her traditional recipes used only local produce and, crucially, only when it was in season. No ingredient travelled further than walking (or at worst, Ape) distance, no throw-away packaging was used, and there was little food wasted. The dishes were wholly connected to the place where they were consumed and had been proven to be sustainable by at least two thousand years of tradition. Seborga was already producing Slow Food, just without the branding.

The visit had also given Ben the seed of an idea.

Marco dropped the couple at the station in time for their train, where they said their farewells before heading their separate ways. The train back was sparsely populated with travellers. So many thoughts were going through Ben's head; this trip had been an education in many ways. The Dean had exchanged emails with Ben and offered to help in any way he could with Ben's research. He was already thinking of how he might exploit this new connection in the plans that were now forming in his mind.

18. TORTA VERDE

The day after their return from their trip to Cuneo, Ben was awoken abruptly by a bundle of folded newspapers landing on his bed and an apparently furious Alessandra standing over him.

"I usually have tea with my newspaper," he joked, half asleep.

"Get dressed now. That scheming daughter of yours has got some questions to answer."

Swinging his lean legs out of bed, he picked up the newspaper and the image on the front page revealed the reason for her mood. There was a grainy colour photograph of Cristiano and Selene apparently hand-in-hand and smiling at each other like star-crossed lovers. The headline did not help; 'Padre ottiene Principessa; il figlio diventa Principe.'

"Bloody hell. If that means what I think it does, it sounds positively incestuous!"

Alessandra was too furious to see Ben's very genuine surprise at this revelation.

"He is only seventeen!" she exclaimed, "she is nearly twenty-five."

Ben started to point out that, in fact, Selene was not quite twenty-four, but realised that it would do nothing to douse the flames of Alessandra's fury.

"I'll talk to her and find out what is going on," was the best he could offer.

"We'll both find out right now," was Alessandra's rebuttal.

Ben decided this discussion was best held in private, and so messaged Selene asking her to come over to Claudio's for coffee.

"OK. Ten minutes," came her almost immediate reply.

Selene almost skipped into Claudio's kitchen, beaming the confident smile of someone now pretty sure of a new career in journalism. When she saw the grim faces of Alessandra and her father, she was alarmed.

"What's wrong?" she asked sensing something was seriously amiss.

Alessandra pointed to the paper.

"This is so very wrong, you deceitful bitch."

The words struck Selene like a slap. She took up the paper, saw the image confronting her, and whispered to herself, "Oh my God."

Alessandra snatched the paper back from the younger woman and read some of the copy.

"Handsome teenage prince falls for charms of sexy blonde English siren. Have you no shame? After the hospitality that has been shown to you and your father. He is only seventeen years old—a child still."

Selene's brain was slowly beginning to piece together what was happening here. She took the newspaper back and looked more closely at the image.

"This is just not true," she insisted, "that photograph must have been faked."

Alessandra sighed. "You would say that."

Ben instinctively sensed that his daughter was telling the truth. He had known her long enough to spot her taller tales, and this did not sound like one of them.

"Just wait a minute, Alessandra. Hear her out," he suggested.

"I would guess that you would take her side in this. The little slut is lying through her teeth. The same photo is also in her own newspaper on-line."

As Ben knew that she was feeding the Tribune their stories, even he now thought this sounded damning.

"It is what? This photo was in the Tribune as well?"

That was enough for Selene, who turned and stormed out slamming the kitchen door behind her.

Ben started to say, “There may be some other interpretation–” but Alessandra cut him off.

“I might have known that when the chips were down, you would take her side,” she hollered at him.

Still trying to defuse the situation he began, “I understand that you are under a lot of pressure, what with the up and coming referendum, worrying about your father and all but I think you could be over-reacting to something which could have an innocent explanation.”

“That tart–” but this time it was Ben’s turn to cut her off.

“Now that is enough,” he bellowed at her, totally losing his composure this time.

“You have been snapping at me for weeks and are now starting on Selene, and probably Cristiano too, I would guess. Your trouble is you are raging at the whole world. You are taking out your problems on the people around you, and I am not putting up with it any longer. You are the one acting like a selfish, childish...” he struggled for the right word but then found it.

“Princess!” with a sardonic laugh and a parting, “Bloody grow up.”

Ben left her in the kitchen, carefully closing the door behind him. Alessandra wrenched opened the door and furiously shouted after him, "And keep her away from my son.”

When Selene called London, “She is busy in a meeting,” was the response from the editor’s PA.

Selene replied angrily, “Tell her that if she doesn’t take this call, there will be no more exclusives or coverage of the Seborga referendum.”

Thirty seconds later she heard the editor’s voice. “Selene darling, what seems to be the problem?”

"You know what the bloody problem is," sneered Selene, "why did you not tell me my photo was about to be splashed all over the newspaper?"

There was a brief pause and a hint of a sigh.

"There was just no time to hold a compliance meeting. We were offered it exclusively in the UK by an Italian Papárazzi barely ten minutes before the press deadline last night, and I had to make an on-the-spot decision. Anyway, I thought that you looked charming in it. And remember, it was you who didn't tell Cristiano about the photos you were sending back to us? Perhaps that's your first valuable lesson learnt in your new role. The media is a many-headed monster which has no qualms about sometimes biting the hand that feeds it."

Selene made a sarcastic mock laugh and asked, "How much did you pay for it?"

There was another pause, as if her editor was reappraising the situation, and then she answered, "Just a thousand euros. But we sold twenty thousand extra copies of the paper today. Why?"

This time Selene laughed out loud for real.

"Good. Because that is like small change compared to the compensation you are going to have to fork out when it's proved a fake."

There was another long silence before Selene heard just one word from her new boss, "Shit," and the phone went dead.

Two hours later the editor called Selene back on her mobile. The conversation was brief and pragmatic.

"OK. We lucked out on this one, but the damage is containable," the editor said.

Selene answered, "You mean it's only Cristiano and me who got hurt. No one too important, or powerful enough, to hire big lawyers."

"Don't go all Carl Bernstein on me, Selene. This is not Watergate. And as the article that you submitted to your university magazine testifies, you're not above interpreting the facts to suit your story."

"How the hell?" followed by a realisation that there was only one way her new boss could have got to see her students' submissions, and this finally brought some clarity to Selene. She said, "Nikki! That nasty cow."

"Now. Now. You need to show more respect to your editors, current and former. But really, having in effect stolen her job, you didn't expect Nikki to just crawl into a hole and hibernate, did you? If I were you, I would keep an eye over my shoulder for her in future."

Four years previously, Nikki had narrowly beaten Selene in a race to be elected editor of the university magazine. Selene had then later submitted a draft article to her for consideration for publication. The piece was a review of the role of social media in getting Barack Obama elected president. Her former friend had waited until a group editorial meeting to pillory Selene's piece publicly. Pointing out every single supposition and erroneous conclusion. She had apparently kept a copy of this article; doubtless filed under M for Morton, cross-referenced L for leverage, Selene imagined. It brought to mind the adage about 'revenge being a dish best served cold'.

Selene winced at the idea of her new potential boss reading something she had written several years ago as a naïve student. However, her pain was somewhat relieved when the editor added, "Paradoxically, your quote about not underestimating the stupidity of the American voter has turned out to be prophetic. It's just a shame you did not do a bit more research and attribute correctly, rather than make it sound as though Barack had said it. Perhaps you are lucky that Nikki didn't just go ahead and print it."

Selene flinched at this damning assessment, but her new boss then went on to add, "However, I loved the fresh angle from which you approached the story and some of the analogies that you chose. It was a truly original piece of work. Unlike anything Nikki ever submitted to me."

Unseen by the editor, Selene was now punching the air in glee at this praise.

"Anyway, none of this changes anything. Mistakes are mistakes. If I have made one in printing this fake photo, we need to deal with it. Now let's talk turkey, as Barack Obama might have said."

Selene found her father at Valerio's having a glass of wine and some of his sister's torte verda Ligure, a light-crusted pie of ricotta and chard. It was just gone noon.

"Bit early even for you?"

Ben looked up without smiling but pulled out the seat next to him and gestured for her to sit.

"I'm turning Italian," he replied with a wry half-smile.

His daughter said, "I can't deny that I am really disappointed you even entertained the possibility I would behave like that with Cristiano, but I can also see the photo did look convincing."

She went on to explain that she and Cristiano had become terrific friends since they had met and she liked him a great deal, but as a kind of kid brother. She revealed that he was desperately sad about what had happened between his father and mother but had no one to talk to about it. His Italian family all hated his father, and his mother did not understand his dilemma at being caught between them.

"He was lonely and found it easy to talk to me, partly because I speak English, am nearer his age, and I am objective, but also because of what happened to you and Mum."

Selene speculated that the photo had been snapped with a long lens just after they had been talking about him coming to London to study cooking.

"We were both happy and joked about the fun we would have together there. From a distance, it might have looked like we were a couple in love, but we were just fooling around. Having a lark. The hand-holding was faked using image manipulation software by an Italian paparazzi. They took multiple shots and then digitally placed our hands together."

Ben was intrigued by the deceit, but was also starting to feel a surge of relief.

"But surely a newspaper of the Tribune standing would know better than to print something like that? They would know how to spot a fake."

His daughter explained that they usually would have had it checked by their in-house graphics people but because of the importance of the story, and the time pressure they were under, they chose to take a chance.

"I am sure the paparazzi timed this offer to coincide with the print deadline, knowing this would likely be the case. The editor also possibly wanted to believe it was true a little bit too much and, in the heat of the moment, that clouded her judgement."

Valerio appeared behind Selene, placing a hand on her shoulder, a slightly intimate gesture which Ben noticed but placed no significance on.

"Drink Selene? Another professore?"

Ben was starting to feel brighter and so ordered another beer and an Aperol spritz for his daughter.

"And will they retract and apologise for their mistake?"

Smiling broadly, she said, "Already done. It was online fifteen minutes ago. And, I have negotiated a premium," she added smugly.

"My new job at the paper is now guaranteed, and I also have a little something for Cristiano to ease his embarrassment at being romantically linked to me. Although, if I'm honest, apart from damaging my relationship with Alessandra, the episode has only enhanced my personal standing. My phone's never stopped buzzing and my Facebook page is on fire."

Vincenzo then appeared from the shadows of the alley opposite, striding towards the bar. He greeted them both and then said to Ben, "Claudio has invited you to the boar hunt tomorrow. I told him it was too dangerous for a man of letters such as yourself, but he insisted I ask you anyway. Shall I tell him you are busy reading or writing?"

The not very thinly-disguised slur on his manhood did not pass Ben by, and he was not in the mood for being humiliated again. Like a man being challenged to a duel, he answered simply, "What time and where?"

19. CACCIATORINI

The sun was still coming up over countries much further to the East, and it would be another few hours before its warming rays reached the North-West of Italy. The cool mist, which often pours down from the Alps in the evenings and shrouds the olive groves at night, had yet to clear.

The loud thumping on Ben's bedroom door had the ferocity of a police raid, but it turned out that it was, in fact, Vincenzo. It was only hours since he had seen him in the bar. How could he be up and about and so bloody boisterous after so little sleep?

"Cinghiale won't wait," he shouted so loudly that Ben imagined it would warn away any boar for miles around.

He had not even slept well, trying to figure out whether to just cut his losses and sneak quietly away from Seborga. His thoughts were interrupted by the honking of a horn below his window. He could now also hear the unmistakable sound of an Ape revving, doubtless producing a cloud of smelly blue smoke. He dressed quickly and, without much thought to the task ahead, ran down the steps to the waiting Vincenzo.

In the back of the Ape were two scruffy dogs barking and showing their teeth as soon as he appeared. One unidentifiable command from their master and they both lay down and fell silent. They were, or had at one time been, white, with large liver brown markings. They looked like a cross between an English Pointer and a Cocker Spaniel but were stockier than both and with coarser coats. The dogs lay amongst a carpet of gun bags, cartridge belts, tall walking sticks, and old green knapsacks. Ben had to find a space between all of this without standing on a trigger and possibly blowing the dogs to meet their maker. Before he had done so, the Ape took off in a cloud of pollution and Ben fell amongst them all and made himself as comfortable as possible. The dogs yelped but then settled either side of him, their bulk providing some stability and warmth. Their bad breath was not quite as welcome, and he pushed their muzzles away from his face. He liked dogs, and generally, they warmed to him. He reflected that, after his latest failure with Alessandra, maybe he should just get a four-legged friend and just avoid women.

The Ape bounced along the road out of the village, passed the sign to the Passo del Bandito, and continued along the valley side towards the mountains. After a couple of kilometres, Vincenzo turned up an impossibly steep track, slowing to little more than walking pace. Just a few hundred metres further he stopped and motioned for Ben to get out.

"You'll have to push over this bit."

The dogs seemed to instinctively know they also had to disembark, while, with the engine still running flat out, Ben helped ease the little truck up the incline. Even Vincenzo was out of the cab pushing, while also revving the engine and steering. Once over the hillock, the terrain levelled a little and Ben and the dogs could all climb back in to continue the journey deeper into the mountains along unmade tracks.

Eventually, a cluster of other Apes and several ageing Japanese 4x4s came into sight in a clearing in the trees. The dogs were out and running before their Ape bumped to a halt. Men in green and brown camouflage stood around, guns draped over forearms or hanging on straps over their backs: nearly all were smoking. Headwear of some type seemed obligatory. These were either small trilby-style hats with long bird feathers in one side, or baseball caps advertising brands, of which only "Barretta" he recognised as the Italian gun-maker made famous by James Bond.

Most of the men waved a cigarette-smoking hand or acknowledged Vincenzo with a gruff 'salve', as he was obviously a man of some importance in an unwritten hierarchy he still did not fully understand. Then Ben spotted Cristiano who could not have been less appropriately dressed in tight jeans, sweat top, glittery baseball cap, and orange training shoes. Strands of dense black curly hair protruded from either side of the hoodie which covered most of his head. They exchanged nods of acknowledgement, but his demeanour was nervous and defensive: apparently, like Ben, he was also in very unfamiliar territory.

After exchanging greetings with most of the men, Vincenzo raised his hand and shouted, "Attenzione!" at which everyone stopped what they were doing.

Ben understood 'professore Inglese' and then 'Cristiano' and something about 'Claudio' but nothing else.

The steaming contents of coffee flasks were now being poured out into tin cups, along with something from clear glass bottles without labels, which Ben was soon to discover contained Gappa. Focaccia and salamis completed the al fresco breakfast.

Ben later found out that the official name of these small salamis is Cacciatorini, which means hunter's sausage. These were the size and weight of squash balls but were irregular in shape. The men also referred to them variously as 'hunters' or 'chubbs'. They looked as though they had been made in a hurry with little care for presentation, possibly even by the men themselves. Women would have made them neater, Ben speculated. Their outer skin was dry, hard, and crusted with a white powder. Ben could taste black pepper and garlic in his first slice, but there were also apparently several other spices and dry white wine in the recipe. Oh, and pork, or cinghiale, of course. The little pink-purple nuggets of protein and fat were joined in links by a rough hessian cord. They were perfect for fitting several into various pockets without adding too much weight or bulk, which might get in the way of the important business ahead.

Each man had his own knife, which they used to carve off thick bite-sized slices. The ten-centimetre blades curved slightly inwards and could be swung back into the handle when not in use. Some of the handles were dark wood and others of some type of bone. All looked well used, but were kept sharp as razors. Vincenzo loaned his knife to Ben to cut off some sausage, which it did with ease.

"Cinghiale," said the hunter pointing at Ben's hands.

Ben held up the salami and questioned, "This is made from cinghiale?"

Carlos pointed again at the knife. "Cinghiale," he said, taking it from Ben and holding it beside his left jaw and putting his right index finger sticking up from his right jaw.

The mime finally registered with Ben; the twelve-centimetre handle was evidentially made from the tusk of a male wild boar.

Ben was slightly hungover from last night, which even now was only six hours ago. He saw the mix of caffeine, alcohol, and protein as a life-saver: the hair of the dog. The sausage had a rich waxy texture. It was darker in colour than regular salami and speckled with much bigger chunks of white fat. At first, there seemed to be little flavour, but after chewing, which it required a lot of, there was a distinct strong meaty taste. He liked it and smiled his thanks and added, "Bella, grazie."

The boy refused everything he was offered and avoided eye contact with the mainly middle-aged men in the group.

Breakfast out of the way, Vincenzo made a simple whistle, and his two dogs came running back to his side; circling behind him and then emerging sitting one on each side. It seemed a well-rehearsed routine. Vincenzo spoke on, apparently nominating individuals for specific roles and issuing unsmiling instructions to men who merely nodded acknowledgement.

Someone arrived with a canvas bag and started taking out day-glow vests of the type used by men repairing roads. All the men took one and slipped it over their camouflaged shoulders. This choice of garment immediately struck Ben as odd, as surely the colour would cancel out any advantage the camouflage might give. The reason for this anomaly became clear later. Vincenzo turned to Ben and the boy and spoke in English.

"You must listen very carefully. Do exactly as I tell you."

He picked up two vests and handed one to Ben and the teenager.

"This is a dangerous business. Life will be taken today. My job is to make sure it is not your life. Wear this vest always, no matter how hot you get."

Although several sizes too large, Ben had already slipped his on, but the teenager held his in his clenched fist and now looked at it with disdain.

"Put it on!" barked Vincenzo, in a tone which brought the dogs whimpering back to his side, and finally made the boy slip on the vest.

"With this, the boars will usually avoid you, and, just as important, we won't shoot you by mistake."

Vincenzo explained that the shooters would spread out in a line about one hundred metres apart, along a clearing that had been cut in the trees of the valley for the purpose. Ben and Cristiano would go a hundred and fifty metres further up the hill, next to where the treeline started again. Here, a raised platform had been constructed from timber from where they could see everything, but remain safe. Under no circumstances must they come any closer to the line of shooters or stray out of either side of the line.

"Were they clear about this?"

They both nodded, although only Ben with any enthusiasm.

The main pack of dogs had been taken to the bottom of the valley by their two handlers and held there awaiting the signal to begin the chase. They could faintly hear them howling in the distance, apparently having already got the scent of their prey in the undergrowth somewhere down below.

Apparently, the cinghiale came down into the inhabited lower valley during the cover of night to feast on the farmer's crops: grapes, olives, vegetables, and rubbish left out. The animal's first instinct, when disturbed, would be to head back to higher ground. The thick, thorny, unkempt undergrowth above the cultivated land was their natural habitat, and they knew all the trails running through it. The vegetation is almost impenetrable to man but not to the short, sturdy dogs and their quarry. The boar's hugely powerful hind legs, and sure feet, mean they can easily out-run the dogs—even going uphill. However, the barking and yelping behind them dissuades the boar from thinking of turning back until they reach the line of hunters. By that time the dogs are far enough behind to be out of danger of being shot by accident. These were techniques honed by centuries of experience.

The mist was just beginning to clear a little, and there was the glimmer of the first rays of sun over the mountain tops. Along the path by which they had arrived, Ben thought he saw what appeared to be a man on horseback emerging out of the mist. A gun was slung over his shoulder. He shook his head to be sure he was not hallucinating. The figure got closer and became clearer as the clip-clop of hooves could be heard on the rough stones of the path. Prince Claudio sat tall and erect on the big horse making for a striking, if slightly surreal, sight in the early morning mist.

"Buongiorno. Buongiorno."

Slipping his feet from the stirrups, he slid effortlessly from the horse, and surprisingly spritely for a man of his age. Although Ben was learning that the Ligurian lifestyle and diet meant that life expectancy was much longer than for most Europeans; there were several people in the village over one hundred years who were still reasonably active. He recognised this horse from his walk with Vincenzo, when it had been grazing peacefully on Claudio's terraces. It looked even larger close-up. It was not the slender, skittish, Arab-type horse Ben was familiar with from England but a powerfully-built, sure-footed and calm creature.

Claudio's hand immediately extended to Ben who took it and shook it warmly. Cristiano greeted him, "Nonno di buon mattino," showing for the first time any sign of respect for anyone present.

He also had genuine affection for, but also some fear, of the old man.

"Also, his first cinghiale hunt," exclaimed Claudio proudly while patting the boy on the top of his hoodie.

"To be a man in our family, he must do this before he is eighteen. His mother does not know he is here. She'd go mad at me if she knew. His uncle brought him from San Remo this morning."

He then exchanged what sounded like very stern words with one of the men. He kept repeating his name 'Carlos', and Ben also recognised the word 'mio nipote' again and then 'professore', his forefinger underlining who he was referring too and emphasising his commands, presumably about the safety of his charges. Claudio then mounted his horse by pulling himself up from the horn of the saddle. Looking over his shoulder, he said, "Ricorda quello che ho detto, Carlos," before trotting off to follow the shooters.

With the horse's extra pace and height, Claudio would work the flank pushing back any boar heading away sideways from the guns. A steep gorge on the other side would prevent them going in that direction. Ben watched as Claudio disappeared along the path which led around the valley, thinking this was like a scene from one of his childhood TV programmes, such as Robin Hood or William Tell. He thought, surely this was not still happening in the twenty-first century, less than an hour from the glitz of Nice and Monte Carlo.

The shooters all settled down in their places, smoked more cigarettes, and awaited the signal. Ben was soon to discover that Carlos was to act as a 'sweeper', picking off any boars which might make it past the line of hunters. He was to be stationed in front of Ben and Cristiano but over a hundred metres behind the line of other guns. He was also, therefore, their 'babysitter'. Both positions were a big responsibility, as he could only take a shot once the boar had passed the line of sight with the men in front of him. Any earlier, and he risked hitting one of the men in the back. If a boar came straight up the middle, he would have to try and either drive it sideways before it reached him, or just let it go past and hope it did not charge him down. Carlos was chosen because he was the most accurate shot with the fastest reactions.

Carlos, Ben and Cristiano sat on a felled tree just below the treeline to await the coming action. Ben had almost nodded off to sleep when the first shot rang out. The rapport was not so loud but echoed around the mountains for a good few seconds. This was very quickly followed by the sound of the dogs barking and howling way below. Ben roused himself and took his place in the enclosure, but Cristiano was hanging back. Carlos quickly gave him a firm shove in the back with the butt of his gun, projecting him in the direction he was to go. The boy scowled at his Grandfather's aide but acquiesced. Claudio had made Vincenzo in-loco-parentis, and he was taking his job seriously.

Waiting for the action to start, Ben had noticed that the ground around the wooden platform had been overturned in clumps here and there: clear signs of cinghiale; just as Vincenzo had pointed out on their walk. Apparently, these woods were rife with them. Looking up he could see why. Oak and chestnut trees formed most of the woods' canopy, and the husks of their fruits littered the ground and crunched under their feet as they walked. Where there are woods such as these, there are usually mushrooms and often truffles, Ben remembered. Fuelled by coffee and Gappa, he was beginning to enjoy this adventure, and he found the countryside truly spectacular.

The noise level from dogs' yelping increased, as the pack had apparently cleared a ridge somewhere ahead of them. Somewhere out of sight, terrified wild pigs were now rushing in the direction of the shooters. The first driven animal emerged from the scrub without any warning, but was hit with several shots before it had covered three metres. It fell in a cloud of steam evaporating from its own perspiration. Such was its forward momentum that, even after being hit, the pig continued tumbling head-over-hooves for another three metres. Other animals soon followed. Some were alone, others in twos or threes. Often two or more hunters were reacting to the same target, meaning that they were hit several times from different angles. Ben saw that the bigger male animals often ploughed a deep furrow in the ground with the momentum of their body weight and speed as they fell. Their snouts and tusks acting like a plough, parting the earth before them.

Suddenly, away to Ben's left, a voice was heard shouting, "Aiuto. Aiuto, Aiuto," which he understood translated as 'Help' and it sounded as though the caller was in some considerable pain.

Carlos started to move off in the direction of the cry, but first turned his head to look directly at Ben. With his spare hand, he pointed to the teenager and then held the same finger under his right eye, in a signal even an urbanite like Ben understood in these circumstances.

The shooters, meanwhile, were trying to keep a wary eye on the line of scrub for any more targets but were also curious as to what was happening to one of their own. They were later to learn that the final man in the line had moved forward slightly from his original position to get a clearer shot and stepped into an illegal gin trap. The metal-toothed jaw had clamped around his boot just cutting through the leather and biting into his ankle. He was trying to stay still but was struggling with the pain and the uneven terrain. The man to his immediate left had come to his aid, but it would take two men to force the jaws open safely. Carlos was by now only metres away from him.

Ben was both horrified and captivated by the events unfolding before him and had failed to notice Cristiano leave the safety of the hide. The boy had slept too late that morning. He had not left time to go to the bathroom when his uncle had called for him to leave. So, during what the boy thought was a temporary ceasefire, he had decided to relieve himself. He headed back into the higher treeline behind the hide.

With two shooters missing, still trying to help their injured friend, there was now a gap in the defensive line. It was into this very opening that the next boar to emerge from the valley had run. It was moving very fast indeed. In normal circumstances, the remaining men further off to each side would have left this one, but now had no choice but to act. Two fired almost in unison, the first hitting the outer fatty layer of the boar's lower belly, the second blowing off half its flapping left ear. Neither of these wounds slowed its pace even slightly. So fast was it moving, that no other man in the line dared make a third shot as the beast was now approaching the prone hunter. The day-glow jackets of the huddle of men were enough to send it veering right toward the wooden hide. Carlos was also far too close to the others to shoot, and the injured animal bolted past him, heading for the treeline.

Ben turned briefly to check on Cristiano only to discover he was now at least ten metres away with his back to him. A small wisp of steam was rising from where he was peeing into the damp undergrowth. Before he could come to terms with the situation that was unfolding, the boar had passed the hide at speed and closed on the boy, who was oblivious to its presence. It struck him on his lower left leg, with a force projecting him both upwards and sideward, like a bowling ball hitting a skittle. Cristiano landed on his side a bodies-length from where he had stood a moment before, his trouser leg already covered in blood.

Ben was not sure whether this blood was his own or the boar's, which was now leaking profusely from its wounds. He could see this quite clearly because the animal had stopped and turned around to face them. It was pawing the ground with one hoof, audibly snorting, and occasionally shaking its massive head. It was, presumably, not only extremely angry at being pursued up a mountain by a pack of dogs, but now also in considerable pain from the two gunshots it had received. Ben judged that it now intended to vent that anger on the prone teenager.

To an animal with poor sight but excellent sense of smell, Cristiano's bright clothing, glittery baseball cap, and an enveloping cloud of men's cologne, made him an easy target. Ben was momentarily frozen by the speed and ferociousness of the attack and his brain scrambling to assess what had just happened. Carlos and the others had seen the boar disappear into the shadows of the treeline and, thinking the danger had passed, heaved a collective sigh of relief. They did not realise the boy had left the safety of the hide and was now eye-to-eye with over a hundred kilos of snorting cinghiale. The beast was bristling with primeval hostility.

Strange involuntary movements took over Ben's legs, propelling him from the hide and towards the forest with the speed and agility of a twenty-year-old. This was taking place while all his rational instincts were telling him to stay where he was, in the safety of the hide. As he closed on where the boy lay, he could see Cristiano's ashen face looking up from the ground pleading with him to make this thing go away. Tears ran down his cheeks and Ben had never before seen anyone so absolutely in fear of their life.

The snorting boar now had them both in focus and, sensing a new challenge, made its decision to charge. Stepping over the boy Ben raised himself up to his full six feet, grasped both corners of his day-glow waistcoat and spread his arms. From the rear, he looked like a giant orange bat. The prostrate Cristiano sheltered in the gap between his legs, gripping the flesh on Ben's ankle so tight he winced.

The combination of fear and anger sent adrenaline flowing through Ben's veins, and he began yelling with all the fury he could muster, "Fuck you, you ugly bastarrrrrrrd!" He spat the words out with a look of murder in his eyes. He then kept repeating this chant at the top of his voice, like a mantra.

The sight of this two-metre square, screaming orange apparition, must have been enough to cause the boar to hesitate for a second, to reassess this apparently much more significant new challenge. It halted its charge after just a few steps. But, before the animal's inadequate brain could see through Ben's bluff, a shot rang out. The boar appeared to hop a few inches into the air before collapsing in a cloud of steaming perspiration. Its head rested facing them, and a full stream of dark blood began to pool around its snout. Its substantial hairy body shook one last time, and then it rolled on its side. A large hole just below its already damaged ear was now also spouting blood like a fountain.

When Ben finally managed to move a muscle, he turned to his left to see Carlos still pointing his gun at the animal, in case it got a second lease of life. The sweeper had sprinted back close enough to the treeline to get a clear shot and fired without hardly halting his stride. He was indeed not only a skilled shot but also a sprinter of some considerable speed. None of the other hunters was anywhere close enough to the ridge even to witness the scene that had unfolded.

Turning back to the still shaking Cristiano, Ben knelt beside him. A cut on the boy's head from where he'd landed against a stump was now also seeping blood down his cheek. He was further taken aback when the stricken teenager threw his arms around Ben's neck and began weeping like a child.

"It's dead," said Ben, "completely dead. There's nothing more to worry about. You are safe."

By now others had arrived, guns un-shouldered, and were shouting questions. Realising that he was clinging to Ben like a five year old and the men were now watching Cristiano loosened his grip and started to compose himself. He wiped the tears and blood from his face and tried to get up but stumbled again. His colour was ashen. Until this moment, the adrenaline of fear had cancelled out the pain from the nasty wound on his left shin. The boar's tusk had gouged a sizeable piece of skin from his leg, which hung like a flap from an envelope. As his fear subsided, so the pain replaced it. Someone produced a first aid kit from a bag, poured antiseptic into the wound, and started to bandage it, carefully folding the flap of skin back into position on Cristiano's leg. The boy winced at the rough treatment but clenched his teeth and said nothing, although he was obviously in agony.

Only then did Claudio arrive at a trot from his outer position, slipping from his horse while it was still moving and letting the reins fall abandoned. He was hollering either questions or instructions: Ben was not sure which.

Ben's brain was racing. He had no idea of what prompted his own reckless reaction. It was as though he had been driven by some unknown force to act in a way that his brain, both then and now, told him were madness. He wanted to move away from the scene and stumbled off further into the trees. He had not gone ten paces before he vomited violently and, in a single gush, emptied the entire contents of his stomach.

Most of the other hunters were busy maintaining their vigil on the line below to prevent the dogs sending other boars careering into them. An occasional shot still rang out as a straggler boar appeared out of the valley. One of the men had gone back to his 4x4 to radio for help. Within a few minutes, someone had bound together three or four straight branches hewn from the forest and turned them into a makeshift seat-come-stretcher. Vincenzo and one of the other stockier men bent down and placed one of Cristiano's arms behind each of their heads and hoisted the boy onto the seat. Claudio walked in front, and they then set off retracing their tracks back to the cars.

On the long bumpy journey back down the mountain, Ben was quiet and reflective. Carlos was jabbering away in Italian and the other two in the jeep were nodding and occasionally joining in. They all pretty much ignored Ben, who just tagged along, still in shock.

It struck Ben that in his entire fifty-plus year existence he had never once before been genuinely in fear of his life. Nor had he ever seen anyone else in mortal danger. Of course, he had seen it in films and on TV, but it never occurred to him before quite what a pivotal moment it would be for him. He pondered the concept of this level of jeopardy and concluded that with few exceptions, people in today's developed world, are seldom out of their comfort zone. Most of their experiences are safe and predictable and, even the ones containing an element of risk, are usually carefully controlled.

In the twentieth century, driving a car used to be the most dangerous activity that most people undertook on a regular basis. Since the advent of crumple zones, airbags, and even lamp posts which deliberately snap on impact, even that is now relatively safe. Going out into the wild to confront an animal easily capable of killing you, is what cavemen did thousands of years ago. Those people did it because they had no choice; it was kill or die of hunger. In the twenty-first century, this is no longer what most people would consider an acceptable level of risk. And yet, without much thought, that is precisely what he and Cristiano had set out to do this morning—to risk their lives for the thrill of the chase. They could have both refused. Although that may have been awkward and embarrassing, no one would have dragged them there. But they now realised, that even with modern weaponry, in the lottery that is man versus nature, sometimes nature wins.

Ben's thoughts then turned to his own reaction. What the bloody hell came over him, he wondered. He had never even confronted anyone jumping the queue at the bar, let alone a furious and injured wild animal. And yet, he recalled the feeling of the adrenalin pumping through his veins like a drug. The fury which he felt inside, and which then flooded from him, manifesting itself in his uncharacteristically foul-mouthed war cry. Perhaps it was fifty years of pent-up anger and frustration? —the final straw after years of looking the other way and turning the other cheek.

Things could have gone even further, because, just for a second, he had felt such fury that he imagined he could even have attacked the boar with his bare hands. Nevertheless, he concluded, thank heavens no one saw or heard him, except the cinghiale. Cristiano was undoubtedly too terrified to look up, and it was all over in a flash. The whole incident can't have lasted thirty seconds and yet he could recall it all, as if in slow motion. What on earth had made him spread his arms like a bird? Perhaps it was something he had subliminally learned from watching Richard Attenborough in his wildlife TV programmes. He did not even know if that was the correct thing to do because he could now vaguely recall something about making yourself very small if attacked by a bear.

Trying to rationalise his actions, Ben wondered what was it in human DNA which informed the instinctive decision-making process when a person has the binary choice between fight or flight? He was clear in his own mind that this had certainly not been a conscious decision. Something, or some alter-ego within him, had taken over his actions in a way that had never happened before. Was this what bravery was? Was it an unconscious rather than deliberate act? The Englishman found himself asking many such questions over the next few days.

He did not know this boy well, or particularly like him, from what little time they had spent together. The teenager had undoubtedly not helped to avoid the situation he later found himself in, by refusing to follow any of the simple instructions he had received. His actions had put them both in real danger. Not bravery then, he wondered but merely self-preservation?

In the absence of any other explanation for his out of character behaviour, Ben latched onto survival as his motivation. His primeval instincts must have calculated that he himself was in danger and, that when the boar had ripped the boy to shreds, it would then turn and kill him too? That was it, he concluded. After all, self-preservation sounded like the Ben he knew and understood. He had not just protected the boy; he had acted to save his own skin.

20. TROFIE

The Osteria was closed. Alessandra was at the hospital down on the coast with Cristiano, who was being kept in after minor surgery on his leg wound. Everyone out and about that night had therefore gathered at Valerio's. Selene was already there and seemed to be spending even more time at the bar than Ben. She used the excuse that she could get a good phone signal from his premises, and it had become her temporary office from where she could file her reports.

"Dad. Thank God you're alright," she said, looking him up and down for any outward signs of injury before hugging him close and not letting go.

"One of the hunters phoned ahead with the news that Cristiano had been injured and that you were with him."

Ben shrugged his shoulders as if to say he didn't understand what all the fuss was about.

"I'm fine, and Cristiano will be soon," was all he added.

With the advance notice of the opportunity, the savvy bar owner had arranged a special 'piatto del giorno' of Trofie al Ragú Di Cinghiale; although this was frozen meat from a boar that had been killed in a previous hunt. The most common sauce served with trofie pasta in Liguria is the classic Genovese pesto, quite often also served mixed with very soft-boiled potatoes. It is the easiest, cheapest, and most filling of pasta dishes but also a culinary triumph if done well, as Ben had discovered from Alessandra.

Ben had heard that today's boar meat had already been shared equally amongst the men. The animal that struck Cristiano turned out to weigh one hundred and thirty kilos, which, even after waste and bones, gave each man several large portions.

Modern hunters have found it is best to freeze the meat for several weeks before eating, as this makes it more tender. Valerio knew that, as the main course, the hunters would want to share the liver from the animal shot that day. They had brought it to him earlier in a cool box and wrapped in hessian sacking. His sister had seasoned it and coated it in flour ready to be fried in olive oil and wine with some mild white onions. As they had already filled up on pasta, this was more a symbolic dish than a sustaining one. It seemed to Ben that it was as if to stick two fingers up at the wild beast and prove who'd come out on top, the hunters would feast on his offal. Then again, why not: nothing would be wasted, Ben rationalised.

He recognised many of the hunters from that morning, including Carlos who offered him what seemed like a grudging 'salve professore' when he arrived. The others turned and nodded but quickly looked away without further acknowledgement. Without Vincenzo to translate, he did not bother trying to join them but took a table of his own outside. He noted that no one offered him any boar liver. He concluded he was not seen as one of them. Not a hunter.

No, he thought, he had in fact been the hunted.

The men already sounded very drunk and full of bravado when Ben had first arrived, and much more wine would be drunk that night. This was unquestionably a post-hunt ritual amongst the menfolk.

Almost before he had sat down, Valerio had a frosted bottle of beer on the table and his opener ready to remove the cap.

"Si," Ben confirmed.

"You will need that after today's fun," offered Valerio.

"That was no fun, believe me," he replied.

"Just a scratch from a pig," offered the barman. "The boy will be Ok. It will help make a man of him."

Taking a long swig and savouring the cold bite as it slid down, Ben enquired on the news from the hospital. Valerio explained what the whole village already knew that the wound looked worse than it was because it was deep and there was a lot of blood. The skin was torn but not lost, and so they were able to stitch it, and it will heal. There would be a small scar.

"He can brag about his boar encounter and show the mark to impress the girls."

He would need a crutch for a week or so, but other than that he would be fine.

"Thank God for Carlos' keen eye and steady hand" offered Valerio.

"Indeed," said Ben noting that there was no mention of his role in the event.

A couple of cousins had appeared to help Valerio on what was going to be a busier than usual night. One was a pretty teenager, with many of the attributes, but not yet any of the confidence, of a woman. She could not stop checking that her hair was straight behind her ears, that her skin-tight, very short shorts were folded to the exact same length on both her thighs, and looking at her reflection in the glass at every opportunity. Despite this, she was charming and attentive to the customers.

The boy was probably about the same age but looked younger. He had a strong family resemblance to Valerio and was also developing some of the bar owner's natural charisma. The two youngsters seemed to be doing most of the food serving: back and forth from the tiny kitchen with steaming plates of pasta, while Valerio looked after the drinks, which were flowing freely.

The events of the morning kept replaying in Ben's mind, but after a couple of plates of aperitivo and another beer, he felt more relaxed. He ordered the ragú and a bottle of Rossese from Valerio's new assistant. Danilo was his name, he discovered, and his English was excellent, having spent much of his time working at his parent's restaurant down on the coast. He had also attended a school near the French border with a mix of international students: Italians, French, English, and Russian, made up most of the cohort.

The young man returned within minutes with a dish in one hand, a basket of bread balanced on his wrist, and the Rossese in the other hand; a glass balancing upside-down on the bottleneck. This was the practised economy of movement that only a nation, where customer service is a national sport, can achieve. His female counterpart could also do all of this, but while also simultaneously checking her reflection in the window glass as she passed the open doors at full pace. It's all about 'bella figura', as they say in Italy.

When the dish arrived, Ben had mixed feelings about eating the cinghiale. The ragú was undoubtedly delicious and the rosemary, sage, and thyme just sang-through the strong meaty flavour of the pig. He just did not feel like the victorious hunter, or like eating his competitor. Let's face it: the boar had out-witted them, out-ran them and, but for happenstance, could easily have been the victor. He pushed the chunks of meat around the plate, ate some of the pasta, and mopped up the sauce with the bread. The passing Danilo said,

"Scarpetta, benne," in his direction and carried on to the next table where he delivered two plates.

Seeing Ben's puzzlement, on his way back, he explained, "Scarpetta, is to mop up the sauce with bread and is a sign of a well enjoyed pasta dish."

"Scarpetta," Ben practised. "I'll remember that. Grazie."

"Prego," answered the young man and went scurrying back to the kitchen with his plate, still containing much of the boar meat. When he returned, he asked, "My mother wants to know if your pasta was not so good tonight."

Realising he had made a mistake in sending back a half-eaten plate of food, which would be construed as a huge insult to the kitchen, he tried to explain.

"I have had one too many close encounters with the cinghiale today, and it has spoiled my appetite. Please apologise to your mother and tell her that the pasta was perfect and her sauce delightful."

He seemed to understand and returned to the kitchen with the good news. Ben was finishing the last of the carafe of Rossese when Danilo returned carrying a plate and glass. With no hint of a choice or expectation or any dissent, he said, "My mother says that you must eat this and drink that. The dolce is good for shock, and the drink will settle your stomach."

As it seemed that this was a proclamation, rather than a suggestion, Ben took up the spoon provided for him. The panna cotta looked like any other, but when he tasted it, a delightful lavender flavour filled his mouth. It was simple but sublime; like the best medicine in the world. The drink was predictably limoncello, but Danilo explained that this was his mother's own, made with organic lemons from the hills around the village where the mountain mists wash over them each day.

"They are the crinkly, odd shaped ones that you will see in the shop here in the village. The supermarkets don't want them, but people here recognise that they are the best. No chemicals or colouring and much more flavour."

The visiting diners and drinkers were thinning out now, and the staff could relax a little. It seemed to Ben that, from his actions in standing and lining up his sights on an imaginary gun, Carlos had retold the story of the shooting of the boar several times. Each time a new audience arrived he did so with increasing enthusiasm when the shot was fired. 'Bang' he shouted louder each time.

Danilo was keen to practice his English and Ben was relieved to be able to hold a conversation without choosing his words so carefully or listening so attentively to the replies. He invited the boy to sit down and asked what he was studying.

"English and business," came the eager reply.

"Both my subjects," Ben replied, almost as eagerly. "Well, I don't teach English, but I did study it when I was at university."

He went on to explain how he taught economics and some other business modules at a northern university in England.

"I heard that," the boy replied.

Yes, of course, thought Ben. Everyone knows everything that is going on in the village; particularly when a strange foreigner was concerned. He decided to turn the tables and extract some information from his new friend. He asked about Cristiano, who he thought would be more or less the same age. Danilo said that he did not know him personally because Cristiano had lived in America all his life. His mother had brought him back to Italy, very much against his will, about a year ago.

"After the big trouble. You have heard about this?"

Ben nodded, affirmatively.

"Since then he has been living most of the time with his uncle and cousins and helping out in their restaurant further along the coast. Everyone says that Cristiano wanted to stay in New York and try to help his father get the restaurant going again, but his mother would not let him. Until he is eighteen, he cannot re-enter America without her authority. Apparently, he is irate about being stuck here thousands of kilometres from his father and all his friends," Danilo concluded, in a tone which suggested that he had little sympathy for the boy's predicament.

"His father now has a drugs conviction and is on probation. He can't leave the United States without permission from the courts, and so Cristiano hasn't seen him in over a year. Also, I suppose, after New York, this must seem like a comedown for him," the teenager speculated.

Ben, on the other hand, was starting to have some sympathy for Alessandra's son, but also for her predicament in trying to keep him away from his evidently feckless father.

The last of the limoncello drained from the bottom of his glass almost simultaneously with the last of his will to stay awake. Although his mind was racing with all he had learned, he needed his bed. He thanked Valerio and his helpers, paid the bill, which did not include his dessert or digestivo, left a generous tip, and headed home to an empty house.

Danilo's mother's culinary prescription had worked its magic, and, after the exertions of the previous day, he had slept soundly and awoke late. He decided he needed some time on his own to collect his thoughts. Calling at the shop for some basic provisions and bottled water, he had decided to explore the hills nearby on his own today. He did so, however, with a newfound awareness of some of the natural dangers.

Retracing the path Vincenzo had taken him along, he went in search of the Templars cave. Despite walking all morning, he could not find the clearing, which had seemed so obvious only a few days ago. A few times he had reached a point at which the view across the valley looked as he had remembered it, but perhaps slightly more elevated, or lower down. He retraced his steps a few times to forks and took alternative tracks but could still not find the rock with the Templar cross. It was almost as if he had imagined the whole thing and, yet, he knew that this was a ridiculous thought. After another hour of walking in the full heat of the sun, Ben returned to the village, the whereabouts of the cave still a mystery.

As he entered the village, all the ladies were sitting on the steps in the shade chatting: their washing fluttering in the breeze would be bone dry in minutes, he thought. Children were still playing nicely without a hand-held digital device in sight: a rare sight in a twenty-first century western country. There was still no activity at the Osteria, and the shutters were firmly down. However, there was a hand-written sign, pinned to the menu blackboard, which read 'Cristiano é all ospedale e esta bene. Apertura questa sera alle 19.00.' He understood, 'Cristiano', 'bene', and '19.00', and could guess the remainder.

Meanwhile, back at Claudio's, things were not so quiet. Apes, Vespas, and bicycles were parked everywhere outside. People were coming and going. Those arriving all carried something on a tray or in a dish, which was wrapped in a tea towel or brown paper. Those leaving all went empty-handed, apart from their baking trays. No one paid much attention to

Ben as he entered the dark hallway and slipped up to his top floor room for a rest away from the heat of the late afternoon. Although, as he passed, it was evident there was much activity on the first landing, presumably where Cristiano had been brought to recuperate. He could hear female voices all competing in speed and volume, including Alessandra's with her slightly different accent; another unwelcome legacy of New York he wondered?

As he arrived at six thirty, Valerio was already knocking the top of a cold Peroni ready for him. Selene was already there and looked like she had been for some time.

"The prodigal son is returned to his family in one piece," Valerio offered for confirmation.

"Si," allowed Ben, but then went on, "Judging by all the food that has been brought to the house for him, they will need to reinforce his crutches to deal with the weight he will put on."

Valerio had walked away still trying to translate his remark but then suddenly turned and laughed out loud when he finally got the joke. With their new-found familiarity, he was tempted to quiz Valerio about Alessandra's covered-up arms. Selene had not yet noticed this quirk and he didn't want her to start speculating about it. He decided not to pursue the matter for now. Instead, he said, "No Danilo and his charming assistant tonight?"

The bar owner smiled and waved his arm to the predominantly empty seats, "With the Osteria open again, I will not need them tonight. It was a good night last night though, thanks to my family coming at short notice."

Ben was learning about the complex extended family networks in Italy and how they provided a mutually beneficial support system, which allowed businesses to survive. These would have long since gone to the wall in the UK. He could not help but be impressed, but also slightly saddened, that he could rely on no such network himself.

Valerio returned to the table and gestured to the seat beside Ben saying, “May I? I feel that I should warn you that Carlos has been telling everyone that you failed to look out for Cristiano and this was the cause of the boar attack.”

He went on to say that Carlos had claimed that Ben had been left in charge of the boy, but had allowed him to walk out of the hide on his own and into danger. Not allowing time for Ben to respond he went on,

“Even if this were true,” he added questioningly, “I am not sure what an unarmed city man such as yourself was expected to do against a charging male cinghiale. Anyway, that is what he was saying. Mind you, Carlos is a cunning fox and will turn any situation he can to his advantage. He will relish being the hero and will secure plenty of free drinks on the strength of it. However, many others will pay little heed to what he says but just be warned in case Alessandra hears his story first.”

Ben did not say anything but looked at Selene to gauge her reaction. Did she think he was a coward, he wondered? His daughter reached for his hand and held it gently in hers. If she did believe it, it seemed that she certainly was not judging him badly for it. But was that because that is what she would have expected?

How ironic, mused Ben. For the first time in his life, he had done something courageous, and he had ended up looking like a coward. Isn’t life unfair?

Whatever the village was being told, there was only one show in town as far as food was concerned, and he needed to eat; so, bring on the circus, he decided. Selene agreed to join him, which pleased him greatly. As they strolled through the alleyways towards Alessandra’s Osteria she said, “It sounds like you and Cristiano both had a lucky escape.”

“Like you, Selene, I am beginning to realise that you have to make your own luck in life. Sometimes you just have to stop accepting what comes along and make things happen.”

His daughter looked at him quizzically, apparently not understanding what he meant by this remark. Was he suggesting that he had acted to save himself, as this Carlos character was saying? She decided that she did not want to discuss this possibility, in case it turned out to be true.

The Osteria was busy. Perhaps it was all the extra people in the village visiting Valerio, or news of yesterday's excitement that had brought the curious to see the now legendary sharpshooter, Carlos. Vincenzo was there, of course, and several of the other hunters. The Dutchman, who he hadn't seen since he first arrived, raised his glass and said, "Buonaserra."

There was as yet no sign of Alessandra, but someone else quickly appeared to take their order and give them a page with the hand-written piatto giorno.

"Another family member, no doubt?" Selene suggested.

The menu was a brief affair, as befitted the lack of time she had doubtless had. 'Bruschetta con funghi, Spaghetti al Pomodoro, semifreddo all amaretto, formaggio di capra.' At least there was no cinghiale he thought, chuckling to himself. He did not know why he felt quite so light-hearted under the circumstances. After all, yesterday he had suffered a near-death experience, the woman of his desires seemed to loathe him, and he was being publicly proclaimed a coward. And that was not counting all his troubles at home.

Maybe it was post-traumatic relief, but the elation of surviving his near-death experience was making him feel invulnerable. He ordered Selene and himself a Prosecco. What the hell, he thought, let's celebrate life. The Dutchman held up his empty glass, and so he ordered him one too. The old hippy moved over to their table and gestured to the spare seat. Ben waved him to sit down.

"Celebrating?" he asked.

"Yes, absolutely," said Ben.

"I heard about the pig."

"You did. Which one?" came his quick-witted retort, "the one with, or without the gun?"

Both the Dutchman and Selene were puzzled by this apparent joke but decided to let it go. Their drinks arrived in large wine glasses, at least double the measure of a usual sparkling wine flute. They chinked glasses.

"Salute," offered the Dutchman.

"Life, in all its forms," toasted Ben.

"Cheers," said Selene.

"Prohst," closed the Dutchman.

Selene asked Rikki how he had ended up in Seborga.

"To get lost," was his somewhat mysterious response.

"If you want to get lost, this is the place to come. Or at least it used to be."

"You sound like you were on the run," she said, only half-joking.

"You could say I was running because of a conversation just like this one. I used to work in oil and gas exploration. You know, they pay you big money to work in all the shitty places in the world and steal the local's natural resources. Well, I got sick of all the bribing of politicians, raping of national assets, polluting their rivers and seas, and one night, over a bottle of tequila and a couple of joints, I told my story to a pretty female journalist."

"You were a whistle-blower?" suggested Selene.

The Dutchman looked puzzled at the expression.

"I don't know about blowing whistles, but this girl blew my mind and so I blew my mouth off. It would not have been so bad if she had not used my name and a photograph."

Both Ben and his daughter winced at the thought of the fallout from his foolishness.

"After that, I was not only unemployable in Holland, or anywhere else in the world where the oil and gas industry exert any influence, but things also got a bit dangerous."

"They threatened you?" asked Selene.

"The companies did not threaten me directly, but it became very unhealthy to be in any bar in Amsterdam, Rotterdam, or The Hague after that. He lifted his upper lip and revealed a denture which filled a gap where several of his top row of teeth had once been. You see, so many people in Holland have gotten wealthy from their expertise in this industry, they did not want anyone shaking their money tree. I should have known that it's best not to piss off people who have survived working in places like the Congo, Russia, Iraq, and on the North Sea oil rigs.

"So, I threw my stuff in the Khubelwagon and drove south to the Riviera but found the welcome not much better on the French side of the border. Then one day, by accident, I stumbled on this place. Me, and the American artist, were the only non-Italians here and, importantly, there were no former oil and gas people. The food's excellent, the wine's cheap, the sun shines, and the police rarely drive up the mountain to cramp my style. It's the perfect place for getting lost.

"I bought the whole building with the shop and two apartments for the equivalent of three months' salary working on the Russian pipeline. I have a few investments, l can live for virtually nothing, and the junk shop pays for all my little luxuries," he said waving his unlit joint and holding up his glass in the other hand.

"You don't get bored, or," Selene hesitated, "lonely?"

"Sure, sometimes but, if I want to find some fun, I just drive down to San Remo. They have a casino and all that goes with it."

When their spaghetti arrived, The Dutchman thanked Ben for the drink and took his leave. After the first taste of the spaghetti, Ben decided that never before had a dish been so under-sold.

"Wow!" he exclaimed. "Spaghetti with tomatoes was all that was offered on the menu; no embellishment or further details."

He told his daughter that this was perfectly cooked pasta, "With just enough bite so you could almost taste the land it had grown on?"

Ben could also see the sauce contained thick green olive oil, tiny capers, pine nuts, red onion, as well as some herbs that he had not yet identified. He thought that it was the antithesis of the current trend for over-emphasising the quality of ingredients, which, in practice, can rarely be distinguished within the dish.

"This is surely the zenith of the philosophy of 'simple things done well'? It is easy to see how in a fancy New York restaurant, where tastes are probably so jaded, it could turn the head of a Michelin judge. Each ingredient is the star in an ensemble performance. It was the Beatles of dishes at the Abbey Road of their careers," he concluded, pleased with his own analogy.

Selene smiled at his unbridled school-boy-like enthusiasm. She was discovering sides to her father that she had not seen before.

"It's certainly very yummy," she agreed without the need for further analysis.

This dish was a lightbulb moment for Ben. In that instant, he understood what Italian pasta sauces were about. They were poverty made tolerable. Hardship made bearable. When people had almost no money and could spare little time away from their labour on the land, with a mere cup of flour, plus whatever grew around you, a dish could be produced which would sustain your body and your sanity. It would cost only pennies and take only minutes, but could taste like a feast and keep you going all day in the fields. The taste of that sauce would stay with Ben for weeks.

With his scarpetta technique now honed to an art form, Ben soaked up the last few drops of rich sauce and sat back in his chair replete. When his plate was removed, he tried to engage the new staff member in conversation with "Molto bene," but she was having none of it.

"Si," was the only response, and that was without a smile. It was as if to say, 'Si. Of course, it's good. We made it, and that's what our customers expect.'

He was by now getting fed up with the sideways looks he was receiving from the hunters and decided it was time to ask Vincenzo what was going on. Before he could rise to move to his table, there was a sudden drop in the noise level, and then everything went completely silent. All eyes were turned to the piazza outside.

Across the stone slabs hobbled Cristiano on a shiny new aluminium crutch, with Claudio by his side in case support was needed. It took him a while to limp across the square, and in that time, total silence had descended on the bar. Most were wondering why he was out of bed so soon after an operation on his leg. Word had certainly reached his mother because she came flying out of the kitchen and was shouting his name hysterically. But her pleas were too late; he was already in the Osteria. Claudio guided him across to Ben and Vincenzo where he paused to steady himself.

"Vai avanti" prompted Claudio giving the boy a gentle nudge in the back.

Cristiano steadied himself, the white bandage of his head a stark contrast to his dark skin, eyes, and raven hair. He held his hand out for Ben to shake. When he did so, the boy grasped it and shook it firmly, so all could see. He began to speak, eyes lowered at first but then looking straight into Ben's.

"I came to thank you for saving my life."

At this point, the boy turned to look at Carlos, who had shrunk back into the crowd of men. He then scanned the room as if to check that he had everyone's full attention.

"We have been told that this man, Carlos", he made a dismissive gesture with his head over his shoulder, without even looking at him again, "claims that we both froze in fear and that he alone saved me from a second charge from the boar. It is certainly true that I froze and that he shot, what was by then, a sitting-duck target."

Alessandra had stopped short of the table and was drying her hands on a towel, taking in her son's monologue. These were the most words she had heard from him in one encounter during the past twelve months. The rift between them had been long and bitter. Most recent conversations between the boy and his mother had been reduced to her lengthy questions and his one-word answers.

The teenager continued, "In New York, I got very used to armed men. I had one at my school gate every day of my education, and I could not walk a block without seeing a cop with a revolver. Guns make men feel brave, even when they are not. You were completely unarmed when you left the safety of the hide and ran towards that boar like a maniac. Just for a moment, I thought that the boar looked as scared of you as I was of it. You alone stopped it in its tracks long before the big white hunter here got back with his gun."

Ben had a strange thought: that the room looked like the crowd at a tennis match; all heads were swinging from Cristiano to Carlos and back again each time his name was mentioned.

"I hope that you will accept my apology for not coming sooner," he paused and smiled broadly at Ben. He had his mother's fantastic smile, realised Ben. Claudio also beamed at both Ben and the boy, like the proud grandfather he was.

Ben could not tell what the expression on Alessandra's face meant. She seemed confused and a little overwhelmed. Everyone seemed to be now looking at Ben expectantly. After a while, he said quietly, "Although I am grateful for your kind words, I think you may have overstated my role in all of this. There was no need to come from your sick bed to tell me this, but I do appreciate that you have. Your mother should be very proud of you for your own bravery tonight."

Cristiano turned and looked at his mother, more warmly than in a long while. Claudio added nothing. He put his hands gently on his grandson's shoulders, turned him around, and helped him out of the door. As he passed the table with the hunters, he briefly glared at Carlos and said, "Chi non ha testa abbia almeno buone gambe. Parleremo domani," of which Ben only understood the last part (We will speak tomorrow).

"What did your father say to Carlos?" Ben asked Alessandra later.

"It's an Old Italian proverb which translates as, 'those who have no head at least have good legs.' It's roughly the equivalent of 'fools rush in etc.' She explained that Carlos had been expressly tasked by Claudio with guarding the rear and forming a second line of defence for his grandson and Ben. There were no circumstances in which he should have left his position. Others could have easily dealt with the man in the trap. In moving from his place, he left them vulnerable and what happened was the direct result of his actions.

"The fact that he then ran back so quickly and eventually shot the boar, somewhat requited his blunder, but his final mistake was when he tried to blame you for his initial failure. When Cristiano told Claudio that, without your bravery in delaying the boar's charge, Carlos would almost certainly have been too late, his grandfather had exploded in rage."

Tonight, Claudio must have received word that Carlos was here in the bar bragging about his actions and it was probably more than he could stand. Alessandra had been already seething at her father for taking him on the hunt in the first place. She was now even more furious that, against doctor's orders, he had marched Cristiano down here to tell everyone what happened and put Carlos in his place.

Alessandra apologised for not being able to stop and thank Ben properly for what he did but would see him tomorrow if that was OK.

After she had retreated to her kitchen to serve more pasta, Selene said, "I would not like to be in Carlos' shoes tomorrow when Claudio speaks to him.

Ben countered, "I'm not sure I'd like to be Claudio's shoes either when Alessandra gets home tonight. I have a feeling he will get a double scolding from her."

Selene looked long and hard at her father before saying, "Well, aren't we full of surprises? You didn't run away. In fact, according to Cristiano, you ran directly at the boar to try and stop it hurting him any further. Where on earth did that come from?"

Changing the subject, "But isn't it peculiar," Ben suggested to his daughter, "that otherwise gentle old man with his grand title, which few outside of the village recognise, and with no legal authority whatsoever, still holds such powerful sway over these people. These men gathered here tonight are not part of any army, and neither Claudio or Vincenzo are their commanding officers. And yet, I believe, that if either man had commanded it, tonight Carlos could have been arrested, marched away, and summarily shot for deserting his post, and not a single voice of dissent would have been raised in this village. Are you beginning to see what an astonishing place this is?"

"I am," she agreed, "but if I wrote any of that in an article no one would believe me.

View from Seborga down the mountain towards the Mediterranean.

Drawing by Linda McCluskey

21. BURIDDA

When he awoke the next morning, Ben found a note had been pushed under his door. It read, 'Please meet me at the Osteria by 9.30am if you can. Dress for a walk in the hills—boots, hat, etc. Oh, and swimming trunks. Alessandra.'

Ben looked at his watch. It was already ten past nine. He had found that even after a nap in the heat of the afternoons, he was sleeping later each morning. He was also sleeping more soundly than he could remember. As he quickly showered, he wondered just what the enigmatic Alessandra had in store for him today: Perhaps a hike to a sheer cliff that she could push him off? Maybe there was a nest of vipers she could lead him into? He was sure that whatever it was, it would not be dull. Perhaps she was going to allow him to change into his swimming trunks before soaking him with limoncello this time. How considerate, he mused.

When he arrived at the Osteria, she was sitting outside with an empty coffee cup and a small backpack on the table. He could not help staring at the long, nut-brown legs, which were revealed by her cut-off jeans. A black linen shirt was knotted-up above her waist, leaving a strip of equally brown tummy and some considerable cleavage but still covering all her arms. Her hair was up and tucked under a wide-brimmed cowboy-style hat, although there was so much of it strands were escaping on all sides. Hiking boots completed what was a look that surely no other European princess would dare go for, he thought.

She asked only, "You need coffee, or are you ready to go?"

Ben had not yet turned completely native. He could still manage to function without at least one, or more likely, two, stiff espressos on a morning.

"No. I am fine. Let's go."

Without further explanation, Alessandra strode off in the direction of Passo del Bandito, a route he was becoming very familiar with. After an initial steep climb, the path levelled out and headed north, apparently into the end of a ravine where the folds of two hillsides converged. They passed the now familiar signs of foraging cinghiale but fortunately, saw none of the beasts themselves, who at this time of day would have been high up in the forest above them. She stopped now and then to point out herbs and wildflowers that were, 'the perfect accompaniment to this and that dish'.

After about a half a kilometre, and once it could go no further without going up or down the mountain, the path headed back east along the hillside. Apart from the occasional slight rise and fall, the route remained parallel with the village. It was mostly shaded by overhanging trees but occasionally, where the ground was just too steep for their roots to get a foothold, exposed to the sky. The sun had yet to clear the ridge above them and so, for now, they were cool; whether in the shade or not.

Without warning, Alessandra suddenly stopped and turned around. She allowed Ben, who was walking with his eyes on where he was putting his feet, to almost walk into her open arms. She then hugged him long and tightly. He was shaken by the sudden intimacy. This was the first time they had been so close since Cuneo, but he could distinctly remember the smell of her perfume.

"That is from Cristiano" she said, kissing him gently on the right cheek.

"That is from his grateful, and very relieved, grandfather," kissing him on the left cheek.

If he was surprised by these actions, then he was astonished when she then kissed him fully and passionately on the lips, lingering long enough so that he could taste her. When she finally broke away, she said, "That is from me, and it was a long kiss because it also includes a sincere apology for my behaviour."

Ben's head was lurching with mixed emotions, but after a moment, he managed to speak.

"If we are settling accounts, I think you owe me two apologies."

Alessandra frowned, hesitated tipped her head to one side and then kissed him again, perhaps even more intensely than before.

"There. Are we even? Can we start over?"

Ben smiled almost from ear to ear, showing off his naturally-even white teeth. His best physical feature, she thought.

"Just one more thing: now that the truth is out I think you also owe Selene an apology," he replied. There was a long pause.

"I know. I know. I'm just putting off dealing with that because I don't think she will forgive me for the terrible things I said, and where would that leave us?"

Ben shrugged, realising that she had a point.

"She knows that she needs you on her side, and so I think that you might find she's more pragmatic than you would imagine. Only one way to find out."

Although she looked less than thrilled at the prospect, Alessandra said, "OK, I'll speak to her."

With that, she turned and walked on; with perhaps just a bit more bounce in her step than earlier.

After several minutes' silence, while they both adjusted to the new reality, she was suddenly more talkative. She asked Ben what he thought about Seborga. He tried his best to articulate his thoughts so far. Superlatives such as extraordinary, astonishing, remarkable, and other-worldly, littered his account of what he had seen and learned during his time there.

"I think I've fallen in love."

Seeing that her stride had momentarily faltered on hearing this remark, he quickly added, "with where you live."

With this, she continued without turning her head. Ben did not want to talk about himself but was very keen to find out more about her life before she returned to Seborga. Feeling more confident about his newfound status – whatever that was – he opened with, "Where is Cristiano's father?"

"Burning in Hell, I hope," came her instant reply.

As she was not going to elaborate without prompting, he continued, "So, your marriage did not end well?"

She stopped and turned, hesitated and then turned back. Walking on she spoke over her shoulder, "There's a shaded area ahead with a fallen tree. We'll stop, take a breather, and have a drink of water."

When they sat, she pulled a bottle from her backpack and offered it to him.

"After you," he offered, and she drank deeply from it.

Handing the bottle to Ben, she continued, "I am sure you have heard enough gossip in the village about my former life to know the answer to your last question."

Alessandra went on to state that her marriage had collapsed with, 'cataclysmic force', adding, and "taking with it my career, my family, and my home."

She explained her view that not only was she betrayed by her husband and her staff, but now even her only son had taken against her.

"As if that weren't bad enough, I also received these as a life-long reminder of my folly."

She had undone her shirt cuffs and turned over her arms to reveal a broad scar the full width of both her wrists. It had not completely healed and looked still raw and angry. Ben now understood her reaction to his jibe about tattoos and felt remorseful. It also went some way to explain the night in Cuneo when he'd tried to undo her blouse.

"I am so very sorry about what I said about the tattoos," he offered.

"You were not to know. It is I who should be sorry for covering you with limoncello."

Ben laughed and began to say, "Think nothing of– " but was interrupted.

"No. Really. That was very special limoncello, and I am very sorry for wasting it like that."

They both laughed out loud at her joke, and Ben put his arm around her shoulder and pulled her closer. When she turned, she was laughing, but tears were also rolling down her face.

"What a fuck up I have become. I am so bitter and angry I could not recognise a decent human being if they hung a sign on him. I have misjudged you badly, and I am very sorry."

"I'll accept another of those apologies, like the one earlier."

She laughed out loud again, her smile spreading outwards like ripples from a pebble thrown in a pool.

"Thank God for a man with a sense of humour. But don't push your luck, I am still partly a New Yorker."

"An Italian New Yorker. What a lethal combination," Ben taunted.

Physically refreshed and emotionally unburdened, they walked on but with a new lightness of step. It was as if the couple had each discarded a heavy rucksack, which had been weighing them down. Leading the way as they walked in single file, Alessandra could fill in the details of her tale of woe without the embarrassment of having to look Ben in the eyes.

She explained that she had arrived in New York aged just eighteen to work in the Manhattan restaurant of a distant relation. Here, she washed pots, chopped vegetables, and mopped floors, for more than a year. When this joy-less hard labour failed to drive her back to Italy, as everyone had expected it would, the owner decided that she was serious about the business and set about training her. She worked her way slowly up the ladder until one day she was allowed to plan, prepare, and cook a staff lunch.

She had prepared her mother's pansotti alla salsa di nocci. The staff had all raved about it, and even the hard-to-please chef acknowledged its extraordinary lightness and subtleness of flavour; praise indeed. When her boss also tried it, he suggested to the Chef that they try it as a lunch special. "Chef's all having egos the size of watermelons, he had to change something to make it his own and so added a faux-walnut on top made of parmesan, breadcrumbs, and truffle oil." The Manhattan ladies-who-lunched there all adored it. They chose to believe that, because it tasted so light, there could hardly be any calories in it and no one pointed out their error."

Alessandra's pansotti became a mainstay of the regular menu and, not long after, she gained promotion to commis chef. One day, several months later, the New York Times food critic came for lunch unannounced and ordered the pansotti; apparently on a recommendation from a girlfriend. When she had finished, she ordered the same dish again. She later explained this was to check:

"A: it was not a fluke; B: the quality was consistent; and C: she was not dreaming."

Her review the following weekend said it was, 'pasta purses seemingly constructed from fairy's wings, with a filling so divine it must have been gathered from the Garden of Eden. All this was bathed in, what surely must be, the essence of an entire forest of walnuts.'

This accolade was the catalyst for a promotion, and later, a series of dishes inspired by her mother's traditional Ligurian recipes but given a decidedly modern twist. This became a very successful formula which would bring them many more accolades.

She explained the formula which brought her success,

"Firstly, portion sizes were reduced by about two-thirds from what one would expect in Seborga. To shield the sensibilities of their prim New York diners; bones, shells, heads, and other inedible elements, were all removed in preparation. This was to disguise the fact that whatever it would finally become, it had once been a living animal. Finally, some ingredients very much in vogue – squid ink, gold leaf, deep-fried leek sticks – were added to bring it right up to date.

"So, for example, the traditional rustic Coniglio alla Ligure; in the original rustic recipe, this is simply a whole rabbit chopped roughly into sections with a cleaver and containing all its bones and certain of its offal. This was simply braised in olive oil, whole taggiasca olives, and wild herbs. The New York interpretation became de-boned rabbit fillets, formed into a Ballantine the size of a small chicken breast, and served in a tiny pool of sauce made with a little garlic, Vermentino wine, cold pressed Ligurian olive oil, de-stoned chopped taggiasca olives and sprinkled with rosemary and garlic crumbs. Reduced balsamic vinegar was then drizzled around the plate."

Ben frowned at what he judged to be an unnecessary refinement of the dish he had come to love but, on consideration, also thought that if he had seen it on a New York menu, he would probably have ordered it. So, he learned, a journey began which saw the young commis chef grow in skill and confidence. One day her uncle and mentor offered her a partnership in a new restaurant he planned to open with another distant cousin, also an emigre from Italy. She accepted. It worked. The two young partners fell in love.

Nearly twenty years, a Michelin-star, and a baby later, they had created two successful restaurants in the up-and-coming areas of New York with all the trappings of prosperity: up-town apartment, Maserati, exclusive gym memberships, etc. Consistent with this achievement, they had both worked twelve-hour days and saw little of each other or their child, who spent much of his time with a succession of live-in nannies and after-school clubs. Their work-rate and pressure kept them both trim, while their celebrity ensured they were always well groomed.

"Externally, at least, we were the perfect American success story. We were featured in glossy magazines and even appeared on a couple of TV talk shows."

Ben was astounded to hear the level of success that Alessandra had enjoyed in her previous life and was also already wondering why on earth she had given all that up. He envisaged her long brown legs swinging out of a shiny Maserati outside the Museum of Modern Art, dressed head to foot in Prada. As an afterthought, now he knew Alessandra better, he imagined that she would probably also be carrying an arm full of borage and a couple of dead rabbits on a string.

Without warning, the path emerged from trees on a bend. It felt as if the perfectly cloudless blue sky were a roller blind that someone had gotten hold of and then pulled it right down to the floor at their feet. The hillside dropped away steeply from the path until it reached a strip of palm-fringed tarmac road far below them. From there, the Mediterranean stretched out to the horizon, although the actual union of sea and sky was hard to discern: eighty per cent of their vision was filled with the most amazing azure blue. When his eyes adjusted, he could see that the otherwise flawless backdrop was pierced only by the occasional spinnaker or foresail of a yacht catching the warm wind coming up from Africa. It was breathtaking, he thought. With this bucolic vision still occupying his mind, Alessandra brought him abruptly back to reality.

"Then that bastard threw it all away."

She explained how he had apparently started using cocaine at parties, but then it had become a way for him to get through the long days, which often went on until the early hours.

"Guests spending five hundred dollars on dinner did not expect to be told when to leave." She went on to describe it as, "The familiar storyline of a thousand movies; buying larger quantities of the drug had brought him into contact with bigger criminals. Some of these were men also visiting their restaurants. When Franco found ready cash was harder to find because more customers were paying with plastic cards, he had been struggling to pay them for his habit. The thugs stopped paying for their food and wine bills. Then they also added exorbitant interest to his debts, and things got even worse. The dealers offered to convert his debts into a loan, with his restaurant shares as security. Without even knowing it, I was in partnership with the Devil. With hindsight, I knew something was wrong, but I did not want to confront it. I stayed in my kitchens and cooked. That was what I was best at. I sleep-walked into a nightmare."

One night after closing, Alessandra had started to drive home when she remembered that she needed something from the freezer in the kitchen of the second restaurant. It was well after midnight on a quiet night, and she had calculated that the staff would probably still be cleaning up after service. Parking her car at the rear and seeing that the lights were on in the kitchen, she went around to the service entrance. The kitchen door was propped open with a crate, as was the usual practice on hot nights. Before she reached the fire door, Alessandra could hear loud banging on the stainless-steel worktop. It sounded as though someone was vigorously tenderising a rump steak, or more likely at this time of night, she thought, kneading some pasta dough ready for tomorrow.

Once through the open door, she could see the back of her husband who had his trousers around his ankles. In front of him, she could make out a skinny, dark-skinned girl dressed in kitchen whites, was bent over the work surface with both her hands grasping a knife rack on the wall.

An empty, clear plastic bag showing traces of white powder and a Black American Express credit card on a chopping board hinted at the foreplay to this seedy encounter. The girl was tiny; her toes were barely reaching the kitchen floor and her arms as thin as sticks. Alessandra recognised her instantly, even from this angle.

"Camila. You disgraceful, ungrateful bitch!"

Alessandra shoved her husband away with her left hand, cursing, and then grabbed the ponytail of her most junior member of staff with her right.

Camila had been offered to them as a subsidised trainee under a Catholic Church program to rehabilitate junior minor offenders who had demonstrated talents in certain areas. Against her better instincts, she had taken her on, partly because of a very compelling letter from her priest about her family circumstances, but mainly because of the extraordinary Hijole Caramba that she had whipped-up at her informal kitchen interview. The girl had seemingly thrived in her new role and had made good progress up the ladder from pot washer.

Alessandra's fury was compounded by what she saw as this betrayal of trust. That this obscenity was happening in her kitchen, and on her pristine stainless-steel surfaces and with her husband, was beyond any other treachery she could imagine. She wrenched the diminutive girl backwards by her hair. She screamed what sounded like Spanish expletives. Instinctively spinning to face her assailant the hyped-up girl swept her right hand ahead of her. There was a brief flash of silver.

It was as if time had stopped. No one spoke. The only sound was a slow drip like a tap had been left on somewhere. Before she could feel or understood anything of what was happening, Alessandra first saw the appalled looks on the faces of, first her husband, and then the now terrified girl. Until this sobering point, Camila had been too high on coke to know, or care, who had entered the room and attacked her. She had instinctively snatched a fish boning knife from the rack in front of her and lashed out with it as she spun around. It had cut deep into both the upturned wrists which Alessandra raised to defend herself.

The blood pulsing from both her wounds reminded her, somewhat bizarrely under the circumstances, of the exact colour and consistency of a rich Barolo. It flowed freely from the cuts on each wrist, dripping and already pooling thickly on the white tiled floor. It later transpired that the scalpel-sharp blade had severed both the ulnar and radial arteries of each wrist. The girl's chef's whites were splattered with it; it was also on her still bare legs, and the panties still around her ankles were soaking it up off the floor.

The look of horror on Ben's face was clear to see as he tried to envisage this terrible scene. He visibly winced at the thought of the six-inch narrow blade striking the bones of Alessandra's wrists.

"By the time they got me to A&E, I had lost over four pints of blood. I almost died. Both of them were completely useless. They were both so hyped-up on coke they could not think straight. The bitch fled. He just sat on the floor and wept. I had to tourniquet my own wrists and dial 911 myself on the kitchen phone to get an ambulance. Can you imagine that?"

Apparently a passing police car also responded to the call, resulting in her husband being charged with dealing and the girl still being sought for a whole batch of arrest warrants.

Ben was struggling to come to terms with this picture of total mayhem. It was, as she said earlier, like a scene from any number of movies. Still, he found it very difficult to conceive that someone he now cared about was the real-life victim. The scars were now much better than they had been. But so long and deep had been the cuts, it had been difficult getting them to heal. By the time Alessandra finished the harrowing tale of the surgery, recovery, the collapse of the business, the bad publicity, and her retreat from New York, the pair had arrived at the road next to the sea.

They had to dodge the usual swarm of motorbikes, scooters, and cars, all now heading home for lunch, but managed to make it across to the beach side unscathed. Alessandra immediately stepped over the small concrete wall, dropping her backpack and hat. In two more strides, she had stepped out of her shorts. In two more her blouse was off. In four more steps and a final dive, her black bikini was disappearing under the beautiful coral-green band of water, which stretched out about a hundred metres from the beach.

Ben watched her swim away with confident strokes before somersaulting and then swimming back towards him, beckoning him to join her. She had obviously planned to make her revelation before she had to reveal her bare arms for the first time. After the long hot walk, his shirt was sticking to his back and his shorts clinging to his thighs. He needed no persuading to peel them off but had to turn back to the road while he slipped on his swimming trunks. His white buttocks prompted a few honks from passing scooters as he wriggled out of his shorts.

His hair was now almost bleached completely white by the sun and just thin enough to see the brown skin of his scalp below. He looked tanned and lean: not in bad shape for a man of his age. The water was at first a shock to his hot skin, but quickly moderated to what he guessed to be about a perfectly refreshing and invigorating nine degrees. They swam and laughed, for no apparent reason, other than it was hard to do anything else in such an idyll. This was a far cry from Newcastle and, after what he had just heard, must seem to her like a refuge from the craziness she left behind in New York. They had both escaped a close shave, he thought.

With no towels, they simply picked up their few belongings and walked along the shingle beach in their swimwear. The hot early afternoon sun and a warm breeze blowing up from the direction of Tunisia soon starting to dry their skin. Hair and fabric would take a little longer. Relaxed and tanned, with her wet unkempt hair, she looked beautiful, Ben thought.

Ahead of them, about half a kilometre he estimated, Ben could see a timber construction jutting out from the land-side towards the sea. Wood piles had been driven into the shingle to support its terrace, from which wooden steps led down onto the beach. A past-its-best yacht mainsail had been up-cycled as a substantial triangular sun canopy. It still carried the insignia of its former boat class stitched into the canvas in huge blue letters. A few customers and staff could be seen – but only as silhouettes – in its shade.

As they drew closer, Ben could see that a single table had been set-up on the beach; almost at the water's edge. A large umbrella planted next to it gave it shade. Someone could now be seen waving from the restaurant terrace, who then started ringing a large brass ship's bell which was fastened to a post. Alessandra waved back.

"My cousin Vittorio," was all the explanation she offered.

When they made it up the dozen sea-bleached wooden steps, Vittorio swept Alessandra into his arms, spun her fully around and kissed her affectionately on each cheek. Ben extended his hand for the expected handshake, only to have it abruptly swept to one side by the powerfully-built restaurateur. He then put both arms around Ben shouting,

"Il professore, the cinghiale hunter," and hugged him like a long-lost old friend.

Ben could hardly breathe as he tried to remember the last time he had so many hugs and kisses. His memory failed him, as he could not recall such an unconcealed display of affection. Very un-English he realised.

After a cooling bottle of beer at the bar, Vittorio suggested they leave their shoes inside and lead them back down the steps to the table on the beach. Vittoria enquired rhetorically, "Is this table okay for you, signor?"

Ben looked up and down the beach, where all he could see was the fine shingle gently washed by the coral, green waters and replied, "It is perfecto."

"There is no such word," Alessandra pointed out. "And yet, somehow it does seem like the appropriate response," she conceded.

No menu was offered, no wine list produced, no preferences or allergies discussed, but within minutes a young man appeared with a wine bucket under one arm, a basket of bread in the same hand, and two plates in the other.

"Polpette. These are my favourite appetizer." Alessandra exclaimed with delight.

Ben smiled but looked puzzled by the small bread-coated spheres. They looked like small scotch eggs, but under the coating he could see a pale green filling.

"Taste first and then tell me what you taste."

He cut through the slightly baked crust of what looked like parmigiana and breadcrumbs and into the soft, warm centre. He ate a mouthful and was very quiet for a while, savouring the subtle flavours that he had guessed were potatoes and zucchini, perfectly cooked and seasoned. Then he answered, "All I have been able to taste since ten o'clock this morning are the lips of an astonishingly beautiful woman who I hope I can now call my friend."

Taken by surprise, a flush of red was almost visible, even on her well-tanned cheeks. There were other signs of her embarrassment: the flicking of hair, fidgeting with bread and avoidance of eye contact. Ben knew his arrow had struck home. Quickly changing the subject, Alessandra said, "These are a Ligurian speciality made with boiled marjoram, zucchini and potatoes, then mixed with egg and rolled in breadcrumbs."

"That was the herb I could not identify. Marjoram," he interjected.

"You can deep fry them, or even better, bake them in a wood-fired pizza oven. Delicious!"

"With a glass of chilled white wine," Ben agreed that this was a perfect primo piatto.

Alessandra waited until Ben had savoured the wine and then asked, "What do you think?" It was sharper with more citrus than the Vermentinos he had got used to.

"Gavi?" he ventured.

She smiled warmly.

"It's a Lumassina. It is a light-skinned grape variety indigenous to Liguria. It's used for both still and sparkling wine but now only made by a few small producers."

Ben sipped some more and swilled it around his mouth.

"High acidity and lots of fruit. Perhaps some honey notes in there? Be great with white fish."

"What about your history, Professore? How is it that you were persuaded to leave your academic ivory tower; especially for such an unknown spot. And to carry out research, that presumably, they could have sent a recent graduate to do? I feel sure that there is more to your story than meets the eye."

Ben began by telling her she was correct; that there was another reason for him being here, but then the pasta arrived.

"Buridda," announced Alessandra.

The dish that arrived was another traditional Ligurian speciality. Fresh fish gently stewed in an aromatic tomato sauce flavoured with garlic, herbs, carrots, onion, and olive oil. Traditionally, Buridda was made with cheap cuts of fresh fish such as dogfish, mullet, anglerfish, drum fish, etc. Vittorio's luxury version contained octopus, clams, snapper, and sweet red San Remo prawns. An Italian equivalent of a French bouillabaisse it is served with toasted garlic bread for dipping. This one was spectacular in proportion and presented in a vast blackened, iron, oven dish. After removing it from the wood oven more large prawns, still in their shells, were laid extravagantly over the top to cook in the residual heat.

"It looks and smells spectacular," Ben commented.

He thought that her sheer enjoyment of eating was very sensual. She would fork several long strands of dripping linguine into her mouth at once, in that unselfconscious way that Italians do. Mealtimes were the only ones when they would put aside their 'bella figura' (I must look my best) mentally. With the pasta gone, so had the last of the Lumassina. They had talked, eaten and drank non-stop for nearly two hours.

Now they seemed utterly relaxed in each other's company, Ben felt he could tell her the truth about how he had come to be here.

"Where to begin?" Ben questioned. "You will doubtless be aware of the growth in the number of millionaires, and indeed billionaires, created during China's recent economic boom? These newly super-rich Chinese have prospered in a culture where, shall we say, corner-cutting and queue-jumping are seen by most as shrewd business practices. Few things were impossible if you had enough money and knew the right person."

Ben went on to explain that part of the legacy of China's former One-Child Policy, was that this generation had a single focus for their affection and newfound wealth.

"So, this generation singlehandedly carry all the aspirations of their parents and grandparents, most of whom did not get the chance to go to university at all. Unfortunately, like generations of other societies who have been brought up in a period when their parents have prospered, this one has had their work ethic bred out of them. Their overindulgent parents seemed to have taught them all about consumption, but little about productivity. Bereft of any economic necessity or self-motivation, both they and their parents see nothing wrong in simply buying, or otherwise acquiring, what they all so desperately desire: the prestige of a degree from an English university. They do little work but will do almost anything else they can to get what they want. The girl who caused my problems was one of these."

"Oh no Ben! Please tell me you didn't. Not a student?" Alessandra almost pleaded.

"No. I most certainly did not! But please hear my story through before you judge me."

Ben began by explaining in some detail, that he had been targeted at the pub near the University, where this perceptive student had observed he always went on a Friday evening. Ironically, he had deliberately chosen The North Terrace pub as his local: partly because students did not often frequent its bar and because it had a better than average wine list. He had been in there since his last lecture finished at 6pm. By nine, after downing the best part of a bottle of Château Laroque, he was a little tipsy but not drunk, although he was feeling particularly lonely and therefore highly susceptible to some friendly female company.

He said that he might not have noticed the Waitrose carrier bag overflowing with spring onion, coriander leaf, and lemongrass, which had been carefully placed near his feet, had it not started to move across the floor; apparently of its own accord. Startled, Ben had looked up from his gloomy stupor to seek out the bag's owner. Seeing the beautiful young Chinese girl sitting at the bar near him, he had quipped, "Miss, your shopping appears to be leaving without you."

Ben vaguely recognised this strikingly beautiful young woman from around the campus, but she was not one of his own students. It was then that he had noticed the killer heels, long legs, and finally, her figure, which appeared to have been shrink-wrapped into something which looked very expensive.

"Oh, Professor Ben," she had said feigning surprise. "I am soooo sorry. It's my lobster. The bands around its claws must have come loose."

Now realising that this was a student, Ben responded to the food story with his customary joke about their usual eating habits. "I thought students only ate things that had been long-dead, severely processed, and then microwaved."

She had laughed, perhaps a little too enthusiastically, at Ben's joke, then retrieved the errant carrier bag, tied it tightly at the handles, and hung it on the arm of the bar stool. Slipping back onto the stool she crossed her legs to show off their impressive proportions, without ever losing eye contact with Ben. They had exchanged pleasantries for a while, and Ben had turned back to his drink. Suddenly, he heard the girl crying and whimpering. She said, "Pardon me Professor, but I could use someone to talk to. My plans for the night, and probably my future career as well, are in ruins. I came in for a drink to console myself as I could not face going home."

Unable to ignore a maiden in distress, Ben had asked her what had happened. The resulting story involved an old boyfriend from Hong Kong. He had promised to help her check the referencing on her research, in return for her cooking him an excellent Chinese supper. This seemed plausible enough. Less believable, thought Ben, was the part about this boy then cancelling a date with this beautiful girl at the last minute, and reneging on his promise, just to go to the casino with his pals.

"When the girl told me about the menu she had planned which included a tuna sushi starter and lobster noodle main course: her boyfriend's judgment suddenly seemed incredibly flawed."

Ben described how he had left his own table and sat on the adjoining bar stool, where they were soon hemmed-in by the lively Friday evening bar crowd. She told him that she was studying for a masters in geology. He was relieved to hear that she was therefore at least twenty-one-years-old and not even a student of the Business School. With this potential conflict of interest removed, he relaxed again. He had offered her a glass of his Saint Emilion and, to brighten her mood, had chit-chatted harmlessly about campus activity.

As he had finished his wine, he had picked up his briefcase and was preparing to say good night.

"I don't suppose you would quickly look over my referencing and I will cook you this lobster in return? I only live around the corner, and my flatmate does not like fish."

This girl had apparently done some research about Ben, although it was not of an academic nature. He loved fish and, especially, Asian cuisine. He had been about to walk back to his apartment for another night alone with an M&S ready meal, while watching a movie on DVD. He admitted that, with hindsight, her last-minute inference that a third-party chaperone would be present, was ingenious: this removed the final hurdle to him saying, what at least part of his brain desperately wanted to say, which was, "Very well. I always try to help a damsel in distress."

It transpired that there was, in fact, no research to check or flat-mate at home, and supper remained firmly in the carrier bag. Everything else, however, was very real, fresh, and apparently available if he had the appetite for it.

In the post-mortem that inevitably followed this farce: she claimed that he had offered his help with her work and then seduced her. He insisted that she had entrapped him and propositioned him, intending to blackmail the University into awarding her a degree. He claimed he left as soon as he realised what was going on. She claimed he stayed just long enough to try to have sex with her.

What she did not know was that they were recorded on the University building's CCTV. Ben was looking inebriated, entering the flat of a pretty young student, carrying groceries and more wine. The girl had slipped her arm under his, as though they were very familiar with each other. Even Ben had to admit that it did not look good. To even the most sympathetic arbiter, it looked at best like extremely poor judgement. To the more cynical observer, it was a damning case for a breach of professional standards.

In mitigation, he went on to explain, that the same camera had also recorded him fleeing the flat no more than ten minutes later. Even the Dean had admitted that he had looked more like a scalded cat than one that had got all the cream.

"However, in a climate where bashing fee-grabbing universities was a favourite sport of the press, even this brief encounter was enough of a media story to make life very uncomfortable for the Dean: particularly at a time when foreign student recruitment could not have been more competitive. The girl intended to use this story to blackmail her way to the MSc that she did not deserve and would not otherwise have passed."

Ben looked suitably contrite as he continued, "Luckily for the Dean, and for me, this girl had already tried to seduce another male colleague several weeks earlier, in one of the reading rooms. He had wisely rebuffed her immediately and reported the incident to the Dean. So close to her finals, and with no real harm done, the Dean decided not to take any action on the matter. But he had checked the library CCTV footage anyway to confirm the story. This time it showed the girl very much as the predator and my colleague as the prey."

Ben outlined how, armed with this trump card, the Dean now intended to expose this student's blackmail and thereby hopefully dissuade others from trying anything similar. He had said that he fully expected her to 'fight dirty' and so wanted to be prepared when the media follow up the story. The Dean said that he viewed Ben's blemished staff record, unmarried status, and fondness for wine, as making him vulnerable to probing journalists and wanted 'the accused' out of the way until it had been settled. One unguarded quote or photograph in a bar with other students, and the case for the prosecution-by-media would be made.

Looking at Alessandra pleadingly he offered, "I know that I foolishly allowed a dangerous cocktail of St Emilion, loneliness, and frankly, vanity, get the better of my judgement. It was weak and stupid in the extreme, but I did not actually do anything wrong. This girl just set me up and thereby threatened what little I had left."

Flawed he may be by his own admission, Alessandra thought, but at least he seemed honest.

"Oh Ben, what a nightmare," was all she could think of to say.

"No. Not at all," Ben replied, smiling. "It's turned out to be far from a nightmare. It's become a dream come true. I'm here with a woman even more beautiful than even this breath-taking setting."

He gestured to her, with his swept hand, as the subject of his admiration.

Ben continued, "No, I love the Chinese and the Dean, without whose pragmatism, I could be looking at a much gloomier view than the one I have here. As it turns out, I kept my job, plus got nearly a year off, paid for by the EU, and Seborga got me. I know who got the worst deal," he joked.

Over a dolce of fresh fruit; cherries, melon, peaches and, finally susine (another local speciality like a plum), all served in a large bowl with a base of crushed ice; Ben completed his abridged biography. As he did so, the first wavelet from the slowly encroaching sea swept over their bare feet. The swell had increased sufficiently to push the water another metre or two up the shingle, and their table was now effectively sitting in the water.

Ben felt like pinching himself. It was just too enchanting. How had he found himself sitting here in this place, feet in the cooling ocean, opposite this beautiful woman, being brought amazing food and wine? Just when he thought it could not possibly get any better, Alessandra slid a small parcel wrapped in muslin and tied with string across the table. Ben was puzzled and stared at it without reacting. When he finally undid the parcel, inside was a gleaming new pocket-knife. It was the type he had seen the hunters use for cutting their meat. There was also a note which read; 'This has been fashioned for you from the tusk of the boar that you saved Cristiano from. It is the best quality Masunin knife, made right here in Liguria. Claudio had Vincenzo change the handle for you. All our love, Alex.'

Sensing a tear welling in one eye, he quickly moved on, using the knife to slice the fruit, while pondering the significance of the gift. The knife felt good in his hand, unfolded precisely, and locked with a satisfying click. Naturally, it was sharp, and the blade narrow so as not to clog in the soft cheese. The trouble that they had gone to in sourcing this special knife, customising it, and presenting it, touched him, and he was genuinely grateful.

But, in the back of his mind, it was the note that was most significant. 'All our love. Alex'. Did she mean 'our,' or did she really mean 'my' but was too shy or embarrassed to write it? He concluded that this was ridiculous speculation. She wrote 'our' because she meant 'our' he decided. But then again, 'our' included her, and so maybe… ? He knew this tendency to over-analyse things had gotten him into trouble before, mainly where women were concerned. He had misread signals so many times that he had pledged to stop looking for them. Indeed, he had concluded that women were such irrational creatures that he would be better off taking these things at simple face value. And yet, where Alessandra was concerned, here he was breaking his pledge. He knew this gift was significant. He just did not know how much so.

More unrequested delights arrived; iced glasses from the freezer and a bottle of a thick, pale green pistachio liqueur. The bottle had also come straight from the freezer and was white with frost. This was a very much enjoyed, and an entirely new, digestivo for Ben.

"Please don't pour any of this over me," he joked. "It's far too good to waste, and I'll never get that green out of my trousers."

They both started laughing out loud and then chinked glasses in a unified 'salute.' Their laughing continued, completely out of proportion to the rather weak joke, until they were almost hysterical. Tears of laughter rolled down their faces as if they had both achieved some long-awaited release from their respective pasts.

No bill was forthcoming for lunch, and his protests about this were waved away. This was another act of gratitude from a family glad to have one of their own back safe. After the excesses of lunch, they were happy to accept a lift back to the village with two of the staff on the back of their motorinis.

Alessandra helmeted-up and mounted the bike with accustomed ease; Ben with far less elegance. Once astride and purring along the road hugging the coast, he started to enjoy the journey. The warm breeze was welcome, and he could see Alessandra ahead of him, strands of escaped hair streaming from under her helmet and her shirt fluttering in the wind. During the post-lunch lull in traffic, his driver was able to pull alongside his colleague, and they sped side by side towards town. He could see Alessandra looking at him quite intently. Then she seemed to be mouthing something that he could not discern. He tried to shout,

"What?" Across the void but was not sure she could hear over the noise of the bikes and the road.

She mouthed the words again which looked like they began, 'I want you to...' and then a car horn sounded behind them and his driver dropped back to allow it to pass. A stream of cars and faster motorbikes kept them in single file until they reached the turn-off to Seborga, where they headed up the much narrower local road. The ride up the mountain to the village reminded Ben of the day that he had arrived, several weeks ago now, in the back of Vincenzo's Ape.

It was still as remarkable a view across the Riviera as it had been that first day, but today without the apprehension that he had felt then. By the time they dismounted in the piazza and gave thanks to their riders, Alessandra was now reminded that her son was lying upstairs recuperating. Ben tried asking her what she had been saying but she changed the subject, gave him a peck on the cheek, and hurried away.

Back in his room, Ben tried to nap but the extraordinary events of the day were swimming through his mind, and he was desperately trying to unravel them.

22. MILLEFOGLIE

The day of the first public debate on the future of Seborga began with unusual weather. Instead of the mist rolling down from the mountains as it usually did, it was gently drifting in off the sea and clambering up the hillside over the olive groves, fruit plantations, and wineries. It clung close to land and formed a blanket over the coastal plain. Where the hills began to rise upwards from the plain the mist filled in the valleys, leaving the higher ground in clear bright sunshine.

From the elevation of Seborga, it was possible to see over the mist and out to a brilliant blue sky beyond the coast. It was like looking down from an aeroplane, Ben thought. He had woken early, unable to sleep with all the thoughts, questions, and worries rolling around in his head; not least, that no one had so far seriously challenged the existence of the Papal charter. As far as he knew, only himself and Selene had physically seen it, and even they were not sure what it was anyway.

There is little doubt that the initial acceptance by the Tribune of Nikki's fact-checking, and the newspaper's subsequent publication of the original story, had given credence to the charter's existence. Because of the credibility of the UK broadsheet news-press, the international media had taken it as fact. In reality, politicians, bankers, and religious leaders, all over Europe were in a panic based on nothing more than hearsay and supposition.

At the core of the story was the questionable ability of a man of almost ninety-years old to recognise a document that he had not seen for more than sixty years. And, verify it from nothing more than a mobile phone photograph taken in the half-light of a cave. It was improbable, bordering on insanity, Ben reflected. And yet, looking outside, he could see news vans, cars, and media people everywhere, all apparently brought here on the strength of his claimed sighting of a charter written nearly a thousand years earlier.

Ben had suggested that Selene got up very early and went with Vincenzo, who would show her some other signs of Templar occupation of the area. Thinking this might be more useful photo material, she agreed, and crept out at dawn to meet him. She climbed aboard the Ape, where Vincenzo had thoughtfully placed a straw bale for her to sit on, and they headed down towards the Autostrada but turning off eastwards before they quite reached it. They bumped and bounced their way along narrow dusty tracks, until they reached a boulder about the size of a wheelbarrow and stopped beside it. Less than a hundred metres away, a constant stream of huge trucks, vans, and cars, whizzed by, heading towards or away from the French border.

"The ancient border of the Principality," said Vincenzo pointing at the stone. "It was placed here by the Templari and marked with their cross as a warning to all that they were entering their territory."

Selene could not help being a bit underwhelmed by a dry old stone; even one which had been scratched on by an ancient Knight. Not much of a story in that, she decided, but she took a few photos anyway to satisfy him. Then a shout was heard, "Ciao Vincenzo."

The source of the voice was about fifty metres away and now walking towards them. Behind the man approaching them, Selene could see two others all busy moving lengths of timber. A third was painting the wood with red hoops over a previously applied white base. There was also what looked like a shed, painted pale blue and white: the colours of the Seborga flags, which flew everywhere in the village. The two men spoke, not only in Italian but also in Ligurian dialect, so Selene had no chance of understanding anything they were saying. There was a lot of gesturing, arm waving, and pointing at the box, when it suddenly dawned on her exactly what she was looking at; a check-point. Effectively, a border post. She looked again more closely, and sure enough, there were 'stop' signs fastened to the posts. She moved closer and started snapping photographs and had taken plenty when Vincenzo said, "Selene, no. No photographs, please."

Barely unable to disguise her incredulity, "You are going to put up a border post check-point across the motorway? Does it really pass through Seborga territory?" she managed to ask.

All Vincenzo would say was, "You have not seen this, OK?"

He ushered her back to the Ape, turned it around and headed back to the village. This suited Selene as she could not wait to get back and start doing some research into her next big story.

After only thirty minutes on Google, she had learned that trade between Italy and France totalled about eighty billion euros per year. Even discounting trade in services, and assuming a small amount of trade was by air and sea, the bulk of it must take, the quickest, cheapest, routes by road. Because of the physical barrier of the Alps, apart from the Autostrada, there are only two other major crossings between Italy and France—both tunnels with expensive tolls.

One of them, the 12km Mont Blanc tunnel, carries a prohibitive tariff of three hundred euros for a lorry. The Autostrada had no toll for crossing the border. It, therefore, did not seem ridiculous to Selene to suggest that trade along the highway, which crossed Seborga, must be valued at somewhere close to fifty billion euros a year, or one billion euros per week. And this does not take into account Portugal, Spain, Germany, Austria, Greece, and all the other EU countries trading across this tarmac, barrier-less frontier.

A tariff on lorries crossing Seborga of just a tenth of Mont Blanc's would still be worth about one million euros per week to the new state's economy. Or, looked at another way, that is a hundred thousand euros per annum for every man, woman, and child in the Principality. This was the next highly explosive story that The Tribune's most recent foreign correspondent would be sending back to London.

Ben had meanwhile met with Claudio as previously arranged and each had updated the other on the events unfolding and discussed the forthcoming debate. Claudio had given the envoys from the Italian Government, European Union, and The Vatican, a courteous but not too enthusiastic reception. The box containing the charter, which Vincenzo had finally recovered from the cave, had been set in the centre of the table. It had been cleaned and opened to reveal the ancient leather-bound document within. A set of white cotton gloves had been laid alongside the box for the use of anyone wishing to handle the contents.

"May I?" asked the Cardinal stepping forward towards the box.

"You may, but please be extremely careful as it is in a perilous condition."

Claudio looked nervous as the Vatican's representative donned the gloves and tentatively folded back the fragile cover. An elaborate illuminated introduction page to the manuscript was revealed. It was badly faded and had some water marking. The Pope's representative had never seen the original but could not fail to acknowledge the age of this charter and could recognise the Latin calligraphy. The Cardinal carefully closed the document, turned to the others, and nodded. He crossed himself and said, "I can see that it is genuine."

Claudio and Vincenzo appeared to share a knowing smile, and simultaneously the prince seemed to begin to utter a sigh but caught himself, and instead stiffened his body back into his big chair. He had told them that in his view his citizens felt betrayed by the people who represented them in Rome and Brussels and he believed they would vote for full independence in just weeks from now. Claudio also told them that he had no appetite for compromise and, in any event, at his age, no time for long, drawn-out negotiations.

Soon he would make a speech to the people setting out the position and options as he saw them but said that, as things stood, he would recommend voting to leave Italy and the EU and declare full independence. He instructed them to report this back to their superiors and tell them that, if they were serious about preventing what he saw as the inevitable, they had better get someone senior here in the next couple of days. Someone who was capable of making big decisions on the spot without having to defer to anyone else. If not, to not bother coming back at all and wait to see the outcome on TV.

As they departed, the Italian interior minister recognised the French envoy waiting in the hallway outside. "Just paying our respects," the Frenchman offered by way of explanation for his presence there.

"Bullshit," hissed the politician as he passed heading for the door. When all the emissaries had departed, Claudio and Vincenzo remained staring at the box containing the document.

"That was a game of poker I would not wish to play again, Vincenzo."

The younger man closed the lid on the box and smiled.

"Don't they say that it's not always a matter of the cards you hold but the way that you play them?"

Alessandra was waiting for Ben when he left the meeting, and she looked anxious.

"Fancy a stroll?" she asked.

Ben was happy to but was not sure where they could go without bumping into TV crews or reporters. She took his hand and led him down some stone stairs that he had been previously unaware of.

"I did not know there was a cellar," he remarked.

"Cantina would be the word," she corrected, "except it isn't one. It is another exit onto a street a level down."

They exited onto a narrow alley, and from there another set of stone steps took them through an arch and out into an olive grove facing west.

"Can you tell me what the Hell is going on? I can see my father is scheming something and that you are in on it but why has no one told me?"

Ben tried to explain that they thought there was an opportunity to create a sustainable future economy for everyone in the Principality. Not just a short-term gain, but one which their children and grandchildren would benefit from without sacrificing their traditions. It was also going to be a very delicate balance relying on many things all coming together, and in sequence. He acknowledged that the chances of pulling it off were only about fifty-fifty and they might have to settle for something less than ideal. Indeed, it was possible that some potential outcomes would leave the citizens even worse off than they are now. If they vote to leave Italy, and therefore the EU by default, then these politicians will extract vengeance. Within days the government could stop paying pensions, and unemployment benefit. The EU will also show their displeasure and cease agricultural subsidies, probably ban exports, and the like. That is before they start on schools, health care, police, fire services, roads, and so on.

"We need to handle this extremely carefully."

Alessandra now realised that she had been so preoccupied with what this meant for her, her son, and the Osteria, that she had not even considered these more significant issues.

"My God. It's even worse than I thought!" she moaned.

Ben tried to reassure her. "We have a feasible plan and, so far, it is working out just as we had hoped. But it all hinges on brinksmanship. The media are vital to getting things done, and under full public scrutiny, so the politicians cannot wriggle out, or move the goalposts later. We need to play the media along by giving them the ammunition they need to hold a gun to the heads of the Church and State. Can you face giving a press conference? They are going to hound you, in particular, until they either get something to print or make it up. You might as well do it on your terms."

Ben argued that she was the one with the international dimension and that she also spoke perfect English.

"But crucially, even after the discovery, you have no power and so cannot decide policy. But you can have personal opinions. You also look fabulous," Ben added, "the media will adore you."

Usually, she would have been embarrassed by that last remark, but today she hardly noticed. Alessandra agreed to think about it and let him know later.

"A press call tomorrow would be ideal," he tested as they parted.

"So, no pressure then?" she countered.

The 11th-century church of San Bernardo, built by the Templar Knights, had not seen such a crowd since the wedding of Valerio's sister. On that day, everyone in the valley knew there would be free wine from the family's famous vineyards for the guests, and the bride would have made her legendary Millefoglie wedding cake for the feast. And so, every villager felt the need to pay their respects and come to the service. Similarly, today, the only citizens of voting age not present were the sick, or those working or studying away from the village.

The media were arranged outside, fanning out across the piazza in disorderly rows. Some were on step-ladders; others had portable aluminium platforms so their cameras could get a better view. The citizens-only rule might keep them out of the meeting, but it was not going to stop them hearing and seeing most of what was going on. The doors and windows were wide open, in an attempt to mitigate the stifling heat, and directional microphones could pick up the sound of a match being struck to light a candle on the altar. The unmistakable images of Knights Templar were everywhere in the frescos and wall paintings, and the setting could not, therefore, have been more appropriate or more picturesque.

Vincenzo and three other men were dressed in their military uniforms, and two of them had brought leashed hunting dogs;

apparently, as reinforcements to keep the journalists at bay but also impress their viewers. Claudio was wearing his white peaked cap, sash, and gloves. He was carrying an impressive gold-topped swagger stick, an embellishment Ben had not seen before. He had to admit that it all looked very imposing. Looking around, he saw that even some of the world-weary hacks were somewhat awestruck by the scene that was unfolding before them. However, the business that was about to take place was less likely to be quite so pretty, thought Ben.

At exactly 6pm, Vincenzo called, "Silenzioso" and then, partly for the benefit of the media, gave Claudio his full introduction of "his Supreme Tremendousness Prince Claudio Biancheri the Third of Seborga, servant only to God, The Pope and his loyal subjects."

A couple of horns or trumpeters might have been a nice touch, Ben thought, as he watched Claudio take his place in front of the podium.

The old man looked regal and confident as he addressed the murmuring crowd and eavesdropping media. Claudio retold the story of Ben's finding of the historic charter and, once again, thanked the 'eminent professore' for his part in that. He went on to remind them that, although he had fought, and his parents had died for their freedom, many things have changed in Italy since then. There was whispering of approval and much nodding in the audience.

"It is bad enough that our role in securing victory over oppression and freedom for Europe has been so quickly forgotten, but now we are ignored by our own government. Now we face new oppressors from the EU."

The murmur of approval turned into gentle applause.

"It is one thing to be neglected by your own politicians but is another being dictated to by foreign powers. That is what we are now faced with."

There was now loud applause and yelling of, "Si. Si. Let's get out."

Claudio went on, "The professore came from Great Britain to help us. His once proud nation has decided to claim back their sovereignty. They stood up against oppression in the last war, and they also fought alongside the partisans in our fight. We were brothers in arms then and could be again."

By now some men were standing, and some were whistling and others shouting, "Brava."

Journalists were aghast at the importance of the story unfolding before them and furiously scribbling notes.

Claudio paused to let his opening remarks sink in and the noise to die down. He then began describing the options facing them. He gave an impartial assessment of what he saw as the benefits and dangers of leaving Italy and the EU, but when he had finished, it was difficult not to be left with the firm view that Claudio appeared in favour of Seborga going it alone.

It was a persuasive and emotive speech. Ben thought that if they'd taken the vote there and then it would have been a landslide in favour of independence. There was a standing ovation as Claudio stepped down from the podium and then someone cried, "Long live the prince."

Others joined in, and it became a chorus ringing around the church. "Long live the prince, long live the prince."

Claudio took a seat that had been set-aside for him facing the audience, and Vincenzo invited anyone who wanted to say something to raise their hands. Nearly every hand went up. Using his intimate knowledge of the Seborga pecking order, Vincenzo started at the top and worked his way down, pointing to individuals whose turn it was next. There was no dissent at his choices, as everyone else also knew their place in the social strata.

The questions were predictable enough: what will happen to taxes, pensions, mortgages, education, hospitals, and so on. This debate was interspersed with the news from one man that someone was going around the village offering to buy options on land 'at a very good fixed price' in the event of independence.

"They say that they will pay ten per cent cash upfront for a two-year option, and we can keep that money if the vote is to stay in Italy and they do not complete the deal. Should we accept?"

One business owner reported they had received four enquiries to buy their shop, "from a Monaco Bank wanting to open a branch here."

People who had houses up for sale in the village, some of them for years, were now receiving offers of cash sales.

"Should they hold out for even more if independence does go ahead?" another asked.

Some voiced concerns about foreigners diluting their culture and their religion. One villager's specific concern was too many Russian, German, and English people buying property. She speculated that, "If we become a tax haven, all we will be able to buy in the village shop will be French Champagne, German sausage, Beluga caviar, and Earl Grey tea."

Then bitter accusations started. Farmers were accusing neighbours of greed in selling good agricultural land next to their own, which would then be built on spoiling their drainage, light, shade, wind, and so on. Others did not want all the houses to become holiday homes, full of foreigners for only six weeks of the year and deserted the remainder. Those with grown children worried that many young people would never be able to afford to buy a house in the village. The crowd were already getting rowdy and even Vincenzo was having trouble making himself heard when the shout of, "Ladro", (thief), was heard.

One landowner was accusing another of stealing land that did not belong to him. Although it did not belong to his accuser either, the rightful owners having not been seen or heard from in decades; it was the principle that he was objecting to. Having rubbed along peacefully enough for years, these two neighbours were now close to blows. There was shoving and shouting from supporters of each man.

Vincenzo had decided that he had heard enough and slammed his hand on the lectern making a mighty thump.

"Silenzio. Domani notte avrete le risposte. Niente più domande stasera."

There was an urgent surge for the exit, as everyone knew they would struggle to get a seat at The Osteria tonight or a place in the bars, where the real debate would continue in earnest long into the night.

News teams quickly edited and filed their reports to make their deadlines. Some headed back down the hill to their hotels on the coast; others would stalk the cafés and bars looking for a juicy comment or snippet of gossip that they could use to differentiate or spice up their version of the story. Many questions began something like; 'What happened to bring the Princess back from New York? Is she in a relationship with the Englishman who discovered the charter? What does the prince think of this romance with a commoner?'

Alessandra had managed to avoid facing the media by making torta verde and focaccia with olives, earlier that morning, offering just these and cold snacks with drinks in the evening. She had also called Valerio, suggesting that he get his sister to offer a piatto del giorno at the bar and this would take the pressure off the Osteria. Nevertheless, Alessandra knew that she could not evade the media indefinitely.

With two days to go until the vote, on this particular morning, the early mist seemed as if it was being drawn back into the mountains, as if someone was pulling the night cover off a birdcage. Ben had slept much better, partly because things seemed to be going as expected, but mainly because he felt more confident that Alessandra was on his side; even if she was not entirely sure which side that was.

That morning, he was awoken by the sound of a helicopter approaching from the East. This was not in itself unusual, as the village was on a direct route from the wealthy cities of the north and east of Italy – Turin, Milan, and Bologna – to both Nice and

Monaco. This helicopter was much lower, however, and was therefore also louder. It also began to hover over the village, blowing dust clouds up in the alleys and flapping washing hanging on lines. It then moved away, but only as far as the Farmer's Co-op depot on the road up to the village. Here there was enough space for it to land in the car park, where a large black Mercedes was idling. Around the car were several men in dark suits and sunglasses who, watching citizens guessed, were not farmers coming to buy fertiliser from the Co-op. This previously unprecedented scene was repeated within the hour, this time, the chopper approaching from Nice Airport. Reporters rushing to see who had disembarked need not have bothered, as they were passed by the occupants heading back up to the village in their blacked-out cars.

The Italian Prime Minister was the first of the day's dignitaries to set foot in Seborga. A relatively young man for such a tough job, he had been voted in by the power of bella figura. Whatever his credentials or experience for the job, he looked great and always gave a quote, so the media adored him, and the women of Italy voted for him in droves. His youth and attendance at popular music events and fashion shows also won him the younger vote. Traditional, older men were more sceptical.

He immediately made a beeline for the cameras of the BBC, NBC, and CNN. Relishing attention from the world's media, he made a huge, exaggerated gesture out of stopping to look upwards at the villages high walls and turning around three hundred and sixty degrees as though admiring the view, saying, "Bella Italia."

Questions were being fired at him from all directions:

"Do you acknowledge the claims of Prince Claudio?"

"How do you plan to keep Seborga in Italy?"

"What about the check-point on the Autostrada?"

One English hack even asked, "Have you brought your passport to enter Seborga, Prime Minister?"

Although relatively inexperienced, the politician knew better than to address any of these questions directly. He had his own firm agenda, which only involved getting re-elected in two months' time. He knew that the next twenty-four hours would be likely to decide the outcome.

"I have long wanted to come to this beautiful and historic Italian village. Now that I am here, I can see that it is more stunning than I had been told. The people of this village fought and died for Italy. They are Italians first and foremost. I am here to protect their rights as Italians. I am sure we can iron out these other minor issues without the people losing all the benefits of being Italian."

Vincenzo and Ben watched from the shadows and both agreed that it was a very shrewd politician's speech for such a young man. Praise the home which they are proud of, acknowledge their role in history, point out the benefits they enjoy, but end with a veiled threat of removing all these things.

"He had ticked all the boxes," Vincenzo acknowledged.

It would have been impossible, they both agreed, for him to have used any more references to 'Italy' or 'Italians' in his address. He was appealing to their national pride.

The La Stampa newspaper was on the table when Ben walked into Claudio's kitchen. A large photograph on the front page showed what appeared to be a rudimentary checkpoint being assembled by a group of workmen. Immediately behind the construction sites, lines of lorries and cars could be seen rushing by, their images blurred by the speed at which they were travelling. Beyond the traffic nothing except the sea and the sky. There was only one place this could be, but just in case anyone was in doubt the headline read, 'Rogue state to close border across Autostrada.'

That news will deflate the Prime Minister's cockiness, he thought.

Similar images with headlines on the same theme were on the Internet, TV, and in newspapers around the world. Ben especially liked the headline in the online version of Paris' La Monde, which he translated roughly as '50 billion euro trade halted by an Italian in a wooden shed'. Ironically scathing, Ben thought, as French farmers, armed with tractors, had been doing essentially the same thing to the British at the Chanel ports for decades. However, the key threat had been made, and the timing could not have been better.

Over coffee and a brioche, Ben was still trying to convince Alessandra that she should speak to the press.

"I did not even like doing PR for the restaurant in New York," she pleaded, "I am a cook, not a front-of-house person. Franco did all that."

Despite her imploring, Alessandra knew she had little choice but to face the media and she finally agreed to do so with nothing but trepidation. All that was required to set up the press conference was for Vincenzo to post another sheet of A4 paper, written in both English and Italian, on the village notice boards. Within minutes, it was being scanned by the circling media. The Italian press was the last to see the notice, as morning coffee and pastry took precedence over everything. In anticipation of her agreement Selene had written out some key bullet points:

Answer any questions about the Charter or how it was found by saying, 'You were not there and had not yet seen it.'

Deflect any questions about what might happen with: 'Claudio is the prince, and you have no authority to make policy'.

Anticipate questions about your life in New York and why you returned home.

Turn the above and any other questions into positive statements about your personal hopes and aspirations for the village.

She suggested that she think through some of the answers and make notes, but you should not be seen referring to them. Alessandra took Selene's list without comment and left to prepare herself. Ben went to meet Claudio and Vincenzo for a final update before their meeting with, what he described as, 'the big guns' from Brussels and Rome.

They had all seen the press and agreed the coverage could not have been better. Vincenzo described the scene in the Piazza earlier and said that The Prime Minister was now touring the village, shaking hands—mainly with curious tourists—providing photo opportunities with business owners, pensioners, and babies. According to Vincenzo, he had been snapped testing melons for ripeness at the grocery store, helping an old lady up some steps with her shopping, and cradling a new-born in his arms whispering, "Bello, bello."

The Pope's emissary, however, was not seeking any attention. He had arrived in an everyday car, without his robes and gone straight into the church by a back entrance for a briefing from the local priest on the mood of last night's meeting. It turned out was not good news. Claudio, although careful not to offend the priest, who he liked and respected immensely, had publicly dammed Rome's role in this affair.

The arrival of the EU Foreign Minister was, in terms of profile, somewhere between her two counterparts. She was happy to be pictured arriving here and reacting to yet another challenge to the EU but, as a not directly elected official, she did not want to be seen grand-standing or appearing to be overly concerned about the turn of events. Having presided over the Brexit talks, she had seen how divisive these events had been. Every disenfranchised faction in the Union, who blamed it for their predicament, now realised that, as in life, 'marriage' to the EU was not necessarily forever. Divorce was possible. Pockets of dissent were everywhere from Catalonia to Germany. A vote for Seborga to leave the Union, however small the population, would be seized upon by the media and certain groups as a vote of no confidence. It could be the crack in the dyke of European unity that many have predicted.

The sharply-dressed middle-aged woman had been a Spanish MEP, but her vigour and ambition, tempered with a gift for diplomacy, had quickly boosted her up the ranks. She had a reputation for problem solving by getting decision makers in one room and not letting them out until a deal was struck, no matter how long it took. It was negotiation by attrition. Her approach was undoubtedly more business-like than political, Vincenzo assessed. Although they each had their own agendas, Ben knew that they had a common reason for making this trip and only one thing would make them go away satisfied. They needed people to vote to stay and knew that the only question was how much that would cost to achieve.

The press conference was set for 2.30pm, the same hour as Claudio's audience with the three dignitaries. The thinking being that this would distract the media from where the real action was taking place; in Claudio's old throne room. It would also mean that it would almost certainly be too late to do much real damage in the event of the interview going badly. It would also not interfere with the Italian media's lunch break and yet still allow them to get their story out in time for the evening news.

The formal dining room at Claudio's had been prepared as it used to look; the dining table pushed to one side and with three smaller chairs facing the prince's huge one. All the windows and shutters had been kept closed, and it was cool compared to outside. When Vincenzo led the two men and one woman in, Claudio had already taken his seat.

As if to underline what he felt was his current status, the prince did not rise when the others entered, and his prominent guests were unsure of how to deal with this apparent challenge to their assumed seniority. The Italian Prime Minister took the initiative and approached him, offering his hand. Claudio shook it politely but unsmilingly. The others just took their seats. Claudio opened with:

"You will forgive me for dispensing with formalities, but I am an old man, and I have been waiting for a very long time for this moment. I do not intend to rake over the past, discuss how we got where we are today, or negotiate where we go from here. You are all busy people, and I do not have enough time left in my life for all of that."

The Italian Prime Minister began to make some placatory remark and was stopped in his tracks by Claudio continuing, "I can save you from the disaster which will probably end your careers and see your names go down in history for all the wrong reasons, but I have a list of requirements which I need you to agree collectively. I have considered them very carefully and, given the circumstances, believe that they are reasonable, deliverable, and require only your individual approval today. The decision must be mutual and without dissent or the whole deal is off. I will not discuss these things unilaterally. You are of course entitled to reject my requirements or walk out now if you cannot agree,"

He paused and then continued, adding, "providing that you believe you can justify your actions to the media waiting outside and, through them, the people who you ultimately answer to."

Claudio then placed his right hand palm down on three other documents on the table next to him.

"To help you focus on the task at hand and fully understand the dilemma I find myself in, I can tell you that I have had two firm offers. One is from the French offering to make us their protectorate, like Monaco, the second, perhaps more interesting and surprising offer, is from an international bank. In return for us offering Seborgan citizenship exclusively to their high-net-worth clients and declaring a zero tax on their incomes, we can claim a one per cent transaction tax on all the funds which flow through a new Royal Bank of Seborga. They tell me this could easily create a tax revenue of a billion euros per year.

"My guess is if they have offered one per cent, we can probably negotiate two, or possibly three per cent. It will still be much cheaper than paying taxes anywhere in the world. But I believe there is an even better solution for Seborga, which will not only give us financial security but also preserve our unique environment and culture for future generations. The latter is my preferred option and the one I propose to you now in this document."

The weary Prince allowed the enormity of what he had said to sink in.

"I will now leave you for an hour while you talk amongst yourselves and make whatever phone calls you need to make before returning to hear your joint answer. If you agree, we can all sign the document and Vincenzo will photograph you doing so, and we can go back to business as usual. We also should agree to a press embargo until after the election results tomorrow, when we issue a bland joint statement of unity, leaving out most of the details of what is in this document. At tonight's debate, I will recommend that my people vote as I advise, something they have not failed to do for seventy years. If you do not agree, then I will bid you Buongiorno and allow you to go and explain to the press how you gave up my small country. My modest requirements are–" and Claudio proceeded to read out a list from the document in his slightly trembling hand, very briefly describing the rationale for each requirement.

In the Osteria, where the press conference was being held, the conversation was not entirely so one-sided. Alessandra had fended off questions about the Charter successfully, and whether she favoured leaving Italy and Europe, but the press pack had turned to her private life. The NBC reporter asked, "Why did you leave New York, Princess Alessandra?"

She started to answer that her father's health had not been very good and that he was on his own, when the reporter interrupted her.

"Was the real reason that your business collapsed amid accusations of mob debt, money laundering, and drug dealing?"

Ben felt helpless and inadequate as Alessandra's face turned ashen and she began fiddling with the cuffs on her blouse sleeves. Faltering, she started to answer and then stopped. Cameras flashed. Lenses zoomed in. Other questions rained down:

"Where is the young Prince?"

"Why has no one seen him here?"

"Does he not want to go home to New York?"

"What is your husband's role in all this?"

"Are you still married to him?"

Alessandra was slowing drowning in fear and shame when another New York accent said, "My parents' restaurant failed because of my father's stupidity."

Unseen, Cristiano had pushed to the front of the reporters and now stood behind his mother and next to Ben. He had combed his hair as best he could (because there was so much of it) and put on a plain white cotton shirt. He looked smart, thought Ben. The teenager went on, "My mother knew nothing of his borrowing, drug taking and worse. He let us both down, and he broke the law, for which he is now being punished. Does that answer all your questions?"

Needless to say, it did not, and now the questions came thicker and faster but now were directed at him:

"What will be your role in the new state?"

"Is the English woman really your girlfriend?"

"Do you think you will get to meet The Queen of England?"

Alessandra had by now composed herself and spoke firmly, "My son is still under eighteen, and so, as professional journalists, you will, of course, respect his position as a minor and address any question about him through me and refrain from taking his picture."

The paparazzi, of course, ignored this plea and the photograph, which would circulate the world, was of the beautiful Princess Alessandra in tears. At one side the handsome young Prince consoling her, and behind, the English professor with one hand on one shoulder of each of them.

When Claudio re-entered the dining room where the politician, the bureaucrat, and the cleric had been left in discussion, the atmosphere was charged.

"You have reached a decision on which you all agree?"

The EU Foreign Minister seemed as though she had acted as a chairperson, and she looked sternly at the other two without speaking. They nodded what looked like a very reluctant agreement. Then she said, "You gave us a take-it-or-leave-it proposal, which under the circumstances we understand. We will give you the straight answer you require and sign your agreement on camera, if you will also understand the political pressures that we each face and agree to one single caveat."

Five minutes later they all left the room, except Claudio who sat blankly staring at the paper in front of him: A tear in the corner of one eye rolled slowly down his wrinkled and tanned cheek to finally drip onto the sheet, like a royal seal.

The press conference descended into a heckling mob, and it was only when Vincenzo and Carlos appeared to shield them were Alessandra and Cristiano able to slip away. They reached Claudio's still trailing insistent paparazzi just as the dignitaries, and their minders were leaving. Inside, the Prince sat alone still staring at the piece of paper in front of him, when Alessandra's yelling broke his train of thought.

"I knew that was a mistake," she screamed.

"And now I see why you did it. I was a bloody decoy while your political manoeuvring was going on. You knew the media pack would tear me apart. You just decided that your scheme was more important."

Ben was taking the brunt of the onslaught, but some of the sentiment was also now aimed at her father.

"You're a pair of dreamers. This whole thing is coming crashing down on our heads while you two scuttle about, making your pathetic plans, which, let's face it, will never become a reality. These people don't care about us. They will sell us down the river for their own ends. You've got nothing to bargain with. They have all the power. Bloody dreamers!"

This last remark was fired off over her shoulder as she climbed the stairs to her room, where they heard her door being slammed. Ben and Cristiano were left standing in the hallway and Claudio was still seated in the throne room, the door wide open. They were all speechless but for very different reasons.

23. CAPPONADA

Ben was up early to get the newspapers from the village shop. When he returned, he tapped gingerly on Alessandra's bedroom door.

"It's me. Can I come in?"

After a pause, she bid him enter but in a voice so quiet he could hardly hear her. She was up and dressed and sat in a chair by the window.

"Good morning," he offered, cheerily, hoping to put yesterday's events behind them.

He placed a copy of La Stampa gently on her lap.

"The press conference did not go anywhere near as badly as you imagined."

A photo of her and Cristiano took up most of the top half of the front page. She scowled,

"I look awful. My mascara is running," she said sullenly.

Ben glanced at it and added, "But look at the sub-headline, 'La bella Principessa che la è regina della cucina.' If my Italian is good enough, that translates as, 'The beautiful Princess who is the queen of the kitchen?' and it's basically the same theme in all the other papers."

It seemed that despite the journalists probing into her past, the editors had decided that the story likely to sell more papers was the positive one. Little, or no, mention was made of Alessandra's past. There was, after all, plenty of bad news dominating politics, religion, and sport. A sexy royal who could cook was better than another financial scandal.

"You are every red-blooded Italian man's dream woman and Cristiano is referred to as 'the brave and handsome Prince', standing up to support his mother. Every teenage girl in Italy is posting stuff about him on the Web."

"But I don't want to be every man's fantasy," she countered, "and I especially don't particularly want thousands of girls lusting after my son. He has enough to cope with at his age."

Although the fury of last night had subsided, Ben was aware that there was a lingering resentment at being thrust into the spotlight, even if the results were ultimately beneficial to their cause. All the publicity had brought tourists in their hundreds—possibly thousands—it was hard for Ben to estimate once they had dissipated into the narrow alleys and numerous piazzas. Added to the media circus already present were now property speculators, politicians, bureaucrats, and lawyers. There was not a hotel bedroom or restaurant table to be had within twenty kilometres. Cars were parked along the approach road to the village for two kilometres. Ben could not help thinking of Eze Village and agreeing that Alessandra had been right about that.

Trying to keep things light-hearted, and make Alessandra focus on the positive outcomes, Ben said, "That boy of yours showed pluck coming to your support like that. What became of the shy teenager who wouldn't say much?" he joked.

"Some pluck?" Alessandra questioned, "You English and your funny old-fashioned words."

Ben made a mock frown and countered with,

"Just because the Americans have dumbed-down our once great language and then re-sold it to the world through movies, does not mean that we should let our standards drop in Blighty."

"There you go again. Where the hell is Blighty?"

They were both laughing now.

"Seriously Ben, is this all going to work out? I am worried about Claudio and Cristiano."

"Let's get away for lunch somewhere and leave this madness for a couple of hours," Ben suggested, "we can take Cristiano with us if he wants to come."

She smiled at this idea.

"I'll go ask him. Why don't you ask Selene to join us and I can try to apologise? If she accepts the invite, I know that I'm at least in with a chance."

It was beginning to dawn on Ben that it was hard enough keeping a new relationship going with only two people in it. The prospect of four strong personalities, each with their own agendas and baggage, was frankly terrifying. Nevertheless, he could not see a way out of agreeing to ask her and called his daughter to extend the invitation.

The four of them drove down the hill past lines of parked cars. One entrepreneurial farmer had set up a stall by the side of the road selling fresh organic lemonade to people making the hot steep climb to the village on foot from their parking places.

"See, that's the kind of spirit we need around here," said Ben, trying to lighten the mood.

After the fifteen minute descent of the mountain, a couple of kilometres drive east along the coast brought them to Ospedaletti. As they approached the pretty seaside town, Selene Googled the name in her iPhone. She said, "According to Wikipedia, it was established by the Order of the Knights of the Hospital of Saint John of Jerusalem... Blah blah blah... to provide care for sick, poor, or injured pilgrims, coming to and from the Holy Land. There is just no escaping those bloody Holy Knights," she added, "their presence is everywhere around here."

The seafront at Ospedaletti looked like any other along the Italian coast. Its prime beachfront had been licensed to family businesses, who ran their own bagnis (beach clubs) with military precision. Identical beds and beach umbrellas were set in lines as straight as vines in a vineyard. Each had its own immaculate shower block, changing cabins, children's play area, and, most importantly, small restaurant. Alessandra's choice was The Regina (Queen).

"How appropriate," remarked Ben, thinking that this was Alessandra's little joke.

"Just a coincidence," explained Alessandra smiling, "it's named after Queen Margherita who was fond of this area. They serve the best seafood around here."

The place was already busy, and it was still only just after midday. The owner already was shaking his head as they approached him and mouthing 'siamo al completo' (we're full). Then suddenly his expression changed completely, and he beckoned them forwards with a, "Mia signora sei la benvenuta. Should I say, Eccellenza?"

All three simultaneously realised what was happening.

"He has seen the news and has just recognised you three," said Selene, articulating in words what the others were already thinking.

Without arguing, they allowed the fawning owner to show them to a table overlooking the sea. Alessandra wondered whose reserved table they had just stolen, but today she did not care too much. Hopefully, it was someone from the media, she thought, smiling. She was enjoying being in the company of the two men in her life and did not want to spoil it. There was also the great food to look forward to.

While Ben and Cristiano took their seats, Alessandra tugged Selene's hand, "Let me show you the view from the most beautiful Ladies powder room on the coast."

Selene responded with only a puzzled smile but followed her anyway.

Alessandra returned after a few minutes seeming contrite. Selene followed a minute later with an aura of righteous coolness. Ben instinctively knew that words had been exchanged – possibly harsh ones – but ultimately, fences were mended.

With the innocent indifference of youth, Cristiano focussed on his choice for lunch.

After examining the menu, and to move the conversation in a more positive direction, Ben asked, "What is Capponada?"

Even Alessandra was unfamiliar with this dish and so deferred to the restaurateur, who explained in Italian that she translated for Ben and Selene. It was a cold dish served in the galleys of cramped wooden ships in bad weather. When the sea was just too rough for cooking, it was still vital to eat sufficiently moist dishes to maintain strength but without causing seasickness. The dish was prepared in advance using ship's biscuits (crackers made from flour, water, and salt), beef tomatoes, and musciàmme; a preserved fish fillet that was eaten on board ships as early as the twelfth century. This was softened in a marinade of extra virgin olive oil and combined with anchovies, black olives, capers, hard-boiled eggs, vinegar, and salt. It was kept dry ready for the worst conditions. It had everything a seafarer required to survive.

Two portions were duly ordered and, when they arrived, Ben and the children all thought it tasted better than it had been described. Alessandra had ordered a local Pigato, and the crisp, chilled wine was the perfect foil for the salty, slightly fishy appetiser.

Ben then said, "Eleven hundred AD. That was about the time–"

But he was interrupted by his daughter laughing, as she guessed, "I know what you are going to tell us; that these biscuits were probably eaten by those bloody Knights travelling to the Holy Land. Take a day off from the Templars, Dad."

They all roared with laughter, even Ben, who was now the target of the joke.

It was a warm day even in the shade, but a slight breeze was blowing off the sea and taking the edge off the heat. Sleek sailing and glitzy motor-boats were moored in the bay, their crews having been disgorged into inflatable tenders to reach the restaurants along the seafront. Two teenage girls, from a family at the next table, had been pointing at Cristiano and giggling. They now approached their table holding out a mobile phone. They wanted their photograph taken with the 'Il Principe'.

Alessandra began to object but then saw the delight in her son's eyes at the attention from these two beautiful young girls and relented. Selene also joined in with, "Oh, go on, let them, Alessandra."

The capricious pair dressed in bikini tops, shorts, and flip-flops, squeezed Cristiano tightly between them and gave their sexiest selfie-pouts to the camera phone, which they had handed to Selene. Then just for good measure, each also kissed him on either cheek.

"It's a dirty job etc." offered Ben.

They all laughed out loud, except Cristiano, who seemed to blush even under his ochre tan. This was the most relaxing and happy day that Alessandra could recall spending with her son in well over a year. He had become a man during this last year, she thought.

Then came a voice, which was instantly familiar to her, from behind the two children,

"Remember me?" in English with a New York accent.

Cristiano rose instinctively and hugged the man with the abandon of a small child, rather than that of an introverted teenager.

"Pappa," he exclaimed but perhaps with just a trace of hesitation and agitation.

Alessandra's eyes narrowed, and she too rose slowly.

"Remember you, Franco?" she almost spat at him. "How could I forget you when every single day I have these to remind me?"

She thrust her wrists forward palms upturned revealing her scars.

"And that's not counting the scars you left inside, you worthless piece of shit. Who the hell let you out of jail anyway?"

Judging by his demeanour, Ben imagined this was not quite the welcome that the stranger was expecting.

"I got parole. I wanted to see my son, who you kidnapped, incidentally."

Ben thought it just as well Alessandra was not in her kitchen because she would have had something potentially more lethal to hand than the bread basket, which she now hurled at him. Chunks of bread rained on tables either side of the unwelcome visitor. The Englishman could see that poor Cristiano was between a rock and a hard place in this row between his parents. Instinctively he put a reassuring hand on the boy's shoulder, something that he just realised was becoming a bit of habit. Franco was backing off now but saying, "I have papers from a New York court granting me access to my son."

He could see that Alessandra was scanning the table and those around her for something heavier to throw at him, so he swiftly backed away and headed for the exit. Franco was waving the papers over his head as he departed saying, "I have the law on my side this time."

What none of them had noticed, until now, were the two men in dark suits leaving with him. They had stayed well back and kept quiet throughout. In fact, they showed no reaction at all, as though violent confrontation was not unusual in their lives.

Alessandra was looking like she might turn on anyone unfortunate enough to get in her way, and Cristiano that he might burst into tears. Selene looked like she had a dozen questions that she was dying to ask, but the stern look and head shake, which she received from her father, dissuaded her from saying anything for now.

Ben suspected that they had not seen the last of Franco and this now worried him greatly. He was not only younger than Ben but also handsome. His new rival had a full head of wavy black hair, showing only a few streaks of grey. Even this flaw, only served to make Franco look even more distinguished. He was also lean and fit looking, perhaps from having time on his hands in jail, Ben speculated. If he had to have a rival for Alessandra's affections, this is the last man he would choose.

24. MELA MARCIA

Claudio was preparing for the final debate at 6pm, when he received a call from Vincenzo to warn of an unexpected and most unwelcome visitor. About an hour later, they had made preparations and Vincenzo let the visitors into the dining room with the cheerless greeting, "I did not think you would have the balls to show your weasel face around here again."

Franco half smiled, half grimaced, and replied, "Nice to see you too, Vincenzo."

The two suited men from the restaurant were a couple of paces behind Franco, still staying in the background and remaining expressionless. Claudio was seated expectantly but offered nothing by way of acknowledgement of the three men. Franco spoke first.

"So, you have finally got your kingdom and your crown Claudio."

He paused for effect and then went on, "Well, I'm afraid that I am here to rain on your little parade. I have a couple of pieces of bad news for you."

He was holding a thick sheaf of papers and went on to explain that they were from a judge in New York granting him access to see his son.

"Me and my boy have a lot to talk about and plans to make."

While he let this bombshell sink in, Franco explained the presence of the two men behind. "They represented the people who your daughter and I still owed money to, a nice Old Italian family as it happens. They leant on someone to get my parole terms relaxed to allow me to travel. They had seen the news about Seborga. They figured that, as Alessandra and I are not yet divorced, and that she is next in line to the throne, then they had a claim over his share of any divorce settlement. They like the idea of owning a bit more land in the old country," joked Franco, "especially if it's about to become valuable real estate."

Claudio had listened without comment or reaction until the younger man had finished talking. Then he let out a sigh.

"You were always full of shit, Franco."

Vincenzo approached Franco and held out his hand as if he wished to examine the papers. He took them, had a cursory glance at the cover, and then with his shovel-like hands tore the fifty plus pages clean in half and dropped the two halves at Franco's feet. The brutal physicality of this action looked like it was the start of something and prompted the men in suits to reach inside their jackets.

Somewhere away to their right, in the gloomy unlit room, two loud clicks were heard by all present. The strangers immediately recognised the first click as a gun's safety catch being released. The second click turned out to be a Zippo lighter lid; the resulting ignition momentarily illuminated Carlos re-lighting the tiny stub of a slim cigar. He was accomplishing this with his left hand. In his right hand was the stock of a double-barrelled shotgun, which he was pointing in the direction of the two strangers. The large barrels were resting on a chair back, precisely in line with the men's groins. Vincenzo smiled at the strangers.

"As I hear that you have some Italian blood and will be familiar with firearms. So, you will, of course, recognise that as a Fausti twenty-gauge shotgun. Carlos here was just on his way to the cinghiale hunt. He can stop a hundred and fifty kilo charging boar dead in its tracks with just one barrel of that gun. You two big guys, look as though you would be about seventy-five kilos each?"

The hands that had been moving inside their suits now fell back to their sides. All that could be seen of Carlos after the brief illumination, was the occasional red glow from him drawing on his cigar, but they all knew his finger was still on the trigger.

"Boys, boys," said Claudio.

"Now we each understand our respective negotiating positions, perhaps we can dispense with the business at hand and you can go home. Firstly Franco, let me explain the new reality. You are now not in America but in the Principality of Seborga, where your lawyer's papers are worthless. I make the law here, and Vincenzo and Carlos enforce it."

He pointed to the pile of torn papers on the ground and said, "That is my reply to your lawyer."

The old man paused to glance at the two men in suits, but then continued, "Like in the United States, we have laws here in Seborga about carrying unlicensed weapons and extortion. What are the penalties for those crimes Vincenzo?"

The big Italian scratched his head and then answered, "Two years in jail plus one hundred thousand euros for each unlicensed weapon, il Principe."

The prince looked at the two men and offered, "What do you say we call it even with the divorce settlement?"

They nodded eagerly in unison. He turned his attention back to Franco.

"Look behind you." The three men turned and looked up at the balcony where Ben was holding his mobile phone, its camera operating light blinking at them.

"A video of this encounter is being transmitted to my cousin, a police inspector in New York, meaning that you, Franco, are now known to be in serious breach of your bail. You certainly won't be taking any trips back there with Cristiano anytime soon. As for you two," Claudio turned to the two thugs, "unless you two are seen by Vincenzo getting on a plane back to America, never to return, we will let both the Italian and French police know about your little guns and your doubtless interesting CVs.

"Well, unless there is anything else, I think your business here is concluded?"

He gestured towards the door indicating that the two thugs should leave. Just in case they had any other ideas, Vincenzo added, "You gentlemen need be very careful outside because the rest of Carlos' pig hunting gang have been waiting around for him in the heat and they might be getting a little impatient for a target. If they were to find out you have been threatening their Prince, who knows what might happen?" Vincenzo followed them outside and made sure they left the Principality.

Claudio returned his attention to Franco.

"I'm guessing today's events only relieves some of your financial pressure and also makes it impossible for you to return to the United States?"

Franco nodded but added, "I still have an Italian passport and family here."

Claudio sighed the sigh of a man who has seen many things and learned the art of pragmatism.

"You are still Cristiano's father, and the boy has a right to see you if he chooses. It is only natural. But it will be at a time and place of our choosing, regardless of any legal papers. And if he decides he no longer wants to see you, that will be the end of it. Do you understand?"

Franco nodded again, but pointed out, "He's eighteen soon and can choose for himself who he sees and lives with."

Claudio terminated this conversation with an abrupt but polite, "Good day, Franco."

A few minutes later, as Carlos was unloading his Fausti ready to leave, the prince said to him, "sei perdonato" (you are forgiven).

Claudio looked exhausted and saddened, thought Ben. Surely, any man who had fought as he had – at first against his own countrymen in a civil war and then an invading army – to lose both parents, his wife and then to have his only daughter and grandson threatened by mobsters, was entitled to some peace now?

25. FRUTTA DEL LAVORA

Claudio took to the lectern at two minutes after five in the afternoon. The press had been told the meeting was at 7pm and, although this little deceit did not keep all of them away, at least they were able to hold the meeting in something approaching privacy.

For the first time, the prince was looking his age, thought Ben. Even his voice was less robust than usual. He had lost much of his healthy colour and looked pale.

"It has been a very trying week for me," he began, "so many things have happened, and I have had some very difficult decisions to make."

There was a long pause, interspersed with coughs and some murmuring amongst the audience.

"You all know how long I have dreamt of Seborga's ancient status being recognised and how hard I have fought to that end. However, the older, and hopefully wiser, I have become, the more I have realised that we are just too small to exist as a truly independent state. Even if every one of us here worked in its governance, it would not be enough to administer even a very small nation properly. In a modern country there are just too many complications, which would require resources we simply do not have. That is not to say that our historical rights should not be acknowledged, and our claims accepted for the truth they have now been proven to be. But, at the end of the day, I also realised that this status could only be the basis for a favourable negotiated settlement to remain part of Italy. There are plenty of precedents for a 'special status' where we could enjoy the trappings of nationhood, allowing us to keep our ancient culture but still enjoy the considerable benefits of Italian citizenship and European membership."

There were many looks of surprise, some of confusion, and even the odd whispered dissent, amongst the audience at Claudio's revelation that he did not actually want full independence. He ignored them and went on. "However, we are blessed to now have a way to restore the fortunes of our people, protect our way of life and create a sustainable future for our grandchildren; all based on the land which we have nurtured for so long."

Claudio took a thread-bare blue handkerchief from his pocket and mopped his brow.

"Some months ago, an Englishman came, at my invitation, to try and help us. Little did I know then, the many ways in which he would help. Ben told me that several weeks ago he had asked Alessandra to write down a wish list of what she desired for our community. This is that list."

Claudio held a scrap of paper torn from a notebook. It contained little more than half a dozen lines of handwriting.

"When I read this, I realised that my daughter is not only beautiful and kind, but also very clever. She had condensed my years of thinking and dreaming into a few short sentences. The Professore also agreed, and he has used this list as the objectives of his economic plan."

Claudio started by telling the audience about Ben's work looking for a better use for their land, other than the olives, from which they could hardly scrape a living. "He has been searching for a crop that is in high demand but short supply. Also, one which would benefit from our unique climate and environment. Not an easy task, as we know.

"In the end, it was fate, serendipity, call it what you will, which had brought him to the answer. Ben's research into the Templar Knights revealed the vital clue to potential future prosperity. He learned that, as well as religious relics, the Knights had brought back many strange plants, seeds, and spices, from the Holy Land, and other places they passed through on their journeys."

He explained that citrus fruits, first cultivated by the Arabs, were found to thrive here in this climate. The monks at the monastery discovered that blood oranges, in particular, prospered at the higher altitude of Seborga. Later, the monks also claimed to have discovered great healing benefits from drinking the juice of the orange which had the colour of blood. This colour was perceived as significant, in both religious and medical terms.

"Both here in Seborga and down in Ospedaletti, where it was used to treat the sick pilgrims and injured knights, often with remarkable results. The relic found by Professore Ben in the cave along with the Charter clearly shows a sick Knight drinking something from a chalice. He now believes this could easily have been this apparently miraculous cure."

Claudio paused to mop his brow for the second time. He looked weary.

"No one is sure why these trees disappeared from this land eight-hundred years ago, but Ben found that references to them stop about the same time as those about the Templars. Perhaps they cut them down in spite when they were driven from here by their persecutors from Rome. Who knows? After that, olives and grapes took over. But as we know, there is now too much competition in the market for olives because there are too many places where they can be grown more cheaply than on our steep rocky hills."

He told the audience about further recent research by Ben which had shown there was science behind the ancient claims for the healing power of blood oranges. They have recently been proven to contain extremely high levels of antioxidants missing in other citrus fruits. Many assertions are made for the medicinal and health benefits of these antioxidants, and so blood orange products are now in high demand.

Some of these claims stem from the rare and very special environments where blood oranges prosper. These are at an altitude and an elevation where they receive very hot sunshine by day but then cool mountain mists by night. We farmers know that it is exactly this climate that has been a curse for many of the crops we have tried here. However, it turns out that our land appears to be perfect for growing blood oranges.

"In the whole of Italy, currently only Sicily has Protected Geographical Status for arancia sanguigna (blood oranges). They grow them on the slopes of Mount Etna because of its southerly latitude, combined with its height above sea level, making it cold at night. These oranges can be made into marmalade, tea, soft drinks, ice cream, cakes, vitamin tablets, and beauty products. All these things carry a premium price because of their extra perceived value."

Claudio paused to let everything sink in.

"Then Ben had a chance meeting with the English owner of a Fair-trade cosmetics company that was already using blood oranges and are looking for more."

Both Claudio and Ben could see the olive farmers in the audience suddenly looking more engaged with the dialogue, while they presumably tried to work out in their minds the viability of all this theory.

"I know that you are thinking; it is all very well but it takes years to grow trees to bear fruit, and that needs long-term investment. Please be patient." the prince asked.

Claudio went on to say that orange trees could be grown to bear fruit in about four years. So, switching production from olives to blood oranges would take investment and time, but not too much time. And ultimately, it would provide a profitable crop and greatly increase the value of the land on which they were grown. Perhaps more importantly, this fruit is difficult to grow anywhere else and so gives us long-term protection against cheap competition.

Claudio looked around at the faces in the room and could see that there was some nodding, chin scratching, and murmuring, but, as yet, no dissent or argument. He continued to try and explain Ben's concept of added-value as best he could.

"The biggest profits are to be had when you make something with the produce, instead of just sending it to market and letting the big companies take the bulk of the proceeds."

He told them that marmalade and concentrate were simple products to manufacture, requiring no great skill, expensive equipment, or factories. There was also a growing market for other artisan produce, especially with a provenance of origin and potential health or beauty benefits.

"Even if all of this is true and possible, what does this have to do with independence, some of you will be asking?"

Claudio put his hand into the trouser pockets of his uniform and turned them inside out. They were empty.

"Money," he said, "unfortunately, it is all about money and – quite simply – we don't have any. Even the blood orange plan I have just outlined would require millions of euros of investment. This week we have seen people with money and fancy suits arriving on our doorsteps. Did you meet any that you would trust?" he asked of the audience.

A ripple of laughter went around the room, despite the audience not really knowing where Claudio was going with this argument.

"It seems that our choice is either to go it alone into independence or remain part of Italy and the EU. The Principality still needs huge investment, either way. Our choice is simple: private investment or public finance?

"The speculators and bankers won't give or lend us money without strings. If we declare independence, they will buy our land and property but when it's sold, so is our children's legacy, our heritage, and our way of life. It's a one-off gain only this generation will really benefit from. Seborga will then surely become a Monaco-in-the-Mountains. The rich and crooked will be sitting up here, avoiding their taxes, drinking their French wine, and dipping their bland supermarket bread in Turkish olive oil."

Claudio screwed up his face at the abhorrent thought of this heresy.

"But Ben has found another way. He has taken Alessandra's wish list and has made it a very real option for us. His Italian is still not yet good enough, and so I will explain it the best that I can."

This was Alessandra's wish list:

A way for farmers to make a decent living from the land.

Skilled jobs with a future for our young people and graduates.

Recognition of our unique history and culture.

Restoration and protection of our historic buildings.

Some controlled, sustainable, high-value tourism.

"Today I have met with the Italian Prime Minister, the EU's senior negotiator, and the Pope's representative, and agreed the terms of a deal, should you decide to accept it. If you vote to stay part of Italy and thereby, also the European Union, I have settled on the following major concessions. This is guaranteed public finance with no other strings attached.

1. A five year fully-funded investment plan to repair all the suitable terraces, re-plant with blood orange trees, with an annual subsidy to farmers until they have a saleable crop. We will then be awarded Protected Geographical Status (DOC) for the produce from Seborga.

2. A grant to convert and extend the Co-op olive processing plant to create a blood orange marmalade and concentrate facility with offices for worldwide sales and marketing of Seborgan produce, creating skilled jobs.

"Already, a world-leading fair-trade cosmetics company has offered a five year purchasing contract to guarantee a market and price for the blood orange concentrate."

3. The Vatican will publicly acknowledge the role of the Templars here and bless the relic found in the cave by Ben. That image with the Templar Knight drinking from the Chalice will become the communally-owned brand under which all produce from Seborga will be marketed. The relic will be placed in a newly constructed museum, which doubtless will become a tourist attraction.

4. The village will be granted World Heritage status, protecting its ancient buildings, providing funding for restoration, and placing very strict limitations on any future development.

5. A grant will be made for the sympathetic conversion of the old ruined monastery into an eco-friendly boutique hotel and restaurant, with an emphasis on authentic cuisine using local produce. To compliment this, provision of tourist signage from the Autostrada and road improvements and parking.

"The same international cosmetic company are also offering to run a spa here, using the blood orange products sourced here. This will create more jobs.

"In the meantime, Professore Ben has also been carrying out his own negotiations, and he can confirm;

6. The creation of an academic research centre in Seborga with ten fully funded scholarships to study the effects of the unique Maritime Alps environment on the produce grown here. The centre would be an English-Italian joint venture between Ben's University in Newcastle and the University of Gastronomic Sciences in Piedmont.

7. As a spin-off from the above, and as part of their course, each month the students must research a historic dish, source the ingredients, and run a pop-up restaurant somewhere in the village. The Slow Food movement has agreed to ask famous chefs to help them prepare these special one-off dinners. Several top chefs have already expressed interest in cooking with the students in this unique environment.

"In total, we calculate that this investment package is worth fifty million euros over five years and we do not have to give away a single metre of land. Indeed, the Vatican who have previously resisted all attempts to do anything with the abandoned monastery and its land, will now gift it to the community for conversion into a hotel."

Claudio also advised those who had already sold options on their land, not to be concerned. If the vote to remain succeeded, the property speculators would not exercise those options if they could not build on the land. The deposits they paid for the options would be likely to be forfeit to the land-owners. Furthermore, those who had already sold land at inflated prices would almost certainly be able to buy it back, for less, after a Remain vote.

"Lastly, I said there were no strings, but that is not strictly true. I must tell you of one caveat which I have agreed to in exchange for obtaining these major concessions. The politician's concern was that if we give up claims of statehood, by default, then there is no Principality and, so it follows, no need for a Prince. They want to draw a line under this once and for all, and if there were generations of potential future Princes, starting with Cristiano, their concern is that the issue would surface again. So, I would become the very last Prince of Seborga. In return, they have agreed that Alessandra will become a Contessa and Cristiano a Count."

Finally, he then sank down into his chair, looking very tired indeed.

Because of the sensitivity of the issues, at the politician's request, Alessandra had not been party to the details of the discussions that Ben, and her father had been having. She was therefore totally surprised and stunned by everything that she had just heard. She turned to Ben, and then to her father, wearing a look somewhere between admiration and disbelief.

On the one hand, she thought, she could not deny the clear ingenuity and apparent logic of the scheme. On the other, such was the audacity, complexity, and uncertainty of it, she had serious concerns that the citizens would not be convinced it would work. Compared to the apparent financial certainty of the speculators waiting in the wings with their chequebooks, this seemed like a leap of faith, despite its obvious appeal to many of the older citizens.

However, Alessandra seemed strangely relieved that she might be finally rid of the title of Princess, which, most of the time, "Felt like a yoke around my neck," she later revealed to her father.

However, she also knew how difficult it must have been for Claudio to give away what he believed was Cristiano's birth-right and end a thousand year dynasty. But she also knew that her son felt the same way as she did about his royal title. Indeed, wondered if he would be even interested in becoming a Count. But these were minor concerns, she realised, compared to the consequences of a vote to turn down this deal.

Vincenzo took questions deferring either to Ben or Claudio for the details that he did not have.

"What about those of us who do not have land on which to grow these lucrative crops?" asked the Dutchman from the antique shop, in English.

Ben answered, also in English because he knew that would make it almost a private conversation. "A fair question, Rikki. But if you sell to the speculators, you only get a one-off gain on the value of your property, which, let's face it, you could easily drink and smoke away in a couple of years. If we all accept the economic development package, your sales of reproduction Templar documents will rocket, giving you a lucrative income forever. Plus, with a sustainable economy, your property will rise steadily in value as well. It's a win-win."

Given something to think about that had previously not occurred to him, the Dutchman sat down.

It was now Carlos' turn to add a note of dissent to what Ben had hoped would be a consensus in favour. "Without any evidence that these oranges will grow here, your plans seem too risky. What is more, it will be a year or more before we know if the trees are thriving. If not, it will be too late."

Claudio rose warily from his seat, looking exasperated.

"Carlos, you know very well that we can grow lemons on our land and have done so for centuries. There is also some evidence that the Templars grew these oranges here. But you are right; it is not entirely without risk. However, compared to the risk of secession, in which our health, fire services, police, education, and pensions, might all disappear overnight, while we wait for these speculators to pay us what they promise us." He paused to let everyone think about this before continuing, "Faced with trusting these jackals, I would rather take a chance on my own farming skills."

Although Carlos sounded less cocky about his questioning, he continued, "But I have seen the cheques and bankers drafts they have given to those who have agreed."

Now clearly despairing with Carlos' naivety, Claudio said impatiently, "Let's say that you vote for independence and, thereby, to effectively declare yourself non-Italian. You could sell your land for development, but in which bank would you deposit your cheque? Also, if there were a vote to leave, Italy would be unlikely to offer new passports to people they will see as traitors. Nor are the EU likely to give you free passage, or any other rights to travel that you now take for granted, as a citizen of Europe.

"And remember, from here you must first enter Italian and then French territory before you can even reach Monaco by road. Finally, without a Seborgan currency that anyone recognises, how would you spend your cash? You would become a paper millionaire, who can't travel anywhere, or buy anything, unless you fly to Monte Carlo by helicopter."

The old man paused to catch his breath. "Personally, I'll take my chances with what we can grow on our land. Even if I can't sell it, at least I will still be able to feed my family. You can't live by eating bank notes."

This sobering assessment of the choices seemed to draw a line under the debate. There was a lot more private discussion among various groups, which continued out into the piazza an hour or so later.

Ben assessed that these groups could be roughly divided into three broad viewpoints:

The 'take the money and runs.'

The 'let's stick-two-fingers-up at the authorities and the interfering foreigners.'

The 'stay in Italy and try to build a new future for the grandchildren based on sustainable agriculture.'

Neither of the first two groups wanted to openly defy Claudio and were now in no doubt what his recommendation was. Those with currently worthless plots of land, and with teenagers wanting to go to university any time soon, still faced a very real dilemma. Claudio was promising jam (or marmalade to be precise) tomorrow, when they were being offered caviar today. Each group had their own agenda and dilemma. There was certainly no consensus, Ben realised.

The academic reflected that perhaps they could have presented a better case? Maybe it was too complicated with too many uncertainties? For some reason, he could not fully explain, Ben felt that the outcome of this vote would also decide where his own future lay. He still had no idea how Alessandra felt about the plan, or a clear picture of her feelings for him.

He did know that the concept of a micro-economy, based on growing and processing high-value artisan foods under a protected brand, built on the back of all the publicity which had come to Seborga, was a compelling one. A complimentary artisan production and food-led tourism business model, like those in Cuneo and Bra, also seemed the perfect pairing. The icing on the cake was the academic research centre, which would keep a body of students and lecturers here: including himself, he hoped.

He also knew just how much Alessandra despised the idea of what Seborga would become in the hands of the speculators, if the vote were to go the other way. It was difficult to imagine Alessandra serving pizza to coach loads of foreign tourists, or indeed salad niçoise to super-rich tax exiles. He felt that a leave vote would just be too much for their relationship to survive.

There was so much hanging on the result of this referendum; it was impossible to overstate its importance to all concerned.

26. SAN REMO PRAWNS

Claudio saw Alessandra at breakfast the next morning. She was distracted but silently going about her usual routine; making coffee and tidying away dishes.

"I did not see you after the meeting last night," Claudio quizzed.

She continued laying out coffee cups, plates, and cutlery, but made no comment.

"What do you think of the plan? You are the generation that will have to implement it."

She had still to make eye contact with her father and remained tight-lipped.

"Are you angry about losing your title – I thought you didn't like it anyway? I know Cristiano hates his."

Still, the silence continued.

"This deal is the best possible outcome for our people, and remember, it's based on your own wishes."

There was a crash as a dinner place smashed on the terracotta tiled floor: it had been thrown, not dropped. Alessandra calmed herself and began to speak quietly and deliberately.

"When I wrote that wish list, I never dreamed anyone would try to make it a reality. But you and Ben now believe it will actually happen. Well, I think you are both dreamers. You want to create your own little island Utopia here in the heart of Europe. Well I have bad news for you, Utopia does not exist. I believe people will vote for independence, regardless of your dream. Not because they want to control their destiny, as you believe, but because of the new riches it will bring them."

She swept her hair back with the hand not holding the drying cloth and revealed the tears that were forming in her eyes.

"They don't care about their ancient Templar roots, Italy, or the European Union. What they want is a modern draught-free apartment in San Remo, an American refrigerator, a new BMW, and university education for their children. Unfortunately, if that means shattering your life-long dream, then as much as they love you, I believe that is what they will choose to do. And maybe they are right."

It was Claudio's time to be silent for a minute before responding.

"Daughter of mine. It saddens me to see what those years in New York, and that idiot that you married, have done to you. While welcoming you home last year was the happiest day since I married your dear mother, you came back full of bitterness and anger. Those scars on your wrists must have cut deep into your heart. You must let them heal. You can't be angry forever. Ben has given the village a chance. He is also offering you a chance—a new start. Can't you see that? But, you must put the old life behind you."

Alessandra only heard the tail end of her father's words as she walked calmly out into the hall and then left the house.

Alessandra knew that she was angrier at herself than she had been at either her father or Ben. She had already resigned herself to the defeat of their plan. Alessandra believed that, most likely, people would vote for independence and sell their property, with all the terrible implications that had for their village. But she was ashamed of how little faith she had demonstrated in her father and Ben, and how little she had done to help them. Far too wrapped up in her own bitter recriminations for things in the past, she had missed the opportunity to rally support for them amongst the villagers. Their plan was a work of genius, she silently conceded, but almost certainly too late to hold back the tide of greed, which had now surrounded their mountaintop idyll and was already lapping at their feet.

The bitterest pill of all was that she, Princess Alessandra Biancheri, who, of all people, should have been setting an example of selflessness, had already acted to feather her own nest. She'd thrown in the towel before the fight really started.

Less than twenty-four hours earlier, Eugene, the Irish chef, had surprised her in the kitchen at the Osteria.

"I told you that I'd come and visit," was his cheery greeting.

They had exchanged pleasantries, he enquired after 'the Englishman', and then he got to the point.

"How would you like to go for a second star?"

Alessandra leant back against the worn marble worktop, completely stunned by this question. Eugene waited while she composed her thoughts and then, gesturing around him with his open arms, added,

"You're far too good for this place."

Alessandra took the stained and battered Bialetti coffee pot off the stove, grabbed two cups and beckoned her old friend to join her at a table.

"Tell me more."

The diminutive chef looked different not wearing his chef's whites; younger and more prosperous. He was dressed elegantly, but not ostentatiously, and sported his trademark bight coloured spectacles and a South of France tan. His white Mercedes convertible was parked outside, roof down.

"The owners of my place in Eze want to open a second restaurant and have acquired a prestige site."

He explained that it was to be in the new tower block built on the former railway track, which once ran through Monte Carlo.

"It will be the highest restaurant on the Riviera with the most spectacular views over the harbour and into both France and Italy. The best apartment in the same building is on the market for two hundred and fifty million euros and might even get bid higher than that. They want a sophisticated Italian theme and so an Italian chef with Michelin credentials. Do you know anyone?" he joked rhetorically.

Even as Alessandra was taking all this in, some of her old ambition was returning, and she could suddenly imagine herself in this shiny new stainless-steel kitchen inventing exciting new dishes. She looked around at her cramped workspace with its ancient old equipment on which she cooked the same dishes week after week.

"We would work together and share some staff with the Eze restaurant until everything was up to scratch, but they want one star by the end of year one and another by year three. I plan to retire in three years, and so you'll be set to take over completely. You would have two stars in Monte Carlo. Think of it."

Alessandra was already thinking about how much longer it would take to get three stars to match the legendary chef at Monte Carlo's Hotel de Paris. The Irishman detailed some more of the package he was sure that she could negotiate, including creative freedom, generous salary, apartment nearby, and a big bonus when the stars were achieved. Alessandra's mind was racing with conflicting feelings but, underlying them, was a desire to re-grasp the opportunity she felt she had been robbed of in New York.

"Can I use local San Remo prawns instead of the tasteless, farmed, Argentinian leviathans?"

The pragmatic Irishman laughed.

"You can use any ingredients you like, but there is a catch," Eugene added cautiously.

"They wanted someone front-of-house with similar credentials and had already found their man."

"That's not necessarily a problem is it?" Alessandra replied already getting a bad feeling.

"It's Franco," he revealed.

Alessandra's cup slipped from her hand and hit the saucer just an inch or two below, spilling much of her coffee into it.

"Before you start, you know he was the best in New York until he fell off the rails. He's also Italian, and he's here and ready to go."

The colour had drained out of her otherwise lightly tanned face. A moment ago, she had been offered the moon and stars, but now she was being told that to get there, she would have to travel there in a rocket with the Devil.

"You mean he'll be raring to go when he's sniffed a couple of lines up his nose?" she hissed with as much bile as she could muster.

"Weekly drugs tests are now obligatory in our restaurants. There is too much investment at stake to risk dope-heads wrecking everything. If he's not clean, he's gone."

Eugene argued that Franco desperately needed this job and knew that the owners were well aware of both his good and bad reputations. This was a five million euro investment. They believed that he'd learnt his lesson and that his experience was worth the risk.

"Plus, he's Italian, handsome, charming, and knowledgeable. They will love him in Monte Carlo, where many of the customers have a bit of a shady background."

Her old friend also pointed out that, like in New York, he would be front-of-house, and she would rule the kitchen. She would be starting work well before him and be home long before Franco had finished serving digestivos. On a day-to-day basis, there would be little need for them to interact.

"At least think about it," he concluded.

"When do you need to know?"

Eugene grimaced. "You've only got forty-eight hours, I'm afraid. Then I have to ask our second choice."

After a hug and kiss on the cheek, the chef departed, leaving Alessandra with the most significant professional dilemma she had ever faced, at the same time as she was wrestling with a range of bewildering personal choices. Eugene's parting shot was,

"Think hard, Alessandra. You can do this, and you won't get another chance like this as long as you live."

She knew that and was already thinking very hard. Why should she not have her life back? She had done her duty by her father, and he was now as well as any other man of his considerable age. Her son was nearly a man and would soon be making his own way in the world. She wondered where that would leave her—slaving over a stove in the Osteria's ancient kitchen, divorced and turning greyer by the day?

And, although Ben could turn on his English charm, was not bad looking, and did have a sense of humour, in a few months he would probably be going back to his university and his old life. He was certainly in love with her pasta, and maybe also had an infatuation with her. But, after all the anger that she'd directed at him during her quarrels with the world, by now he would almost certainly not be quite so keen on anything resembling commitment.

She was being offered a new start, even better than where she had left off two years ago. Almost as if the nightmare had never happened. It was the opportunity of a lifetime for anyone working in her industry. She would be cooking for, if not the most discerning palettes, certainly the deepest pockets, and she could use any ingredients she wanted without worrying about the costs. Surely, she concluded, she would be crazy not to go for it.

Alessandra did not believe that Claudio's and Ben's plan would win over the people of Seborga at the referendum. It was too ambitious, too long-term, and too risky. The citizens would vote for independence and then take the money being offered to them by the property speculators. It was a bird-in-the-hand, and a big juicy bird at that! When that happens, Seborga will turn into Monaco anyway, and the life that she had come to appreciate will be destroyed forever. She may as well join them on the coast before they come marching up the mountain with their diggers, cranes, and American Express cards.

And what about Franco? Alessandra pondered. Did she have any feelings remaining for him after all those years? After all, they were a successful team; the best in New York. He still looked good. But it was really only their business relationship that worked well. Outside of work, the couple were not so compatible. The marriage only lasted because they were at home together so little, she had concluded. In her heart, she knew that they married because she was pregnant following a champagne-fuelled romp, after celebrating their first Michelin Star. They were flying high, and, in that moment, it seemed the natural way to cement their partnership.

Earlier that day, Franco, wearing a yellow hard-hat, eye protection, and high visibility jacket, was being shown around the debris-strewn forty-ninth floor of the new Tour Odeon building in Monaco by his new boss. He got straight to the point. "And how would you feel about the idea of reuniting with your ex-partner? Any unresolved issues that might get in the way of your working together?"

Franco took his time answering and chose his words carefully.

"The problems my wife and I encountered were all to do with my cocaine misuse, which I know that you are well aware of. I have been clean for two years now, and your drugs tests will confirm that. You have nothing to worry about on that front."

The French businessman beamed with pride as he surveyed the vast expanse of floor space starting to fill up with bars, wine racks, and tables. Although the external glass had only had an initial clean, it was already possible to get an idea of the breath-taking views over Monaco harbour and out to sea. The world's biggest super-yachts lined up below them looked only the size of bath-time toys from this height.

"Do you think your wife will be impressed?" the entrepreneur asked.

"Honestly, she will not. Alessandra is only concerned with food and not interest in how or where it is served. She is totally focused on being the best at what she does. And, that's what you want, isn't it? I, however, feel that same passion about the dining experience, presentation, and customer service. That's what made us the perfect team."

If Alessandra would not have been impressed by the location, her teenage son certainly was. Following closely behind his father and listening intently, Cristiano already thought that this would be a very cool place to begin his career in the restaurant business. His father had warned him beforehand to keep quiet and speak only if directly spoken to.

Cristiano could see the distant helicopters landing and taking off in a steady stream from nearby Font Vielle Helipad, on the edge of Monaco. They reminded him of bees leaving and then returning to the nest carrying pollen. Except the cargo, in this case, was millionaires, multi-millionaires, or even billionaires; their potential customers for this new venture.

In a culture where the bigger, the bolder and the brasher, the better, the highest restaurant in Monaco would hold a trump card which was hard to beat. The owner explained to Franco, "We have even created one table on an elevated, slowly rotating platform. One lucky customer and his or her guests can claim to be a couple of feet higher than all the others in the highest dining room on Monaco. If they prefer to enjoy this privilege in privacy, there is a screen which can be electrically raised and lowered to shield them from the other diners."

Franco could easily see how this would appeal to this clientele, and also imagined the generous tips he would secure for allocating it to his favoured VIPs.

27. CIBO D'AMORE

Ben had gone looking for Alessandra, on the pretext of showing her a video clip that Vincenzo had taken that morning on his mobile phone. It confirmed the departure of the American thugs from Nice Airport. What he actually wanted was to talk to her about their future. If indeed, there was a future for them.

She had not been at the house or the Osteria, and so Ben started looking around the village. He eventually found her on her father's olive groves. She was sitting, apparently deep in thought, on an upturned plastic tub; one of those used to collect the olives at harvest time. She was leaning against her father's old stone Rustica, from which she had removed the temporary seat.

The clip that he had downloaded to his phone clearly showed the two Americans, who had threatened her father, passing through Nice airport security, being escorted—none too gently—by six heavily-armed French National Gendarmerie.

"Apparently someone," Vincenzo had told him, with a knowing smile, "we do not know who, warned the French diplomat who came to see Claudio that two dangerous American drug dealers would be passing over the border into France from Italy today; possibly armed. The informant gave them good descriptions. They were later intercepted, have now had their passports stamped as 'undesirable aliens', and were walked onto an aeroplane. Franco's two friends will not be setting foot in Europe ever again."

Pre-empting the speech Ben had prepared, Alessandra unleashed a lightning bolt, "I've been asked to work alongside Franco to set up a new restaurant in Monte Carlo."

She had not begun to think about how he might react to the news, but she was not expecting him to look like he might vomit. He rose and walked over to the edge of the terrace and looked solemnly out across the valley.

Turning to face her, he asked, "Just so as I am not misunderstanding this; you are telling me that you are considering leaving the Osteria, moving to Monaco, and working alongside the husband who destroyed your previous career, ruined you financially, and was the cause of the scars you will wear for the rest of your life?"

She started to say something, but Ben continued before she could get the words out. "And you are going back on all you preached about ethical, sustainable, and local food. What about tradition and heritage? What about the Slow Food ethos?"

Alessandra tried again to offer some mitigation, but Ben saw her lips forming words and headed her off with, "You are willing to shatter your father's dream, abandon the people who look to you for guidance, and expose your son to his father's dubious influence?"

He paused. "Well, congratulations on your news. I wish you every success," before setting off along the terrace back towards the village piazza.

Alessandra sat back down on the tub, drowning in the misery of her own guilt and doubt. She was already well aware that everything Ben had just told her was true. He had merely articulated what she already knew in her heart but did not want to acknowledge. It was even more painful to hear it from someone else, she thought, particularly someone who she cared about. What was the matter with her, she wondered? At precisely what point in the last few days had she lost sight of what was important. Something was clouding her otherwise good judgement, but she was not sure what it was. There was so much happening in her life at the moment, it was difficult for her to figure out exactly what was confusing her so utterly.

She had run away from Seborga as a young adult and then retreated back there in mid-life. Now she was contemplating running away again, but from what, and to where? This was what she couldn't decide.

At that moment, Ben suddenly reappeared behind her, having done a U-turn halfway back to the village. He looked furious; so angry that she thought for a moment he might even strike her. As it was, he took both her hands firmly in his own.

"Listen to me. Your father needs you here in Seborga, Cristiano needs you here and, although they might not know it, the citizens need you to make this deal work. But far more importantly, I need you desperately.

"I've spent most of my life bumbling along, rudderless and without any real motivation. Suddenly, out of the blue, I found this extraordinary place and you. Now for the first time in my life, I know exactly what I want and, more importantly, how to get it. I want to make your dream – and it was your dream for Seborga, remember – a reality. What's more, I believe, that with your help, I can do it. And, when that happens, perhaps you will make my dream a reality?"

Ben pulled Alessandra into his arms, held her firmly, and kissed her passionately.

It seemed as if someone had opened a valve, releasing two years' worth of accumulated angst. Her body relaxed as all the tension drained out of it. Ben supported her lightly at first, but she continued to melt into his embrace, almost as though she was fainting. So, Ben swept her up into his arms, and placed her on the pile of folded olive nets stacked in the Rustica. Feeling the warmth of embrace after so long on her own, rather than let go of him, she pulled him down with her onto the bed of netting. Her muscles then tensed as she became aroused. Her movements were frantic and jerky as she tore at Ben's shirt, sending buttons scattering.

At first, surprised and confused at this turn around in events, Ben quickly allowed his pent-up longing for her also to take over his own actions. The final act was wild and ferocious, but ended in a tender embrace, which seemed to go on for hours but was, in fact, only minutes. Although spontaneous and extraordinary, their intimacy seemed overdue and somehow accustomed, Ben sensed.

After this momentary loss of inhibition passed, they were both suddenly aware of their surroundings. They were almost out in the open, in broad daylight, and not a hundred metres from the village. Nevertheless, they both lay back on the nylon olive nets, contemplating what had just happened. As they looked out across the valley, the house martins were darting and weaving through the afternoon sunshine, collecting insects as they flew.

"They will be gone before too long, back to their home in Africa. Is that what you'll do Ben? Go home before winter?" she asked.

"Like them, I'd stay if I could be fed all year round, especially by you." Smiling, he stroked the back of his fingers down her cheek, wiping away the tear which had suddenly run down it.

Gesturing to the landscape before them he added, "Look at this place: why would anyone leave it?"

Her beautiful smile returned, but it now had something which Ben had not seen before. More relaxed. Much warmer. Not so strained, or tense.

"So, it's just the pansotti and the view keeping you here then?" she teased.

"Add to that great wine and sex with a beautiful princess, and you've got a pretty compelling attraction," he joked. She laughed out loud.

"If Claudio gets his way, in a couple of weeks you might have to settle for liaisons with a lowly Contessa."

28. SLOW FOOD

Following the public debate, the apparent division of opinion had alarmed Ben. It had also shaken the self-confidence he had recently rediscovered. He had believed that his vision was one that the citizens of Seborga would nearly all share with him. And, although it was clear that some did, he could not ignore the reality that the draw of immediate wealth was more appealing to many. This rejection of his argument saddened him. Not just because it was a rejection of his hard-fought concessions, but also because it seemed symptomatic of a more general attitude of selfish short-termism which was now prevalent in so many of the developed nations of the world.

It seemed to Ben that peoples' attitudes had never been so polarised and that this was being reflected in current political events. Extremely right, and left-wing political parties, which had been marginalised for decades, were enjoying a resurgence. Behind much of this movement seemed to be a fortress mentality; a growing feeling that protectionist and isolationist policies would protect people from the effects of globalisation. Several other once-independent regions and nations were campaigning for secession from their 'parent' country. Britain was exiting the EU, and the viability of the European dream was being seriously questioned. It, therefore, should have been no surprise that many Seborgans felt the same way.

However, there was a sizeable, growing number of people who cared desperately about the environment, fair trade, sustainable agriculture, artisan production, and so on. Ranged against them was another growing group who were equally, if not more, vocal about solving their own current problems and concerns at any price. Any price that is, so long as it was not them, or their generation, paying it. It occurred to Ben that the

Seborgan independence dilemma seemed like this tug-of-war being played out in miniature—a simple choice between instant or delayed gratification—fast food or slow food.

The final and most hurtful part for Ben was that even Alessandra appeared sceptical that they could deliver on the plan. And ironically, it had been her ideas that he had based it upon. It seemed that the only person who believed in him was Claudio; a ninety year old man who claimed to be a prince but couldn't prove it. Ben had to admit that to any objective observer, Claudio had begun to look like a crazy man on a personal crusade.

Ben began to wonder if his objectivity had perhaps been blinded by a drive to fulfil his personal agenda; to solve his own problems, just like everyone else wanted to. After all, mostly, he wanted to gain Alessandra's love and respect. He also longed not to return to Newcastle, but to remain here in this beautiful place. He just needed a role and revenue that would allow him to do that. It could be, that this whole plan had been contrived only to achieve these selfish goals. That would make him no different from those who wanted to take the developers' bank drafts. He wanted what suited him and was prepared to gamble an entire community's future on getting it.

Then he remembered Cecily's global, fair trade, cosmetic company, the University in Bra, the Banca del Vino and the foodie micro-economy in Cuneo. This 'Slow' movement involved millions of people all over the world. The ethos was real, Ben thought, and tens of thousands of customer-facing businesses were based upon it. What's more these were not only sustainable businesses but profitable ones, in which people enjoyed working. These organisations, in turn, support sustainable farming and production all over the world. Although still small, it was an alternative economy and lifestyle which worked. Why not here in Seborga? What better place?

He then speculated about the possibility that the plan might be accepted but that Alessandra did not come as part of the package. Would he want to stay in Seborga without her by his side? In fact, that would be unbearable, because if he did not have her, the place was so small that he would still see her almost every day.

Worse still, what if she chose someone else? Franco? Or, even Vincenzo? Ben now realised that without Alessandra, he could not remain here. He needed to know where he stood with her before the vote. If she rejected him, he would have to tell the citizens that he could not stay to implement his own plan.

Ben realised that giving Alessandra an ultimatum would be a risky strategy. Given her recent unpredictability, violent mood swings, and temper, anything could happen. He hoped that this less attractive side of her personality would improve once there was some stability in her life. Considering he had received so many rejections, he began to wonder what had kept him chasing after her. He had never run after a woman in his life. In fact, he had mostly been on the run from them.

He smiled at an amusing thought entering his head; Alessandra often behaved like the wild boar that attacked Cristiano, snorting and pawing the ground in anger and frustration. Also, similar was his reaction to this threat. When all his instincts told him to flee the danger, here he was being drawn towards it again. He laughed out loud at the vision of Alessandra as an angry cinghiale but decided that he would not share the joke with her.

29. BONÊT

The day of the referendum dawned clear and bright. The mountain mists and sea frets had decided to take a day off. There was a slight breeze coming from the Alps, which left the air fresh and crisp. It was so clear that, from the edge of the village, it was possible to see along the French coast as far as St Tropez—over one hundred and fifty kilometres away. By 8am, the central piazza was already buzzing with activity. The broadcast media had already staked their claims on the best vantage spots.

Today another sizeable modern vehicle was vying for parking space with the satellite broadcast vans. Not one to miss a marketing opportunity, Cecily had despatched a mobile promotion vehicle from Paris. It had driven through the night and arrived in Seborga before dawn. The shiny white van had a collapsible side with an awning, which created a pop-up beauty salon complete with make-up chairs and a retail counter. It was stocked with her range of blood orange products and staffed by uniformed beauticians, according to Cristiano, "All look like supermodels."

A small queue of curious female journalists was already forming under the awning, and two TV anchor-women were lounging comfortably in chairs having products applied. More importantly, thought Ben, the villagers were picking up the products from the counter and discussing them; almost certainly focussing on the prices, he assumed. At an average of forty or fifty euros each tub, Ben hoped that the people might now realise how lucrative their olive groves could become if they grew blood oranges. This point was underlined when some of the journalists were seen leaving the unit with bags bulging with the rare creams and lotions. Even some of the male TV presenters could not resist a quick makeover from Cecily's well-chosen sales staff.

It had been agreed between Claudio, the EU, and the Italian government, that a simple majority was all that was needed to decide the referendum one way or the other. Claudio would have a casting vote in the event of a tie. With only around five hundred citizens in the Principality, and a fifth of those being too young to vote, it would not take long for the count. Those who had already cast their vote remained to wait for the announcement of the result; taking seats in the Osteria or standing talking in groups in the Piazza. Ben had heard that balconies overlooking the Piazza had been rented from residents by TV companies for exorbitant fees; a sign of things to come, he wondered.

Roving journalists were conducting their own exit poles amongst those voters willing to talk to them and relaying their conclusions back to their newsrooms by mobile phone. Vox-pop interviews were probing villagers hopes, fears, and expectations. These were as varied, and therefore inconclusive, as it was possible to be. This would be a close-run thing, was their conclusion.

Vincenzo had brought Claudio's big chair-come-throne from his house and placed it at the rear of the counting table. On each side were stationed members of the Seborgan armed forces, in full dress uniform.

Ben was joined by Rikki, dressed in his brightest waistcoat and bow tie. He leaned in toward the dapper Dutchman and whispered, "Did I uncover treasure or trouble in that cave?"

Rikki winked and whispered back, "You found the makings of a curse, but between us, we have transformed it into treasure worth five hundred-million euros to our community. Not bad for a couple of days work."

They shared a knowing smile before Rikki added, "That original leather cover went a long way to convince the Cardinal it was the complete document, but the restored inside cover and faked inner pages produced by my American artist friend, clinched it."

Ben winced at being reminded of this blatant deceit and said, "The new pages did look remarkably authentic. The calligraphy was a masterpiece. Thank the Lord that the Vatican sent someone to negotiate who had never seen the original. I'm still not entirely comfortable about being party to the faking of a document with such far-reaching political implications."

The Dutchman laughed out loud.

"I don't see why? You found the true, original charter and its contents were real enough back in time, and all the parties involved knew that. The fact that a thousand years had reduced its pages to dust doesn't change the truth it once contained. The Church and the scheming politicians all knew it had existed and that the independence it confirmed was valid. That's why they haven't seriously questioned its existence or checked its contents too carefully. They arrived here already believing it existed and all we did was reinforce that belief. Previously, they were just happy to think that the Seborga copy had been lost forever."

Ben frowned when he recalled that most of what they had found inside the cover of the Charter was powdered paper and dead insects. Only the first page, which damp had bonded to the leather outer, was legible. What remained beyond that was past salvaging and therefore would have proved nothing about the independence claim.

"It would have mattered, if anyone who actually knew what was in the Vatican's copy had looked inside our copy," Ben countered.

Rikki gave a dismissive wave of his hand and said, "It's just a game of poker but with higher stakes than usual. You don' let them see your cards and keep a straight face." He also pointed out that neither they nor Claudio had made any actual claims about the contents of the document, "Only the media did that."

Vincenzo had seen the two talking in whispers and joined them, guessing the subject of their hushed conversation. He said, "Have you heard that a platoon of crack Italian Alpine troops has arrived in a couple of jeeps and a small armoured car? They have parked at the border of Seborga territory. They are not stopping cars but easily have the capacity to do so if they are so instructed. It's a show of authority. Calling our bluff."

Ben was not surprised, and neither was Vincenzo.

"The Sergeant is a cousin of mine and so I knew that they were coming yesterday. I have arranged to have coffee and canestrelli sent down there to keep them awake," he added, as though that was the expected thing to do when threatened with an invading army.

He also reminded Ben and the Dutchman that,

"It was just as well the politicians agreed to Claudio's offer to 'make the charter disappear' immediately after the election; always providing that independence is rejected. They do not want any evidence of it to remain, in case the independence claims ever resurface in the future. However, if the vote goes in favour of secession, and that process gets started, someone is sure to want the document examined independently. Your clever scheme would all come unravelled then, and we will have a problem for which we currently have no solution."

Ben looked worried. He had not really wanted to be reminded of this flaw in their plan. The crafty Italian offered him some assurance saying, "I am confident that another earth tremor is due any day now. I understand that the wine cantina, where the charter is being stored, has an unsafe vaulted stone ceiling which could collapse at any time. Such a catastrophe would surely crush the remaining unstable pages, as well as soak any remaining fragments in vino rosso from the dozens of broken demijohns which are stored in there with it."

Ben still looked concerned at the audacity of their deception.

"It will only be poor wine though. No Rossese, Professore," Vincenzo teased.

An hour before the voting cut-off deadline, a clip-clop of hooves on stone slabs could be heard in the near distance. Everyone around the piazza, except those in uniform, turned to see what fool was bringing a horse into the middle of the village with all these people here. As the sound of hooves grew ever louder, the crowd on the fringes of the piazza began to part. The four soldiers stood to attention and saluted. The tall black stallion entered the piazza baring Claudio in full uniform, including gold-topped swagger stick. Ben thought that it was almost possible to hear journalists' jaws dropping, even over the sound of their cameras clicking and whirring.

"Very impressive," said Ben out loud to himself, with no one else listening.

A spontaneous round of applause broke out – strangely beginning in the ranks of the media—causing the horse to whinny and step backwards. The stallion reared, momentarily raising both its front hooves like a Lipizzaner dancing horse, providing yet another fantastic photo-opportunity. Claudio firmly shortened both reigns and spoke softly to it, and the horse settled immediately. Ben thought that if his plan for the Principality was accepted, no amount of money could have bought this level of global publicity. The Seborga brand would be more widely known than Monaco, and for better reasons, he concluded. Vincenzo marched forward purposefully and took hold of the horse's bridle while Claudio dismounted. Claudio gave a little wave to the crowd, and the cameras all clicked again.

He had timed his entrance perfectly. The Italian Prime Minister had arrived earlier in the day flanked by two naval officers in extraordinarily flamboyant uniforms. One was the Admiral of the Italian fleet, the other the Captain of the Cavour, the most modern of Italy's two aircraft carriers. This extraordinary party were surrounded by male and female naval ratings dressed in immaculate white shore uniforms, all handing out Italian flags. Italy's thirty thousand ton pride of their navy had made the short journey from its home base of La Spezia, just along the coast, and had moored in the bay off Seborga during the night. When the citizens awoke that morning, the aircraft carrier was visible from all over the village, dwarfing every other yacht or ferry in sight. Just in case anyone had not noticed it, pairs of F-35 Lightning jets took turns in roaring from its deck and screamed over the village before peeling off over the Alps. It had put Ben in mind of Theodore Roosevelt's oft-quoted negotiating strategy, 'talk quietly but carry a big stick'. It was a stark reminder that becoming a nation-state comes with a responsibility to protect your citizens, defend your borders, and enforce the rule of law.

It was 5.30pm and the voting deadline had been set for six. As the local election officer knew everyone in the village and judged that they had now all voted, he started the count early. As he did so, two piles of voting papers, placed face down, began to rise higher, but no one except the counting officer and his assistant, knew which stack was which. For a while, one appeared considerably higher than the other, but then that status would reverse. It took just fifteen minutes to count them all twice, and he still ended up with two piles looking almost even. He then added the twenty or so proxy votes from those unable to attend in person. Writing down some numbers on a notepad, he showed the totals to Claudio.

Looking at the paper, the old man appeared visibly deflated, as though the last bit of strength had just drained out of him. The number of votes to remain part of Italy was one hundred and ninety eight. The number to declare independence was one hundred and ninety nine. Even Claudio's vote would only make it even. He asked them to count again.

Selene had been standing hand-in-hand with Valerio on the edge of the crowd watching the drama unfold. Cristiano had joined them there just before his grandfather arrived on horseback. At 5.45pm Alessandra made her way through the now packed piazza and stood beside Cristiano, placing her arm around his shoulder and pulling him close. He smiled at her but looked embarrassed and pulled away, gesturing to the watching cameras all around them.

"How is it looking?" she asked.

"Judging by the two equal-sized piles of ballot papers and Claudio's expression; too close to call" answered Valerio.

Selene told Alessandra, "Cecily's product demonstration and your last-minute plea to all the citizens by text message seems to have prevented a landslide victory for the leave vote, but may not have been enough to swing it completely the other way? The lure of the riches that an independent tax haven would create was apparently stronger than we anticipated."

Alessandra suggested to Cristiano that they go and stand beside Claudio and Ben in a show of unity.

Ben greeted her with, "Is this our Bonêt?"

Alessandra looked puzzled. So he explained:

"Like the dessert, we had in Cuneo. You taught me that Bonêt meant the last thing to enjoy before leaving."

She half-smiled but did not answer.

The third vote count was complete, and the clock was approaching 6pm; the prime-time television slot across Europe. Claudio would soon have to announce the result, and that looked like being a win for Seborgan independence by a single vote. The property speculators had triumphed, and one more island of ancient culture was about to disappear under the rising tide of globalisation.

Before Alessandra could move, her son held his hand to her ear and whispered, "I realise that, with all that has been going on, you have been very busy. And so, I want you to know that I understand why you forgot. And that I forgive you. But I became eighteen today and so, later tonight, I would like to go out to a club in San Remo with some friends to celebrate if that is okay with you and Grandpa?"

Alessandra looked dismayed; not about the nightclub but, that in the frenzy of events she had forgotten her only son's eighteenth birthday.

While his mother began to weep quietly, Cristiano continued, "Last night Ben showed me the video of those men brought here by my father. It showed them demanding money from and threatening my grandfather. I can see now that I have been foolish to believe that my father will ever change. This morning I messaged him and told him that now I am eighteen, I choose to stay here in Seborga with you and Grandpa. I would like to study to be a chef, like you."

Alessandra then suddenly took Cristiano's hand and pulled him roughly towards where the dejected Claudio was seated, contemplating the demise of the nation he cherished. The crowd murmured, dogs barked, the media stirred, and a frenzy of cameras began clicking. Then silence fell as everyone present strained to hear what the Princess was saying.

"Father, there is one more citizen to count. Your grandson turned eighteen today, and so is entitled to vote in the referendum."

BOOK 2

UNLIKELY PAIRINGS

One of the alleys leading out of Piazza San Martino

Drawing by Linda McCluskey

1. CAPRA CON FAGIOLI

"At the resting place of the Holy Grail, a new prince will be crowned this week" was the extraordinary headline of a press release that was bound to obtain a reaction (even if that reaction was mostly incredulity followed soon after by derision). Most of the journalist recipients of the email marked "*NEWS CONFERENCE OF THE CENTURY*" quickly dismissed the writer as a crank and moved on to perhaps more mundane, but at least not fake, news.

Nevertheless, the invitation to attend a media briefing contained within the press release had brought a dozen or so curious freelance and local journalists to the tiny, disputed Principality of Seborga one airless, sultry Saturday evening. This would-be micro-nation, with its self-declared monarchy, sits at the junction of three recognised sovereign states. Its strange history and quirky politics had previously provided many colourful stories when hard news was in short supply.

From its five hundred meter elevation, Seborga looks out across the Mediterranean. Below it, on the coast, is the Italian town of Bordighera, the French harbour of Menton and the Monaco district of Monte Carlo. This pivotal location has placed Seborga at the crossroads of a thousand years of political turmoil, leaving it rich in culture, but poor in tangible assets.

Most of the journalists present at the briefing were Riviera-based freelancers of the multitasking, multi-media variety, taking notes by recording sound and filming video on their phones and iPads. They were reporters trying to make a name for themselves, many as yet without a salaried job and therefore no official press accreditation. No major newspapers or TV channel were represented, but this didn't matter to the instigator of the event. As long as the coverage ended up somewhere on the Internet, it would be picked up by those who needed to know.

Earlier that day, two miserable French delivery men had arrived in Seborga complaining bitterly. After an unexpected trek up the mountain, which had involved navigating fifty or more hairpin bends, many with dangerous drops, the driver and his colleague were behind schedule and furious. The client had told their employer that the job would involve a simple short trip from Nice, thirty kilometres over the border into Italy. It should have taken no more than an hour each way, in which case they would be back in time to see the kick-off at Nice on TV. Now forty-five minutes behind schedule, they were still carrying trestle tables down ancient alleyways too narrow for their large van, into the tiny but breathtakingly beautiful Piazza San Martino.

The piazza was no larger than a tennis court, with a pink stucco church crowding all of one side. The villagers who had built this church sought to disguise its small size and the modesty of its construction with an elaborate façade. It was adorned with faux columns and beautiful frescos painted in bold colours. Gables were topped with stone urns and cherubs, leaving no surface or space without unnecessary decoration. The effect was of a wedding cake made for a princess in a fairy tale. Only its ancient weathered chestnut doors, bleached and cracked by the sun, indicated the church's actual age; they sagged on their blacksmith-hammered hinges, which were held in place with iron studs the size of plums. They looked like they could withstand a siege and at times may have had to do so.

It was early evening and most of the piazza was now in shadow. The amber stones of the other buildings were radiating warmth from the residual heat of the day's sun. The two Frenchmen set-up the tables and dining chairs according to the detailed plan they had been emailed. A single, elaborate, high-backed chair was placed at one end, with its back to the frescos painted on the wall of the church. Two heraldic standards were erected and hung behind the large chair and a white canvas bag was placed on the seat. Meanwhile, caterers from San Remo were waiting to cover the tables with white cloths, lay cutlery and place four elaborate candelabra at even intervals along the table's surface. Glasses, water jugs and wine bottles were the final pieces of the jigsaw. After this was complete, the caterers received a call on their mobile phone. They lit the candles and retreated to their van to enjoy a much-needed cigarette.

Francois de Payen strode into the piazza shortly after seven pm, towing an entourage of media behind him like a popular politician on a campaign trail. The Frenchman was short, with a slim build but unusually broad shoulders, making him look somewhat top-heavy. His build was a legacy of his younger days when he had been one of France's best swimmers. He was gesturing flamboyantly towards the many architectural features of the buildings around him, giving a running commentary in his native language to the journalists who seemed to be paying him little attention.

It was less than four years since many of the same journalists had been here covering another significant news story, where an English academic walking in the hills had stumbled across an ancient cave. The cave had contained an eight-hundred-year-old document, which proved that the Pope had given the lands of Seborga to the Knights Templar. The long-missing deed was the evidence that finally proved Seborga's claims of independence. It also bestowed authority on its monarchy, who had up until then been recognised by no outside powers.

It was after this discovery that the de-facto Prince Claudio and his daughter Princess Alessandra offered to give up their crowns. This voluntary sacrifice of their short-lived official status was in response to a deal offered by Italy and the EU. It was a high price, but one which father and daughter were willing to pay to create a sustainable future for their subjects.

At the recommendation of their Prince, the people of Seborga narrowly voted to give up, once-and-for-all, not just its monarchy, but also its long-running claim to independence.

In doing so, they agreed to fully become a part of Italy and therefore also the European Union. This decision came with the sweetener of tens of millions of euros in economic development grants for their community.

Italy's contribution to this sum was what its politicians were willing to pay to avoid even a small part of their country seceding. The European Union were providing the bulk of the funds to prevent something that would have looked to the world like another Brexit. Neither party wanted the world to see a very public vote of no confidence in them.

"So, who is this French clown?" one of the Italian reporters asked of no one in particular. They were about to discover that, although this was indeed something of a circus, Payen was no clown.

It was not an accident that the date that Payen had chosen for this event was the weekend of the lavender festival. Until about thirty years ago, lavender had been grown commercially in Liguria in areas of sheltered pasture high in the mountains. Before motor vehicles, it was a long walk to reach the crops, so it had become a tradition for the whole village to make the journey up the hills together for a few days each year to gather the blooms. The bunches of tiny purple flowers would be brought back by donkey and turned into expensive French perfumes. Inevitably, after the lavender harvest, a celebration would be held, during which there would be much feasting, drinking and dancing. The lavender festival was taking place that very weekend and most of the village was attending. This exodus had left the streets of Seborga largely deserted, apart from the very old and the remaining few parents of young families with children too small to make the journey.

The party of media visitors now entered the tiny piazza which housed the equally small church of San Martino. This ecclesiastical facade was to be the backdrop for what turned out to be the evening's bizarre events. It was surely not a coincidence that the ancestors of the former citizens of Seborga had chosen a warrior saint for the patron of one of their churches.

The even older Templar-built church on the outskirts of the village had been named after San Bernado of Clairvaux; it was in this town in France that the Templar organisation had been founded. The village's tangible connections to this once-powerful but mysterious medieval organisation seemed hewn into the very fabric of its architecture and woven into its unique culture. No other community in Italy could claim stronger links to the men who fought in the Crusades of the Holy Wars.

As darkness fell, the architecture of the medieval building had been illuminated by candlelight. It was an impressive sight, even by Seborga's aesthetic standards. The light was emitted by the large candelabra’s, which had been placed on the dining table and on tall stands placed around the piazza and also by the numerous single candles set on convenient outcrops of stonework.

The two delivery men (who were now dressed in the costumes of medieval courtiers) held flagpoles in one hand and elongated brass horns, from which hung heraldic banners, in the other. When the reporters were all present in the piazza, the men in costume held the instruments to their mouths and a loud fanfare sounded. It was apparent to all that this sound was recorded and being broadcast over nearby speakers. Nevertheless, it was good quality sound and well-timed, which added to the theatricality of the scene. The piazza looked and sounded like a set from a big-budget Hollywood feature film; it was very imposing.

During the fanfare, Payen took his seat at the head of the table. On one side of him sat a slightly older man and on the other, a woman of Asian appearance. Both appeared to be in their early thirties, and they were not introduced.

Only after Payen and his two guests were seated did the host gesture for the journalists to take their seats. They did so, chattering loudly amongst themselves, whilst carefully ensuring not to give away any insights they might have gained to their competitors.

Payen's eyes met in turn directly with each of his guests. Silence fell. One of the caterers appeared carrying a large platter on which was a single but enormous focaccia loaf, which he placed in front of the Frenchman. Another waiter followed with a dozen or so empty wine glasses on a tray. With the platter on one side of him and the tray on the other, Payen began tearing off pieces of bread, filling glasses with red wine and proceeding to pass them along the table. Seeing bread torn and wine poured in this way by the host seemed peculiar to most of those present. However, a few of them began to grasp the symbolism of this act. It appeared that what they were witnessing was an astonishing re-enactment of the Eucharist, with Payen casting himself in the role of Christ.

Most of those present had joined this press-call viewing it as nothing more than a media jaunt with some free food and drink. Also, the invite had come at a time when real news stories were in short supply. The more optimistic of the reporters thought they might get a small story to publish in a local Riviera news outlet. However, this was already turning into something much more interesting.

Nothing so far had been said about the crowning of a prince. The man and woman either side of Payen were providing an effective barrier to him being interviewed, by fielding any questions directed at him with, "All will be revealed very soon. Enjoy your supper." Even the choice of the English word "supper," rather than dinner, seemed deliberate.

By the time dishes of figs, marinated olives and green Taggiasca olive oil arrived, most of the journalists were already suggesting joke headlines for their stories. Even some of the kinder reporters were discussing using terms like "crackpot, crank and fantasist." The harder-nosed ones smelled a financial motive, although they could not yet identify what that might be.

Capra con fagioli (goat with beans) arrived at the table next, a traditional stew using white beans from neighbouring Pigna, braised in olive oil, Rossese wine, rosemary, thyme, oregano and a single bay leaf. So far, all of the food and wine appeared to have been traditionally Ligurian, cucina bianca. Any of those present who had a little historic culinary knowledge would also have noted that these were versions of ancient Eastern Mediterranean dishes that could easily have been served at the last supper.

Many of what had become the staple foods of the Northern Mediterranean had supposedly originated from the Holy Land, brought back by the Crusaders. Even the grape used to make the Rossese wine that they were drinking was believed to have had its origins in Palestine. If so, it was probably introduced by the Crusaders and, some say, tended by Saracen prisoners they brought back with them.

As the significance of the choice of setting, food, wine and the language began to sink in with the guests at the dinner table, Payen played his masterstroke. The two courtiers carried a huge gilt-framed painting into the piazza and placed it on an easel next to the Frenchman. The scene depicted on the canvas was one of a prostrate and injured Templar knight drinking from a green glass goblet while angels hovered above him. Payen now rose from his seat, gestured to the portrait and announced,

"Ladies and gentlemen of the press, please allow me to introduce you to my ancestor, Hugues de Payen, the first Grand Master of The Knights Templar."

Pausing briefly to allow this link with their setting to become established, he then continued, "You will see that he is pictured holding the precious glass chalice recovered from the battle of

Caessarea in 1101. The same Sacro Cantino which now resides in the Cathedral in Genoa and is widely acknowledged to be ... the Holy Grail."

Uproar ensued as a dozen excited journalists all shouted questions at once, but Payen's aids stood and waved away questions with the appeal, "Please be patient, and all your questions will be answered."

When the noise quietened down, the diminutive Frenchman continued, "The painting, of which this is merely a print, has hung in our family home for centuries, but my ancestors have always been very private, seldom talking about their links to the Templars. This painting has never before been shown in public. Those of you who covered the English professor's discovery of the Templar cave will note that this scene is remarkably similar to the one depicted in the wall painting he found there. In this depiction, the detail of the chalice itself is much clearer. What you see is unmistakably the hexagonal shaped glass of the Sacro Cantino."

More questions were shouted down the table. These queries were ignored as Payen talked-on, raising his voice above theirs in the manner of someone used to commanding an audience.

"In the eleventh century, Pope Gregory VII instigated the First Crusade, encouraging the noblemen of Northern Europe to recapture the Church of the Holy Sepulchre taken by the Seljuk Turks. He offered all kinds of inducements, not least eternal salvation, but also more worldly benefits such as land owned by the Church. The land on which we now stand was a quiet monastery community, but was gifted as a military base for the Knight's campaigns. Included in this gift was independent nation status, with my ancestor chosen as its first prince. Seborga, the name he chose for his principality, is derived from the word sepulchre, meaning a place where the most valuable relics are kept."

Getting straight to the point, one of the gathered media shouted, "Prove it!"

"After eight-hundred years, you'll be lucky," another replied.

Undeterred, Payen continued, "I am about to provide you with the evidence that you seek, if you will grant me a little more of your time. During the Holy Wars, when the Holy sites looked like being overrun by the Saracen armies, Hugues de Payen did what he saw as his duty to the Church. He rescued what could be carried and returned the priceless holy relics to their base here in Seborga. The significance of the name now becomes clearer, does it not? However, in making that long and arduous sea journey, he paid a heavy personal price. Even the Pope's blessings had failed to deflect all the arrows aimed at him during his campaigns and by the time he arrived here, he was close to dying from his many injuries. However, his very survival of the severe wounds he had received in battle and his endurance of the three-month journey home was considered miraculous. None of his fellow knights thought he would make it back to the boat, let alone survive the sea journey. His comrades put this down to their leader regularly sipping fluids from the Sacro Cantino, which he kept with him at all times.

"The cup kept him alive only long enough to safely return it and other Holy relics to Seborga. Here he knew they would be safe in the caves guarded by the Knights Templar garrison. After what he saw as the Knights' failure to protect Palestine, the Pope had little further use for the Templars, declaring them persona non grata. Snubbed by Rome, the Templars collected their spoils and returned to their lands in France. There, the Sacro Cantino was seized by King Philip IV of France, who had heard claims of its life-preserving qualities. The holy relic disappeared from records for many years. It is believed that the chalice was later traded to the Genoans for a vast fortune in gold, plus several warships. It remains in Genoa to this day, but I believe it should be returned to its rightful home in Seborga."

Payen's aids were now handing around a file to all the journalists. Amongst other documents, it contained colour copies of the portrait before them with selected areas enlarged and highlighted.

"I acknowledge that this painting is not, in itself, definitive evidence. However, much of the story that I have told you about my ancestor is recorded in historical research. I am sure you will wish to check for yourselves. You will also see from these detailed photographs that there are several physical traits that I share with my ancestor. These are acknowledged hereditary characteristics and the chances of finding all of them in two people without a direct blood link are a million to one."

The first image showed Hugues de Payen with detached ear lobes, as Francois Payen demonstrated that he too had detached earlobes by folding his own outwards. Attention was next drawn to the fact that the two also appeared to share freckles and dimples, although this was less clear from the painting. Payen then held up his glass in his left hand, mirroring the grasp of the man in the image behind him.

"Most of my ancestors were left-handed. As am I. Finally, let me quote to you from one of the contemporary texts. Here, Hugues de Payen describes the relic he had brought back from the Holy Land. He says it was, 'Egyptian blue glass the colour of the Sea of Galilee.' He was quite clearly colour blind. As too am I. You all know that the Sacro Cantino is bright emerald green and has always been described as such by others. Only Hugues de Payen ever described the chalice as blue."

Having created, what he saw, as sufficient a body of circumstantial evidence to make his link to the man in the painting, Payen moved swiftly to the next phase.

The so-far un-introduced man on his right produced a blue and white silk sash and passed it over Payen's head. The lady on his left extracted a golden jewel-studded crown from a canvas bag. She held it in front of Payen with both her hands. The two courtiers raised their horns to their lips and once again a fanfare blasted. The extraordinary night seemed to be evolving fast, indeed, more quickly than many observers could come to terms with. Most appeared to be utterly astonished at what they were hearing and seeing.

"I hereby reclaim my birth-right as Prince of Seborga and declare that I am the sovereign ruler of this ancient Principality."

Payen took the crown from the woman and placed it on his head. Every single camera, phone and iPad present dutifully recorded the event for posterity.

"I further denounce Claudio Biancheri, who previously claimed to have been the Prince of Seborga, as a fraudster and nothing more than an opportunist. He used the chaos of the Second World War and his position as leader of the local partisans to take over the throne of Seborga. It therefore follows that the Biancheris had no authority to give up the nation status of this land. Lands granted to my ancestors by the Pope and acknowledged in the charter found four years ago by the English professor. The deal signed back then between Biancheris, Italy and the European Union is thereby invalid and has no legal standing. The EU has wasted their money."

The entire speech and much of the lead-up had been recorded on an array of mobile video devices, which would be analysed in more detail later. For the journalists, now was their chance to fill in some of the many missing pieces of this jigsaw. A barrage of questions rained down on Payen, including;

"What's this got to do with the Holy Grail?"

"You are saying that your ancestor brought the Holy Grail here to Seborga?"

"Do you want Italy to give the Holy Grail back to Seborga?"

"You claim the multi-million euro deal with the EU was a fraud committed by Prince Claudio?"

All of the questions Payen parried with a politician's guile. Un-noticed, a large black Mercedes arrived at the only road exit from the piazza and the Frenchman was quickly bundled into it, still clutching his crown, and whisked away. The members of the media looked more than a little stunned at what they had just witnessed and more than a little frustrated at all their unanswered questions. They then seemed to all agree, vocally at least, to dismiss the whole thing as a farce, although many were secretly thinking that their first-hand account of this event may give them a significant career boost. A similar situation four years previously had done just that for the English journalist who had broken the Seborga independence story.

Once again, a serious question mark had been raised over the status of the former Principality of Seborga.

2. PORCHETTA & FAZZINO

Delicate yellow zucchini flowers filled with a mildly-savoury cheese and marjoram mixture may at first seem an unlikely culinary marriage, but compared to Ben and Alessandra, they would be considered Romeo and Juliet.

This would be Ben's third year helping with the lavender harvest. Although the tradition survived as a festival in Italy, only a few local artisans were remaining who could distil the flowers into the precious lavender oil. It no longer made commercial sense to collect lavender on such a small scale. Often used as the base of many perfumes, lavender was now grown on an industrial scale mainly in much flatter Southern France. There it could be harvested by machine and processed in factories.

The hand-picked flowers were so fragile, that if harvested in Seborga, they had to be transported carefully down the mountain in small bundles in the back of Apes (pronounced, ah-pays), which are the scooter based, three-wheeled trucks that were ubiquitous in those parts. The delicate bundles also couldn't be piled too high, or the valuable scent would be crushed out of them before they could be processed. All of this effort would only make sense if the farmers were getting paid a large percentage of the couple of hundred euros that one of the end products (a tiny bottle of designer perfume) would cost shoppers down below them in Monaco, which they were not.

The Englishman, however, had come to understand the reasoning for the villagers' enthusiasm for this annual outing. Once they climbed the narrow twisting roads past the initial peaks and into the higher valleys, the atmosphere was remarkably different. The air was somehow purer: it seemed to Ben to be almost medicinal, as though each breath he took was making him healthier. He drew each breath deep inside and savoured it. The Maritime Alps form the beginning of a natural, high altitude corridor from the Mediterranean through the Carpathian Mountains, almost reaching the Black Sea. It is some of the only remaining wilderness in Europe.

A decade of long, summer holidays from school spent at his grandmother's cottage in Kent were the fond memories brought flooding back to Ben by the smell of the lavender fields. The gentle old lady smelled of it, as did her bedding and towels. That smell triggered more memories; of apple pie made from the fruit of her own orchard, grilled brown trout from the stream that ran through it and cucumber salads.

While they were camping up there, if he were ever to wake in the night and listen carefully, he was greeted with pure silence, only occasionally broken by the sounds of animals. Goats munching Alpine grass could be heard hundreds of metres away. Wild boar grunting in the distant woods sounded as close as neighbours snoring in a house next door. In the far distance, the eerie howls of dogs. *Or were they wolves*? Ben had often wondered. The lack of background noise exaggerated every small sound, as the sides of the valley they bounced off amplified them, which made it difficult to ascertain the direction of the source.

Ben also enjoyed observing the customs and rituals that the villagers went through. Each villager had their own special lavender shears or a curved blade knife, which had often been passed down from a previous generation. Chestnut or bone handles were worn smooth by the calloused hands of their previous owners. Sometimes, these tools were so old that it was possible to see the hammer marks where a blacksmith had beaten the blade from a piece of white-hot steel. The villagers would stop work and spend what seemed like hours, but what was probably no more than ten minutes, sharpening these tools before continuing to harvest.

There was something quite magical about these mountain passes that drew the people of Seborga here each year to pick lavender for no wages, their only reward being some grilled meat, wild fruit and rough wine.

"I love this place," Ben suddenly announced as they drove.

Alex turned her head towards him, "What is it about the mountains that you like so much?" she asked incredulously.

Ben thought for a while before answering, "Seborga exudes an atmosphere of other-worldliness, like it's somehow lost in time. The mountains are wonderful in a different way; I think it's because they're remote and so completely wild. I know that there are tales of wolves returning to these mountains, but I wouldn't be surprised to read that previously undiscovered species have been found up here. It's as if we've arrived on a different planet from the one in which the cities below us on the coast exist."

Ben had fallen under the spell of the mountains and the feeling of peace that always returned when he was up there. This trip in particular had been therapeutic to Ben and Alex's relationship; their problems and tensions being briefly left behind in Seborga. The atmosphere in the car lightened with every hundred meters of altitude gained as the fresh air worked its magic.

"You English are such romantics," Alex laughed. "They are just mountains. Sure, the air is cleaner, which heightens the senses and that's why the food seems to taste so much better up here."

"And the wine," Ben added hurriedly in order to finish her sentence. "The same bottles that I love and that you bring with us from the Osteria acquire much greater intensity when I drink them in these hills. How can you explain a phenomenon like that other than magic?"

"Let's not try to explain it. Let's just enjoy it," she responded.

They made love that night in their tent for the first time in several weeks.

During the harvest they had time to talk. The previous night had reminded Alex just how much she loved her husband and of his passion for her home village and its people. She reminded herself that she should not be jealous that his work drew heavily on his time and attention, when it was Seborga's survival and prosperity that had become his raison d'etre. In that, and in taking care of Alex, he had effectively taken over from her father. The late Prince and the Englishman had become great friends in the short time they had known each other.

With some rare time together away from the village, Ben also realised just how distracted he had been. The timeless grandeur of his surroundings and the wonder of nature had put his concerns into perspective. Being here with Alex made him realise that this was all that was really important and that they must not lose sight of that. He had escaped what seemed like a life sentence of mediocrity and found himself in his personal heaven. He knew he should celebrate his good fortune every day and not dwell too much on things out of his control.

"Are you happy living back here in Seborga? Don't you miss the high-life of New York?" Ben asked his wife.

When Ben met Alessandra, she was a princess: not as in the modern-day parlance for a spoiled woman with delusions of grandeur, but the actual daughter of a prince. Before Ben had recovered from this initial shock, he discovered to his cost that this Italian-American princess had the aggressive, confrontational manner of a seasoned New Yorker. Even more extraordinary, under the tutelage of her uncle in Manhattan, Alessandra had earned a Michelin Star for her modern Italian cooking.

There was a long pause while Alex thought about this unexpected question, during which she bent and cut stems of purple lavender.

"I am happy here with you if that's what you mean."

"You know that's not what I mean," Ben said, frowning at her avoidance of the question.

"But, it's like asking if you miss kippers, or warm brown beer and Yorkshire puddings. I know you do. So sure, I sometimes miss not being able to buy fresh coriander, or hand-dived scallops, or French beans out of season. And yes, I occasionally miss going to see a show and then eating supper in some trendy downtown restaurant, cooked by someone who I've trained. New York has a buzz that's hard not to like and even harder to forget, but the bad memories still overpower the good ones for me."

After her former husband's arrest in New York for drug offences, she had faced a rigorous police investigation. The authorities had alleged that she had allowed her premises to be used for narcotic dealing and that her restaurant business was a front for money laundering. She had been cautioned, searched and then interrogated for four hours before the detectives realised that she was not knowingly involved in either and released her. It was her first, very brutal, brush with the law and Alessandra was determined to make it her last. Even if Italy had a reputation for bribery in the past, she was going to make sure that she would not be the one to perpetuate it here in Seborga.

Added to this, Ben could tell from their conversations that she still felt guilty about dragging her son, Cristiano, back here to Seborga. She always wondered if she had done the right thing in taking him away from all the opportunities New York had to offer a young man. As a minor, Cristiano had no choice but to accompany his mother to Italy, a place he had only previously visited briefly for an occasional family wedding. He appeared to despise her for it at the time.

At first, Cristiano was deeply unhappy about being uprooted from his friends and from the city of his birth, which he loved. He also struggled to acknowledge his father as the total villain in his parents' marriage split, despite the overwhelming body of evidence to support this. However, after a little time acclimatising and then witnessing a particularly unsavoury encounter between his then recently paroled father and his beloved grandfather, Cristiano finally accepted the truth. He had also since discovered a passion for his mother's profession and had grown to love Seborga. He and Ben's joint encounter with the boar had cemented their relationship and he greatly admired the Englishman's daughter, Selene, who he now saw as a cool big sister.

They continued cutting bunches and placing the blooms carefully in a basket.

Ben was the product of one of England's less-renowned boarding schools: polite, thoughtful and complex, but also perplexed by life in the twenty-first century. For a failed banker with no teacher training or particular affinity with young people, lecturing had not been an obvious choice. In reality, it was not so much a career choice, as the first parachute available when his career and personal life went into freefall. Although teaching may have helped to break his fall, Ben often felt as though he had landed in a strange ocean and was now cast adrift, alone and rudderless. Although he never cooked, his only passion was for French food and wine. As for Italian cuisine, Heinz ravioli was the nearest he had been to it.

Yet, although the pair had apparently nothing in common, this moderate, conservative Englishman and feisty, explosive Italian had been married within a year.

After the dust settled from their initial sparring encounter, they had discovered joy in reversing roles. Alessandra became teacher, educating the Englishman in Italian culture, food and wine, while Ben relished being her willing and adoring student. However, instead of the peaceful existence in a bucolic setting which they had envisaged, the couple had been drawn into almost daily political wrangles. These disputes most often related to the economic regeneration plan, which they themselves had set in motion four years earlier.

"You know what's weird?" Alex asked, "I railed against being a princess all my life. When I was a child, I wanted to be just like everyone else. As far as I could see, my title brought me no benefit whatsoever. In Seborga, having the prefix of Princess in front of my name was like having a big question mark hanging over my character. My friends assumed that because my father was Prince that I was different in some way. It was part of the reason I ran off to America as soon as I left school. There, only my uncle knew the truth about my background and I swore him to secrecy. I never used the title when I was in New York and it was like a weight was lifted from my shoulders. I earned my Michelin Star as Alex Biancheri, not as Princess Alessandra of Seborga."

"That's not so weird," Ben empathised.

"No. What's weird is that now I can't use the title, I miss it."

"What!" Ben replied, astonished at this revelation. "From our very first encounter you resented the accident of birth that gave you that title and never stopped complaining about it."

"I know. That's what's strange. I've been trying to rationalise it, but it still makes little sense to me. No one in the village treats me any differently than they did before. In the company of strangers they still refer to me as 'la principessa' just as they have always done. The agreement that we signed with the government means nothing to them. Yet, something doesn't quite feel the same now. I feel robbed of it."

Because she had given up her royal title as part of a deal with the Italian government and the EU, Alessandra no longer held any official role in the village. However, in the eyes of the citizens, she was still their de-facto leader. Regardless of titles, Alex remained single-minded about protecting Seborga's rich heritage, culture and architecture. She was also adamant that none of the public money they had secured in the deal should be misused by paying inflated prices to 'connected' contractors or 'oiling the wheels' of bureaucracy through bribes.

In contrast, Ben's frustration at the lack of progress was turning him into a pragmatist. If it meant something moving forward, he was willing to sacrifice some of his principles; in his view, he was merely becoming more 'Italian' in his attitude. The difference in their respective stances was leading to arguments, which were becoming increasingly fractious. It was a situation that didn't suit Alessandra's fiery temperament.

Over the previous year, Ben had witnessed a change in Alex where her confidence had waned. He had guessed that this was connected to the outcome of the referendum, but still didn't believe that this was the sole cause. More likely, Ben guessed, the root lied within her loss of status as a New York chef and restaurateur. In New York, she was not merely a princess in title, but the queen of her kitchen, with the Big Apple's foodie courtiers bowing and scraping to get a rare table. Italian chefs are expected to be good and so usually receive little by way of pay, thanks or esteem for their talent when compared to their French counterparts. There had been any number of French restaurants in New York with Michelin Stars but virtually no Italian ones. Alessandra had broken through this invisible barrier and lifted Italian artisan food to another level. Returning to the tiny hillside community of Seborga, she had left all the glamour behind.

If Ben's star had risen, arguably Alex's was in decline. Not only had Alex lost the prestige of her job and, to some extent, been usurped as leader of the village, in Italian eyes, Ben was now also the head of their household.

Ben caught his wife's attention by throwing a small bunch of lavender in her direction as she stooped to cut more of the stems.

"Alex, you do know that no matter what happens, you are my princess, my favourite chef and a better parent than I have ever been. Nothing will change that."

For a moment, Ben wondered if he had said the wrong thing. He could see tears beginning to creep from the corners of her eyes. She suddenly dropped her basket and ran at him, only dropping her blade at the last moment. Alessandra threw herself at her husband, wrapping her arms and legs around him, sending them both sprawling into the uncut lavender, respectively laughing and crying as they fell.

"That's why I love you. You crazy fucking Englishman. You can convey more sincerity in one sentence than an Italian man would in a lifetime of bullshit."

The other lavender pickers were now hooting, whistling and clapping at the pair rolling around in the meadow. After the harvest was complete, they washed in the stream and Alex started helping the others prepare dinner outside of the communal mountain house the villagers used as their summer base. Someone had started this process at breakfast time by lighting the wood oven, which had taken over an hour to reach its optimum operating temperature.

Before they left Seborga, the porchetta had been boned, stuffed with wild fennel and liver, rolled and tied with string. Its skin rubbed with oil, salt and crushed fennel; it had remained marinating in a cool box for almost two days. After seven hours of slow cooking, it was ready to be joined by the Fazzino - soft potato bread, like a muffin, which was typical of the mountain villages where flour was hard to come by. Made with seasoned olive oil and onion, it requires a long fermentation which produces a pocket-like cavity inside. It is the perfect food for eating outside when there are no plates or cutlery. The bread was filling, easily absorbing all the juices from the fatty porchetta, yet subtle in flavour, so it did not detract from the rest of the dish. It was the perfect pairing.

The smells from the stove were drifting around the camp, causing the men to chant, "Bella porchetta" while they drank their beers or wine. It was the feast everyone had been anticipating and it would soon be ready. It would be another remarkable night, as memorable to Ben as the three that had preceded it and he was already looking forward to next year. Once the food was served, Alex joined Ben and they sat close to one another, eating, chatting and laughing for the remainder of the night.

One of their neighbours came around pouring a pale green digestivo from an unlabelled bottle into paper cups. It was made with fresh mint, sweetened with sugar and tasted extremely potent. With a generous cup of the strong liqueur, all their worries and problems in Seborga seemed to melt away. After a second night making-love in the open, they lay enjoying the warm night air and scanning the stars, so bright in the unpolluted sky, it was as if they could reach out and touch them. Ben turned to Alex and said,

"We're a great team, you and me. We can take on the world if we stick together, but I need you to give me confidence."

Alex kissed him tenderly but fleetingly,

"You are right my love, but every team needs a leader and you are mine. I am too hasty. My heart rules my head. I trust you to make the decisions in your cool, deliberate English way. As for giving you confidence, that is easy, because I love you so."

3. FIORI DI ZUCCA FRITTI

The next day, all of the citizens of Seborga returned from the lavender festival. The rumour quickly circulated around the village about the strange Frenchman who had held an outdoor dinner party with members of the press in attendance. Without permission from either the Church or the Commune (local council), the stranger had simply taken over the piazza for his own purposes. No one except an elderly dog walker had seen or heard what had taken place. *All the more reason for the locals to speculate wildly*, thought Ben when he was told about it.

At around ten o'clock in the morning the day after they had returned from the festival, Ben's phone rang. He was sitting with Alessandra having coffee and freshly baked focaccia outside the Osteria. Before he could answer, his wife's phone also started buzzing. They looked at each other puzzled and then both put down their coffee cups to pick up their respective handsets. They answered almost in unison,

"Si, pronto."

Ben's Italian had progressed only to the essentials of everyday conversation. For everything else, he still relied upon Alex to translate. However, there was no need for his new-found faltering Italian because this caller was speaking English. Both calls had the same effect on their recipients - silence accompanied by an expression of abject horror. The phone calls were from journalists who had been present at Saturday night's press conference in the piazza. Their simultaneous timing was a mere coincidence, but their questions were essentially the same.

"What do you know about a Frenchman's claim to be the true prince of Seborga and his accusation that Claudio was an opportunistic fraudster?" Then, impatient for an answer. "What do you think will be the political consequences, if these allegations are proven to be true?"

It was a classic journalistic technique to hit a subject with a critical question, getting straight to the point when they least expected it. The less time the interviewee had to prepare themselves, the more honest the response was likely to be, resulting in the best quote.

Ben recognised Alessandra's expression changing to one he knew all too well. He grabbed her phone from her hand and pressed the red button just before her well-practised New Yorker's expletives passed her lips. He then also pressed 'end call' on his own phone before he said anything in response.

Turning off her phone had not stopped the tirade that Alex had been about to unload on the journalist. Instead, Ben and several other customers at the Osteria were on the receiving end. Fortunately, her husband was the only one who understood her American/Italian-accented English. He knew it was best to wait and let her get it out of her system before speaking. Focaccia crumbs, which had been on her lips, were sprayed over the table as Alex riled at the unseen callers, whilst Ben scrambled to make some sense of what they had just been told.

It was a few minutes before her husband's lack of visible reaction finally caused Alex to stop shouting and allow him to speak.

"Try and ..."

But before Ben could said any more, she was off on another rant.

"The sneaky French have been a thorn in our sides for generations. Moving the border, stealing our land, robbing our farmers and now we have to put up with them coming to our restaurants asking if our steaks are horsemeat, if our wine is Sauvignon and can they have some Dijon mustard."

Ben sipped his coffee and waited, a response often inclined to make Alex even more furious. She failed to understand how the English could remain so calm in the face of so much provocation. In truth, it was one of the things she loved about her husband. His English reserve was like a breath of fresh air after a life full of over-heated Italians and antagonistic New Yorkers, both of whom shouted a lot but were seldom moved to action. Faux-rage at people queue jumping, cutting-someone-up in traffic or crossing the street on a red light, most often resulted in nothing more than a dismissive hand-wave and a ‘pah’ in Italy, or a ‘fuck you’ plus a single finger in America. She knew that Englishmen rarely got genuinely angry, but when they did, someone could easily get hurt.

For his part, Ben had also come to realise that it was his wife's passion for the things that she cared deeply about which caused her to be so emotional about them, and he had come to admire this absolute commitment to her chosen causes. Not least because he knew the same passionate support also applied to him. God help anyone who criticised Ben's dedication to Seborga or his actions in trying to make his plan work. Alex would almost literally bite off the head of any of the more cynical locals who were foolish enough to question his motives within her earshot.

When there was finally a break in her speech, Ben asked,

“What would anyone possibly hope to gain from making these claims? It makes no sense whatsoever.”

Alex’s face began to colour again, but before she could speak, Ben held his finger to his lips and then a palm down waving gesture as if patting a dog on the head.

“Basta (enough),” was all he said to her before continuing in his quiet manner.

“Let’s face it, your late father devoted his life to this place, receiving nothing but worry and pain for his trouble. You could have taken over where he left off but chose not to because you knew just that. The crown of Seborga is a job which comes with enormous responsibility, not least the expectations of its citizens. Then there is the administrative burden, as well as the pressure on your private life and your free time. All this for what? There is no palace, no lands to speak of, no priceless jewels and no salary. Who would want such a job? You certainly didn't at the time."

Alessandra, now thinking instead of shouting, had to agree. This claim made no sense.

"Especially for a Frenchman," she now realised. "They hate being away from their native land, their cream sauces, smelly cheese and their strong wine. Italy is an anathema to them. The only thing they like here is the low prices."

But she added, not all-together convincingly,

"They have been stealing our land for as long as anyone can remember. Much of what they call their Cote d'Azur should be our Italian Riviera dei Fiori."

Ben was beginning to conclude that the mysterious event in the piazza needed further investigation.

"I think there is something we're missing here. We're taking this claim on face value when it seems more likely there is another agenda we are not aware of."

"But what could that be?" questioned Alex.

"I have no idea." Ben admitted.

Ben was aware that he had, to some extent, taken over his father-in-law's role in the village. He was known as 'il professore' and the one who had taken-on and out-foxed the Italian government and the European Union. Ben was seen as being wise in the ways of the world, if not so much the workings of nature or agriculture. Any problems in the village, whether to do with property, money or even relationships seemed to end up at his door, or more accurately, at his table in the Osteria over a glass of wine. He was often found there sat with Vincenzo (who was supposedly translating, although Ben suspected also adding his own opinions) dispensing solicited advice over glasses of Rossese wine.

Vincenzo had been the late-Prince Claudio's closest confident, protector and enforcer, although the last two roles were rarely required. In this region, it was sufficient to know that should either task prove necessary, there was no more competent man for the job than Vincenzo. He had always occupied a position of respect amongst the other citizens; his presence was enhanced by a natural air of authority he seemed to have possessed since childhood. He was also, physically, an imposing man, standing taller and weighing more than any of his neighbours. He was not quick to judgement, but was resolute when his mind was made up.

His day job, like most of the men in the village, was working on the land, tending to whatever crop was in season and keeping the Osteria supplied with produce. When required, he would don his smart Seborgan guard's uniform and officiate at any public event going on in the village.

Vincenzo had admired Alessandra from a distance when they were both teenagers and had been secretly heartbroken when she left for America before he had made his feelings known. When she returned, he became aware of the problems that she had endured as a result of her husband's drug problem. With her father dying not long after, Vincenzo saw himself as her protector from all external threats.

Vincenzo had initially seen Ben as one such threat and so the relationship between the two men had not got off to a good start. Since then, Ben had proved himself worthy to Vincenzo by saving Alex's son from a charging wild boar during a hunt and by devising a plan to save the whole village from economic decline. Even if he secretly thought that the Englishman had ruined his second chance to woo Alex, he had earned enough respect to be forgiven.

Ben was aware that his wife had gone through a lot during the past few years; her whole world had been turned upside-down. Everything she thought was secure had turned to dust - her husband, her business, her life whole in New York.

Returning to Seborga and meeting Ben had at first seemed like a fresh start, but then her son had been unhappy about being brought to Europe. He had been whisked away from his father, all his friends and the world he knew at such short notice. Alex had given up their royal titles and heritage in a political trade-off. Soon after that, her father had passed away.

On top of all this pressure, Ben was beginning to have grave concerns about the welfare of the new blood orange trees. The trees, recently planted with some of the EU money from the deal, were a key part of the former principality's economic regeneration plan. This coming year should be the first commercial crop of oranges delivered to their single customer, the PURE Fair Trade Cosmetic Company.

However, those villagers who had chosen to grow the unusual oranges were beginning to express serious fears about the percentage of the blossom that appeared to have been pollinated. Roughly only five per cent of the blooms appeared as if they would mature into fruit. This rate of productivity was less than half of what had initially been expected and the crop seemed as though it would fail. If the villagers' fears turned out to be realised, then calculations for this years' revenues would be lower than planned and the company which had contracted to take them would have a shortfall.

Four years ago, Ben's chance encounter with Cecily, the English cosmetics entrepreneur, had given him the idea for the planting of the orange trees. She had mentioned that her company was struggling to source sufficient blood oranges to make a new product which was selling well. The restorative qualities claimed for blood oranges, combined with her company's Fair Trade ethos, was proving a winner with wealthy women all over the world. This conversation had been the catalyst for Ben's big idea.

Olive trees had dominated the Liguria regional agriculture for centuries, but their fruit was difficult to harvest and even harder to make a profit from; blood orange trees, in contrast, had seemed to be the way forward. It was not just that blood oranges were in high demand and short supply, their unique characteristics meant that they only thrived in special environmental conditions found in only a handful of places around the world.

It was also the case that these rarefied conditions were what imbued the fruit with its antioxidant qualities, for which many health and beauty claims were now being made. Providence had it that Seborga found itself at the centre of just such a micro-climate. It was next to the warm Mediterranean Sea but also remarkably close to the snow-capped Alps, from which cooling breezes regularly flowed down, meaning it was often hot during the day but cool at night.

Seeking a solution to Seborga's farmers' economic woes, this conversation and the few facts he had read about blood oranges had solidified into an idea. A bit of further research quickly confirmed that Seborga's climate, geography and soil conditions were similar to the places where the rare red fruits already grew successfully, in the high altitude areas of Sicily and Northern Spain. The biggest challenge would be financing the massive change in agricultural practices, which would take years to achieve.

That problem was overcome when, during his research, Ben accidentally stumbled upon a long-lost charter from a 13th century Pope unequivocally proving the Principality's independence. This discovery gave Seborga the political leverage it needed, allowing it to obtain the significant public investment required with which to ensure the community's economic revival. Italy's Prime Minister, who was then facing an election, could not countenance losing any part of Italy, no matter how small. Similarly, the European Union were desperate not to see a possible, tiny, Italian version of Brexit. Italians were already disenchanted with the dream of European unity, and if Seborga succeeded in exiting it would be the straw that broke the camel's back. The fears of both these parties had been assuaged in the deal and Seborga was now seeing – quite literally – the fruits of their labours flowing from these negotiations.

Following his appraisal of the blossom, Ben, somewhat reluctantly, determined that he should speak to Cecily and forewarn her of his concerns about the forthcoming crop. He was also hoping that with her recently acquired experience with blood orange crops, she might have some insight into what the problem might be. In any event, she needed to know as soon as possible that she may not receive the quantities from this first harvest that she had been anticipating. He at least owed her that.

Ben decided it would be best if Cecily saw the trees for herself and so emailed her with a lunch invitation in Seborga. Cecily was a foodie who loved Alessandra's cooking. It was the time of year for the first zucchini flowers and Ben knew how much Cecily loved his wife's version with its secret stuffing. *How does that woman stay so slim*? Ben wondered. He mentioned the zucchini in his email and also that the Osteria Alex now ran had received some fresh porcini, knowing that this would induce their friend to accept his lunch invitation even if she already had other plans.

Cecily was due to arrive at around twelve thirty. Ben had first met the successful entrepreneur onboard the classic sailing yacht that she called home. He had accompanied Alex to its mooring on the harbour at Menton to deliver some of her father's precious olive oil. For some years, Prince Claudio had been supplying his best product to Cecily's onboard chef. Cecily loved telling her dinner guests the 'royal oil' of Seborga story. Olive oil had been Claudio's and Seborga's only cash crop. However, their organic, cold-pressed Taggiasca olive oil did command a premium price in the right markets, and so it was still worthwhile income.

Cecily's fair trade cosmetics business had been started in her kitchen in London. Under her astute leadership, it had snowballed to become a global market leader in little more than fifteen years. Her knack of spotting trends and her speed in sourcing products to meet new demands had resulted in her pioneering blood orange range. The scale of the success of this new range had surprised everyone and left her with the problem of obtaining more and more supplies of the rare red oranges.

Lunch had been arranged with Cecily and now Ben had another dilemma: should he tell the sole buyer for their new agricultural product that, not only was this years' harvest estimated to underperform, but that all future ones might be placed in jeopardy by the Frenchman's claims?

As it turned out, that decision was taken from Ben, as Alex blurted out the news before Cecily had even received a welcome hug and a kiss on either cheek from both of them. Such great friends they had all become that the idea of keeping secrets from her now seemed ridiculous to Ben.

Although they were great friends, Ben still thought Cecily was something of an enigma. She was beautiful, successful and charming, yet she appeared to have few friends and no love life: at least as far as they could see. She also never talked about her family and was vague when questioned on her upbringing. She had confided that she had been married once, but that it hadn't lasted long and that no children had resulted from it. She had also added,

"I prefer not to revisit the past. I live in the present and deal with the day-to-day. I look forwards, not backwards."

With the focus of a potential investor assessing a business opportunity, Cecily assembled the facts from Alex's angry summary, analysed them and quickly concluded that she concurred with Ben.

"This bloody usurper must have an, as yet unseen, agenda, although I admit that I also have no idea as to what his motive could be. His story has more holes than a sieve. I can't believe that he thinks that he can get away with such deception."

However, Cecily did harbour an unspoken concern that it might have something to do with the lucrative blood oranges; she pondered whether a French agent in Paris could be acting for a significant competitor and trying to cash-in on their work.

The cosmetics market was one of the largest and most profitable in the world, approaching that of pharmaceuticals in the value of its sales. In the lucrative world of beauty, underhand tactics were not unheard of, especially when it came to the development of innovative product lines and the capturing of new markets. Cecily concluded that she needed more information and she was determined to get it.

The news that the orange trees were not yet as productive as they might be was less concerning to Cecily.

"I am well aware that fruit crops can vary wildly from year to year, also that there are remedies for many of the natural challenges that affect these plants. I'm playing a long-game and another twelve months will not make that much difference."

She further put Ben and Alex's minds at rest on this point by adding,

"I will call someone I know in Sicily and ask for his advice. He is one of my main suppliers of blood oranges. His land has reached its capacity and there is no more to be bought, so he often has time on hands. I am sure he will at least advise us what the problem might be."

Returning to the question of the challenge to the crown on Seborga, Cecily agreed that this also needed further investigation.

"Ben, why don't you call Selene in London and see if she's heard anything about this guy at her newspaper?" she suggested. "I'll make some enquiries of my own, and we can talk again on the phone later tonight."

Ben agreed to make a call to his journalist daughter after lunch. Selene was already well aware of the unusual status and strange politics of Seborga. It was she who had broken the story about the discovery of proof of its independence to the world's media four years prior. Ben delayed the call, as one of the things now ingrained in his psyche was the Italian rule that everything stops for lunch. Nothing is more important than sitting down to eat with your loved ones for a couple of hours in the middle of the day. It was sacrosanct, especially when Alex was doing the cooking.

Stuffed zucchini flowers arrived with cold, crisp prosecco and the opera that was lunch began on a high note. For the contorni, porcini had been prepared four ways: as a delicious light mouse, pan-fried in oil and garlic, raw with pecorino and stuffed and finally dipped in breadcrumbs and deep-fried. A cold sauce made with fresh wild cherries and a hint of mint poured over milky panna cotta completed the performance. It received a seated ovation.

Cecily departed on the pillion of their 'boat bike' ridden by one of her crew. It was a tatty, non-descript scooterino she kept for general running around when they were in harbour. Despite the age difference between rider and passenger, to a casual observer, Cecily, in her helmet and sunglasses, could have been his Italian girlfriend being taken back to work after a lunchtime liaison, mused Ben.

"Does she look so young because her products actually work?" questioned Ben.

"Yes, that, and she looks after herself and doesn't spend all her days in a hot steamy kitchen chopping onions like me."

"I thought women paid fortunes to visit spas where they were put in steamy rooms and had vegetables put over their eyes," taunted Ben.

The last crust of left-over bread bounced off of Ben's brown forehead and landed on the Osteria floor; he knew that this discussion was over.

4. LUTEFISK

Ben had not spoken to his daughter in several weeks, although they had exchanged regular, all-be-it brief, messages on WhatsApp. Her job at the newspaper kept her busy and she also now had a column in a monthly glossy magazine. Life was good for her at the moment, possibly partly because Ben had heard from her brother, Tom, that there was a new love in her life.

Selene's big break in journalism had come about from a hike she had taken with her father into the hills above Seborga four years earlier. After a sudden, massive storm had caused a landslide, they had accidentally stumbled across a long-hidden cave, whose entrance must have been covered for centuries by previous land movements. Inside, they had found the long-missing agreement between the then Pope and the Knights Templar proving that Seborga was an independent state. Breaking that story and her subsequent deft handling of the news that flowed from the discovery had earned Selene her present job with a well-established London broadsheet newspaper.

The story had everything: religion, royalty, politics, even sex. Well, at the very least it had love interest, in the shape of a beautiful Italian princess that any red-blooded man would kill for and her handsome teenage son who every young girl in the world would die for. Selene's reports had been syndicated around the world, giving her a reputation greater than her age or experience would generally merit.

Valerio, who she had met in Seborga four years previously, had briefly followed her back to London, but things had not worked out and he had returned to Seborga heartbroken. According to Ben's son, her new love was Danish and, he was told, more than a match for Selene in strength of personality. Ben loved the idea that his daughter might have finally met her match.

Selene was surprised but also slightly worried when she saw her father's number ringing her mobile while she was at work.

"What's up, Dad? Everything okay in Neverland?"

Ben disliked her continuous disparaging remarks about Seborga, mainly because he knew deep down that she loved the place, yet she could not resist suggesting that it was somehow unreal.

"Well, everyone is fine. Maybe not everything. How are you? Still loved-up?" he teased.

"I'm fine," she answered, avoiding his probing dig.

"Have you heard anything from Tom? He'd said he might come and visit us this summer, but I've not spoken to him since that call a couple of weeks ago."

"That's because he's been here in London, dossing on my couch, getting pissed, researching Estonian courting rituals and avoiding getting a job. I guess he'll come and visit you when either I kick him out or Miss Tallinn 2019 kicks him into touch. My guess is the latter will happen first because he's a slob. A handsome slob with a great bod, but still a slob."

Ben laughed, but behind this bravado he was also seriously worried by his son's seeming reluctance to join what he referred to as the 'real world' and act like a responsible adult. Only a few years away from thirty and no permanent job, place to live or any signs of a life plan, Ben wondered what his only son would end up doing.

"Was there a reason for the call, Dad, because I have a five o'clock deadline and still a day's work to do?"

Ben got straight to the point and explained the events of earlier in the day - the two phone calls they had received as well as subsequent unknown number calls which they had ignored. He also expressed his bewilderment as to what was going on.

Selene had been making notes as he talked, underlining the name 'Francois de Payen' twice and circling the words 'Knights Templar.'

"Let me make this deadline and then I'll start doing some digging. I'll call you back later tonight or in the morning before work. A doppo (later)."

Ben laughed at her Italian salutation, obviously learned from Valerio, said his own goodbyes and pressed end call.

Immediately after her father hung-up, something stirred in Selene's memory. She typed "Payen" into the search bar of her email account and one matching result came up. The bizarre press release had indeed also been sent to Selene, amongst the countless others that she received every day. After a glance at the headline, she had dismissed it as nonsense and moved on. Now she had more information on which to base some research. She flagged it 'unread' to deal with later and got back to her deadline.

What his son Tom had also told him, but which Selene had yet to, was that she had been in deep trouble at work. Her editor had received a complaint about something she had written and the individual that she had written about had threatened to get their lawyers involved. The accusation was that in one of her columns, she had placed a high profile actor in a restaurant at the same time as an actress with whom he was currently making a feature film. There had already been speculation in other media publications that there was an illicit relationship going on, although Selene's piece did not refer directly to this.

According to Tom, it transpired that this actor was actually on set, filming three hundred and fifty miles away in Scotland at the time Selene placed him in a smart London restaurant eating lutefisk. The celebrity was furious because his wife now believed the rumours. Their children were even being teased about it at school. Both injured parties were baying for Selene's blood.

Her editor had despatched Selene to the home of the star bearing flowers, a full apology and the offer of an unequivocal written retraction. Luckily, this had worked. The actor, having been down this path before, had no appetite for civil litigation, as he knew it could drag on for months or even years, would undoubtedly cost a fortune and result in little recompense. He just wanted to get on with his life and a prominent retraction and admission of the mistaken identity would take the heat off of him and allow him to do just that.

Tom seemed to have taken some pleasure from his sister's misfortune. Lately, he had noticed that her attitude toward him was superior and that she treated him mostly with contempt. This treatment spurred him to tell his father the further details surrounding Selene's situation. The source that had told Selene about the actor's dinner was her Danish boyfriend, a partner and front-of-house staff member at an upmarket Scandinavian eatery in Clapham, which was currently very much the place to be seen trying their signature dish, lutefisk.

This traditional Scandinavian dish was made with stockfish (air-dried cod), which was pickled in lye and rehydrated over several days to create an intensely fishy and gelatinous food that according to Selene, "Only the Scandis' could love." To her, it appeared as unappetising as it smelled and tasted, but the trendy Clapham-ites were lapping it up. Tom told his father that the men saw eating the odorous gloop as a macho challenge. Women, on the other hand, thought the trend for Scandinavian cuisine, started by the Copenhagen restaurant, Noma, meant that lutefisk was highly sophisticated.

One of Selene's colleagues had re-read several previous weeks of Selene's columns and pointed out to the Editor that there were no less than three other references to extremely famous people being seen at this same, otherwise unremarkable, Clapham venue in recent months. This frequency might have been accepted as just a coincidence, if it hadn't been common knowledge in the office that Selene's boyfriend was one of the proprietors.

"Perhaps this could be why this place is doing so well? They're getting free advertising in our publication," was her editors opening remark as she thrust the four clippings across her desk towards Selene. Head bowed, Selene looked submissive but inside she was fuming with anger, partly at her boyfriend, but mainly at her own stupidity. She'd been under pressure to meet several deadlines and had taken the titbits of gossip from Victor because it was great, easy copy.

"I've dumped the selfish Danish shit and put his best suit in bleach," Selene told her editor. "I've made a big mistake which won't happen again."

Not wishing to lose the opportunity to knock Selene down a peg or two, her boss reminded her of where she came from and the dizzying heights to which she had risen in such a short time. Gesturing to the busy newsroom outside her glass office walls where a dozen journalists toiled over laptops, the seasoned newspaper-woman began,

"You cut out a lot of the hard slog that most of your colleagues had to endure to get to this level on a national newspaper. Unfortunately, your fast-tracked career has meant missing out on making these kinds of mistakes early on. The others will have made these errors when it didn't matter too much. If you'd been reporting for the *Muddy Boot Mercury* then there would be no threat of anyone getting divorced and you wouldn't be facing getting the sack. We would have just had an angry mum and a couple of tearful children. You would, however, have received a dressing down like this one, which you would have remembered all your career."

Selene stood, ready to face the brunt of the verbal beating that she knew was coming, but hearing this self-evident truth did not make it any more palatable. She had even started to imagine how she could use her column to get back at the person who had caused this. She arrested these thoughts before they went any further, now very aware that this was precisely the same unprofessional journalism for which she already stood accused.

"You could have caused a divorce, broken up a family and got us sued. At this level, Selene, you only get one chance and that was yours. You've just had it. If anything like this ever happens again, your career is over at this newspaper. And remember, in this game, everyone knows what everyone else gets up to. No other editor would ever trust you again. I'd see to that."

Tearful but still angry, Selene turned to leave, with the following words following her out of the door,

"Check your sources or get your coat."

5. CONIGLIO ALLA LIGURE

Cecily waited until her call was picked up, which took several tension-building rings. When the call was eventually answered, she was greeted by silence.

"Roman? Is that you?" she said softly.

Immediately recognising her voice, a quiet man's voice confirmed slowly and deliberately,

"Si, Cecily," gradually picking-up enthusiasm the hesitant voice continued, "How lovely to hear from you. It's been a while."

"I have wanted to call every day but waited two months to allow you time to grieve and get things in order."

"That's thoughtful. It has been a difficult time. Anyway, how are you and where in the world are you?"

The pair exchanged small-talk and caught up on each other's lives before Cecily finally got to the reason for her call. Today's events had provided her with the perfect excuse to call, as she had wanted to do for weeks. Being able to disguise initiating contact with Roman as a plea for help could not have been better for her. She explained her predicament, emphasising that the blood orange trees under-production in Seborga were not only a problem for the principality itself, but for her also.

"Please come and help. It's less than an hour's flight. I am sure that you need a break, to get away from all the sadness. This little favour will be the perfect distraction. We need your wise counsel."

There was a long silence before he answered.

"OK. I'll check the flights and let you know when I will arrive."

After dinner, Cecily called Ben to tell him that she had an expert on blood oranges coming from Palermo who she was sure would be able to help with their problem. She said she would arrange a meeting, hopefully in a few days. While they were talking, Ben saw Selene's number come up on his phone and explained to Cecily that he would have to take this call.

"Bloody unbelievable," was Selene's opening.

"What is, darling?" Ben replied.

"This guy is some piece of work," she continued.

His daughter explained how she had found the press release inviting the media to the event in Seborga sitting in her junk email folder, which she had ignored when she received it a week before as the headline had sounded like a hoax. Once she had read the message, it provided many of the details that her father had not been able to supply. Most of this information had not been that much help. She had been able to confirm that Hugues de Payen had indeed been the first Grand Master of The Knights Templar. Also, that he had fought in the battle at Caessarea in 1101. Finally, it was following this conflict that the Holy Grail had been 'liberated' by the Templars. She also pointed out that any sixth-former with an iPhone and access to Google could have put that story together. After that, everything else sounded like a fairy story.

"However ... I did spot one tiny detail which turned out to be very telling indeed. The email address from which the release was sent belongs to a French company with a very interesting director."

The savvy journalist revealed how she had looked up the company, Exportations Bourguignonnes SARL (Burgundy Export Company).

"This outfit turned out to be a bit of a smokescreen for a Monaco registered company called, Vins Royaux SARL."

"Royal Wine Company," Ben translated for his daughter's benefit.

"There are only two controlling directors of this company, a man and a woman - the man owns ninety five per cent of the shares and is by far the most interesting. Flavien de Paine, who I believe is masquerading under the alias of Francois de Payne, is allegedly a notorious con man. Before that, he was a shadow director of a string of dubious companies who extracted cash from the EU and the French government for agricultural schemes, the outputs of which were never delivered."

Ben seemed unsure whether the news that this pretender was a con man made it easier to dismiss his claims, or just made him a more dangerous adversary. Either way, it was unsettling news.

"What do you think your colleagues in the media will make of his story?" Ben asked.

Selene paused to consider the very different agendas of the various news outlets and then replied,

"I don't think the mainstream media will touch the story, even considering the interest it generated four years ago. Any decent journalist would be immediately suspicious of the nature of his wild claims, which would make their fact-checking even more rigorous than usual. The fraud is alleged and not proven; also, it is a relatively small-time commercial crime, so I doubt they would report that either. That said, the more sensational online media might see something in it and Riviera press will almost certainly print something, as it's of local interest. I think it will be out there in the online media jungle but not in any high-profile way."

Ben thanked Selene for her help, said his goodbyes and hung up. When he ended the call with his daughter, Ben was utterly deflated. One of the many things that he loved about being in Seborga was that it was like being on a peaceful island. Here, he was shielded from nearly all of the pressures and stresses of the twenty-first century. Now all of a sudden, waves of unwanted problems were crashing down on them. Just when he thought he had found some peace, trouble seemed to be seeking him out again.

On his way to the Osteria to have dinner, Ben made the decision not to say too much to Alex about what he had learned from Selene, at least not until he had more facts and a better grasp of what was going on. He need not have worried because, as well as the normal local evening trade, Alex was working flat out serving another party of foodie visitors on a gastro tour of Liguria.

Thanks to the world-wide publicity generated four years ago, an increasing number of companies were now offering guided food and wine tours to Seborga. They were generally small groups of discerning, well-off visitors. It was good business for the Osteria and the village as a whole. The guests ate here, often slept in the B&B's and then bought local food and wine from the shops to take home. It had been the first tangible success of their economic regeneration plan and it made everyone feel that they were headed in the right direction.

Alex brought Ben his aperitivo: a fresh cold spina (draft) beer and a couple of stuffed zucchini flowers. She had no time for anything more than a brief,

"Hello, dar-r-r-ling," which she purred, drawing out the word.

Alex had begun calling Ben 'darling' soon after they were married. She thought he would like it because it sounded to her "so very English." In fact, Ben was slightly embarrassed about her expressing her affection so publicly, although he knew that that her use of the word was genuine and so said nothing, just in case she was offended. Also, the locals did not understand it and so part of him enjoyed it as something private between them.

He took a cold drink of beer and set about his zucchini. The visiting party of gastronomes had requested the traditional Coniglio alla Ligure (Ligurian rabbit with olives) and so that is also what Ben received. He used several slices of fresh, rustic bread to soak up the red wine sauce. The semolina flour scattered on the surface of the crust gave this local bread the contrast of hard and soft textures he liked so much. He was hoping for panna cotta, but the party had asked for Alex's baked susine fruits; a small local plum filled with an almond filling and marsala wine. By the time Alex was finished and the restaurant cleaned up, all she wanted to do was sleep. The conversation Ben was dreading was therefore avoided for now.

6. TONNO DI POMODORI DE MENTA

Cecily was waiting at Nice Cote D'Azur Airport where Roman's flight from Palermo was delayed forty minutes. She spent the time looking at the newspaper racks in the airport shop for signs of the story about the French pretender prince. There were small pieces in both the French *Nice Matin* and Italian *La Stampa* and a larger story with several photos on page five of the English language *Riviera News*.

The tone of the stories was factual, stating what took place and what was said, but they all made it clear that they were dubious of the claims. The articles were scattered with words such as "claimed," "unsubstantiated" and "alleged." Cecily knew that the same stories would have more detail, photographs and videos in their less costly online versions, which she would check later. Significantly, they all showed the Frenchman wearing his sash and crown with trumpeters either side of him, looking, worryingly, every inch a prince.

She grabbed copies of each of the newspapers and took her position at the arrivals gate alongside the drivers holding up notice cards, and these days, also digital tablets with clients names displayed on them. How many of those names were made-up, she wondered, to avoid unwanted attention for those too famous for their real names to be displayed in public? Cecily knew that journalists chasing a hot story were known to hang around the Cote d'Azur airport looking for famous names carelessly displayed by chauffeurs so that they could pounce on their unsuspecting targets. She needed no such notice for her guest.

Roman exited early, as he was travelling without hold luggage, and came striding straight towards Cecily. He wore his trademark straw fedora, faux tortoiseshell Ray-Bans and a smile not quite as broad as she had hoped. He was nevertheless clearly pleased to see her. They kissed on each cheek, both with a single hand on the others shoulder, with warmth but outwardly no more than that. To any onlooker, they could have been nothing more than work colleagues.

Cecily had brought the Bentley but not a driver. Roman hated being chauffeured, especially in what he described as a conspicuous open-topped car. Cecily knew that by Riviera standards her sapphire blue Mulsanne was reasonably understated, a thin white wall on the tyres being the only non-standard and arguably slightly pretentious feature.

Once in the car and with no driver to listen in, they could speak properly for the first time of months.

"God, I've missed you so much" Cecily gushed as soon as the car was rolling. She turned briefly to the passenger seat to gauge his reaction, but there was little.

"How is business?" he asked, changing the subject altogether.

She now regretted rushing things, although she had been longing to go further than she did. What she had actually wanted to do was to embrace her passenger and to kiss him long and passionately. Not doing so was a potential disaster averted, she realised.

"Business is great except that we can't get enough blood oranges to meet the demand for our new cosmetics range. On the other hand, the shortage has meant we haven't had to discount prices or spend money marketing and so profit margins are high on what we are selling."

"May all your clouds have such silver linings," he responded, now more affectionately.

A comfortable silence filled the car as she drove. After a while, she asked,

"Do you want to talk about the funeral?"

There was a short silence as Roman considered his answer.

"It went as expected. There were hundreds of people, most of them locals. Of the girls, only Patsy spoke to me properly and afterwards they both flew back to the US. I can't say it was easy, but I've had nearly a decade to prepare myself and there were no surprises."

"It can only get better from here," Cecily offered.

Roman sighed, turned to her and replied,

"I know that you are right, my friend, but it seems like a long climb up from down here."

Detecting his deep sadness and changing the subject again, Cecily proposed,

"I thought we would have a quiet supper on board the boat tonight and then drive up to Seborga in the morning. The sea temperature is lovely just now and you could have your swim when we get back to Menton. Tomorrow, after Ben has taken you to visit to see the orange trees, Alessandra is planning a fine lunch for us all."

She took Roman's silence as acceptance of her plans. The remainder of the short journey to Menton was conducted mainly in silence. Conversation in a convertible can be challenging, even a Bentley.

The boat's chef had been told to prepare Roman's favourite dish, something he had done many times before. The tuna linguine contained several ingredients that both French and Northern Italians would think odd. The sauce was made with cherry tomatoes, capers, mint and a good deal of fresh chilli. This hot sweet combination was a vestige of its Arab roots, Sicily being only a short boat ride from Tunisia and Libya. The fresh tuna steak was added only in the last few minutes so that it was just cooked through when the dish was ready. More fresh mint leaves and a few whole capers were scattered over the dish when it had been plated. Served with an ice-cold Sicilian Grillo white wine, it went some way to lift Roman's mood, believed his hostess.

The following day they drove to Seborga, this time on the boat's scooterino rather than in the Bentley, with Roman upfront. Whilst he was driving, Cecily briefed him on the situation,

"As far as Alessandra and Ben are concerned, you are a long-standing supplier of blood oranges from Sicily. They will no doubt have guessed that we must also be friends for me to get you to come all this way and help them. How do you want to play it?"

"Let's just leave it at that and see how things go," was his non-committal response.

When they had crossed the east-west running Autostrada on the climb up to Seborga, Cecily tapped Roman on his shoulder and gestured for him to pull over. They each took off their crash helmets and she pointed up to where Seborga sat perched atop a peak, still eight kilometres away and fifteen-hundred-feet higher. Roman had to squint in the light, but could see its pale pink, yellow and tan painted houses shimmering in the sun and its green ceramic capped church bell tower piercing upwards out of its centre.

Although he would soon learn that this was not the case, it appeared that nothing more than wild green countryside surrounded the village. Most of the land higher than Seborga was uncultivated mountain slopes and forests and was the home only to wild boar, eagles and snakes. It was land that had remained mostly unchanged for thousands of years. Above the village, it was too high and too steep for most things to grow and it could get very cold at night when the mists rolled down from the Alps. A few roads penetrated into these areas, but only so far as to lead to remote stone houses. The folk who lived in these homes presumably sought solitude and were hardy enough to pay the lifestyle price to get it, or were those too poor to afford anything better. Either way, there were not many people left living up there.

"It's certainly remote, but it's beautiful, at least it seems so from down here. It's easy to see why the Templars would choose it as a place to defend," he mused.

"Or, in the case of some more recent visitors, as a place to hide?" she offered.

Roman flashed her a knowing smile, the first sign of his mood lightening.

Fifteen minutes later, when the scooterino pulled into the village's main piazza, Ben could be seen sat on a bench under the shade of a tree. While reading messages on his phone, Don Gateau, Seborga's well-known three-legged cat, had slinked over from where he had been dozing in the shade. The colourful feline rubbed past Ben's trouser leg seeking a stroke, which Ben was happy to oblige. The cat was something of a metaphor for the village itself, Ben thought. Born a stray without much future, he was later further handicapped by a car accident which claimed one his front legs. However, Don Gateau was a survivor who made the best of what he had and managed to still appear cheerful and friendly. The villagers fed him, stroked him and he enjoyed a good life in the sunshine. He could even occasionally outwit an unwary rat or mouse.

Ben looked drawn, worried and absorbed, thought Cecily, as he sat there stroking the stray cat. She wondered if Ben and Roman would make for heavy-duty company at lunch in their current depressive moods. She stepped off the scooter, removed her helmet and shook loose her well-coiffured hair in one seamless movement, like a teenager from a Fellini movie, thought Ben. He was always impressed how easily she moved between her very different worlds: equally at home on a scooter or in a Bentley; in Michelin Star restaurants or with the gnarled old farmers in the Osteria.

As the Sicilian was introduced to Ben, he shook his hand firmly, but was clearly not paying much attention as he looked past him towards the cliff edge.

"Che bello! What a view!" he exclaimed, leaving Ben with Cecily and walking closer to the southwest edge of the piazza, which opened to the valley below.

"Is that the Bay of Nice down there?"

Ben confirmed that it was, "Before Nice, you can see Monaco, beyond it Cap Ferrat and then the Bay of Cannes. On a clearer day, you can see all of the Cote d'Azur to St Tropez. That's one hundred and seventy kilometres."

"It's extraordinarily beautiful," Roman said, turning to Ben. "I apologise, I must seem rude, but I have never seen a view quite like this and it took my breath away."

"Completely understandable. It had the same effect on me the first time I saw it."

Roman shook Ben's hand again as if to start their introduction over, this time fully engaged and smiling broadly. Gesturing for Ben to take Cecily's place on the seat behind him on the scooterino, the two men set off back out of the piazza. The Englishman gave hand-sign directions out of the village towards the new orange groves, while Cecily walked to meet Alessandra at the Osteria.

Only a few hundred meters out of the village, Ben pointed down a track off the road and Roman turned, slowing to little more than walking pace. When Ben indicated to pull over, they found themselves amongst a sea of fruit trees in blossom. The saplings had been planted equally spaced between the stumps of felled olive trees, the decaying matter shed by the former occupants helping to feed the new arrivals. The expectation was that the oranges would extract different minerals from the land and so thrive as a result of a type of long-term crop rotation. It was an unusual scene for Roman, whose trees were mature and growing on land where, for as long as he could remember, they always had. His property, however, benefited from volcanic soil thrown out by Mount Etna and so needed little fertilising.

Roman wandered slowly along the terrace, gently reaching out to hold a branch and inspect the delicate white flowers. He turned and looked at the land all around them and then up above them into the forests before announcing,

"Apes (bees) are your problem."

Ben looked alarmed and then confused.

"Vincenzo's Apes are damaging our trees? What, by driving down the terraces?"

Italian scooter maker, Piaggio, gave their tiny three-wheeled commercial vehicle the name Ape (bee) because its engine sounded like a buzzing insect. These cheap utilitarian vehicles first created after the Second World War had become ubiquitous in Italy, where they can navigate the narrow streets and farm terraces with ease. The Sicilian shook his head, realising that he was not explaining himself very well. He took off his hat to wipe his brow.

"No. You misunderstand. Not the vehicle Ape, but the honeybee. There is a shortage of wild bees to pollinate the blossoms."

Roman explained that he had read that an infestation of Asian hornets had spread into Liguria from France. These migrants attacked native bees, eventually weakening each colony until they could no longer defend their hive. The outcome was a decline in native bees and a consequent reduction in the pollination of many plants and trees. He also explained to Ben how climate change was impacting bees in various ways in many countries,

"It's a worrying problem."

Ben's heart sank at this news. He envisaged all his efforts, the huge investment and the hopes of the community, being thwarted by flying invaders from the East. He would be ridiculed by his neighbours who had put in all the hard work, castigated by the politicians who had put up the money and, worst of all, he would have betrayed Alessandra who had put her trust in his big idea. It was total humiliation. How had he not discovered this threat in his research, he asked himself?

Seeing his despair, Roman smiled broadly and quickly moved to reassure him.

"We can counter this problem with two simple solutions, but we need to move fast to help this year's crop. You must plant roses."

Ben was beginning to wonder if this crazy Sicilian had been brought here to torment him.

"We have spent four years growing orange trees and now you are suggesting we plant flowers? Why? To make our useless trees look pretty?"

"Yes. Exactly. Buy the most fragrant roses in flower and plant them at the end of every few rows of trees. These will bring in whatever wild bees are left living in the forest above. They will move from the roses onto your trees to collect more pollen. It is known as companion planting."

Beginning to feel a little more optimistic at this explanation, Ben asked,

"And the other solution?"

"Rent bees. Commercial bee-keepers – probably from France – will bring you hives and leave them near the groves. The roses will also help with getting them to work more quickly. The bee-keepers will be keen on your orange blossom in their honey and so shouldn't charge too much."

"This sounds like it can all be done quickly?" Ben asked him to confirm.

"Si. A week at most to get bees here if you get on the phone Monday and push things along. You can buy roses already in flower locally and plant them next week in readiness."

Ben could barely contain his relief. His instinct was to hug the Sicilian, but he thought better of it. This problem had been losing him sleep since it was first brought to his attention by the farmers. The problem was, although they carried in their heads many generations' knowledge of growing olive trees, they knew nothing about oranges.

Ben placed his hand on Roman's shoulder,

"This calls for a drink," he suggested.

Alessandra had set out a table in the shade of one of the big olive trees next to the Osteria and prepared a fine lunch. Bunches of lavender had been picked and set in glass jam jars and a bowl of fresh lemons had been placed at the centre of the table to help keep mosquitoes at bay.

A cooling salad of roasted beetroots, ripe peaches and crushed walnuts started things off, accompanied by one of Ben's prized bottles of Rossese. He had produced the wine himself using the vines owned by Prince Claudio. After much reading and experimenting with winemaking methods, he was now producing an aromatic red with good colour and finish, with a bite of earthy acid. Cecily liked it very much and thought it an improvement on many of the other local versions.

"Well done, Ben. From rough beginnings, that's a pretty good wine. It puts me in mind of a decent Burgundy."

Roman agreed with her.

"I also like it very much. It's perfect with this beautiful fresh salad."

Ben nodded in genuine surprise and gratitude for the compliments, but he still wondered whether it seemed slightly impertinent for him, as an Englishman, to be making Italian wine; like an Italian blending Earl Grey Tea. To make matters worse, he had been required by the European Union to register as an official Italian agricultural producer: effectively a farmer. This seemed like excessive bureaucracy to Ben, but without it, he could not sell a single bottle.

Prince Claudio, Alex's father, like most of the men in the valley who owned suitable land, had produced a small quantity of his own wine for family consumption. In reality, apart from his title and inhabiting the largest house in the village, the prince's life was little different from anyone else. He grew or hunted almost everything the family needed and sold surplus olive oil to pay for anything else. Without recognition of Seborga's independence, his royal title meant little. He could not raise his own taxes and so had no revenues. A principality in name only, Seborga's leaders had all the responsibilities of power, but none of the benefits.

Cecily emerged from the kitchen triumphantly carrying two more large plates. This time, sliced tromboncini with a salty white cheese from nearby Triora and a plate of fresh bread. Almost every bit of the white tablecloth was now covered in the most extraordinary colours; bright yellow lemons, dark purple beets, bright oranges, red peaches, pale green tromboncini and violet lavender flowers.

"It looks like Monet's palette," observed Cecily.

Roman was providing Ben with even more tips on how to get the best out of his orange trees while they waited for the two women to take their seats.

"No more talk of business until after lunch," ordered Cecily. "You have Roman's advice. Now he has earned his lunch in peace."

"He's earned more than his lunch," added Ben with a smile. "He may well have saved this year's crop and my reputation in this community along with it."

With Ben's sprits somewhat restored, Cecily became aware that Roman was beginning to relax in this new environment and the amiable company, as they all enjoyed a delightful lunch. Alex busied herself serving her main course of the classic rabbit with olives, which Roman declared was the best thing he had eaten this year. Panna cotta and coffee inevitably followed and chairs were pushed back to allow better digestion.

Ben had quickly begun to feel comfortable around the Sicilian. He exuded a quiet strength tempered with a natural charm. Alex noted that three bottles of wine had been consumed over lunch, not to mention the prosecco to start.

"Roman seems the perfect name for an Italian fruit grower," Ben ventured with newfound familiarity, fortified by Rossese.

Cecily seemed startled by Ben's out-of-the-blue statement and froze as if expecting an adverse reaction. She turned her body very deliberately and noticeably towards her male friend to witness his response.

Roman returned her stare for a second expressionless, but then turned to face Ben.

"My given name is Raman. I was born in Sicily, but my father was an Arab. My mother is Italian."

Cecily looked astonished. Roman rarely revealed any part of his past to strangers. Indeed, she had done business (and been sleeping with him) for a year before he had revealed this fact to her. While he was in this candid frame of mind amongst supportive friends, Cecily ventured a question that she had longed to ask but had previously dared not to. Conscious that to question an Italian man's or woman's dress sense was to risk a sharp rebuke or worse, she proceeded cautiously.

"As we are all being open and frank," she said wearing her best broad smile, "can I ask why, when you are in Palermo, you dress like a typical Sicilian businessman, but whenever you are away from home, more like an English gentleman?" As she spoke, Cecily gestured to the tan suede loafers, soft sage linen suit and plain white cotton shirt he was wearing.

Roman looked embarrassed by the question and a little agitated. He squirmed in his seat, adjusting the seam of his trousers. His lack of any immediate response made Cecily a little bolder and prompted her to drive home her point.

"Last time you greeted my yacht on the quayside at Palermo, you were wearing stiffly-creased white trousers, penny loafers with a gold bar and what looked like a Hawaiian shirt. It was so bright I could spot you the moment that we entered the harbour. You stood out like a beacon."

The Sicilian gave her a look somewhere between a grimace and a half-smile, but knew that she had him cornered and he would have to respond. He paused a little to choose his words but then spoke quietly,

"In Sicily, to them, I am still a foreigner in a strange land. Never completely one of them. And, when you live amongst wolves, it does not pay to dress like a lamb."

For a few seconds, Ben and Alex looked puzzled, but then quickly guessed what their new friend meant. Cecily laughed out loud at the idea that Roman had been conducting this deception all these years, but he remained stony-faced. He knew that he would now have no choice but to explain to Ben and Alex how he came to be in Sicily.

"You see, my father was a young fisherman from Tunis. When the Allies were preparing to invade Sicily from Africa in 1943, the Americans enlisted the help of the Mafia to organise partisans to divert the enemy. They even released a few influential mobster family members from jail and shipped them from New York to organise local resistance ahead of the Allied landings. My father was paid to covertly bring such a party of convicted gangsters from Tunisia to Sicily. Their journey, it turned out, was an exceedingly difficult one."

He described how the Allies had chosen the cover of bad weather for his father to make the crossing through the heavily patrolled waters, but the wind turned out to be far worse than anyone imagined. For twenty-four hours his father had battled with the wheel of his small boat, as the wind blowing up from the Libyan desert threw a relentless barrage of waves at the stern. Rolling-in from behind, each new breaker that appeared suddenly out of the darkness seemed taller than the one that went before it. The wall of water towered above the boat and each wave looked as though it would overwhelm them. Always at the last minute, the surge of water would lift the tiny fishing vessel high into the air, where it momentarily balanced on the crest before sliding down the other side of the wave. This terrifying rollercoaster had lasted all through the night.

The pampered Italian Americans were not used to threats they could not deal with using violence. Nature, it seemed, was harder than even the toughest mobster. A couple of them begged him to turn back to the mainland. One was so terrified that he was in tears and threatened to end it all by jumping overboard rather than face any more seasickness.

All the passengers had feared for their lives. They were, to some extent, reassured by the resilient, calm Arab who wore what seemed like a permanent grin, although Roman admitted this expression was more of a grimace. He was as scared as they were, but he also knew that to turn around into these waves would be suicide. No skipper of a small boat would usually have been out in such a storm, but he knew that he must keep the waves behind them and run with the sea.

"Miraculously, after nearly twenty-four hours non-stop wrestling with the helm of his boat, my father finally brought the crime bosses all safely into the harbour in Pantelleria. Once ashore, they kissed the earth and praised the Virgin. My father now found himself in another tricky position, which could have gone either way for him. On the one hand, he had witnessed these supposed tough guy mobsters reduced to tears of fear, something they could not risk him revealing to the locals, the Allies or anyone else. On the other hand, his skill and resoluteness had undoubtedly saved their lives and brought them safely back to their motherland. They were alive, out of jail and back in Italy. They had good reason to be grateful and had grown to like the smiling Arab. Their solution was to keep him close by them and prevent the boat from returning to Tunis."

"Your father was kidnapped by the Mafia?" stated Ben, summarising what he had been told in a few words.

"I suppose," answered Roman. "It was firmly suggested that he marry a nice girl from one of the families to ensure his silence further, as well as cementing his place in the community. Tunis had been ravaged by war and the people were starving. Sicily was beautiful and relatively prosperous by comparison. All of which was a long way round to explain why I call myself Roman and, as my ex-friend unkindly pointed out, I sometimes feel I have to dress like Al Pacino in the Godfather."

They all laughed, including Roman, who also made his hand into a mock gun, pointed it at Cecily and pulled the trigger finger.

"I will speak with you later," he added.

Alex tried to give Ben a secretive quizzical look, but she could not catch his eye.

"Sorry to be the bearer of bad news, but you will note that I have waited until we are about to leave so as not to ruin our visit," Cecily said, as she retrieved some folded newspaper pages from her large straw shoulder bag.

"I picked these up at the airport and, as far as I could see, they were the only coverage of the troublesome French guy pretending to be the Prince of Seborga. Frankly, there's not much to read and the tone is broadly dismissive" she summarised.

Ben's recently acquired euphoria quickly evaporated. For a couple of blissful hours, he had forgotten about the pretender-prince and the threat of his claims undoing all their hard work. Ben reached for the newspapers, but Alex put her hand on them to prevent him from opening them.

"Let's not spoil a lovely lunch. Just say goodbye to our old, and our new, friend and deal with that later."

7. CAPPON MAGRO TERRINA

Ben told Alex what Selene had discovered about Payen's background. As they each read the press clippings, they both confirmed that his daughters' journalist instincts had been correct: the bizarre briefing had generated virtually no significant media interest. There was more detail of the event online, which had drawn some surprised comments from the public, but it all seemed to have been a bit of a pointless exercise. If Payen's plan had been to mount something of a coup-d'état via the media, his first attack had been refuted by hard-nosed news editors. Nevertheless, it still left the question of why: why would someone go to so much trouble with no apparent return? As the couple both had things to do, they agreed to return to the issue later.

Ben's thoughts shifted to the renovation of the boutique hotel and spa on the edge of the village, a project which should have been completed by now, but was not. Thankfully, the skeleton staff at least had access to a working kitchen and the hotel was the only part of the project that required a substantial new building. Strategically-located just before the road from the coast opened into the piazza, it had previously been the site of two large old family houses. These had long been abandoned and were about to collapse in on themselves. Now demolished, the local stone was being reused to clad the front of the hotel and some of the ancient old wooden beams would become architectural features in the new reception.

Adjacent to the site were the ruins of a tenth-century monastery, built by the monks of the nearby St Lérins Islands in the Bay of Cannes. It was from this very building that the Order of St John had run their hospital for the sick knights and pilgrims going to and from the Holy Land. If the legends were true and the injured Hugh de Payen did bring the Holy Grail back to Seborga, this is where he would have been treated and therefore where the fabled relic would have resided.

The builders of the time were inclined towards functionality over aesthetics and so the monastery was robust but not architecturally decorative. The beauty lay in its simple craftsmanship and the history contained in each hand-picked stone. Building without modern mortar, its structural integrity relied entirely upon the choice of the perfect shaped stone to rest upon, with each stone aligned in perfect formation adjacent to its neighbours. The resulting jigsaw of odd shapes and subtle earth shades was indeed beautiful in its own right and Ben had grown to appreciate it.

What remained of this monastery needed to be very carefully preserved and incorporated into the new structure, which would allow it to function once again as a modern commercial building. This brief was tough to achieve; planning consents for the convergence of the various elements of Ben's complicated economic strategy had unravelled against a combination of Papal conservatism and Italian bureaucracy.

Students who would study and work in the kitchen of the completed hotel were arriving at the end of autumn. To get the funding for this element of the project, at least part of the hotel had to be ready by this time, as the student's degree courses and subsequent careers were not on a flexible timescale.

Tables and chairs had been set up on wooden decks amongst the remaining ruins of the monastery. These were sheltered by temporary awnings made out of recycled yacht sails, tied in place with old ropes which were weathered white with age, an idea Alex had stolen from her cousin's restaurant at Ospedaletti.

The tables with their white tablecloths looked like an archipelago of small islands floating, surrounded by cliffs made up of the ancient Templar ruins, with the sails as the final component of the nautical feel. Any incomplete building works were screened by cheap white cotton, drawn tight over wooden frames and fixed at strategic points. At night, lights were placed behind these screens, which gave a soft light and showed the details in the ancient stonework around them.

As pop-up restaurants go, this was a pretty cool one, Alex had decided. A blend of the permanent with the temporary: of ancient and modern. Until it was finished, this restaurant was going to have to be quite literally a moveable feast. The decor was mostly for the expected foreign foodie tourists, as Italians do not place much importance on restaurant interior. They are far more concerned about the quality of their ingredients and the cooking.

Alex's only son, Cristiano, was one of the junior chefs already working at the restaurant. A good looking boy, he had lots of female attention but only seemed to be interested in cooking. After four years of training, he was already showing considerable talent and had acquired good skill. He had inherited his mother's passion for cooking and learned some of her technique in the reinvention of classic Ligurian dishes. His specialities were derived from inventive ways of preparing and presenting locally caught fish. He was still experimenting with what he saw as his signature dish, a cappon magro terrine.

Cappon magro is a traditional Ligurian fisherman's salad, made with cold cooked vegetables and whatever fish and shellfish are to hand. It is a fiddly, time-consuming dish to prepare and difficult to make attractive on a plate. Cristiano's idea to create a layered terrine using the same essential ingredients was not only more economical and more pleasing on the eye; it also meant it could be prepared beforehand in quantity, kept cool and sliced as required. He was still testing versions with various side sauces and pickles, but the coloured layers in each slice already looked fabulous to Ben, who had been tasting them for him.

Although he had been reluctant to come to Italy, Cristiano had now embraced the culture and lifestyle. Only seventeen when he was lifted from the liberal streets of New York City and dropped into a conservative macho culture, it had been a baptism of fire. One minute his most significant threat was being knocked down by a car crossing the street, the next he was nearly killed by a charging wild animal. Without his mother's permission, his grandfather, Prince Claudio, had taken him on a boar hunt – seen as a right-of-passage in rural Liguria.

A know-it-all teenager, he had ignored all instructions about safety and found himself face-to-face with an enormous and angry wild boar. Ben's action of placing himself between the boy and the boar had saved the boy's life and had bonded and strengthened their relationship.

Cristiano's father, having served a short sentence for drug-related offences in the USA, was now clean and working as maître d' at one on Monaco's best restaurants. Father and son saw each other infrequently but were on reasonably good terms. Good that is, considering the trouble that his father had initially brought with him from America.

A couple of American goons working for one of his father's former drug suppliers had arrived threatening his mother and grandfather, trying to extract some of the money they claimed they were still owed. Vincenzo and his guards had dealt with them in a way only they could – quietly but effectively. Seeing how his father's selfish actions had brought real danger to the people he loved had changed the way Cristiano saw him.

Alex had turned down the opportunity to head-up the kitchen of the new restaurant, partly because she anticipated a potential conflict of interest with her son's position there, but also because she had begun to value the freedom of not being tied to a competitive commercial kitchen with lots of staff to manage. She was content in an advisory role at the hotel, as long as she continued what was effectively a one-woman show at the Osteria.

Alex had recommended someone else for the job, who had previously worked under her in one of her own restaurants in New York. Ecstatic about the idea of cooking real Italian food in Italy, the head chef had flown over, been interviewed and promptly landed the job. At the moment, Renata was still in New York working her notice before she could relocate to Europe. She would not arrive in Seborga to fill her new position at the hotel for another five days.

In the meantime, Alex was overseeing preparations for a soft-opening that would precede the official public launch, which would be in less than two weeks. Cristiano had everything well in hand as far as the kitchen was concerned and Alex only had to concentrate on front-of-house. Although this was new territory for her, everyone agreed that, considering they were working in a building site within a ruined monastery, she had done a fantastic job.

Ben was on his way to see what she had been doing at the monastery when a big black saloon almost struck him, passing far too close and travelling far too fast for the narrow road. The car then turned suddenly across his path, forcing him to step back out its way. The driver swerved into a parking space just ahead, leaving the rear of the car protruding a metre into the narrow road, barely wide enough for a single lane of traffic.

The aggressive driving had somewhat shaken Ben and he was annoyed at the total lack of consideration for any other cars that might need to get past. The driver and passenger stepped quickly from the vehicle without even acknowledging Ben or the fact that they had almost hit him, as if he were invisible.

The smartly-dressed Asian woman made the first mental connection for Ben to the events of the weekend in Seborga. From the descriptions he had received, this man must be Payen and his partner. The pair were now walking quickly away towards the central piazza, entirely oblivious to his existence.

“Excuse me!” Ben called while walking after them.

“You are Francois de Payen?”

The Frenchman turned quickly and faced his accuser with a challenging, arrogant look.

"Who wishes to know who I am?"

"My name is Ben Morton. My wife is Alessandra, daughter of the late Prince Claudio of Seborga."

Payen smiled and took two steps towards Ben. The woman looked slightly concerned.

"So, you are the son-in-law of the fake prince?"

The driving, crazy parking, the sudden realisation that he was facing his potential nemesis and now this insult was all too much for Ben. His instinctive English reserve was evaporating more quickly than he could come up with a plan to deal with this confrontation. The Frenchman stood hands on his narrow hips, waiting for a response, broad shoulders compensating for his lack of height in terms of a perceived potential threat.

Before Ben could speak, he became aware of another vehicle approaching at some speed from behind him, its rough diesel engine revving noisily. All of a sudden there was the sound of an almighty crash, like an explosion. He turned to see that an old squat truck had collided with the rear of Payen's car. The impact had pushed the black saloon further into the parking space, which it had not adequately occupied previously. The force of the impact had also smashed its rear lights and severely damaged the rear bodywork. The truck's thick steel bumper was grazed, but the vehicle looked as if it had already endured a hard-working life, with plenty of signs of previous scrapes and dents.

Slowly, the familiar imposing figure of Vincenzo lowered himself down from the cab. Claudio's former right-hand-man was an unusually tall Italian at almost two meters. Although he was somewhere approaching sixty years old, his work kept him fit and his expressionless confidence made him a menacing presence. He casually looked at the front of the truck and then briefly at the Mercedes' rear end. He appeared unruffled by the collision and displayed little concern for the damage to the

Mercedes. He began shaking his head slowly back and forth as if to demonstrate his displeasure with something.

"Quale idiota ha parcheggiato qui (What idiot parked that there)?"

Ben could barely prevent himself from laughing out loud.

Vincenzo pulled himself to his full height and walked towards the Frenchman as if he knew whose car it was. Payen had both his hands on his head and was shouting angrily,

"Merde. Merde. Merde!"

Vincenzo stood in front of Payen and unsmiling he reverted to French, before introducing himself as "Chef de la Défense Civille (Chief of Civil Defence)." The distraught car owner started to speak, but Vincenzo held up his hand to silence him.

"Ne dites rien qui puisse nuire à votre défense (Don't say anything to harm your defence)."

"Défense? Défense?" The Frenchman repeated, now clearly apoplectic with rage, his face red with anger.

Again, Vincenzo held up his palm to silence and began his verbal assault. He slowly and quietly explained that parking in front of the fire exit from the town hall was a serious offence and that leaving a vehicle where it could also cause an accident was significantly worse. He informed Payen that, under Seborgan law, there were fines of one thousand euros for both offences, before they got started on the damage to his truck.

The Frenchman now completely lost control and started shouting and swearing at Vincenzo, who firmly took two steps forward in response. Suddenly, realising the disparity in their sizes (Vincenzo towered over the Frenchman), Payen took one step back. Point made, Vincenzo turned his back on him, walked away, got back into the cab of the truck and started up the engine. Payen, thinking he now had him in retreat, followed at a distance, still babbling unintelligibly. Vincenzo began a manoeuvre which would eventually see the truck facing back the way it had come.

Rather than drive away, Vincenzo drove the truck straight at Payen, forcing him to dive out its path and fall roughly on the road. Narrowly missing its driver, the rust-covered truck slammed into his car again—this time in the passenger door. The Frenchman picked himself up and now stood in stunned silence, his black suit covered in dust and torn at one knee. A second aggressive reverse manoeuvre from the old truck caused Payen to realise that a third collision was imminent.

Payen was now waving frantically to try and prevent another impact, but to no avail. The front wing of the car was hit just behind the headlight, breaking the glass in the lenses and leaving glass shards on the ground. After three collisions, Payen's car was severely damaged. The front and rear lights were broken, rendering the vehicle illegal, as the Frenchman would discover before he could exit Seborga.

Now with a clear exit to drive away, Vincenzo stepped down from the truck's cab once more, smiled thinly and handed Payen a piece of paper before adding,

"Just to keep this completely legal, this is my name and address for your insurance. My cousin at the Carabinieri will discover where we can find you."

He turned and looked at his handiwork on the black car and said quietly so only Payen could hear,

"Oh yes, one more thing: that was a royal decree from the late Prince Claudio."

It looked as though Vincenzo was daring, and perhaps even hoping, that Payen would throw a punch or try to seek retribution in some way. For a moment, he looked as if he was thinking about it, but he did not. Vincenzo stepped up into the cab and drove slowly away in the direction from which he had come. Ben had watched all this drama with a mix of astonishment and amusement. Payen's female friend looked terrified. The Frenchman returned to where she was standing still staring at the piece of paper in his hand.

The clearly shaken pair then continued walking, unspeaking, in the direction that they had previously been heading, stunned by what had just happened and completely ignoring Ben. He watched them enter the Town Hall and he wondered what possible business they had there. As there are no secrets in Seborga, Ben would be sure to find out later. He would doubtless also hear more from Vincenzo tonight in the Osteria, but not too much more, as he had learned that Claudio's former right-hand man and royal degree enforcer dispensed information only on a need-to-know basis.

8. STOCCAFISSO ACCOMODATA ALLA LIGURE

The events of recent days were going around in Ben's head like clothes in a tumble dryer; some tangled, others floating free, but nevertheless moving together in the same muddled orbit. No matter which way he looked at the facts, Ben could see no pattern emerging; no two socks seemed to match. The newspapers brought by Cecily had provided no real information that they were not already in possession of.

At the same time, the Englishman was trying to deal with the potential crisis emerging in the blood orange groves, as well as keeping things moving forwards with his economic development plan. Ben couldn't remember a time when he had more to think about. He constantly worried about the consequences of things going wrong and felt under enormous pressure. His first job at a bank had come with a little responsibility, but nothing whatsoever on this scale.

Ben was not nearly competitive or brutal enough to have ever become a highly successful banker, but if he had not been photographed at the office party kissing the Chairman's daughter somewhat too enthusiastically under the mistletoe (kissed by, he claimed), he would likely still be in his job.

After that fiasco, Ben began teaching at the university where all he had to do was turn up, fill out the paperwork and collect his salary. No one ever questioned his performance and he certainly had no real responsibility, other than a nominal duty of care to students. This reminded him that in some people's eyes, Ben had failed even in that simple responsibility. The second accusation of inappropriate behaviour had made him look like a serial workplace lothario. Although that accusation was later proved false, Ben felt that some mud had stuck. His confidence and self-esteem had both been incredibly low until he met Alex.

Ben's university employer had sent him out to Seborga on a research project, to get him out of the way of the UK media while they dealt with the accusations against him. Although they now knew these accusations to be false, at the time the matter was potentially damaging to the University's reputation until their lawyers had negotiated a settlement. His resulting temporary sabbatical was now approaching its fifth year, as events took an unexpected turn when Ben met and fell for Alex.

As Ben's mind struggled to cope with the barrage of thoughts both past and present, Vincenzo arrived at the Osteria and headed straight over to his table, looking even more severe than usual,

"I must apologise. I did not wish to alarm you today with the truck, Professore. I received a call on my mobile phone to say that that French crook had been seen heading up the mountain road to Seborga and I immediately set out to prepare a reception for him. However, I had to drive over from Negi where I was working and so they arrived just before me."

"And the help you gave him with the parking. What was that about?" Ben asked.

"I must confess to being a little angry about what Payen has been saying about my beloved prince, Claudio. My head was controlling the brakes, but my emotions took over my accelerator pedal."

Ben looked a little concerned but offered,

"It is understandable under the circumstances, but won't there be repercussions?"

Vincenzo described how his cousin in the Carabinieri, along with a colleague, was waiting at the Seborga border for the damaged black Mercedes. Payen was stopped and given tickets for a total of eleven breaches of motoring law, two more for failing to carry all his documents and received a caution for being rude to a police officer, for good measure.

"As for his complaints against me, he was told to drive to Genoa and file a written report in Italian, but only after getting his car made one hundred percent road legal. That will keep him busy for a while until he cools off. I think he got the message."

Ben was smiling and trying his best not to laugh.

"He certainly got your message from Claudio. So, what do you think he is up to, Vincenzo?"

Vincenzo paused for a moment and then confessed he had no real clues as to what was going on except that,

"At the office of the Commune, Payen registered the purchase of some land in Seborga."

"Land? What kind of land?" Ben asked.

"Poor farmland. Land that no Italian in his right mind would buy. It was an old vineyard that has been left for decades without care. There was no market for wine grapes; the terraces were also too steep and narrow for anything else to be grown."

"Worthless," was Vincenzo's summary assessment.

Another 'odd sock' going around in the already full tumble dryer, thought Ben.

Alessandra arrived with a plate of aperitivo and two cold beers. She placed her offering on the table, gave her husband a peck on the cheek and her old friend, Vincenzo, an affectionate squeeze of the shoulder, before returning to the kitchen to get on with cooking for the eager diners. Ben's eyes followed her back to the kitchen door as he wondered how much she knew or cared about all this when there was food to be prepared. He knew that, come time for service, his wife had a knack of being able to leave all other thoughts aside and focus on the food. The result of tonight's intense concentration in the kitchen was stockfish stew, her particular version, with an addition of a pinch of chilli flakes added to the usual ingredients of tomatoes, potatoes, pine nuts and olives.

Stoccafisso (stockfish), whose name derives from the Norwegian stokkfisk (meaning stick-fish), are air-dried cod, perhaps a strange ingredient for a Mediterranean country, as cod are caught only in cold northern waters. The freshly caught cod are gutted and dried in the open on a wooden pole. It is not to be confused with another Northern Italian staple, bacalao, which is also cod, but preserved in salt. Preserved fish is invaluable to seafarers as a way of providing protein to sustain long voyages. Genoans, being famous traders and navigators, brought preserved cod to Liguria from the north many centuries ago. The inventive Italian cooks found ways to make the otherwise unpleasant stockfish flavour into a sought after dish to this day, something which Alex was especially good at.

9. MUGGINE ROSSA ALLA LIGURE

The perfume of orange blossom wafted up from the grove driven by a slight breeze from the sea far below. An almost imperceptible salty edge gave the sweet smell a dimension that Ben had never before encountered. He wondered if Cecily was aware of this phenomena and if it translated into the products made from the fruits. He made a mental note to discuss this with her later.

The white beekeepers suit Ben had been given to wear was making him feel almost as uncomfortable as the thought of encountering the insects themselves. Although not especially concerned about bees in the singular, the prospect of fifty thousand stinging insects all jealously protecting their queen filled him with dread. However, he did not feel quite as much trepidation at the prospect of the bees, as at the thought of facing the community of Seborga if his blood orange plan failed. So here he was, dressed head-to-toe in protective clothing on an unusually hot windless morning.

A spot had been found at the side of one of the orange groves where a beekeeper, who had driven the two hours from Provence, could unload the six hives. Smoke from a canister had been circulated to calm the bees down so they could be lifted carefully and placed on wooden pallets stacked there for that purpose. Other hives were transferred one at a time to Vincenzo's Ape for a short ride to terraces further around the valley.

The previous few days had been spent planting fragrant white roses at the end of every third terrace of trees. These would need daily watering, but this was a small price to pay for their contribution in attracting wild bees from the forest above, something that had already been seen happening. Combined with the addition of the captive bees, the plan would hopefully boost orange blossom pollination and ensure a much better crop that year. The hope amongst the locals was that the wild bee population might recover and preclude the need for the mercenary French imports. Ben and Cecily were less concerned about the relatively small cost. They both knew that there was virtually no price barrier in the global industry of beauty and age-defiance, which is where most of the oranges would end up being used.

At Cecily's request, Roman had returned from Sicily to witness the event and see that all went well. In contrast to Ben, he wore no protective clothing and could be seen waving away the occasional bee with his hat, showing little or no concern. Roman had another reason for his return trip, which he had yet to share with either Cecily, Ben or Alessandra. He had, however, suggested another lunch in Seborga on the pretext of tasting more of Alessandra's cooking, a claim which was not entirely without substance.

Ben was glad to be out of the white beekeepers suit, but desperately needed a shower, so sent Roman ahead to the Osteria to meet Cecily. She had arrived fifteen minutes earlier and was in the kitchen, helping Alex prepare lunch. Cecily had – by arrangement with Alex – gone to the quayside market at Menton early that morning. There she had bought fresh red mullet, anchovies and squid from a fisherman who they both used regularly.

Alex had treated the sliced squid and small fish to a shower of Menton lemon juice and then to a coating in seasoned flour, before laying them out on paper towel ready to fry. The mullet would be pan-fried in olive oil with garlic, cherry tomatoes and

Taggiasca olives, with some flat-leaf parsley thrown over before serving. A mixture of fresh summer vegetables from her orto had been drenched in oil, seasoned and then griddled before being left to cool. A final squeeze of lemon and a drizzle of oil would freshen these before serving.

Alex did not know how long it would take to unload the bees and get things settled, so she had chosen a relatively easy lunch to prepare, one which would only require ten minutes to cook at the last minute. Everything was in place so that the two couples could share a glass of wine and update each other on their lives.

Since their previous lunch, where Ben and Alex had met Roman for the first time, Alex had been longing to ask Cecily more about the mysterious Sicilian and specifically, if their relationship was strictly professional. However, she did not feel they knew each other well enough yet and so was waiting for her to bring it up first. Cecily was equally desperate to talk to someone like Alex about Roman, but dare not until she was sure that the careful Sicilian would not object to a third-party being in on their secret. She knew he would be angry about his private life being discussed behind his back and so dare not risk him finding out. Consequently, they both stayed on safe ground, talking about restaurants, food and Cecily's beauty products.

Roman stuck his head around the kitchen door as if requesting permission to enter. He was given a smile, a cold beer and was then shooed-away by Alex with the absolute authority only a former Michelin Star chef could muster. Ben found him sat outside drinking his beer in full sun at just after midday; clearly, a man well used to the heat, but perhaps not the emotional temperature that could currently be found in Alex's kitchen.

"No bee stings?" he enquired as Ben approached.

"Not one. The French bees seemed to know that we were all foreigners and kept to themselves."

Roman laughed out-loud at what he saw as Ben's old-fashioned, English sense of humour.

“Shall we move to our table in the shade?” Ben suggested, gesturing towards a table set up under the canopy, with jam jars filled with fresh flowers and a basket brimming with two types of freshly baked bread. The two men settled naturally into chairs next to each other, looking for all-the-world like they had known each other all their lives.

For a man who had not known much close male friendship, Ben felt instinctively at-ease in Roman’s company and yet, on the face of it, they had so little in common. They shared neither nationality, religion, career, nor status. Roman was an Italian Arab and so Muslim by default if not by choice, and clearly a man of some wealth and prestige in his native Sicily. Furthermore, Ben had not been separated from his father’s homeland and his birth family. What did they possibly have in common? Why did they both seem to have such an affinity with one another, Ben pondered.

The sounds and smells of frying fish broke both of their quiet trains of thought. Moments later, a large oval ceramic bowl, which had been Alessandra’s mothers, appeared from the kitchen carried in two hands by the chef herself. Cecily followed close behind with two plates of roasted vegetables. The pale blue bowl was piled high with crispy fried fish; the anchovies had curled in the heat and were interlocked with the circles of squid. Large wedges of lemon were placed all around the edges of the bowl. Alex pointed Ben towards two bottles of chilled Pigato nestled in an ice bucket on a nearby cabinet, which he retrieved and set on the table.

Roman sat up in his chair and placed both hands on his stomach as if to prepare it for what was to come. Surveying the table before him, he announced with genuine enthusiasm, “Well worth a plane ride from Sicily.”

Two hours flashed by with talk of bees, oranges, face creams, ways of preparing anchovies and even a brief comparison with Ben’s beloved kippers, a food product dismissed as primitive by both Italians and the only other

English voice. Ben and his kippers were out-voted by those in favour of the anchovy as the king of preserved fishes.

Coffee arrived signalling that the lunch was drawing to a close. Roman cleared his throat and sat up straight as if to gain everyone's attention for an important announcement. On seeing this, Cecily looked as though she might jump to attention. She appeared simultaneously perplexed, terrified and excited, but all three of these emotions quickly evaporated and she seemed physically deflated as the subject of Roman's revelation became clear.

"I have been doing some digging into your French interloper, and I have some bad news."

He stalled, hoping this pause would help Ben and Alex to steel themselves for what was to come.

"I'm afraid signor Payen is a much more dangerous man than you might have imagined."

Cecily sank back into her chair, looking, Alex thought, at once both relieved and crestfallen – it was hard to tell which.

Ben's response on the other hand could hardly have been more evident. He looked like he had been kicked in the gut by a horse. When Alex saw her husband's eyes darken and sadden, she instinctively reached for his hand.

"My contacts in Sicily quickly found out what he has been up to because he has dirty money which is surprisingly hard to hide, clean or spend, but they are the experts in that area."

Roman also admitted that his contacts had a certain admiration for Payen's exploits, considering him a clever man operating an innovative scam. Ben listened with growing alarm at the prospect of an adversary that was admired, by what sounded like, the Sicilian Mafia. Whatever it was they liked about Payen, their admiration could not possibly be a good thing, he quickly concluded.

Under a descending cloud of doom, the three listened as Roman disclosed what he had found out.

"Payen has made millions over the last couple of years from faking fine French wines."

Roman's story was beginning to sound familiar to Ben, who had spent most of his adult life savouring and learning about French wine.

"Is this the guy who sold thousands of bottles of fake Romanee Conti right under the noses of the growers?"

"The very same," confirmed Roman.

Ben's memory came flooding back to him. He continued,

"A couple of years ago, a man rented an unbelievably beautiful old chateau from one of the Romanee Conti family growers. The house was their original family home but had become too expensive to maintain and heat in the winter, so they had built a modern house nearby and rented the old one to wealthy foreigners during the summer. He was there for several weeks over two summers, during which time many foreign guests came and went.

"Whilst they were staying with him, he arranged tastings for his guests with the grower who had rented the house. They were said to be tasting real Romanee Conti, in genuine vine groves, with experts.

"These guests were all Chinese and only Payen had an interpreter to understand what was being said between the winemaker and the tasters. Both the growers and the potential buyers were in the dark, totally reliant on what they were being told by a very sophisticated and charming Chinese woman."

"The woman who has been seen with Payen?" Alex blurted out.

"Almost certainly, the very same," confirmed Roman.

The three were starting to join up the dots in the story, as Roman continued with what he had learned,

"Payen had targeted high net-worth individuals because they were looking for big-return investment opportunities. They knew nothing about wine but liked the idea of owning a prestige, classic, western, branded product."

“And they could speak neither English very well nor French at all,” guessed Alex.

Ben cut-into the conversation, now beginning to understand the audacity but also the simplicity of the scam,

“No, but they could read a Google map and search for a wine label. They wouldn’t have been entirely stupid if they could afford that kind of investment. They would know that they were in Romanee Conti, France, at an easily identifiable chateau, sampling a genuine labelled product. Plenty of photographs had been posted on Facebook and Instagram showing Payen with the Romanee Conti chateau in the background. It seemed for all the world that they were buying a sound investment direct from the grower, cutting out the wine merchants and auction houses.”

Roman told them that there was now a warrant out for his arrest in France as they wanted to question him about this fraud, which was estimated to have earnt him tens of millions of euros.

“I am not surprised,” replied Ben. “One bottle could be worth up to five thousand euros, so just two hundred bottles sold would net him a cool million. A scarce vintage could be a half-a-million for one bottle. Also, the excellent stuff is seldom actually drunk and so few people in the world would know what it tastes like. It’s an untraceable and portable investment. Its value is all in the perception. Anything, like this scam, which undermines that perception, is a serious threat to investor’s values and the brand owners.

“So now that we know what he does,” Ben concluded, “what possible connection does any of this have to Seborga?”

Roman summarised the remainder of what he had discovered. It seems that it had taken a while for the warrant to be issued because the French police were unsure that there was a criminal case to answer. However, the Romanee Conti society and the enormously powerful French wine growers lobby had pressured the Government to act. He explained that de Payen had indeed faked the Romanee Conti, but that the scam itself – the execution, the victims, the transactions – had all been made overseas and the money never came back to France. His company is registered in Monaco. No French citizen had complained of being conned, and indeed, no foreigner had made a formal complaint in France.

"What was the crime? Where was French law broken?" Roman summarised.

The authorities in Monaco were unlikely to be suspicious of a company registered there receiving large sums of money from abroad, as there was hardly anything unusual about that. The French could not even prove any deception at the Romanee Conti villa tastings because the wine they drank was the real thing. If there was a crime, it was committed outside of France and the direct victims were not French.

"You have to admit that it's pretty clever," proposed Cecily. "He used their own house, staff and product samples to defraud them."

The winegrowers claimed all types of brand infringement and copyright breaches, but the police pointed out that these were all civil matters and thereby outside of police jurisdiction. The winegrowers would have to get Payen into a civil court to press that claim and that seemed highly unlikely. In desperation, and to avoid the accusation that they weren't doing enough, the police came up with an obscure law about selling wine without a license, exporting without a license and failing to keep records of overseas transactions. The arrest warrant sighted these three charges.

"I think I might have found something significant that might explain his fleeing to Seborga," Roman finally revealed. "None of the charges in Payen's arrest warrant are serious enough to be pursued under a European arrest warrant; so long as he stays away from France and remains in Italy, their police won't be able to touch him. He's also got lawyers in Paris fighting the warrant and, because the charges are flimsy at best, they might eventually even get them dismissed."

Cecily then further speculated: Seborga was within thirty minutes of Monaco where his business was based and less than an hour from the French border and neither had border passport checks. If he needed to, he could quietly visit either place with little chance of detection. Also, even if the French pressured the Italian police – between whom there was apparently no love-lost – they would probably view arresting someone who claimed to be a member of the royal family of the disputed principality of Seborga as far more paperwork than it was worth.

Cecily questioned, "If you were Payen or Paine, or whoever he is, where would you go?"

"No one has seen him or heard from him since Vincenzo customised his car for parking in the wrong place," Ben responded.

At least Roman had provided a potential motive for a man on the run for coming to Seborga, which was a start. Ben also now knew that this man was both cunning and potentially dangerous to the village, having no qualms about breaking the law. Ben's biggest concern by far was how the politicians who had promised grants for Seborga's regeneration would react if they heard this news. He would not have to wait long to find out.

10. FRITTO MISTO

Salvatore Benigni had been appointed as the civil servant handling the Italian government's support for the Seborga Rejuvenation Scheme, as he had himself titled it. His appointment to this role had been arranged rather than achieved on merit.

Benigini had trained as an accountant, but had become a career bureaucrat because, although the pay was less in the public sector, the hours were better – much better. In truth, he was only in his office for around four hours, four days of the week. Ben had come to learn that the only time he was able to contact Benigni at his office in Genoa was between the hours of 9.30 - 11.30 am and 2.30 - 4.30 pm, Monday through Thursday. Even during those times, Ben had found that there was only a fifty per cent chance of obtaining a response, which is why he was astonished to receive a call from Benigni's office at 8.30 am.

"Professore Morton?"

The Italian sounded highly agitated but was still maintaining strict formal protocol despite the two men having now spoken several times a month for over three years.

"Salvatore. How may I help you?" answered Ben, already anticipating and dreading the answer.

"I am extremely concerned to see several local media stories about a Frenchman who claims that he is the true prince of Seborga. Furthermore, he claims that the late Principe Claudio had no legal right to hold the referendum. It was that vote which ultimately led to my government's substantial and ongoing investment in Seborga. Exactly what do you know about this man?"

Ben had anticipated this call. He was also aware that if he did not handle this well a similar, but probably less polite, phone call would soon follow from Benigni's French counterpart in the EU office in Strasbourg. However, he had a plan to deal with Salvatore. During the past couple of years, Ben had also learned the reason for the civil servant's regular absences from his desk. He liked to eat well and often. Ben also suspected, but could not be sure, that the unmarried, overweight, bald and boring civil servant might also linger at the more louche bordellos to be found in the same district as some of the absolute best eateries in Genoa.

"Why don't you come to lunch at the Osteria tomorrow and we can set your mind at ease on this crooked French conman? We can call it a site visit for a progress report. Alessandra is preparing your favourite fritto misto and trofie pesto."

"Excellent idea, professore. I happen to know that there's a train that gets into Bordighera at 11.30 am. I will be on it."

Ben knew that once Salvatore had Alex in his sights and her pasta in his belly, he would be putty in her hands. She knew precisely which of his Italian male buttons to press. He would go home brim-full, half-drunk and dewy-eyed, having forgotten why he had come in the first place. However, he also knew that if the news of the pretender to the crown reached his EU counterpart in Strasbourg, it would be quite a different matter.

In the meantime, Ben had pollination activity to check on. At the orange groves, he found Vincenzo and some of the other growers standing around staring at the hives.

"The last French bees are on strike," was the assessment of one his neighbours.

"They refuse to come out and work," confirmed another.

"The roses seem to be doing their job however," added Vincenzo. "There are more wild bees about but still not enough to do all the pollination on their own."

As well as all his other roles, Vincenzo was a farmer like almost everyone else in the village. He had his parcels of land to look after, as well as a self-appointed and unpaid role overseeing that which was inherited from Claudio by Alessandra. In his mind, Claudio had tasked him with overseeing the care of his daughter and her inheritance. Vincenzo had as much, if not more interest in the success of the blood orange trees as anyone else.

Ben recalled that the beekeeper had warned that the bees might need a few days to settle into their new surroundings, but try as he might, he could not convince the gathered farmers that their hired-in bees were not just indolent, work-shy French socialists. He finally agreed to call the beekeeper in the morning if they had not shown themselves for work that day.

As he was walking towards the groves the next morning for a bee roll-call, Ben saw something that stopped him in his tracks. The colossal crane, which had become a fixture of the skyscape since the renovation of the monastery had begun two years earlier, was being dismantled. Several sections of the steel framework had already been lowered to the ground and were being loaded onto a truck. Men in yellow hard hats scurried around, pulling on ropes connected to pulleys. Ben changed track and approached the crew, honing-in on the man with a clipboard.

“Where are you going with that crane? The job is nowhere near complete.”

Ben was answered with a shrug and a palm-upwards gesture that he knew meant that the man had no idea.

“Il capo (the boss),” was all the man had to add, pointing to a car in which a besuited young man was busy talking on a mobile phone. Fortunately, the man spoke some English and with the help of Google Translate on his mobile, Ben was able to obtain the explanation he feared. Their European Union paymaster had told the crane operators that their contract was on hold until further notice. That the crane cost a thousand euros a day and the company could not afford to have it standing idle when they had paying work for it elsewhere.

Ben was devastated. The EU had turned-off the money tap without warning or consultation. He was well aware of what some of the EU bureaucrats in Strasbourg thought of his economic plan. He had also learned from Benigni that one of them referred to it privately as the 'Italian ransom' and to him as the 'English dreamer.' Delon viewed the money that he was tasked with distributing as little better than blackmail: a ransom for not shining a spotlight on the current view of many to leave the European Union (and a costly ransom it was, at that). They were hoping to find some excuse to stop paying out for what they saw as an Italian agricultural fantasy.

They were not, however, expecting their prayers to be answered by a French conman, but they were more than happy to accept this unexpected gift. The officials had found work for a graduate intern who they set-to scouring the internet for any source of scandal which involved anyone connected to the Seborga project.

What the EU bureaucrats expected they might find was either bribery or contracts not awarded on merit, which would allow them to delay the project budget until it fell apart completely. Something as significant as a pretender to the crown who could undermine the legality of the whole deal was better than their wildest dreams. Ben imagined them in their glass towers in Brussels or Strasbourg dancing a jig while toasting each other with Champagne.

Delon was expecting Ben's call,

"Monsieur Morton. Quelle surprise. And what can I do for you on this wonderful day?"

"Monsieur Delon. You know very well why I am calling. What I want to know from you is, how widespread is this suspension of spending? Is it just the crane you are stopping or are you planning on wreaking more havoc? There are farmers and families here whose entire livelihoods are at stake."

"You English academics are so unlike our own. A French professor would have skipped around a subject for hours, while you get straight to the point. I like it and so I will be equally candid. I have introduced a total and indefinite block on all spending. Indeed, if it turns out to be true that your scam – excuse my English – I meant plan, had no legal basis, we will look to recoup the money already paid from those we deem responsible. Furthermore, I don't give a centime for your grubby Italian peasants or their idiot scheme of growing oranges for make-up."

Ben hung up, knowing further dialogue was pointless and he didn't want to give the arrogant Frenchman the satisfaction of hearing him squirm. He could not, however, miss the irony of his situation. His grand plan seemed likely to be unravelled by a conman and could result in him being slandered with that name himself. Ben felt as though a Chernobyl-like cloud was hovering over his head, ready to rain poison on his plans for the village, his neighbour's livelihoods and possibly his marriage as well.

In an internal audit of his own folly, Ben totted-up the likely outcomes that could be lain firmly at his door:

Number one, he had persuaded the village to switch from olive production to blood oranges, which may possibly never bear enough fruit and was an agricultural decision that would take years to reverse.

Number two, a brand new orange production, packaging and marketing plant had been built, but had no product to process.

Number three, an ancient Templar monastery was only half-way converted into a hotel and catering school, into which students were already waiting to enrol.

Number four, his wife and step-son had forsaken their royal heritage going back eight hundred years.

Number five, twenty-plus million euros had already been spent and the EU might now try to claim it back from Alex and himself.

All Ben could think was that the horrors his wife had endured with her first husband would seem like a minor hiccup compared to this total disaster. His immediate instinct told him that the only sensible course of action was to run away before the whole thing imploded. But to where? He asked himself.

Seborga viewed from the approach road.

Drawing by Linda McCluskey

11. CANNOLI WITH EARL GREY TEA

The original events which had led to the current crisis in Seborga had coincided with the election of a new government in Italy. In order to secure the deal to rejuvenate Seborga four years earlier, Ben had played upon the then incumbent Prime Minister, Antonio Mazzon's concern the debacle over independence would detract from his core election strategy. He was happy to pay to make the Seborga problem go away quickly. His opponent, Sergio Mastroianni, wanted to negotiate a form of partial independence that would see Seborga a Principality within Italy but outside of Europe. Mazzon later acknowledged that he believed that averting the loss of Seborga from the union was a turning point in his overall campaign and key to his eventual victory. Whether that event actually played a part, no one can be sure, but Mastroianni seemed well aware of the role that Seborga appeared to have played in his failure to become Prime Minister. With hindsight, he recognised that he had underestimated the symbolic power of the underdog in winning over public opinion.

Ironically, many of the media channels avidly covering what became known as 'Seb-exit' had been owned by Mastroianni. The threat of the tiny principality of Seborga voting to leave both Italy and Europe had been seen as a microcosm of broader dissent in Europe. The street corner newspaper vendor from Genoa had built a billion euro fortune from taking over and redefining failing mainstream media organisations. Unfortunately, in this particular race, he had backed the wrong horse. It was a mistake that he was determined not to make again.

Mastroianni was politically about as far right as it was possible to be; at least privately if not always publicly. At the time, he had wanted to see Seborga gain recognition of its Principality status and for its royal family to continue. Not just because that was the opposite goal of his opponent, but also because he could have his very own Italian version of Monaco right on his doorstep; a puppet state with him pulling the strings.

He also liked the idea of being cosy with his very own royal family and saw this as a clear statement to the world of his power and influence. The newspaper mogul envisaged himself being regularly photographed attending a dinner with a princess or boar shooting with a prince. For a lowly street vendor, it would be the pinnacle of his career. It was the kind of credibility money could not buy.

One of Mastroianni's primary weapons on his rise to power had been an extensive network of family and friends. Himself one of nine children, he had over thirty nephews and nieces and had himself lost count of the offspring of his many cousins. He had six children from three different wives, some of whom now had grandchildren. He shrewdly invested in their education, engineered their employment and their promotions, then waited to reap his harvest. There was virtually no walk of Italian life into which the tendrils of his family web did not penetrate.

The savvy street merchant-come-media-mogul had also built another network of people who 'owed' him, by pressuring his editors to thrust those individuals craving publicity into the limelight but keeping those who wanted to avoid it, out of it. He had the power to make or break careers, marriages and businesses.

Mastroianni was also a brilliant self-publicist with a knack for getting himself in the right places with all the important people and could orchestrate careers and success for those he favoured. However, if he helped you to the top, you had a debt to pay. He played the long-game and was happy to let rising stars have their moment in the limelight, knowing that the taste of success would make it even harder to give up.

His willingness to throw away the rule book for independent unbiased reporting and play fast and loose with media monopoly regulations had also made him some powerful enemies. The traditional press and the educated political elite despised him, but by-and-large the Italian masses adored him. He was a self-made man who had proved that being a poor boy from Genoa did not mean that you couldn't succeed. If he felt like showing off his wealth with brash extravaganzas in the company of beautiful young women, who could blame him? At least, this was what the average Italian appeared to think. Bending the rules to suit the circumstances was all part of the game of life as far as they were concerned.

The call that Mastroianni had on-hold from one of his numerous nephews was expected, but the timing was unwelcome. It came as he was enjoying his afternoon tea and cannoli. This 4 pm tradition had originally consisted of coffee and canestrelli, the sweet biscuit of choice for poor Genoans. This habit changed in the seventies when the then up-and-coming businessman watched The Godfather movie and thought that the Sicilian's favourite, cannoli, was more befitting for the power-broker role he envisaged for himself. Around the same time, he had also watched the original movie of Ocean's 11 featuring the Rat Pack, of whom Dean Martin was the character he identified with most. Martin was an infamous womaniser and hard drinker of whiskey, but also less well-known for his love of English tea. After that, at 4 pm every day, he enjoyed the peculiar international combination of Earl Grey tea and cannoli, which he now saw as his trademark.

"How is your mother, my sister and her commi husband? What can I do for you?" The second question arrived before the caller had a chance to answer the first.

"They are both fine, uncle. You asked me to keep you informed on the Seborga project. I have big news."

The civil servant waited a while, assuming that he would have piqued his uncle's interest in this conversation.

"Get on with it then," the politician urged.

"I had been keeping a close eye on things in Seborga, as you requested. My diligence paid off when I discovered some small articles in the local media that few others seem to have noticed."

"No doubt you have done an excellent job, Sergio. Now, what the hell is this about? I am a busy man."

"I know that uncle, but you will find this interesting."

Family or no family, Mastroianni's patience was wearing thin.

"I will be the judge of whether it is interesting when you tell me what it is. Now get on with it, or I'm going to hang up."

"A Frenchman claims he is the true prince of Seborga," Sergio blurted out.

"A Frenchman, you say? Tell me what you have learned."

The civil servant repeated the conversation he had had with Ben and Alex about the alleged conman turning up in the village and claiming the crown of Seborga as his own. He explained how Ben had reassured him that it was just a hoax: a stunt to deflect attention from the Frenchman's other misdemeanours in his home country.

More importantly, he told Mastroianni, very soon after his visit, he had received a call from his counterpart at the EU. The official had informed him of what he already knew about this French pretender, but crucially that he was immediately suspending all expenditure on Seborga until the situation was clarified. "He made it clear that he did not expect clarification to be any time soon, if ever. He went as far as to suggest to me that 'you Italians' would be wise to stop any further investment in Seborga until there was an enquiry."

The Italian government had agreed to fund only those elements of the overall plan relating to education and tourism. These made up less than twenty per cent of the total budget. Most of this investment would not be made until the infrastructure to house them was in place, so little of Italy's money had yet been spent. The bulk of the funds used so far had come from the EU, which had gone on the big agricultural and construction projects. Salvatore still held more than ten million euros from Italy in reserve, waiting for the completion of the works now underway.

"Monsieur Delon in Strasbourg has made his dislike for the Seborga project very clear to me, he is revelling in shutting it down."

After a short silence, Mastroianni asked,

"Who have you told about this?"

"Only you, uncle."

"Good. Keep it that way. Well done, Sergio. You're a good boy. You did very well."

Although his nephew thought "good boy" was a strange way to address a man of forty-five years, a compliment from Mastroianni was worth a little embarrassment.

Mastroianni's ability to acquire state intelligence and even pull some of the levers of government, despite losing in the last election and having no official role except as leader of the opposition party, showed just how dangerous he was.

The canny politician knew that the game was now in play.

12. ROMANEE CONTI & COKE

During his two summers entertaining Chinese buyers in France, Payen had learned some surprising things about them. Firstly, they saw no problem in investing in expensive wine, although few drank it (at the tastings many said they just did not like the flavour). On one occasion, a Chinese billionaire even brought along a can of coke to dilute the wine before tasting. It was an act of savagery just too much for their sensitive French hosts, who refused to pour any further samples into the Coke. Payen only managed to rescue the situation by lying that the man had a medical condition affecting his ability to process alcohol at that strength.

Nevertheless, the Chinese enjoyed the ritual and ceremony of the tastings and revelled in joining in the strange traditions: the sniffing of the cork after careful extraction, the pouring and swirling of the red liquid, holding the large glass up to the light to examine the colour, more sniffing and finally the loud, exaggerated slurping of the wine (which they thought hilarious). The Chinese could not, however, countenance spitting out the residue into a stainless steel bowl. Such a base behaviour was a cultural leap too far for the men from the reserved East.

After their immersion in this pool of European wine culture and hearing about the annual yields on previous investments, the wealthy businessmen ordered cases of what they had tasted – or bottles that looked just like it, as it turned out. Their business rationale saw it as a sound investment, but like many such things, it was as much about personal bragging-rights. When back socialising in China, being able to mention that their

Romanee Conti had gone up thirty per cent in a year made them appear both smart and sophisticated. The fact that the supposed ten thousand dollar case of wine was sat in a temperature-controlled cellar in Switzerland or London and would likely never again see the light of day was not important, except to Payen. This last fact was particularly important to him.

However, some of the wine was later shipped to China to be given away by the buyers as gifts to ingratiate them with potential business partners or government officials. They would present a beautifully boxed bottle of wine in a formal ceremony. The giver would not describe the gift as a European might, as "a bottle of Romanee Conti Marey Monge from 1967," as the implication was that the recipient would be educated in such things and understand the value of such a rare item. Instead, the wine was more likely to be introduced simply as "a fifteen hundred dollar bottle of French wine." Implicit in this statement was the knowledge that the purchaser had travelled to France, understood the wine's value and could afford such an expensive gift.

These were the worrying bottles as far as Payen was concerned and he had tried to discourage this kind of generosity by suggesting that the wines did not travel well and would spoil. The last thing he wanted was for there to be any chance of these wines ending up being tried or carefully examined by someone who knew what they were talking about. He had gone to great trouble to ensure the bottles, corks and labels were perfect copies, even the wine he chose to put inside was not cheap rubbish, as greedier criminals may have used. He had sourced acceptable quality wine blended as close as he could to the supposed product in question. Close enough to fool most, but certainly not a genuine expert in fine wines should one ever be offered some to taste. Nevertheless, in China, Payen guessed that this eventuality was unlikely and so far he had been correct.

One potential buyer mentioned that he been on tasting courses in Burgundy, Bordeaux, California and Barolo. He also bragged about holding several cases of wine with Cull & Porter in New York. Payen paled visibly when he heard mention of New York's leading investment wine merchants. They were also known in fine wine circles as the 'Petrus Police' for the ability to literally sniff-out and unmask fakes of famous French labels. This type of more informed buyer was later told that there was a sudden decline in stock and that the bottle he had requested would not be restocked for the foreseeable future; he would have to look elsewhere.

The final thing that had surprised Payen was how many of his buyers were practising Christians, particularly those living in Hong Kong. The revelation came to light when some of them recognised the often religious iconography on the wine labels. In France, it is common to name wines after saints or other religious icons. Wine labels often depict scenes from biblical tales: the logo of Taittinger Champagne is a Knight Templar on horseback and the name of the most expensive wines in the world, Petrus, is derived from St Peter. The links between wine and Christianity go back to the Old Testament.

Before this, Payen had assumed that, if any faith were still practised in China after a hundred years of religious suppression, it would be of the Eastern persuasion: Buddhism or perhaps Hinduism. He was shocked, not only that Christianity had existed in China since the 7th century, but also that it had remained so strong today.

The explanation came from his Chinese girlfriend, who explained that early Jesuit missionaries in China were from the educated upper classes. Their followers and ancestors enjoyed similar advantages in access to learning and so often prospered in business. Even under the communist rule, they were smart enough to keep their faith under-cover. However, their knowledge and skills were sufficiently in demand by government for their private practices to be over-looked, provided they kept them low profile. In more recent years, the Chinese Christians' greater understanding of western values had also meant they were adept at trading with Americans and Europeans and so had prospered even further.

For Payen, this further explained the propensity for this successful group to be interested in the investment in fine wine, while having little, if any, experience consuming it. It had also informed his targeting of future potential customers and after this, he had focused on Christian groups and organisations in China. The Frenchman was a sharp observer and quick learner, prompting his girlfriend to often speculate on what he might have achieved had he stayed on the right side of the law. She also knew that, like many Chinese men, for Payen, it was all about winning. Not content with winning in the business transaction, he also savoured taking on the law and beating it. His one hundred per cent success so far in keeping one step ahead of the police had made him arrogant and perhaps even complacent, she feared.

13. CINGHALE CON GAPPA

Ben was in the orange groves watching the French bees begin to explore outside of their hives. He wondered what they made of this new Italian landscape: more mountainous with a greater variety of flora and fauna than they were used to. Italy's subsistence farmers have had far less impact on the land than their larger and more mechanised French neighbours. One only had to look around to see the variety of cultivated crops around Seborga, above which was only wild forest, compared to the monoculture of the adjacent Provence. More insects, wild birds and mammals had survived in this more varied Ligurian landscape. Except, of course, for the very thing Ben needed: bees!

With reinforcements from the French, perhaps this part of his plan might yet survive, he allowed himself to hope. Even if it did, Ben also knew it would not be enough to get him out of the seemingly bottomless hole currently being dug by Payen. He had been there for almost an hour trying to think of a way to break the news to Alex. He had not found one.

After he had discounted running away, not least because he had nowhere to go, he had considered asking Vincenzo to beat the shit out of Payen, drive him over the border and dump him at a French police station. This was a task he felt the big Italian would gladly undertake and with some enthusiasm. He also wondered whether he should enquire of Roman how much it would cost to take a contract out on the Frenchman's life with his Sicilian associates. While these had been pleasing distractions from his problems, Ben knew that they were not the answer.

Ben was not aware of how much time had passed and suddenly realised that he had been out, pacing up and down in the groves for most of the day. His wallowing in self-pity ended abruptly when he heard voices approaching. Vincenzo was walking down the dusty track from the village and alongside him was Carlos, followed by a handful of other men from the village. The men all appeared to be berating Vincenzo, who was handling things in his usual way: saying nothing but doing something. Before he reacted to his neighbours questioning, he wanted to seek an explanation from Ben as to why they were taking down the crane. It seemed as though they all sensed something pivotal was happening.

For many in the village, Ben's dream was almost too good to be true. Italian pessimism about anything promised by those in power was well-founded. The post-war generation had endured a lifetime of marginal government, making it almost impossible to get anything significant done. Any proposal for change that leaned even slightly too far left or right was torpedoed by the factions holding the balance of power. It was a stalemate in which politicians learned to set their expectations low but keep their promises high, or at least, slightly higher than their competitors. Then, when nothing got done, their unfilled pledges were little worse than those they had stood against.

The initial erection of the enormous crane, thrusting ever upwards into the blue sky, towering over Seborga, had seemed like a sign that maybe things could actually change. Perhaps someone would finally deliver on a promise? One farmer had suggested holding a crane festival in celebration.

But now, having watched the hundred-meter tower be reduced to a short metal stump barely taller than the buildings around it in just one morning, the dream seemed to be deflating before their eyes. The bubble of hope in which most had existed for three years had finally been pricked, as it had seemed to many old-timers it inevitably would. Now the cynics were looking for someone to whom they could point out "we told you so" and Ben was that man. There seemed little point in him putting off talking to Alex. If Seborga's citizens were aware of what was going on, so soon would she be.

Ben pleaded with Vincenzo to buy him some time while he spoke to Alex. He was unsure what he had told the group of men, but the level of their berating went up in volume several notches. At least now they were all engaged in passionate arguing and questioning of Vincenzo, meaning Ben could sneak off to the Osteria.

On the hot, sweaty walk back up the track to the village, Ben looked down and noted the pristine new orange groves, below which were ancient, gnarled olive trees and beyond that, grapevines already heavy with early fruit. The Mediterranean created a sparkling azure carpet, meeting the sky at some undiscernible point and thus creating the effect of a seamless blue backdrop to the cornucopia of green vegetation. Looking inland and up past the tinder-dry forest to the first line of pine-covered peaks, Ben could just make out snow-covered ones in the far distance. Above the ridge, a lone eagle circled on thermals of hot air rising up from the valley below. In a frenzied, often despoiled world, Ben was reminded of just what an amazing place this was. No matter what happened, he could not give this up, he resolved.

As he entered the piazza, Ben saw Alex standing outside the Osteria with her back to him, looking up at the skyline holding her hand to her eyes to shade them from the late afternoon sunshine. She was watching as section by section of the crane disappeared below the warm terracotta rooftops. She appeared to wipe her face with her kitchen apron. She was crying, he realised.

The steps that he now took across the cobblestones were the most difficult he had ever made. Each one felt like a step nearer to the edge of a precipice. What was more, it seemed that he was walking down an ever-increasing slope towards the edge of a cliff. At any point, his feet might slip from underneath him and he would tumble helplessly into the abyss.

At this moment, Alex turned and saw him. Her face immediately lit-up, a thin smile quickly becoming a huge grin. She laughed through her tears. She held out her arms as though he was a soldier returning from a war that had kept him away for years. Ben was perplexed. This display of affection was not the greeting he had been expecting. She was still crying, but now her tears ran over the creases in her smile formed by her laughter. Nothing was said at first as he walked into the outstretched arms of his wife, as she hugged him close and held him there.

Finally, she mumbled between the tears and laughter,

"I thought you'd gone."

At which Alex fully sobbed and went slightly limp in his arms.

"Gone?" was all Ben could think of to say.

"I had a strange premonition that you'd run away from us. I was chopping tomatoes and a feeling suddenly hit me that you were leaving. It had all become too much responsibility and you had fled back to England. Come inside, and let's talk."

Ben was now thoroughly ashamed to admit to himself that this thought had briefly crossed his mind, which must have been precisely the time Alex had her premonition.

It was too early for aperitivo and the Osteria was empty. The couple took a seat in the shade, away from the earshot of any passers-by, although there were none.

"I thought you had left me" Alex continued tearfully. "Do you think that I don't know what's going on? I have seen all the same signs that you have. From the moment I heard about the Frenchman and his claims I knew that we were in trouble. You must be worrying as much as I am about what will happen next."

"But you don't know about the conversation I have had with Delon," he confessed.

"I can easily guess how that snake would react to news about our misfortune and, unless I am very much mistaken, I can see the results of Delon's actions before my very eyes," Alex said, gesturing to the skyline where the crane had previously been a prominent feature.

Ben confirmed what she had already suspected about the crane and also told her word for word the warning the French bureaucrat had issued. Once again, Ben was astonished by her reaction.

"Fuck him. You can't drink wine from an empty bottle. If Seborga's rejuvenation is stopped, then we have nothing worth selling. How is Delon going to extract twenty million euros out of us? By the time I had found out what my ex-husband was up to, he owed plenty of money to several New York drug dealers and the IRS, so Monsieur Delon doesn't frighten me. We have all we need here. We have the food from the orto, grapes in the vineyard, boar in the mountains, a roof over our heads and no bank loans. We might grow tired of cinghale con Gappa, but we will survive."

This was not at all the type of conversation that Ben was expecting to be having with his wife on this particular afternoon. Alex's unfaltering expression of solidarity combined with his scenic walk up to the village had filled him with new vigour. In less than a few minutes, her unwavering support had raised him from the depths of despair to a feeling of hopefulness once again. The only good news he could contribute was that the new bees were out scouting for food and might well now pollinate all the blossom.

Alex smiled gently, "There you are. Cecily will get some blood oranges and the farmers will get some money. We can live without a hotel and the other things until this gets resolved. Maybe we can invite the French conman and his countryman, the paper-pushing prick from Strasbourg, to the Osteria for dinner where I can poison them slowly with the wrong type of fungi."

“An easy mistake to make, I hear,” joked Ben.

As they laughed at their own joke, the name Salvatore Benigni flashed up on Ben’s phone for the second time in a week and the device began the buzz.

“Benigni again,” Ben said to Alex. “I’ll wager that Delon has phoned him to twist the knife in the wound.

“Salvatore. How can I help you today?”

Ben’s face easily re-told the conversation to Alex, as the civil servant confirmed that his counterpart had indeed contacted him at the EU office and that they had advised the Italians to follow suit by cutting off funding.

However, his frown began to turn to puzzlement as the greedy Genoan proposed another lunch.

“I have, perhaps, some better news for you. I would like to introduce you to a potentially powerful ally in your battle with Delon and Payen. Tomorrow would be good for you?”

The last statement seemed to Ben more of an instruction than a question. Ben agreed, mouthing the words “lunch tomorrow” to Alex and receiving her nodded response.

“Can you not tell me more about this good news and who this ally might be?” Ben asked.

“All I can say is that things might not be quite as bleak as they appear right now, but make sure it is a good lunch to impress our guest. He likes to eat well, as do I. Oh, and he’s also from Genoa, so loves to eat fried fish. Anchovies are his passion.”

14. ANCHOVIES E PAPRIKA

They would usually be far too tired after a late shift at the Osteria, but that night, Ben and Alex had gone home and made love. Rather than create a fracture as Ben had feared, their perilous predicament had somehow welded them even closer together. The next morning, they had slept later than most of the villagers and were awakened just after 8 am by unusual sounds outside. There was a crowd of chattering people gathered in the piazza, some of whom had started clapping as a noisy diesel engine coughed into action. Alex went to the window and peered into the early sunshine.

"Ben. Ben! Get up and come look."

Ben threw off the single summer sheet and stood naked beside her looking down into the piazza. It seemed half the village was out there and they were all looking up at the rooftops. From this angle, the couple could not see what everyone else could. Alex shouted down to one of her neighbours, asking what all the commotion was about.

"The men came back and are re-erecting the crane. They say it was a misunderstanding which has now been cleared up. They say the crane will be working again tomorrow."

The couple were as mystified as they were elated.

"I will go to speak to the engineer in charge and see if he knows what's going on," Ben offered. "He seems like a nice guy and speaks great English because he worked for a year in London helping build The Shard."

He could not help but think that this was somehow linked to the call from Salvatore. Alex, meanwhile, had an important lunch to prepare. Salvatore had informed them that he would be arriving by train as usual, which meant that someone would need to go to Bordighera to collect him. His mystery guest would be coming in his own transport, they had been told. This news at least meant that Alex could order fresh fish to be collected, along with the rotund civil servant. She rang her favourite fisherman, the son of an old friend of her father's.

"I have swordfish, red mullet, San Remo prawns, squid, big octopus and anchovies. All fresh this morning," he told her.

"I'll take four mullet, two kilos of anchovies and a kilo of red prawns. Vincenzo will collect them at 11.15 am. Grazie, Simone."

She knew he would over-weigh and send more than she had ordered, plus probably half a kilo of octopus or whatever he thought was the best day's catch. Simone knew that when he came to visit the Osteria at festa time to taste Alex's famous rabbit with olives, porcini tagliatelle or wild boar with Gappa, he would be compensated for his kind investment. Fish ordered, Alex set-to preparing the remainder of the courses that she would serve to the mystery guest.

Ben came into the kitchen just as she was finishing the call to Simone and told her,

"The engineer has no idea why the sudden change of heart. He says that he received a phone call at home late last night from his managing director ordering him back here at daybreak this morning. He has been told to have the crane back up and working in twenty-four hours. Frankly, he looked terrified. Like he would lose his job if it were not done on time. He's out there shouting at his men to work harder, saying no coffee breaks until it is done."

"I'll take the workers coffee in paper cups that they can drink on the job," said Alex, knowing little progress would be made without it.

"And maybe some fresh brioche to keep up their energy levels," suggested Ben.

With a couple of hours to go until lunch, Ben decided to check on how the orange blossom pollination was progressing.

He knew that the peace and seclusion of the lower terraces would give him space to figure out what was going on. Ben found that being alone in the countryside always made it easier to think. Back in the UK, he always had his clearest thoughts in a nice hot bath with a glass of Bordeaux. In Italy, baths were rare and those that existed were short, stubby things in which it was impossible to lie-back and relax.

Ben's analytical mind quickly concluded that, except for the pollination problem, Payen was at the core of all the others. It was the arrival of the French pretender to the crown that had sparked uncertainty and led to punitive action by the EU, with further potential sanctions from Italy very much on the horizon.

If Payen's claim could be shown to be fake, they would have to reinstate the agreed funding, Ben reasoned, but what they had learned about his past suggested that the Frenchman would not be easy to dismiss. He had already demonstrated some resilience to pressure. So long as he was around, Ben knew there would be no peace in Seborga and therefore no respite for him.

Alex and Ben heard the powerful motorbike winding around the countless hairpin bends that led up to the village. Its guttural exhaust increased in volume and pitch during its acceleration and then deepened into bass as the rider braked. Up and down the sound went as the bike conquered the fierce corners, growing steadily louder as it neared the village. The sound reverberated and echoed around the valley, disturbing the otherwise peaceful serenity of the mountains. This was the sound of someone pushing the bike to its limits between corners and downshifting when braking to make it around the tight bends. Either a rider in a hurry or someone feeding-off the adrenaline.

Bike enthusiasts of all flavours—man-powered and motorised—relished the ten-kilometre climb to Seborga. Its eighty corners were a challenge worth attempting, not just for the spectacular views along the journey, but also for the potential culinary reward at the summit.

As the motorbike approached the walls of the village its sound was momentarily shielded by the bulk of stone and earth, but then its throaty roar burst into the piazza like an explosion. The visual assault was almost as imposing as the audible one. The deep red petrol tank boasted white ‘Ducati Corse’ graphics that contrasted with the riders shiny black leathers. Slowing the bike to a walking pace, the rider’s visored, black-helmet panned back and forth, up and down, appraising the architecture and surroundings. Spotting the Osteria, a quick blip on the throttle brought bike and rider to the entrance where a press of the stop button finally silenced the beast. All that remained was an occasional metallic ‘pinging’ noise as the hottest metal parts cooled following their exertions.

Only now were Ben and Alex able to observe the bulk of the rider. There was a large and somewhat out-of-shape man squeezed into the black leather suit. In the crouched riding position, supported by the bulging petrol tank, his paunch had been less noticeable. Now stood upright he looked quite absurd, they both thought. He dismounted and pulled the heavy bike onto its stand with assured ease. He undid the chin strap and pulled back the helmet revealing the sweat covered, mostly bald, but well-tanned head of a man of some maturity. He appeared to be around sixty, perhaps even seventy years old, they both quickly assessed. When he finally removed his sunglasses, they immediately recognised their visitor as the outspoken and outlandish head of Italy’s leading opposition political party. His face was seldom out of the news.

Alex’s inner amusement at the sight now before her was masked by a look of astonishment that this particular man was here at all. Sergio Mastroianni was one of the most famous — some would say infamous — men in Italy. He was seldom out of the papers and so easily recognisable even in this somewhat dishevelled state. The rider did his best to straighten his remaining hair and brush away beads of sweat. He then realised that he could hardly offer his sweaty hand in greeting. He smiled broadly, but in a somewhat forced and unconvincing way, Alex noticed.

"Mi scusi altezza reale. I am in no state to greet a princess, but I will be very soon."

He glanced over his shoulder just as a black Mercedes van swept into the piazza going far too fast and heading straight for the Osteria, screeching to a halt outside.

"You're late, you idiot. I have been here five minutes," Mastroianni shouted at the driver who was already down from his seat and sliding open the side door with its blacked-out windows. Inside the pale leather-lined interior there was a dark suit with a white shirt on hangers and what looked like expensive shoes in a cloth bag. An array of men's' toiletries was set out in neat rows on the back seat.

"It will take me but two minutes to change. Please excuse me," Mastroianni requested, sliding the door shut behind him and disappearing behind blacked-out glass. The driver turned his back to the door, standing firmly in front of it as though barring the way to imaginary interlopers.

Alex looked at Ben, lost for words. Ben mouthed, "Mastroianni – the politician and media mogul?" She could only manage a nod in confirmation.

Sure enough, a little more than a couple of minutes later, the big man stepped from the side door of the van transformed into the more familiar figure they had seen on television. A smart blue suit of shiny wool was cut rather too tight for a man of his bulk and age, so it gaped to reveal a crisp white cotton shirt which looked like it had never been worn before. His thinning hair was combed flat over his dark brown scalp and the wrap-around sunglasses had been replaced with gold-framed Ray-Ban Aviators.

He approached Alex once more and simultaneously bowed his head and clicked his heels together saying,

"Your Royal Highness, it is my absolute privilege to meet you finally. If I am not too bold, can I add that you are even more beautiful in real life than in photographs? As happy as I am to meet you, I am deeply saddened that I never got to pay my respects to your dear father, the late prince Claudio. Perhaps if the election result three years ago had not gone against me, we would have met and been good friends."

Alex was suddenly aware that she was wearing an apron stained with fish guts, her hair was bundled-up on top of her head like a birds nest and she was wearing no make-up whatsoever. She had little choice but to accept the hand offered to her and shake it gently, trying to leave as few fish scales as she could from her own. She frantically collected her thoughts, knowing that she had to restore some equilibrium to this increasingly bizarre situation.

"Senior Mastroianni. First of all, I am no longer a princess. I gave up my title after the referendum and so there is absolutely no need for any formality. While I have not prepared for a VIP guest; you are very welcome to my Osteria. This gentleman is my husband, Ben Morton."

Mastroianni turned to Ben only briefly and nodded to acknowledge he was there, but his eyes quickly reverted to Alex. It was a strange and unsettling look somewhere between a smirk and a leer. Whatever his intention, it did not feel comfortable. He also leaned in far too close, assuming an intimacy that was at odds with his display of deference. He was wearing so much aftershave Alex could feel it invading her taste buds. She did not like him, she decided on the spot.

During this verbal exchange, his driver had manhandled the motorbike onto two metal bars protruding from the rear of the van. A hydraulic lift then hoisted it up off the ground and it was secured with webbing straps to a chrome rack. The Ducati was not being ridden back down the mountain. The chauffeur drove his van with the bike attached to the edge of the piazza, turned off the engine and slumped down in the seat to wait for his boss.

Alex made her excuses about having to return to the kitchen and finish preparing lunch.

"Ah, yes! The cooking countess, as she has become known in a certain few of my newspapers. We will have to see about elevating your status," he added, somewhat cryptically. Alex shot him a puzzled look over her shoulder and left Ben to deal with their guest.

"You're the mysterious guest that Salvatore told us to expect," Ben said, to steer the conversation in a direction that might shed some light on what was going on. Mastroianni finally focused on Ben, as he began to explain that Salvatore was his brother's boy and that it was he who had brought the current plight of Seborga to his attention.

At that moment Vincenzo arrived, driving the flustered and over-heated civil servant in his cramped and ancient Cinquecento. The car had no air conditioning and a passenger window that would no longer wind down. Salvatore was deposited outside of the Osteria, his suit crumpled and sweat-stained. He looked like the antithesis of his restyled uncle, who seemed less than impressed by his appearance.

"Salvatore, you look like you've been sleeping rough. Don't the Government pay you enough for a decent suit?"

His nephew thought about defending himself and deferring some blame to his hosts choice of transport, but knew that his explanation would be pointless. He said nothing and tried to smooth out some of the wrinkles in his trousers with his palms.

Ben indicated a table that had been set aside for them in the shade. Here they would benefit from any breeze blowing up from the terraces below and along the narrow alleys. Ben decided to get straight to the point and began by asking the reason for their visit.

"I wish you no disrespect, signore Ben, but I would like princess Alessandra to be present when I explain why I am here. I am a busy man and don't want to have to repeat myself."

While superficially stating that he didn't want to undermine Ben's position, Mastroianni simultaneously managed to display as little respect as it was possible to do. Ben decided he did not like this man either. With little left to say, Ben excused himself and went to the kitchen to see if he could help carry out anything for their lunch. Alex had brought in her son Cristiano to help her in the kitchen and he had plated the appetisers just as Ben entered.

"What a bloody rude man," was Ben's greeting to the young chef.

"Yes, mama said he was a fat, arrogant fool, so you seem to agree. His reputation is not a cool one," Cristiano added.

"Where is your mother by the way?" he asked, as he realised that she was not in the kitchen as he had expected.

"She said that she had to go home for a moment but would be back very soon."

Ben took the two large plates of fried anchovies out to their guests. As he did so, he saw Alex appearing from the other side of the piazza. Alex had quickly slipped into a light cotton day dress that was buttoned up the front, brushed her hair out and quickly applied some lipstick. She cannot have been away more than ten minutes, but the transformation was remarkable, even to Ben, who had seen her do this many times. She had also adopted the swaggering walk that she did so well. Her entrance gained the attention of all three men at the table, as well as every other man in the piazza. Already a small crowd of locals had gathered to admire the brand new Ducati and to see if the rumours were true about its famous rider.

Mastroianni stood and bowed again, but much lower this time, or at least as far as his paunch and tight trousers would allow.

"Princess Alessandra. It is true what they say. You are a truly remarkable woman."

Without responding, she took one plate from Ben and squeezed the lemon quarters, that had been placed on the side, over the crisp fried fish.

"From the Bay of San Remo. Fresh off the boat this morning," was all she said about the dish.

Ben poured glasses of cold, crisp Vermentino from a fridge-frosted bottle and lunch began in respectful silence for the food they were about to receive.

Only unintelligible murmurings of appreciation were heard for some time until Mastroianni finally wiped his mouth with his napkin and spoke.

"Those are the best anchovies I have had in many years and probably the best I've ever had outside of Genoa. What is your secret, Princess?"

"If you will cease calling me princess and start calling me Alessandra, I will tell you."

The big politician looked squarely at her as if to check how serious she was.

"OK. I concede that you gave up your title to help your subjects, but you are still a princess to me and I hear also to most of the people of this region. However, if it is your command that I call you Alessandra, I will be your humble servant and comply."

"It is my command if you wish to put it like that. Paprika is the answer. I put a little paprika in the flour coating."

"Not very Ligurian but I like it. Yes, I can see now that there was the very slightest kick to cut through the coating.

"You're correct signore Mastroianni. Frying flour in oil can be a little cloying on the palette. The acidity of the lemon and the spice of the paprika allow the fish to shine through. A little trick I learned in New York."

"If I must call you Alessandra, you must call me Sergio."

"Agreed. Sergio, it is," she answered, offering up her glass in a toast.

Ben observed the apparent warming of this new relationship and was intrigued to know what was going on. His wife was now openly flirting with this man, who represented everything she despised. He had so far proved to be everything the moderate media said he was, a brash, boorish, right-wing misogynist and yet none of this had stopped him from becoming one of the most powerful men in Italy, if not Europe. It was then that Ben realised that his wife had guessed what was going on and had decided to play the politician at his own game. *She was born for the role*, Ben thought.

Mastroianni counted foreign heads of state, billionaires and celebrities amongst his acquaintances. He dared to say the things most public figures did not and to take on those who appeared beyond accountability or above reproach. Both the Church and the European Union, in particular, had felt the sharp edge of his tongue, the power of his chequebook and the wrath of his media empire.

In a moment of clarity, Ben suddenly understood. Alex had realised that sat right here was an ally who was more than a match for Delon and his bosses in Strasbourg. He was possibly the only man in Italy who would take on the might of the EU and who might even win. She had begun her charm offensive and Sergio looked as if he was already poised to wave a white flag of surrender. By the time he had eaten her dessert, Mastroianni would be her willing subject; resistance would be futile.

The question that neither he nor Alex knew the answer to was what did Mastroianni want out of this relationship? He was certainly not a philanthropist. They did not have to wait long to find out. The grilled octopus provided both the catalyst and an analogy for the conversation they were waiting for.

"The EU is now like the octopus. Their tentacles reach into every aspect of our lives. While we're watching two apparently benevolent legs right in front of us, two others are picking our pockets, another is stealing our food and a fourth is giving you the finger behind your back."

Mastroianni raised his middle finger in an unnecessary illustration of his point.

"When Salvatore told me what the Euro-commies were doing to you, I knew that I had to help. Someone has to stand up to these bullies and thieves. They can't be allowed to steal the very livelihoods of Italian — apologies Seborgan — farmers and get away with it. Severely reducing the power of the EU, or ridding ourselves of it completely, is the main pillar of my political campaign."

Here finally was the answer Ben and Alex had been searching for. Mastroianni understood that Italians would view Seborga's struggle as a microcosm of their subservient position in the European Union. This cause was to be a sparring match during the election campaign in which he could be seen flexing his muscles. If he were elected, he would then be in shape for the much bigger battle against the EU, the ultimate objective being an Italian exit. Ben was immediately reminded of UK Prime Minister David Cameron's promises to extract similar concessions from the EU. Although he had ultimately failed to do so, it did get his party elected and made him PM, at least for a while.

The octopus before them on the table was beyond picking anyone's pocket. It had been seasoned, marinated in olive oil, garlic and oregano, before being pre-cooked in boiling water with lemons and finally flash-grilled. Served with the left-over marinade and lemon wedges, it looked wonderful.

"Have you seen how the locals who fish from the quayside dispatch any octopus they catch?" Mastroianni asked.

Alex pulled a face to show her repugnance at the very thought of it but replied, "They put it in a bag and bludgeon it to death on the rocks."

Mastroianni smiled in agreement. "Well, that's what I'm going to do to the EU."

While the politician tucked into his octopus with ever-increasing delight, Ben could not help envisaging Delon stuffed in a sack with Mastroianni swinging him around his head before crashing the bag to the floor. It would take another two more of Alessandra's Ligurian dishes before the businessman-turned-politician finally revealed any detail of his plan.

"I am not an educated man, professore. I did not go to university like you. I see what I see and then I know what I know. I know that today, a princess can only be a princess if the people accept that she is. In the same way that any leader can only lead those who want to be led and rulers can only rule with the will of their people. You may have given up your title, but the people still think of you as their princess and so you are. Monarchy has become democratic. No?"

Alex pondered the incongruity of the apparent worldly wisdom of this Genoan street trader. Perhaps it was just this adroit analysis of matters that had allowed him to prosper in a world full of better educated but less street-smart men. In accord with her guest, Alex responded,

"The Americans certainly decided they did not want an English King and so threw him a tea party in Boston."

"Yes, and in doing so encouraged the French to have their cake and eat it," was Salvatore's little joke and only contribution to the conversation. Mastroianni shot his nephew a withering look that left him in no doubt that he did not understand and that any further contribution from him would be unwelcome.

Alex countered with,

"Italy's Savoy family might still have been on the throne of Italy if they had not allowed another autocrat onto the stage. Especially one as dangerous as Mussolini. Any ship with two captains is heading for disaster."

The diners arrived at a kind of epiphany, as they mentally assembled the ingredients in the pot: a continent-wide swing towards right-wing politics and away from European centralisation, combined with a yearning for inspirational, celebrity figureheads.

In a nutshell, Mastroianni's goal was Italy's withdrawal from Europe, leaving him in an expanded presidential-style role, with Alex as a kind-of token royal family for all of Italy. She would provide a popular figurehead under his control and offer legitimacy to his scheme. As crazy as it sounded, those present seemed to acknowledge that it might just work. However, at least two of them were asking at what cost to themselves.

The 13th century San Bernardo church was built towards the end of the Templar era.

Drawing by Linda McCluskey.

15. CIMA ALLA GENOVESE

Alex had not heard from Cecily for a couple of weeks when she received a phone call, considerately made, after her lunch service at the Osteria.

"Hi. Where have you been?" was Alex's greeting delivered with exaggerated surprise at receiving the call.

"I can't wait to tell you. Can we have aperitivo in Sasso this evening?"

"Yes. I also have very, very interesting news."

The urgent rendezvous was agreed to be at the only café bar in the small hamlet of Sasso, half-way up the mountain road from the coast. The chosen location made the journey a short one for both of them and also meant that they could talk in relative privacy. Alex knew Ben would not mind as he had taken to spending an hour or so early in the evenings watching the bees returning to their hives. It was as though he was counting them back safely, as if fighter pilots returning from a sortie over enemy territory, she thought. Roman's initiative seemed to have worked and pollination-en-masse was taking place in the orange groves.

Cecily arrived first by scooter and found a quiet table on the terrace, as far out of earshot of the bar as it was possible. The view from the café terrace almost rivalled that from Seborga. Because the tiny community of Sasso was at a lower elevation it was not possible to see much beyond the promontory of Monaco, but being several kilometres closer to the coast, the panoramic view of the sea was amazing. Alex was ten minutes late, having had to negotiate a fallen tree blown down by strong summer winds blowing off the mountains. The two women kissed each other's cheeks and Alex ordered a Dubonnet and soda.

Before Alex had even sat down Cecily blurted out,

"He's finally made a commitment. He's moved in."

She was clearly unable to contain her happiness at this turn of events. Alex's brain struggled to get into the right gear and up-to-speed with what she was being told before querying,

"Who's moving ...? Oh I see! Roman is moving in with you?" she said, not at all sure that she had got this right.

"Yes, Roman has moved onto the boat. He's just flown to Sicily to collect some of his things and is driving back in his precious old car."

In the four years, they had known each other, Alex had never seen Cecily so ebullient. She was acting like a teenager in love and glowed with happiness.

A plate of aperitivo arrived and was placed between them. Cecily realised that the kitchen must have got word that Alex was in their restaurant because the offering was far grander than that being served to the locals at the bar. It consisted of a wide selection of wild boar sausage (cacciatorini), lardo, cheese and olives, accompanied by dried olive-flecked flatbread that spilled over the sides of the large oval plate. It was the cima alla Genovese that the other locals in the bar were jealous of, a speciality of this bar that was only reserved for special occasions or VIP guests, such as Alex.

Cima was traditionally a way to use up leftovers, but today was an artisan Ligurian delicacy. It is made from any combination of used vegetables, mushrooms, rice, potato and eggs wrapped in a blanket of sausage meat that has been minced from offal and cheap cuts of veal. The main seasonings are minced garlic and marjoram. The stuffed loaf is held together in a muslin sack, boiled slowly and then left to cool under a weight. When cooled it is sliced thinly, revealing a centre speckled with colour from the vegetables in the stuffing, encased in an outer ring of finely-minced pink meat.

Once the owner who had brought this feast was out of earshot, Cecily continued,

"Ten years. Ten years I have waited. Putting up with snatched encounters, flying visits, or worse, last-minute cancellations after weeks of planning. It's been torture not being able to talk about it. To tell you."

Alex was finally beginning to assemble the components of an, until now, secret relationship. This fact finally helped to put many other things about Cecily's life into better perspective. Gaps remained in the picture, but her English friend was about to paint in the detail.

"How did you meet Roman?" Alex asked.

Cecily explained that before acquiring her current boat, she had occasionally chartered smaller yachts for regular sailing holidays. At the end of a long and rough voyage from Sardinia, she had finally motored into the calm of Palermo harbour, tired, wind-burned and covered in sea salt. As they approached the only mooring space on the otherwise busy quayside, she noticed a striking looking but oddly dressed man closely observing their arrival. It was as though he had been waiting for them.

When they were within a few metres of land and ready for a crewman to jump ashore with a mooring, the man gestured to throw him the rope. The man caught the line but only put one loop around the bollard, to bring the boat to a halt and allow the momentum to swing it alongside.

"Best if you do not moor here," suggested the stranger holding the rope.

"According to my pilot book this is the public quay, and this looks like the only space available," the French charter skipper shouted back, apparently quite sure of his rights.

"This is Palermo my friend, not Antibes. I am waiting for a man who has reserved this space. He is coming back from the mainland after three days away and in all that time, no one has moored in this space. If you think about it, I'm sure that you will understand that there is a good reason for that."

The stranger finished his advice with a smile whilst also drawing his forefinger across his throat mimicking a knife cut. The skipper turned to Cecily and shrugged as if to say that he had little choice but to move on. The man was very charming and said that he would gladly show them to another mooring nearby, which was also right outside the best fish restaurant in the harbour. They all now assumed that this must be his own restaurant and that this was simply a ploy to drum up trade.

"There was something about his eyes, Alessandra. They were pale green, large and mysterious. They seemed to smile even when the rest of his face did not. Even when he was talking to the skipper, his eyes never left me, even though my hair was a rats nest and my nose glowed red from the sun and wind. I had worn my T-shirt and shorts for two days and no one had showered. The sea was too rough to attempt anything other than keeping the boat upright and on course."

She explained that the stranger had gestured that he come aboard and when the skipper nodded, he released the rope and in a single movement stepped deftly onto the deck. Directing them to the other end of the harbour, he took out his phone and had a brief conversation in dialect with someone. As they motored closer, they saw three small fishing boats being hastily repositioned. They were placed bow to stern, instead of the side to side arrangement they had been occupying. This action had created a space just big enough for their 38-foot yacht to reverse into.

When safely moored, the stranger introduced himself and invited Cecily and the crew to join him for dinner in the restaurant that was to be their new temporary neighbour.

"He was wearing a very obvious wedding ring and was far too handsome to be single, so I thanked him but declined before the skipper could say yes, as was his inclination."

The man they now knew as Roman, countered the refusal by saying,

"Without my advice, you might have been forced to move your boat again later tonight in the pitch dark and to who knows where. While all Palermo was enjoying dinner, you might even have had to sail back out into that storm. Why would you risk eating in a bad restaurant, in the wrong company, when my advice so far has proven reliable? Also, tonight is my birthday, and my restaurateur friend has prepared a special feast of fish fresh from the sea today. The best of the day's catches from all the boats in the harbour."

Realising that this was not their benefactor's own restaurant, a popular show of raised shoulders and eyebrows from the crew indicated that they thought the invitation should be accepted. Cecily finally nodded, a time was agreed and while the crew tidied the decks, she enjoyed a long-overdue shower.

"Cecily, can you please fast forward? Please spare me more yachtie or foodie adventures. I want to hear how you two got together."

Cecily laughed at Alex's abruptness, "It was really quite simple. Despite all the raucous people filling the restaurant we hardly took our eyes off each other all night. If he was married, no wife appeared for his birthday. No more than a few words were exchanged between us, but something clicked. I went to the bathroom and when I came out, there he was waiting. He just kissed me right there in the busy corridor with waiters hustling by carrying plates and bottles. I didn't resist. I just melted. Next thing we were across the quay on the yacht and waves were lapping gently against the hull while the crew partied the night away."

Alex looked stunned.

"You hardly spoke to him, he kissed you and then you're in bed? This news is all too much to take in. It sounds nothing like the you that I have come to know. I was expecting a surreptitious note to be passed under the table suggesting another meeting, followed by weeks of gentle courtship. Not a smile, a kiss and hit the sack. Wow."

Cecily blushed.

"When you put it like that it does sound impulsive, but I just knew. And I was right. As we got to know each other, Roman explained that after years of mutual unhappiness he and his wife had agreed to part. At that point they had been living separately for eighteen months."

Cecily went on to explain that the very next day and at the drop of a hat, Roman agreed to join Cecily on the remainder of her holiday. They sailed from Palermo, through the Strait of Messina and into the Ionian Sea. Without a firm itinerary, each morning they let the prevailing wind determine their destination, by making use of it to chart a swift, smooth route. The first night found them at Melito di Porto Salvo, the southernmost community of mainland Italy.

"This was where Garibaldi first landed his forces on the mainland in the war that eventually united Italy under a single flag. When we landed, I immediately recognised the smell of bergamot which is used a great deal in perfume and cosmetics. The area was perfect for the cultivation of these valuable fruit trees," Cecily explained.

The next day, after raising a billowing pale blue spinnaker, they let a south-westerly wind blow them to Syracuse and were back on Sicily's east coast in swift time. Here they had visited the extraordinary Roman amphitheatre and the Orecchio di Dionisio, a limestone cave in the shape of a human ear.

"We tried an unusual stretchy bread made with hot tomato oil, which I proceeded to drip all over my espadrilles," she laughed.

For the final night of this trip, they made it to the small island of Favignana just off the northwest coast of Sicily. Here they dined on fresh tuna steaks which had been marinated in oil, lemon and capers before being flash-grilled so still slightly pink in the middle. Although they did not know it then, this was to be the first of many visits to this island which turned out to be their favourite destination for their clandestine meetings.

"Roman would drive to Marsala or Trapani and I would be waiting in the harbour to collect him. It was a relatively short crossing to remote Favignana where we could be away from prying eyes. It was blissful," she remembered, smiling broadly. "It is the happy memories of those times that has kept me sane the past few years.

"Several more encounters followed quickly and he flew to London for a few days. Then we met in Sorrento just a couple of weeks later. We grasped every opportunity to be together with vigour, even if it was only for one night," Cecily recalled.

It could not have been more perfect, until one day Roman received a call from his eldest daughter to tell him that his soon-to-be ex-wife had been diagnosed with early-onset dementia. Then, for reasons he was unable to explain to anyone adequately, he decided that he could not go through with a divorce under these new circumstances. He told Cecily to move on with her life and forget him. That for him, it could be a sentence of twenty years or more caring for the mother of his children.

"It was over almost as suddenly as it began, but I just couldn't leave him, despite the apparent futility of the situation. Don't get me wrong I did try to move on, but I just couldn't give up on the hope that I might regain what I had lost. I kept remembering Favignana."

She admitted that, although it was maddening, his stoicism and loyalty to his wife and children had, if anything, made her love him more. Alex nodded in understanding at her friend's reaction.

"How many men would do what he did in the face of such difficulty, especially with such an attractive, easy way out?" Alex empathised.

"You only know half of what he eventually suffered," continued Cecily.

She explained that, after only a few months, his wife's mental health deteriorated significantly. The bitterness about their failed relationship spilled over daily and morphed into fantasies of Roman having led a lifetime of unfaithfulness. Everyone was accused of affairs, from the cleaner to her closest relatives. It was not an easy time for his family.

While she had been in good health, his wife had never learned about the one relationship he really did have, but one of their daughters had. The eldest girl had listened in on a long telephone conversation he had with me before confronting him, and Roman being Roman, he did not deny it.

"His daughter agreed not to tell anyone, including her younger sister, on condition that Roman put the land and the house in Sicily in trust to them. If Roman were ever to meet anyone else, the daughter wanted to exclude any future partner or children from inheriting anything. He said this was easy to agree to because, unknown to her, such a trust was already in place.

"Her other condition was not so easy to agree on, but he did nonetheless. His daughter asked that her father and I would never be seen together in public on the island of Sicily. This exclusion was supposed to avoid her mother the pain of hearing such news, although his wife's imaginings were far worse than anything taking place."

Cecily explained how this condition had restricted their ability to meet very often, as he could not be too far away from the farm for too long.

"I couldn't meet him on Sicily and so we had to make do with short trips. I would pick him up from the quay at Palermo and sail to mainland Italy, or out to the neighbouring islands of Marettimo, or our favourite, Favignana. That is how I came to own and live on this larger yacht. It was the only way to get to see the man I love regularly."

"Wow," exclaimed Alex. "That's commitment. He must be some guy to merit moving your life to a boat. Even if it is a beautiful one," she added quickly, to avoid any perceived slight to Cecily's incredible yacht.

"He is," she agreed, nodding for emphasis.

Alex now understood why Cecily appeared to have few close friends or a family of her own. She had spent over a decade floating around Europe, conducting her business in-between fitting in short clandestine meetings with Roman whenever the opportunity arose. "Was his wife's death a release of sorts for both of them?" ventured Alex.

Cecily nodded. "There's still a lot of sadness about what happened and I know he feels terribly guilty about his daughters, but yes, there's an enormous relief that we can finally make plans."

Alex felt compelled to give Cecily a long hug. On reflection, the huge burden that she had carried all this time had been evident. Now, she seemed unchained, and she was ecstatic about it.

"Well, I thought my news was momentous, but it now seems somewhat prosaic compared to your story," Alex said, smiling.

Try as she might to look serious and more attentive about her friend's forthcoming revelation, Cecily could not wipe her own smile from her face. Neither did her thoughts ever stray too far from the life she was now planning with Roman. However, she managed to make a good impression of interest and intrigue as she prepared to listen to what Alex was about to tell her.

Alex began by telling Cecily about the dismantling of the crane and the threats from Delon at the EU. She then went on to describe the overweight, balding seventy-year-old who arrived on a red superbike. When she finally said his name, Alex immediately gained her full attention.

"Mastroianni. The famous bumbling billionaire bum-pincher. Bloody hell!"

"The very same. And, my latest fan," she added with a smirk and a wink. "Although I'm not sure whether it's my pasta or my ass he desires most."

The two women almost collapsed laughing with relief at the unburdening of the absurdity of their respective situations.

Their happy snorting and giggling had brought them to the attention of the staff and customers at the bar and they quickly regained composure, realising that they needed to be careful not to be overheard. These were, after all, small communities where news travelled fast. Things in Seborga were already complicated enough.

"So, what else does he want in return for saving Seborga?" was the question that immediately sprung to Cecily's mind. "No disrespect to your ass," she whispered conspiratorially, "but Mastroianni seems to have access to a hareem of options in that respect."

"No offence taken. Well, maybe a little offence," Alex joked, making a fake frown. "He says that he wants to give the EU a bloody nose and that he thinks the Seborga case is a cause that the average Italian will support."

"So, in other words, it will win him votes."

"Exactly."

Knowing that Cecily was the perfect person to counsel her, Alex became much more serious as she went on to express her genuine concerns about cooperating with such a notoriously exploitative figure. She also explained the pressure that this had placed on Ben: how he was struggling to cope with potentially failing crops, the cessation of work on the hotel and other buildings, as well as the latest threat of being pursued to repay millions of euros. She even told her friend that she had briefly feared that Ben might leave Seborga because of it, at which point, Cecily decided that she needed another drink.

When the refilled glass was before her, she asked,

"So, what's the deal?"

Alex explained that Mastroianni's opening demonstration of power was the crane. Delon had ordered it stopped. Mastroianni ordered it re-started.

"Round one to Mastroianni," Cecily summarised.

Alex continued by explaining that Mastroianni was, through his nephew, effectively in control of nearly ten million euros of the funding allocated to Seborga. This amount was not enough to complete all of the elements of the plan but, with careful management, it was sufficient for works to continue on all the essential parts.

"He is promising that any shortfall will come further down the line, by which time he expects to be in power and promises to make up the difference from central government."

"Most of the opinion polls agree with his prediction about the election," added Cecily.

"He wants to make a show that Italy doesn't need any more EU hand-outs."

"Now that they already have had most of them, he surely means?" quipped Cecily.

Cecily said that she accepted that this was at least a plausible plan, which on-the-face-of-it, appeared to get everyone – except the EU – what they wanted. She could not, however, help pointing out one potential flaw.

"If it succeeds, it leaves Mastroianni pulling the strings on your little puppet show."

"I know" answered Alex, visibly squirming at the very idea. "But what choice do we have? We discovered that we had gotten into bed with the devil when we accepted the money from the EU, who have proved every bit as evil as the empire builder that seeks to replace them. I may not like Mastroianni any more than them, but I do understand him. Rather than a bureaucratic machine, he is at least human and therefore predictable."

"And he's a man," added Cecily.

"Exactly, and a very vain one," Alex concurred with a knowing smile.

"That's our ultimate lever," she continued. "After power, what Mastroianni really craves most is social acceptance. Despite his billions, he is despised by many in business and by the quality media outlets. The old-money Italian families think he's a new-monied moron. Finally, no one knows better than him, that the current new breed of celebrities is as shallow as he is. He feels that only acceptance by the old noble families or royalty can afford him the status and credibility he craves. Oh, and he wants a noble title of course, to cement his new standing."

"A title!" Cecily blurted, almost spraying her drink over her friend as she tried to contain her laughter. "You mean like, Lord Sergio of Genoa?"

"Actually, Sergio, Duke of Seborga" Alex replied with a straight-face.

The two women could no longer contain their feelings at the utterly bizarre ridiculousness of this situation and fell into fits of uncontrollable giggling. Both took some comfort from the fact that here was a person whose life seemed to be more complicated than their own. When the laughing died-down to the point that they could speak, Cecily asked,

"But, are you allowed to just create a Duke?"

"Apparently I am, if I am Princess of Seborga once again."

"But surely you gave up that title and any privileges that went with it?"

The conversation now took a more serious turn as Alex explained Mastroianni's rationale. The politician had pointed out that it was the EU who were proposing the Frenchman's claim should be taken seriously, potentially making the referendum invalid, which was their excuse to stop any further money. The savvy schemer also calculated that the referendum had been a constitutional quagmire anyway because it depended on whose laws you applied; Italian or Seborgan.

"He argues that if the referendum was invalid as the EU claim, the deal with them is void, which means I am still Princess of Seborga but back under the jurisdiction of Italy and in a few weeks, he could be the Italian head of state."

Cecily looked astonished but could not fault the logic of this analysis. Alex further revealed, that Mastroianni planned to provoke the EU between now and the Italian general election into officially announcing that the agreement was invalid. He believed they would retaliate with demands to recoup the twenty million, but in reality, they knew they would never get this back. Delon would be happy to have exerted his authority and saved the balance of money they would have had to pay had the deal continued. Mastroianni's spies had determined that after a career in obscurity, the French paper-pusher wanted one last hoorah before his retirement.

"Mastroianni claims that he can easily get rid of the crooked French usurper Prince one way or another. Italy will then officially recognise the Seborga principality and grant some level of fiscal independence. This legislation would not only allow the Principality to raise revenues, but also to create a unique tax environment attractive to high net-worth Italians."

"Like Mastroianni, you mean," offered Cecily with a cynical smile.

Alex squirmed a little at Cecily's astute analysis and merely nodded in agreement of her conclusion.

"However, on the plus side, Seborga gets everything that was promised in the EU deal, plus some significant other benefits, without giving up the principality status my father fought for all his life."

"In other words, all of the good bits from the referendum and none of the bad ones," summarised Cecily.

"The only fly in the ointment is Mastroianni himself," added Alex, before Cecily had a chance to. "Il Duca (The Duke), if you don't mind," she joked, trying to make light of the issue.

Cecily had to think hard to see a flaw in this overly complicated scenario. Thinking out-loud she rationalised,

"So, it's only the EU and Italy who have a direct interest in this issue, of which only the latter is a sovereign state able to make a law directly affecting Seborga. So, if the EU effectively walk away from the deal ... OK, I understand his thinking. After the Italian election, he will ultimately end up back in control of the whole show. No one outside of Italy and Seborga gives a damn."

"Exactly," confirmed Alex. "And it will doubtless bring him brilliant publicity, turning his current marginal majority in the opinion polls into a possible landslide victory at the ballot box. If he wins a big enough majority, he will be able to do as he pleases."

"Especially when his own editors put their boss's unique spin on events," Cecily suggested.

"It is cunning, manipulative and morally dubious but possibly just-about deliverable," she concluded.

"It is also very clever," Cecily grudgingly added.

"As for this French thief who we thought was going to be our nemesis, he now looks as though he might have been our saviour from that vindictive EU bean-counter."

The two women kissed and parted both their heads, both swimming with speculation brought about by their respective news.

16. VITELLO TONNATO

The old Mercedes squeezed into a space on the quay. The driver parked between a petrol tanker, which was in the process of refuelling the luxury yacht in the berth next to Cecily's, and a local baker's van delivering fresh bread. The sixty-year-old Mercedes Ponton was built for the type of long, arduous journeys this one had just undertaken. It was fifteen hundred kilometres from Palermo to Menton, a trip which took Roman four days to complete.

This driver, however, did not see it as an arduous task. Roman was on a journey to freedom; the great escape he had been dreaming of for years. Each new stop along the road north was like an adventure. Each kilometre took him further away from painful memories and brought him closer to a new horizon.

Having been warned of the new arrival by one of her handful of crew, Cecily was on deck before Roman had turned off the old but reliable diesel engine. She thought the pale green saloon with its faded tan leather interior, made in the same decade that he was born, suited Roman. It was classy and robust but in no way pretentious or frivolous. It came from an era when Mercedes cars were built to achieve a standard of quality and reliability. Only when their pedantic engineers had achieved those objectives did the accountants work out the price. This policy was the reverse of all later construction practices.

This post-war thinking often resulted in Mercedes list prices being almost double those of their competitors, which in theory should have made them unsaleable, yet it did not. People who could afford it paid the extra for a variety of different reasons, not least because everyone knew if you drove a Mercedes, it said something about who you were. In this case, in Sicily, it signalled that you were connected, therefore no parking problems, no speeding fines and God help anyone who scratched or dented it.

This car had been Roman's father's: a gift from his Mafia boat passengers on the day of his wedding in further gratitude for their safe delivery to their homeland. The Ponton had the added advantage of what seemed like acres of space inside and a spacious boot from which Roman was now removing his battered weekend bag and a vibrant yellow bunch of sunflowers, collected from the market in Menton. The remainder of the car was filled with wine boxes, vinyl records, a carrier bag of fruit from his farm and several suit hangers; the accumulated belongings of one man curated down to a single carload. Looking at it like that, it was almost sad to see, Cecily suddenly thought.

However, the way he crossed the quay and strode purposefully up the passerelle, Roman looked in no way sad, she assessed. Neither did he seem tired from his long road trip. He seemed glad to be here and back with her and that was all she cared about.

"Permission to come aboard, Captain?"

Cecily took the flowers from him and pecked him on the cheek.

"This is your home. You don't need anyone's permission. Oh, and I have rented you a garage in Menton for your precious car. It's safe and dry, plus just ten minutes' walk from here."

"But if this is my boat, then that is also your car. You can get rid of that Bentley now and share the Ponton with me," he offered, knowing she would not.

"Ummm ... maybe not. I like the Bentley and it's a useful signal of success when I'm going to meet buyers and suppliers. To use an analogy that I heard recently from a wise older man, if you are meeting with wolves, it is best not to go dressed as a lamb." She laughed and he returned her smile. "So, for now, I won't exchange my lovely car for your 1950's classic but thanks for the offer."

"Why not? You were willing to trade your freedom for this 1950's classic," he said, pointing to himself.

"Ah yes, but you're more reliable, comfortable and refined than that one parked over there. Although now that you mention it, you do both smell of oiled-wood and leather, which I guess isn't a bad thing."

They laughed and hugged like young lovers, oblivious to the despairing looks from teenagers sunbathing on the deck of their neighbouring yacht.

"Alain has prepared vitello tonnato for dinner. Why don't you go and change for a swim and let the guys unload the remainder of your baggage?" Cecily requested and Roman did not argue. The water looked inviting after a long drive without air conditioning.

They had previously enjoyed many such dinners on board, with only a couple since the death of his wife, yet this one felt like something quite different. It was the start of a new sort of relationship, one that involved commitment and therefore responsibility: it was a fresh start for both of them. Roman scanned the boat's interior wondering if this really could be his new home.

Cecily had chosen vitello tonnato because it was an unusual coupling of strangely foreign ingredients much loved by the English and Italians. Tuna and capers from Sicily, veal from nearby Piedmont and mayonnaise from France. It seemed to neatly sum-up their own pairing and their new life together. Henceforth, it would become a regular meal on board. They also both agreed that the chef had created his own absolutely delicious light-supper version served on slices of garlicky bruschetta bread to give some crunchy bite to the otherwise silky rich dish.

After a dessert of fresh fruit, they slumped into their soft white linen sofa and Cecily snuggled close to Roman, who deftly switched his drink between his hands so he could wrap his arm around her shoulder.

"I've been thinking about a new job for you."

Roman jerked-up in his seat, totally taken aback by this unexpected announcement.

"New job! I only retired from my old one four days ago! Cecily, I have a new partner, a new home ... oh, and a new garage for my car. That's too many 'news' for one day. I'm not ready for you to send me out to work already!"

"Hear me out. I think you'll like it. It's a lot like your old job, but without the risk and responsibility."

"And therefore presumably without the rewards?" the canny Sicilian guessed.

"That's not strictly true. There is a small salary, the chance to help a friend in trouble and the perk of Alex's Osteria as a staff canteen."

Cecily could see that he was intrigued, if not yet entirely sold on the idea.

"Ben is struggling with managing orange production. It is not his skillset managing farmers; he doesn't speak their language and currently has half a dozen other pressing projects to oversee. You would only be an advisor because, ultimately, each farmer is independent and so responsible for their own trees. If they ignore your advice then it's their problem. Well, and mine, I should add."

She could see that he was at least considering it.

"Anyway, I don't want you sitting around here all day while I work. You will get fat and grumpy. You need something to do."

"It sounds like you have made up my mind for me. Is that the way it's going to be from now on?"

"Well, we might as well start as we mean to go on," she joked.

Joining in the joke, he asked, "When do I start?"

"I don't know, I haven't discussed it officially with Ben or Alex just yet. I'll get back to you on that one," she grinned.

"The job you have just talked me into doesn't yet exist! What a woman. Now I remember why I love you. Some people talk about doing things, but you make them happen. OK, I give in. If Ben and Alex need and want my help, then count me in. I guess I was already bored with retirement."

17. TAGLIATELLE AI FUNGHI PORCINI

Mastroianni's election campaign was planned like a military operation. He had learned the lessons of his past and knew that he needed to fight several adversaries on multiple fronts, without being out-gunned or outflanked. A team of advisors were brought in and suggested that he offer a highly paid sabbatical with a big success bonus to senior journalists from each of his newspapers, in return for acting as his dedicated public relations experts. All but one accepted his offer. She sighted concerns about the conflict of interest undermining her journalistic integrity. She discovered that integrity was a commodity without value to Mastroianni and the unfortunate woman was now looking for another job.

Mastroianni would need to leverage his capitalist credentials for the right-wing voters, his working-class roots for the socialists and try to acquire some environmental credibility to appease the greens. Of these groups, only the relatively small green vote was keen on the EU, who the others collectively hated. Seborga offered a cause with which to garner support from all three factions in one neat package. There was even the bonus of considerable financial and social gains for him if he could pull it off. He would make the Europeans look like back-stabbing cheats by restoring an Italian royal family, protecting poor agricultural workers and helping to create a ground-breaking, environmentally-sustainable community in Seborga. In doing so, he would create headlines for every political flavour of the media. It was a masterstroke that would allow Mastroianni to micro-manage these issues with relative ease. What is more, none of these issues had yet to appear on the radar of any of his competitors in the Italian election. He would catch them all unawares and he already had his ace card up his sleeve.

At the heart of his manifesto was the pledge to reduce the power of the European Union or to take Italy out of it. The success or failure of the first part of this promise was entirely subjective and so would doubtless be measured in retrospect by Mastroianni's flexible standards. At seventy years of age, this experienced streetfighter was concentrating on feathering his retirement nest and shaping his own obituary. The author of any history of his life would have no choice but to refer to him as a billionaire businessman, former-prime minister and Duke of Seborga. He was not especially interested in the long-term consequences for the people of Italy. Indeed, he was more interested in the medium-term prospects for Seborga, as that was where he planned to shelter most of his money from the taxman.

No one had to wait long for the opening shot in the battle. It came in the shape of a headline in *La Republica*, a centre-left newspaper ultimately controlled by Mastroianni, but through an intermediary company which read, "*Community of artisan workers ditched by EU accountant.*" It was designed to please almost all factions using just four words. Everyone wanted 'community' and now loved anything 'artisan.' On the other-hand people hated the EU and loathed accountants. The sub-heading drove the knife firmly where it was aimed, "*EU's bean-counter recorded calling Italians grubby stupid peasants.*" The end of this day would see the termination of that jumped-up French bureaucrat's career, Mastroianni was sure of it.

It did not matter that Ben had not recorded the phone call he had with Delon about him cancelling the payments. He had accurately recounted the conversation to Mastroianni, who was not too bothered if it was accurate or not. He also didn't care if it was true because he knew the French did not record their phone conversations, as one of their privacy laws strictly forbade it.

A Frenchman working for the EU calling the Italians ignorant, dirty peasants had the predictable effect. By lunchtime, the Italian broadcast media, from far left to far right, had universally voiced their outrage. It was too late for the other daily newspapers, but they joined in with even greater fervour the following morning. The most outraged citizens took to the streets, standing to shout outside EU offices and even the French Embassy in Rome waving Italian flags. Ben even spotted a couple of Seborga flags being waved in TV footage from Turin; no doubt young ex-pat Seborgans at the university there.

At the heart of the story in every outlet, was Seborga's simple aspiration to save their failing agricultural economy and unique culture from the ravages poured down upon them by big business and globalisation. A modest aspiration now being bullied into submission by European bureaucrats based in France. Seborga was Michelangelo's David to the EU's Goliath, but with the added advantage of Mastroianni loading poisoned stones into their slingshot.

Mastroianni could not have been more delighted with the outcome of his intervention. He had phoned Alessandra to gloat, but she had missed the call. He left a message on her voicemail and despite their agreement on referring to her as the princess stated, "Princess, Mastroianni does what he promises". Alex played the recording to Ben, who commented sceptically, "Well, this time he has."

Mastroianni's initial attack on the Eurocrats had deliberately played-down their actual rationale for holding back Seborga's funds and concentrated on the human consequences it would have. His follow-up campaign a few days later would endeavour to link the French pretender for the crown to the EU themselves, even going as far as to suggest that they were in league together. He would not, however, go as far as to dismiss Payen's claim as without substance. He needed a credible question mark to hang over the legitimacy of the Seborgan referendum for its outcome to be undermined.

The politician spun the story to suggest that the EU had promised the money to get rid of the Italian royal family of Seborga, only to replace them with a French version under their control. Although the story was preposterous when the facts were scrutinised, with the current mood of the average Italian being very anti-French and anti-EU, it was one he believed that they would swallow. They did.

"FRENCH GUILLOTINE SEBORGAN ROYALS" was the headline plastered across the front of the *La Stampa* newspaper, predictably stoking the flames already burning under Ital-Franco-Euro relations. A sister-publication went with *"EU COUP OUSTED ITALIAN PRINCESS."* Both papers went on to infer that EU motives were to replace Alessandra with their own puppet Prince and ensure the troublesome enclave near the French border was forever subdued.

Inevitably, as soon as these stories were out, the media began trying to contact Alessandra for comment. As Mastroianni had not consulted her at all about what was happening, she was caught completely unprepared. She knew, just like last time, she could not put off the media indefinitely and she needed to prepare some response. She turned off her phone until she could talk to Ben and concentrated on her trofie pasta that she was making for the piatto giorno.

"We need to talk about a response to these news stories. The media are hounding me," was how she greeted Ben as he arrived at the Osteria.

"We don't," Ben disagreed. "We let Mastroianni make all the claims and allegations. If we keep quiet, we can later distance ourselves from anything that backfires on him. If we comment, then we will be attributed with a stance on the issue, probably that we are in alignment with him."

"So, it's no comment?" Alex said.

"Better still, turn your phone off, be unavailable and keep your head down."

Ben had little thought of anything other than Mastroianni's proposals since his visit to the village. Like Alex, he had assumed they were just that—proposals—which would require acquiescence from them before he proceeded. The pair had been unfamiliar with the workings of billionaire media moguls, but now they understood how he worked.

The prospect of undoing all the agreements that he had worked so hard to set up to secure Seborga's economic future filled Ben with dread. The many uncertainties that came with re-establishing Alex as Princess, not least where that left him, troubled him almost as much. What concerned him more than any of these things was the prospect of getting into bed—politically speaking—with a man whose reputation for ruthlessness preceded him. This furore had already demonstrated Mastroianni's willingness to ride rough-shod over their wishes in the media.

On the other hand, Mastroianni had demonstrated his ability to get things done and work continued unabated on the Seborga infrastructure project. There were even signs of progress speeding up. Ben, in particular, was aware that he was being asked to attend fewer meetings because unforeseen problems had occurred. It was almost as if all the previous issues had gone away; things that he had previously been told were impossible, suddenly seemed easy. Ben guessed that the construction companies and their contractors had a new unseen project manager, someone with far more power than Ben and to whom they were unwilling to say "no" or make excuses to.

Try as he might, Ben could not think of any other way forward. Without the elusive French pretender renouncing his claim to the throne and the EU doing a U-turn, they would be destined to live in a half-built Seborga surrounded by immature orange trees, with no farmers left in the village to harvest them. Mastroianni turned up like a genie out of a bottle and was offering to grant all their wishes, provided that they climbed aboard his magic carpet for a ride to who knows where. It was a prospect that terrified them both.

Ben was greatly cheered by the sight of Alex emerging from the kitchen with steaming plates of pasta; there were few things in life that could not be made better with the application of good food and wine. With the bees now doing their job, the huge crane re-erected and work continuing at a pace on the monastery, the locals had returned to talk of more important things. Only Ben and Alex saw the clouds gathering on the horizon.

Porcini was the Ligurian food topic of the moment in the bar: specifically, the best places and conditions in which to find them, of course, without actually giving away any exact location. Indeed, some of the wilier foragers deliberately gave out misinformation. They would claim to have seen vast caches of enormous fungi, “high up by the old water mill,” or “down in the bottom of the valley by the waterfall,” all in the hope of getting the naive hunters following the wrong trails. Then came the more heated discussion of mushroom magnitude: when it came to exaggerated claims of length and girth only fishermen told taller tales, Ben observed.

When finally, Alex sat down with Ben to enjoy a drink together, they had much to discuss but little appetite to do so. Before Ben could say anything, Alex surprised him with,

"Why don’t we go away for a few days? We both need time to think and we’re not going to get it here.”

“But ...” Ben began to speak but was interrupted.

“The summer season is coming to a close and so it’s quieter here in the Osteria and Renata arrives tomorrow to take over at the new kitchen. Cecily and Roman would like us to accompany them on a short cruise to celebrate them finally getting together.”

Seeing the look of despair on Ben’s face at the idea of leaving all his projects, his trees and his bees, Alex quickly added,

"It's just a few days along the coast to visit the Cinque Terre. You can pick Roman's brains about orange trees and anyway, he has something that he wants to talk to you about."

"Cinque Terre? Five lands?" Ben quizzed.

"Yes, five small coastal towns spread over five hills and valleys, famed for being some of the most beautiful in all Italy. Just a day and night sailing."

She paused to see if he was still resistant and as he opened his mouth to object she interrupted with,

"I've already said yes to Cecily. We leave first thing in the morning the day after tomorrow."

"It sounds like you've got it all worked out," Ben responded with resignation. Only to himself did he acknowledge that his wife was probably right. Some distance from Seborga, with space to clear their heads, would probably be the best thing at the present moment, as would Alex being uncontactable by the media.

While Mastroianni had his minions scheming his way to power, Ben had also briefed his own PR expert, his daughter, Selene. She was going to monitor all media activity related to the election which mentioned either Mastroianni or Seborga. From this, she would try and distil his political strategy so that they would not be wrong-footed and could plan their response. Selene, like most journalists both inside and outside Mastroianni's organisations, despised everything he stood for. Picking apart his strategy to potentially undermine it would be a pleasure.

18. SANGUINACCIO

A week or so earlier on a sunny Saturday evening, Ben and Alex had been on their way home from Bordighera when they stopped off at the bar in Sasso for an aperitivo. The bar served several local rustic wines which Ben had not heard of or tried. The burly owner wore a bushy white beard like Santa Claus and had a convivial personality to match. Pleased with the Englishman's interest in his collection of wines, he offered him samples to taste. Inevitably, the locals all joined in with their views of which was best, but none could agree.

A craggy-faced, deeply tanned man in working clothes known as Turi was one of the few English speakers in the bar. He wore a bright coloured baseball cap which he tipped in deference to Alex. His unkempt beard left little of his countenance exposed, meaning that his expression was hard to read. Smoke from thin roll-your-own cigarettes created an almost permanent fog around his head, making him look mysterious. Turi offered a colourful anecdote for every new bottle the barman produced to try, beginning with,

"Pah ... that stuff is rubbish. The best Ormeasco comes from above Arma di Taggia. Luca's land has the best angle to the sun and the perfect slopes for it. His soil is half sand from the bottom of the ocean, pushed up by volcanic activity millions of years ago." He announced his thoughts with such authority that no one argued with him.

Ben absorbed all his stories like a sponge, slowly building his already extensive knowledge of viniculture. When it came to tasting a very local Rossese di Dolceaqua, Turi judged that finally, he had the best local wine available in his hand. "This

Rossese comes from right there," he said, pointing through the osteria's window and out across the valley to where the entire opposite hillside was covered in rows of well-cared-for vines.

Turi translated his summary of each story and the Englishman's response to his pals in the bar, soliciting a range of reactions from disdain to laughter. The bar owner brought out two plates and placed them on the bar amongst the drinkers, one containing lardo and the other sanguinaccio. Turi helped himself to a plateful of the boar fat and blood sausage before continuing,

"The east-facing slopes below Soldano are the most ideal land for Rossese production in all of Liguria. The name Soldano itself comes from the word Sultan, because the men who tended the vines were Saracens brought here as slaves by the Templar knights. They had captured the Arabs during their battles in Palestine and brought them back along with plants and seeds from their native lands. It is said they brought grape varieties which had not been grown here before, but which thrived because the conditions were so similar and the Arabs knew how to get them to grow well."

Although well aware of Soldano, Ben had not heard the story about the origins of its name before. The red wine and Templar connection prompted Turi to recount another local legend,

"Let me correct myself, that Rossese you are drinking is indeed a fine wine, but not the best that could be had from around here. Crippled Lorenzo made the best red. A blend of Rossese and Dolcetto with a special ingredient."

Knowing that he had the Englishman's attention, Turi allowed this teaser to work its magic. Ben looked expectantly for the answer, but Turi just held up his empty glass. Finally getting the hint, Ben bought another round of the bars' best Rossese so the story could continue.

"Although he passed more than thirty years ago aged one hundred and twelve years, Crippled Lorenzo was remarkably fit. Although he had been born crippled, he was cured when he reached adulthood and was in better shape than most men half his age when he died. If it had not been for the hand brake failing on his Ape and it rolling-off the mountain with him in it, I think he would still be here today."

Turi translated and the men in the bar all murmured in agreement and raised their glasses to Crippled Lorenzo. Ben was now beginning to think that Turi and his friends were poking fun at him and was about to challenge this ridiculous story when Turi held his up hand, indicating that he was ready to continue the tale.

"Crippled Lorenzo had inherited a small vineyard on the west-facing slope of the valley above Seborga. Significantly, the land lay beneath the cave high up on the hillside, where legend says the Knights Templar had kept their most valuable treasures. The land only produced a few bottles of wine each year because the spring which irrigated it was little more than a trickle and water did not spread far, but crucially, it never completely dried up, even in the severest droughts."

It became clear to Ben that even some of the local men in the bar had never heard this story before. Like him, they were all enthralled by Turi's tale.

"Why did this land not pass to his family and then this famous wine would still be available?" asked one who was cynical about Turi's story.

"Because the small earthquake which sent Crippled Lorenzo's old Ape tumbling off the cliff also cut off the underground source of the spring. The water dried up completely and no grapes have been harvested from the land since. Nothing but weeds will grow there now."

"I don't understand. What was the connection between the wine and the Knights Templar's cave?" Ben asked.

At this point, some of the younger men who had been listening walked away. They had heard enough of these old wives tales, but Ben was still intrigued.

"Did anyone else here ever taste this legendary wine?" he asked, looking around the bar. Vincenzo now translated this casual question for Ben, apparently making it sound like an interrogation because nearly all of them shook their heads immediately. Ben looked back at Turi for further evidence of his outlandish claims. Then a small voice from an older man who had been sat in the corner said,

"Ho Bevuto il vino di Lorenzo (I drank Lorenzo's wine)."

The men all turned as the old man rolled up his sleeve, exposing his wrinkled brown arms.

"Here are the scars from multiple snake bites I received while helping Lorenzo weed the terraces – it must be fifty years ago, now. One snake bite is no big deal. You are ill for a few days and then usually make a full recovery. This was a nest of vipers and they struck me several times. I slipped and fell onto the nest in shock after the first bite and the others joined in biting me."

Ben could see everyone in the room wincing at the prospect of the scenario the old man was describing.

"In those days, it was several hours journey to the nearest hospital. With so many bites, it was unlikely I would have survived, even if I had made it there: it was too much venom for the human body to fight. I thought I was doomed, until that is, Lorenzo brought a bottle of his wine from the Rustica where he stored his tools.

"'Sip this slowly. It will help. Not too much though,' Lorenzo said.

"I thought this was to be the last drink I would ever take and all Lorenzo seemed to be worried about was that I left some wine for himself, but then he poured a little more of the wine onto the wounds on my arm."

Unable to contain his curiosity one of the men at the bar urged,

"And did it save you?"

The others all burst out laughing, but the man speaking looked perplexed.

"Of course it saved me, you fool! I'm standing here telling you this story, aren't I?"

More laughing ensued, with the questioner now also joining in the laughter, but the man continued resolutely,

"My bite wounds stopped bleeding almost immediately and none of the normal symptoms of viper venom ever took hold of me. In half an hour we were back weeding, as by then the snakes had all scattered, but I have these scars to prove my story. Lorenzo then told me the story of the spring and the Sacro Cantino."

Several of the older men crossed themselves and muttered "Sacro Cantino" under their breath.

Ben, who had been listening spellbound asked them what was meant by that. As they understood no English, Turi interjected and explained,

"They refer to the holy grail. The green crystal chalice that is now in the Cathedral in Genoa was kept in that very cave. Legend has it that the Templars removed it from its hiding place when they fled Seborga, having been denounced by the Pope. As they did so, a spring erupted from under the rock where it had rested. That water flowed unabated for eight hundred years until Crippled Lorenzo died."

As they drove back up the hillside to Seborga, Ben thought about the extraordinary story they had just heard in the bar. It swirled around in Ben's head; the information felt like an answer searching for a question. And then he had it. He sat bolt upright in his seat.

"Alex. That must be it. The reason for the Frenchman's arrival in Seborga and his subsequent land purchase. He must have heard the story of Crippled Lorenzo's wine. The fabled wine and a Templar connection all points to another Payen wine scam."

Alex appeared to be puzzled by Ben's conclusion,

"Surely not. That's just one of the tall tales the old men tell in the osteria. Lorenzo may well have made good wine and claimed wonderful things for it. Probably, over the years, the story has grown and grown until it has become a legend. And anyway, how on earth would Payen ever get to hear such a story. He doesn't even speak Italian."

Ben could not get the story of Lorenzo's wine and the Holy Grail out of his head. He later telephoned a contact that he had met a few years ago at the University of Gastronomic Science in Piedmont. He asked where he might find any old records of wines from Seborga and the valleys around. He was told that the university building had been the summer palace of the Savoy's, the former ruling power in Northern Italy. The University basement had held the most extensive collection of wine in all of Italy and their archive still contained all its books and records. The Italian professor asked what he was looking for and offered to ask their librarian to see what he could find out.

Ben waited five days before he received a call to say that the professor had found an entry in the Savoy inventory for a small batch of red wine from Seborga, to which a lengthy note had been added. The message explained that this wine was a gift from the Bishop of San Remo who claimed miraculous healing powers for it. The note told of a local legend. It described how, when the Templars returned from the Holy Land bearing the Holy Grail, they had hidden it in a cave near Seborga. When the chalice was finally removed from this hiding place, a new spring of freshwater emerged from the rock beneath it.

The entry in the books went on to state that the locals who drank this water were cured of long-standing illnesses, barren women became fertile and old men were rejuvenated. The farmer whose land this was began to plant vines on the newly irrigated slopes and the resulting wine had similar apparent miraculous qualities.

"The wine of the Holy Grail!" shouted the elated Ben down the phone.

"It's just a second-hand story from a priest, doubtless wanting to ingratiate himself with his King and in doing so gain some advantage. I would not place too much store by it," his academic friend warned.

One of the many narrow alleys that wind between the piazzas.

Drawing by Linda McCluskey

19. ARANCINI CON PIZZA FOCACCIA

Vincenzo was waiting with the engine running on his Ape when Ben arrived in the piazza for their prearranged rendezvous. He heard the distinctive rattily engine and smelled the fumes before he had turned the corner into sight. The old hunting dogs were in the back, as usual, but they had long-since ceased growling at Ben when they saw him. Ben noticed that Vincenzo had brought along his gun.

"I see that you are prepared for any hunting opportunity that might come along."

Vincenzo shot him a look that said no one in their right mind would go walking in the hills without their gun; why miss the opportunity of filling the freezer for free? Vincenzo's stomach was also never far from his thoughts, the Italian noticed that Ben was carrying one of Alex's legendary packed lunches.

Although it was still some months until hunting season, the odd gun-shot still rang out around the valleys. Farmers in the bar were always claiming their prizes were a result of a shot purely in self-defence. With wild boar being a plague to anyone with a garden or orto and no witnesses and few officials who really cared anyway, no one ever got charged with hunting out of season. Unless that is, some innocent bystander got shot, which was not entirely unheard of.

Ben had remembered to talk to Alex about Vincenzo when they were alone one evening. He had previously been told that when they were at school together, Vincenzo had feelings for Alex, which the then shy teenager never articulated. For her part, Alex said that she had been oblivious of his affections. As soon as she finished school, she had left for America, where she would stay with her uncle and work in his restaurant.

Before his death, Prince Claudio had told Alex about Vincenzo's crush on her and what happened to him after she had left Seborga. Vincenzo and a group of other young farmers had gone to San Remo on a Saturday night and got into a fight with some local boys. In the fracas that followed, Vincenzo had punched one boy and knocked him out cold. One of his friends had dealt a similar hard blow to one of the other city boys, but he had fallen badly, hitting his head on a granite kerb. The other boy never woke up from the second blow to the back of his head.

They were all arrested. Vincenzo's friend was charged with involuntary manslaughter and he with affray. Because the two serious incidents were linked in one trial, they both received heavy custodial sentences. Vincenzo spent both his nineteenth and twentieth birthdays in prison in Genoa. Worse still, while he was there, his grief-stricken father died of cancer; some said that his illness had been made worse by his son's incarceration.

Alex had told Ben previously, "If Vincenzo sometimes seems dark and distant, now you can perhaps understand why. Apparently, he is racked with shame and guilt. Sometimes he has spurts of anger, directed at no one in particular, but at the cards life has dealt him. Although I don't think he has ever seen a doctor, I suspect he suffers from depression. Any New Yorker would have had years in therapy."

She explained that when he returned to the village, many had shunned Vincenzo as an ex-convict and blamed him for leaving his mother a grieving widow.

"But my father took him under his wing. Claudio treated him like the son he never had and that patronage also earned Vincenzo some standing again in the community. Although, that took at least a decade. His mother, who had never got over the trauma of her only son being jailed and her husband's death, became a recluse, staying home with Vincenzo as her only company. He still devotes his life to his old mother to this day. Perhaps in light of this, you can understand why the men in the village treat Vincenzo with respect mixed with uncertainty and fear? Women are also wary because of stories they have heard about him, despite them being only gossip and tittle-tattle. They fear he would be a violent husband. I do not believe so. He hides his many troubles behind a mask of toughness. I believe he is a gentle giant."

Ben had found himself genuinely touched by what his wife had told him. It was so far removed from anything he had been expecting. He now felt guilty about making judgements about Vincenzo based on what little he knew of the man. If he was sometimes irritable, short-tempered and uncommunicative, he had good reason.

"Poor bloke," was all Ben could add.

The short journey took Ben and Vincenzo as far as the Ape could manage. They continued on foot a further five hundred meters or so until they reached a point where the path split. Vincenzo looked down at the photo-copied plan that Ben had brought along. He turned it one way and then another to check his orientation before announcing,

"From here, all the cleaned land, above this path heading to Negi and to the left of this one heading up to the peak, is the plot the Frenchman has bought." As he spoke, Vincenzo also gestured with his hands in the direction of the boundaries.

"The uncleaned land to the right of the path leading upwards used to be Lorenzo's. It is twice the size of the Frenchman's plot."

The "cleaned" plot referred to land which has been well maintained to keep it free of the long grass and weeds that can cause a fire to spread. In this area, it is seen as the duty of all landowners to ensure that they keep their terraces clear, even if they are no longer harvesting the trees or vines. Failing to do this bi-annual job risks you being shunned by your neighbours, as you put their houses and gardens at risk of the wild-fires, which are regular and highly dangerous. A combination of accumulated dry leaves, brash and trees with hot, dry winds make for a tinder box awaiting a spark.

"So, the Frenchman has actually bought the land next to Lorenzo's, not his actual old vineyard?" asked Ben rhetorically. "But why?" he added, looking utterly bewildered.

"Maybe it was a mistake? As you can see, the boundaries are not clear and the maps in the Commune office use a small scale. Hundreds of tiny plots, no two the same size or shape are hand-drawn on a map. It's not exactly precise."

Ben nodded in acknowledgement of Vincenzo's theory, the basis of which he knew to be correct, but was still not entirely convinced.

"Or perhaps they could not trace Lorenzo's family, but by then he had already seen that Luca's land next door was being kept cleared?"

Strimming land to 'clean' it is the unofficial national sport of Liguria. In summer, the rasping two-stroke strimmer engines start somewhere in the valley around daybreak and continue almost unabated until sunset. Ben would see a strimmer protruding from nearly every passing Ape, car or scooter. He often joked that the Italians should propose synchronised strimming as an Olympic sport, as they would certainly be the unopposed world champions.

The larger plot was totally overgrown and stood buried under a metre and a half of weeds, brambles and self-seeded saplings. It was evident that no one had cleaned this land in many decades. Ben was aware that such land was of little value and that there were hundreds of similar small plots which had been on sale for years without finding a buyer. In fact, these plots were higher, steeper and more remote than most of the others, surely meaning they must be even cheaper, Ben assessed.

"How much do you think Payen paid for his land, Vincenzo?"

"I know how much the French idiot paid Luca for the big plot — a few thousand euros. The owner, Luca, was still dancing a jig a week after he banked the cheque. He could not believe anyone would ever want it. As for the bigger plot, I can't be sure because the family who owned it no longer live in the area, but I'm guessing five thousand at most. I would not give you the price of a bottle of wine for it, because I'd then be responsible for cleaning it. It would take one week's strimming about twice a year to keep it safe. What would be the point?"

By any other standard in Europe, a hillside wide and long enough for a ski slope with views of the Mediterranean for less than the price of a second-hand car would surely sound like a bargain, but then again, he reasoned, as there was apparently nothing that would grow on it, why would someone pay anything at all for it?

Ben had come out to the mountain hoping to find some answers for Payen's motivation to invade their life and disturb their peace.

"Higher above here is where we found the Templar chest containing the charter, isn't it?"

"Si, si. This is one of several paths that would eventually take you to that cave," confirmed Vincenzo.

Ben realised that Vincenzo had not been paying much attention to what was being said. His dogs were busy tracking back and forth through the undergrowth following the smell trails of boar. Their master was keeping a sharp eye and a keen ear out for anything suddenly sprinting out of cover. He knew that this would likely be preceded by furious barking and yelping from the dogs, but his instinct was to be ready just in case.

"OK, there's nothing much to gain from looking any further. Let's head back to Seborga," suggested Ben, resulting in Vincenzo looking deflated at the thought of no picnic lunch.

Ben had turned so he was walking in front of Vincenzo as they descended the hill down a more direct route. Halfway down and without warning, Ben felt a sharp shove in his back which sent him diving head-first into the brambles. Before he had a chance to recover his thoughts, a loud shot rang out that was so close it seemed as though it had been aimed at him. The combined pain from the poke in his back, the cuts from the bramble thorns and the shock from the sound of the gunshot made Ben momentarily think it was he who had been shot, but then there was another loud bang and this time he knew he had not been hit.

Struggling to turn himself around without receiving more cuts from the brambles, Ben finally saw Vincenzo above him holding out the butt of his gun for him to grab. Using it, he was able to pull himself upright, but his hands, lower arms and face were all cut and bleeding. The dogs were going crazy, barking and snarling.

"Professore, I am sorry. I did not think. I had to act quickly."

Ben looked down to where he had been about to step. There was what looked like a tangle of ropes smattered with blood. On closer inspection, he could see that the brown and black skin was that of a snake. The two dogs were still standing guard over the spot snarling.

"A pair of mating vipers aspis," their nemesis explained. "They were oblivious to you and you were about to step into their love nest. One of these on its own is bad news. Two unsatisfied lovers would be very pissed off."

Vincenzo used the barrel of his gun to unravel the bloody mess. Each of the vipers was about as long as his gun and the thickness of a zucchini. Their brown skin had irregular shaped black markings the length of their bodies. The first shot had almost severed the body of one, the second decapitating the other. Pointing to the severed head, Vincenzo warned,

"Do you see the arrow-shaped head and the elliptical vertical slit eyes like a cat? Those characteristics tell you it's probably poisonous. Most of the snakes around here are harmless and they have slimmer heads and round eyes with horizontal pupils."

He turned back to Ben, assessing his injuries.

"I can only apologise. There was no time to warn you."

Ben was finally regaining his composure and coming to terms with what had just taken place. This man had possibly just saved his life. They were far away from the road and even there they only had an Ape capable of a maximum of about twenty miles an hour. He calculated a hospital was probably more than an hour away if he was lucky.

Vincenzo was holding his gun in one hand and brushing grass and thorns off Ben's clothing, while still apologising. Ben finally managed to say,

"Vincenzo don't worry about the scratches. I will survive those."

He pointed to the dead snakes and added,

"But I might not have survived those. Are these the descendants of the vipers that bit the old man from the bar, do you think?"

Vincenzo screwed up his face indicating doubt about that connection but said,

"I suppose it's possible, but these snakes are quite rare. Or at least they are rarely sighted. I have not seen one for many years. This land is so wild and overgrown I guess it provides good cover from the eagles and makes excellent hunting ground. They would usually have known we were coming from a hundred metres away and disappeared unseen. They do not seek an encounter with anything that is not edible prey. These two were just preoccupied."

They set off to continue their journey back down the hill, Ben now being very aware of where he was treading. At the Ape, Vincenzo emptied the chamber of his gun and put it in the back, where the dogs were already laid out waiting to leave.

"We are not having lunch?" Vincenzo asked, nodding to the package still in the front seat.

Ben never ceased to be astonished at Vincenzo's preoccupation with his stomach.

"I think I need to get back, get some disinfectant on these cuts and have a stiff drink," Ben responded impatiently.

As the Ape bumped and rattled back down the hillside, Vincenzo was mumbling in Italian about his wasted trip and lack of lunch, with not even a pig to show for it. Ben could hardly hear anything above the noise of the engine, but this didn't prevent Vincenzo from complaining. He cursed Payen for causing him yet more trouble. His only consolation was that it sounded as though the Frenchman had been robbed by the local who had sold him the worthless land.

Switching to English, Vincenzo added, "Even if Lorenzo's spring had still been flowing his land was hardly worth cleaning. Unless I suppose, you were mad enough to believe the old-timers claims about the Sacro Cantino."

"Sacro Cantino?" questioned Ben.

Another one of Vincenzo's withering looks proceeded this explanation of what he clearly believed was the blindingly obvious,

"The Holy Grail."

"Vincenzo please stop. Stop the car. I need to talk to you."

As soon as the Ape stopped moving, Ben got out and walked away from it, taking the packed lunch with him as he knew this would ensure Vincenzo's full attention. He found a spot away from the noise and fumes of the Ape, where he had a line-of-sight back up the hillside from which they had just descended. He beckoned Vincenzo to join him and now that he could see Ben had brought the food parcel from the Ape, Vincenzo followed him willingly.

Ben opened the carefully folded paper to reveal huge focaccia pizza slices with anchovies, capers and olives. To accompany the traditional cheese-free Ligurian pizza, Alex had made some golden brown arancini stuffed with boar ragu. The two men sat on a rock facing one another. Each took a slice of the cold pizza and a drink.

This scene reminded Ben of the day, several years earlier, when Vincenzo first told Ben about the Knights Templar occupation of Seborga. They had hiked to a place in the hills where Vincenzo wanted to show him a large Templar cross, along with some mysterious letters & numbers that had been hewn out of a granite boulder. That day, they had also sat eating a picnic prepared by Alex while speculating about the meaning of the symbols left in the rock. Ben recalled that Vincenzo had suggested that they were some kind of coded directions to continue to another site.

Returning to the current mystery, Ben asked,

"So, you too have heard the story about the wine with restorative qualities? Tell me everything you know about Lorenzo, the spring water and the Holy Grail. Then, explain to me what, if any, connection there is to the cave where Selene and I found the Templar charter, because if I'm not mistaken, that land is somewhere below that very cave."

Ben rose to his feet and pointed up towards the hillside, where he believed the cave to be. He asked, "Have you been up there since you removed the Templar's charter from the cave?"

"No," answered Vincenzo, "I had no reason to go back. And anyway, the rocks are always collapsing and the ledges shifting. It's dangerous."

"How long would it take us to walk back up to the cave?"

"No more than thirty minutes," Vincenzo replied. "Better on a full stomach."

Ben got the message and handed Vincenzo the parcel to pick what he wanted for lunch, while he retrieved two beers wrapped in a cool, damp towel from his knapsack in the Ape.

As they hiked upwards again, Ben told Vincenzo that there had been no sign of any water in the cave for years when he and Selene had discovered the Knights Templar chest. Everything in the cave was covered in dry dust and looked as though it had been for many years.

The local pointed out that these hills were thrown up from the ocean floor by the Earth's shifting plates many millions of years ago. The shale layers are unstable and contain many crevasses and caves, often linked together inside the hillside. Rivers of water can be found flowing down through them but they are completely invisible from the surface. Also, as he had seen, they remain unstable, with small earthquakes being commonplace.

"When there is earth movement, some old caves open-up and others disappear. Watercourses shift inside the mountain and springs can pop-up where previously there were none."

They reached the spot where Ben had uncovered the charter which proved that Seborga had been gifted to the Knights by Pope Gregory. Little seemed to have changed in the intervening four years, except that more undergrowth was gradually covering all signs that the cave mouth was there at all. Ben looked down the hillside and tried to get his bearings.

"So, Lorenzo's land is below here as far as the path leading to the road and extends left further up the valley as far as that big oak?"

"Si."

"The land Payen has bought is slightly right from a line below us and continues down the valley?"

"Si. More or less. Old Lorenzo's land gets the morning and evening sun but is shaded in the late afternoon. Better for growing. Many parts of the Frenchman's land will have sun most of the day and has views down the valley to Monaco. Not so good for growing."

Vincenzo picked up a stout stick and wandered off, using it to peel-back undergrowth as if seeking something hidden behind it. He climbed higher up the hill above the cave and continued poking around. Ben also climbed higher to see what he was up to. After ten minutes Vincenzo called out,

"Professore, come and look."

Ben joined him where he was holding back brambles to reveal another cave entrance. Gesturing for Ben to hold the stick, he took out his Zippo lighter, bent and tucked inside. It transpired that he did not need the light because sunlight was coming from a source further inside.

"It's light in here. Come on in."

Ben jammed a stout stick into the bush to keep the brambles back. As he did so, thorns scratched the back of his hand, adding to the others he had already received and drawing a small amount of blood. He wiped the blood on his shirt and followed Vincenzo into the cave.

"There must be another opening further up the hill because rays of light are flooding down from it."

They could both now hear water flowing. Venturing further in, there was a stream appearing from under a hefty piece of rock. The water flowed across the cave floor in a channel it seemed to have eroded over many hundreds of years. It turned abruptly when it reached a boulder the size of a suitcase which blocked its path, yet the original channel looked as though it had once continued on the other side of the rock. This route was now dry and filled with dust. The rock appeared to have fallen from the roof of the cave above and blocked the channel of water. The stream's path interrupted, the water took the line of least resistance and turned down a slight incline. After travelling just a meter on the surface, the water disappeared down a crevice back into the hillside, from whence it had come.

"Where is that stick?" Vincenzo asked Ben.

Ben went back to the cave entrance and retrieved the stout post. While Ben levered the boulder with the stick, Vincenzo tried to roll it out of the channel with his hands. The wood bent under the strain and finally snapped, but not before they had moved the stone sufficiently to see water trickle under it and create a damp patch in the dried-up stream bed heading in the original direction.

"There's the answer to the missing stream," announced Vincenzo proudly. "A small quake will have dislodged this boulder. It fell, blocked the water and so it flowed away back inside the hill. Simple as that. One more man and maybe an iron lever and we could turn this tap back on."

Ben looked incredulously at his damp, dusty hands and in an almost reverential whisper said,

"So, this is the water Crippled Lorenzo used to grow his life-enhancing wine? Possibly the same water that is recorded appearing from the rock after they removed the Holy Grail, probably from this very cave. Holy water?"

"I guess so," Vincenzo confirmed matter-of-factly.

Ben dipped his hands into the stream and scooped water onto the scratches on his face and arms, washing off the dust and now dried blood. He was quiet for several minutes. He had had an idea.

20. INSALATA DI POLPO

Once well clear of Menton harbour and any other sea traffic, the skipper turned the big yacht into the wind and stopped the diesel engine. After heading directly away from the shore, they were now turned parallel with it. All the villas on the hillsides outside of Menton had shrunk to matchbox size and somehow had become even prettier from a distance. The green lawns, whitewashed walls, terracotta roofs and palm-fringed pools seemed idyllic as they glowed in the early morning sunshine.

Roman and the older crewman moved around the boat, pulling up fenders, untying ropes and unfurling sails. The remaining younger members began winding chrome winches, which in-turn began hoisting the mainsail and mizzen up the tall wooden masts. Cecily received the slack rope from behind one of the winches and skilfully coiled it neatly on the deck; she was a hands-on boat owner.

The sails flapped loudly as the stiff breeze blew across their width but did not yet fill them. As the winch man hauled the sail closer to the top, the fabric became tighter and the energy needed to fill it became greater. The triangle of sail was now almost entirely open. The bulge in the sailcloth which formed a pocket for the wind tightened, stitches straining and guide ropes groaning.

One of the crew turned to the skipper and gave him a thumbs-up. The skipper called out, "Coming about," and began spinning the stainless steel, wood-rimmed wheel. The skipper explained to Ben that this turn would bring the bow of the boat to "a close-haul on a port tack." He added that the wind was blowing about twenty-miles-per-hour from the east, but Ben had no idea what any of this meant.

Ben was not prepared for the severe lean that the boat now took, tilting about twenty five degrees from horizontal, which had him stumbling until he found something substantial to hold onto. The sail filled with wind and after more brief fretting of the canvas, the fabric became tense and quietened.

Ben could feel the surge of the movement forward as the breeze pushed the boat into the sea. It seemed as if the powerful engine had suddenly been put into full throttle and yet there was no mechanical noise. Several loud creaks and groans could be heard as the boat's timbers adjusted to the new strains that they were under. Without the diesel noise, the boat settled into a rhythm of natural sounds consisting mainly of wind and waves punctuated by the occasional rope tightening grind from a crewman on a winch.

His first time on a wooden sailing boat, Ben thought that it seemed almost alive. Its timbers, each chosen for its specific qualities, were toiling hard at their respective jobs. Although theoretically lifeless, it was far from inanimate; the wood stretched and bent before returning to its given shape, bestowing an organic feel to the manmade structure.

It seemed to Ben as if the groans and creaks were the planks and spars complaining about their workload. He ran his hand over the teak deck, feeling its grain and admiring the workmanship that created it. As he did so, he noticed that all the scratches on his hands from the bramble thorns had disappeared entirely. It had been two days, which seemed to Ben to be remarkably quick healing. *Lorenzo's holy water*? He allowed himself to speculate, before quickly dismissing the idea.

There was something remarkably peaceful about the atmosphere on board now that the engine had been cut. There was still plenty of other noise, even apart from the complaining timbers. Sales fluttered, ropes strained and waves slapped against the bow as it cut through them. They were all unfamiliar sounds to Ben but seemed completely natural to him; he felt at once disconnected from the ties of the land and at one with nature. He also felt an unexpected but powerful connection with all sailors and explorers that had gone before him; with nothing more than the wind for fuel, they could now travel anywhere in the world from this location. It was the ultimate feeling of freedom, he mused, and it felt good.

Course set, the boat, crew and passengers settled into a routine. Apart from the adjusting of ropes to stiffen or slacken the sails to accommodate any changes in the winds, the crew could concentrate on other duties, which included lunch. Alex and Cecily were stretched out on cushions on the focsle and chatted out of earshot of the men. Roman was reclined on a bench in the cockpit. He had a cushion behind his head and was already deep into a well-thumbed copy of The Leopard. Ben had settled with his back to the mizzen mast. He was transfixed by the waves being made by the boat as it scythed through the water.

His head empty of all other distractions, Ben once again tried to make sense of the Payen situation. He knew enough about wine to know that, as much as he personally loved Rossese, it was never going to be good enough to be passed off as Romanee Conti. Even if wine fraud was the Frenchman's plan, why did he need to be Prince of Seborga to carry it out?

Then there was the land. Surely, he could not bring even the most naive visitor to that tiny patch of scrubland and convince them it was capable of producing any worthwhile crop? And yet here he was, claiming the crown was his; a known conman whose modus operandi was fine wine scams buying land in Seborga – what possible other explanation could there be? The call of "lunch" finally broke Ben's fruitless analysis and he parked any conclusions he had had for now.

Alex had been conscious of Cecily's chef possibly being uneasy by her presence on board. She understood that he would know about her former Michelin Star status. There exists a strict hierarchy in the world of kitchens and within it, everyone knows their place. To ensure Cecily's chef understood where Alex saw herself in the hierarchy onboard this boat, she knocked on the side of an imaginary door to his galley. Addressing him as 'chef' in explicit acknowledgement of his seniority in this situation, she addressed him,

"I just wanted to say that, if you are short-handed with the extra guests on board, it would be a privilege to chop some vegetables or do any other prep that you need. Cecily has told me many times of the fabulous work that you do for her and Roman and I are really looking forward to tasting your menus."

The chef stopped what he was doing, "It is kind of you to offer, but as you can see, space is limited. Thank you, though."

"I can't imagine how you can work in such a cramped space and produce the dishes Cecily describes."

Pecking order established, egos massaged and a culinary kinship formed, Alex retreated from the chef's territory with a cheery,

"OK. Looking forward to lunch."

While they were under sail, with the boat heeled-over and a fresh breeze blowing across the deck, lunch was served below in the saloon. A delicious spaghetti of fresh clams was followed by chef's own version of capon magro, where sliced octopus replaced the white fish. Alex observed,

"I think the firmness of the octopus works better in the salad than fish, which tends to flake into tiny shreds so that you lose all the flavour. It also goes perfectly with the prawns."

Alex made a mental note to tell Cristiano about this interpretation of the dish.

Roman had brought some Malvasia wine with him in the car from Sicily that he explained was, "Strong in colour, flavour and alcohol and wonderful if well chilled."

As he was pouring the remnants of the bottle into Ben's glass, he said,

"Ben, I have a favour to ask you. I am used to being active. The fruit farm kept me busy seven days a week. Only a week or so has passed living here on the boat and I am already feeling bored and a bit useless. I know how busy you are with your various projects, would you allow me to help you with the orange trees? It would make me feel useful and allow Cecily to get her work done here."

Cecily could barely contain her grin. The crafty old negotiator had turned her suggested offer of charity into a plea for Ben to help him. Putting it this way made it much more palatable to the Englishman. He was no longer seeking help but giving it. Before he could accept, very willingly, Roman continued his pitch.

"I am officially retired and so can't accept any payment; however if Alex were to offer me the occasional lunch when I'm working in Seborga that would be worth more than any salary. It could be just until the trees are established and producing fruit. By then, I might be ready to hang-up my pruning shears."

Alex spoke for both of them when she answered,

"Roman, that would be fantastic in so many ways, I can't tell you how grateful we would be. The farmers would respect and listen to you. They have put Ben under a lot of pressure, but mainly because they have no one else to turn to. You would be the answer to all our prayers."

"No. I insist that it is you who are doing me a favour," Roman countered.

"No, it is I who will benefit most," added Cecily. "He's already getting grumpy from boredom and I can't get any work done with him moping about the boat looking for things to fix, replace or varnish. I think the crew are ready to mutiny."

With an enormous load lifted from his shoulders and half a bottle of wine consumed with lunch, Ben slept through much of the afternoon stretched out on a deck cushion. His dreams were dominated by trying to work out Payen's motives, the rationale for his claims and his reasons for buying the supposedly worthless land in Seborga. He was sure there was some connection to the Knights Templar legend of the Holy Grail.

The sudden activity on deck woke Ben with a start. The yacht was entering the mouth of Portofino harbour. The sun was setting behind the church, which was high on the hill above the town. The Chiesa di San Giorgio had served the spiritual needs of the fisherman of this tiny enclave since the time of Templars. Now, it is the number one aspirational marriage venue for international football stars, models, rappers and oligarchs. Not least because of the church's proximity to the fabulous Hotel Splendido, which is next on the wish-list of must-haves for the perfect wedding party for those who don't need to ask the price.

However, the picturesque church and the fabulous belle epoque hotel are mere bookends to what must be the prettiest harbour in all of Italy, and therefore surely all the world. Rows of tiny shops, restaurants and bars line the narrow east quay, which at one point was little more than a couple of meters wide. Above the canopies keeping the late sun from the customers' Aperol spritz, brightly coloured apartments and a few private houses cling to the hillside, their foundations barely above the waterline. The coloured patchwork of houses are stacked up the hillside until it becomes too steep, from there the forest of the National Park takes over.

The broader western quay was the now shaded setting for just a handful of larger restaurants, before the cliffs rose steeply up towards the church. Where the two quays converged, a slipway of stone slabs emerged from the crystal clear waters and sloped up towards a piazza filled with people enjoying their passeggiata (evening stroll). A few children played on the water's edge, dabbling their toes in the cooling sea. More open-air restaurants, including the Splendido Mare, a satellite waterside branch of the famous hotel, were cut through by narrow lanes leading off into the old town behind.

There is only one narrow, two-lane road into Portofino and the same one heading out. It is a dead-end for vehicles. Less than a dozen narrow streets make up the entire village and with land so valuable, there is limited parking. As a consequence, it is gridlocked in summer; walking, bus or water taxis are the best way to arrive – or by yacht, of course.

The sails had been dropped on Cecily's boat and the crew were furling them on the decks, deftly knotting ropes to keep them shipshape. Blue fenders were being lowered over each side to avoid any unwanted scrapes as the boat closed on its new, temporary neighbours. The diesel engine spluttered into life again and began its slow churn, pushing the boat purposefully towards the mooring where several others were already at anchor.

Assessing the scene in front of him, Ben wondered if the half-dozen-or-so boats permitted to moor here each night were chosen based on their aesthetic qualities. He imagined some kind of fantastical, artistic harbour master selecting pretty boats for his pallet of applicants in some sort of bizarre nautical beauty pageant. The best sizes, shapes and colours being carefully placed against an azure blue canvas to make this already unbearably bucolic place look even more attractive. Illuminated at night with downlighters from their masts and stays, these boats completed a vision that was almost too perfect; a picturesque scene, which was photographed and digitally circulated throughout the world by tourists hundreds of times every evening.

Although some of the boats were new, many were older than their owners, most of whom seemed to Ben to be quite mature. What they had in common was that they were all sleek sailing boats with classic lines and considerable length. Sailing boat pecking-order is measured in their length by feet, even in Europe where the metre has always ruled.

Mass production yacht model names will usually carry a suffix as 38 or 52, which refers to their length in feet from bow to stern. These boats were all past the 52-foot range. There were also a handful of big fibreglass motor cruisers that were common in marinas around the world. There was limited space along the quayside, which was less than 100-metres and Ben could see less than eight boats currently moored in the harbour.

Yacht Cecily's sleek lines, tall masts and white canvas slipped into this scene like a well-manicured hand into a glove. Dropping anchor, Ben was to discover, was quite the event and it required the assistance of several pairs of hands and eyes. In such a small harbour, the boats cannot be allowed to swing on their anchor in the shifting seas, they must be secured front and rear to prevent them from colliding with their neighbours – who were often multi-million pound, floating assets.

The technique involved sending out the tender to pick up a line with which to secure the rear. With a rope attached to this mooring line, the boat would motor forward before dropping anchor some twenty meters out in front of its final resting place. It was a manoeuvre fraught with potential problems. Most common of these faux pas' was to lay the anchor chain over that of any of your neighbours, thereby preventing them from moving off before you have retrieved yours, a task that was easy in these crystal clear shallow waters but not always so simple in deeper, murkier moorings.

"An owner or skipper wanting to set sail at dawn to be in Monaco by the next evening, would be very angry to find his anchor trapped, perhaps while the culprit slept off a hang-over in the Splendido Hotel," explained one crew member.

With this scenario in mind, Ben asked if the raising of the anchor was as noisy as lowering it, as the thick metal links clattered out of their locker and the sound echoed around the harbour. At dawn, this would be a rude wake-up call, he imagined. The crewman confirmed that it was almost as loud, but also pointed out that seafarers were usually early risers.

As soon as the skipper was confident that everything was secure, the boat's shore tender was pulled alongside the ladder. The youngest crewman was holding the small inflatable boat firmly against the hull so that it was pushed away with the force of passengers boarding from the ladder. Roman climbed down and then held up his hand for Alex to follow. With a person at each end and one in the centre, the small rib was more stable, allowing Cecily and Ben to join them. They were all carrying their shore shoes to prevent damaging the inflatable boat. Once his passengers were settled, the rower steered for the slipway just thirty metres away.

Ben trailed his hand in the water while he admired the other boats they were passing. Alex watched, marking how relaxed he seemed after only a day at sea, away from the pressures of Seborga. The wind and sun's reflection from the sea had coloured him, giving his tanned skin a healthy glow that contrasted with his almost white hair. In his tortoiseshell Ray Bans, Ben could be the wealthy owner of any of these yachts, she thought.

Cecily had suggested that they eat on board that night. She said that the restaurants ashore would all be packed with tourists, and the food would be expensive but not necessarily that great. Ben and Alex agreed that, if lunch under sail were anything to go by, Chef could no doubt work wonders while stationery. Going ashore for aperitivo allowed them to have a look around Portofino while dinner was being prepared and the table on deck laid.

Cecily suggested to Alex that she'd like to walk up to see the church. Roman countered by suggesting to Ben that he was ready for a cold beer and so the pairs went their separate ways. They agreed to return to meet at the nearby Café Spinnaker where the east quay met the piazza in about half an hour or so. In any event, as you could reach almost everywhere in Portofino from the piazza and there was only one road in and out, it was practically impossible to lose anyone for too long.

Entering the narrow Bar Italia on the restricted east quay, Roman was greeted warmly by the short, muscular owner — a fellow Sicilian it later transpired. He was a younger man by at least a decade, Ben guessed. The Englishman, clearly benefitting from the association with his southern countryman, was given a similarly familiar welcome. The greeting included a finger-crushing handshake and firm slap on the upper arm that made his recently tanned skin sting.

Rocky and Roman obviously knew each other from Palermo, Ben now realised, and as the Sicilian had headed straight here ignoring all the other watering holes, he had clearly known that this man was running this bar. Cold Sardinian beer was poured from a tap into thick glasses which had been frosted white in the freezer. The old friends exchanged news while Rocky cut chunks of chilly-flecked hard cheese and pink salami with what looked like a large hunting knife. When he was done, the blade was firmly stabbed into the chopping board, where it remained upright and seemed somewhat menacing, Ben thought. The two men took stools at the narrow open-sided bar, from where they could see across the harbour and up to the church above.

"What an amazing place!" Ben said, not expecting any contradiction.

"Just perfect, isn't it?" agreed his friend.

After the initial pleasantries, with Roman introducing Ben to Rocky, Roman got to the point of their visit.

"What have you heard about a Frenchman called Francois de Payen? Sometimes Monaco based. Fine wine fraud is his MO."

Rocky scratched his chin, then his scalp and finally the lobe of his ear, as though trying to massage his memory into action. Then, his expression changed, as if a lightbulb had come on.

"Oh, yes. I hear he's climbed quickly up the ladder. I could not recall the name, but his work with fine French wine I do remember. A couple of years ago no one had heard of him and now suddenly he's a face. He did well for himself, so far, without getting caught."

"A face?" Ben queried.

Ignoring Ben's plea for an explanation, Rocky continued to address his answer to Roman.

"Bit of a mystery man, but one who I hear has powerful allies in high places in Italy. Not much else to tell. What's your interest?"

Roman explained briefly and asked the bar owner to keep his ear to the ground for any more news. He wrote down his mobile number on a beer mat and gave it to Rocky before draining his glass. He took out some euro notes but was waved away by Rocky with a cheery,

"I'll stick the beers on the next Russian guy's bill. They never tip but can't add up."

Ben was slightly disappointed that they were departing, as he could easily have sunk another of Rocky's excellent cold beers. Roman pointed him to a place at the end of the quay, which looked much more sophisticated, but less appealing and certainly more expensive. Ben acknowledged that this was probably more to Alex and Cecily's taste, as they had gone to some trouble to dress up.

As they walked, Roman explained that Rocky had left Sicily at short notice. He had been tipped-off that he had been accused, wrongly Roman was certain, of being a police informant.

"Bar owners trade in beer and banter, but I know Rocky. He was too smart to be bribed and too tough to be threatened by the authorities. There is no way he was a grass. More likely, some little upstart with big ideas but no brains was offended by him throwing him out of the bar. The punk will have then put Rocky's name about in the wrong places and as Rocky was not one of the old Sicilian families, he had no support network and had to leave."

"Still. It doesn't look like things have worked out too badly for Rocky," Ben suggested.

"No. He has a nice enough life here, but he is from the south and so will never be seen as an equal in the north. Plus, he will always have salty Sicilian blood pumping through his veins, making him sometimes a bit abrasive for the fine, gentile folk of Portofino. That knife stuck in the bar should act as a warning to the unwary."

Everyone in Portofino was dressed like they owned or worked on a yacht crew, Ben realised, and yet, that was impossible as there were no more than a dozen boats in the whole harbour. If every boat held ten people, they would only fill one of the twenty-plus restaurants now packed to the gunnels. Nevertheless, deck shoes, shorts and nautical tops were the uniforms of nearly every group of people they passed. In fact, when he looked around them, their party of four looked the least like seafarers.

When the two men arrived, Spinnaker bar was full. All the tables were taken and there were people three deep at the bar. Looking around for anyone who looked like they might be leaving soon, they heard a shrill whistle. The source of the sound was the four crew members from their boat, who the skipper had shrewdly sent ashore for a well-earned beer and to hold Cecily a table. As the four young men rose to vacate their seats, Ben took their bar bill from under the ashtray where it had been left.

"We will get your beers. The very least we can do," Ben announced.

Ben and Roman took two of the four now-vacant seats at one of the best tables nearest the water's edge. As he sat, Ben recognised the distinctive Geordie accents of natives of Newcastle upon Tyne amongst the crowd of half a dozen men two tables away. They were quite loud and getting slightly boisterous, but all seemed good-humoured, Ben assessed. Before they had managed to catch a waiters attention, one of the two older men in the loud group came over to their table and asked,

"These chairs taken, mate?"

"Yes, they are," Roman answered.

"Are you sure? We are neighbours, after all," the exuberant Geordie pressed.

"Neighbours?" Roman queried.

"We're on the Sunseeker opposite you. We watched you mooring earlier. Which one of you lucky gentlemen owns that beautiful boat?"

Roman looked at Ben, before answering,

"Neither of us. We are merely house guests."

"I own it, but there was no luck involved in acquiring it. Simply hard work." Cecily said.

The two women had arrived back from their walk and were standing behind the stocky stranger waiting to take their seats. The now embarrassed Geordie stepped aside holding the empty chairs ready for them to sit. Undeterred, the stranger explained that his son was getting married here that weekend.

"Tonight is a gentle warm-up. My son's a bit of a lightweight in the party department. He does have a first-class degree in business, however, so you can't have everything," he joked.

"And are you in business?" Cecily asked, feeling that the Sunseeker and stag party in Portofino had probably already provided the answer to that question.

"Aye, I have ten Hotels with Spas from the Scottish borders to Yorkshire. Two of them have Michelin Star restaurants. My son is now the operations director."

"Is that so?" Cecily replied. "I supply beauty products to most of the best spas in Europe and North America. Perhaps we should have a chat sometime. Do you have a business card?"

The man turned and shouted across the bar,

"Warren. Business card," holding up his thumb and forefinger ready to receive one. The young man brought it straight over, but seemed very keen to leave again and not get involved in the conversation. The Geordie handed the card to Cecily and said his farewells which included the reassuring,

"Don't worry, I'll make sure that they keep the noise down when they come back to the boat later."

Roman smiled, but looked displeased with Cecily and said,

"You can't stop doing business, can you? We're off duty now."

Ben had come to learn that Italians are stricter than Northern Europeans about separating business and private life. If business has to be discussed out of office hours, it is done by employing subtle techniques and less obvious language. Sensing some tension between Roman and Cecily over this topic, Ben tried to move the conversation on,

"I hope our Geordie friend has a good financial director keeping an eye on the cash, because I suspect that his son might not be entirely trustworthy."

They all looked astonished, but it was Alex who felt the need to defend the young man's character.

"How can you tell he is untrustworthy from his appearance? He never even spoke to us."

Ben shook his head and revealed,

"He avoided me in particular because he recognises me. He was my student at Newcastle. Even though all students are told that we use copy-checking software, he was caught three times submitting work where over eighty-five per cent of it was plagiarised. A record that still stands in the Business School to this day, I believe. I also strongly suspected, but could not prove, that he paid someone to write his final submission. It sounded nothing like any work he had done before."

"That tells us two things about him," offered Roman. "He is not only a cheat but also a not very clever one. Best avoided I think, Cecily," he advised.

Cecily said nothing.

Alex deftly steered the conversation back on course with,

"I'm dying for an Aperol spritz."

"Me too," added Cecily.

Tired of waiting, Roman got up to go and find a waiter.

Their table was in the best possible position for both people and boat watching. Their view was over the entire harbour, both quays and most of the piazza. Almost everyone strolling about in the evening sunshine had a camera or phone and was snapping photographs or panning video footage.

"This was not the place to come if you wanted to avoid being seen," Alex suggested.

Cecily looked around to see all the iPhones being used and said, "You stay in the Splendido if you want privacy. There are no phone cameras allowed on their grounds. You look down on this scene from up high, away from prying eyes. We could have gone for aperitivos, but it's a cab ride to get there and there is more atmosphere here."

At that moment there was a commotion and some squeals of delight coming from the piazza. A pair of white doves had fluttered up into the evening sky, having been released from a basket. It became clear that it was a bride and groom posing for staged photographs with a Portofino backdrop. The watching crowd enjoyed the show, and there was much clapping, cheering and photo snapping. Their drinks had just arrived, when Cecily pointed out the time, they were due to eat at eight thirty and it was already twenty past.

Climbing the ladder onto the yacht, they could see the table laid out on the deck under a temporary canvas bimini. The canvas sheet sheltered the table from the late sun. It also provided some privacy from people in nearby boats and the promenading tourists on the quay. If there was a more idyllic setting for a dinner, Ben could not think of it. It was certainly more attractive and almost more comfortable than any of the restaurants they had seen tonight where everyone was crammed into the minimum of space.

Chef's dinner menu reflected the region and the fact that Portofino was once a busy fishing port. Neighbouring Santa Margherita still maintains a sizeable fishing fleet. It was to here that the chef had gone to get tonight's key ingredients of Santa Margherita shrimps, San Remo red prawns and swordfish. Ben read through the menu which had been carefully handwritten on the boat's letterhead paper.

The Santa Margherita shrimp had been marinated in ginger, served with pumpkin cream and topped with black truffle. The San Remo prawns were grilled with seaweed and served with blood orange sauce—a nod to her guests, Ben assumed. There was a mid-cheese course or Agnolotti with white truffle, Jerusalem artichoke and anchovy sauce. The main event was roasted swordfish, salmoriglio sauce, with sautéed potatoes and local mushrooms.

Spotting some Lagiaccio biscuits on his travels - a local sweet delicacy in Santa Margherita - the chef had decided to use them as the basis for a special type of tiramisu made with a local liqueur nocciolino (hazelnut liqueur). The biscuits were a speciality of Lagiaccio, a district of Genoa where once there had been a manmade lake. They were told that this had long since been drained and built upon. The long-lasting biscuits were originally made for ships to take to sea but were now just a rich buttery treat to have with coffee.

"Bravo!" exclaimed Alex loudly, marvelling at both the ambition and invention of the menu.

"There are combinations of ingredients on here that I have never tried before! On paper, prawns, seaweed and orange sauce should not work and yet I am guessing that Chef knows that it does. Same with cheese and anchovy, a combination that I suspect might get a chef arrested in Paris. It sounds fabulous and I can't wait."

Prosecco was poured, the first course arrived and the happy group settled down for a long night of complete indulgence. It was a windless, cloudless night and the sky was a mass of stars. The scene from Ben's dining chair could not have been prettier, he decided. As darkness descended, the lights from the bars and restaurants danced on the water. The sounds of conversation and cutlery on china could be heard all around the harbour. They were luckily the only boat dining on deck and so had the harbour to themselves, or at least until other owners returned from dinner ashore. Opposite him sat Alex, tanned, groomed, smiling and looking incredibly beautiful.

"How lucky are we?" he offered to his dinner companions.

Roman raised his glass to propose a toast.

"We have a saying in Sicily. 'Love is like a cough. It is impossible to hide.' So, I toast lovers, young and old."

"Lovers," they all joined in, with Cecily adding, "but less of the old, thank you."

By the cheese course, their conversations had diverged into the men's and the women's. Roman was curious to know more about Ben's children, as Cecily had already told him that, like him, he did not see that much of them.

"Your daughter arrives soon? She is a journalist in London?" Roman prompted.

Ben explained how Selene had struggled for years to get a job in her chosen career, but then serendipity intervened in the form of their discovery in Seborga, which had got her the break she needed and she had done a great job maximising the opportunity. She leap-frogged several rungs of the career ladder and more than made up for the lost years. Ben did not reveal that he worried that this short-cut into journalism may now be proving to be her Achilles heel.

"And your son, what is he doing?" Roman asked.

"Tom is where Selene was five years ago. A bit lost and rudderless – but he is charming and handsome and so he survives."

"We were all young and foolish once, eh Ben?"

"Some of us are still a bit foolish now," was Ben's response.

"And you have two girls about the same age as my two?" Ben said.

"Caroline and Patricia, both have been living in America where they went to college," Roman answered, looking slightly uncomfortable.

"The eldest, Caroline, is like her late mother." He made a cross with his finger on his chest, out of habit. "She's quick to judge, long on opinions and short on temper. Her boyfriend, Ross Garret, is some sort of broker in New York." Roman leaned in towards Ben so the two women could not hear and whispered,

"He's a wanker, but has a business degree from Harvard and makes millions. Frankly, I would not hire him to pick oranges, never mind look after my money."

Ben was surprised but flattered that Roman felt comfortable sharing such confidences.

"Although they look very much alike, Patsy's a different sort of person. She's a gentle soul, but maybe too much so. It makes her vulnerable to chancers and a sucker for victims. Her current project is a penniless musician with few prospects but a winning smile. Daniel, at least, seems like a decent boy. He's just not a great musician and his lyrics make no sense – at least to me they don't."

Ben realised, not for the first time that he only had to talk to another parent to realise that almost everyone had their challenges.

Dishes came and went, wine was drunk and the chat was amiable. It was a wonderful night and only closed because the sea air had made them all tired. (Or was it the wine?) In any event, they were all in bed well before midnight.

21.BURRIDA

The following morning, a brisk north-westerly wind filled the sails as soon as they left the shelter of the harbour at Portofino, conveniently pushing them briskly in the direction of the Cinque Terre. Cecily had told them that it was impossible to find a temporary berth in any of the five pretty villages that made up the Cinque Terre. The plan was to cruise slowly along the coast until they found an anchorage with a good view. After a lunch ashore, they would take a tour of some of the villages. In the early evening, they would return to the boat and sail south to a berth in the port of La Spezia, home of the Italian navy.

The five communities that make up the Cinque Terre are not extraordinarily different from many other villages along the Ligurian coast. However, their west-facing location, leaving them clinging perilously to the steep west-facing rocky coastal hills, has prevented any overdevelopment. Stacking-up from the shore until it was just too steep to build any further, almost every house in each town is visible from the sea. Each property could be differentiated by its colour, chosen from a seemingly endless palate; the fishermen who lived in them would have been able to pick out their own homes from a couple of kilometres out in the Liguria Sea.

The steep hillside drops straight into the sea, with little by way of beaches or flat coastal strips as there are to the west on the south-facing coastline. That topography has dictated what could be built and also restricted expansion, leaving the villages looking almost exactly as they would have several hundred years ago. There are many other pretty villages on either side of the Cinque Terre, yet these five, so perfect and grouped so tightly together, have come to represent the traditional image of coastal Liguria.

It had taken less than three hours at a speed of around ten knots to cover the distance to the first of the five Cinque Terre. The amount of sail had been reduced so that they could alter course into the bay in front of Monterosso al Mare. The slower progress also allowed everyone to enjoy the breath-taking views. With the north-westerly wind still brisk, this sizeable sheltered bay was probably going to be the best option for a calm mooring, the skipper explained.

Unusually, this town also had a small sandy beach to make landing the tender easier. The skipper found a suitable place for the boat about three hundred meters off the beach. He ordered the sail to be dropped and the anchor let go. Once the anchor chain had all rattled-out, the boat stopped. The remaining breeze swung the big yacht on the anchor until it was almost pointed back from where it came and it settled to swaying gently.

After a morning in the sun and salty wind, Roman suggested a swim. Ben and Alex agreed immediately, but Cecily declined so she could make some phone calls and send some emails. The boat had been out of phone signal for much of the journey but had now arrived in the range of a communication mast. When the swimmers climbed the ladder from the bay, Cecily was waiting for them wearing a perplexed expression.

"The strangest thing," she said. "I have just received a text message and an email from Sergio Mastroianni, a man I have never met in my life and yet he has my personal phone number and my email address."

Roman quickly pointed out that firstly, Mastroianni was immensely powerful, and secondly, he owned a large piece of Italy's largest mobile phone company.

"I'm guessing he could get the contact details of anyone he chose and more besides if he wished."

"But he also speaks to me as we've known each other all our lives. 'My dearest Cecily' he begins. 'I hope that you are enjoying the Cinque Terre. Monterosso al Mare is pretty at this time of the year when the bougainvillaea is in bloom.' How the bloody hell does he know where we are?"

"Once he has your number, Cecily, he will be able to know where you eat lunch and how long it takes," Roman pointed out. Cecily frowned and gasped in horror.

"Remind me to change my telephone number when I get back to France, Roman."

Ben and Alex had immediately guessed that this unwelcome contact was in connection with their previous encounter with the manipulative Mastroianni.

"Anyway, after his smarmy preamble, all he had wanted from me was to get Alex to contact him urgently — as soon as you get this message. He told me to use these exact words: 'The future of Seborga might depend on your actions in the next twenty-four hours.'"

Roman laughed out-loud, beginning to see a funny side to this. He gestured to Cecily saying,

"Does the secretary to the Princess have an official title like 'lady in waiting?' or is she just a menial office worker."

They all saw the funny side of the millionaire entrepreneur taking messages, but Alex also looked slightly embarrassed and apologetic.

"That man is unbelievable. What a nerve, tracing your number and calling you here. I am terribly sorry, Cecily."

She smiled and winked at Alex.

"I don't mind keeping your male admirers at bay. And anyway, who knows, if he does become the next Prime Minister, he might be an especially useful contact."

Cecily gave Alex a slip of paper with Mastroianni's number and she went below to change and make the call. The men dried off and opened some bottles of beer. When Alex returned ten minutes later, she looked ashen. She outlined what Mastroianni had told her.

"His bear-baiting of the EU in the media has finally pushed them into declaring that the entire Seborga project is being stopped. Not put on hold, but permanently cancelled.

"Furthermore, Mastroianni's opponent in the election had engineered a big swing in the opinion polls by claiming that the EU has provisionally agreed to the bold spending plans in his manifesto. Because Brussels knows that Mastroianni is anti-EU, they do not deny his opponent's claims. They have gifted him this political advantage, despite apparently having no intention of ever agreeing to his ridiculous left-wing spending plans.

"In short, we have been abandoned by the EU, so if Mastroianni loses the election again, there will be not a single euro more for the only half-finished work. The whole project will be doomed, like so many others in Italy that were left as abandoned building sites after the last banking crisis. He wants me to go to Genoa for a press conference in the morning. He has an idea that he believes will turn things around."

Ben scowled, "So, even if we despise him and everything he stands for, our only chance is to help him win? Bloody marvellous! What is his next grand plan?"

"He is sure that if I tell our story to the media, the Italian people will back us."

"Back him, you mean, as the two things now seem intrinsically linked," chided Ben.

Neither Roman nor Cecily could think of anything positive to say about the situation. Cecily called to her skipper who was busy on deck sorting sails,

"How long to sail to Genoa?"

"If the wind stays like this, I'd guess ten to twelve hours."

The weathered French sailor asked for five minutes to go below to check the forecast. When he came back on deck, he revised his ETA for ten hours from departure because the wind was due to move to a more normal south-westerly.

Alex looked pained at the idea that she was interfering with Cecily's trip.

"Firstly, I have not yet agreed to go, although Mastroianni has assumed I will and says he is arranging a driver to come to whichever port we are in to collect me. More importantly, I can't spoil everyone's holiday because of my problems in Seborga."

"They're also our problems, Alex. We now all have a vested interest in the survival of Seborga. If we leave later this afternoon, we could be in Genoa in the morning. A night in La Spezia, or a night sailing. It's the same difference."

Cecily looked determined and before anyone could add to the discussion, took control of the itinerary.

"We still have time for a nice lunch here. The crew will need to rest if they are to sail through the night. This afternoon we could get the train from here along the coast to the other four villages of the Cinque Terre. After a light supper on board, we can sail overnight for Genoa and arrive at dawn."

Cecily knew precisely where to go for lunch. She was only hoping that they had their signature dish, a Ligurian fish stew known as burrida. From their table, they could look out and see their yacht swinging on its anchor in the breeze, its position already having changed to face northwards. Water, bread and wine arrived. Trying to lighten the mood, which had become somewhat gloomy, Ben said,

"Alex and I had this dish at her cousin's beach restaurant in Ospedaletti. It was amazing."

"It was our first real date," she added, without sufficient enthusiasm.

Keen to try the local wine from the vines they could see on the hillsides around them, Ben ordered Cinque Terre Sciacchetra DOC, made from Bosco, Albarola and Vermentino. The waiter explained that the terraces in which these grapes were grown were so steep, that they could only be harvested by hand. Each box was then carried to a miniature railway line bolted to the hillside from where they could be extracted to the winery. The waiter was perhaps telling this story to justify the price tag, which was high for what was essentially just a blended Vermentino. However, it was distinctly different and likeable they all agreed, and so well worth the experiment.

The phone call from Mastroianni had cast a shadow over their weekend that was proving challenging to lift. Both Ben and Alex could not help feeling as though they had been ensnared by the wily businessman-turned-politician. He had arrived like a white knight to save them from their enemies, but now held them imprisoned in his web of deceit, using them as pawns in a game for which only he knew the rules.

The excellent food and wine did eventually lift the mood. Roman steered his conversation with Ben towards the crops they could see growing on the hillside in the distance. Cecily, meanwhile, engaged Alex with lists of sites, galleries and shops she was going to show them later in the afternoon.

Monterosso al Mare railway station, like many in Liguria, looked like it had not changed since it was built sometime in the middle of the 19th century. Were it not for the palm trees, it could easily have been used as a set of spaghetti western. Original station buildings from the Victorian era had rooves adorned with fancy fretwork, elaborate cast ironwork detailing and stained glass windows.

The rail line through the Cinque Terre winds in-and-out of tunnels, through the protruding rocky outcrops, before opening up into the inlets where the towns are perched. From the coast looking inwards, each trains' progress looks like a needle threading through folded green fabric, looping in and out of the mountainside. Viaducts are sometimes required to carry the trains through the villages, often passing close to the windows of some of the houses and sometimes even over the rooftops of others. Like the villages themselves, the railway seemed more beautiful for its chaos and apparent lack of planning.

The train makes slow progress, but no village is far from its neighbour and so journeys only take a few minutes. Road access to the Cinque Terre is challenging and so the trains are packed with both tourists and locals, the two groups being easily distinguishable. The four friends had to stand as all the seats had been taken. However, from this position, they had a better view of the breath-taking scenery as the train emerged from each tunnel. The pleasures of lunch in good company and now the excitement of the scenic day trip provided some temporary anaesthetic for the pain of Ben and Alex's many concerns. They stepped off the train at Vernazze onto the narrow station platform and were swept along with the tide of passengers filtering into the narrow streets of the small town.

Cecily had never seen the Cinque Terre so busy. Thousands of mainly American and Asian tourists filled small shops and cafés, munching pizza slices and drinking from plastic bottles.

"A victim of its own success," Cecily observed. "It's a shame because it is so pretty without all these people."

"Yes, and the type of success we must fight hard to avoid in Seborga," Ben added. "These day-trippers and cruise ship passengers have the maximum negative impact, for the least financial gain for the economy. You only need to look at Venice and Rome to see how it has changed their economy and way of life. We want people to come and stay in Seborga, to shop for local produce to take home, to eat food and wine in our restaurants that has been grown by our farmers. That type of tourist can sustain our economy and protect our culture."

"Fewer but better," agreed Alex.

After an hour fighting through the crowds and warding off-street hawkers in the rising temperature, Cecily finally said, "Let's get out of here. It's just too busy." No one argued.

22. BRIOCHE ALLA CREMA

The sound of water rushing past the hull, less than the thickness of a paperback book away, was the unfamiliar sound that Ben awoke to. It took his brain a while to adjust to his strange surroundings. He turned over to find Alex already wide awake and propped up against her pillows, staring out of the porthole at the sky.

"Trouble sleeping?"

She nodded and rolled over towards him, her long wavy hair flicking onto his face. He brushed it to one side to avoid it making him sneeze.

"I'm terrified about this press conference. I know I am going to be ambushed again, just like last time when the media came to Seborga."

Ben didn't know how to respond and so said that he needed coffee to clear his head and would go and bring some from the galley. When he reached the foot of the stairs leading to the deck, he could see that although it was still dark outside, Cecily and Roman were sat at the table. He emptied and then refilled the Bialetti coffee pot and lit the gas ring under it before joining his hosts on deck.

"Early risers all?" he offered.

"When we're sailing I like to see the sun come up over the ocean. There is something very magical about it out at sea," replied Cecily.

Roman rose from his seat and offered,

"Coffee, Ben?"

Ben sat opposite them and told them that the pot was already heating up on the stove. Roman relaxed back into the cushions with an arm over Cecily's shoulder. They were a handsome couple, Ben thought, and already so amazingly comfortable in each other's company. He had to remind himself that although he had only known them as a couple for a few weeks, their clandestine relationship had previously gone on for many years.

"We have been chatting about this press conference, Ben. If you don't mind us saying so, we think that you need to readdress the balance of power. Mastroianni seems to have been running the agenda from day one, with you and Alex running to catch up. Today is another example. You have no idea what you are walking into or what his plan is, but there is one thing that you can be sure of and that is that the main beneficiary will be Mastroianni. Everything and anyone else will be seen as collateral damage. Maybe you shouldn't go?"

Ben was simultaneously relieved at the idea of avoiding the media lion's den doubtless waiting for them in Genoa, but perplexed by how running away from it could help them.

"What can we do? Mastroianni always seems to have us backed into a corner."

"Except that this time it sounds as though it is he who is on the ropes in the corner and you two are relatively safe outside the ring," suggested Roman.

Cecily began to explain, but the Bialetti pot started hissing loudly to warn that the coffee was nearly ready. Ben suggested that he go and get Alex so that they could all chat over coffee.

When they were seated and cups filled, Cecily explained the plan that she and Roman had devised. The morning air was still cool and they were travelling at a good speed in the fresh breeze. Steam rose from the cups but was then wafted away in the slipstream. Alex hugged her cup in both hands, enjoying its warmth as well as the aroma of coffee.

"We have been outside of mobile signal most of the night. We turn off our handsets now, so even the phone company can't know where we are. Although we have it installed, a yacht this size is not obliged to have AIS, so we can turn that off so we can't even be seen on satellite tracking. We can simply disappear into the ocean."

Roman then pointed past Alex and Ben to where the first glimmers of sun were starting to show on the horizon in the west.

"We change course and sail into the sunrise, straight past Genoa, leaving Mastroianni to fight his own wars today. It will wrong-foot him and gain some time. He will know that you are not his puppet."

He went on to elaborate on the strategy, which was to buy some space to understand the situation and then to devise a plan to take back control of the agenda.

"Before we talk, the first important decision is, do we change course now before we approach the entry to Genoa harbour?"

Ben looked at Alex, who hesitated for a moment and then nodded firmly. He turned to Roman and Cecily.

"OK."

Before they turned the boat away from the coast, Cecily sent a text message to the number Mastroianni had called her from, the day before. It read, 'Electrical problems onboard affecting navigation. Cannot safely reach Genoa Port. Alex will not make rendezvous.' She then turned her phone off and took out the battery.

Genoa is the largest port in Italy and so the shipping lanes on its approaches are extremely busy with ferries, freighters and cruise ships. In theory, under the rules, sea boats under sail have priority of powered vessels. In practice, it takes a long time to stop or change the course of a large tanker or cruise ship. Sailing boat skippers know it is safest to assume it is they that will have to get out of the way. Before plotting his course to cut straight across the shipping lanes, he needed to check the radar to see who was in the area, the course that they were on and the speed they were travelling. When he was confident it was safe and the crew were all at their stations, the skipper called,

"Coming about."

The skipper spun the wheel at the helm and the big yacht started to turn. The masts moved from twenty-degree tilt to the north-east, to almost upright. The sails all flapped furiously at the unsettling winds. The ship's lean then continued to the opposite side, causing everyone to adjust their footing to keep their balance. After a little more flapping and some fine adjustment of ropes by the crew, the sails tightened again and continued pushing the ship forward, now in a westerly direction.

Even after the momentary excitement of the turn, the crew all maintained their stations on deck to keep a close watch for other vessels and channel marker buoys. It would be another hour before they were past the busiest shipping lanes and out of immediate danger. The sun was now over the horizon, but only just. Its golden rays danced and glinted on the waves of a sea being chopped-up by the strong breeze. Ben took in a big breath of sea air and savoured it.

"I like sailing," he announced to no one in particular.

Claude, the skipper, heard him and smiled.

"Did you know that your English forebears borrowed their flag of St George from the Genoans to keep them safe when they were sailing in these very waters?"

Ben looked puzzled and felt slightly put-out that this Frenchman should be in possession of such an important fact about English history, of which he was evidently ignorant. His brain scrambled to imagine that the symbol, that for him was so intrinsically linked with the Crusades, The Knights Templar and King Richard the Lionheart, could be Italian. Cecily smiled. She was aware of this story, having heard it many times passing along this coast. She decided that this might be news made more palatable coming from a fellow countryman, rather than her French skipper.

Cecily explained, "The red cross on a white background was the ensign of Genoan merchant ships from the tenth century. It was a sign of wealth and strength much respected in these waters. During the Crusades, it was Genoan ships that the Knights Templar often chartered for their voyages and these already flew the red cross. Thus, it became the emblem associated with the Crusaders by both their friends and enemies. Only later was it adapted onto their robes as part of their uniforms. After the Holy Wars, back in England, it became associated with the heroes of the Crusades through contemporary depictions of the battles. It was eventually adopted as the national flag of England."

Both amazed and fascinated, Ben determined to carry out some of his own research into this gap in his knowledge. The skipper told them that breakfast would be postponed until they were safely out of the channel, so the four returned to their cabins to shower and dress.

The smell of warming brioche brought everyone to the table hungry after being up for many hours with only coffee to keep them going. There was also fruit, bread, salamis and cheese. The boat was healed over at too much of an angle for plated food. The sun was now fully up; the air was warming and the breeze dying down somewhat. The skipper estimated that they would be back in Menton by mid-afternoon if they did not stop anywhere along the route. They ate more or less in silence; each of them was also digesting the events of the previous day and trying to understand what was happening.

It was Ben who began the discussion by asking Alex,

"What exactly did Mastroianni say had happened to necessitate the press conference in Genoa?"

Alex wiped the croissant crumbs from her chin with a napkin and leaned back in her seat, trying to recall his exact words accurately. She repeated what he had told her about the EU formally announcing what they already knew to be the case that the funding would stop. More important was the information that it would be a permanent halt to the funds, not a temporary one, which there was no way back from. The second part, about

Mastroianni's opponent winning in the opinion polls, seemed opaque. The media mogul attributed it all to this issue of an unrealistic proposed spending spree being rubber-stamped by the same fiscal authority who had removed Seborga's entire regeneration budget. This move appeared to be counter-intuitive.

Roman, who amongst the four was the most familiar with the workings of Italian politics, was more sceptical. In his adult life, he had lost count of how many political parties and prime ministers he had seen come and go, sometimes two or three in a year.

"Italian opinion polls are not an accurate measure of public opinion. They are more a kind of barometer of daily mood, which could change several times a week. If the weather is nice, the pressure goes up. If it is raining and the men can't get out to play petanque and drink Gappa, there will be a low. If Mastroianni puts his picture in his own newspapers getting into the latest Maserati with a new pretty girl on his arm, his rating could be back where it was the next day. Unfortunately, they also choose which party to vote for using the same flimsy criteria."

Cecily deployed her analytical business brain to the problem and proposed drawing a mind-map to try and understand what was going on. She went below and returned with a notepad and pencils.

"What do we know to be fact?" Cecily asked pencil poised to write.

"The EU have definitely withdrawn all funds." Alex reconfirmed.

"We need verified information," Cecily declared. "Ben and Alex, you check out the EU side of the story using Ben's English mobile phone, which is less likely to be shadowed. Roman, you use the ship's PC to look into Mastroianni's claims about the opinion polls. I will use my iPad to talk to some of my banking contacts in Monaco and see what the markets make of Italy's political situation. When we are all ready with some facts, let's reconvene to discuss our findings and options."

It was Cecily who was first to uncover new revelations about Mastroianni from her broker contact in Monaco. Drew was a larger-than-life Englishman; a former banker who had lived in the tax haven for over a decade. Drew's wife, Katy, was the principality's most sought after society photographer. She was also one of the best walking advertisements for Cecily's beauty products, the entrepreneur believed. Between them, the couple knew everyone and went to all the best parties. Cecily thought that Drew had a good handle of what was happening across all sectors of commerce. If an individual, market or business was growing hotter or cooling off, he was Cecily's thermometer of choice.

He told her that there were many rumours swirling around Mastroianni's media businesses and so everyone was nervous about recommending their shares. Also, that his various companies were all highly leveraged, Mastroianni having sucked any available cash out them. Property assets owned by the businesses had been moved into a property holding company and all other capital assets into his leasing arm. These were then rented back to the companies at inflated monthly payments.

Furthermore, the Government's pensions authority was looking into several dubious transactions made by the company's pension funds. In short, he might personally be a very wealthy man, but the sources of his income all looked murky and his businesses shaky. They relied too heavily on cash-flow at a time when advertising revenue for traditional media was dwindling as more people moved online. Drew concluded his summary by adding,

"That's why he so desperately needs to win this election. If he can get control of the government, he can get the pension people off his back and add a much-needed veneer of respectability to his business empire. The prestige would help his share prices and ability to borrow, so he could invest in new media channels, but I think he's left that too late."

Ben knew it was hopeless calling Delon at the EU because the Frenchman would be unlikely to take his call. He decided Mastroianni's nephew, Salvatore, would be more likely to be forthcoming with information, especially if Alex were to ask him. Salvatore had met Alex on a few occasions and was smitten with her, as well as her cooking. All previous formal contact had been with Ben, never had Alex phoned him directly.

"Salvatore," she said warmly as soon as he picked up. "Thank you for taking my call. I know that you are an especially important and busy man."

Unseen by anyone, the overweight bureaucrat had unconsciously sucked in his tummy and pulled himself up to his maximum potential height at the sound of Alex's voice.

"Princess Alessandra. How lovely to hear from you."

"Now, now. We are old friends, Salvatore, you know I don't use that title, even if I were allowed. You must call me Alex."

Salvatore revelled in this level of intimacy with a woman who was not only beautiful and a fantastic cook but also acknowledged by most Italians as being of a higher social class. He had been rendered suitably malleable in just a few sentences and so she got to the point of the call.

"I have heard several different accounts of what the EU has said concerning Seborga, but I knew only you, in your unique position of authority, would have the full picture. The true story."

Salvatore hesitated and then replied,

"It is not good news, Prince... sorry, Alex. I know that I can speak to you in the strictest confidence. My uncle has stirred up a hornet's nest in Strasbourg and they are looking for someone to sting. This Frenchman who claims to be prince has lobbed a hand grenade into the already angry nest and what's more, he's now evaporated in thin air, so his claims can't be tested. It's not a great outlook for the project. However, my uncle says that I am not to concern myself. He is confident all will be resolved when he is elected and that the Frenchman was nothing to worry about. 'A mere pawn in the game,' were his words."

Roman did not bother looking too deeply into the opinion polls, but instead emailed an old friend in Sicily, who in turn called another one of his connections before responding with his assessment. From his raised eyebrows, it was not the answer he was expecting.

"Whales!" shouted Claude from on deck. "A pod of sperm whales off to starboard."

Everyone rushed to the deck to witness the majestic site of what must have been five or six huge blue-grey whales taking turns to surface and blow waterspouts.

"I had no idea there were whales in the Mediterranean," Ben said in astonishment and obvious delight.

"Many different types," Claude confirmed, "including Orcas occasionally. We would normally have to be further out at sea, but in this bay in front of Genoa sightings are quite common closer to shore. They come for the squid."

Passengers and crew all watched, transfixed by the enormous mammals that were cruising along at speeds close to that of the yacht. After five minutes on the surface, the colossal whales dived below the water and were not seen again.

The boat continued on its journey toward Savona, but the departing whales left Ben feeling slightly sad. His being momentarily so close to such a natural wonder had touched a part of him he had previously been unaware of and left a void. He was determined in that moment to try and sail more.

"Have we all got some new information to share?" asked Cecily, taking a seat at the big dining table as the others joined her. A crew member came to offer drinks, but they had all had enough coffee for one morning. In turn, they shared what they had been able to find out from their various contacts and online research. When they had finished, Cecily summed up the situation as she saw it.

"Although Mastroianni may not have been the catalyst for Seborga's problem, he has certainly fanned the flames to suit his own ends. His businesses could be in major financial trouble unless he wins this election. As prime minister, he gains control over the pension regulators."

"We might be feeling a little heat, but his pants are on fire," was Ben's analogy to sum things up.

Roman contributed what he had learned.

"His political rival appears to have offered some kind of deal with the small but vital green party in return for their support. Initially, Mastroianni's anti-EU stance on the lack of support for small organic farmers had brought them into his camp, but they are now more concerned about other environmental issues. A recent study has shown that the newspaper industry is still a huge polluter through their insistence on using bleached white paper, as well as printing inks containing potentially harmful trace elements. The media mogul's environmental credentials are not helped by being continually pictured in those same newspapers getting off powerful motorbikes and out of expensive cars, helicopters and jets. The greens now feel they can't be seen as supporting such a man and his opponent has swept them up."

Alex gave a small laugh and said,

"So, it sounds like Mastroianni needs us even more than we need him."

"That's it in a nutshell," replied Roman. "You might effectively hold the balance of power in Italy."

"That's way too much responsibility!" exclaimed Alex. "I sometimes struggle with feeling responsible for the few hundred citizens of Seborga."

Ben appeared to be trying to get all the facts straight in his head; he was making notes on the piece of paper in front of him.

"If I understand what Roman is telling us, the mainstream pro and anti-Europe factions are fairly evenly split, but the Greens, the far-right and a few other groups can tip the balance.

Seborga's plight would instinctively bring supporters of the right-wing parties, who are extremely anti-EU. If the Greens are key to this, how can we get them on our side?"

Cecily suggested they go back a few steps, pointing out they had all been lulled into assuming that their side and Mastroianni's were the same. She pointed out that it would be far more palatable to the Greens to support Seborga's cause than back Mastroianni. Similarly, the Nationalists would be likely to be sympathetic to some token restoration of royalty, if only because it would infuriate the communists.

"Although Payen's claims to the throne started this debacle, Mastroianni himself seems to have become a bigger problem. It's his personal profile, not his party's policies, that people dislike," concluded Cecily.

Alex scowled.

"Yes, he seems to have succeeded in pushing the EU over the edge at the same time as pissing off the Greens, and the only tangible thing Seborga has to show for it is a crane partially reassembled."

"Without the rest of the funding that crane will soon have nothing to lift," Ben pointed out.

"And what do you make of Mastroianni saying that Payen is nothing more than a pawn in the game?" Alex asked.

The skipper interrupted the discussion to say that they were not far from Savona and that the crew needed to rest for a couple of hours after sailing through the night.

"Would you like to go ashore for lunch, Cecily? There's a good marina at Varazze with restaurants and bars." Claude suggested.

Cecily agreed and Claude returned to call the harbour master at Varazze to check if a berth was available before returning to his charts to plot a course. In the hour it took to reach the marina, Alex had agreed on a short-term strategy based on their findings and discussions. All that remained was to enjoy their lunch and a quiet sail back to Menton dozing in the afternoon sun.

Alex concluded the discussions with, "Thank you all for your wonderful support and advice. For the first time since this crisis began, I feel like I now have a full understanding of what is going on. I am armed with information with which to make decisions. I'm going to take this fight to Mastroianni and Payen and start playing by some of their rules."

"God help them," muttered Ben under his breath.

The Osteria of my story is a fictional amalgam of the real-life Trattoria San Bernado, and this, Osteria del Coniglio.

Drawing by Linda McCluskey

23. SARDENARA

The boat had arrived at Menton harbour just as the town was bathed in late afternoon sunshine. Wispy white clouds were blowing out from the mountains behind the town, casting the occasional fleeting shadows on the water. While the crew stowed the sails and tidied the decks, Ben and Roman walked to one of the marina-side bars for a cold draught beer. Alex and Cecily popped into the shop next door where they picked up a selection of newspapers. There was no mention in the media about a press briefing in Genoa.

Any stories mentioning Mastroianni took the usual form, either putting him on a pedestal or trying to knock him swiftly off one, dependant on who owned the media channel with the story. Ben and Alex took this as confirmation that the so urgently convened press conference in Genoa was just another device of the scheming politician aimed at controlling the agenda. They were sure that only his own news media would have been invited and that any stories reported would have been of his own making.

They all reconvened at the marina bar and Cecily spread out the newspapers on the table.

"Nothing to report," she told them.

"That man is bloody unbelievable," Ben riled. "He feels not an ounce of guilt at the prospect of dragging us all away from our holiday and having you travel overnight all the way to Genoa, all for a mythical emergency of his own concoction."

Alex agreed, "We seem to have wrong-footed him for now because he has not been in touch for two days."

Cecily and Roman went to the bar to order drinks and there was a long pause as Alex and Ben contemplated the situation. Suddenly, Ben asked,

"Are you sure that you are okay with the plan that we hatched with Roman and Cecily? It is risky and there's a lot at stake."

"I know, Ben" Alex responded, "but we all concluded that we had no choice. And if we can pull-it-off, it fixes everything."

"And everyone," Ben added.

Alex smiled at the images this inspired.

They agreed to change the subject and make plans for the weekend. Ben brought Alex up to date on the details of his daughter's pending visit to Seborga. Selene was arriving at Genoa airport on Friday morning but had several meetings booked in the city before she could drive to Seborga. She would be there in time for a family dinner. Cristiano would have the night off so that he could join them. The Seborga National festival would be on Saturday night and the young chef was due to a night of rest before the preparations began. Mastroianni had been officially invited to the festival but had yet to respond.

"Do you think he'll come after I didn't show up for his press conference?" asked Alex, knowing that his presence was necessary for their plans.

Ben smirked knowingly.

"For Mastroianni, being seen in Seborga with you fits perfectly with his agenda and he knows that it will make a wonderful photo opportunity. He needs good PR desperately. I think he will not be able to resist. Plus, he will want to try and find out why you ignored his plea to go to Genoa. I am sure that he will have guessed that the electrical fault on the boat was just an excuse."

After considerable pressure, Cecily and the others had persuaded Alex that, under the circumstances, she needed to start playing-up to her new — but hopefully temporary—role as Contessa di Seborga; specifically, that she began dressing like a royal for the press at public events.

Cecily has suggested that she take a leaf out of her late father's book and start to play the part of a royal overtly. Claudio had never shied-away from dressing-up when the circumstances required it. He knew the effect that a bit of pomp and ceremony could have in swaying people to his way of thinking. Alex had squirmed at the idea, imagining satin dresses and formal suits, but had finally agreed to a compromise of Ben's invention.

Alex still occasionally rode her father's old horse for exercise. Despite his considerable age he still looked very imposing, at over seventeen hands high with an almost pure black coat. Prince Claudio had a fine-looking saddle made and a beautiful headdress of embroidered white cotton that covered the horse's ears. He looked handsome when brushed and with his tail and mane platted. When he rode into the piazza on the day of the referendum four years ago, the world's press was collectively wowed. That image was one of the most used in the following global news coverage.

Ben suggested a pseudo-military outfit, similar to the one Queen Elizabeth used to wear for the changing of the guard in London when she was Alex's age; essentially formal riding attire but with some grand military embellishment. Cecily arranged for her and Alex to visit a dressmaker in nearby San Remo, someone she had used for special occasions when she needed things altered. This lady also made uniforms for officers at the naval base in La Spezia, as well as cassocks for bishops and cardinals in the Catholic Church.

"She's good with braid and bling," Cecily summarised.

While they were in San Remo, they had agreed to have lunch and then both go to the hairdressers. They took a table outside a busy bar on the main pedestrianised shopping street and ordered a pizza slice and a glass of Vermentino each.

"Sardenara," corrected the waiter. Alex smiled at him, acknowledging her mistake.

"Si due Sardenara all San Remo."

What the locals called Sardenara was, in fact, the same as what passes for pizza in the remainder of Liguria, but in San Remo, of course they claim theirs to be superior. A soft focaccia base is smeared with tomato sauce and sprinkled with Taggiasca olives, whole garlic cloves, capers, oregano and anchovies. It is a simple and delicious snack.

'Faded grandeur' was a phrase that could have been invented for San Remo. The names of some its remaining hotels — Grand Hotel Londra, Royal San Remo, Grand Hotel des Anglais—tell a story of more affluent times. It even has a casino, although not one with the same prestige as Monte Carlo. In Victorian times, aided by the spread of railways, the monied and aristocratic families of Europe flocked to the Riviera for the better winter climate. They occupied the Italian side of the border as much as the French side and soon influenced the architecture and popular culture of both. Precisely why the cities of Nice and Cannes on the French side have retained all their glamour and prestige but San Remo has lost most of it, no one is sure. In economic terms, it would appear that in the battle of the Rivieras, France has fared better than Italy. Italians would counter that, in terms of retention of their identity and culture, they have won hands down.

Alex told her friend the details of Ben's daughter's impending arrival, including that she would be staying for a further four days after the festival. Cecily was keen to know what more she had managed to dig up on Payen and Mastroianni. Alex told her that she assumed that the meetings Selene had set-up in Genoa were in connection with the media mogul. This guess was based on nothing more than that being his birthplace and the headquarters of his media empire.

Although she had known Alex for many years, Cecily had only become closer friends with her since she married Ben. She was yet to meet Ben's daughter.

"What's she like — Selene?" Cecily asked over lunch. "Second wife and stepdaughter relations are the stuff of legend."

Alex took a second to choose her words carefully.

"We did not always see eye-to-eye. As you told me with Roman's girls, it was a situation which was guaranteed to foster suspicion and distrust on both sides. Such a starting point can make misunderstandings easy to occur and quick to escalate."

The details of early encounters, before Ben and her married, was the material for the next half hour or so.

Alex concluded, "Since the wedding, Selene and I have been fine. She can see that her father is happy here and she has somewhat fallen for Seborga herself. Selene has been back at least once each year — sometimes two or three times. She often now joins me in the kitchen to learn a bit of Italian cooking. We get on pretty well. Cristiano adores her. She is the big sister he always wanted and she spoils him."

"Have you met her mother?" Cecily couldn't resist asking. "Does she look like her?"

Alex explained that Ben's relations with his ex-wife, which had never been good, had almost completely broken down now she no longer received maintenance for the children. They have no reason to interact and he never hears from her. Alex said that, although she had only ever seen photographs of Ben's ex-wife, Selene did not particularly look like her.

"She has much more of Ben I would say, although anyone might easily mistake her for your daughter, Cecily. She's an English rose; all fair and pale."

"My sister, you surely mean," laughed Cecily.

"Of course. My mistake," said Alex laughing along.

Alex brought her up to date on Selene's meteoric career rise since the Seborga discovery scoop. Also, how her single-minded approach, combined with an ability to see subjects from a different angle, had made her a respected journalist in her field. She had gained hard-to-get interviews with some of the most media-shy subjects.

"She seems to have a knack of knowing what readers want to hear and the persuasive powers to get subjects to talk about exactly that. I admire the drive that has allowed her to achieve so much in so short a time. In that respect, she is very much like her father — driven, but in a subtle, quiet way."

"Gosh, I'd better watch what I say in front of her," Cecily joked again.

To qualify her assessment, Alex added the caveat that Selene's job was not that of a hard-hitting investigative journalist. Nevertheless, she had taken up this particular challenge with Mastroianni with enthusiasm.

"I suspect that, as well as her desire to help her father, she also knows that finding dirt on the reviled Mastroianni would score her a lot of kudos amongst her colleagues in the quality media."

More probing from Cecily had revealed that Selene had been through several boyfriends in the years she had known her, none of them lasting very long. Alex suggested that her job seemed to take priority over everything and she was pretty unforgiving about anything that got in the way of her career. She did not seem to need anyone in her life and was quite happy with her own company and her work.

It did not seem like the time for Cecily to reveal to Alex that she had now found herself in her own father/daughter and de-facto-step-parent situation. Roman's younger daughter, Patsy, had begun phoning him on an increasingly frequent basis, something that she had seldom done before her mother's death. If Cecily happened to answer, she had tried to be pleasant to the girl, offering sincere condolences, but received only curt instructions to put her father on the phone.

Nevertheless, both women seemed pleased with the results of their day in San Remo, as though they were now ready to face the forthcoming festival looking and feeling their best. Cecily was more relaxed about the idea of meeting Ben's daughter and their discussion had allowed Alex to crystallise her own feelings on Selene.

24. RICCI DI MARE

Roman was awoken at 5:30 am by Cecily's alarm going off. Although she had leant over and silenced it quickly, this was the third time in a week he had had his sleep interrupted by Cecily leaving or arriving in the middle of the night. He cursed quietly under his breath and rolled over to try and go back to sleep.

"I'm sorry, darling. I have to be on the 7 am flight to New York. See you tomorrow night."

"You mean I'll see you tomorrow in the middle of the night," Roman grumbled from under the covers.

The sun was rising over the Mediterranean, its rays streaking across the sea and into the cabin portholes. After Cecily left, Roman couldn't get back to sleep, which put him in a foul mood. Following a lifetime as a farmer and several years as a caregiver, Roman had been looking forward to some peace and relaxation. He had not bargained on living full time with an entrepreneur running her own international cosmetics business.

Cecily's fair-trade brand had been a success in almost every country in the world, which necessitated her visiting far-away places fairly frequently. Distances and time differences meant that she was leaving or arriving at very unsocial hours. When she was single and only seeing Roman for an occasional couple of days, this had worked well enough for both of them, but now they lived together their conflicting lifestyles were proving problematic.

Finally, Roman gave up trying to get back to sleep and sat up in bed.

"It's like living with an airline stewardess. You've been away five days out of the last ten which wouldn't be quite so bad if you worked nine-to-five, but this is a terrible life. When you're here, you're suffering from jetlag; you're sleepy while I'm wide awake and, if you're not travelling, you are on that bloody phone every ten minutes."

Cecily was listening whilst also rushing about getting ready, because this was one meeting that she could not afford to be late for.

"Roman. I am sorry. I know it is not particularly good at the moment, but it will get better. I promise. I have to go now, but we will have a long chat when I get back."

"If you can stay awake, you mean."

As much as she wanted to stay and explain, Cecily knew that she had to be on that flight. She kissed him gently on the forehead and left, leaving only a cloud of Chanel No.5 and some traces of lipstick on his forehead.

Already too awake to get back to sleep, Roman decided to get up, have coffee and to fish from the bow of the boat. Sea fishing was his new hobby and he had already had some success. Their mooring was close to the harbour entrance and so in casting distance of open water. Predator fish often came close in looking for the smaller pray who inhabited the calmer waters inside the harbour wall. Recently, the fisherman's patience had been rewarded with a barracuda of some three kilos, which the chef had made good use of.

Cecily returned from New York a little earlier than planned. Roman's words still ringing in her ears, she had pushed her meeting forward an hour and caught a direct flight to Nice, rather than the one she had booked via Paris. This decision had got her back twelve hours earlier than she had initially planned. When she phoned her chef to arrange a special supper for her and Roman that night, she was told that he was no longer on board. He had left early in the morning. The chef did not know anything more and the skipper had gone to Marseille to get spares, so he could not ask.

All her worst fears came raining down on her as Cecily walked towards the car park at Nice Airport. In her fretful state, it all made perfect sense to her. Roman was not happy with their new arrangement. Things were not as they used to be. She imagined that he was also missing the farm and his children. Then they had rowed. Patsy had called and he had left immediately afterwards. He must have gone for good, Cecily concluded in a blind panic. She called Roman's number, but it went straight to voicemail.

She called Claude, the skipper of the yacht, but his number was unobtainable. After a few minutes, she tried again. What Cecily could not realise, was that they were both travelling through the same chain of tunnels that stretch along the coast between Menton and Nice but in opposite directions. At any one time, one or other of them was out of range of a phone signal. The drive from the airport seemed to take twice as long as usual. Tears were running down her face when she arrived back at the quay in Menton.

Back at the boat and in her cabin, Cecily checked the wardrobe. Some of his clothes were missing and his holdall. She redialled Roman's number but received the same voicemail message. She found that it was even painful hearing his voice speaking in that detached manner that people use when they do not know who the listener might be.

"He's left me," she whispered to herself before subsiding into a helpless flood of tears and throwing herself on the bed.

She called Alex.

"Roman's left you? Are you sure?" was Alex's reflex response.

She realised that, although rhetorical, this was a stupid question, as Cecily would know whether he had gone or not. Why and whether he had gone for good were more relevant questions. Alex had never known Cecily less than totally in control of things. She always seemed invulnerable to the usual ups and downs of life.

"I can't leave the Osteria otherwise I would come down there to see you. Do you want to drive up here? You can stay with us tonight?" Alex offered.

Cecily thanked her but declined the offer. She explained the circumstances, how Roman often complained about her busy work-life. That they had rowed before she left for New York, but she had to dash for the flight with things left unsaid. And finally, how she had returned to find him gone, clothes missing, with no message or explanation.

Alex tried to apply some calm rationale to what she had heard.

"In the short time that I have known Roman, he does not strike me as a man who would run away from anything. He did not run away from his wife when many men would have given the circumstances. I am not saying there's nothing to worry about, it sounds as though you have some issues to resolve, but I do not believe Roman would leave you without some discussion."

Cecily thanked her friend for her reassuring words, which had made her feel slightly better. However, she could not help feeling that she had blown-it with Roman. After all those years of waiting and hoping for them to be together, she couldn't believe she had allowed her own greed to ruin things. If not greed, then it was undoubtedly her compulsive habit of always try to negotiate a better deal than the good one on offer. Not entirely just for the money, but because she was good at it and felt that she should, Cecily concluded.

"What a fucking idiot I have been," she said to no one but herself.

Roman was sitting down to dinner with what the restaurant owner said was the most beautiful woman in all of Sicily. He could only agree with his old friend's assessment and glowed with pride at the vision before him. Patsy and her elder sister looked remarkably alike. In their younger days, many asked if they were twins. Their lustrous, straight black hair set off the olive complexions and large, dark, almond-shaped eyes. It was only Caroline's propensity to frown and Patsy's to smile that set them apart. The former always looked cross and the latter elated and indeed, that seemed to Roman how they had been for most of their childhood. Caroline seemed perpetually angry at her little sister and the rest of the world, while Patsy did not notice, which made her elder even crosser.

As dinner between himself and Patsy progressed, the story that he heard filled Roman with dread. Caroline's husband had persuaded his wife that they should sell parts of his farm for development. Despite Patsy's strongly expressed reservations about carving up her family's farm, the American had gone ahead and appointed a surveyor, as well as an architect to draw up plans. His response to Patsy's pleas to at least consult their father before continuing, was to tell Patsy that her share would be one-point-five million euros. His flawed assumption was that this was an amount of money that would assuage any reservations, but he did not know Patsy. Her early morning phone call to Roman had brought him reluctantly back to Sicily.

"I don't know why they want to sell the land, Papa," Patsy urged. "They don't need the money. I am hoping that I can persuade Daniel to move back here with me and run the farm. He would love this life and it would be a wonderful place to bring up children. I'm tired of cities, the ceaseless rushing about, pollution and pressure to meet the rent."

For a moment, Roman allowed himself to envisage future grandchildren running around the outside of his old farmhouse, with Patsy standing at the door calling them in for lunch. The very house that his father had built with his own hands. He knew that, under the terms of the trust that he had already set up, neither sister could sell anything without the agreement of the other.

However, he also knew that, unlike her sister and her husband, Patsy had little money other than her share of the modest income from the oranges on the farm. Also, that she effectively kept her long-term boyfriend, who earned even less than her. If the slick Harvard salesman who her sister had married could swing Patsy to his side, the farm might indeed be carved up and any grandchildren might grow up in the USA. Over a spectacular dinner of ricci di mare (sea urchins), followed by red snapper, Roman reassured his daughter that he would resolve things.

Cecily was the only foreign woman who Roman had ever met who was willing to tackle sea urchins. Even amongst committed foodies, they were an acquired taste. Indeed, there was no food that the Englishwoman would not try, at least once, one of the many reasons they got on so well. This rare private moment seemed like the right time for Roman to tell Patsy exactly how he felt about Cecily.

He had already accepted that he was unlikely ever to change her big sister's point of view, but Patsy at least knew the meaning of true love. She would not have stuck with Daniel otherwise. He explained to her how much her demonstrations of indifference towards Cecily hurt him. He proposed that they all needed to accept what had happened in the past and move on. Patsy agreed that it was childish and promised to try harder to get to know Cecily in the future.

That morning on the boat, in his rush to pack after receiving Patsy's phone call, Roman had left his mobile phone charger. The battery now depleted, he had to seek to borrow one from his hotel. Cecily was not due back from New York until the early hours of the morning and so a text message sent now would still arrive before she landed. With the little power in the phone, he quickly typed, 'Patsy called. I had to return to Sicily. I will call in the morning' and then turned off his phone for the night and left it to charge.

The next morning, Patsy told Caroline and Ross that Roman had arrived in Sicily the day before to clear up some business affairs. She had told him about their plans and he had persuaded her to at least think about it. They were surprised, both by Roman's sudden arrival, but even more so by his reaction to their plans. By way of explanation, Patsy told them that their father was aware that she needed the money and that this could be enough for her to buy a house and save paying out rent.

"He would like to meet Ross today at the location so that he can explain further his plan."

After a couple of phone calls to locals, Roman had already discovered the sites Ross had in mind. He had also learned of the predictable anger of his neighbours whose land abutted the plots or was overlooked by them. Roman made his plans.

He realised that in all the morning's planning and running around, Roman had not phoned Cecily to explain why he was here. He stopped the hire car and dialled her number. She picked up before the first ring was complete.

"Roman. I'm so sorry. I am an idiot. Forgive me."

"Wo, slow down. What do I have to forgive you for? What exactly have you done?"

A tangible sense of relief was surging through Cecily's veins as she began to realise that things were not as bad as she had imagined. Feeling slightly faint, she sat down on the bench in the salon, where previously she had been dozing fitfully from effects of jetlag. She composed herself.

"Roman, we need to talk. When can I see you?"

"In about 5 hours. The flight arrives back at eight. Anyway, should you not be still on Air France over the Atlantic?"

Cecily just managed to blurt out, "See you there," before she hung up and fell sobbing into the cushions on the sofa.

When Claude the skipper arrived in Marseille, he saw Cecily's missed calls. He called her back to explain and pass on Roman's message that he had flown to Sicily to sort out some family business but would almost certainly be back before she was home from New York.

Later that night, over their favourite onboard supper of vitello tonnato, Roman and Cecily had a long overdue and frank discussion about their respective hopes and aspirations. To Cecily's delight, they agreed on much more than they disagreed. They were both adamant that their relationship was the most important thing and that that was where their mutual happiness lay. Not-with-standing Roman's family responsibilities, which Cecily acknowledged, he agreed that it was time for his daughters to run their own lives and make their own mistakes. Roman was able to do so, with reasonable certainty that his most recent intervention should not ever need repeating.

Mid-morning the following day, Roman received another call from Patsy. She sounded genuinely perplexed.

"What on earth did you say to Ross when you met him yesterday?"

Roman tried to sound equally puzzled when he replied, "Nothing very much. Ross did all the talking. I just listened. Oh, and then I introduced him to some of our neighbours who I thought might offer him some local advice about what he was planning, which they were only too glad to do."

This answer sounded evasive to Patsy and went no-way to explaining the extraordinary turn of events. She was still puzzled and quite sure that her father was not telling her the full story.

"Ross arrived back at the farm late yesterday afternoon looking very pale, as if he was ill or had received a nasty shock – a car accident or such. He went to his room and did not see either of them until this morning."

"Maybe he had sunstroke or heat exhaustion having been outside all day. He's a pale city dweller unused to being in the countryside."

Patsy then described how, at breakfast that morning, Ross had announced that after having seen the land he had decided to scrap the whole development idea. He had said something vague about the site been unsuitable because of some geological problems. He told her that they were flying back to New York ahead of schedule and said they had no plans to return in the foreseeable future. Then he had said to her that she could do as she liked with the farm, so long as they get their fair share of any profits."

Not totally convinced that she saw the whole picture, Patsy was so happy with the outcome that she was willing to accept things on face value.

"Well, that's just what you wanted, isn't it?" Roman offered.

"Yes, it is. But it is not what I expected."

"Well, my advice is to accept your good fortune and start working on persuading that boyfriend of yours that his fortune is unlike to be found in his guitar case."

25. TROFIE NERO CON PESTO

Roman had reluctantly agreed to be driven to the festival in the Bentley. Cecily had explained that it would help the Seborgan cause for the event to look as prestigious as possible. The fear of losing Roman that had been stalking Cecily was abating, but she was determined not to repeat the mistakes of the past.

Cecily's phoned pinged with an incoming email. Roman scowled and shook his head in dismay when she pulled over to the side of the road to read it.

"Not again? After our conversation last night."

"Just this last one. If this is the news I am expecting, I think you would like to hear it."

"It's always just one more. You never stop working," Roman replied somewhat resigned to these interruptions.

Cecily put the phone down and said,

"That's it. It's sold."

"What's sold?" Roman asked, "Another container of cosmetics?" he proposed disparagingly.

"No. I've sold my Company to D'Monde."

Roman looked astonished.

Well, most of the Company. I've kept the blood orange range. It's small and manageable and I can run it all from here. Everything else has gone.

He questioned, "What no more midnight flights to Tokyo? No more lunch meetings in London?"

That last trip to New York was the final negotiation. They've signed and paid the money to my bank. I'm out."

"Are you sure about this?" Roman asked.

"I have been wanting to sell the company for a few years now, but I was waiting for the opportune moment and the motivation to sell, which you've provided me with. I want to enjoy life without pressure; I have proven my success and now is the time to make time for myself and for us."

Roman put his arm around her and pulled her close as they drove along in the warm evening air.

"However," she joked, "I will still need regular meetings with my favourite orange grower in Italy."

Their laughter mingled, dissipating into the fragrance of the bougainvillaea plants which formed a purple corridor leading up the hill and nothing more was said on that matter.

After a while, Cecily asked, "What exactly happened to Caroline's husband to make him change his mind?

"I'm not certain that I can remember exactly," was Roman's evasive answer.

"But you introduced him to those men, so you know who they were," Cecily probed a bit further.

Sensing that he was going to have to offer some kind of explanation, Roman said,

"Just a few local Sicilian farmers like me. They probably pointed out the impact that such a development would have on the local community, and Ross had a sudden change of heart. Maybe he has a conscience after all?"

"We both know that's a crock of shit," commented Cecily uncharacteristically bluntly.

"Look. I can't recall what was said by who or what effect that had. All I know is that the matter is concluded. No one was hurt, and most people got what they wanted. Let's leave it at that."

Cecily knew that there was no point in pursuing this any further and she passed the remainder of their short journey in silent speculation.

The trestle tables had been set for the festival in the usual manner, ready to seat upwards of four hundred people. They radiated-out from the performance area that would later be filled with families celebrating, children playing and couples dancing. One unusual addition was a long table for the expected VIP guests which had been placed on a raised platform to the left of where the band had set up their equipment. As well as the usual white paper tablecloths, this table was draped with two large flags of Seborga. The same blue and white flags flew from every pole on all the buildings surrounding the piazza. It was as if to announce the revival of the claim for independence.

Mastroianni's acceptance of the invitation to the event had come at the eleventh hour. It arrived by way of a text message to Alex saying that it would be him 'plus one.' Ben had laughed at the confirmation of his prediction. It seemed the politician could not resist an opportunity for this kind of publicity so close to the election. Regardless of his acceptance, Alex and Ben had already received advance notice of the attendance of Mastroianni when TV vans and journalists from Genoa and Milan started arriving in the early afternoon. It appeared that they had been tipped-off by Mastroianni's office about the potential for a good story with fantastic images.

Cecily had engineered something of a coup, by getting Serge Philippe, Monaco's Minister for Business & Commerce, to agree to attend in his official capacity, but more importantly also as her guest. His presence represented a quasi-official, and arguably international, recognition of Seborga's status. Her successful global cosmetics business had an office in Monaco, creating valuable jobs in research and development as well as marketing. Revenues also flowed through the principality and so hers was precisely the type of high-value, low carbon footprint business that they wanted to attract there. It would have been hard, but not impossible, to refuse Cecily's invitation. His presence at the event wearing his red and white sash of office would not go unnoticed by Mastroianni or by the media. It would lend an extra level of credibility to Alex's position. It was also the case that the previous Prince of Monaco had always acknowledged Seborga's status, the history of the two nations not being so different.

All around the piazza was a swarm of activity. Vans were arriving and departing like bees around a hive. Cases of wine and beer were wheeled across by men with sack barrows. Temporary signs were being fastened above the individual food service areas and huge cauldrons steamed behind the preparation tables of the outdoor kitchens.

Cristiano had been busy with preparation since lunchtime, with the help of his new assistant, Marius. He had lit several grills and braziers, but these were still at the stage where they produced too many leaping yellow flames and thick smoke. Later, as the wood turned to charcoal, they would settle down and glow white-hot in readiness for the meat. Because events like this happened regularly in the summer, it all worked like a well-oiled machine. Everyone knew their job and got on with it.

Flag throwers practised their routines, sending the tools of their trade higher than they would in an actual performance, just to test their skills while no one was looking. This added enthusiasm meant they would occasionally fail to catch one; something that never happened during a show. A flag being allowed to touch the ground in performance would today mean humiliation for the thrower; in medieval times these flags were the emblems of local aristocrats and dropping one in the dirt might have resulted in a flogging, or even in death.

Early festa-goers had arrived to claim the best seats at their desired tables. Many would have driven from as far away as France, others were local Italians from the coast. The revellers were usually a mix of Italian and French, with some Monegasques, plus a smattering of foreign tourists.

Cecily was pleased to see Monaco's Minister, and his wife, Marie, arrive in a black official Mercedes, complete with government pennants fluttering on the wings. Drew and his glamorous photographer wife Kate had also been invited by Cecily. They had just been dropped off on the edge of the piazza by a taxi. Roman spotted Ben walking across the piazza with Selene on his arm. He nudged Cecily and nodded in their direction. She smiled broadly and turned back to Roman.

"Wow!"

Roman also smiled and nodded in agreement and added,

"Well done, my dear. Good choice."

Needing something to wear at the last minute, Selene had consulted Alex and she had called her friend and new royal fashion consultant. Cecily had persuaded designer Isabell Kristensen of Monaco to loan Selene a dress, hinting at the potential for fantastic international publicity. The garment that was the cause of so much admiration was a pure silk crepe de chine day dress, which looked as though it flowed like liquid over Selene's hips and thighs, stopping just at knee height. The fitted bodice revealed enough to be suggestive but not so much as to invite comment. As she turned to receive introductions to other guests, Roman could see it was also backless but for the straps from the bodice which were tied in a bow at her neck, their ends hanging between her shoulder blades.

"It is perfect," commented Cecily. "She looks stunning."

The media had also spotted Selene and photographers were homing-in on her from all directions.

Their party of eight now complete, Cecily made the necessary introductions and they headed for their seats at the top table. Vincenzo had drafted in some reserve guards and two of these in their new Seborgan uniforms and blue berets escorted them through the piazza.

The distant roar of a helicopter engine announced the arrival of Mastroianni and his mystery guest. The engine note was soon drowned out by the noise of the rotor blades slapping the air. The blades were fighting-off the forces of gravity, while the helicopter pilot navigated to a vertical landing on the five a side football pitch.

Before the blades had even started to slow, two male passengers were out of the cockpit, heads bowed and striding purposefully up the gradient towards the piazza. Two burly security men who had been waiting on the sports pitch were having to half-run to keep up with them. All four were wearing sunglasses, although it was already dark in Seborga. They fielded questions from journalists at they walked, their responses jokey and avoiding anything of substance. Mastroianni was saving the juicy stuff for later.

In the piazza, one of the Seborgan guards was waiting to show the VIP guests to their seats, one either side of the centre, where a chair for Alessandra was still vacant. Mastroianni began by introducing his newly-appointed deputy, Andrea Cassini, who most had already recognised from TV and newspaper appearances. He was memorable, not least because he was so young for such a senior politician, but he was also strikingly handsome. Cassini had very wavy fair hair, a characteristic of some of the people of his native Sicily. He also had an athletes' physique. It looked as though the sleeves of his immaculate blue suit were only just sufficient to constrain his muscular arms and yet he was slim without an ounce of fat.

The party had barely all sat down when a single military drum started a roll, which was the precursor to a furious crescendo of drumming performed by upwards of ten young men. The noise echoed around the piazza, drowning out the conversation of anyone who had not already stopped talking. The flag throwers emerged from several different sides of the piazza waving their standards before launching the poles high into the night sky with a deft flick. The flags fluttered upwards and then hung in the air for a split second before tumbling back only to be caught on the feet of the thrower. The dexterity and skill of this tradition required considerable dedication and many hours of practice to master. It was kept alive by the fact that it never failed to impress an audience, none more so than the guests now sat at the VIP table.

The finale saw all ten flags sent high, but at an angle, so they landed on the outstretched foot of the thrower opposite, just as the last drum strikes sounded. The timing was impeccable. The flags were then draped in two lines and at a forty five degree angle, creating a corridor a couple of metres wide leading to the centre of the piazza. In the silence created by the sudden stopping of the drums, the distinct sound of metal horseshoes could be heard slowly clip-clopping. Between the lines of flags, a huge black horse appeared, its head cloaked in white embroidery leaving only its eyes uncovered.

Alessandra arrived mounted on her father's old stallion. A blue silk sash swept across her black military-style jacket, which was complete with epaulettes. Azure blue jodhpur-style fitted trousers fitted into black knee-high leather boots with faux-gold spurs. Her raven hair was pulled back in a ponytail and she was immaculately made-up; something rarely seen, even by Ben.

Spontaneous applause broke out all around the piazza, as people rose to a standing ovation. At first, Ben was unsure how much of this tribute was for the flag throwers. He soon realised it was mostly for Alex. The clapping continued and grew even louder as she approached the tables. Vincenzo had been walking alongside the big horse looking resplendent in his uniform, only his burgundy beret differentiating him from his foot soldiers.

The media, who had attended many such festivals before, had so far appeared underwhelmed. Even the flag throwers had failed to stir their cameras into action. When Alessandra arrived, they were tripping over each other to get in the best position to capture the fantastic images.

When she could ride no closer to the VIP table, Alessandra gently brought the huge horse to a halt. She passed the reins to her aide-de-camp, Vincenzo, and slid deftly from the polished saddle in one seamless movement. Alessandra gave the horse's nose a gentle stroke before Vincenzo passed the reins to another guard who led it slowly away. The crowd were still clapping when she greeted the now standing guests at the table. Vincenzo made introductions from a list he had written on his hand.

Cecily thought Alex positively radiated charisma, charm and, well, royalty. She looked every inch a Princess of Seborga, as if she had been living the role all her life, which her friend knew that she had not. She also knew that underneath this show of confidence, Alex was probably screaming to be somewhere else: most likely, in her comfort zone of a busy commercial kitchen where she knew the rules, was in control and confident of her ability.

For the villagers, this was also a revelation. Used to seeing Alessandra going about the village in her working attire and rarely having a night off for which she might have dressed-up, they were reminded of who she actually was. Most of the rest of the world might not acknowledge her status, but here in Seborga she was still their Princess. They also knew her to be generally modest, reticent and under-stated, unless angered that is, when she could become formidable and fearless. They had not seen this apparently bold and quietly confident side to her. This person was an Alessandra no one had seen before.

Even Mastroianni, not a man usually stuck for words, looked amazed and said nothing. He simply nodded, apparently in approval of this change of image. No one except Cecily had seen Alex's outfit and even she was not prepared for the full effect with her on the horse in all its finery.

"Simply regal," she whispered to Roman.

"She does look very much the part," agreed Roman.

Cecily thought that Alex must have whispered something similar to Selene during their brief embrace, because the younger woman blushed and bowed her head to try to hide it. The band started playing, which was the signal for the festival feast to get underway. People queued at stations serving all the classic Ligurian dishes: black trofie pasta with pesto, rabbit with olives, goat with beans and so on. Other stations sold bottles of wine and beer on-tap. Only the VIPs would be served by waiters from a special menu prepared by Cristiano in the Osteria. Their food courses would be held back until everyone else was seated. In the meantime, they were brought aperitivo and prosecco.

Ben began chatting to signore Cassini, who insisted he called him Andrea. Ben pulled back his chair a little so that Roman, who was sitting to his right, could join in the conversation with Andrea. The three men seemed to have a lot to talk about and the atmosphere appeared convivial.

To his left, Alex was engaging Mastroianni in a similarly intense discussion, following a carefully worded script that they had all worked on prior to the event. Both parties appeared in one moment quite serious and then very smiley. It made the conversation seem as though it was a series of peaks and troughs in a debate, as points—perhaps contentious—were raised, argued and then finally agreed or conceded.

Occasionally, Mastroianni glanced past Alex to look at Selene, both women assuming this was just the man living up to his lecherous reputation. After a few minutes, the two separate intense discussions seemed concluded. The party leader and his junior then reverted to the job at hand: winning votes for the forthcoming Italian general election.

Mastroianni spotted a couple of the cameramen filming him in close-up and so offered Alex his glass to chink, reinforcing their apparent good relations. He also caught the eye of any other guests looking admiringly in the direction of the glamorous VIP guests and raised his glass to them as if they were all old friends. These potential voters were astonished at being acknowledged by the famous man who might soon be their prime minister.

Mastroianni would have liked a photograph of himself with Monaco's ministerial representative, which would be viewed as an inferred endorsement of his campaign. The savvy minister, however, was well versed in the art of avoidance of such compromising photographs. He had well-practiced techniques if all attempts at simply distancing himself failed. He would sometimes turn his head away at the critical moment and look at someone else, or raise his hand to scratch his nose, or even adopt a scowl to show that he was not pleased to be in the company. All three, plus a couple more, had to be deployed to prevent anyone obtaining an image which appeared to show that he was happy to endorse the determined but questionable Mastroianni.

While Mastroianni had been staring at Selene, she had been looking past him to the tanned younger man talking with her father. Cecily had noticed and said,

"Handsome, isn't he?"

Selene was slightly embarrassed at having been so transparent about her interest and tried to deflect it by answering,

"Who is?"

With no intention of continuing any pretence, Cecily simply ignored what she saw as a rhetorical question and continued,

"And single."

Cecily qualified this by adding,

"Well, at least he's no longer married, which is almost the same thing. He married and divorced when too young. He has a son of about 12 years by his ex-wife, who's now remarried. His name has been mentioned along with several beautiful women but none for very long."

Selene concluded that there was no point in feigning disinterest.

"He is gorgeous, isn't he? And his fair wavy hair, it's just so un-Italian ... but I admit I would like to run my hands through it," Selene whispered conspiratorially.

The two women laughed at their private joke.

Cecily pointed out that,

"Fair hair is not so unusual in the far south of Italy. On the island of Favignana off the coast of Sicily, there are many men with curly blonde hair. Some of them wear it long and curly because they are so proud of it."

After everyone had had their fill of the feast, Vincenzo took the microphone from the stand on the stage and brought it to stand behind Alex. He tapped to check it was working and then his baritone boomed out across the piazza,

"Honoured minister, monsieur, madame, signore and signora, per favour, taci per Contessa di Seborga, Alessandra."

Alessandra hesitantly rose from her chair, as though she was not relishing the speech that was to come as she took the microphone from Vincenzo. Speaking in Italian, she welcomed everyone, thanked the minister from Monaco, Mastroianni and his deputy and members of the media. After a pause, she continued,

"Just four years after the most important day in the almost thousand year history of Seborga, our small community find ourselves once more at a momentous crossroads. The European Union who promised so much, have now reneged on the agreement we reached with them. Based on nothing more than the word of a French imposter, who claims to be the rightful heir to the throne of Seborga, the EU has withdrawn their promised funding. Without it, we cannot now complete our agricultural rejuvenation and architectural restoration projects."

Some boos and jeers could be heard amongst the crowd, but most listened intently.

"My son and I agreed to give up our birth-right. Seborga pledged to cease its claim of independence, which my father had fought for all his adult life, and in return, we would be given the resources to save our community's economy. Despite all this, at the stroke of one EU bureaucrat's pen, this agreement has been broken."

Mastroianni was revelling in this attack on the EU, it was playing right into his hands. He beamed as he looked around the crowd gauging their reaction to Alex's speech.

She continued,

"It was a dark day indeed when we received this news. Within twenty-four hours workmen were taking the down this crane."

Alex gestured in the direction of the tall yellow metal structure still looming in the backdrop to the village, lit with small red lights to warn aircraft of its presence and for tonight, draped with the flag of Seborga.

"Light was brought back into our lives by the Tricolore Party. They have taken up our cause and given us hope that this project can be saved."

Mastroianni was irritated that she had referred to his party and not to him by name but, as Alex was not reading from a script, thought this was just an oversight. She went on to thank them for ring-fencing the ten million euro Italian contribution. Then she turned to Cecily.

"Tonight, we can further announce that a further one million euros has been donated by our guest Cecily and her PURE Fair-Trade Cosmetic Company. Please show your appreciation."

Cecily stayed in her seat but bowed her head and gave a slight wave to acknowledge the applause. She turned to Roman and began a conversation to divert any further attention. Cecily had achieved what she had set out to.

Although she was sympathetic to her friend's cause, this donation was not entirely a philanthropic gesture. It would be a tax-deductible expense from the proceeds of the sale of her company. Cecily also knew that she had gained international publicity for her blood orange range. Simultaneously, she had cemented relations with the citizens of Seborga, thereby ensuring her on-going supply of the valuable fruit. This investment seemed like shrewd insurance against any competitor company trying to poach her supply.

Mastroianni's face turned red and he looked as though he was about to explode with anger at the revelation of this donation. Alex invited Cecily to stand, at which point she held up a cheque and handed it over to Alex. This turn of events blind-sided Mastroianni. He suddenly looked furious and reached into his inside pocket, fishing for something. He was then seen scribbling something on a piece of paper.

Alessandra then concluded her speech with,

"Signore Mastroianni, leader of the Tricolore Party, has told me that he would also like to say a few words."

With a gesture of her arm, Alex invited Mastroianni to take the microphone. Vincenzo took it from Alex and handed it to him.

The old politician pulled himself up to his full height, sucked in his stomach and drew a hand over his thinning hair to make sure he looked his best. He waited until silence fell.

"Once again, the EU is on the take. They've taken away our freedom to decide our destiny, stolen our fish, made us pasteurise our cheeses and sucked all the cash out of our economy to bail-out French vineyards and German car plants. Then they dare to tell us that we have to sell their bloody subsidised Bollinger and BMWs in our supermarkets."

Cheers went up all around the piazza as Mastroianni was striking a chord with these voters.

"This action against Seborga is typical of the way they pick on the weak and most vulnerable. The artisan growers of the village were already victims of EU policy. They could no longer make a living from olives because the EU allowed inferior Greek and Spanish oil to be mixed with cheap Turkish oil and to be sold as 'produce of the European Union'. Enough is enough. When we win the upcoming election, we will be having a conversation with the EU that they will not like. We will take back control or we will take us out!"

Wild cheers now rang around the piazza, with only the French visitors refraining and appearing suddenly slightly nervous at the turn of events. They were expecting the usual summer festival, not a political rally. Conscious that Mastroianni was turning this into a party-political broadcast,

Alex rose and turned to him expectantly. He got the message that he had said enough and finished with his parting shot.

"I will not see the EU steal Seborga's cash. As well as the ten million I have already ring-fenced from the government, my private company will contribute a further two million euros to see that this vital work continues and Seborga's people are saved."

He pulled out the now creased cheque, waved it over his head several times and finally handed it to Alex. A glance at it revealed what she suspected, that the one million had been altered to two million and initialled by Mastroianni. He could not bear to be seen to be outdone by Cecily, thought Alex. Their plan had worked. Seborga now had nearly thirteen million euros available, not enough to complete everything as per the original plan, but then that had always been a very ambitious programme. A scaled-down version could see all the major works completed within that budget.

If the Tricolore Party were now elected and they fulfilled Mastroianni's promise to make up the difference from central government, then that would be the icing on the cake.

"I promise," concluded Mastroianni, pausing for effect.

"I will give you back your pride in your nation and create a future for your children."

Alex took back the microphone as Mastroianni basked in the applause and cheers, as the cameras clicked all around.

Alessandra acknowledged the gift, "We thank the Tricolore Party for their support and this extremely generous gift."

Alex held up the cheque just to reinforce Mastroianni's commitment in full view of the media, thereby making it almost impossible to go back on. The politician was once again irked by further references to the Tricolore Party, rather than to him or his company personally. It felt to him almost as though he was being side-lined.

Ready now for the coup-de-grace, Alessandra gestured to the men either side of her,

"These men, who it now seems likely will be running Italy very soon, gave me some reassurances earlier tonight. To avoid any further external bureaucratic interference in the Seborga project, we have tonight agreed that these funds should be placed into a not-for-profit trust administered by the Slow Food Movement. As an already registered international charity, they are above party politics and beyond the reach of the EU."

Alex smiled in the direction of Mastroianni who had little choice but to smile and bow in acknowledgement of his own apparent wisdom in this move. He knew, however, that he had been out-manoeuvred with this statement. It was true that Alex had floated the idea of a charitable trust early in the evening. He had paid lip-service to the merits of the idea, but he was a hundred per cent sure he had not agreed to anything.

The politician also noted that Alessandra was now speaking as though she were already the official head of state of Seborga when this was not yet the case. Her official role was now somewhat in limbo. Mastroianni himself had floated the idea that if the EU deal was off, then the monarchy could be restored and possibly even officially recognised by Rome. All, of course, subject to him being elected. Alex seemed to assume that this now a done deal, despite no details having been discussed with him. Were they all so naive as to think this would just happen without some further negotiation, Mastroianni wondered?

The billionaire also failed to understand why his second-in-command, Andrea Cassini, was enjoying so much of everyone's attention. In his view, he was little more than an ignorant southerner, dirt poor and without any real political clout. He might be young and handsome but he, Mastroianni, was quite clearly the real power broker here, yet he had seen Alex deliberately place herself closer to Cassini, actively inviting the media to photograph them together. Did Alessandra believe that this good-looking young man would be interested in an older woman, even if she were a princess, he wondered? He struggled to imagine what other motives she might have in courting this upstart.

In Mastroianni's eyes, everyone had ulterior motives and a selfish agenda. He was unsettled by anyone in his orbit whose ambition he could not understand. The events of the evening had left him puzzled but not altogether dissatisfied. In the main, he had achieved what he had set out to and was confident that the news coverage would nudge him further ahead in the race to become prime minister.

Selene excused herself and made her way back to the Osteria to use the bathroom. The restaurant was closed to the public, but its restrooms had been made available to Alex's guests. As she emerged a few moments later, she was surprised to find Mastroianni waiting in the narrow corridor leading to both the men's and women's toilets. There was very little space and the imposing politician did not give way, forcing her to back-up to the wall as she tried to pass. Although he was wearing his broadest smile, the big man appeared menacing. Suddenly he grabbed both of Selene's wrists and held them firmly down by her side. Unable to move, he pressed his considerable frame against her body, squashing her against the wall. Their faces were so close she could feel his warm breath on her cheek. He was still wearing his forced smile.

"My spies tell me that you have been snooping around my affairs; that you have visited Genoa asking questions, stirring up gossip and speculation. If you want to know more about me, I thought this would be a good opportunity to get to know each other better. I have left my security outside the Osteria so that we will not be disturbed. Think of it as an exclusive, one-on-one interview. Up close and personal."

Selene had no idea what to do and could not even muster a response. She was shocked and frozen in fear.

"You have been talking to disgruntled former employees and collecting lies about me. I also heard about your enquiries at the Department of Pensions. You have even interviewed one of my former girlfriends. Did they tell you how great I am in bed?"

Mastroianni paused to let all this sink in and then pressed himself harder against Selene's body. It was becoming more difficult to breathe, as when she exhaled emptying her lungs, he pushed himself further against her, making the next breath even harder. She could also now feel that he was getting aroused. The gap between pressure and violence had been crossed and he appeared to be turned on by it. She was terrified.

"You see, nothing gets past me. I have my people everywhere. Now, what exactly is your little game my English rose? Do you want to be my girlfriend or my enemy? I could easily accommodate you as either."

He suddenly froze rigid and raised his eyes to the mirror behind Selene. In the reflection, he could see a young man in chef's whites wearing a red bandana around his forehead. He was almost as close behind Mastroianni as he was to Selene.

He spoke quietly, but clearly and deliberately,

"That cold object that you can feel supporting your testicles is my Berti boning knife. Luckily, I was in the kitchen here sharpening it, ready to go and cut open some goats when I heard your voices. If I were to remove that knife suddenly from where it currently rests, it would slice through the crotch of your beautiful suit and God knows what else as well. So, I would suggest that you now turn slowly and very carefully away from this young lady and let her breathe."

Seeing the seriousness of the situation, Mastroianni complied, only for the chef to deftly switch the point of the blade to just inside the politician's left nostril. The pain caused him to tilt his head back so that he could not look his assailant in the eye. Selene looked like she might faint and Cristiano nodded for her to leave. Once on their own, without pushing on the knife any harder, Cristiano twisted the blade just enough so that a tiny amount of blood started to trickle from

Mastroianni's nose, over his top lip and into his mouth, where he could feel the bitter metallic taste.

"Now, I don't know what this was about, but I do know that you are an unbelievably bad man who finds himself currently in a very bad position. I also have another advantage aside from this exceptionally fine knife. I once again find myself Prince Cristiano of Seborga. We both know that you need Seborga and therefore my compliance to win this forthcoming election. After that, you also want my mother to bestow a grand title on you.

"So that you can be sure all this happens, you and I need to agree to keep a secret. I am going to forget that this happened, but you are going to stay a very long way away from that girl, my step-sister. I would also like to make you apologise, but frankly, I don't think she could bear to be in the same room with you while you did it. Come to that neither can I, so just say you agree and then go and collect your gorilla from outside and go home to Genoa while your balls are still in their sack."

At this, Cristiano took a white cloth from his belt and stuffed one end into Mastroianni's mouth where it started to soak up some of the blood. He then removed the knife and followed the politician to the Osteria door. As the door opened the security looked aghast at the sight of his boss holding the bloodied cloth under his nose, but Cristiano quickly said,

"I think your nosebleed will stop very soon, Signore Mastroianni. Keep pressing that towel on it. Probably just the extra altitude or that helicopter journey."

Selene had gone to the Osteria bar and helped herself to a glass of water. Her skin was almost white, which accentuated the mascara-tinged tears running down her face. She still looked terrified.

Cristiano appeared beside her. "He's gone now," he said, opening his arms to offer a hug, which she accepted gladly. Selene began to sob, then said,

"That bastard. I knew he was a crook and suspected he was a misogynist, but I had no idea he was that evil. If you had not come in, I dread to think what he was capable of. God only knows what horrors he has forced on women before."

"And apparently got away with," added Cristiano.

"Until now," Selene said with some self-assurance returning.

"Speaking as a chef, I can tell you that revenge is a dish best served cold, so for now just take some deep breaths. Let some blood get to your brain and regain your composure."

As she reflected on the events of the previous thirty minutes, Selene was astonished at the assured way Cristiano had reacted. He had not thrown himself at Mastroianni and pummelled him into submission, as he doubtless could have, the smaller man had managed to apply a more menacing threat and achieve greater control but through the application of less actual violence. He had stopped her assailant in his tracks, humiliated him and sent him packing with his tail between his legs, but there would be hardly any visible evidence that would require explaining.

"Weren't you Mr Cool in there?" Selene complimented him. "Where did you suddenly acquire your street skills?"

Cristiano reminded her of what she seemed to have forgotten; that he grew up in New York and had travelled the subway almost every day. The districts that he had lived and worked in might now be fashionable, but back then, they were still waiting to be gentrified. His first school had an armed guard at the gate, he told her.

"When my parents set-up their first restaurant in Chelsea, Mayor Giulliani was still trying to clean up the streets with his zero-tolerance policy. New York still had numerous muggers, street gangs and rapists. I've seen experts perform low-key, maximum-threat mugging; they don't want to draw too much attention to what's taking place, otherwise other people get involved – that's when the shooting starts. They just want the wallet or purse and to quietly walk away, free to keep on working."

Selene had already been extremely fond of Cristiano. The way that he had not hesitated to step in and protect her had made that bond even stronger. When the young chef had visited her in London, they had enjoyed evenings out and then long chats late into the night. Cristiano had confided in her some of his most personal thoughts, which caused her to worry about him returning to Seborga. She was not convinced that his destiny lay here, believing that his dreams seemed unlikely to be realised in such a small conservative community.

Most guests at the festa had by now finished eating and were dancing, drinking and socialising. Cristiano's work had mostly been done and he could afford to leave what remained to others. He phoned Marius and explained that something had come up; he told him to speak to Vincenzo and ask him to get some guys to start to shut everything down in the outside kitchen.

The pair then sat in a booth in the Osteria, the young chef clutching Selene's hand to comfort her. The journalist in her slowly began to realise the significance of what she had just experienced. She held on to that thought, as it gave her reassurance that it would eventually be worthwhile. Although Selene now had some colour returning to her complexion, after the shock of the assault, she was still shaken. She stood up, excused herself and turned to visit the bathroom to splash some water on her face. When she returned, Cristiano said that he would walk her home.

Things were winding down in the piazza. Most of the public and VIP guests had left. The media had long since returned to their bases, to get their stories ready for publication. Alex sat alone with Ben; he assumed that Selene had decided on an early night after a frantically busy few days. Satisfied with their night's work and relaxed after several glasses of Rossese, Ben was in a reflective mood. Alex leaned her head on his shoulder while he talked.

"When the speeches were taking place tonight, it dawned on me the fundamental difference in thinking between the likes of us and the Mastroiannis of this world. We believe in building a sustainable future by creating real, tangible value. For him and his type, it is just about gaining an advantage over someone weaker, slower or poorer. There's no real added-value and so no sustainable future. It's just an endless series of small wins, or losses, where you are only as good as your wits hold out. That goes for his personal life as much as his business dealings. It must be exhausting," Ben concluded.

Alex did not respond and when he looked down she was sound asleep in her chair, her head resting on his shoulder.

26. BRIOCHE ALLA MARMELLATA DI ARANCE ROSSE

The morning sun was just creeping over the bell tower of the Chiesa San Martino and beginning to heat up the stones of the piazza. It was one of the cloudless, breezy mornings which cleared the air over the coast, allowing for spectacular views along the Riviera. On the best of such days, it was possible to see almost as far as St Tropez, a hundred and eighty kilometres west into France.

Alex had been experimenting with using blood oranges in her cooking. Over a breakfast of coffee with brioche filled with a jam made from the red citrus, Alex and Ben assessed events of the previous few days.

Mastroianni had gained maximum exposure from the event in Seborga in the media. Even the centre-left press covered it. However, the opposition media applied an entirely different agenda to their reporting. The big politician was pictured handing a big cheque supporting poor farmers to a glamorous princess; most Italian voters loved the idea of the poor-boy-made-good mixing with aristocracy on equal terms. If he could make that transition and close that gap, there was hope for their children and grandchildren. Mastroianni's poll rating had soared again as a result.

Andrea Cassini was portrayed as the loyal lieutenant to Mastroianni, his role more measured and diplomatic. The photograph of him with the Minister from Monaco was widely used. Roman had explained to Ben that Cassini was ‘yang’ to Mastroianni’s ‘yin’ and appealed to an entirely different demographic of voters. He represented the new generation and spoke not just to the young, but also the more educated and liberated female voters. Crucially, he was a union man at heart, a leaning previously unthinkable in traditional right-wing politics.

Traditional political divides were shifting in Italy, as they were in other parts of the world. Sections of the demographic that would have once been guaranteed to vote in one way, were now drifting in the opposite direction. Children of relatively well-off parents had concerns about the environment and social injustice and were voting left. Those of the poor who had clambered a rung or two up the economic ladder shared concerns about immigrants taking jobs and receiving benefits and were leaning to the right.

Andrea Cassini’s meteoric rise to power in Italian politics had been fuelled by fishing and family. He was the chosen candidate of the Italian fishing union, a body naturally aligned to the left but also fiercely anti-European Union and increasingly nationalistic. His father had led the Union all his adult life until his recent retirement, but was still a legend in every port in Italy. With no part of Italy far from a rich, easily navigatable sea and possessing a coastline of over eight thousand kilometres, there were a lot of voters relying on fishing and a lot of Italians who loved what fishermen brought home.

When Cassini senior’s son, Andrea, moved into politics, his first aim was to fight for the fishermen’s cause, and the union-backed him to the hilt. The younger man was also an environmentalist who recognised that the traditional Italian methods – using small boats to catch a wide variety species – was a more sustainable practice than the industrial fishing methods of their European neighbours.

He was indeed the man of the hour and he now found himself just one step from the power to make a real difference. Mastroianni had chosen Cassini precisely because he was so different from himself. He was already proving to be the ace in his hand. When combined with Princess Alessandra, he surely had the royal flush that would finally see him prime minister. He would not have long to wait, as his end game was now in play.

The day after the festival, during which Mastroianni had assaulted her, Selene had emailed her editor to tell her that she was on the brink of an enormous story, with many newsworthy angles — sex, crime, politics and royalty. What's more, she had an exclusive that could bring down a prime minister. She asked for more time and an extension to her stay was agreed until three days after the election.

"The story had better be good and your expenses modest," had been her editor's parting shot in their telephone conversation.

A couple of days later and the election was a landslide for the Tricolore party. At least it was a landslide by Italian standards, in that the party won a workable overall majority, greater than fifty five per cent. In recent memory, every previous election had resulted in marginal parties, often several of them, having to be co-opted-in to form a majority with whoever held the lion's share. These ill-fitting alliances usually resulted in a stalemate, where little change of any significance was ever achieved and the status quo was pretty-much maintained. In-fighting and back-biting between the factions would sooner or later result in one or more faction changing sides resulting in the government's collapse. The whole crazy circus would then begin over again.

On hearing the final result, Mastroianni was beyond ecstatic. He stood on the balcony of his headquarters in Genoa, waving and blowing kisses to a vast crowd for forty-five minutes. It was in one sense also a victory for the Genovese, who saw Mastroianni as their own man. Once a powerful and wealthy city-state, Genoa had fallen on hard times and Mastroianni gave them their first real home-grown hero since Christopher Columbus. OK, he might sometimes be a bit brash, but he was one of them. A man's man. A Genoan.

In Brussels, emails were flying around to arrange urgent meetings to coordinate a response to what they saw as a threat to their very existence. They knew that Mastroianni had won this election on his anti-EU stance and that the Seborga debacle had helped him over the line. One email between senior EU colleagues did not pull any punches or avoid apportioning blame.

"If that moron, Delon, had not taken it upon himself to withdraw funding for the Seborga project, we would not be in this mess. He thinks he saved us twenty million euros but in reality he may have cost us billions to pay off Mastroianni. That crook will blackmail us until we give him what he wants. The alternative is an Italian version of Brexit, which will probably be the end of the European Union and our careers."

Delon had been quickly pensioned-off as soon as his original folly had been exposed to his superiors. By then, his unilateral decision was in the media and it was too late to backtrack without looking like they were weak and had caved-in. Delon, aged just fifty, was now living very comfortably on his very generous final salary pension in his seaside home not far from Narbonne, oblivious to the carnage unfolding. His selfish intervention had been driven by little more than the pursuance of his personal dislike of the Englishman and his so-called princess wife.

Monsieur Bisset had been Delon's line manager at the EU department and he had already suffered the deflected consequences of his subordinate's decision, as it was said to be a result of his lack of oversight. He was now looking for blood and to claw-back some credibility. He had instructed investigators to trail through Delon's expenses claims, emails and computer files looking for some dirt to stick on him, to distract from that now landing on himself.

Bisset was also angry about the role played by their fellow Frenchman, Payen, in triggering the debacle in Seborga. It was this wanted criminal's outlandish claims of a royal lineage that had prompted Delon to withdraw Seborga's funding. The senior bureaucrat was pulling every string to bring pressure to bear on the authorities for Payen's extradition and arrest on the existing charges, plus any new ones they could think of. Bisset wanted revenge from the two idiots who might have cost him a lucrative promotion, and he was not too bothered how he got it.

One of several boundary stones with Templar engravings found in the hills around Seborga.

Drawing by Linda McCluskey

27. BRANZINO ALLA LIGURE

The election result was greeted with mixed emotions in Seborga, where they were aware of the part that they had played in Mastroianni's victory. Alex and Ben reassured each other that they have done what they thought was best for the people of Seborga. They would have to wait and see how that turned out. The intervention by Payen had triggered a chain of events which had taken them down a route that they had no wish to follow, but it seemed as though they had had little choice.

"I wish I knew what Payen's game was and why he has now just disappeared. I am not sure whether we'd be better off if he stayed away or if he came back so we could get some justice by proving his claim to be false," Alex said, clearly seeking a focus for her wider frustration with events.

"If all goes well now, this election might also be the saving of Italy as well as Seborga. Only time will tell," Ben speculated. He continued, "For myself, I'd be happy if we never heard from Payen again, but I somehow doubt that will be the case."

Selene did not bother filing a report to her office in London on the election, which she knew would be adequately covered by the news agencies. Anyway, she had more important fish-to-fry, she had told a colleague. She was absent from Seborga during the days preceding the election, offering no explanation to her father as to her whereabouts other than that it was work-related.

The un-named mystery English girl had been a last-minute guest at a private party in Rome when the election victory was announced. Most of the other guests were not politicians or VIPs but owners of small fishing fleets, fish merchants and a few union officials from all over Italy. An English speaking female researcher from the Tricolore party had been assigned to look after Selene and translate. Over a supper of fried anchovies followed by Ligurian style Seabass, the invited guests watched the counting taking place in town halls all over Italy.

From what she was told, Selene understood that there were genuine misgivings about their Union's move to support Tricolore. The centre-right party was an alliance only brought about by their Union's leader entering into the election on this side of the political divide. They were mostly deeply distrusting of Mastroianni, with many members openly questioning their leader's wisdom.

Selene had spent the evening listening to the mostly male guests passionately explain why the best fish dishes came from their locality. She received countless invitations to visit and try these dishes in restaurants up and down both the Mediterranean and Adriatic coasts of Italy. On the big TV screens, Mastroianni's electioneering was turned down to a minimum because the blonde, pale Englishwoman was the star of this show.

Selene had weighed-up the merits of reporting Mastroianni's assault to the police but had decided against it. Any evidence was too circumstantial and he was too powerful a figure to be brought down by the uncorroborated word of a foreigner, particularly that of a woman. He would doubtless turn the tables and claim she had tried to seduce him in the narrow corridor and Selene would end up on the wrong side of the story. How many times before had this happened, she wondered to herself? How many women had he threatened and molested and gotten away with it?

Mastroianni, on the other hand, had given the incident not a single further thought, other than to make a mental note to bide his time before taking some revenge on the cocky young chef. Even if Selene had complained, he knew most voters would believe his version of the story, that a foreign journalist seeking a big story had used her sexuality to try and compromise him.

Alex and Ben were well aware of the critical importance of the timing of the next sequence of events. They had taken a big gamble in backing Mastroianni in the run-up to the election, but had tried to mitigate that support by trying to focus the attention on his Tricolore Party. The presence of Andrea Cassini had made this much easier, as he was a figure with whom they could more easily identify. The more Alex and Ben had learned about his sustainable marine policies and his support for traditional artisan fishing practices, the more they liked and respected him.

It was Cassini who, in his new role of deputy PM, arranged the transfer of the Seborga Rejuvenation funds from the Italian government into the trust to be administered by the Slow Food Movement in Piedmont. Of the many issues Mastroianni had delegated to him, he had quietly prioritised this legislation, along with the drafting of an act to recognise Seborga's special status.

Under this new act, Seborga would become a state-within-a-state, something akin to the Vatican. It would be part of Italy, administered by Rome, but would enjoy some of the autonomy of a principality, including maintaining its current full royal titles and its own flag. Any subsequent honours could be granted only by the reigning royal on an emeritus basis. The special status granted under the act would allow Seborga to maximise its commercial and tourism potential, as well as claim unique branded providence for its produce. One slightly worrying aspect for Cassini, was that Mastroianni had told him to wait for a special taxation clause that was being drafted by specialist lawyers in Monaco and would be added in before submission to parliament.

After the election result, Mastroianni had not wasted time in contacting Alessandra. His pretext for the call was to congratulate her on the impending official recognition of her royal status, to which her reply was,

"Thank you signore Mastroianni, but I did not need it. To be sustainable, royalty can no longer rule by decree — only by consent. My father and I held on to our titles only because that was the will of the citizens and that support was all we needed to do our jobs. Any ruler who thinks that they can cling to power because they have the job title is in for a shock, look no further than Italy for evidence of that."

The barely disguised parallel with Mastroianni's position was lost on the ebullient politician who was still gloating at his historic victory. The pretext out of the way, the new Prime Minister got on to the real purpose of the call. He told Alex that his assistants had started preparing his official diary for the coming months and he wanted to know when to schedule the ceremony at which he would be awarded his title of duke. He reminded her that the first part of the arrangement had been delivered: the government money was now in the trust and out of the reach of any interfering third-parties. When the recognition of the Principality of Seborga document was complete, it would be rushed through parliament where it would pass largely un-opposed.

Alessandra stalled by offering, "No more than a few days and we should be able to have a party in Seborga and make the announcement."

She explained that it would take her a little while to arrange everything in Seborga and invite appropriate VIP guests. She offered to call him back within forty-eight hours with a firm date. Reluctantly, he accepted the need for proper preparations to take place if he were to maximise the publicity from this honour.

"I also wanted to talk to you about getting the plans for my house fast-tracked," was the next bombshell Mastroianni was to drop on Alessandra. "I have negotiated to make the most of that big crane and all those construction workers while they are in Seborga. They might as well build me a villa while they are there. I'll get the drawings sent over."

When she recounted the conversation to Ben, his response was less than pleased.

"What? That man is unbelievable. He wants planning fast-tracked, in other words, rubber-stamped. He wants to divert our contractor who is being paid out of public funds to build him a house, presumably at little or no cost to himself.

He paused.

"Wait, does that mean he already has land in Seborga? How could that happen without our knowing?"

Alex shrugged her shoulders, the horror of this revelation only just beginning to sink in. It had been one thing interacting with him to achieve what they needed for the village, but the idea of having him as a neighbour filled her with dread. Things seemed to be going from bad to worse and the pressure was beginning to get to Ben.

"What have I unleashed, Alex? If things don't go exactly to plan now, this could all fall apart before our eyes. What if there are more revelations like this?"

Alex responded, "We need to get out of here into the hills to clear our heads. I'm going to the Osteria to give instructions to Cristiano while you find our hiking boots."

28. PIZZA SEGRETA

Strada della Villa led inland from the village in the direction of the mountains, but rather than uphill as the topography might suggest, sloped down towards the floor of the valley to where the Nervia River flowed. This was the watercourse into which eventually the entire valley drained. Only eight kilometres from the sea, the river would grow a little in volume before reaching the coast at Bordighera.

The source was only another kilometre upstream. From this point, the river dropped steeply in its rush to the sea. Most of the time it would be little more than a steady trickle, but after rain in the hills it transformed briefly into a raging torrent. These flash floods washed away most of the small stones, leaving much of the riverbed consisting of little more than the smooth stone slabs; the very fabric of the mountain itself. Only the occasional boulder that was too big and slow to shift remained stuck in the channel. Eventually, even these would be eroded to a size where the force of the water could move them on downstream, although that might take another millennium. Here today, the river could be crossed easily in a couple of strides between suitable rocks.

Once on the other riverbank, Ben and Alex began the steep climb towards the tiny hamlet of Negi. For a community of fewer than sixty people, Negi has three named suburbs, Peverei-Negi, Tegui-Negi and Fumei-Nehi. The collective facilities of this community consist of an olive mill and an eating place, which was not an official osteria. The eating place, known locally as the Secret Pizza, was merely an agriturismo with a couple of letting rooms and an open-air dining area.

When guests were staying in the letting rooms who also wanted dinner, the owners might fire-up their pizza oven, but this was not very often. The process of getting the brick oven up to a temperature of five hundred degrees took so long and used so much firewood it was not worthwhile for just a small number of people. To justify using this much sought-after olive wood, a 'Secret Pizza' text message is sent out to a select band of locals. It announced that their wonderfully thin and fluffy-crusted pizza would be available that night. Alex had received the text earlier in the day.

Everyone around knew or had heard that these were the best pizzas to be had in the area. The difficulty was getting membership to this exclusive club. The family who ran the agriturismo grew or hunted most of the ingredients and foraged the remainder from the hills around. They also milled the olives and made the wine. Only flour for the pizza and pasta was bought in from outside.

It would take at least another hour of uphill hiking to reach Negi from the valley floor. First, the couple would have to cross another small tributary, this time over a small arched bridge thought to date back to Roman times, although no one was sure. These paths were not only routes between the villages, but part of a network connecting this valley to the next and then continuing back right into and over the Alps. The paths were used principally to trade salt out from the coast and flour in from the plains of Piedmont. Later that trade would temporarily turn into arms for the Italian partisans in two world wars. Today these routes were only used by locals and a few adventurous tourists.

On the ground, there were signs of wild boar everywhere. Freshly turned-over earth, especially under trees, was the very obvious sign of their omnipresence. There were also cloven hoof marks from a species of small deer known as chamois. Paw marks that looked like dogs could easily have been a fox and other prints with long claw lines that were distinctively badger.

Occasionally, discarded used gun cartridges were a sign that any of the former could have been the quarry of the hunter who had left these in his wake.

Through occasional clearings in the otherwise dense forest, the pair caught glimpses of their destination clinging to the hillside above them. Constructed with little more than the stones found laying around the hillside, these villages would be perfectly camouflaged were it not for their terracotta tiled roofs and copper drainpipes. The colour of the stones matched perfectly with their surroundings and only the patchwork pattern of the dry walls gave away the hand of man in their making.

Alex's footing was momentarily lost as her boot slid off one of the slimy stones. She began to topple backwards, grasping for anything with her arms that would prevent her fall. She need not have worried, as only two paces behind Ben steadied her with both his arms while she regained her foothold. While they were momentarily in an embrace, she turned and kissed her husband gently on his forehead.

"Grazie gentiloumo."

As they finally drew slowly closer to their destination, the couple could see the wood smoke issuing from a gap between the houses, a clear sign that pizza was in the oven. The terrain was too challenging for very much conversation. They both needed all their breath to make the climb up the steep paths.

There was also a single track tarmac road to Negi that wound around the valley side. As Seborga was at only a slightly lower altitude, this road was longer, but much easier to walk and that would be their direct route home.

Finally, tired, out of breath and a little sweaty, the pair stepped up from the trees onto the road on the outskirts of Negi, now just metres from the Secret Pizza. The thought of a cold beer had kept Ben going for the last forty minutes and now it was almost within his grasp. It was still early and only a few other guests from the agriturismo were seated on the raised stone terrace, which made up the open-air dining area. Scandinavian visitors, guessed Ben by the propensity of blond hair and lack of pretence or formality, happily waved at the complete strangers now entering.

Alex had gone straight to the family's semi-open-air, summer kitchen to say hello to the three generations that she knew she would find there. She also helped herself to two cold beers from the fridge and the old nonna scribbled a note of this sale on a pad with the stub of a pencil. Formalities complete, Alex joined Ben on the terrace, handed him a beer and held up her bottle to offer a toast. She also invited the visitors next to them to join in, which they did with enthusiasm raising their own glasses.

"To professore Ben Morton and all that he has done for Seborga And, all that he has done for me," Alex announced.

"What have I done?" Ben said in complete surprise. "Do you mean changing centuries of agricultural practices, putting livelihoods at risk and possibly landing us with a twenty million euro liability?" Ben suggested.

The Scandinavians, who spoke perfect English, looked puzzled and a bit embarrassed.

Alex stood up, addressing the group of strangers directly and pointing across the valley said,

"You see the many terraces filled with healthy young orange trees in blossom?"

They nodded, said that they had already been admiring them and added that they look beautiful. By now, many of the host family had come out of the kitchen to listen to Princess Alex's impromptu speech.

"And there on the edge of the village, the old Templar monastery now almost restored, which until a year ago was a complete ruin?"

Again, the group acknowledged that they had visited the monastery and that it was a triumph of incredible restoration.

Alex then pointed further down the valley where it was just possible to pick out the roof of the former COOP agriflor.

"Down there was an ugly former industrial warehouse, now transformed into a modern, low-carbon building clad with local stone and wood, so that it sits almost hidden in the landscape. It's now not only a beautiful piece of architecture, but will soon be creating many valuable jobs for local people."

The slightly puzzled audiences nodded in apparent praise of such a fine piece of building, although they could hardly see it.

"Well, this man you see before you, Ben Morton, in just four short years has almost single-handedly created all this. With no formal training, armed only with ingenuity and determination, he formulated the plan, raised the money and project managed the whole thing. What is more, he did it all for me and for the village, asking nothing for himself."

By now, the half dozen young strangers were on their feet and along with the host family were gently applauding and calling, "Bravo." Ben was speechless. Alex took her seat, chinked his glass and they sat back to enjoy the view. Rudy the spaniel, who belonged to the agriturismo, trotted up to say hello, closely followed by one of the children bringing them a bottle of water and a basket of bread. As the child departed, so did Rudy.

There is no menu at the Secret Pizza. What is on offer will depend on what is available. What is available will depend on the week of the year and the weather. Some aperitivo would probably, but not certainly, arrive as they were quite early. When the other seats were filled, salads, side dishes and pizza would arrive in waves until everyone said they were full. Two colours of wine, without labels or corks, were placed on tables and were replaced as required and charged for if consumed. It was a beautifully simple formula. Bills were small, hugs were bountiful and everyone went home happy.

It had been the tonic Ben needed. The teenage son of the host family drove them back to Seborga sat on the back on the family

Ape, their legs dangling with boots just above the tarmac. He began hooting furiously at a group of boar crossing the road as he sped along in the night air. Not for the first time, Ben quietly marvelled at his good fortune, in arriving in Seborga and finding Alex. Without the need for Internet dating apps, their unlikely pairing had spanned cultures and continents to bring them together. Alex's unwavering faith and loyalty was all the fuel he needed to keep going. The end of this part of the journey seemed to be within their grasp.

29. TURLE CON SALSA COZZE

Roman was due to meet Ben at the Osteria for breakfast and was on his way from Menton. Afterwards, they were going down to the orange groves where they would check on the trees. Cecily had arranged to drive up with him to meet up with Alex; she wanted to see how the cookery school and hotel projects were progressing. Work had been restarted on these again, now that funds had been secured and Alex wanted her friend's advice on a couple of things. Cristiano greeted them at the entrance and was suspiciously chirpy for a young man at this time in the morning.

"Why so smiley this morning?" Alex asked Cristiano.

"Why not. It's a beautiful day and I'm going to spend it in the kitchen."

When inside, the reason for Cristiano's good cheer became apparent. The first intake of students at the cookery school had arrived for a visit from the Slow Food University. Although their first term in Seborga would not start until the end of the summer, they had come for a 'taster session,' to meet the staff, to look at accommodation options and receive instructions as to what equipment they would require. Three of the six students were girls and none of them could take their eyes off the handsome young Cristiano in his immaculate chef's whites and his red bandana.

Renata, Alex's former second-in-command at her New York restaurant, had finally arrived to take up her place as head chef. With her from the early days of her first restaurant, Renata had started with Alex as one of the troubled kids on a government-subsidised employment scheme. They were kids, usually from illegal immigrant families, who looked like they were heading for trouble with the law. Singled-out by their teachers or preachers they were thrown this lifeline, in the hope they would use it to pull themselves up.

They started as kitchen porters, before graduating to pot washers and then to the dizzying heights of kitchen prep. Less than one-in-five stayed the distance and those that did make it needed a lot of managing. However, in the early days, they were a cheap source of labour for Alex and the ones that made it usually stayed loyal. Staff turnover was a huge problem. It took a long time to get people trained to turn out dishes at Alex's standard, so loyalty was a highly valued commodity.

The two embraced, both delighted with their respective choices. Alex knew that the new cookery school and eventually also the hotel kitchen would be in safe hands under Renata. The New Yorker was a child of parents of Mexican and Italian heritage, which gave her an unusual insight into the two most influential cuisines in North American cooking. Alex had taught her everything she knew about Italian food and in her opinion, Renata could turn out some of the finest Ligurian cuisine in New York, despite never setting foot in Europe until this week.

Renata could not believe that after a rocky start in life, with little prospect of getting out of the ghetto, that here she was fulfilling what she had thought was just a pipe dream. She would be running her own kitchen in Italy and cooking pure unadulterated Ligurian food with local ingredients. Alex also knew Renata would not suffer any nonsense from Cristiano and that he would learn a lot from her.

To achieve the earliest possible opening, the building had been restored from the inside out. All the original stones that remained from the old monastery were cleaned and returned, with no new stone added. Some parts were almost complete, restored to how they would have been in the twelfth century, whereas other parts were little more than ruins. They did not want to over-restore or recreate anything false, to avoid the finished building looking like a brand new version of the original; the process was meticulous and was therefore time-consuming.

A temporary tent was constructed over the whole building. This cover allowed work to continue inside and the kitchen to operate. Now an ultra-modern structure of glass and wood was currently being constructed to enclose the whole building. From the outside, new solid timber sections were built to fill in the missing stone parts, clearly defining what was old and what was new. The glass sections allowed the old stone to be viewed as it would have been. The completed whole would create a part real, part virtual illusion of a building of the original scale and shape.

Cecily asked, "Who was the architect? A local guy?"

"Do you need an architect?" prompted Alex.

Cecily had been planning to tell Alex this news over lunch today, but the conversation had led them naturally to this point.

"I bought the boat so I could follow my love. Now I have him in one place, we can look for a house."

"And will that be in Monaco or Saint-Jean-Cap-Ferrat?" Alex teased.

"If it were, I think I'd quickly be on my own again. Roman is a Sicilian farmer. He hates that kind of lifestyle, almost as much as I do. We are thinking about something here in the valley between Bordighera and Seborga. If your Highness will have us, that is?"

The two women embraced and laughed.

"In that case, yes, I can give you the name of the architect. It's a woman."

The women left to let Renata and the kitchen get on with preparing a lunch that the new students would observe and then later enjoy. A long table had been set up so that Ben and Roman could also join them when they had finished in the groves. Alex knew that Cristiano would want to impress both Renata and the new students with his skills. She was also aware that Cristiano was about to be out-shone by Renata, who could out-cook him with one hand tied behind her back; this was a lesson he needed to learn so that he knew his place in the pecking order. This combination would make for a lovely lunch; Alex was confident.

The adjacent new hotel and spa building was little more than a shell at this stage, but the roof was on and so it was watertight. Builders swarmed over every facet of the building, doubtless spurred on by the knowledge that Mastroianni was now one of their paymasters. Progress would now be rapid if this pace were maintained. The design was a product of the same architect so therefore incorporated the same sympathy for the landscape and local materials. Cecily was pleased to see that it would be a place that she would be proud to showcase her products.

Lunch was Turle pasta, a highly localised Cinque Terre version of pansotti that Alex had discovered on their trip there and taught to Renata. It was a slightly different shape, but contained the same basic mixture of ricotta and wild mountain leaves. This version was served with a mussel sauce, rather than the nut version which usually accompanied pansotti.

Ben had also brought back some of the Sciachetra white wine that he had tried and loved in Monte Rosso. Too sweet and rich for the pasta course, they would have this with dessert.

Ben and Roman arrived from the terraces looking hot and thirsty. It was the first time the four had met since the previous weekends' festival. Alex thanked Roman again for his suggestion of having a conversation with Andrea Cassini and for making the crucial introduction.

"How did you know him?" she asked. "You didn't say."

"I did not know him personally, the suggestion came from a friend when I was making enquiries about Mastroianni. I did, however, know his father well enough for me to be able to make that call and get through to him."

Roman turned to Cecily.

"Do you remember the day we met in Palermo? You were going to moor in that empty space on the quay and I advised against it."

"How could I forget that night?" Cecily confirmed with a wry smile.

"Well, that was signore Cassini senior's mooring place. Andrea's father was head of the powerful fisherman's union. He toured the coast in his boat visiting all the union offices at ports and meeting the members. He had a mooring saved in every fishing port he wanted to visit in Italy, from Venice to Portofino and God help any cocky yacht owner who thought it was first come first served for mooring places. They would come back to find their precious yacht blocked in by trawlers and probably smattered with smelly fish guts."

They all laughed at this image, but knew there was a serious edge to this story.

"Well, it's our luck that you did know him because Andrea was a charming antidote to Mastroianni."

"Not to mention a bit of a dish," added Cecily.

"Not to mention the key to our future," Ben concluded.

30. FRITTURA MISTA DI PESCE

“You cannot visit Genoa without going to see the Sacro Cantino and we are almost passing by the door,” local journalist, Lucia Rossi, had told Selene. From the hotel car park where they rendezvoused, the casually dressed Genoan woman in her thirties had led Selene through the huge intersection that was Piazza de Ferrari.

They skirted around the magnificent fountain creating its dome of water that somehow seemed to refresh the air around it. The ancient city of Genoa was a bustling rabbit warren of old narrow streets. While relatively modern majestic avenues stretched away into the northern suburbs, to the south, only much older, narrow, curving alleyways led downhill towards the port area.

The district was a melting pot of commerce and culture, with businesses looking as if they may have been trading when Columbus was looking for supplies for his voyage to the Americas. These sat alongside trendy eateries that looked as if they had been created last week. There were a couple of streets where, officially or not, sex workers openly plied their trade. Yet even though there was an ‘edge’ to this city, Selene never felt threatened. It seemed frantic but pretty safe, much like New York.

Just five minutes’ walk from Piazza Ferrari her guide said, “Here we are. Cathedral San Lorenzo. Home of the Genovese Holy Grail.”

“Genovese Holy Grail? There are others?” queried Selene.

"The Spanish claim to have another, but this is the real one," Lucia stated, but Selene judged that she was speaking here as a proud Genoan rather than an objective journalist.

The twelfth-century structure was wedged in amongst the crowded commercial and government buildings of the regional administrative centre. It had a striking facade of horizontal bands, layers of contrasting black and white stone slabs guarded by two huge marble lions; even after nearly a thousand years of exposure to the elements, the façade still looked as striking as it must have done to the Crusaders returning from the Holy Land with their precious chalice, Selene imagined.

"An annexe to the side of the central nave contains several extraordinary religious treasures — a huge silver arc, golden plates and more — but the main attraction sits in a dark cave-like alcove carefully lit by spotlights," Lucia explained.

Selene was surprised at how overwhelmed she was by The Sacro Cantina. She noted that if she were to move her head, even slightly, the translucent emerald green dish seemed to emit pulses of light as though its source was somehow active or alive, an illusion which Selene found fascinating but also slightly eerie.

"It is breathtakingly beautiful," confirmed Selene to her temporary guide. She made a mental note to return when she had more time and to bring her father with her.

Conscious that they were not on a tourist jaunt, the reporters cut their visit short and continued deeper into the streets that appeared to be getting narrower the further they descended towards the quayside. Few of the lanes were straight, so a person could not see the end or where the lane was leading. Selene was told this layout was designed to confuse attackers arriving from the sea and give advantage to the defenders who knew their way around. To this day it still intimidates visitors.

Even before they exited the shadows of the tall buildings on either side of the tapering alleys, the smell of fish frying drifted up to them from the harbour side below. Lucia looked at her watch to confirm what her stomach was telling her: it was lunchtime.

"You must try some Genovese mixed fried fish (frittura mista di pesce)," was her direction, rather than a question, as her new friend pulled Selene in the direction of a street corner stall. They left with two paper cones overflowing with crisp golden morsels of fish, of which only octopus, anchovy and squid could Selene identify. Whatever it was, it tasted wonderfully fresh, hot and satisfying, Selene thought. The light lunch was the perfect antecedent for the meeting they were about to have.

After a short walk along the harbour side, they cut back up one of the side alleys and immediately into the doorway of an apartment building. The entrance had an open area about a meter square to allow residents to access their keys without being swept away by a speeding Ape or scooter heading down the lane. They rang a buzzer, a greeting was made in Italian and they were let into the stairwell. There was no lift and it took eight flights to climb the four floors to Albina's two-room apartment. It was a cramped and dark space, although it did have a window opening to the sea that was closed and shuttered, "To keep out the noise and fumes from the traffic," the old woman explained.

"This is Selene. The lady reporter from London who I told you about," Lucia explained slowly to the slightly deaf, Albina. Selene estimated the old lady to be in her eighties or even older, although she still had great skin, she noted. It appeared as though she suffered from a curvature of the spine, causing her to stoop and to have to raise her head to one side to make eye contact. Her eyes were warm and kind, but contained a hint of fear, Selene thought.

Selene had been told Albina's story by Lucia when they had both met on the day she had arrived from London. Lucia had told her about the victims of Mastroianni's plans and Selene had requested this interview. She wanted to see for herself how the pensioners of former print workers were living. Albina's husband had been a typesetter, a highly skilled man during his working career. Luckily for him, his retirement had coincided with the demise of manual typesetting which was soon to be replaced by digital processes in the nineties.

With their state pension topped-up from the print workers fund that he had paid into for fifty years, at first they had lived a reasonably comfortable existence. However, since the death of her husband, payments from the print workers fund to his widow were reduced to just twenty-five per cent of what they were, which was barely enough to live on.

"Now that fat, greedy, womaniser Mastroianni wants to take even that away from me," Albina almost spat.

Selene was taken aback that such a tiny, frail, old lady could muster-up so much venom, but understood her grievances. From her own research, she knew that not only had Mastroianni moved the whole pension fund into an investment vehicle of which he had control, but he was also looking for ways to cut outgoing payments.

"He now claims to have found a loophole in the clause that allowed spouses of deceased print workers to continue to draw a proportion, all-be-it a small one, of their pensions until their death," Albina explained. She continued, that this provision had not been in the original pension scheme but was added years later after protracted negotiations with the union.

"Mastroianni now claims that this clause was invalid because of some procedural error. He wants to end such payments," she concluded.

After much more digging around, Selene had also discovered that it was the pension fund which owned many of Mastroianni's lavish private properties. The fund had bought them, at his direction, and then leased them back to him at a fraction of the market rental. His yacht and helicopter were also 'investments' made by the pension fund and rented by the man who controlled it. What is more, his management of the fund also came at the price of a million euro per year salary for Mastroianni. It was because of this, plus the purchase of these poorly returning assets, that the fund was evaporating quickly and he was looking to cut costs by cutting payments to widowed pensioners.

Albina opened her cupboard to show Selene the contents. Flour, polenta, salt, olive oil and several jars of home-made preserved vegetables were all that she could see. In a plastic basket were two bulbs of garlic, one onion, some carrots and a few potatoes. These were the basics for making her own pasta and polenta, plus a simple sauce. There were no cans or packets or indeed anything that looked like it came from a supermarket.

"My nephew brings me the vegetables, olives and oil from his orto in the hills once a month. I buy cheap fish from the market once a week and fry it in oil. Last time I had meat was Christmas Eve. Such is my life. At least I can get all I can afford without going too far. The prices here in the city are so high. My rent takes half my income."

Selene could feel tears welling in her eyes at hearing Albina's story. She wanted to give her money on the spot, but was not sure how that gesture would be received; with horror and embarrassment, Selene feared. The journalist was, however, now absolutely determined to see justice for Albina and the other pensioners. Selene thanked the frail old lady, kissed her gently and left, as angry as she was saddened by her story. She thanked Lucia for the suggestion of meeting her and the two journalists parted.

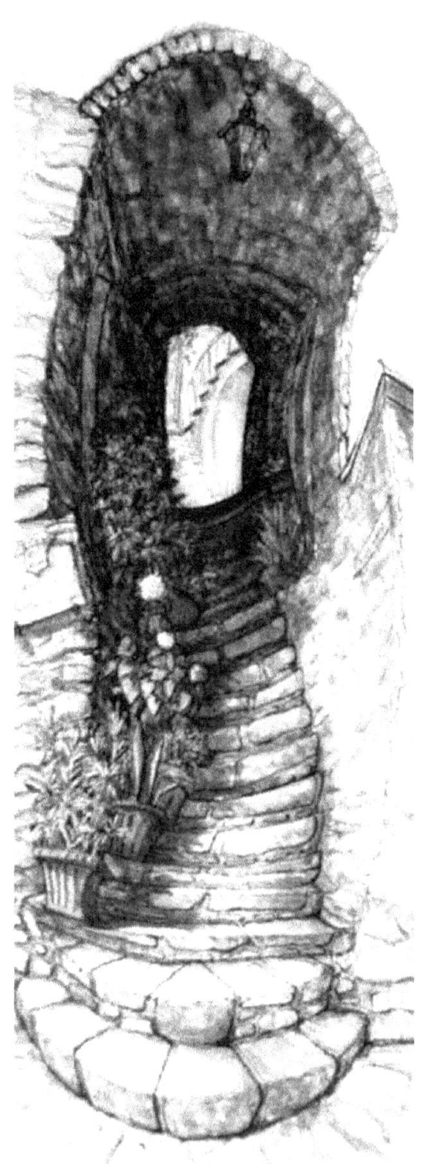

Vaulted arches of local stone support buildings often many stories high.

Drawing by Linda McCluskey

31. MOROCCAN CHICKEN WITH LEMONS AND OLIVES

It had taken Ben, Vincenzo and Cristiano a whole week to clean the land that had once been Lorenzo's. First, they had used a chainsaw to attack the thickest branches and then machetes. They soon realised that lurking beneath the brambles, thicket and self-seeded saplings were many of Lorenzo's old vines. Despite most of them looking completely lifeless, having been starved of light by the undergrowth and lacking water, Vincenzo believed they would revive with care.

The first thing was to clear the growth around them and then protect the stems with plastic sleeves. That would allow them to clean the land around them using strimmers. Ben had taken a chance on cleaning the land when he did not yet own it, but Vincenzo had said that in the unlikely event of anyone challenging them, they would say they were just creating a fire break.

Ben had already learned a little about local viniculture practices from caring for the late Prince Claudio's vines. This vineyard was on the outskirts of the village, on land that Alex had inherited from her father. The vines had been somewhat neglected after the Prince's death and needed a severe pruning before they produced a decent crop. At least Claudio had maintained all his terrace walls over the years, replacing sections bulldozed by wild boar or collapsed by earth tremors. Each terrace already had the metal posts to carry the wires that would eventually support the grapes. On Lorenzo's land, all the stone terraces were in disarray and no other infrastructure was in place, but it did now have a water source.

Vincenzo had brought with him a long steel bar to use as a lever and they had returned to the cave. Cristiano had never visited any of the Templar caves before and was astonished by what he found there. He was struck by the enormity of time that had passed since the legendary knights had used these caves. Almost a thousand years seemed too long a period for the young man to imagine.

"So, it's over eight hundred years since anyone else set foot in here?" Cristiano asked.

"Apart from Vincenzo and I a few days ago, yes, that's probably the case," Ben confirmed.

"That's awesome," the young man said while videoing the scene on his iPhone. "And you think that this is where they kept the Holy Grail? What happened to it after that?"

Ben screwed up his face as if uncomfortable with either confirming or denying what was after all only legend. However, he offered Cristiano the facts as he saw them so that he could make his own conclusions.

"It is documented that the Sacro Cantino, now in Genoa, was taken from Palestine by the Knights Templar and brought to Europe. We also know that the Templars were based here in Seborga for at least two hundred years. So, the idea that they brought the chalice here is not too much of a stretch of the imagination. There is also a long history of Islamic pirates, often known as the Barbary corsairs, raiding these coastal towns during that same period. If you lived in Seborga, where would be the safest and least accessible place to hide a valuable Holy relic?" Ben proposed.

Cristiano looked as though he could hardly take it all in.

"I thought the Holy Grail was just a myth. I never for a moment thought that it truly existed."

"Enough talk. Let's work," was Vincenzo's only contribution to the discussion.

With Ben and Cristiano pushing from each side, the three of them easily rolled the boulder out of the channel where it had been blocking the steady stream of water. With the stone removed, the water immediately flowed back down its original course and sloped towards the cave entrance. After just five minutes, it was issuing from the hillside and starting to trickle. The dusty soil was thirstily soaking up the water; it would take days before any of it started to irrigate the land further below.

"In a week or so it will spread across most of the vineyard," predicted Vincenzo. "We might need to use some plastic pipework to create a couple of aqueducts and channels if we are to make sure it gets to all parts of the terraces, but that's easily done."

Alex had made enquiries and found some of Lorenzo's relatives living in nearby Perinaldo. They were in touch with the other beneficiaries of his will who were living in Piedmont. As none of the family knew the land even existed, they were glad of some money for it. After not much negotiation, they agreed to sell it to Ben and Alex. Ben used cash still in his UK bank from selling his old Audi, topped up with some of his teachers' pension savings. The pair would soon own an ancient vineyard in a remote part of the valley. Vincenzo still thought he was a crazy Englishman and told him so regularly.

Every time Ben thought that his relationship with Vincenzo had moved a little closer towards friendship, the quiet Italian would abruptly pull back. It was as if he was still wary of the Englishman, or perhaps it was just a suspicion of all strangers, Ben wondered. He certainly did not treat Ben much differently to anyone else outside of his immediate and small circle. Nevertheless, Ben was never quite sure where he stood with the mercurial Vincenzo.

They finished working on the land earlier than usual the day Selene returned from her trip because Alex was preparing a special supper for them all. It had been almost a week since Ben's daughter had arrived and yet they had hardly seen her. She was due back in London in a few days and so they all wanted to catch up. Alex and Cristiano had worked all day helping to prepare food, but tonight Renata and the students would run their first service alone. Cecily and Roman were invited, as was Vincenzo and a Romanian labourer who had been helping Vincenzo work on the land.

Marius had turned out to be much more than the poor Romanian migrant worker he first appeared to be. Aged only thirty, his weathered, dark skin, dishevelled clothes, unkempt long hair and beard made him look ten years older. After chatting, they found out that he held a master's degree in agriculture from the prestigious Bucharest University and could speak English, French, Italian and, of course, Romanian.

Marius was knowledgeable, good company, an extremely hard worker and had a great sense of humour. Although thin and wiry, he could wield a machete better and for longer than any Italian Vincenzo had ever worked with. Vincenzo had heard that Marius had been looking for work at the farms in the valley. He had recruited him to work in the vineyard for just forty euros a day. At this paltry daily rate, Ben did not feel right not inviting him to eat supper with him and his extended family.

Selene looked tired when she returned in the hire car at around six that evening and Ben was concerned. He suggested she take a siesta before dinner and she needed no further persuading. Tonight's meal was being served in the Monastery dining room and was to be a real dress rehearsal for when it opened commercially. Alex tried to put Renata at ease by telling her that this was just a dry-run to test equipment and systems. Although she pointed out that the guests were all family and close friends, not restaurant critics, she still knew that her former colleague would see it as a test of her cooking and management skills.

Cristiano seemed to have become friends with Marius while they were helping out at the vineyard and the two sat happily chatting and laughing over a beer waiting for Selene, Cecily and Roman to arrive. Roman had ridden up on the boat's motorcycle with Cecily on the back. At Alex's suggestion, they had deliberately dressed down to try and take the pressure off the new chef. Apparently, Selene had either not received the message or just forgotten; when she finally arrived ten minutes late, having overslept, she looked stunning. Cristiano applauded her entrance and Roman joined in.

"Brava, bellissimo, bella ragazza," Cristiano called with enthusiasm.

Looking around at her fellow guests, Selene seemed to realise that she had forgotten Alex's prompt about dressing down. She wore an emerald green satin dress that showed off her figure and her blonde hair wonderfully. The hem was just above the knee, with an open back and plunging neckline. It was just the right side of respectable but definitely not suitable for church, was Alex's assessment.

"I'm sorry. I have been so busy and preoccupied. I completely forgot. I'll go back and put on some jeans."

Ben stood, put his hands on her shoulders and sat her sat next to Cristiano.

"You're fine. You look beautiful. Relax and let us enjoy our dinner and tell us, where have you been?"

Selene briefly described a route that had taken her to Rome, Milan, Genoa and finally, into Nice this afternoon. She described to Cristiano the wonderfully fresh and light fried fish she had enjoyed in Genoa and the North African chicken with lemons and olives at lunch today in Nice. Being around cooks, she realised that she had become like her father, punctuating all her description of places with dishes, rather than landmarks.

Finally, Selene said to Cristiano, "And who is your new friend?"

Cristiano apologised and introduced Marius as his new multilingual friend. Seeing how much Cristiano appeared to admire the stranger, Selene tried to put him at his ease. She asked her step-brother to change places so that she could sit between them and be able to better converse. This also placed her opposite her father, from whom she was keen to hear all news. Ben poured Selene a prosecco from a bottle in a cooler, and she took a big gulp, as though she had just emerged from a trek across a baking desert.

"I needed that Dad. Thank you."

Selene seemed to finally relax, almost melting into the chair as if an ordeal were finally at an end. Or at least, an end was in sight. Ben assumed that she was probably tired from all the travelling and was glad to have her home safe. He suddenly realised that he now automatically thought of Seborga as home, although if anyone asked him, he always said that he was English, despite not having had a home or a base in the UK for four years. Would he ever feel fully integrated he asked himself: think Italian, act Italian? Probably not, he concluded. But there was nothing much wrong with things as they were. In many ways, he had the best of all worlds.

Ben looked over at his daughter, sat between two transfixed young men, she radiated confidence and charisma. What a difference four years had made. The strange quirk of fate that had brought him to Seborga and changed his life had resulted in her following him, which had then transformed hers.

She had been rudderless, demotivated and not a little angry at the world. Now here she was, focused and driven. A professional journalist, she had leap-frogged others her age still clambering up the greasy media pole trying to make a name for themselves. But it was not just the luck of being in the right place, he knew that. She had seen the story in what was taking place in Seborga long before anyone else. It was her telling of that story and the way she instinctively knew what people would be interested in that had made it go around the world. She had made her own luck and she made him feel incredibly proud.

Ben might have been less at ease had he known about the ordeal that Selene's presence here had recently exposed her to at the hands of Mastroianni. He would almost certainly have felt extremely guilty about his part in asking for her help with the Payen problem. As it was, Selene had sworn Cristiano to silence about Mastroianni's assault until she had, "all the pieces of the jigsaw in place."

The young chef was smart enough to understand that there was a bigger picture than just a misogynistic, perverted bully and that it would be worth waiting to get the best result.

For someone who had never visited Italy and therefore never tasted any genuine Ligurian cuisine, Renata's dinner menu was fascinating to Alex. She had taken several of the recently gentrified versions of traditional Ligurian dishes Alex taught her in New York and returned them to their roots.

Alex had spent years refining rustic 'cucina povera' recipes to ensure they would satisfy the adulterated palates and specific tastes of New York's diners, also so that she could charge more. In doing so, she effectively turned the dishes into the opposite of what they started out as. She had used the same basic flavours that she knew worked so well and kept the pasta shapes and sauce combinations, but removed heads, tails, bones, skin, stalks, or anything that would cause offence to rich ladies who lunch. It could be an animal, so long as it did not look like one. Poor farmers food had been gentrified; it worked and earned her a Michelin Star.

Conscious that she was returning to the home of this cuisine, Renata had been doing her homework. Having read about the traditional dishes and practised late into the night, the Mexican had created hybrid versions. These were dishes that had been on a journey of invention from rustic to Manhattan and back again. They were highly refined, more intense versions of the originals. However, Alex detected some ingredients in them that were simply not to be found in Italy, let alone Liguria, which she would have to discuss with her. While Alex had no problem with the innovation of these classics, she believed it was vital to maintain the authenticity of indigenous ingredients.

For Alex, tonight felt like an important meal in so many ways. It was the first meal service in the Monastery restaurant. It might be the last with Selene before she went back to London, having once again proved herself invaluable to Seborga. Tomorrow night, the no doubt gloating Mastroianni would return to Seborga as the victor of the election, holding his long-sought-after job title of Prime Minister of Italy.

Then, as if his ego were not inflated enough, Mastroianni had invited the media to witness Alex declare him Duke of Seborga. No one had yet spotted the irony that the Italian version of duke, Il Duce, was the title also given to the dictator Benito Mussolini, or that he also rose to power from within the newspaper industry. Their respective fates might yet turn out to appear prophetic, Alex mused.

Selene approached carrying two glasses of Champagne and handed one to Alex, raising hers in a toast,

"The Principessa di Seborga. Restored to her rightful place."

Alex blushed a little but accepted gratefully before proposing her own, "London's finest investigative reporter."

The two began to laugh out loud now realising the enormity of what had just happened. The two women turned to look at the other guests, all laughing, joking and drinking.

Selene said, "We seem like an all-conquering army celebrating a famous victory against overwhelming odds."

Alex smiled and replied, "Selene, that is exactly how I feel and I think the others are all the same. It's good to see Cristiano so animated and happy. He seems to have acquired new confidence this week since meeting Marius."

Selene looked quite serious for a moment as if wrestling with a dilemma. Finally, she said, "You do know, Alex, don't you?"

Without hesitating Alex replied, "You mean that Cristiano is gay? I'm his mother. Of course, I have known for many years. At least a couple of years before he did."

Selene looked entirely relieved, as if a huge burden had been removed from her. It had been three years since Cristiano had revealed his sexuality to Selene during his visit to London and he had told her that it was not known in Seborga. She thought that he was struggling to come to terms with the reality that attitudes in rural Italy were not the same as in New York. It was causing him much concern, not least because of his mother's position as head of the community.

During the time since his visit, Selene had been weighed down by this confidence, wondering if, when, or how to eventually have the conversation with her father and Alex. Seeing him so happy with the charming Marius tonight, Selene could no longer bear the strain.

Alex could see that Selene was more comfortable unburdened from what she thought was her secret. She used the moment to share one of her one with Selene. Nodding in the direction of Vincenzo, she brought her attention to something she had been witnessing.

Alex whispered, "Perhaps even bigger news than your revelations is that Vincenzo seems to have found a love interest."

Selene looked over to the tiny, slim Renata and the strong, tall Italian deep in conversation. Neither Alex nor Selene had ever seen Vincenzo smile so much.

"In the twenty years I known her, I have yet to see Renata show much interest in anything that she could not cook and eat and yet tonight she looks like she might devour Vincenzo whole."

Selene watched for a moment picking up the nuances of body language. As she watched, Alex filled her in on some of the troubled background of both Vincenzo and Renata, which she thought might go some way to explain their unlikely, mutual attraction.

"I have to agree with your analysis; they do look smitten. That seems to be everyone happy, then," Selene summed-up.

"Except you, maybe? You've never mentioned this Scandinavian guy in London once. Is that completely over?"

Selene told Alex the short version of the story, about him putting her career in jeopardy, or rather, that she had put her own job on the line by believing what he had told her was true without checking. In the new spirit of family bonding, Selene revealed to Alex that there might be someone new on the horizon.

"But I already have real concerns about it," she confided. "Things happened so fast, we have nothing in common, there's all kinds of complications but ..."

"But what?" Alex probed.

"I know it's way too soon, but I think I love him. But that can't be right. It's too good, too quick, too easy and ..." Selene paused mid-sentence, "we're just too different."

They were both quiet for a while. Then Alex laughed and suggested, "Your description of this relationship sounds like a summary of your father and me, but that has worked out."

Selene turned to Alex and began to smile in her realization of the similarities, "I guess you're right," she mused, "Maybe we too will be another unlikely pairing."

32. OYSTERS GILLARDEAU

Mastroianni had intended to invite his entire family, from his countless nephews and nieces right up to his ninety-something year old mother. He has seen it as an opportunity to enshrine his place as patriarch of the family and cement their loyalty. Alex had told him that for the ceremony to be valid under the constitution, it could only be conducted in the old palace throne room, the size of which would severely restrict the number of people who could attend.

The former palace of Seborga that was now Ben and Alex's family home, although the largest house in the village, was not very grand at all. What was now the dining room had, over the centuries, been used as a stateroom to receive knights, bishops and visiting princes and although it was generous by Seborgan standards, it could not hold more than twenty people. It did, however, still contain a substantial throne-like chair, emblems of heraldry and the other paraphernalia of Seborgan state.

The new Italian Prime Minister had adjusted his expectations for VIP guests to just his girlfriend, four adult children, mother and favourite sister. By the time Alex had included Ben, Vincenzo, a representative from each of the Carabinieri and Polizia di Stato, plus the priest to do the blessing and an official of the Commune to take an official record, the dining room was set to be full. The Carabinieri officer who would be present was Vincenzo's cousin; the same policeman who had been waiting for Payen as he drove out of Seborga in his damaged Mercedes.

This meant that there was only room for six press passes. All of these Mastroianni allocated to his own media channels. Alex, however, had two more press passes made and had given both of them to Selene without telling anyone but Ben. Mastroianni had quickly forgotten about his encounter with the pretty English reporter, assuming that if there had been any fall-out from it, he would have heard immediately afterwards. He had previously dealt with worse accusations than any Selene might come up with and emerged unscathed.

Not to be deprived of maximum exposure to his moment of glory in joining the ranks of the former ruling classes, Mastroianni had arranged for the live footage to be captured by one of his reporters. The event would be shown live on huge screens he had arranged to be erected in the piazza. It would also be streamed live on the internet. The remainder of his family, friends, business associates and the remaining media could watch the whole event outside live as it happened. He would finally have it all: wealth, power and status in society, with the entire world as his witness.

The car parks were almost full by early evening. When they were full, cars began parking along the roadside and these now stretched half a kilometre out of the village. The Osteria was fully booked and Mastroianni had arranged a grand buffet at the new Monastery restaurant for his guests. Alex had concerns about Renata accepting this booking, but on reflection, said that she should, but only if pre-payment was made.

Vincenzo had called up all his reserve guards and had also recruited the highly capable Marius. Two of the regular men were mounted, their horses dressed in their most beautiful saddles, bridles and headdresses. Seborgan flags fluttered everywhere. If they had to pander to this man's ego, they might as well maximise the opportunity to promote tourism to Seborga, was Alex and Ben's view.

Come the hour, the now-familiar sound of Mastroianni's helicopter could be heard approaching over the mountain. As it came closer, the mounted guards had to calm their horses who were spooked by the slapping rotor blades and the hissing jet engine. Finally, the new Prime Minister came striding up the hill with the vigour of a younger man, his bodyguards trotting to keep up, while looking profoundly serious and panning the crowd for potential trouble. The big, over-tanned politician was waving and smiling, his very obviously whitened teeth glowing in the lights on the TV crews. The Mastroianni family had arrived earlier on a luxury coach from Genoa and were all dressed in their Sunday best.

Alex had decided not to greet him personally, so to create as few as possible moments when they could be photographed alone together. Instead, she waited in the throne room while Vincenzo escorted the party to the palace. She was feeling more than a little nervous about the event to come. There was no protocol for creating a duke in Seborga as it had never been done before. She was going to have to fake a ceremony as best she could for a long as necessary and try to look convincing.

Mastroianni spent a good thirty minutes shaking hands and kissing women and children in the piazza. He was revelling in his moment and wanted to milk it for as long as possible. Finally, Vincenzo lost patience and said,

"Primo Ministro, la Principessa sta aspettando."

At the eleventh hour, Mastroianni had instructed that his bodyguard should remain outside creating space for two more of his guests. He was surprised but flattered to have received last-minute acceptances to his invitation to attend from the leader of the French right-wing opposition party and Italy's most senior judge. Both were men he knew could be useful to him. Now virtually every level of Italian society and international politics would bear witness to his finest hour.

Alex had arranged for the priest to say a few words and prayer before the proceedings got underway. The room became hushed as the cassocked Don Appo stepped forward to a lectern set up by Vincenzo for this purpose. He had consulted with them beforehand and Matthew 5:5 had seemed an entirely appropriate choice to Ben and Alex. So, he began,

"Blessed are the meek: for they shall inherit the earth ..."

Just as the priest reached the part,

"Happy are those who are humble," Selene stepped out of the shadows and finished the line for him,

"They will receive what God has promised."

The crowd stared blankly at her in shock, as they tried to establish whether this woman's conclusion of the passage was part of the ceremony.

"I apologise for interrupting," Selene continued, "but I am here to try and give God a hand to sort the wheat from the chaff. If you grant me five minutes, all will become clear."

A solid metallic clunk was heard as Vincenzo shoved home the big iron bolt on the front door making sure that no one would now be able to enter or leave. Selene was holding a folder of documents in front of her. She placed them on the lectern in front of the priest. Not understanding what was going on, the priest moved aside for her.

Mastroianni appeared utterly mystified as to why this English journalist had been allowed in and what exactly was now taking place. It was the first time anyone present had seen him lost for words. He even looked a bit paler under his tan. Selene was keen to maintain the momentum for the sake of the recording cameras. She pointed at Mastroianni.

"This man, Sergio Mastroianni, has conspired with others to create a threat to the throne of Seborga. He has done so only so that he could appear to step in and save it. He blackmailed this man," she paused to let Payen also step from the shadows into the lights, indicating towards him with her spare hand.

"Pressured by our new Prime Minister, Francois de Payen, made false claims which cast doubt on the validity of the agreement between Seborga, Italy and the European Union. Mastroianni then stood by laughing, as the EU withdrew their funding, building work stopped and an entire community's livelihoods faltered. He then stepped back in, appearing like a white knight, offering to cut them free of the net which he himself had cast over them. He did all of this to appear to be the hero, the defender of the underdog. What's more, on the back of that deceit, he has mislead the voters in the Italian election and as we now know, his lies did help him win."

Selene patted the documents in front of her.

"In this folder is the evidence, including Payen's written statement and these are all now also available on my newspaper's website for all to see."

Mastroianni was beginning to see that he had been ambushed. Now aware that everyone was watching him, he was trying to regain some composure, but as he looked around the room, all he saw were disbelieving angry faces. Outside was a similar situation. Onlookers, expecting a spectacle of pageantry followed by a party, were instead witnessing what amounted to a combination of crime drama and a political coup d'état being broadcast live. They were also aware that what they were viewing on the large screens in front of them was taking place just the other side of the large wooden doors. General confusion and a sense of unrest became evident amongst the crowd.

A few minutes earlier, Marius, wearing a Seborgan guard's beret and high-visibility jacket, had run up to Mastroianni's bodyguards. He told them that there was a security incident and the door had been locked from the inside. However, everything was okay because Vincenzo had whisked their Prime Minister out of a back door and was heading with him to the waiting helicopter. He told them that their instructions were to reach the helicopter, gain a safe height and hover out of gunshot range further up the valley. They would be contacted when it was safe for Mastroianni to be evacuated. Chaos ensued on the ground and in the air. The pair sped off through the crowd and out of the piazza drawing their weapons as they ran. When they arrived at the helicopter, the mere mention of gunshots sent the pilot off into the far distance out of harm's way.

In reality, Vincenzo and Ben were both still present in the throne room and had moved to either side of Mastroianni just in case he tried to make a move.

"This man, Payen, is a wanted criminal in France. A known conman. You can't believe a word he says," offered Mastroianni in his defence.

To show that they were not reliant on Payen's testimony, Selene then added, "Also online, is CCTV footage recorded at the Osteria in this very village, which records Sergio Mastroianni physically assaulting and threatening me because he knew what I might uncover about him. As you can see in this footage, I was only saved from an even worse fate by my step-brother."

Now it was Ben and Alex's turn to look at each other shocked. On hearing this, Vincenzo took Mastroianni's forearm and twisted up his back. The big man cried out in pain. Vincenzo released the pressure but held the arm in restraint. Ben smacked his hand on the big politician's shoulder just to let him know that any resistance was now futile.

The representative of the Carabinieri and Polizia di Stato realised that everyone was looking at them expecting them to act and that they would have to make an official response. It was the Carabinieri officer who stepped forward and started leafing through the folder Selene had presented. He found and removed a signed statement by Payen and thrust it at him asking, "Is this the truth?"

Payen confirmed that it was.

The policeman looked at Vincenzo, "Are you sure this is all true, Vincenzo?"

"On our grandfather's grave, I would swear it is."

"That's good enough for me."

The officer from the Polizia di Stato (state police) realised that his position was being undermined by local crime officers and also joined in to show his authority.

"On the face of this evidence and the statements made here tonight, there appears to be potentially both criminal and state conspiracy offences here."

Each police officer took out his mobile phone and called their respective second in command sat in the two vans on the edge of the piazza. The other witnesses to the events unfolding, both inside and outside the room, were absorbing the news more or less in silence. Some of the women in Mastroianni's family were crying. Some of the men were protesting his innocence. Vincenzo had warned his men and instructed them to close in on any groups who looked like trouble, using the horses to corral them if needs be. However, demonstrating a lack of faith in their own conviction, they did little more than pay lip service to their relative's innocence. After all, they all knew what he was capable of.

Selene was not quite finished with the man who had forced his ageing sweaty body against her, crushing the air out of her lungs and breathing his stale air in her face.

Ben had moved to the door and drawn out the bolt. He now swung it open and in came a dozen old ladies, headed by Albina from Genoa, all carrying banners bearing slogans. Selene's new journalist friend had driven them to Seborga in a hired minibus. They were shouting the slogan written on their banners with as much fervour as their frail voices could muster. Although even collectively, this was not very loud, everyone else was silent and so the message was heard clearly.

"Mastroianni's stealing our pension. Mastroianni's stealing our pension. Mastroianni's stealing our pension."

Selene raised her arms to signal them to stop, which they were reluctant to do. Albina had the last word.

"Ruba ai poveri."

As quiet descended Selene continued, "Albina is indeed correct. Mastroianni steals from the poor. I have uncovered unequivocal evidence that the new Prime Minister has robbed his newspapers' pensioners to pay for his several grand houses, his many fancy cars, his yacht and even that helicopter in which he arrived here today. Albina and her friends here are widows of his former employees, they are the ones who really own those things but they are not much use to them. What they need are bread, fish and vegetables, but Mastroianni thinks his needs are greater."

Mastroianni gave one of his white-toothed grins, as if there was some kind of fantastical joke, except that no one else was seeing the funny side. Boos and jeers were now issuing from the crowd outside, many of whom were his own journalists whose pension funds they now realised he was plundering. Vincenzo realised the crowd were starting to turn ugly. For a moment he considered shoving Mastroianni into the hands of the angry nonas and the baying journalists. Knowing that justice would only be served and Mastroianni truly brought down by proving all this in the courts, Vincenzo reluctantly led him away with the two policemen walking ahead of them.

Alex and Ben had been quiet throughout, doing a good impression of not knowing anything about these revelations. They managed on camera to look as shocked as everyone else. Quietly, they were both heaving a sigh of relief. With the considerable help of Selene, they had saved the Seborga project, got their EU paymaster off their backs and regained their principality status. It seemed like they and the community were better off now than they ever were under the original agreement. At that moment, Alex's mobile phone vibrated in her pocket.

"Pronto," she answered.

"Many congratulations Principessa," the voice offered.

"Many congratulations to you, Prime Minister," Alex replied.

"Not quite yet, but thank you all the same. I have been watching the whole thing unfold live on TV as have half of Italy. The other half will get the soundbites on the Internet later. I must say that I thought the angry nonas were a masterstroke.

The beautiful English reporter did a great job. Please pass on my best regards to Selene and tell her that I look forward very much to thanking her in person soon."

"Yes, it might be acceptable for an Italian politician to be a lothario, liar and even a thief, but when they threaten someone's nona, it's game over," Alex summarised.

She also wondered if she did not detect something cryptic in Andrea Cassini's message to Selene. As far as she knew, they seemed unlikely to meet again before she had to fly back to London. Before she had time to dwell on this, Cassini continued,

"Mastroianni's a dead man walking, as we say in the south. I'm sorry I have to go. The phones are going crazy. Government ministers, civil servants and judges will all be queueing to turn their knives in Mastroianni's back. It's astonishing how a man can make so many enemies and still get elected."

"Respectfully, I would not advise adopting that as your strategy, Prime Minister."

They both laughed and then rang off.

"By tomorrow morning Italy should have a new leader," she said to Ben.

"Well today, Seborga has their Princess back, thirteen million euros in the trust and more help promised. Add to that prime-time TV coverage which will be syndicated around the world and I would say that that was not a bad day's work."

"Yes, and one of London's finest journalists has the second major scoop of her short career," Alex added. "We should celebrate."

"I think I know where there might be some chilled Champagne and a fine buffet going uneaten at the Monastery," Ben replied.

Mastroianni was charged and taken away. The Polizia Stata pacified and stood-down his official bodyguard. After the story Marius told them of the security breach, they were just relieved at not having to explain to their boss that the PM had been assassinated on their watch. Having him arrested was embarrassing, but his death would have been career-terminating. The helicopter had hovered for only ten minutes and then used the excuse of getting low on fuel to return the safety of Genoa where the crew would learn about what had happened on the TV news.

Roman and Cecily were watching the events unfold on television in Menton harbour and enjoying seeing Mastroianni squirm. Cecily noticed that even his stereotypical, young, model girlfriend could not contain a smirk when Selene had unmasked him as a misogynist, bully and sexual predator.

"How do you feel now about your part in his downfall?" Roman asked.

"What about your part? If your Mafia friend had not suggested the connection with Andrea Cassini, none of this would have been possible."

"Excuse me. My friend is not Mafia. He is just well informed and pragmatic about the networks needed to get things done. Anyway, you pulled a few strings with your man, Drew, to get Selene the dirt she needed on his shaky companies. Don't tell me all that information was in the public domain and that some bankers did not have to overlook some data protection rules."

"OK. Let's agree that we did what we thought was best, but it worked out well I think. Tomorrow we will have a southerner — a Sicilian — as Prime Minister. That must feel good?"

Roman appeared to consider this for a moment before answering, "More important than where he comes from is that we have an honest man running our country. A young man with some integrity and vision. With the majority the Tricolore party now has, he might be able to make a tangible difference."

"And he has lovely hair and skin," Cecily added laughing.

"You're the expert," Roman conceded.

"I might try and sign-him-up as a brand ambassador for my men's range."

"Well, that might be the first test of that integrity and I bet you a dinner with Oysters Gillardeau at Mirazur that he says no to you, just like Alex did." As he made his wager, he had gestured across the water to the renowned three-Michelin Star restaurant sitting up above the Marina.

Cecily pointed out that Cassini had already demonstrated his willingness to be pragmatic. He had agreed to offer Payen some protection from extradition by granting Italian citizenship in return for testifying to Mastroianni's conspiracy.

From his confessions, they learned that Mastroianni had heard about Payen's lucrative wine fraud and that the Frenchman was effectively exiled in Italy, avoiding charges at home. Also, that he was seeking to base his operations near the French border. Mastroianni saw that he could use Payen's situation to gain leverage over Seborga. The media magnet paid some Genovese thugs to lean hard on the Frenchman. They told him that his exploits had come to the attention of the Mafia. That their bosses liked the sound of his business and thought they could use it to do something similar with high-value Italian wine. In short, they scared Payen into believing he needed an even more powerful ally on the Italian side of the border.

Once again playing the role of saviour, Mastroianni had then stepped in, offering to take Payen under his wing and protect him from the Mafia. He was told that all he had to do in return was to play a part in some subterfuge by claiming the throne of tiny Seborga. Payen said that he thought it all sounded like good fun and even had a few ideas of his own to embellish the subterfuge. He was hugely relieved to get what he believed to be the Mafia off his back. Mastroianni furnished him with the faked painting of his ancestor and the plausible storyline. Inevitably, his role was enlarged to include acting as a front to buy land for a vast villa in Seborga on Mastroianni's behalf.

"It just doesn't sit comfortably with me that this crook Payen, who is wanted in France and without whose cooperation none of this trouble would have been possible, walks away from this unscathed. He has all the money from his wine scams and now looks like he might even get to keep the land Mastroianni paid for because it is in his name. With dual citizenship, he can probably avoid French justice and have a nice existence here in Italy."

"I know that it doesn't seem right, darling, but sometimes you've got to concede the odd skirmish to win the bigger battle," was Roman's answer to this.

Templar iconography adorns many of the walls of Seborga.

Drawing by Linda McCluskey

33. ACCOPPIAMENTO IMPROBABILI

Cecily's skipper, Claude, motored into the bay mid-morning and used his GPS to navigate to a carefully chosen anchorage not far off the beach at Balzi Rossi. By late afternoon there would be several more boats — mainly motor yachts—from Monaco and San Remo moored at this beach resort. It is a restaurant and bar well-known for great food and live jazz. Its beach was small, but sandy and well-kept, with a private jetty where yacht tenders could drop passengers without getting their Manolo Blahnik's or Jimmy Choo's wet. Security was good, as the beach club could only be accessed through the restaurant where there was always a sturdy doorman.

Cecily fussed about getting the table ready for dinner in the salon later than evening. There were to be themselves plus four guests and they had been warned to come around six and bring swimwear. The plan was to meet on the beach, enjoy a swim, have aperitivos at the bar and then dinner on the boat.

The boat's chef had prepared a new dish that he had been working on and wanted to try it on Alex, Cecily and Roman. He had found an old Ligurian novel which contained a recipe described as anchovies with oranges. After more research, he had also found some variants of it from other areas further south. The version he finally settled on was a salad of fresh whole anchovies, blood orange segments, capers and figs. At first, he and everyone he told about it believed that this was a flavour combination that would not work. Yet when he tried it, somehow it did.

He described it to Cecily as, "An amazing riot of flavours."

Alex and Ben arrived first, dropped their clothes into a canvas bag on the beach and went straight into the water. They waved over to the boat, where Cecily and Roman had been looking out for them. Roman took a spectacular swan dive from the deck into the clear water, while Cecily descended the teak steps and swam after him.

As they were both swimming-in, two security men in black suits appeared though the restaurant and descended down the boardwalk onto the sand. One of the men incongruously carried what looked like a seaman's kit bag that had been made from an old boat sail. It still had a dinghy's insignia stitched into it. The men went in opposite directions, apparently checking to see who was already in the area. One then spoke into his lapel microphone indicating the all-clear and a few minutes later the new Prime Minister of Italy appeared in nothing but his swimming shorts. Alex waved to him from the water. Andrea Cassini took just a few long strides to cross the sand and then shallow dived into the water stroking smoothly towards them.

"We only await the guest of honour," Andrea said with a confident smile.

"How did you get him to come alone?" Ben asked.

"It was Cecily's idea to say that their yacht could not accommodate any more people under its safety certificate. That's some clever woman Roman married. I could use her in my cabinet."

Meanwhile, Alex and Cecily had swum gently out into deeper water for a private chat.

"God, how can somebody be that handsome?" Cecily whispered to Alex.

"Shhh ..." Alex admonished her. "You can't say that about the Prime Minister. And anyway he's far too young for us."

"Well you definitely couldn't say it about any of his predecessors, so I think we can make an exception in this case."

Their final guest then arrived at the top of the boardwalk; Payen's appearance had Cecily and Alex giggling. He was wearing a black dinner jacket and tie, with shiny patent shoes. In one hand he had a bouquet and in the other what looked like a wooden wine box.

"I confess that this was my doing," admitted Cassini to Ben, well out of ear-shot of Payen. "I wanted to be sure that he would want to get changed and get in the water. I will simply tell him I made a mistake about the dress arrangements. He isn't going to leave without what he came for."

One of the Prime Minister's bodyguards produced a pair of swimming shorts from his boss's bag and offered them to Payen. He pointed to a changing room along the beach. Looking very confused, the Frenchman went to change out of his formal attire. When he returned, Ben could see what Andrea had told him was true. Payen had a swimmer's physique, slim waist but powerful square shoulders. This build was the legacy of a decade as one of France's best freestyle swimmers and one-time Olympic competitor. Even now in his late-thirties he looked like he trained regularly, Ben thought.

A waiter from the restaurant appeared with a bottle of Taittinger Champagne in a wine cooler and six glasses and set them up on a beach table.

The party converged. Payen returned, glad to be out of his suit and feeling a little more relaxed, although still holding the flowers and wine. He handed the flowers to Cecily and the wine to Roman and thanked them for hosting the dinner. Formalities over, Cassini grasped the Champagne and started twisting the cork, saying,

"I wouldn't normally order French Champagne, but as Francois might not be seeing so much of it after he becomes a resident of Italy, I thought we should treat him to one last glass."

Payen looked genuinely touched by this gesture. He thanked him and offered, "Salute," and then asked nervously, "Should I read any significance into the fact that the Taittinger logo on the wine cooler is a Templar Knight?"

"Cheers," Cecily added to change the subject.

"Chin, chin," replied Cassini.

"You have the document?" Payen asked Cassini.

"It has been drafted by lawyers in Rome and will be hand-delivered here. I have already heard that their plane landed at Nice airport half an hour ago. It should be with us before dinner. We can sign, Princess Alessandra can witness it and you will be officially Italian before dinner is served."

After just a little more small-talk, Roman turned away from the beach and looked out towards the promontory where someone was waving to him.

"Our lobsters are ready to collect," he said, putting down his glass and pointing to an Italian flag now fluttering at half-mast. There was a man in swimming trunks standing beside holding the rope. As soon as Roman signalled back with a wave, the flag was returned to its full height. To reach the end of the bay overland would have meant a trip back up the hill to the main road and a drive out to the promontory. Roman then announced that he had planned a leisurely swim over as his evening exercise and that anyone who wanted could join him.

Andrea Cassini interrupted, "Signore Roman. With all due respect, swimming all the way out there is one thing. Swimming back with a sack full of lobsters is another matter. It is surely a young man's job and I am also a fisherman's son. I can be there and back in no time at all. Why don't you finish your glass of Champagne and entertain your other guests? I will do the fishing."

Andrea could see that, as he had hoped, Payen was positively itching to offer to show off his prowess and thereby regain some standing amongst this high achieving group.

The Prime Minister turned to him and challenged, "Francois, we're about the same age and build. What would you say to a race? Last one to the flag to get the lobsters pays for the Champagne?"

Without even answering, Payen was running down the beach, with Andrea Cassini soon on his heels. Andrea had longer legs and so they both hit the clear blue water at about the same time. For the first two hundred meters, Payen only gained a little on Cassini, who was also a strong swimmer. As they passed halfway, Payen started to pull ahead and looked comfortable doing so. The Frenchman reached the beach about a minute ahead of Cassini.

A tanned young man and a woman were waiting on the beach by the flagpole. They were both in swimwear, carrying flippers, masks, snorkels and a tote bag. At their feet was a net containing six squirming blue lobsters. Payen then realised that he had no money to pay for their supper and so turned to see where Cassini was, assuming that he would have brought payment.

When he turned back, the two young people had donned blue baseball caps from their tote bag and slipped chrome police badges into the elastic of their swimming costumes. Momentarily frozen with confusion, he turned once again to Cassini, but all the Italian did was shrug as though he was equally mystified. The woman held forward the bag containing the lobsters and as Payen reached to take it, the policeman snapped one part of a handcuff over his wrist. He then clicked the other end over his own wrist binding the two of them together.

"Flavien de Paine also known as Francois de Payen, we have a warrant for your arrest," the policewoman said.

Payen seemed flustered but not unduly concerned. It took the Frenchman a minute to speak and then he answered, "You may well have a warrant, but as I am currently in Italy, you cannot conduct a French arrest here."

Both officers smiled. "Over there you were in Italy at Balzi Rossi." The woman said, pointing back to the beach where they had set off. "Here you are in France," she said, now pointing to the ground at her feet.

Payen now looked angry. "Look up, you idiot. Is that not an Italian flag?"

"Indeed it is monsieur, because this is an Italian restaurant as are many of them in Menton. You have just swum over the border. Welcome back to France."

An inflatable motor tender was heading towards them at speed with Roman at the tiller. He skimmed up onto the sand and strode over.

"I think they are my lobsters."

"Oui monsieur," said the male officer. "Compliments of the Commissaire."

"Please give this to your Commissaire with my compliments." He handed over the wine box that Payen had given him on the beach. "I am fairly confident this is one of Payen's fake bottles of Petrus, doubtless with his fingerprints all over it. It might prove useful as evidence. I think our business here is complete. Would you like a lift back, Prime Minister? Chef is waiting for these," he said brandishing the net.

The two men pushed the tender back into the water, threw in the net of lobsters and climbed aboard. It was a little while before their outboard motor drowned out Payen's insults and the three figures on the beach gradually disappeared.

Once dried and changed, the remaining five guests took places at the dinner table. While in the shower, Ben had heard the tender leave again, presumably heading to the restaurant on the beach. Chef must have needed something that he had forgotten to buy. A sixth place was still set at the table as a reminder of the guest who would be dining alone in a cell tonight. No one made any attempt to clear the place, which Alex thought odd. Indeed, as Cecily knew the outcome in advance, she wondered why it had even been set.

The three men joked that they were glad that they had not needed to use their plan B, had Payen not taken up the swimming challenge. It would have been far riskier if he had been allowed to board the yacht for dinner. They would have been forced to quietly untie the mooring line and wait for the current to gently drift the boat across the French border Although the skipper had assured them that where they were was now less than a few metres from French waters, the tide was not always strong. It could have taken as long as an hour to be sure that they were across before they could bring the waiting Gendarmes on board.

Andrea Cassini spoke, "Payen was never going to back away from my challenge. It was a safe bet."

Roman asked Ben how he knew that the wine was one of Payen's fakes. Ben explained that Cecily opened the wine box that Payen had given her and had looked astonished. A single bottle of 1985 Petrus would have cost about two-and-half-thousand euros. This was too generous a gift for a dinner invite and that made him suspicious. Looking more closely, Ben saw the security hologram on the label.

"Ah, I've heard about this hologram, but surely that proves it to be authentic?" Cecily suggested.

"If it had been a later vintage, we might have been sat here enjoying it, Roman. But Petrus had not started adding the holograms until 1986. Anything prior to that date with a hologram could only be a fake, but the crook just could not resist another flourish."

Roman replied, "That raises an interesting question, Ben. If you had not spotted the fake bottle and we had drunk the contents thinking it was genuine, do you think we would have savoured it as the real thing?"

"It's a good question. After nearly forty years in that bottle and depending on many factors, including where and how well it had been stored, the contents could have easily been spoiled. The wine could have tasted wonderful or woeful. Either way, it could not have been more enjoyable than the taste of justice that we have witnessed, which tasted particularly good to me."

"You might know your wines, Ben, but you must admit that you were completely wrong about Payen running a wine scam from Seborga," Andrea Cassini teased.

Ben acknowledged that he had not spotted that Mastroianni had been the puppet master behind the Frenchman's declaration that he was Prince of Seborga. He had, not unreasonably, assumed that he had come here looking for another wine product with which to con people.

"I was looking for a complicated explanation when it turned out that it was a simple blackmail. When I heard the tale of Lorenzo's vineyard situated below the Templars cave, I was convinced that must be it. When he bought the land next door, although it was confusing, it seemed like just too much of a coincidence."

Andrea Cassini told them that he planned to make sure Payen would not get to keep the land that he bought on Mastroianni's behalf. He said that he was confident the money would have come, all-be-it indirectly, from the printworkers pension fund and that he was determined that they would get it back. He would use the Proceeds of Crime legislation, brought in two years ago to target the Mafia and the land would be requisitioned and sold at auction.

"Ben could bid for it and add it to his neighbouring plot," Andrea added, making it clear that there would be no favours.

Cecily had overhead Ben mention Lorenzo's vineyard and shifted her attention from the conversation she had been having with Alex to join in with the men.

"No matter what Payen's motives were, I think you have stumbled on something with this wine Ben. There is a unique and utterly amazing story behind the wine from your vineyard. Some of the best brands were founded on accidents. We need to talk about it when this is all over."

With perfect timing, the chef came to the table and set his extraordinarily colourful anchovy and blood orange salad in the middle. He explained that when he came across the recipe, it was not with blood oranges, but with clementines and that this was his own interpretation in celebration of the new Seborgan crop and Cecily's successful products. He also pointed out that the dish was a marriage of cultures: Italian anchovies, Sicilian capers and Arab dates,

"With respect, I have named it in honour of you all: Accoppiamento Improbabili meaning 'unlikely pairing'".

They all heard the small boat returning and bumping up the ladder hanging from the deck.

Andrea said, "Ah, perfect timing. Actually, all of our 'parts' are not here yet. I think the boat engine signals that my surprise guest has just arrived from Nice airport."

Ben looked bemused, "But surely you didn't really have someone fly here with the papers for Payen ... what was the point when you knew that you were never going to grant him Italian citizenship? That was surely just a rouse to get him here?"

Andrea did not answer and Selene then stepped into the saloon wearing a pale green linen suit and a huge smile. Ben's face lit up as he saw his daughter. He stood but was hemmed-in by the other guests at the banquet, so he could not extract himself to hug her. He gestured a hug and Selene blew him a kiss, along with another to Alex.

Looking more than a little smug, Andrea said, "I apologise. I did not think we could celebrate properly without the woman who was key to the success of our bold venture. And anyway, we had a spare place at the table right next to me."

After exchanging continental air-kisses with Celine and Roman, Selene took her seat next to Andrea, who had his right hand on the stem of his white wine glass. Mostly hidden by the huge salad bowl, Selene surreptitiously placed her left hand over Andrea's right. She held it there, while almost imperceptibly massaging the tanned skin on the back of his hand. The act was virtually invisible.

Ben was saying how delighted he was to have his daughter back so soon and asked her about the reaction to her inside story, which he described as "the unseating of Mastroianni, Italy's shortest-serving Prime Minister," when Andrea interrupted, "Surely you mean the story of the meteoric rise and surprise appointment of Italy's youngest-ever Prime Minister?"

They all laughed, and as he spoke, all eyes were on the handsome Sicilian, but none as intensely or for so long as his eyes were on Selene. Nothing much evaded Cecily's attention and she spotted the clear signs of tenderness. She gave Alex a gentle nudge with her elbow while nodding in the direction of their hands, which were still touching on the table mostly hidden by the salad bowl. Alex had been distracted by events unfolding around the table. She had been holding her wine glass about to take a sip when she was astounded by what she saw. In total surprise, Alex attempted to put the glass down on the table too quickly, but it settled on her cutlery. The small amount of prosecco remaining in the glass spilt onto the tablecloth, causing a minor disturbance. Flustered, Alex had begun to apologise when Selene guessed the cause of the upset.

"Is there a special reason for your surprise visit?" Cecily asked, offering an opening for an explanation for the unexpected arrival and recent turn of events.

BOOK 3

RECIPE FOR A NATION

An old Ape, like Vincenzo's,

at the annual Vallebona Ape & Flower Festival.

Drawing by Linda McCluskey

1. CAPRA ARROSTO

Rare on this Earth are places where one can witness such extremes from a single vantage point. Opulence usually likes to keep a safe distance from impoverishment. Beaches and snow-capped peaks are seldom comfortable bedfellows. Domestication is tetchy with wild nature. And yet, from Seborga it is possible to watch a farmer toil all day to harvest olives worth less than a tip given to a valet parker a couple of dozen miles away in Monaco. Pampered pooches sit on their own chairs at restaurant tables, while wild boar that could fell a man forage in forests nearby. Although contradictory and irreconcilable, here it is—a ninth-century anomaly, persevering against all odds into the twenty-first century. Perhaps Seborga is the yin that gives yang a point of reference?

Seborga teeters precariously upon a mountain top, where ancient stone buildings cling to the terrain like swallows' nests. Rather than battle against nature, homes absorb the rocky terrain. They hug the topography of the mountain like children hugging the mother that nourishes them.

Houses appear stacked upon one another with their staggered roof lines. A labyrinth of ancient alleyways snakes by houses on various levels, each home uniquely fitted with windows of oak and doors of chestnut to fit the architecture of the terrain. Buildings of rough stone are rendered and painted from a palette of autumn leaves.

The concept of town planning is as foreign to the Italians as American fast food. Like their cuisine, homes are shaped by their locations, using only materials readily to hand. Any perceived aesthetic value which emerges from this chaos is nothing more than a fortunate accident. The result is breath-taking, with its natural beauty born of simple function.

In legends of the past, told within these homes, the Holy Grail travelled the road up the mountain from the coast to Seborga. Known to Italians as the Sacro Cantino, the treasured holy relic was believed to have first made this journey on horseback under the protection of the Knights Templar almost a millennium ago.

These crusading knights made Seborga their southernmost base in Europe for most of the Holy Wars. They sailed from this coastline in ships bound for Palestine. After two hundred years of fighting all the Europeans had returned, bringing with them relics recovered from the holy sites, including the Sacro Cantino. In the centuries that followed, the legendary chalice was lost to the imagination until it finally found its way back to Genoa.

Nearly one thousand years later, and now more widely known as the Holy Grail, it made its way up the mountain road to Seborga once again. In the place of horses and knights, this homecoming involved a bank security van guarded by Italian soldiers. The van, the type employed for collecting cash from supermarkets, was escorted by soldiers of Italy's crack Alpini-troops in armoured personnel carriers, with automatic weapons at the ready.

Anxiously awaiting its arrival in Seborga was an elite group, including a cardinal, a bishop, members of parliament for both Imperia and Genoa, government ministers of both culture and tourism, the Prime Minister of Italy, the Mayor of Bordighera, Princess Alessandra of Seborga, and her English husband, Ben. Looking on were representatives of most of the world's media.

"Quite a reception for an old bowl," Ben joked to no one in particular.

Alessandra said nothing in response to Ben's flippant remark about the Sacro Cantina, but reached down and squeezed his hand—a gesture of affection and reassurance, knowing that he was as nervous as she was, and that joking was his way of dealing with it. She could still hardly believe that this was finally happening. For as long as she could remember, stories had circulated amongst the villagers about the Templars having brought the Holy Grail here to Seborga. Princess Alessandra would be fulfilling her ancestors' dreams in seeing it return.

Most historians acknowledged that the holy warrior knights were based in Seborga, so it seemed logical that this was where they would bring their most treasured relics from the Holy Land, she rationalised. And yet, these strange tales were always told in hushed tones by the villagers. It was as if the mere mention of the Holy Grail out loud might risk the wrath of God. No other single relic of the world's largest religion is held in such awe. No icon has inspired so many rumours, wild speculation and such fantastic conspiracy theories.

Quite how an agnostic Englishman, with a less than unblemished personal reputation, had persuaded the Vatican to allow this to happen, still left many locals baffled. And yet, here it was—the Sacro Cantina, which most Italians and many others of faith believe to be the Holy Grail—being carried, very carefully, from a black van parked in Seborga's piazza Martiri Patrioti. Overlooking this scene was the near-window-less church of San Bernado, which was built around the time of the Templars.

"Had these weathered stones of this ancient church already witnessed a scene similar to this one around the time of King Richard I of England?" one American TV presenter proposed to his viewers back home.

At first sight of the Perspex crate holding the distinctive green glass chalice, a joyful cheer went up among the crowd. Hundreds of villagers and thousands of outside visitors had turned up on this bright autumn day to witness the historic event. The Grail's arrival was being recorded by at least one film crew from almost every Catholic country in the world. There were three competing TV stations from Brazil, two from Mexico, and four from the United States.

Only the Spanish media was conspicuous by their absence, the Spanish having their own Chalice of Dona Urraca. Their glitzier jewel-encrusted vessel, perhaps more in keeping with the popular perception of the Holy Grail, is kept in the Basilica of San Isidoro in León. However, claims that the Spanish chalice was the real Holy Grail have been met with scepticism by historians and scientists. Yet, these doubts has not stopped thousands of pilgrims flocking to see it. Ben and Alex had hoped that the arrival of far-better-provenanced Sacro Cantina would bring even greater tourism to Seborga and place it firmly on the tourist map. If today was a taster of things to come, it seemed to be working.

Five years prior, Ben had been sent to Seborga by his UK university employer on the pretext of a research sabbatical. In reality, his dean had wanted him out of the way while they investigated potentially damaging allegations against Ben. By the time the investigation established his innocence, the Englishman had fallen for the Princess Alessandra and she for him, but only after a fractious courtship.

A few months after arriving in Seborga, Ben inadvertently stumbled upon a cave that a recent landslide had uncovered. On the rock walls were paintings that appeared to depict scenes from the Holy Wars, suggesting it had been used as a shelter and hiding place nearly a thousand years earlier. Inside, he discovered an ancient charter apparently issued by Pope Gregory in 1079. It was later claimed that this legal document granted Seborga its independence under the Knights Templar rule. Under its terms, the principality was also allowed to choose a prince from amongst its ranks.

The Templars ruled Seborga for over two hundred years, using it as a staging post as their knights travelled to and from the Middle East fighting the Holy Wars. From the Christian perspective, these military campaigns were all about protecting the region's holy sites and the relics they contained from Muslim forces.

A church and a monastery were established in Seborga. Nearby, a hospital was built to treat and convalesce the returning wounded, which became great in number as the course of the war went against them. Despite their considerable wealth, power and influence across Europe, the Knights Templar failed to win a decisive victory in the Holy Wars. When a strategic withdrawal from Palestine became inevitable, it was probably to this very place, close to the Pope who had called for the conflict, that the Templars brought any treasures recovered from holy sites.

With Jerusalem lost to the forces of Islam, the usefulness of the Knights was brought into question. This, coupled with their rising power and popularity amongst the people of Europe, made them a potential threat to both heads of state and even the Pope himself. These incumbent powers conspired against the Knights. False accusations led to their being excommunicated from the Church and warrants being issued for their arrest in France, from where many of the Knights originated. Seborga was abandoned to its fate and the Knights melted away across Europe, their treasures disappearing with them.

Based on this history, the people of Seborga have tried several times to re-establish their independence from Italy and be recognised as a sovereign state once again. However, a copy of Pope Gregory's original document granting independence, which would back up their claims, could never be found. Until Ben's accidental discovery of the charter, the church in Rome had consistently denied all knowledge of its existence, despite knowing that they had a copy safely secreted in their archives. It had simply not been politically expedient for the church to take the side of tiny Seborga in its claimed independence from Italy. The discovery of this long-lost evidence left the current Pope embarrassed over yet another apparent cover-up at the Vatican.

The eleventh-century cathedral in Genoa, where the chalice had rested for nearly seven hundred years, was badly in need of repairs. Its trustees had been trying for years to raise the three million euros needed to renew its leaking roof. Economic hard times in Italy made fundraising difficult. By having the project cost recategorised as tourism development, Italy's new Prime Minister, Andrea Cassini, had cleverly squeezed most of the money for the roof out of the European Union (EU).

Ben had then pointed out that removing the roof for these major works would make the Holy Grail highly vulnerable. He reminded the church of what had happened during the recent renovation at Notre-Dame in Paris, when it nearly burnt to the ground. This valid concern, along with some regret over his predecessors' cover-up, was the final leverage in convincing the Pope to sanction the Sacro Cantina's temporary relocation to Seborga. The village-state had been transformed from a rural backwater on the brink of extinction as a community into a thriving model for sustainable tourism in less than five roller-coaster years. This remarkable metamorphosis was almost totally down to the efforts of Ben and Alessandra.

Princess Alessandra of Seborga did not live in a palace, ride in a chauffeur-driven limousine or have many of the trappings of royalty. With the principality's status still unrecognised, the royal line had no wealth or revenues. Unlike some royal families, however, the princess did enjoy the wholehearted support of nearly one hundred percent of the three-hundred-plus citizens. The problem was that in a community so small, most of whom were still scratching a living from the land, no taxes could be raised to fund jewels or other finery associated with being a royal princess. Alessandra inherited all of the responsibility of a head of state with none of the trappings that usually accompanied it.

So, as soon as she was old enough, Alessandra did what most of her teenage contemporaries were doing at that time. She left Seborga, seeking a more exciting future with better prospects overseas. In the princess's case, this meant going to live with relatives in the United States. Once there, she dropped her worthless royal title, learned to cook, and eventually earned a different kind of accolade: that of a Michelin Star chef. Claudio, her later-widowed elderly father, was left to rule Seborga alone.

By the time Alessandra returned twenty-plus years later, to care for the ageing prince, things in Seborga had deteriorated even further. There were so few young children living there that the school had closed. Former homes of deceased elderly residents remained empty and unsold, with many falling apart. Much of the agricultural land had been abandoned and was returning to nature. Brambles and weeds were strangling once productive olive trees. The village was in danger of going the way of other small mountain communities in rural Italy, and being completely abandoned in favour of city or coastal living.

The economics of artisan olive growing on slopes too steep and narrow for machines no longer made financial sense. Too much cheap olive oil was available from Turkey and Greece and other big mono-culture producers, and the villagers didn't have the marketing know-how to justify their higher costs. There was a much easier, better living for farmers to be had tending trees and shrubs in the manicured gardens of the wealthy down on the Riviera.

With the recent revival of the fortunes of Seborga, a few of these exiled residents were returning. Not yet a flood, but certainly a trickle. Perhaps more significant, younger would-be farmers were joining them. Some of these were well-educated professionals who had grown disillusioned with modern corporate life, or people who just wanted to get away from the pollution and stress of city living. In some cases, they kept their high-paying jobs but worked from a laptop in Seborga with only the occasional visit to an office or meeting. Others made the full commitment to trying to live off the land.

Attracted by low property prices, clean air, a lack of crime, and a lower cost of living, the village's empty houses were being reoccupied and restored. This inward investment of youthful vitality was beginning to revive the community. There were now sufficient parents of young children to lobby for the school to be reopened. The post office and the village store were thriving.

The chalice was safely installed in its temporary home and the Alpini troops had taken up the guard duties, which they would continue to perform for the remainder of its time in Seborga. The platoon of the elite soldiers would be barracked in the village and run round-the-clock security patrols. This was something that the prime minister had offered in order to persuade the Pope to agree to the chalice's loan.

Ben and Alessandra were relieved to have the burden of responsibility for the chalice's security taken from them. The presence of the Alpini in their traditional uniforms with the distinctive feathers in their alpine hats added to the prestige of the principality. When off-duty, they were also twenty more customers for the restaurants and bars.

In the kitchen of the village's new cookery school, preparations were almost complete for the feast that would now be served to their VIP guests. Renata, also new to the village, had cooked for movie actors, musicians, sports stars and politicians in Alessandra's New York restaurant. But this lapsed Catholic, child of a devout Mexican family, had never before fed a cardinal and a bishop.

"I suppose Devils on Horseback will not be going on the menu?" she had quipped to Alessandra when she had seen the reverential guest list.

"In celebration of the arrival of the chalice, we are going to steal an idea from my recent nemesis, Francois de Payen, and serve a twenty-first century reinterpretation of the Last Supper."

Renata looked both slightly perturbed and intrigued by the idea of recreating Christ's last meal.

"Is that even legal in Italy?" she asked, only half-joking.

"That's your challenge," offered Alessandra, knowing full well that Renata would not balk from it. She only hoped that she would invite her son, Cristiano, to contribute some of his ideas to the menu. Cristiano was already an incredibly talented sous-chef, Renata was now his mentor in hopefully achieving even greater things. Like all young people, he was impatient for success, but he also recognised the American's superior experience and skill. He knew that under her tutelage, he could rise to the very top.

The final menu for the Banquet of the Holy Grail was an inspired fusion of Middle Eastern and Ligurian cuisine which read.

Primi-mixed Meze

- Garlic baba ganoush with sesame crackers
- Beetroot falafel with whipped minted yoghurt
- Saltfish beignets with tomato, olive and ginger salsa
  Contorni
- Whole roasted goat 'Porchetta' style-stuffed with wild fennel, apricots and cracked wheat, served with a cauliflower and broccoli Fattoush salad

Dolce

- Warm poached stuffed figs with pistachio, honey sorbet and golden tuille
- Coffee with Baklava, halva and dates

"Bravo," exclaimed Alessandra. "The ingredients of the Bible with the methods of the moment."

With everything looking well in hand for the celebration feast, Alessandra returned to her Osteria.

"Alcuni dicono che sia maledetto, Principessa." (Some say it's cursed, Princess.) Alessandra stopped at hearing the old lady's announcement. She sat on her doorstep, nipping the heads of dead flowers in pots on either side of it. Viola, Seborga's oldest resident, spent most of her waking day sitting on this same step. Here she held court, chatting to neighbours and interrogating strangers as to their business there. Nothing passed her by or escaped her attention. There was no snippet of information too small for her to absorb. She knew who had received letters, and often even who had sent them. Most parcels were left at her door because it was easier for the delivery drivers, and she invited them to do so. Also, because Viola was always in when others were out at work.

"Why would it be cursed, Viola?" the princess questioned the white-haired, chestnut-brown-skinned, stooped old woman, who was suffering from obvious curvature of the spine.

"They say that the Arabs in Palestine cursed it, foretelling that it would bring heavens crashing down on the infidels who took it from them. Certainly, several boats containing the returning Knights Templar were sunk in storms on their way back from the Holy Land. When they got back to Seborga, their fortunes changed dramatically for the worse. They say that the Templars were glad to finally get rid of it."

Alessandra was fond of Viola, as were all the village. She was one constant in a community that had seen much social change. She watched over the children playing in the piazza, acted as referee in their disputes, administered sticking plasters to grazed knees and issued small sweets to those with tearful eyes. No one could imagine life in Seborga without her, although they knew they would have to before too many years passed. However, Alessandra also knew that Viola had another, more personal reason, for perpetuating the myth of the grail being cursed.

Not wishing to contradict or undermine her kindly elderly neighbour's assertion, Alessandra tried to gently sidestep it. "The Templars were a long time ago, Viola. The Sacro Cantina has been safely in the Cathedral in Genoa for hundreds of years without any signs of a curse. I don't think we need to worry too much."

Viola shrugged her shoulders and turned to go inside, leaving Alessandra with a parting remark, "Ride bene chi ride ultimo."

'The biggest laughs come from those who laugh last,' was an uncharacteristically gloomy warning from someone usually so upbeat and so it stayed with Alessandra, lingering like a tiny but persistent cloud in an otherwise flawless blue sky.

2. BISCOTTI QUARESIMALI

At five hundred metres above sea level and miles from any major conurbation, the air was both clear and clean in Seborga. After years of working in London and then Newcastle, just breathing it in seemed both medicinal and therapeutic to Ben. Now that most people had gone home, the loudest noise was the croaking of frogs, of which there were hundreds in the undergrowth around the village. After five years this noise had become the familiar background to evenings in the piazza, pierced only by occasional voices, the chinking of glasses or the clatter of plates at the Osteria.

The banquet had been an outstanding success. Alessandra thought that everyone's high spirits were a mixture of elation at pulling off such a coup, and sheer relief that the chalice had been transported safely from Genoa and stored away without any hiccups. She certainly felt the sense of one weight being lifted from a shoulder, but a similar burden was still resting on the other. Despite the formidable presence of the Alpini troops, Alessandra still felt that she and Ben were now responsible for the safety of one of the world's most important Christian relics.

Long before midnight, most of the guests had departed or retired to their hotel rooms down on the coast. The proud villagers, full of roast goat and Rossese wine, were in their beds dreaming of the crowds of visitors that would soon be bringing euros to the tills of their businesses. A few staff and some new students were cleaning tables and wiping down catering equipment that needed returning to the kitchens. Some were smoking much-needed cigarettes as they worked; a concession

Renata would never have allowed in New York, Alessandra thought. She was already having to make cultural adjustments.

Earlier, Ben had witnessed the prime minister standing down his bodyguards to enjoy a private stroll home with Selene in the safe streets of Seborga. They did not follow the couple, but neither did they leave the piazza. Instead, they positioned themselves at the entrance to the street down which their boss had disappeared, and kept scanning the now almost-empty village for imaginary assassins, terrorists, or worse, Italian Paparazzi.

Cristiano had brought an ice-frosted bottle of homemade limoncello so he could share a digestivo with Ben and his mother. He also carried a small plate with three orange biscuits.

"Quaresimali, how wonderful," his mother guessed correctly. "You know, these were originally made by nuns to be eaten at Lent," she explained to Ben.

"I have practiced making them, and think finally I've got it right. Blood orange and almond," Cristiano expanded.

The three sat on a wall at the edge of the piazza, looking out over the valley and enjoying the cleansing citrus flavours. It was a luminous and clear night with an uncountable display of clearly defined stars. The smoke from the dying charcoal under the spit roast mingled with the scent of orange blossom drifting up from the terraces below. The lights of Monaco twinkled brightly, outshining those of its near neighbour, Nice, a dozen kilometres further along the coast. Some strange phenomena made the silhouette of the mountains opposite appear a deep indigo blue, as they often did at this time of night.

"Look. The outline of hills against the sky looks like a reclining Templar Knight who has been laid out for burial, his hands clasping his sword to a shield covering his chest," Alessandra proposed. With her index finger she traced a line from the knight's imaginary feet to the head, as Ben and Cristiano tried to isolate the shape that she was describing.

After just a moment, "So it does. How extraordinary," agreed Cristiano.

"My father pointed it out to me when I was a child, and now I am telling you so that you can recount the story to your. . ." Realising her mistake, Alessandra let the sentence trail away but knew that the harm was already done.

Cristiano smiled. "It's OK, Mother. You do not need to worry about saying the wrong thing. Anyway, who knows-I might have children at some point. There are ways, you know."

The young chef sank the remainder of his limoncello, collected all three glasses and bid the others goodnight. After he had gone, Ben took his wife's hand.

"It must have occurred to you that the chances of an heir to the royal title looked unlikely when Cristiano accepted that he was gay?"

"Well, that wasn't my first concern, but yes, it did occur to me that my family line would probably stop with him. You and I are too old to consider starting a family, even if it were medically possible. Which, let's face it, is a long-shot."

Ben feigned being hurt and replied, "Are you suggesting that I'm past it?"

Alex smiled, and squeezed his hand but otherwise avoided the question.

"Cristiano might be able to adopt, but that solves nothing in terms of an heir. A surrogate mother would, I suppose, provide a bloodline, but constitutionally sounds like it would be a nightmare. And this ignores the fact that Cristiano is even less inclined to take over the reins of power than I was. I'm sanguine about the situation. He's healthy, happy and has a good life ahead of him in a career he loves. I have no wish to burden him with the responsibility of being Prince of Seborga. For the sake of my father, I will do what I can to make the principality great again, but after I'm gone, the citizens will have to find a new leader."

Ben stood up. "Speaking of children, my very own prodigal son arrives tomorrow. I need to be awake and away to the airport to pick him up. You need to kill the fatted calf for the welcome feast."

"It will be lovely for you to spend some time with your son. I am really looking forward to meeting him."

To temper his wife's expectations, Ben reiterated that their father-son relationship since his divorce had often been fractious. He told her that every meeting since then had ended in a row, or at best someone walking away. His wife's bitterness at what had happened only served to pour fuel on the flames of the teenager's anger. In recent years, things had got a little less volatile, but Ben wondered if this was more to do with their not speaking very often and being distanced. The prospect of finding out where they now stood during two weeks of living in close proximity filled Ben with a strange mix of hope and dread.

Alessandra looked sad at hearing of Ben's obvious pain about his father-son relationship. She rested her head on her husband's shoulder and linked her arm in his as they walked back across the piazza. Two Alpini soldiers on sentry duty clicked their heels and saluted when they saw the princess. Alessandra smiled and gave a brief wave.

"Quite nice to have them around, isn't it?" Ben smiled. "Now you have two armies at your command. Not many girls can say that."

The prime minister had to be out in time for a 9 am photocall with local children and their teachers. They would be carrying out a plastic waste survey as part of their environmental studies program. The idea was that Selene would attend with him, but in her official capacity as a journalist, and together they could enjoy a pleasant walk in the hills. She was almost certain any other press in attendance would not walk too far. They would most likely get their quotes from the PM, stage their photographs at the outset, and then return to their offices to file their material. That would leave the couple some time to themselves.

"I'm surprised to hear that there is much plastic waste in and around Seborga for the children to find," Andrea commented to Selene. "These hills around here always appear to be so pristine. I know that there is plenty of plastic thrown away along the Autoroute and down at the coast, but I'd be surprised to find a big problem up here."

"Let's ask the teachers," Selene suggested.

"It's a slightly different problem in the hills," one of the teachers explained. "It's true that there are not so many plastic drink bottles and sandwich wrappers. Up here, we find the plastic sheeting used to cover crops, off-cuts of water drainage pipes, discarded seed and pesticide bags, and other waste linked to agriculture. The other type is fly-tipping of domestic and building waste. It's a long drive to the nearest official recycling centre, and some people are too lazy, or think they are too busy, to make the trip."

"But surely the children do not pick up these types of things?" Selene said with a look of horror. "There must be so many health and safety issues."

"No, it's a lesson in what is out there and why it's so wrong. We collect small items that can be picked up with one of these," the teacher said, pointing to the metre-long rod with a sprung claw at one end. "They count, estimate the size of, and record the presence of the other waste, which we report to the local authority."

The party did not have to go very far along the road before excited children were competing to be the first to point out a red plastic screw top from a cola bottle on the road itself. Further along, in the ditch beside the road, was a fertiliser bag filled with plastic plant pots. With a clipboard with a pencil attached to it on a string, one little boy recorded each entry and its location using a GPS device.

When they thought about it for a moment, Andrea and Selene realised how many aspects of learning this exercise covered. It was not merely an environmental lesson. There was numeracy, estimating volume and scale, map reading, record keeping and working as part of a team. The teachers had devised a scale of deterioration of the plastic from one through to five, easiest to measure on bottles with thin walls. The lowest number was attributed to newly discarded bottles with no wear. The other end of the scale were bottles worn down by cars running over them or from being washed down the rocky stream beds, which were beginning to break down into plastic microbeads even before they reached the ocean.

The fascinating lesson came when the children were asked where they thought the plastic bottles' missing bits had gone. The teachers had brought some harmless coloured dye, into which they mixed some granules of sugar to represent the plastic microbeads. They filled several of the bottles they had collected with water from the stream, and the teachers added the other ingredients. On a given signal, four children poured their pink liquid back into the stream and watched as it was swept away down the hillside toward the river they could see far below. When it was pointed out how that river ran into the not-too-distant sea, the children's hands were shooting up as they wanted to be the first to answer questions.

These simple but powerful lessons were not only influencing the children's thinking, but they were also having a profound effect on Andrea and Selene. What had previously seemed such complex and distant challenges suddenly appeared clear and immediate threats to the environmental legacy being created for these children.

3. SARDENARA

Were all of the western world's airports designed by one firm of architects? Ben wondered, as the glass doors slid silently open to Nice's Côte d'Azur. As an English Francophile, he had taken only a few international flights in his life, but every airport he had ever been in looked exactly the same. Using almost identical materials, construction, layouts and palettes of colours, they were simultaneously familiar and yet disorientating.

Familiar meant he could find his way around airports easily, but once inside these buildings he always felt detached from the city, country or continent they were situated in. He had often thought that if he inadvertently got on the wrong flight thinking it was to Bordeaux but ended up in Bangkok or Bogota, he probably wouldn't notice that anything was amiss until he got outside of the airport.

Airports seemed to him to be exciting places because they were filled with expectation. For those departing there was the expectation of new horizons–holidays to be enjoyed, business deals to be done, or even new places to be lived in. For others there was anticipation of the arrival; of much-missed family, lovers, colleagues and old friends. For almost everyone there, a visit to an airport was not an ordinary day.

Ben scowled when he saw the arrivals board. His son's budget flight from Gatwick to Nice was delayed by thirty minutes. He had arrived at what he thought was the last minute and parked in the expensive short stay car park. Vincenzo had recommended that he bring Alessandra's car with Claudio's private number and diplomatic number plate, allowing Ben to park anywhere.

It went against his English sensibilities to use an advantage he did not believe he deserved. Ben had told Alessandra's chief guard–only half-jokingly-that it would be tantamount to queue-jumping, a crime second only to murder in an Englishman's eyes. Now, with at least an hour to kill and the parking metre ticking, he regretted his decision. Ben bought a copy of the Nice-Matin newspaper and a café macchiato to pass the time.

He had lost track of time when he heard some commotion further along the airport concourse. Passengers hauling cases to and from flights were scattering to allow four French paratroopers to pass through them, running at full speed. A couple of women screamed and grabbed their children in panic at seeing the armed troops primed for action. Several family groups started heading for the exits at a half-trot. With all the recent terror threats in France, everyone was extremely jumpy. One hundred metres ahead of the human projectile of green combat fatigues, dark sunglasses and claret berets, Ben could now see a uniformed customs officer. He was waving with one arm, and with the other holding open a door through to the airside area of international arrivals.

The four soldiers with their automatic weapons burst through the glass door, nearly knocking the customs man off his feet. No alarms were sounding in the airport, and with the door firmly locked behind them people began to go about their business again, but with perhaps a bit more haste and heightened awareness, Ben thought. Like him, most guessed that the scare was probably nothing more than someone leaving their hand baggage unattended while they used the toilet.

When Ben looked back at the arrivals board, his son's flight was flashing as 'Arrived.' A few minutes later, a flurry of passengers began emerging onto the concourse. He wondered how it was possible for him to know with reasonable certainty that this was the London flight. After all, their faces were not all pale, they were not all carrying Marks & Spencer carrier bags, nor were they drunk and singing football songs: the usual stereotypes of the English abroad.

But then again, this was the Nice Côte d'Azur Airport, where 'tourist' is a dirty word to the thousands of wealthy British ex-pats who pass through it regularly. These travellers all looked well-off but in an understated way. There were few artificial fabrics to be seen. They wore linen, cashmere and leather, but without any overt branding. They all looked self-assured but without any swagger. Their appearance made a statement, but in a whisper rather than a shout. Whatever it was that gave them away, the passengers being greeted or rushing out the doors to waiting cars were for the most part Brits, Ben concluded. As the numbers dwindled to a trickle, there was still no sign of Tom.

Ben caught sight of himself reflected in the plate glass and realised that he blended right in with the passengers he had been observing. A few short years ago it would have been hard to pick him out from the hundreds of other commuters trudging to work up Grey Street in Newcastle. Pale-faced and with his scarf pulled up over his neck to stave off the biting wind whipping up from the River Tyne, he had also blended in there. His handmade shoes had long since seen a cobbler and the seat of his Saville Row suit was now shiny with wear. A navy cashmere coat was still an effective windbreak, but it was shabby at the cuffs. At a distance, Ben might once have passed for chic, but on closer inspection he was now very definitely shabby.

Transformed by a new lifestyle, weather and wife, Ben was today just another Riviera ex-pat. His hair was longer–much longer in fact. And whiter. Or was it the deep tan which made his hair more of a contrast? He was unsure. Deck shoes, shorts, and button-down Oxford shirt were the uniform of the Côte d'Azur and all you needed to get into some of the best restaurants in the world. Not that Ben ate in such places because his wife ran what he, and many others, considered the best restaurant in Liguria. It was there where he would be headed for lunch as soon as he could collect Tom.

Another thirty minutes passed before the opaque glass doors from arrivals slid open again. The four paratroopers emerged, causing everyone around them to move well back out of their path. One soldier was on point and another was bringing up the rear, their eyes scanning the concourse for anyone who might be foolish enough to challenge them. The other two soldiers each had an arm under the elbow of a man whose bound feet were dragging behind him. His wrists were fastened together in front of him with the same plastic ties and his head was bowed. He looked barely conscious. From his sturdy build and the shock of unkempt blonde hair, Ben at once recognised him as his son.

Instinctively Ben slipped from his stool and rushed toward the approaching paratroopers, but even as he was doing so, realised this was an ill-judged move. The soldier on-point shouted, "Arretez!" in a manner that sounded as if he was certain his command would be obeyed. The lead trooper simultaneously levelled his automatic weapon at Ben and clicked off the safety catch.

Ben did as he was instructed and stood stock still, as did every person within about one hundred metres. The two men carrying Tom dropped him unceremoniously on the floor, where he hit his head on the polished marble and groaned.

While Ben was interrogated, the other three turned to form a protective circle, weapons levelled and eyes scanning back and forth.

"Identifiez-vous immediatement mais ne bougez aucun muscle."

Although not a fluent French speaker, he understood this instruction 'to freeze' clearly enough.

"Je Suis son pere." His brain fogged by what was happening, Ben had to think hard for the next sentence. "Je suis ici pour le recoperer."

There was what seemed like an interminably long silence while the trooper assessed the threat. After glancing around to check on his subordinates, the officer mentally downgraded the threat and spoke more softly.

"You are also English?"

"I am, and that is my son arriving from London."

"Put both your hands on your head and do it now." Ben did as the soldier told him.

Some imperceivable communication passed between the leader and the soldier furthest away, who now swept around the group towards him. He swung his weapon over his back to free his hands and started patting Ben's thin summer clothing. He could feel his fingers probing his skin like a masseur, leaving no crevice unsearched. When he was satisfied there was no threat, he told Ben to lower his hands.

"Marcher. Walk," the soldier corrected himself, indicating with the barrel of his gun in the direction of the exit doors. The two soldiers who had been carrying Tom picked him up again and continued dragging him along, with the fourth soldier operating as rear guard.

Once outside in a designated security area, it took Ben fifty five minutes of persuasion and a last resort phone call to his daughter's boyfriend, the Prime Minister of Italy, to finally get himself and Tom released. They were escorted back to Ben's car and watched out of the airport, but only after Ben had paid thirty euros in parking charges. They had instructions to head straight for the French border and into Italy, from where Tom would need to exit and return to London via some route other than Nice Airport. He was effectively banned from the Côte d'Azur.

There was silence in the car for the first few kilometres. Once they had passed the road toll and were on the autoroute that sweeps around Nice towards the French border with Italy, Ben finally felt calm enough to speak.

"Bloody hell, Tom! What planet have you been living on for the past five years? You haven't heard that France is on a virtual war footing after numerous terrorist incidents? Or that French paratroopers are world-famous for their lack of a sense of humour? They eat nails for breakfast instead of croissants. Getting pissed on a flight, threatening a French immigration officer and refusing to open your hand baggage in this tense climate was only ever going to end one way."

Ben glanced across at Tom to judge his ignominy level, only to realise that Tom was sound asleep. A little trickle of dry blood ran from the corner of his lip. Bright red weals had appeared around his wrists where the soldiers' plastic ties had bound them together. His left cheek was swollen, presumably where he'd received a blow from a rifle butt to shut him up, Ben assumed. His clothes looked neither washed nor ironed, and his trainers had no laces. The age of his stubble was indeterminable but certainly older than a week. He looked like a homeless person, his father thought. How could he take him home to meet his new wife and pass his neighbours with him looking like this? he pondered.

In the thirty minutes it took to reach the Italian border, Ben had come up with a plan. He took the first exit in Italy down to Ventimiglia while Tom snored like a pig. Parking the car at the large Carrefour supermarket, he left his son sleeping while he went inside. Ben paused in the foyer to message Alessandra, who was expecting them for lunch. He told her that the flight had been delayed–partly true, he justified to himself–and that he would call when he knew their ETA, but that they were unlikely to make it for lunch.

Ben's mental shopping list consisted of two long-sleeved shirts, sandals, a pack of white t-shirts, a pack of boxers, jeans, joggers, a towel, and a sports bag to put them all in. He guessed Tom's size to be one greater than his own. They were about the same height, but Tom was bulkier, especially since he appeared to have lost some of his muscular tone since Ben had seen him last. At school, he had been a pretty good rugby player. Tom had continued to play until a couple of years ago when he was kicked out of the team for repeatedly not showing up for matches.

When he returned to the car, Tom was still asleep, his body apparently having gone into partial shutdown to recover from the alcohol and the beating he had received. Ben drove to the seafront and parked next to one of the beach showers. He pulled, shoved, and bundled the reluctant, drowsy young man onto the beach and turned on the shower of cold water.

"Fuck. Fuck. Fuck...," was all he heard for about two minutes while the cool drenched Tom's hair and clothes. Yet, he did not attempt to move away from the spray of water. Instead, he revolved his head, letting it into his ears and eyes–even into his mouth.

Ben shook his head in apparent despair. "It's gratifying to see that a hundred thousand pounds' worth of private education has at least endowed you with a varied and colourful vocabulary."

The shower did the trick. After a few minutes, Tom sounded more like himself and started to make eye contact with his father. Ben decided it would be more effective to repeat his earlier reprimand from the car some other time, when he was more receptive and might take in the enormity of his stupidity. Ben held out the towel. Tom went to grab it, but it was pulled back from his grasp.

"Clothes off and then the towel," was Ben's offer. Without any thought or sign of embarrassment, Tom peeled off his wet t-shirt and dropped his cargo pants, under which he was ironically commando. Ironic, because Ben could now see the clear imprint from a soldiers' boot on his left buttock. Either he was stood on, or non-verbally encouraged to move forwards. Throwing the towel at him, Ben picked up the wet clothes and wrang the bulk of the water out of them.

Food and coffee were next on Ben's agenda, and they didn't have to go far to find them. On the other side of the seafront was an array of restaurants and cafes, including one with the unmistakable smell of pizza, called Margunaira. As a hangover cure, this would be almost as good as an English breakfast, Ben decided. After wrapping the wet clothes in the towel and placing them in the car, Ben guided his son across the street, which was busy with Italians whizzing by at speed as if they had a reputation to keep up. Tom limped slightly, suddenly aware of the emerging bruise on his buttock.

During the rapid demolition of a large pizza with prosciutto and salami, little was said. Ben sipped sparkling water, not wishing to order alcohol under the circumstances. He had one of best slices of sardenara he'd tasted anywhere outside of his wife's kitchen. The base was light and almost crumbly—the tomato sauce, rich and slightly spicy. Fragrant and piquant capers, along with Taggiasca olives, were scattered unusually liberally on the top.

"What's that you're eating? It looks good," the now revived young man commented.

Ben explained that it was a local speciality and asked if he would like to try some.

"But of course. I'm still starving."

Two slices of sardenara and two americano coffees later, Tom started returning to what Ben remembered as his usual self. It was at this point that Ben was reminded that his normal self was not always very nice. So far, he had treated the waiter with disdain and blatantly ogled the young waitresses. His first words approaching a conversation were neither a thank you, nor an apology, but a complaint.

"These plastic chairs are a bit cheap and nasty. I thought you'd be eating in nicer places than this now since you're married to a princess."

Ben held his temper until he was in the privacy of the car. The remainder of the thirty minute journey to Seborga consisted of shouted rallies of accusation versus recrimination, and allegations met with retribution. It was not pleasant listening for either father or son, and certainly not a way to rekindle their relationship after a five year break.

When Ben had been asked–nay instructed-to leave his family home by his then-wife's lawyer, Tom was only in his early teens. Much of what was said harked back to what Tom saw as his abandonment by his father. This male vacuum in his life was inadequately filled by his mother's new partner, a man to whom Tom took an instant dislike which only grew stronger with time.

A few years older than Tom, his sister, Selene, had only had to endure less than a year in the new family unit. Against all predictions, she won a writing scholarship to become a residential boarder during the sixth form, from where she went straight to university. After graduation, Selene moved directly to London, rarely returning to the family home.

In stark contrast, Tom's schoolwork went downhill-only his skill at rugby saving him from expulsion, and assisted in gaining him a place at a university where sporting prowess counted more than qualifications. He spent several bitter and miserable years there, during which time he rarely spoke to or saw his father. Failing to gain a degree at his first attempt, he scraped through in his fourth year. The resulting low pass mark in sports science was unable to help him into a career, and he bounced from one casual job to the next. His strongest family bond was with his sister who, although continuously exasperated by his behaviour, always forgave him quickly and offered a sympathetic ear when he was low.

By the time the car turned into the main piazza of Seborga, several long-buried demons had only been partly exorcised and there remained a tense silence. Both men had reached a state of contrition about things they had either done, not done, said, or left unsaid. As unpalatable as this confrontation had been, both now had a clearer understanding of the other's position. It was a platform upon which they could perhaps start again, Ben hoped. The air was clearing, if not yet entirely cleared.

Tom would be staying at the apartment above a shop which his sister had recently inherited from a man who everyone in the village referred to as the 'Crazy Dutchman.' Her brother never questioned this strange nickname because his insanity was evidenced by the fact that he had given an entire building to his sister, someone he hardly knew.

Selene and Rikki–the erstwhile Crazy Dutchman–had met during Ben's daughter's first visit to Seborga. Despite apparently having nothing in common and being almost a generation apart, they had become unlikely friends, albeit nothing more than that. Or at least, there was no prospect of anything other than friendship as far as Selene was concerned. She rented the flat above his shop when she stayed in Seborga two years prior and borrowed his strange yellow VW Kübelwagen Jeep if she needed to drive anywhere.

The odd couple could often be seen having a coffee, a drink or a meal together when Selene was in the village. She found the charismatic, eccentrically dressed, dope-smoking, fifty year old Dutchman was easy company. He seemed to have no personal agenda and so made for entertaining, unthreatening male companionship. The journalist in her was fascinated by his dramatic stories of drilling for oil in wild, faraway places, dealing with local bandits and paying off corrupt politicians. It was possible that some of these stories had been his ultimate downfall. Ben assumed that Rikki had spent so many years in the company of hard-drinking, tough-talking engineers, that the Dutchman simply craved female company and Selene was easy to talk to. Whatever it was, they both seemed to get something from their odd relationship.

About a year later, Rikki went off on one of what he called his 'RnR' trips, which everyone understood to be his periodic need to get drunk and/or high in 'colourful' female company. San Remo was his usual local RnR destination, but he was also known to fly much further afield. Having worked for oil and gas companies all over the world, Rikki knew many people in a lot of exotic places. The problem was that many oil and gas people did not like him because he had turned whistle-blower on some of the industry's shadier practices later in life.

He had never returned from the last trip overseas, and no one in Seborga knew what had happened to him. His store remained locked, its mailbox filling up with post, and his strange old car sat for the time accumulating dust. Almost a year later, a letter arrived in Seborga addressed to Selene, care of her father. It was from a lawyer in the Hague informing her that Rikki was deceased. The letter informed her that he had left his property in Seborga, including the Kübelwagen and his extensive vinyl record collection, to Selene. There was no further explanation.

Looking down on
the bay of Bordighera from Alta:
a scene also painted by Monet.

Drawing by Linda McCluskey

4. PANSOTTI CON SALSA NOCCI

Ben sat at his favourite table under the faded canvas canopy of the Osteria. From here, he could see out over the valley towards Negi, and get advance warning of any weather fronts approaching over the Alps. He could also watch all the comings and goings of people in the village. There was only one road up to, and down from, Seborga, and all streets radiated off the Piazza Martiri Patrioti. The Osteria was literally and socially the hub of village life.

When Ben answered his phone, the prime minister's first words were, "The bill has been passed."

"Wow. To put that in context, that is the first new law specifically relating to Seborga since the Knights Templar ruled this land more than nine-hundred years ago," Ben observed.

He was told that legislation to give Seborga the power to create unique local taxes, planning laws and inward investment rules had been passed without serious opposition.

"There was a bit of bleating from the left-wing parties about perpetuating outdated autocratic regimes, but they did not put up much of a show," Andrea added. "The Green parties supported us because of the environmental aspects of the legislation."

"Thank you, Andrea. We can use this opportunity to both fast-track Seborga's economic recovery, and hopefully find a suitable model to revive other hilltop communities facing similar challenges."

The PM responded, "You understand that I did not do this just for Seborga but for the greater good of Italy? It will be a ground-breaking experiment in sustainable living."

Andrea Cassini had become Italy's youngest-ever prime minister after his predecessor's sudden arrest on corruption charges. It was unlikely that the handsome Sicilian would otherwise have been elected to lead the conservative centre-right party.

Cassini was not an obvious candidate for Italy's top job, due to his age and because he was what many of them saw as a 'loathsome southerner' in a country still harbouring an irrational north-south divide. What's more, Cassini was the son of a union man, he was an environmentalist and, most recently, a champion of women's rights. Ironically, his predecessor had chosen him for precisely those reasons, believing that he would mop up enough votes from these groups to tip the balance of power. It had worked. However, as his boss's deputy, Andrea got his new job by default. He was now seen as just too popular amongst the voters for the conservatives to get rid of-at least by most, if not all, of his colleagues.

As soon as they heard the news, Alessandra called a meeting of the ministers of Seborga to enact their pre-prepared tax legislation. The documents had been drafted in Rome by Andrea's civil servants. The new laws created highly attractive zero-tax windows for inward investment into targeted areas of Seborga's economy. There were some stringent criteria to be met to weed out money-laundering, green-washing, and other nefarious schemes which had emerged in recent times. But for those who could tick all the right boxes, these were ground-breaking incentives.

One such business in London had been alerted to the opportunity by Cecily Noble, the English entrepreneur and recent friend of Ben and Alessandra. The multi-million-dollar, international fair-trade cosmetics business which she had built up single-handedly had recently been sold, although Cecily retained a small niche product line based on blood oranges to keep her busy during her premature semi-retirement. This rare fruit, with its antioxidant properties, had more than ten years earlier brought her into contact with Roman, a Sicilian orange grower who would later become her lover. An experienced sailor, Cecily chose to live aboard a large, renovated, classic yacht so that the couple could conduct their then-secret affair in out-of-way destinations.

Their clandestine affair was a compromise which allowed Roman to care for his wife, who was suffering from early-onset dementia. The Sicilian was married with two teenage children who were at that time still in education in America. The couple had previously separated and were in the process of a divorce when Roman had met Cecily.

However, on hearing of his wife's out-of-the-blue, and ultimately terminal diagnosis, Roman had taken the decision that he could no longer leave her, and his daughters, alone under these new circumstances. As difficult as it had been, he had encouraged Cecily to forget about him and get on with her life. Instead, she had settled for meeting as and when they could, and then basing herself on the boat made that distanced relationship easier.

Cecily's home port for her yacht was Menton, the nearest French harbour to Monaco, where her commercial office was based. The port provided easy access to Nice Airport, from where she could fly anywhere in the world. The pretty harbour town with its regular market offered quite a different lifestyle to that in Monaco. Although just inside the French side of the border, it was more Italian in appearance and atmosphere. It was to Cecily's boat in Menton that first Alessandra's father, and then later her and Ben, supplied their artisan olive oil to her onboard chef. This relationship led to the two couples becoming friends and Ben learning about the high commercial value of blood oranges.

Cecily had been one of the founding members of a small private club in London. A dozen years ago, it had been set up to fill the gap between the oversubscribed Groucho Club and the other stuffy, old-school gentlemen's institutions. It was hipper, more egalitarian and served better food, but was still strict on privacy for its many celebrity members. The Club had quickly attracted a new kind of customer from digital media and other emerging technology sectors. The Club grew to open a dozen such venues in major cities around the world. They had even started to branch out into out of town, country club-like destinations with food and rooms. Cecily used the Club's city venues as a drop-in office and meeting place when she had business abroad.

The Club's directors had been watching an emerging hospitality trend in Italy and France for something that had become known as Albergo Diffuso. This type of deconstructed hotel had emerged in a few ancient hilltop villages, like Seborga, which were also facing depopulation. The model made use of small, abandoned properties scattered throughout villages to breathe new life into the communities.

Rather than all the hotel rooms all being in one building, a central reception provided a hub where guests checked in, but the accommodation radiated throughout the village in individual properties. These often quite different units were all renovated to a consistent, exacting standard and equipped with twenty-first century features such as high-speed broadband, air-conditioning, and so on. To blend into their communities, they looked like traditional village houses but inside had luxury hotel standard features and services.

Alessandra thought that the Club's marketing director had summed up their approach well when he described it as, "A kind of contrary back-to-basics approach, where things are designed to appear rudimentary but are in fact just understated opulence."

The major factor driving the phenomena was a growing desire for a more authentic holiday experience. The properties were all fully immersed in the community in which they were situated. Guests lived alongside the locals and enjoyed experiencing their culture up close. For the community, the Albergo Diffuso model brought construction and service jobs, rejuvenated neighbourhoods, and filled seats in local restaurants and cafes. The affluent visitors also tended to buy plenty of local produce to take home with them.

The Club's CEO and a couple of directors visited Seborga, held meetings with Ben and Alessandra, and viewed some of the potential properties. The directors and investors were very excited about the new opportunity. They saw the Albergo Diffuso model as an opportunity to diversify their offering, attract new members, and expand their asset base without the high costs of city centre sites.

Since first hearing of the opportunity, the slow pace of Italian bureaucracy in drafting the tax legislation had allowed the Club's directors the rare luxury of time with which to plan. They had used the year to fully assess the scheme, draw up proposals and have the investment in place. They were ready to proceed as soon as the legislation that would facilitate it was passed. A local surveyor and a notaire had been appointed to act as their agents in the property transactions, and an Italian subsidiary company had been set up to hold the freeholds.

The tax 'carrots' for the investors included no local property rates and zero corporation tax on profits for ten years, allowing them to keep their overheads down and allowing quicker recovery of their investment. Ben pointed out to the doubters in the village that they were only giving away tax revenue they would never have received had these properties remained empty and the Albergo Diffuso not been there. He had explained that the village got many of its vacant and dilapidated properties renovated, jobs created, locally grown produce sold, and spin-off tourism revenue generated. It really was a win-win.

When they received the news that the bill had passed, the Club instructed their agents to make their first purchase offer. To everyone's surprise, this offer was to Selene for the property; the one that had been bequeathed to her by Rikki, the Crazy Dutchman. They wanted this purchase agreed first as it was the only traditional property in the village with a shop front that could be used as the reception for the Albergo Diffuso.

They also wanted this property because they had discovered that the shop was still packed to the ceiling with Rikki's stock of local antiques and bric-a-brac. There were numerous brass bed heads, copper pans, granite sinks with brass taps, crockery, old coffee pots and almost everything they would need to achieve the authentic, rustic Italian look they wanted for the new guest rooms. Rikki had once sold all these items at hugely inflated prices to foreign holiday homeowners on the Riviera for their retro-chic kitchens. The Dutchman had revelled in the idea that the stone sinks and brass taps which Italians saw as old-fashioned junk, the wealthy northern Europeans thought to be the height of stylish vogue.

When Alessandra heard about the unexpected offer, she put her head in her hands and exclaimed, "What a disaster. All that planning and we are tripped-up at the first step by that Crazy Dutchman. Even from the grave, I bet he's laughing at this."

The phrase, 'just slightly above market-value offer' at once rang alarm bells with Alessandra, who recognised that it could look like nepotism on two counts. Firstly, Selene's father was the instigator of the inward investment initiative. Secondly, it was her own lover, the prime minister, who had pushed through the legislation of which she was to be the first beneficiary. It did not look good from any angle, she concluded.

When Selene had learned about her surprise inheritance, she was delighted about the idea of having a holiday home in the village she had come to love. However, she did not have any money to carry out any of the renovation work required, or to convert the ground floor shop into living accommodation. However, if she sold the property now and pocketed the cash, it would look like profiteering.

Summarising what he saw as their dilemma, Ben said, "The Club needed this property to make their business model work, but if Selene sells it and anyone finds out the parties involved, it could scupper our whole ship before we've got underway."

Alessandra's frustration at one hurdle appearing after another was beginning to boil over. "Scupper. Scupper. What the hell does scupper mean? You bloody English and your insistence on using language from your colonial power days. Well, if you haven't yet heard, Britannia no longer rules the waves and Spitfires do not control the skies over the White Cliffs of Dover. Welcome to the twenty-first century."

Ben knew that in normal circumstances, Alessandra loved his quirky Englishness and revelled in his funny old-fashioned sayings. But this was clearly not one such time.

"Let's speak to that guy, Richard, in London; the commercial director of the Club who, like me, loves your pansotti con salsa nocci so much. I'll explain our dilemma and see if he has any ideas."

Ben made the call and was promised a call back within twenty-four hours. It only took an hour and a half before Richard phoned back with a proposal, which Ben relayed first to Alessandra and then to his daughter. He openly admitted that they knew that Selene's property was pretty much a deal-breaker, so they had set aside a generous budget to acquire it. They had also put a rough estimate on the market value of the furniture and antiques inside the shop.

"We see this as a true value that we can justify to our investors. It is not a gift or a bribe. However, I see how it could be misconstrued."

During their visit to Seborga, the Club's director had been shown a smaller property on the edge of the village that the owners had already renovated. It was a two bedroomed place with about the same floor area as the shop with its flat above which Selene had inherited. Whilst they liked this property, they had discounted it from their list for several reasons-mainly its distance from the village and their desire to use it to provide reception services. Their proposal was that the Club acquired this ready-to-move-in home, but then simply swapped it with Selene's property without any cash changing hands.

"That way everyone gets what they want, and only we know how," Richard had reassured Ben.

Ben later rationalised to Alessandra that Rikki had no family in the village and so no one knew the contents of his will, or indeed, at the moment, even that he was dead. The whole village knew that Selene had stayed in the place many times in the past and was also often seen driving his quirky old car. For now, Tom staying there and driving the Kübelwagen would not in any way look out of the ordinary. When the Club became the official owners, the news of Rikki's death could be revealed, and everyone would assume that the Club had acquired his shop and flat from his heirs. No one would connect it to Selene's acquisition of a house outside the village.

Once the arrangement was put to her, Selene looked online to view the property they proposed to offer her in exchange and fell in love with it. It had an airy first-floor bedroom with a Juliette balcony which provided wonderful uninterrupted views across the valley. Outside were a stone-paved terrace and a small garden in which there was an ancient, gnarled olive tree, plus two others of lemons and cherries. It had all been newly renovated and painted in neutral colours. The asking price was only slightly more than the Club had offered for her run-down property in the village and the contents. It could hardly have been more perfect for her circumstances. Without speaking to Andrea or visiting the property, she agreed to the exchange.

5. FRISCEU DI BACCALA

From her Clapham flat, Selene could be at London's Gatwick Airport quicker than going into her office. From here, there were several flights every day to most of the major airports in Italy with a journey time of an average of two hours. She could leave home at 6 am and be having coffee in Milan by 10 am. From her newspaper's office it was an even shorter journey to London City Airport, albeit with a more restricted number of departures and destinations.

Selene was spending regular weekends in Italy. She was able to take budget flights on Friday nights to wherever the prime minister was working in Italy and be back at work on Monday morning. He would arrange press passes for her to gain access to whatever function he was attending. The events were seldom in the same place twice. Any public guests would be different each time, and so only the PM's closest staff and colleagues would know what was going on.

The mainly Italian journalists who attended several such events would not think it too odd that they saw a familiar face with a press badge. Reporters seldom interacted much, for fear of giving away some vital snippet of information to a competitor. Andrea and Selene had conducted their blissful international love affair for almost a year in this covert way. It was Rome one weekend, Milan the next, and even the occasional few days in Lake Como. Prime ministers worked long hours but get many invitations to some lovely places, she had learned.

The couple had first met at a festival in Seborga when Andrea had only just been appointed as second-in-command to the notorious head of the then opposition, Tricolore Party. The leader was an entrepreneur with a murky past, who soon after was elected Prime Minister of Italy. In a few short weeks, Cassini moved from being a low-level local Sicilian politician to the land's second-highest office. Before they had time to make that nameplate for his office door, Andrea Cassini would himself be promoted to prime minister. The chequered past of the man who had briefly been his boss finally caught up with him and he had been arrested.

Mastroianni had spent a lifetime scheming, manipulating and cheating his way to the top; first in business, and finally politics. He had appointed the young, liberal Andrea Cassini because he was the antithesis of everything that he himself represented. The Sicilian's youthful sincerity put a shine on Mastroianni's otherwise much-tarnished image. For Cassini, it was a pragmatic, if not an altogether comfortable, partnership, which would in time move him into a position where he could get things done. At the time, he had no idea just how quickly that moment would come.

The initial attraction between Andrea and Selene was immediate, and it had grown into them being completely besotted with each other. When he and Selene were attending public events it was very difficult for them to resist touching each other, something they more than made up for when on their own later. Their future together had been discussed but any prospect of marriage quickly put aside. There were already too many potential conflicts of interest. Andrea had previously played a key role in supporting her father's initiatives in Seborga, and continued to do so. Her role as a journalist on a UK national newspaper could be compromised by too obvious a connection to a foreign country's PM. They would just have to wait until either he left office, or she gave up her job. Neither of these events looked in the cards for the immediate future.

The next event in the couples' hectic and exotic calendar was the launch of a four hundred foot super yacht in Genoa, as the guests of a specialist Italian boat builder. Italy ranked amongst the most prolific superyacht builders in the world, and many of those built in other northern European countries were brought here to be fitted out. The small European nation still led the world in luxury goods exports and its designer brands, from cars to clothes, were some of the most desirable anywhere.

Andrea had told Selene that, "The world apparently can't get enough designer bling, and we are very good at providing it."

Since her first work-related visit a year ago, Selene had become very fond of Genoa. This trip would also allow her to visit her father and brother in Seborga. It was less than a two-hour drive along the Italian Riviera to the mountain village where her father now lived with his new wife, Alessandra. They could all enjoy an Italian Sunday lunch together, and she could get a flight back from Nice on Sunday night, or even early Monday morning.

Selene had envisaged the huge yacht sliding down a slipway into the waiting sea after having had a bottle of champagne smashed over its bow. In the event, the glistening white and metallic black boat was already sitting waist-deep in the water, and the prosecco was merely poured over its nameplate to avoid knocking a chunk out of its shiny new plastic skin.

Although the launch itself was something of a damp squib in Selene's eyes, the party was a chic affair. The client, whose name no one had so far been allowed to mention, was there-albeit in a roped-off area away from the press and most of the guests. Even from thirty metres away Selene could see who it was. Two waiters appeared simultaneously, as though they had been poised in the wings waiting for a customer. One was proffering prosecco in frosted glasses from a tray, and the other canapes.

"What are they?" Selene asked of the waiter, but it was Andrea who answered.

"Frisceu di baccala, fried cod fritters. A delicious local appetiser made with dried cod, potatoes and herbs."

"Wow. This is an A-list gathering," Selene exclaimed.

"You mean the rapper?" Andrea asked. "They had to explain to me who he was and the names of a couple of his hits. Music that you certainly won't be hearing played in my car," he joked.

"Do you have to go and meet him?"

"Apparently, I do. And tell him that I love his work. I might tell him that my journalist friend is his biggest fan and has bought all of his downloads. What I am really going to do is get him to sign up to my Green Seas Charter."

"This is the pledge not to discharge untreated waste at sea?" Selene remembered Andrea discussing this idea a few months earlier.

"Well, yes. That, and to only use biodegradable materials on board. Superyachts often use harmful chemicals and then discharge their waste tanks into the sea. It's very damaging to the oceans."

"My bet is that he doesn't give a damn and won't do it. Or at least, he will agree to it here in public but then forget all about it afterwards."

"You are such a cynic. That is the journalist in you. You just watch me at work."

Andrea strode purposely in the direction of their famous and outrageously dressed host, causing consternation amongst two respective sets of minders. The rapper's men bristled and bulked up their frames as a signal to the approaching strangers. Andrea's bodyguards spoke into their lapel microphones and unbuttoned their jackets just enough for people to glimpse the weapon holsters. These signs were sufficient to identify them as the prime minister's party, who they had been expecting. No one else would be allowed to be armed in public.

Andrea sidestepped the Ukrainian rapper's extended hand and went in for the more physical bear-hug he knew that Eastern European men preferred. He placed one hand over Zeno's right shoulder and the other around his waist in what looked the precursor to a wrestling hold. It was easy to see how this greeting had come about as a way of testing the strength of a potential ally or opponent. This completely un-politician-like greeting somewhat disarmed their usually ultra-sure-of-himself host. Andrea kept up the initiative with his opening greeting of, "Big love from me and all your fans in Italy. A style ambassador for Versace would only choose one place to have their yacht fitted out. She looks fabulous."

As he spoke, Andrea reached back for Selene's hand and pulled her gently to his side.

"Speaking of looking fabulous. This well-known English writer is also a huge fan, but told me that she was too shy to approach you. Selene, meet Zeno."

"Truly beautiful, man. Italian politicians, their babes and even their policeman are more stylish than anywhere in the world. I bet your bodyguards have Armani gun belts. I love this place, man," the rapper replied, with more than a tinge of an accent giving away his ethnic origin.

Any potential frost had melted in this possible cultural no-man's land. They both knew the reason that the prime minister had agreed to attend the opening was because the boatbuilder had told him about its unique recyclable construction methods. Zeno was also smart enough to know the environment was a growing cause of concern and would tick many boxes with his fans. Both men would benefit from the photographs now being taken and shared around the world on social media.

"That was very slick," Selene conceded. "You really are a Sicilian fisherman. You certainly hooked that one."

"Of course. I also caught you, didn't I?" Andrea tried to whisper above the noise of rap music resonating from the Bose sound system. "But unlike him, I won't be throwing you back."

"Throwing her back to where?" asked a voice which was suddenly far too close.

"Ah, Amara. You are never far away from a conversation that you shouldn't be listening to," chided Andrea in a way that was supposed to sound jokey, but which also hinted at his displeasure.

The raven-haired, underdressed, over-heeled Junior Minister for Culture seemed to Selene to be omnipresent when Andrea was on official business.

"Exactly what is the connection between superyachts and culture, Amara?" the PM asked.

"Ah, that I can tell you. These floating status symbols are designed by the highly cultured and discretely well-off for the distinctly uncultured, vulgarly super-rich. Ironic, don't you think?"

The woman, who was perhaps a couple of years older, and currently two inches taller than Selene—mostly due to the heels-was striking looking. If she were describing her in one of her columns, the journalist might say something like, 'Beautiful in a uniquely Italian way. Like a Ferrari; both highly desirable and potentially menacing.'

Selene was uncomfortable about the degree of familiarity between Andrea and his Tricolore party colleague but was determined not to let that show. Although, she suspected that Amara had an inkling that something was going on between her and Andrea. She was always hanging around them and, according to Andrea, was a world-class gossipmonger and political manipulator.

When pressed about Amara, Andrea later admitted that five years earlier, there had been a one-night -stand after a party to end a highly successful party conference. When the regretful Andrea had sobered up and then failed to call her about another date, she had sent him abusive messages. Next time they had met, she had confronted him and made a big scene in public. He had told Selene that he was contrite about his role in the affair and that it had been a judgment failure. To his credit, he apportioned no blame to her. He said that he had acted badly and that she had deserved greater respect.

Now that their respective careers had taken off and they found themselves public figures, they were always looking over their shoulders. Relatively minor misdemeanours in the past had a habit of coming back to haunt politicians. They could be either leverage for the needy, or weapons for the angry. Amara unsettled Andrea. Despite ostensibly being on the same side, he couldn't help feeling she was waiting for payback and wondered just when it might come.

"You looked dressed for dinner somewhere far better than this, Selene," Amara probed, looking the Englishwoman up and down and then gesturing around at the crowd made up of the rapper's hangers-on, local bureaucrats, and journalists.

"You're quite right. From here I am going to meet an old friend in Genoa. We have a lot of catching up to do."

Resisting the urge to wink at Andrea, Selene kept her eyes on Amara, avoiding his gaze as he was also trying hard not to give anything away. "In fact, if I don't leave now, I will be late. So, you will have to excuse me, Prime Minister. Amara, it's interesting to have spoken to you."

With no more than a polite wave, Selene backed away from the two politicians and disembarked from the boat via the neon-illuminated walkway. After another fifteen minutes at the party shaking hands and being photographed with the other guests, Andrea also made his excuses and left. When he got back to the car which was parked out of sight of the yacht, Selene was already inside behind the blacked-out windows. It was early enough for them to drive to their destination in the ancient city and have a relaxing dinner.

6. ARANCINI AL RAGU

After saying goodnight to his son, Ben's parting advice had been for him to put some cream on his wrist wounds and sleep off his hangover, adding that he would see him the following day. Assuming Tom still possessed a rugby player's appetite, his worried father arrived at Selene's apartment the next morning carrying a parcel of Alessandra's focaccia plus a couple of brioches. When he let himself in through the unlocked door, there were no signs of life except for lights, apparently left on from the night before, and clothes were strewn around the floor. There was also a distinct smell of marijuana and some suspicious-looking butts in a foil food tray.

After filling the Bialetti coffee pot, he turned on the gas ring and went to wake his son. Asleep under a mop of unkempt blonde hair, Ben was briefly reminded of happier days when Tom was a young schoolboy. When awoken, however, Ben was reminded that the little boy had turned into a belligerent young man.

"What the hell? What bloody time is it?

"Ten o'clock European Central Time or nine am in London, from where you arrived twenty hours ago."

Having been roughly frisked and nearly arrested at Nice Airport, Ben had been forced to cancel both the lunch and dinner Alessandra had prepared especially for him. It had cost him over two hundred euros to equip his son with a basic wardrobe of clothes. Soon he would have to explain to his wife and his neighbours why Tom looked like he had just played in a rugby scrum against the All Blacks. Then, when this holiday ended, he would not be able to drop his son off at nearby Nice but would instead have to drive several hours to an Italian airport, where he would doubtless also have to pay for a new return ticket. Ben was in no mood for diplomacy.

"Now that you are twenty-five and supposedly an adult, I am finally going to start treating you like one. If you don't like what I have to say and are unwilling to behave responsibly, you need to leave. I will drive you to the train station, pay for your tickets home and, reluctantly, say goodbye. You decide."

There was a long silence. Tom leaned forward and took a sip from the coffee his father had brought to his bedside.

"I can't go back," Tom mumbled, barely audibly.

"What do you mean, you can't? I've just told you that I will take you and I will pay for your tickets."

Sitting on the edge of the bed, Tom looked his father in the eyes, knowing that this would hurt him.

"I can't go back," Tom repeated louder this time. "People are looking for me."

"People are looking for you. What kind of people?"

"Bad people. People I owe money to. At least two different bailiffs and a Turkish drug dealer."

The young man's head dropped again, and his sad eyes stared into the cup of coffee. Ben realised he was close to tears. He could not remember his son ever looking so totally defeated. Instinctively, Ben dropped onto his knees and hugged his son. Tom's muscles resisted at first but then relaxed as he started to sob quietly. They stayed in this position for a minute or so. It seemed longer to Ben, as his knees had begun to ache.

"It will be OK, Tom. We will work something out. I'll speak to your mother and..."

"I wouldn't if I were you," the young man warned, now sitting bolt upright.

"Why on earth not? You're still our joint responsibility. At least morally, if not legally."

"That's what one of the bailiffs told her when they turned up at her house threatening to take away her jewellery if she didn't pay them two and a half grand on the spot."

Ben screwed up his face at the thought of his ex-wife confronted by a couple of neanderthal bailiffs threatening to enter her house and take away her prized belongings. A part of him also wished he could have been a fly-on-the-wall to witness that scene.

"And she paid?" checked Ben, assuming she would have.

Tom explained that his mother had rung him straight away when it happened, but that he saw her number come up and had not answered her call.

"She screamed a message into my voicemail about my never setting foot in their house again until I had repaid the money in full, as well as apologised to her and her new husband." His red eyes were growing angry again and Tom added, "Two things that are just not going to happen."

"Bloody hell, Tom. That's just not taking responsibility for your own actions, once again. You can't keep running away from the consequences of what you do. Where will you run from here? This is the last stop at the end of that line, Tom."

There was a pause before Ben asked, "How did you end up owing all this money, anyway?"

The young man's anger mellowed to contrition when he had to face up to the unavoidable fact that he had borrowed from a couple of payday loan companies and gambled most of it away online. With the interest compounding daily, he'd looked for another way to get out. He had accepted some dope to resell to friends, but then gambled the proceeds so couldn't pay back the dealer.

When it all started coming home to roost, he had fled to his sister's flat in Clapham. But then somehow, the dealer had heard he was living in South London. Someone must have spotted him in a pub, he rationalised, and now they were looking for him. Not wanting them to find out where Selene lived and drag her into it, Tom had rung his father, finally taking him up on his offer of a free holiday in Seborga.

"Faced with the prospect of telling you and your new wife, the princess, my sorry tale, I got off my face on duty-free booze between checking in at Gatwick and arriving in Nice."

Ben's mind was already racing through the various scenarios, possible best and worst-case outcomes, and searching for potential solutions.

"So, bailiff number one was taken care of by your mother?" Tom nodded.

"Bailiff number two is still looking for you and wants how much?"

"With costs and interest, I think it's risen to eighteen hundred pounds and some change. Say another £2k"

"And I dread to ask, but the dope dealer?"

Tom looked indignant and pleaded, "He only gave me two hundred and fifty quid's-worth but says he wants four times that back because of the wait and collections costs. He's a thieving Turkish bastard."

"That's why he is in his chosen profession," Ben observed. "So, the sum of your current indebtedness is three thousand pounds, plus the two that you now owe your mother. Is that correct?"

Tom hung his head again and went quiet while he weighed up whether to reveal the full scope of his stupidity. After a few minutes more interrogation, it turned out there was also unpaid rent at his flat. He had simply walked away, ignoring bills for council tax, utilities, and two credit card balances. There were also overdue repayments on a designer watch he'd bought on credit and later pawned for cash. All-in-all, the extra debt was another seventeen hundred pounds.

"So, by my calculation, you need to earn something over ten thousand pounds just to clear your current debts."

The young man looked angry and frustrated again. "No, just short of five K."

Ben sighed. "Tom, firstly, to end up with seven after tax, you need to earn ten. Tax is how adults pay to keep the world around us working. Secondly, you seem to have discounted repaying your mother, or more likely your stepfather, the two thousand. My first condition for agreeing to help you is that you do just that."

"But he's...," Tom started to argue, but his father stopped him mid-sentence.

"Tom, you can only negotiate when you have bargaining power, and you currently have none. This is a take-it or leave-it offer. I will help you on my terms or take you to the station. You decide. I'm now going to tell Alessandra your tale of woe and ask her if she is willing to help me with this. If she agrees, I will return, and you can tell me if you wish to stay here with our support or go back to London and face the consequences of your actions on your own."

At this, Ben left the forlorn young man with his emotions interchanging between embarrassment and resentment as he sought someone else to blame for his predicament. But even Tom found his rationale for each potential contender flawed, and had to absolve them all from blame. In the meantime, Ben called Selene on her mobile, and it rang with a reassuring overseas dial tone. This sign indicated that she was in Italy this weekend as she had told him she would be. Explaining what had happened to her brother, the anxious father asked her to make a couple of phone calls to London on his behalf.

Alessandra took the news about Tom with the sense of resignment that only a betrayed employer, wronged wife, or disillusioned parent could. It occurred to Ben that you needed a strong emotional connection with someone to feel a deep sense of disappointment and feeling of hopelessness at their behaviour. The misdemeanours of strangers are viewed in isolation and not as part of a greater malaise. Without the background of previous transcreations, people seem more capable of redemption. Also, when you have weathered the challenges that Ben and she had during the last five years, Tom's seven thousand pound indiscretions seemed like small change. Alessandra agreed to help unreservedly. Ben remained more circumspect.

After making some phone calls of his own, Ben returned to the flat to speak to his errant son. In the first sign that things might improve, he had picked up and roughly folded the new clothes. Tom was wearing the new denim jeans and the long-sleeved Oxford shirt. He looked presentable and possibly even handsome, Ben thought.

"I can see why you bought this now," Tom said, holding up the buttoned-up sleeves so that the red welts on his wrists just became visible. He still had that winning cheeky smile that seemed to make men forgive him, and women melt, which would no doubt come in useful when he finally met Alessandra. Tom had not attended their wedding or even replied to the invitation. These were actions which had hurt and had upset her at the time.

Ben explained that Alessandra was busy working in the Osteria at lunchtime, but that they would meet tonight. Selene was driving over from Genoa later, and they would have a family dinner together.

"I have brought a packed lunch and you and I are now going for a walk." Ben dropped his own walking boots at Tom's feet. Both men wore the same size, so Ben had put on some old trainers that he used when working in the fields. Tom began to argue against unnecessary exercise but Ben just ignored him and turned towards the door, waving the prospect of lunch over his shoulder.

"If you want to taste the best arancini al ragu in Liguria, you had better catch up."

With Tom's appetite whetted from the amazing focaccia and pastries at breakfast, he pulled on his boots without bothering to lace them and traipsed after his father. The latter was already going down the stairs into the shop below.

As they passed through the ground floor shop, Tom asked, "What's with all the junk?"

"These antiques were the stock-in-trade of the deceased Crazy Dutchman." Ben gestured with his arms to suggest the whole building, "He left all this to Selene in his will. I'll explain as we walk."

"Bloody Hell. If my sister tripped in the street, she would land on a twenty-pound note."

Ben countered with, "Your sister will also have inherited the Dutchman's hashish stash, which you have apparently found and smoked. So, you now also owe her for that as well. But you will know the going rate for dope," he added with more than a hint of sarcasm.

Tom had no reply. As they crossed the piazza heading for the road north out of the village, the young man's blonde head panned around taking in all the sights he had missed when he had arrived the previous day, still half-drunk. He realised how high the village was, as the land dropped away steeply on all sides, except for the ridge they were walking along heading north. He could see the red-tiled roofs of houses scattered on the other side of the valley, nearly all of them at a lower elevation.

Ahead of and above them, there were few signs of habitation. Above the line of the road was little except a wild forest of mixed pine and some deciduous trees. Below, were the silver-green leaves on twisted branches that even Tom recognised as olive trees. Nothing further was said by either man until they reached the Passo del Bandito sign when Tom guffawed aloud.

"I speak no Italian except Birra Moretti, but that sign must surely mean, Bandit Street?"

"That's precisely what it says. This path, and many other trails leading into the hills, are thousands of years old. They were used to move between villages but also for trade over the mountains. They are so remote that they were almost impossible to police. Robbers were able to attack traders carrying goods or money and disappear into the hills. During the last two wars, thousands of partisan soldiers hid up here and fought a guerrilla war for years against the Nazis."

The younger man was surprised at how his father was striding ahead while his own breath was getting short. It seemed as if Ben was deliberately pushing the pace to make conversation more difficult. He wanted them both to have time to adjust to their respective changed perspectives and think about a way forward. During regular pauses to look around him, Tom began to acknowledge the natural grandeur all around them.

Ben felt encouraged that this outing looked like being a good idea. He had always found that these walks helped him to put things in their right places. When you are sitting looking down from what seems like the roof of the world, big problems seem smaller somehow, he had learned. It was now Ben's turn to halt progress. He removed two chilled bottles of water from the backpack. Only when he saw the bottles did Tom realise just how desperately thirsty he was. Partly it was dehydration from yesterday's booze, but mostly it was the exertion of the hike.

They both drank deeply but said little, conserving their breath as there was no sign of an obvious endpoint for this upward sloping path. They soon reached a fold in the hillside. Here, a narrow stream flowed down and under the path, emerging from a stone arch on the other side. Ben ducked under a tree next to the main trail and held up the branch for his son to follow him down. Now, under the canopy of trees, they could see a trickle of water descending a gradient more than double that of the trail they had been walking on. Using the stream bed as a path, Ben started to climb.

"Be careful-the wet stones are slippery," he warned.

The larger exposed stones of the riverbed created a natural, if irregular, staircase, without which the slope would have been almost impossible to climb. There was little more than a drizzle of water flowing off the mountain at this time of the year. Even

Ben, who had done this many times before, had to drop onto all fours for some of the more challenging parts. It took fifteen minutes to reach a flat grassy clearing which had sunlight streaming through sparse leaves. Tom collapsed on his back on the grass, breathing heavily. Ben remained sitting on a rock, for he too was a little breathless. One word at a time, Tom asked, "How. Much. Further?"

"Another thirty minutes but with much less incline now. That was the hardest part."

Without the watch he had pawned, or his mobile phone that had been cut off for unpaid bills, Tom had no idea of the hour of the day, except that his stomach told him it was lunchtime. As his father had promised, the remaining walk was more leisurely, but still took a further forty-five minutes because of Tom's slower pace. As they reached the end, the trees became thinner and expansive vistas began to open up around them. Azure blue skies with the occasional wispy cloud formed a stark contrast with the green all around them. An occasional passing passenger jet left its smoke-grey trail across the blue.

At last, they reached their destination and a clearing opened on one side to a rocky ridge. A boulder about a metre in circumference and two metres long looked as if it had been rolled from the mountain into the centre of the grassy plateau. Here, someone had set about carving symbols into it, including a large cross, with two numbers on one side and a letter on the other.

"Boundary markers of the Knights Templar," Ben offered as an unsolicited explanation. "The numbers indicate the distance to Seborga and the letter the direction, S for south. Carved nearly a thousand years ago."

It was not the most impressive ancient ruin Tom had ever seen, but the view from the ridge took his breath away even more than the climb had. He had been at this kind of altitude before whilst skiing, but not in clear sight of the sea. The coastal ribbon of human development scored a clear horizontal grey line between the green and the blue in the middle distance. Beyond that, the azure sea blurred into the sky without a visible join.

From reading some of his sister's coverage of events in Seborga, Tom was broadly aware of its history and the recent tumultuous events. He still found it hard to believe her luck at being right there when the document proving the principality's independence was discovered-a piece of good fortune that had kickstarted her career in journalism. Not content with that, in Seborga she had since met and was now dating the Prime Minister of Italy. When Tom recently heard about her inheriting a house from a virtual stranger, he resigned himself to believe that any good fortune in their family was clearly destined to be hers.

However, much as he envied her, begrudged her prosperity and hated her smugness about it all, his love for his sister had been brought home to him last year when she was threatened. Tom had witnessed the security video, where the former PM, Mastroianni, assaulted her and was apoplectic with rage. If he had been there, and not Cristiano, he had told anyone that would listen, the 'fat pervert' would not have escaped with his manhood intact, as was the case.

Ben shuffled himself up to sit on the Templar stone and, with tapping his hand on it, indicated for Tom to join him. Out of the knapsack he extracted two small bottles of beer which he passed to his son. Four packages appeared from the bag, neatly wrapped in greaseproof paper. Ben deftly popped off the bottle tops on the rock and let them fall onto the grass.

"Pick those up before we go, Tom. We will leave this place as we found it."

Ben passed him two packages with the advice to open them and spread the contents on their rock table. Amazingly, the arancini were still slightly warm, making them soft and moist inside. The rich red ragu almost dribbled out like jam from a raspberry doughnut when they bit into them. The clean mountain air amplified the meaty smell. There also was a homemade frittata, freshly baked bread, a wedge of hard cheese, prosciutto and peaches.

"So, these are the famous arancini?"

"They are. And your verdict?"

"Well, obviously, I am not yet an expert, but these are the best I have ever tasted."

"Good. Tell Alessandra that, but leave out the bit about not being an expert, and all will be well in her world."

They ate the remainder of their lunch in silence, both considerably calmed by the serenity of their surroundings. Before they set off, Ben bent down, picked up the previously discarded bottle tops and placed them in the knapsack without comment. The alternative route back was circuitous but not as steep, allowing more opportunity for conversation. After more than six years with minimal contact, there were many gaps in Ben's knowledge of what his son had been up to. Most of what he learned on their journey only fuelled his concern. With each kilometre, Ben's frustration, and the weight of Tom's guilt, grew until neither were happy with their burdens.

Selene was expected to arrive in Seborga at about five thirty. She was to meet Tom at the apartment before bringing him for dinner at the Osteria. He had been instructed to wear the long-sleeved shirt his father had bought to hide the wounds on his wrists. It struck Ben as an extraordinary coincidence that now his son and his wife each carried evidence of violence on their respective wrists.

Alessandra's scars had been inflicted in a drug-fuelled rage by one of her kitchen staff who she had caught having sex with her now ex-husband. The girl had lashed out at Alessandra with a boning knife that she had grabbed, leaving deep scars on the undersides of both wrists. The scars left her looking like she had attempted to take her own life, making them doubly embarrassing. She had finally come to terms with this disfigurement when in the company of friends, but was still uneasy about it in front of strangers. Ben did not want her attention drawn to it by having to explain his son's own version.

Alessandra dearly wanted to make a good impression on Ben's son. She was overcompensating for his assumed lack of experience with traditional Italian cuisine by selecting the most anglicised menu she could think of. It consisted of bruschetta, spaghetti pomodoro, Bistecca Fiorentina and tiramisu, served with Ben's Rossese wine. She had run it past Selene in a text message, and she had replied, "Spaghetti, steak and tiramisu. Tom will fall in love with you, as his father did." But at once she qualified this response with, "Well, maybe not quite in the same way," accompanied by a smiling and winking face emoji.

Selene was not very sympathetic to her brother's plight. She was horrified to learn that his drug dealer had people looking for Tom in Clapham while he had been crashing on the couch at her flat. Over the years, Tom had acquired a habit of turning up on her doorstep when he fell out with their mother, stepfather, flatmates, or had just run out of money. Selene had previously been forgiving of her brother's teenage angst but when he got into in his twenties, her patience, like their father's, wore thin. His falls from grace had become increasingly serious, and now it seemed that they were beginning to threaten her personal life.

Andrea had only stayed at her flat on two occasions, but one of them was quite recently. On those nights he had been able to sneak away from official meetings in London, but there had not been enough notice for her to arrange time off work and a discrete rendezvous location. So, the Prime Minister of Italy had worn a baseball cap to disguise his distinctive blonde, wavy hair and taken an Uber to her flat, so they could grab a few precious hours together.

What if this Turkish thug had turned up during one of these liaisons demanding his money, she had agonised? Andrea certainly would not have paid him, even if he'd had been carrying the cash on him to do so. She envisaged the international headlines following what would have been the inevitable fracas between the Italian PM and a London drug dealer taking place at the flat of a British journalist. Tom's shameful behaviour had to stop, she decided.

After an uncomfortable conversation with his sister, Tom turned up for dinner at the Osteria in a foul mood but wearing his best smile and a white t-shirt, despite his father's instructions. Selene thought that her father looked like he had aged since they'd last met just a month or two ago. Tom held out his hand to shake Alessandra's, and she immediately said, "Oh my God, what happened to your wrists?"

Ben had decided that, along with the debts and running away from them, the incident at the airport was one too many disasters to burden Alessandra with all in one go. Tom's explanation of what happened was at variance with his own recollection, but he was in no mood for another confrontation before dinner. He would tell her later. Cristiano, who was helping in the kitchen so his mother could have the night off, came out to say hello. The junior chef was in his clean, pressed whites wearing his trademark bandana to hold his black wavy hair.

Cristiano greeted Tom with a huge smile and open arms, offering a bonding hug and, "Great to finally meet you. Welcome to Seborga." In stark contrast, Tom barely managed a smile, which to Ben looked more like a smirk, while proffering an unenthusiastic handshake and nothing more than, "Hi. Any chance of a beer?"

"Well, this is going well," Selene said to her father under her breath.

Alessandra decided that food was needed to improve the atmosphere, and everyone was happy for the distraction of her handing around bruschetta. Ben used some of his frustration wrenching the cork out of a bottle. Selene started telling Alessandra about her weekend in Genoa, about meeting Andrea, and the dinner they'd had after the yacht launch. The mood lightened somewhat, and Ben poured wine into everyone's glass.

"These are the last two bottles of my first ever vintage, from two seasons ago."

Tom took his glass held it up to the light, sniffed it briefly and then downed it in one gulp. "Pretty good stuff, Dad. Anymore?"

Ben took a second to gather his thoughts. He decided that he'd really had enough of Tom in the last twenty-four hours.

"Yes, Tom. There is another bottle. I believe it's thirty euros per bottle here at the Osteria. Oh, but I forgot, you don't have any money, do you? Which fast-forwards us nicely to the conversation that I was going to save until after dinner. My wife, your sister and I have discussed your self-inflicted perilous situation and are willing to help you, but only if you agree to some simple conditions.

"We will pay off your current debts if you agree to stay here in Seborga and work to pay us back, and then make enough to repay your stepfather. We think it will take about six months, but you will have gained some much-needed work experience for your CV and be out of debt. You will be able to go home, where hopefully things will have calmed down. We will give you somewhere to live and feed you while you are here."

Tom stared into his empty glass as though wishing he had sipped it. "What kind of work?"

"I don't think you are in any position to be picky about your employment, but it might be working in the orange groves, cutting wood, or washing pots for Cristiano in the kitchen. Whatever needs doing that someone is willing to pay you for."

Tom stood up, pushing his chair backwards until it tilted and fell. "Washing pots for Cristiano? I don't think so. Does your first offer still stand?"

"Which first offer?" Selene asked, looking puzzled.

"A lift to the train station and a ticket back to London."

Without hesitating, Ben confirmed that it did. Tom grabbed two handfuls of bruschetta from the plate, said, "I'll take that offer," and stormed off in the direction of Selene's flat, dropping pieces of tomato and basil leaves as he went.

After a moment, Selene observed, "Well, that was a total disaster."

7. OYSTERS AT BENTLEY'S

Back in London, Selene exited from the rear of Kings Cross station, the final part of Selene's daily commute was a pleasant ten-minute stroll alongside Regent's Canal. It housed a strange breed of narrowboat dwellers who were now familiar figures, with the detritus of their minimalist lives often laid out for all to see. In Central London these upcycled steel, floating homes had become the most affordable real estate in the city.

As she walked along holding her takeaway coffee, Selene often wondered what it would be like to live aboard. Certainly, in terms of square meters, it did not appear to be much smaller that her Clapham flat and would save her almost two hours a day on her commute to work. As she walked and pondered life afloat, her phone vibrated with an incoming message. "Are you screwing a Prime Minister?" was the first WhatsApp message of what would turn into a steady stream from her work colleagues over the course of Selene's day.

The first message had been from her editor in with a link to Instagram post clearly showing Selene in a restaurant, with who the author suggested looked 'remarkably like Andrea Cassini, the dashing young Prime Minister of Italy.' The image of the person sitting opposite her was far from clear. The baseball cap pulled low over his brow cast a shadow over most of his face. However, the man clearly had Cassini's build, with locks of wavy blonde hair protruding from under the hat. There was no denying a likeness.

Andrea had chosen 20TRE (twenty-three), a restaurant in the backstreets of Genoa. It was close to the historic Via Giuseppe Garibaldi, a UNESCO World Heritage site. The decor was intimate with moody lighting and had plenty of pillars to hide behind. He had also heard that the food was amazing. Their deconstructed take of the classic Genoan dish of cappon magro was famous amongst the city's discriminating foodie elite, as was their millefoglie with chocolate mascarpone cream.

The restaurant was run by one of a new generation of entrepreneurial young restaurateurs serving modern, reinvented versions of traditional Ligurian cuisine. However, it was hard to get a table, especially if you could not reveal that you were the prime minister. Andrea had booked it through the Minister of Tourism who had said it was for a magazine restaurant critic who insisted on the utmost discretion.

Selene was tagged in the post, indicating that the author knew exactly who she was. She had already weighed up the possible consequences if this went any further. After all, Andrea was an unmarried man, who was young and handsome with a track record of being seen with beautiful women on his arm. Nobody would think there was anything remarkable or controversial about him being out to dinner with a young woman. No one except the diners who found themselves on a nearby table, who must have thought they recognised Andrea. For them, it must have seemed like their moment in the spotlight.

Selene decided to make light of it and typed a reply to her editor, "You know that there is nothing I would not do to get a scoop for our newspaper, and if Mr Cassini so much as looked in my direction, rest assured I would jump into bed with him." Selene could easily justify this statement if pressed because it was pretty much what had happened. She edited a slightly different version of this same story for other friends and colleagues who had seen the post. She hoped not to hear much more about it.

Still dealing with the fallout from her brother's financial fiasco, Selene received a similar sarcastic message from one of her older male colleagues who worked on the news desk. Seeing the reporter's name gave her an idea. She called him, joked about the Instagram photo, but then moved to ask a favour of their newspaper's new crime correspondent. Briefly explaining the background, she asked if he could find and contact the Turkish dealer looking for her brother.

From the detailed description Tom had given, the seasoned reporter was sure that there was a fairly good chance he could find him. Selene said she would transfer a thousand pounds to him but asked that if he had any leverage he could apply, to try and negotiate a deal closer to the actual debt. With something of a crush on Selene and so relishing her personal challenge, the journalist agreed. He said it was better not to make a traceable bank transfer. Instead, he would use his own funds and get it back in cash from her later.

"Can you do it sooner, rather than later?" Selene pressed.

"I can get on it today, but it will cost you a lunch of oysters and fizz at Bentley's," came the reply.

"Agreed," she confirmed, happy to spend an hour dodging her colleague's advances to get rid of the even-less-wanted attentions of this Turkish criminal.

By the following day she received a message saying he had identified the dealer. Later that night, another message read, "Met him. Done deal. Almost half price. Lunch soon."

Concert for the locals by Yannick.

Drawing by Linda McCluskey

8. CACCIATORE

The rattle of a metal-wheeled trolley on the flagstones outside the window told Ben that the time was gone 8 am, when the shop opened. Every item sold in Seborga's few shops had to be pulled by handcart from the piazza, which was the closet any vehicle could get to the narrow alleys of the village. Each truckload might need several journeys back and forth using the trolleys, providing a wake-up call to those who needed it.

Most older villagers were already up and about. Sitting with a coffee, or even a glass of Vermentino, watching the drivers from the cities arrive, manoeuvre around the narrow bends, fight over limited parking spaces and argue over trolleys, used to be a welcome spectator sport in an otherwise uneventful day. However, with the arrival of the Grail, its Alpini guards and the return of tourists, the old men now had plenty of other distractions.

Ben hardly slept the night after what he had hoped would have been a wonderful family reunion. His emotions swung from anger at his son's behaviour-embarrassing both him and Selene in front of Alessandra and Cristiano—to terrible guilt for any contribution that he might have made to his son's apparent feelings of isolation. Ben rationalised that leaving the family home when Tom was at a difficult stage of adolescence had not been his choice, but rather his then-wife's insistence. He also had no control over her moving in a new partner so soon after he'd gone.

Ben subsequently wondered if his wife's relationship with this other man was already going on behind his back and whether his own much-exaggerated misdemeanour was just the perfect excuse to get him out of the house. Ben had no factual evidence for this theory and would probably never know for sure.

Ben tried to keep in touch after he moved out, but Tom was so upset and angry that their phone conversations usually ended with the boy hanging up without saying goodbye. His subsequent move three-hundred miles away to Newcastle must have seemed like the final desertion, he now realised. So, the long night had passed with him going over and over ways that things might have worked out for the better, without coming to any conclusion. He must have finally fallen asleep because Alessandra woke him with a cup of his favourite Earl Grey tea at gone eight o'clock.

"How are you feeling?"

Ben thought for a moment. "Sad, angry, disappointed, let-down, despairing and frustrated," he listed.

His wife replied, "Tom too, I suspect. Plus, maybe, abandoned, lacking confidence, and worst of all, desperately lonely."

Ben scowled. "If you're lonely, you don't push people away. If you're offered support, you don't throw it back in the faces of the people who clearly love you enough to make it."

Alessandra set on the bed and leaned back, close to her husband. "Ben. Ben. You can't just apply your English academic logic to human emotions, especially where family are concerned. It's much more complicated than that. Cristiano and I went through something remarkably similar to this when I took him away from New York, leaving his father 'to rot in prison,' as he saw it. Later, I brought you into his already upside-down life. Fortunately, you were kind, generous and forgiving, and eventually won him over."

Ben began to argue his point, but Alessandra interrupted him, "You're a pragmatic problem-solver, Ben, and there's no one better at that. But in this case, you are focusing on the effects of the problem and not the cause. That is like building flood defences against climate change. Failing to deal with the root cause only moves the problems somewhere else. It's a treatment, not a cure."

It was hard to argue with his wife's analysis or her conclusion, but Ben was simply bereft of ideas of where to start.

"If he insists on still leaving this morning, let me take Tom to the station. I'll see if I can talk to him. At the very least, I will try and get him to call you and set things straight. You can't part not speaking to each other."

What Ben didn't know was that after he had gone to bed early last night, still fuming from the ruined dinner, Alessandra had taken a plate of the leftover food around for Tom. They had chatted, cautiously, for nearly an hour, and Alessandra came away feeling she had gained a degree of trust. However, Tom insisted that he wasn't staying to be a kitchen slave to someone his own age.

"Did you know that he has real issues with gay people?" Alessandra asked.

Ben looked surprised. "No. I had no idea. What makes you say that?"

"The way he treated Cristiano last night. He looked like he thought that he was shaking hands with a leper."

"That would be that bloody snobby school they sent him to after I was gone. It was part boarding school, and there are always polarised factions of the rugby guys versus those few boys still figuring out their sexuality. Teenagers can be cruel and brutal. Later, if they go on to play club rugby, where they're always immersed in that very macho environment, those prejudices are perpetuated."

Alessandra sighed. "This is the twenty-first century. Tom needs to get over it."

"That and a lot of other things," Ben added, looking forlorn.

The couple agreed that Tom had two generous options in front of him. Also, that it was time that he stood on his own feet and accepted responsibility for his actions and decisions.

Alessandra would drive him to the station, but Ben would come and say goodbye before they left.

Unlike Ben, Alessandra could see what she thought was the root cause of Tom's anger. She believed that he had been made to feel homeless and rejected by all his family. He felt that his father had abandoned him to his fate. His sister had left home soon after his stepfather moved in, and he was then sent to boarding school and had not been made particularly welcome if he went back for holidays. For a teenager, already coming to terms with so many other changes in his life, this was just too much uncertainty.

Alessandra picked Tom up from Selene's flat in her late father's old Fiat. Selene had left very early in the morning to get her hire car back to Genoa Airport and catch her flight to London. When Alessandra drove by her own house a few minutes later, Ben was sat outside on the doorstep looking glum and stroking Don Gateau, the friendly three-legged cat. The cat was arching his back and rubbing up against Ben's leg. When Alessandra's car came around the corner, he stood and tried to put on a brave smile. His wife got out of the car, but Tom stayed firmly in his seat with his seatbelt buckled. The windows were down as it was already hot inside. Ben gave Tom an envelope containing some cash and then offered his hand. Tom shook it with only slightly more sincerity than he had Cristiano's the previous night.

A quietly spoken and grudging, "Thanks," was all he would offer in return.

"Take care."

After a peck on the cheek from his wife, the pair set off for Ventimiglia. Ben looked at Claudio's battered gold watch, which she had given him after her father died. It was only 8:30 am and there would be no train until 10:30 am. He assumed Alessandra must have some other errands to run in town. Sitting back down on the doorstep, the cat, who had been lying in a sunny spot, retuned for some more attention from Ben.

"It seems that you're the only one who needs my affection today."

Ben decided to spend the day in the vineyard where the work usually made his troubles evaporate. When he arrived, Vincenzo and Marius were already hard at work in the early morning sunshine. They had spent over a year gradually repairing the terraces on Ben's vineyard in between their other jobs. The stones which had been scattered over several decades by foraging cinghale (wild boar) were first gathered into heaps. Then the painstaking work of rebuilding the dry-stone walls began.

Starting with the biggest stones-many too big for one man to lift–a solid base was created along a runner line of string which was stretched between two points to ensure a straight line across the terrace. Inclined wooden lathes placed every few metres gave the wall a uniform, slightly backwards tilt. This design would ensure the weight of the wall offered resistance to the ground pushing against it. These were techniques practised over thousands of years. For a similar amount of time the hooves and snouts of wild boar, most weighing much more than a man, had been ploughing the walls down. It was a never-ending battle, until the advent of electric fences. But even these were not fool-proof.

After an hour or so, Vincenzo's mobile phone rang with his easily recognisable and much-too-loud Nessum Dorma ring tone.

"Pronto. Si," followed by a long pause with some head nodding and shaking and then, "Princepessa. Si. Si. Si. Abiento."

After pocketing his phone, the big Italian bent back down to his work. Apparently, no explanation was going to be offered, and so Ben did not ask for one. Forty-five minutes later Alessandra's car appeared on the track below the vineyard. Two figures got out and Ben could see that she had brought Tom back with her. Taken aback, he ran through a mixture of emotions including delight, trepidation, and finally relief. His wife stayed at the car but handed Tom a neatly wrapped package which Ben at once recognised as lunch. Ben now looked to Vincenzo for an explanation of the phone call.

Alessandra's right-hand-man shrugged his shoulders as if to ask, 'What was so surprising?' "She asked if we could use some help. I said that we could. She asked me if I would teach him, I said that I would. She said not to tell you who'd called, so I didn't."

Ben smiled at Vincenzo as if acknowledging his dilemma. He set off to meet his son halfway, in a gesture of compromise that was instinctive rather than planned. In the minute it took to walk a hundred metres down the sides of the terraces, Ben decided just to start over as if last night had not happened.

"We are glad that you decided to stay and help us. This is a mammoth task. So long as you're here to take my place, I'll take a lift back with Alessandra. I have other things to do. I'll leave you to get on with it."

Vincenzo waited for Tom to reach them. Marius introduced himself and started showing him which stones to collect and where to stack them. There was half a pile already in place from which Vincenzo was placing stones in the wall. Marius also started building further along the terrace, but they quickly ran out of the material. When Tom came back to the pile carrying just one medium-sized stone, both men stood with their hands on their hips.

Realising that his collection speed was limiting their progress, Tom stopped daydreaming about the morning's events and stepped up the pace. His efforts were still not providing enough stone for two men laying it, so Marius went back to building his own pile. After just ten minutes, Marius had accumulated a pile more than twice the size of the one Tom had created for Vincenzo.

It was past eleven thirty in the morning and the sun was approaching its highest point. Tom's back hurt, he was getting blisters on his thumbs, and his t-shirt was soaked in sweat. Not long after, they could hear the sound of church bells from across the valley. Without checking the time, Vincenzo and Marius knew by the bells' peel that this was noon and so lunchtime. With both piles of stone almost depleted again, they stopped work. Vincenzo turned on a tap which he had rigged up at the end of a pipe fed from the spring up above them. Both men washed their hands and splashed water on their faces.

"Come and have your lunch, Tom," Marius invited.

Being competitive by nature and realising that he appeared to be losing this race, Tom declined. "I've not long had breakfast, so I'll work through." His thinking was that if he could build up some stocks of stone, he could get ahead of their work rate. He took off his shirt, revealing his pale skin, now with reddened arms.

"I'd put that shirt back on, take a rest and have a good drink of water," Marius advised, but Tom ignored him.

After their lunch, Vincenzo and Marius made themselves comfortable, pulled spare shirts over their heads and napped in the midday sunshine. Tom worked on, collecting and piling up the stones in heaps along the terraces. Despite the discomfort, he was finding solace in the work which caused his worries about problems in the UK to dissipate into the heat of the afternoon. After almost exactly an hour had passed Vincenzo stirred from slumber, as some internal clock knew it was time to get back to work. In what seemed like no time at all, the piles of stone had disappeared into the terrace walls and Tom was struggling to keep up again.

The last hour seemed like three to the young Englishman, and when Vincenzo finally stood up, straightened his back and said, "Abbastanza," Tom was nearly ready to collapse. He looked at his now burst blisters on his hands and could feel the tightness of the skin of his back. His back ached and the muscles in his arms throbbed, but strangely, he felt better than he had a long while yet in a way he could not really explain. There had been virtually no conversation during the day, yet so much had been communicated between them.

Tom learned that Marius worked with an economy of movement that it made it look like he was not doing much, despite the all the evidence proving otherwise. The dark-skinned Romanian deferred to Vincenzo in all matters, despite appearing to know as least as much about everything they were doing as his elder did. Vincenzo conveyed that he thought Tom was lazy, weak and feckless just by his body language. Marius seemed more friendly and less judgemental. Tom liked his quiet confidence, he decided. He seemed like a young man much more comfortable in his own skin than he was.

Together they travelled back along the valley in Vincenzo's Ape. As they bounced along the road in the back of the old pickup, Tom took in the scenery of the mountains above and the breath-taking views down to the coast. The sea looked very inviting, and he would have given almost anything to run down a beach and plunge into it right now. He finally opened the lunch package Alessandra had given him earlier. Inside was another of the wonderful arancini, this one filled with soft cheese and ham. There were also some small salami sausages, cheese, and a big slice of salty focaccia.

Tom saw Marius looking at the package and so reluctantly offered up the package to him. He shook his head, causing his long, curly hair to shake from the bandana he'd been wearing. He deftly caught the blue cotton handkerchief in one hand before it blew out of the Ape on the breeze. Declining the offer of food, he reached into his pocket and handed Tom his pocketknife to cut the salami.

"Cacciatore," Marius said, nodding at the wild boar salami. "It's our way to get back at the cinghale (wild boar) who knock down our walls and eat our crops. We make them into sausages."

Tom managed a half-smile, cut some chunks from sausage and offered the knife back. Marius said, "Keep it. You will need a knife every day, and you'd have to go all the way to Bordighera to buy one. I have another at home for myself. I can bring it tomorrow."

The Englishman began to decline this act of generosity but was stopped by a simple raised hand gesture. "I insist," was the end of the matter.

Vincenzo pulled up outside Selene's and waited for Tom to climb out which he did with some difficulty, his muscles and burnt skin now tightening up. Although Alessandra had told him that he could eat twice daily at the Osteria, Tom could only think of his bed.

9. PANINO CON VERDURE ARROSTA

On this occasion, it was Selene who spotted herself in a photograph with Andrea in the Instagram post before her colleagues did. Someone had snapped them at the rapper's boat launch in Genoa, just at the moment she was introduced to Zeno. It was the only time that she and Andrea had touched, at a public event, as he had reached back for her hand and pulled her forward to meet their host. But in the photograph it looked like they were hand-in-hand, smiling like star-struck lovers.

They might have been able to explain this photograph away had it been in isolation, and not deliberately linked to the image posted the day before showing Selene having dinner with a man who also looked like Andrea. They were clearly wearing the same clothes, except for Andrea's ineffective baseball cap disguise, indicating that these images were probably taken only hours apart.

Selene knew that these photographs were going to achieve a massive audience in Italy. In Andrea's brief time in office, he had gone from being an unknown local politician to the most popular PM in living memory. A movement for change was in the air and his policies were striking a chord with voters on both sides of the political divide. His support for environmental issues and women's rights had won him fans who would previously never have supported a centre-right government. But it was his battle with the European Union over sustainable fishing that was his cause celebre.

Even those who were indifferent about the fishermen's plight liked the idea of him standing up to the EU. This made for some previously unthinkable alliances with the Green parties. As a responsible father, being seen to be doing the right thing by his ex-wife and child, even the traditionalist Catholics forgave him for his now ten-year-old divorce.

Giving the media almost as much access as possible, always stopping to provide a photo-opportunity and giving a quote, they had so far treated him kindly. He was also happy to flirt with any female celebrities he met at events which provided endless material for the gossip columns. It also had, so far, distracted any attention from his actual relationship with Selene. Outside and inside his party, his opponents were furious about his golden boy image and a seemingly endless honeymoon with the media.

Was all this about to hit the buffers, Selene wondered? It had been the most wonderful year of her life, and she did not want it to end. The taking and publishing of these photographs could have been just a coincidence, but Selene had an uneasy feeling that someone had a malevolent hand in it somewhere. She just could not think of who or why, although she acknowledged that there would be no shortage of candidates with Andrea being in politics. Anticipating an escalation of interest, Selene rang him to suggest a cover story and then she rang her editor to obtain the backup for it.

Andrea pointed out that the cover story's problem was that, if the whole truth came out, they would look worse than if they just admitted it now. The journalist could see his point. A cover story, if blown, would look like they really had something terrible to hide. However, if they went public, Selene's newspaper's coverage of anything related to Italy would appear to be undermined. She would probably be asked to resign. Andrea's continued support for her father's Seborga projects would suddenly be seen in a new light, and likely retrospectively scrutinised. It seemed that they were damned if they didn't and damned if they did.

In the end, they agreed to go with the cover story that Andrea had given her newspaper's Sunday magazine supplement-a UK exclusive focussing on 'the man behind Europe's best-loved politician.' This gave a very plausible cover for Selene being seen with Andrea outside of his political appointments, but the big problem was that this excuse would come to an end when the feature was finally published.

Although she could probably spin it out for a while in order to obtain her editor's backing for her story, she would ultimately have to deliver a substantial article. At least a few more months of privacy was worth it, they calculated. By then, all the Seborga initiatives would be in place and Andrea could back away from any public connection to the principality. Her colleagues had assumed that her regular trips to Italy had been to see her father, and now she had gained the added justification of the property she had inherited there.

She had barely got the agreement in place for the exclusive magazine feature when the first Italian journalist rang Selene at the office. Sat at her desk, she had taken one bite from a verdure arrosta (roasted vegetable) focaccia sandwich from a new Italian takeaway near her office. Their delicious produce reminded Selene of San Antonio's panettiera, her father's favourite lunch stop when he was in Bordighera.

"Selene Morton? My name is Carina Esposito from La Stampa newspaper. I want to talk to you about the photographs that appear to show that you and our prime minister are in a relationship."

Selene did her best to muster a convincing laugh and then countered the accusation with, "I wish. Isn't he just gorgeous? As flattered as I am that anyone thinks he would be interested in me, I am just like you, a journalist doing my job."

Selene told herself that although this was a highly misleading statement, it contained no facts that could not be justified. She was indeed flattered by his attention, and she was doing her job when she met him. Before she could explain the cover story she had rehearsed in her head, the Italian dropped her bombshell.

"Your father is Professore Ben Morton and his wife Princess Alessandra of Seborga, are they not? Is it also the case that between them they have been the recipients of millions of euros in grants from Senor Cassini's government?"

Selene hung up.

10. BAGNA CÀUDA

The Fiori Autostrada (highway of flowers) snakes along the coast between the French border with Italy and the city of Genoa. It is one of the most spectacular driving routes in the world. As the Maritime Alps were pushed up from the floor of the Mediterranean Sea millions of years ago, they formed dramatic folds of rock along the coast. In some places, these rock protrusions continued pushing upwards until they formed the highest peak of Mount Argentera at over three thousand meters.

The dips between these ridges rising out of the sea became sandy bays around which fishing villages sprang up. Many of these have today grown to be bustling seaside towns with working harbours and pleasure marinas. To traverse this, the undulating terrain more prosaically known as Autostrada 10 alternates between tunnels, bridges and viaducts, twisting and turning along its route to follow the coast.

One moment travellers are in a kilometre-long tunnel through a mountain, the next they suddenly exit into bright sunshine one hundred meters in the air. Implausibly high concrete columns support a roadway that often appears in the sky above towns and villages. It is as spectacular as it is sometimes alarming, but the views are also breath-taking and the driving exhilarating.

After forty-five minutes on the Fiori Autostrada, it was mid-morning when Alessandra and Ben arrived at the tiny hilltop hamlet of Colletta di Castelbianco, located halfway between Seborga and Genoa. Although the village was situated at a similar elevation to Seborga, it was several kilometres further inland and so did not enjoy the same views of the Mediterranean. It was also even smaller than the tiny principality that the couple now called home, with fewer than thirty houses.

What was strikingly different, now they were up close to it, was just how uniform the buildings' condition appeared to be. That is to say, the houses were all unique in size, shape, and elevation outlook, but their exteriors looked to have been recently restored, apparently using their original materials. There were no partly rendered and painted walls, only beautifully hand-laid stone ones. No plastic windows, modern extensions or replacement roofs using modern materials - only old clay pan-tiles, copper gutters and oak window frames could be seen on all the houses. There was not a satellite dish anywhere to be seen.

The use of copper as a waterproof, and rustproof, material in roof architecture goes back to the Romans. In highly industrialised northern European communities, it was later replaced by cast iron and finally by plastic. In remote rural Italy, where people often had to build and maintain their own houses, materials were chosen because they could be formed by hand. Copper can easily be bent into almost any shape and sealed with solder without much expertise or the need for anything but basic tools. For reasons lost in time, in Seborga the ends of copper gutters are sometimes formed into elaborate dragon head shapes by local artisans. When it rains, they look as though these mythical beasts are spewing out water.

One of few common features were the green wooden louvre shutters on all the windows. Each leaf of the side-hung shutters contains another top-opening panel. The purpose of these is not obvious until someone has lived in these houses during summer. By noon, these shutters are closed to keep out the baking rays of the sun. The smaller inset panels are often opened slightly, their carefully angled louvres still offering shade but also catching any breeze and directing it upward into the room. Although today, new shutters are usually made of green-painted aluminium, this cleverly evolved design feature has been retained.

Like all the others in this region, this community would have grown and evolved over hundreds of years. It had probably never looked quite this pristine at any time in its history. It was as if it had all been built within the same couple of years by one builder, using identical specifications. In fact, that is almost what had happened there a few years ago, it would later be explained. Already in economic and social decline, the entire village had been abandoned after an earthquake sometime in the fifties. It had been left to deteriorate even further in the intervening half-century. Twenty years ago, a visionary architect had raised funding to restore the entire village, sticking strictly to traditional materials and practices.

When finished, the unique project became a destination for architectural students: almost a place of pilgrimage for those favouring sympathetic restoration over new build. To meet one of those very graduates was the reason Alessandra and Ben were here today. Alberto Cannavaro was now based in San Remo and was the London Club's chosen architect behind the Albergo Diffuso planned for Seborga. He had invited them here to show them what he planned to do with the buildings his clients were acquiring there.

Like everyone else, the couple had to park outside the village as it was now entirely pedestrian, apart from some small electric carts used to transport baggage, for maintenance, or for any medical evacuation. All the tarmac and concrete paths had been replaced with stone slabs and cobles. The young architect pointed out the black marble door heads, steps and windowsills used on all the buildings. Also, the traditional-looking windows all had triple glazing and integrated internal shutters to maintain the internal temperate-winter or summer.

"It is wonderful craftsmanship," Ben acknowledged.

The young architect then took them out to the perfectly restored and maintained olive groves surrounding the hamlet for what he called his mentor's piece de resistance. He stopped and asked, "So, what do you think of this feature?" A gurgling noise could be heard, and there was a slight chemical smell, but otherwise there was no clue what he was referring to.

"Of which feature?" they both asked, almost in unison.

He urged them both to stand on the tips of their toes and look over that terrace wall. Immediately on the other side was a swimming pool that had been entirely invisible until now. It was long and narrow because they had limited it to the three-metre width of the original terrace. It had just enough width for a couple of people to swim lengths for exercise. Everything was either hidden at sub-ground level or made to blend in with the surroundings. The shower looked like a garden hose with a sprinkler on the end casually slung over the branch of an olive tree. In fact, it was permanently fixed and connected to a water supply heated by the sun on the roof of a nearby building.

"It is all mightily impressive," Ben acknowledged. "Of course, in Seborga we will not be renovating every single building, so the effect will not be so uniformly immaculate as this."

"Maybe not a bad thing," observed Alessandra. "Although undoubtedly very authentic, this does look a little too clinically organised for Italy."

"I tend to agree," the architect acknowledged. "The Club wanted their guests to stay in an authentic environment and not in a museum. But you get the idea of a sympathetic, light-touch restoration?"

They all agreed that there were plenty of buildings in Seborga that would benefit from this treatment. After his tour, Alessandra and Ben thanked him for his time and they parted company. Now approaching lunchtime, Alessandra suggested a slight diversion to San Lorenzo al Mare, where there was lovely restaurant that she knew called Emy, next to a tiny beach. Like her own Osteria, it was run by a female chef. Ben, of course, took no persuading.

They ordered the spada (swordfish) because they were told it was fresh and local, plus some Bagna Càuda and vegetables to start. Two glasses of local Vermentino would go down well with this, they decided.

"Bagna Càuda?" Ben queried, reading it from the menu. "That's another new dish for me."

"The Piedemontese claim it as their own, but there has been a Ligurian version for as long as anyone can remember. It is simply anchovies blended with olive oil and garlic."

"Surely Piedmont is a landlocked region, and so isn't this much more likely the invention of coastal people?" Ben suggested, in academic support of the Ligurian claim.

Although reluctant to concede the advantage to their near-neighbours, Alessandra acknowledged, "We tend to eat our fish fresh after the catch, but anchovies preserved in salt, from which this dish is made, have always been traded with Piedmont for their wheat and pasta, so their claim that it is their invention is not entirely without merit."

When the small bowl of brown dip arrived, Alessandra tested the temperature of the contents with her finger.

"If it's cold then it's probably been made previously in a big batch and kept in the fridge. Warm means they just made it fresh." It was served with slivers of raw peppers for dipping, plus some crusty bread. Ben declared it, "Another triumph for the Ligurian less-is-more philosophy."

While they munched their salty vegetables looking out over the picturesque Italian seaside scene, conversation drifted back to Seborga.

"Tom appears to have settled down and be adjusting to his temporary home, don't you think?" Alessandra suggested.

Ben looked thoughtful for a moment and then replied, "He's so exhausted when he finishes work that he can't get into any trouble or upset anyone at the moment. He gets home, eats and sleeps. What keeps him going is his determination to prove Vincenzo wrong and match or even surpass Marius's work rate. It was the same with sport when he was at school. If a coach replaced him in a team, he would train and train until he could beat that person and win his place back. Having then done that, he would lose interest and stop turning up for matches. As he saw it, he'd made his point. So, I'm not celebrating yet," Ben added.

"People are motivated by many different things, Ben. You should know that."

He smiled, "You proved that when you got him to stay after everything he'd said about leaving. It was an inspired idea, offering to take him to the beach in Ventimiglia for breakfast. He'd go anywhere for food. Then choosing the beach where all the young waitresses go to swim and sunbathe before starting their shift was just genius."

"It's true. I can't deny it," Alessandra said, laughing. "After an hour of watching them arrive on their scooters, undress, swim, shower and then apply sun lotion, Italy was looking far more attractive than rainy old London, even if staying meant that he had to eat his words. There's a carrot for every donkey, as my dear father, Claudio used to say."

As well as the weather forecast for London, Alessandra had said that she was concerned about how he would avoid the people looking for him and where he was going to live, questions to which he'd had no answers. She had flattered him about his athletic physique, saying that it would not only impress the girls, but could eventually get him a better-paid job here working outdoors. After all, to date these girls he would need transport, plus money for petrol, drinks and pizza, she had pointed out. That was when she had phoned Vincenzo to check he would take him under his wing.

"So, it was essentially the same offer that I made him, just in better packaging?" Ben observed, wryly. "And it's me who's supposed to know about marketing," he joked.

Their spada steaks arrived with big chunks of fresh lemon, slightly caramelised on the surface from being placed on the grill. They smelled of the sea and olive oil.

Squeezing lemon over her fish, Alessandra concluded, "It was you who taught me to work out my customers' needs and wants, so I applied that same logic. And what does a twenty-five year old single man want?"

"Exactly what you offered him," Ben conceded.

After his first mouthful and murmur of pleasure, he remembered, "I had a message from Tom's mother this morning, saying that she had finally tracked down the other bailiff who was looking for Tom and paid them off as well. I will send her the money for that today. She only agreed to do this after I personally guaranteed that she would get back the previous two thousand pounds within six months."

"So, with Selene taking care of his drug debt, he is now solvent and no longer on the run?" said Alessandra, sounding relieved.

"As far as we know," added Ben, sounding sceptical. "But let's not tell him just yet. I don't want him thinking the coast is clear to run back home. I'm determined to make up for the time I have lost with Tom. I want to see if I can change his ways before he gets into real trouble."

"Remember needs and wants," his wife taunted.

"And the appropriate carrot for the donkey in question," he joked.

For the remainder of their lunch, the couple returned to the subject that had brought them there. Impressed with what they had seen at Colletta di Castelbianco, Ben wondered if they could not adjust the rules of their inward investment zero tax scheme for Seborga. He proposed that they could include some regulations to promote sympathetic restoration and the use of more environmentally friendly materials. He knew that in UK National Parks, they had similar rules about using such materials and even paint colours. He said that he would ask Andrea, who he felt sure would welcome such an initiative.

Alessandra pointed out that without forcing residents to restore or rebuild in exactly the same way, the new Albergo Diffuso buildings would 'set the bar high' and give them something to aspire to.

Alessandra said, "I believe it will drive up standards, albeit slowly, this being Italy. When is Selene moving into her new house?"

"As soon as the paperwork is complete. Well, it's Tom who will be moving, because Selene is too busy to come at the moment. Maybe less than two weeks. The Club wants someone to get in there and start work the next day. I thought I might ask Richard if there was work for Tom."

"Better still, why don't you suggest Vincenzo to Richard as a contractor for building work? No builders are living in Seborga, and he has stonework and basic construction skills. He can always use some extra money. During Richard's visit, he told me that the Club pays well and offers early completion bonuses. If they accept, let Vincenzo offer Tom that carrot, keeping his new mentor as the one holding the reins. Distancing the job offer from any perceived interference by us will also sit better with Tom."

"You are good at this parenting thing, aren't you?" Ben said, only half-joking.

"Where men are concerned, maybe," Alessandra allowed, "but I'm not so sure I could handle girls quite so well."

Ben gave her a knowing smile and then washed the last morsel of swordfish down with the remainder of his Vermentino.

"A nap on the beach before we drive back?"

11. CARDI ARROSTA

With no previous business experience and just a second-class degree in History of Art, Cecily was both a reluctant and an unlikely entrepreneur. Her first husband had left her for a younger woman he had met on the Internet and moved to live in America. Left with a mortgage she could not afford, she had been forced to try and make some real money or move out of the garden flat in Chiswick that she loved.

Looking south over Kew Gardens and guarded on three sides by the snaking River Thames, the London Borough of Chiswick is an enclave of smug affluence. Some of its 18th century inns actually deserve the label 'gastropub'-unlike the hundreds of formulaic pastiche versions that have bred like rabbits in neighbouring boroughs but would never dream of putting 'bunny' on the blackboard menu.

Working from home, is another term that might have been invented in Chiswick by an earlier generation. Populated by media-tech foodies with flexible hours and high disposable incomes, residents meet in its West End cafés with East End post-industrial décor to discuss their next must-have kitchen implement. If Clapham is where those starting their clamber up the greasy pole begin, Chiswick is where those who make it come to raise families. If all goes well, the next and final stop is Chipping Norton in the Cotswolds.

An Olympic-standard networker with a can-do attitude, Cecily had soon mobilised a small army of her time-rich neighbours. They helped sell her homemade, chemical-free soaps and shampoos to their friends and family. Before she knew it, she was working twelve hours a day making and wrapping orders. Other products soon followed, and later her kitchen table was replaced by an outsourced factory while she concentrated on marketing.

Cecily's years of experience of growing her fair-trade cosmetics business had given the elegant Englishwoman an in-depth understanding of exactly what went into modern beauty products. She had spent her waking hours avoiding the types of toxic ingredients that her environmentally aware clients would find unacceptable. Banning the inclusion of ethanolamine, parabens, formaldehyde, and other harmful chemicals also gave her products a genuine point of difference from her mainstream competitors.

After leaving London to live on her yacht in the Mediterranean, Cecily applied the same rigorous environmental controls to everything used onboard. She knew that, like all boats, the waste from the drains ended up in a storage tank, along with any chemicals and plastics used in the products themselves. Skippers could legally open valves to discharge this waste into the sea, but responsible ones only did this in the deep open ocean, at least five kilometres offshore. So long as all the tank contents were purely organic material, this is an acceptable practice. However, most modern discharges contained harmful chemicals, microbeads, sanitary products and cotton buds – all of which are clearly harmful to the environment and the wildlife. This meant that even a boat made from wood and powered by sail, like hers, could still leave a disastrous environmental trail in its wake.

During the last year, Ben and Alessandra had learned about the poor environmental practices of other ships from Roman during several short sailing trips with the couple on Cecily's boat. Cecily, already a seasoned sailor, was well aware of the importance of respecting the nature of the ocean. Cecily's unconventional relationship with Roman had been the catalyst for her to purchase the classic ketch and to take up permanent residence there. It gave her the ability to stay close to Monaco with the perfect mobile office and provided a rendezvous location for her secret meet-ups with Roman while he was still committed to his cataleptic wife. Roman now a full-time resident, brought his eco-friendly practices learned from lemon farming to the vessel as well. Their combined knowledge proved to be a treasure trove to Ben and Alessandra in their own search for balance with agriculture and the environment. With the passing of Roman's wife, he and Cecily could look towards the future and were making plans to build a house somewhere between Seborga and Menton in close proximity to where the boat was moored. This would give Ben and Alessandra even greater opportunity to pick Roman's brain for more helpful environmentally sound practices.

Roman had also been asked to join the new Seborga environmental working group because his expertise as an orange farmer in Sicily was deemed extremely valuable by Ben. His friend had declined, citing that 'committees were not really his preferred way of working.' However, he did offer to provide advice whenever it was needed, channelling that through Cecily. He further conceded that, if his attendance were thought to be vital at a meeting, he would come along, with the proviso that Alessandra was cooking lunch afterwards.

The prime minister had floated the idea of using the new limited legislative independence of the tiny principality to experiment with untested environmental policies and practices. His thinking was that he could experiment with small-scale, low-cost, and therefore reduced risk, Green projects without making changes to national law. Any which proved successful could be rolled out across Italy. Cecily seemed like precisely the kind of person they needed as part of an advisory group.

Having recently sold the bulk of her cosmetics business, keeping only a small niche range using blood oranges, she had some time to spare. Because some of the rare oranges she needed were now coming from Seborga, Cecily also had the motivation to look after the environment in which they grew.

Even without a vested interest, the multimillionaire entrepreneur would have been happy to help her best friend, Alessandra, and new friend, the Prime Minister Andrea Cassini.

This morning was to be the inaugural meeting on the Environmental Committee of the Principality of Seborga. It would take place in the Osteria, after which everyone would enjoy lunch there. Everyone except Andrea, who could only join them via video from Rome, much to his own disappointment about missing Alessandra's pasta. They had invited Alain Cassel, a young marine scientist from the Monaco Oceanographic Institute, and the chairwoman of a Riviera environmental group. A representative of the Slow Food Organisation in Piedmont and a couple of their students who were now on placement in the village would also be joining the group.

Ben was acting as chairman and already had quite an agenda of things to discuss, and that was before any additional matters were raised by the other members. Today's objective was to come away with a list of potential policies to be researched and costed, ready for the next meeting in thirty days. Before the meeting, the members were asked to provide a list of what they believed to be their main environmental concerns, in order of priority, and any suggestions for tackling them. Ben then aggregated these into the agenda. Andrea was to open the meeting with a few words about his aspirations.

"Almost uniquely, you have the opportunity to reshape the community in which you live. By adjusting taxation, we can reward, punish and eventually cajole people into acting in certain ways. It can attract, but also exclude, certain types of economic activity. What you have to decide is the type of place you want to live in and how its economics will work."

The politician paused to let this sink in.

"Let me be clear that I accept that some of these experiments might not work. After all, that's what experimentation is. But, to borrow a phrase, let us fail fast and often until we find something workable. I don't know how long I will have in the office of the prime minister–historical precedent suggests not that long. I want to try and make a real difference in the time I have."

"Let me get this straight: you're asking a chef, a winegrower, and a food-loving cosmetics expert to reinvent a nation and change the habits of its citizens?" replied Cecily, only half joking about the enormity of the task.

"Exactly. We need to create a recipe for a nation. One that makes the most of local resources, can be created quickly, is sustainable and will attract diners to partake in it. In effect, we will be cooking up a country."

Cecily thought it was a clever analogy, given the audience, underlining once again what a natural leader Andrea was. He would have excelled in business, she mused, had that been his calling.

"If I am to roll out any of the initiatives during my term in office, what we try here needs to show measurable results in months, not years. Please do not propose anything that will take four years to build, a billion euros to fund and a decade to show results. Small-scale, short timeframe, and therefore limited cost projects are what we want, but within those parameters we can afford to be bold."

"I think you'd be better with an alchemist, a wizard or a genie in a bottle," Cecily joked.

"Or a fairy-tale princess and her knight in shining armour," Andrea countered, smiling broadly.

Ben decided this was a good time to wrap things up. He thanked the prime minister, conscious that, as his daughter's secret partner and potential future husband, Andrea probably also had other worries about people's perception of their respective roles in this, should they became widely known. Nevertheless, the members pressed on with the meeting and ninety minutes later had what Ben thought was an excellent shortlist of potentially feasible, economically-sound environmental initiatives.

Cecily had proposed a trial using some of the personal hygiene and domestic liquids on her boat. They were supplied in large containers which could be decanted into smaller reusable glass or stainless-steel bottles available from the village store. This would have the dual effects of significantly reducing single-use plastic bottles and preventing harmful chemicals from being discharged into the land through the soak-away drains and septic tanks still widely used in the village.

"These toxics and plastics will eventually end up in the olives, oranges and grapes that we otherwise think of as organic, and the bottles end up in landfill, or worse, in the ocean."

Andrea said this was precisely the type of initiative they wanted and immediately suggested a zero rate of purchase tax rate on products with no plastic packaging sold in Seborga. Cecily advised them that the loose product already cost less, and with a further twenty-two percent tax removed, customers should not need much more persuasion to try it.

Alessandra said that she would speak to the people behind the new Albergo Diffuso to ask if they would commit to using the refillable organic toiletries. She was confident that it would appeal to their customers' sensibilities.

Anticipating some Italian conservatism and resistance to change, Alessandra proposed an initiative to get the school's children involved - a slight modification to the curriculum to cover specific local environmental issues which would build on the annual survey of discarded plastic in the vicinity of the village. She argued that the children would educate their parents and shame those not complying into good practices.

"When parents and grandparents hear the children's heartfelt concerns about the planet that they will inherit from them, it will move even the most die-hard traditionalists to action," she predicted.

There was much discussion around private car use, and the potential of electric vehicles in particular. Everyone knew that there was currently limited employment in Seborga and only one food store, making regular journeys to the coast essential. However, even those working in Monaco only had a thirty minute commute, which was within the range of most electric cars. Most residents' journeys were only as far as the town of Bordighera, just twelve kilometres and all of that downhill on the outbound leg.

Ben advanced the idea that with the village open to the sun during all daylight hours, solar panels might provide much of the power needed to fuel these journeys. Alain, the scientist, said that these cars were now extremely popular in Monaco, but warned that the cost of acquiring them might be prohibitive to the average Seborgan.

"Then there is the solar infrastructure needed to recharge them," he added.

Andrea said that the government was already in talks with Italian car manufacturers about their industry's future. Without promising anything, the prime minister said that he would speak to Fiat about this problem and also to someone from a green energy supplier before reporting back.

Ben moved on to the problem of all the new construction going on in the principality. He had no previous experience of this building industry but could not help noticing all the plastic materials being used, concrete being poured, and tarmac being laid. The marine scientist added that the latter could increase the potential for flooding by covering previously porous surfaces with impermeable drives and carparks.

Not having even thought of that aspect, Ben added, "When we get storm rain rushing off the mountains around us, the informal network of gulleys that must carry it out of the village and down to the river below already become overwhelmed. The consequences of any further strain on the existing ad-hoc infrastructure are completely unknown."

The incidence and severity of rainstorms had increased, even from the first years that Ben had been in Seborga. The first intense storm, not long after his arrival, had caused the landslide which led to Ben's discovery of the charter given by Pope Gregory to the Templars. In a cave revealed by the landslide, he and Selene had found the long-lost document which proved the principality's independence from Italy. That event had started a chain reaction, leading to Seborga's partial-autonomy, and ultimately to this meeting today.

No one from the Slow Food organisation had so far made any contribution to the meeting, and Andrea was keen that they should be involved somehow. The truth was that the young academics were somewhat in awe of the charismatic Italian leader, the first ever with a clearly stated environmental agenda. They were more used to fighting to have a voice for their cause but now that they had one, they had gone strangely quiet.

The PM said, "Ben is restoring vineyards in Seborga and encouraging other villagers to do so, by joining a wine cooperative. He tells me that one barrier is that the land is often poor or has either been neglected or overworked by people raising other crops. What is needed is a natural fertiliser. This terrain cannot sustain grazing animals that would produce manure. So, I would like you, Slow Food guys, to come up with suggestions to revitalise the land, without compromising the organic status of the end products. Can I leave that modest task in your capable hands and look forward to a report with outlined proposals by the next meeting?"

The Slow Food spokesperson agreed that they would investigate fertilisers.

On hearing about the revival of wine growing, the representatives from Slow Food were also prompted to describe a recent phenomenon they were aware of known as 'crowd-farming.'

"It might be something that the new wine growers could investigate to help fund their initiatives," they suggested. They explained that the model leveraged social media to facilitate the advance purchase of products by individuals from growers who used sustainable methods. Using the analogy of investment brokers who trade commodity 'futures' to provide investment, they pointed out that it reduced all parties' risk.

He explained that funding typically came from city dwellers bereft of access to the countryside who felt too distanced from the source of what they ate and who had environmental and food integrity concerns. This new breed of consumers could connect with individual farmers almost anywhere in the world, whose food ethics they supported, and order part of a future crop–a box of oranges, litres of olive oil, wine cases, and so on. When it was harvested, the produce would be delivered directly to their homes by a carrier. It offered a direct connection to an artisan grower where people could invest in their success and share their produce, they explained. Customers shared a small part of their risk in return for a percentage of their crop.

"Consumers feel as though they are part of something worthwhile, and it makes a great dinner party story when they finally eat or drink the produce they have invested in. It's a global initiative that is growing exponentially," the student spokesman added.

"Armchair farmers who don't even have to get their hands dirty," joked Andrea. "I love it."

Ben was making notes, already highly excited by this crowd-farming idea and determined to find out more. Only his lack of prowess with Internet technology was casting a shadow over his ambitions. He wondered if Tom might be able to help him in exploiting this idea.

Lunch was roasted cardoons in bechamel sauce with a parmesan breadcrumb crust which had been baking slowly for over an hour.

"A member of the artichoke family, the cardoon can be found wild and cultivated in Liguria and so is found in traditional recipes of the region, but little used these days," Alessandra explained to her now-hungry diners.

12. LINGUINE AL RAGU DI COZZE

The Osteria's shuttered kitchen window looked out over the valley towards the sea. A three-generation-old stone sink with a copper and brass tap had been placed in front of the window. The glass panes were perpetually obscured with stains of splashed pasta water and so during the day were usually open. It was there Alessandra worked on her food preparation, looking out over the landscape which produced the ingredients.

Cecily had arrived early for their meeting, so had taken over scrubbing mussel shells under running water while her friend ground a paste in the mortar and pestle.

"Not a bad view from your office window," Cecily observed. "What are we cooking?"

"La cucina di strettissimo magro (lean recipes). This dish was created many years ago by a Ligurian priest to make on 'sacrifice' days when the congregation were forbidden to eat meat. The pasta sauce I'm cooking is the result that one might expect from an Italian coastal community. It includes mussels, anchovies, pine nuts, garlic and a lot of olive oil, with a little parsley to finish. It is perhaps a sign of changing times that this is a rare dish these days. Only a few small places are keeping old Ligurian recipes like this alive, and here at the Osteria we are one of them."

"Roman will be so cross when I tell him about this dish, Alessandra. It is exactly the type of thing he loves."

"Good," she replied, joking. "Maybe that will persuade him to attend future meetings."

Ben had found some equally unusual rosé wine made with the Rossese grape in Piedmont which he was keen for everyone to try. Rosé wine was something he was eager to experiment with. Italian rosé is often quite different from the light pink wines of the south of France. It is usually darker, stronger and drier. Until recently, little had been sold in Italy and even less exported, although that was changing as they acquired a better reputation. Ben thought that if he could create a Ligurian rosé with more of the Cote de Provence characteristics, he might find new markets for it. Regardless, he was enjoying the research.

A week earlier, when Ben and Alessandra had eaten spada (swordfish) for lunch in San Lorenso Mare, she had noted that they had used a liberal sprinkling of small capers in the sauce, which seemed to work well, adding some sharpness to the otherwise simple fillet. That morning, her fisherman friend had offered her freshly caught albacore tuna so she decided to try her own version, including a splash of Ben's rosé wine for extra aroma. Ben declared it to be sublime and no one present disagreed.

Alain congratulated Alessandra on choosing one of the more sustainable fish for her dish, pointing out that swordfish had been overfished in the Mediterranean in recent years. However, he also acknowledged that the Italians were not the worst culprits in this depletion of Mediterranean fish stocks. He explained that their smaller boats generally used traditional nets, keeping and selling almost everything caught. Virtually nothing was thrown overboard and wasted. These methods were far less damaging than the larger, industrial-scale trawlers favoured by other nations.

The young scientist from Monaco said, "You have a real opportunity to create something unique here. You have an unspoilt area that has changed little in hundreds of years. Traditional farming practices have been gentle on the land. That is why I was delighted when I was asked to join this group. Andrea Cassini has a genuine will to try new and better ways of doing things. His willingness to take risks to get quick results does not sit too comfortably with my scientific training, but I also understand the need for him to see measurable progress."

Alain now turned to Cecily, saying that she must be aware of the use of harvested seaweed and algae in cosmetics. Mid-way through a mouthful of tuna, the Englishwomen was caught off-guard and could only nod her agreement. Alain explained that, although what had become known as ocean farming had been taking place for hundreds of years, it had always been an informal industry. Coastal farmers desperate for nitrates to reinvigorate their land had always used seaweed washed up on the shore to bring life back to the soil.

"It seems to me, that although a landlocked nation, Seborga needs to look to the nearby ocean for means of sustainably strengthening the make-up of the soil."

Ben could immediately see this suggestion's logic, but any obvious method of putting this into practice eluded him and almost everyone else around the table. However, Cecily seemed to enjoy a light-bulb moment and quickly washed her food down with a gulp of wine.

"There are many thousands of boats moored along the Côte d'Azur, all of which need de-fouling every few years. My own boat was done last year and what looked like a ton of algae was scraped off the hull. This was just washed back into the sea."

Ben interjected, "So your yacht is cruising around the ocean unwittingly harvesting algae as it goes?"

"Mine and every other yacht. If you don't clean your hull below the waterline regularly, the drag that it causes gradually reduces your speed under sail and increases fuel consumption under power. Surely that algae could be a source of fertiliser? It's free, and boat owners want rid of it."

The marine scientist had already spotted the flaw in this theory. He explained that it had been the general practice for many years to paint boat hulls with antifouling paint below the waterline. This coating often contained potent chemicals to discourage the algae from attaching to the hull in the first instance. This antifouling paint had previously been identified as a marine hazard. Power-washing off the algae would inevitably take with it some of these chemicals, thereby rendering the algae tainted.

He acknowledged the merit of the idea in principle, but suggested that they discount it, for now at least adding, "Once again, man's attempts to resist the forces of nature has solved a human problem, only to create an environmental one."

Over dolce, the conversation turned from future initiatives to what had already been achieved. Alain complimented Ben and Alessandra on their achievements so far.

"In just a few years you have almost transformed this village from a failing community to a thriving one, with lots of projects as-yet unrealised. Farming oranges is now a sustainable business, with a spin-off benefit of raised brand awareness for the remaining olive growers. Winegrowing has been reinstated, and the resulting products are showing promise. The Slow Food outreach cookery school and restaurant are up and running. By the time the hotel and spa are finished, this community will be unrecognisable from what it was."

"Not to mention now being the home, albeit temporarily, to the Holy Grail," added Ben, putting aside his usual British understatement and natural modesty for a brief spell.

As much as Alessandra relished a moment of self-congratulation, she was keen to focus on the remaining challenges. No one was more aware than she how the fickle hand of fate could suddenly throw plans out of the window. While Andrea was in power and very much fighting their corner, she was determined to capitalise on this situation. She raised a glass and offered a toast, "Like our English St. George, we Templars can slay these environmental dragons with courage and cunning."

Those around the table raised their glasses while a chorus of "San Giogio," was mixed with, "Saint George," responding to Alessandra's toast.

Gianni delivering his zucchini flowers to local restaurants on his trusty scooter.

Drawing by Linda McCluskey

13. SCIUMETTE

A wooden box overflowing with canary-yellow flowers balanced on the footrest. With nowhere to rest them, Gianni's long legs hung over each side of his Vespa, his trainers skimming the stones of the piazza on his way to the Osteria.

"Fiori di zucha?" Ben asked as he disembarked, balancing the box on one arm, his helmet dangling by its strap from the other. The obligatory headgear was permanently dangling from his arm and never seen on his head-as if the mere act of having it about his person fulfilled the letter of the law.

"Si, Professore. Your Italian is getting better," he complimented, adding, "but slowly."

"So, I need to, veloce?" the Englishman suggested.

"Più veloce," Gianni corrected.

The pair had been going through this ritual most mornings for nearly five years and Ben's Italian was still woefully inadequate for a permanent resident. One of the problems was that although he spoke English, Gianni only supplied vegetables. Their short conversations were therefore limited to what grew in these hills, the seasons, the weather, and the elderly Vespa that served as his delivery vehicle. The meat supplier and fishmonger spoke little English, so his guesses at the names for the contents of their deliveries usually went uncorrected. Despite this, Ben had acquired invaluable restaurant Italian, and could now at least translate almost any menu with reasonable accuracy.

Only ten days after their initial discussions with Richard, a director of the London Club considering creating the Albergo Diffuso, an agreement was in place. Vincenzo could now begin work on converting the shop, which Selene had owned briefly, into the reception. This was an unfeasibly fast process by Italian standards but the project was already fully funded, and the decision-making team had been small. The Club was used to rapid decision-making, were good at delegating, and were willing to rely on email to record any initial agreements. However, they were yet to encounter official Italian bureaucracy where success is measured by the volume of paperwork generated and progress is more often counted in months, not days.

Ben had allowed all three men to cease their restoration of the vineyard terrace walls. They had made much progress but it was not urgent work, and Ben was running low on resources to pay them, having unexpectedly had to finance his son's debts. The Club was paying the men a far better rate than he could afford, and the more Tom earned, the sooner he could repay everyone who had loaned him cash. The young Englishman was now fit again, had calloused hands, and had acquired some basic construction and masonry skills.

The conversion of the Crazy Dutchman's former antique store into a reception for the deconstructed hotel concept was not a complicated job. They would first have to remove all the contents into a shipping container delivered to a nearby carpark as temporary storage. It was then merely a case of supporting the floor above before demolishing all the internal walls and removing the stone residue. It was physical, dusty, but not incredibly skilled work which Tom was now equipped for. The work required little more than a sledgehammer, a shovel, a wheelbarrow and some muscle.

Vincenzo knew that these works required a building inspector's consent but were also aware of the consequences of asking for permission in terms of the timescale. The Club had offered a twenty percent success bonus, based on each phase meeting its projected deadline. It was a sizeable incentive.

Vincenzo had explained to Ben, who had in turn told London, how he suggested they proceed.

Vincenzo had learned from the San Remo architect that the Club wanted all work done to the highest standards and using best industry practices. This meant they would build everything to at least meet, and more often than not exceed, the minimum building regulations. If they stuck rigidly to the rules and took photographs of all critical work in progress, they knew that they could not fail to obtain retrospective approval, even if that meant it would ruffle a few feathers among officials later.

This way of working meant that the construction and the application could proceed in parallel. However, it was a strategy bound to create friction with the bureaucrats whose jobs it was to administer the process. Alessandra and Richard had agreed that they would manage the human factor using tried and tested methods. Ben would previously have had all kinds of ethical concerns about the plan, but after all he had witnessed in recent years he had learned to keep those concerns to himself and be 'more Italian' in his approach. He justified his stance in knowing that no corners would be cut in construction, and no one bribed, at least not with cash.

The Club was making informal invites to those officials involved to attend an official ribbon cutting of the first phase in just six months' time by non-other than the prime minister, who was also their ultimate boss. Between now and then, Alessandra would host a monthly update meeting at the Osteria which would take place prior to a fine lunch. The inspectors could still produce all the paperwork that they wanted for their superiors, albeit retrospectively. They would just be doing so after a good working lunch every month. Ben had to admit this plan had managed to combine both carrot and stick neatly.

Although he had yet to admit it to anyone, Tom was enjoying the construction work. He found it emptied his mind of any worries he might have, and that being physically fit again felt empowering. His fair skin had adjusted to the sun, and he could now work in shorts without a shirt and not get sunburned. He was getting along well with his workmate, Marius, and even beginning to respect Vincenzo, if only for his physical strength and purposeful character. Alessandra had been exceedingly kind to him, bringing him free beers on an evening and making him packed lunches. She had even been dropping him at the beach on a Saturday morning so he could take a swim and chat with the locals while she went shopping for ingredients in Ventimiglia's famous food market.

Ventimiglia sits just on the Italian side of the border with France. The inevitable cross-border trade meant that the produce on offer blurred the respective cultures. Goods are available in Ventimiglia market that one would be unlikely to find elsewhere in Italy. Also, the disparity in wealth and taxation rates between the French Riviera and the Italian meant that things were often cheaper there. More than half of the customers at the food market were French people looking for bargains. It was a bustling, vibrant cornucopia of flowers, food and wine. Alessandra loved it.

Tom's evening meal arrangement's informality meant that he often ended up chatting to his father during dinner at the Osteria, or over an aperitivo afterwards, without either of them explicitly arranging to meet there. By learning to avoid talking about his mother, his debts and his future career prospects, they had even managed to get through several evenings without disagreeing over something. Both men were finding the process restorative, and Alessandra was feeling pleased with herself for her role in the peace process.

It was after one such enjoyable dinner which went on too late for his father, who had already gone home, that an attractive young woman entered the Osteria and ordered a drink. Tom enjoyed the last scrapings of what Alessandra had told him was Sciumette, or 'floating islands' dessert, another old Ligurian recipe.

"The islands are made from meringue floating in a sea of custard, flavoured with pistachios," she explained.

When Alessandra took the young woman's order, she spoke in English, which promoted Tom to say, "Hi." Although it turned out that she was Italian, the girl spoke excellent English and chatted for a while. She said that she was a journalist drafting a story on bringing the Holy Grail to Seborga.

Tom's response to hearing the subject of her work was to ask, "Do people really believe all those stories about the Holy Grail? It sounds like a fairy story to me. Yet another myth perpetuated by the Church to keep people putting money in the donation box, in my opinion."

The pretty reporter had the most enormous dark eyes that Tom could ever recall seeing, and she kept them engaged with his own continuously during their conversation. So enamoured was he that he did not notice that, after his dismissive opening, she asked very few questions about the Grail. However, she did want to know a great deal about all the restoration and building projects that were going on. She wanted to know who was involved and how that came about. Tom told her what he knew, which was extraordinarily little. Then, to appear more knowledgeable and seem more important, he embellished the facts with things he'd assumed or made up. The more he talked, the longer she stayed.

When Tom had run out of things to say about Seborga, he turned his attentions to what he saw as far more important matters and asked the girl to come back to his place for a digestivo. The flirtatious reporter suddenly transformed herself into a 'good Catholic Italian girl,' feigning modesty. She did leave him her business card and asked him to message her if he remembered anything more about the Seborga projects. Before she had left the Osteria, Tom was already trying to think of an excuse to call her.

"She was pretty," Alessandra offered when she came to clear the table. "A new friend?"

"I would like to think she could be. She's a reporter here to write about the Grail," Tom explained.

Alessandra pulled a face at hearing she was a reporter, as they were not her favourite group of people. That said, through Ben, she had learned that they could be manipulated, always provided that you were aware of the rules of engagement. In such matters they both now deferred to Selene, who had become adept at acting as both poacher and gamekeeper, as Ben would say.

Alessandra looked puzzled. "The Grail has been here for weeks now. The story has died down everywhere else. She is a bit behind the curve for a reporter."

Tom shrugged. "Who knows? Well, grazie and buona notte," he said, practising the little Italian he had learned on Alessandra.

As he left the Osteria, he spotted Marius and Cristiano entering the piazza from the other side. They were laughing and joking. He was then astonished to see that they were holding hands, although they dropped their grip as soon as they spotted Tom. The embarrassed Englishman looked away and walked on, not acknowledging that he had seen them.

Shocked, it had never occurred to him that Marius might also be gay. The Romanian fitted none of the stereotypes Tom had formed over the years. He was annoyed at his own naivety of having grown to like and trust his workmate, enjoying his company during and after work. He had no idea what he would now say to Marius when they next met.

14. SARDE A BECCAFICO

Unusually, Alessandra had a morning to herself. There was no preparation to do for the Osteria, as Cristiano was stepping in for her today. Ben had gone to meet Vincenzo at the vineyard where he wanted to show him some slight signs of blight on the vines furthest from the water supply. He was proposing they put in more irrigation to feed water from Lorenzo's Spring—as it had become known locally. Alessandra used the time to care for own neglected plants on her doorstep and veranda, as well as tidy the house in case Roman and Cecily came back later that afternoon.

Cecily had invited Ben and Alessandra out to lunch. Their hosts would pick them up, and they were told it was even less informal than the Osteria and so to dress casually. Roman drove up to Seborga in his old Mercedes Ponton, partly because it had been stuck in the garage for weeks and needed a run to charge the battery, but also because it had four doors and generous luggage space. They arrived to collect their friends from the Osteria at noon. From the time chosen, Ben had guessed that they weren't travelling far.

"Why the mystery tour? It can't be a new restaurant because I would have heard on the chef's grapevine by now," Alessandra quizzed.

Ben was correct about the distance; they had not travelled a kilometre out of the village when Roman steered the immaculate old car onto a dirt road and parked. Alessandra had also been correct, in that this was not a restaurant. It was a parcel of ground, flat for the first twenty metres or so, then dropping steeply away into the valley below.

Roman opened the boot of the Mercedes to reveal a picnic table and four folding chairs. He invited Ben to carry what he could manage, and he followed with the remainder. Cecily lifted out a cool bag and handed it to Alessandra before taking the large bamboo basket that remained. Ben had noticed with curiosity that a garden spade was also in the boot.

"A picnic in a bramble patch. How lovely. We can pick our own dolce," Alessandra said with a sardonic smile.

The two women had become the absolute best of friends, which was strange considering how little they'd had in common in their lives until recently. However, what they had shared was a focus on their respective careers that had made making and keeping friends difficult. What had finally broken the career cycle for both was finding new love at a time in their lives when they were starting to question what was important to them. It was probably no coincidence that this opening up to a new partner also resulted in their finding new friendships.

Both Cecily and Alessandra had worked extremely hard but had also enjoyed success early in their twenties before either woman had much self-confidence or experience. Some level of fame and money had brought with it people whose motives were not always what they seemed. Both had fallen foul of this. These bruising encounters had caused them to retreat from the limelight and busy themselves with work, which, ironically, brought even further success.

Today was to mark a significant milestone in Cecily's journey. After ten itinerant years, she had finally put down roots with her man in a new country, as a neighbour to her new friends. With the table laid and glasses at the ready, Roman removed the champagne bottle from the cooler and expertly poured four glasses.

In his wonderful English with a Sicilian accent, Roman proposed, "A toast to our first home, my soon-to-be wife and our good friends." To which Cecily quickly added, "And our new princess."

It was all too much for Alessandra to take in. She burst into tears and hugged her friend, seeking acknowledgement from her own lips, "You're getting married?"

"We are," Cecily confirmed. "And building a house right here where we are standing. Roman, get the spade. We have work to do."

Ben had shaken Roman's hand, but the Italian had decided an embrace was more appropriate. The Englishman's stiff upper lip was quivering a little and he too was a bit teary, but he hoped no one had noticed.

"I'll get the spade," Ben offered, welcoming the diversion. "You top up the champagne."

Roman dug the spade into the ground and placed Cecily's hand on the handle under his own. They lifted a pile of earth and then passed the spade to Ben and Alessandra to do the same. With a permanent marker, Roman wrote his own, and Cecily's, names, along with the date on the champagne cork. Cecily took a small tin from her bag and placed the cork in the container along with a little soil from each spade full.

"Our little time capsule which we will bury under the house. Right; let's eat. We have a wedding to plan."

"And a house to plan," Ben added.

"It's all planned," Roman announced. "Cecily and the architect that you introduced us to have been working on it for weeks. After lunch, I will show you the drawings, and my soon-to-be wife has a virtualisation on her iPad."

Roman rolled out the paper plan and then turned it so that it aligned with the house's actual position in the landscape. There were two main structures to be built in an arc following the contour of the land. One would sit above and behind the other, mirroring the terraces into which they would sit. On the lowest level, a wide but narrow pool followed the same curve. In the front elevation drawing the stonework was drawn to match that of terraces on either side, as well as above and below it.

"From just metres below the whole structure will be almost invisible. Looking up from Bordighera no one would know it was here," Roman said with some satisfaction.

Ben and Alessandra stood imagining themselves looking out from the terrace above the pool. The view was down the valley, slightly east of the village and out over what was known as locally Fisherman's Beach. It derived this name from being immediately beside the small harbour of Bordighera. This made the aspect of the house south-east, meaning they would enjoy a sunrise over the coast and have sun most of the day until the early evening when it would dip behind Seborga.

"That evening sun bakes the house in the summer, and the residual heat makes for uncomfortable nights," Alessandra pointed out, trying to be helpful.

Cecily looked slightly smug and said, "That will not be so much of an issue because this will be a Passivhaus, where the temperature inside is carefully controlled with extremely high standards of insulation and clever climate control technology. The triple glazing has a coating to reflect the heat and will also be shielded by programable vertical louvre shutters."

"Sounds expensive," Ben commented, but then realised that this was unlikely to be an issue for Cecily.

"The structure is being built in a Czechoslovakia factory, so not as expensive as you might imagine," Roman countered, not wishing to seem extravagant. He explained that it would be made of engineered timber, with specially laminated sections to create the curves. He also acknowledged that the expensive parts were the windows, doors, heating, and cooling systems, which cost more than the structure itself. "The windows alone cost most than the average house in Sicily."

"What did I work eighty hours a week for and rack up tens of thousands of airmiles if we can't spend our money on some comfort and enjoyment in our retirement?" Cecily admonished her partner. "Anyway, enough of houses. It's lunchtime. Take those plans off the table."

Cecily's onboard chef had prepared the picnic which she was now unpacking from the basket. There were Sicilian arrancinette mignon–small rice balls filled with prosciutto and mozzarella. Roman's favourite dish from Palermo followed this; sarde a beccafico–rolled sardine fillets stuffed with breadcrumbs, raisins, pine nuts and anchovy.

After two southern Italian classic dishes, the pudding was, like their hosts, an English/Italian affair: summer pudding made with Valpolicella wine – strawberries, raspberries and blackberries cooked in vanilla flavoured wine and placed in a stale bread-lined bowl until the juices turned the casing red. Alessandra picked four juicy brambles from the nearest bush and some nearby wild mint, placing this garnish on each portion.

"It's just perfect," Cecily announced. "I could not be happier." Just then, her phone rang.

"Don't you dare answer," said Roman, looking suddenly cross.

"It's Selene. I'd better answer."

Cecily's smile instantly evaporated. "She's been trying to get hold of you two," Cecily said, looking glumly at Ben.

Ben explained that they had both purposely left their phones at home so they could enjoy an uninterrupted lunch. Cecily handed the phone to Ben, who listened, nodded, shook his head, and finally closed his eyes as though he had a headache.

"I'll take a look and call you back," was all he said before turning to his wife and announcing, "It's out there on the Internet. Andrea Cassini is in a relationship with the daughter of the recipient of millions of euros of government money. In another report, Selene is also further implicated as the recipient of a free house from a developer with interests in Seborga. She believes that both their careers are about to fall off a cliff."

15. BASTONICI DI POLENTA

The city of Rome sat baking in the Tiber basin, smouldering in a heat wave. The old, pale cream stones of the ancient buildings retained the warmth of the sun, releasing it again at night so there was no respite from the cloying heat. With few of the covered walkways of Turin or Milan, most Romans went about their business in the city in the full rays of the sun. Still, Italians dressed like it was spring. The care they invested in their appearance suggested they were heading for a first date, or the most important interview of their careers. Even the traffic officers all looked like poster models for a police recruitment campaign.

Amara sat in her air-conditioned office in the city centre, savouring the consequences of her actions and anticipating future outcomes with glee. She calculated that she had earned an indulgent treat and so had picked up some Bastonici di Polenta (polenta sticks) dipped in Fontina cheese from the deli near her office. Munching on these delicious snacks, she watched the media acting like sharks in a feeding frenzy, snapping at any snippet of information relating to the PM, Selene or Seborga. The wily Minister for Culture had several such tasty morsels ready to toss into the pool whenever the media interest looked like it was waning. For now, Amara was happy to let them chew on this feast of intrigue.

The journalist she had tipped-off about the relationship enjoyed her scoop, her newspaper publishing, and creating a Twitterstorm amongst Andrea Cassini's supporters and detractors. Amara had briefed her allies to re-tweet and share the stories. She had supplied the journalist with the first photograph of them together at the yacht launch. The second snap of the couple taken later the same evening was just a lucky break. It had persuaded Amara it was time to go public with her suspicions.

The second photograph had been taken by a friend of one of their Tricolore Party junior colleagues at a birthday celebration. The young researcher had attended several events during the last year with the PM, at which the English journalist was also present. Selene's pale skin, blonde hair and English clothing style made her quite noticeable. She spotted the Englishwoman in a friend's Instagram post, and after closer examination of the photograph, she also thought that she recognised her boss. Initially, she had not considered the frequent attendance of this foreign journalist particularly significant. She knew the PM to be single, and that Selene was in Genoa that day for the boat launch. Why should they not be having dinner, she had thought?

The next morning, when chatting to Amara at the coffee shop, she mentioned the photo her friend had taken in the restaurant. She knew that Andrea and Amara had worked together for a long time and, from the way she looked at him, suspected that Amara held a candle for the prime minister. Her superior asked to see the image, but then contrived disinterest and told her colleague that she did not believe it to be their boss.

"However, it does look a bit like him," she added as an afterthought. "Please forward the photo to me and I will tease Andrea about it later. Just between us though," she had added, holding one finger to her lips. Later, to distance herself from its public release, Amara would claim that she had shared it with other colleagues in her office. "And from there, God knows where it got sent," she would later say.

Even the media at the centre and right of the political spectrum struggled to see how to put a positive spin on the breaking news. It only took a few minutes of cursory research on Google to tie Selene to her father and him to the substantial Seborga cash grants. From there, the money trail led back to

Andrea. At best, it was a grave error of judgement for a PM to expose himself to such obvious accusations of appearing to be handing out personal favours. If Andrea eventually acknowledged the relationship with the English woman, he was surely handing his opposition a stick to beat him with. Their reactions would be predictable, and Andrea's fate would be sealed.

For many in the opposition, as well as some in his Tricolore party, Andrea was just too young, too radical, and far too handsome for his own good. For the media, he had also been annoyingly squeaky clean up until now, with no apparent skeletons in his closet and so little of substance to write about. Cassini's only apparently newsworthy aspect seemed to be his left-leaning policies, them being somewhat at odds with the leader of a traditionally right-wing party.

Andrea Cassini simply did not generate the kind of juicy gossip that provided journalists with salacious copy to write and sell newspapers. Most political reporters would rather have seen the return on a Mastroianni-type character, who created a new scandal almost weekly. For all the reasons that his detractors disliked him, the public loved Andrea Cassini. No prime minister in living memory had garnered such high approval ratings and been so well respected.

He had spoken to Selene only very briefly on the telephone since the news broke. She had been in tears for most of the short call and he was due into an urgent meeting with his press secretary. He was being bombarded with phone calls and messages, essentially asking the same question: was it true?

They both knew that it would not take much investigation to place Selene in the same place as the PM on at least a dozen occasions over the past year. A little further digging would probably find a member of staff at a hotel or restaurant that the couple had visited who would tell all to the press for a moment of fame. Denying the relationship now would only make

Andrea's position untenable when the truth finally came out. And it would. Of that, they were both quite sure.

The press secretary's meeting did not take long, mainly because the civil servant did not have a viable proposal to offer his boss. The best he could suggest was to say that his personal life was his own business, that he was a single man and had nothing to hide as far as Seborga was concerned. Even as he said it, the press secretary knew that he would be crucified in the evening news and tomorrow's daily papers if they went with this. After a few minutes, the PM instructed that a news conference be called at 6 pm that evening, at which he would speak live to the Italian public.

"That's just three hours from now," his press advisor pointed out. "That is not enough time to draft a statement, get it agreed by the party or for you to learn it."

"I don't need a statement, and I certainly don't want to speak to anyone from the party. Just call the briefing. I will adlib. The truth is clear. It's only lies that are difficult to remember."

The press secretary looked ashen at hearing these instructions, now certain that this would be his, and his boss's, last day in their jobs, with no lucrative PR job in the private sector to follow for him. Henceforth, he would be known as the press secretary who oversaw the downfall and public disgrace of two prime ministers in a single year. Quite a record, even in Italy.

Amara could not hide her joy at hearing the news about the press conference. She was convinced Andrea was going to offer his resignation. She had even started drafting her own press statement distancing herself from the prime minister, his policies, and his actions. The scheming minister had already pulled strings to have the junior researcher who gave her the photograph of Selene with Andrea promoted to her own Department of Culture – a promotion which came with a sizable salary uplift. This should ensure her loyalty and silence, Amara calculated. In her new role, the young girl's first job was to fact-check the press release she had prepared and get it ready to email out to the list of favoured journalists.

However, the press briefing had somewhat wrong-footed Amara, as she was expecting official denials to drag on for days, or even weeks. She had heard about the imminent press conference from her journalist friend, rather than unusual internal government channels. Slightly panicked that events were running ahead of her; Amara instructed her newly appointed assistant to email her the edited press release and make another Instagram post at 5:50 pm. She wanted to attend the briefing in person and witness the PM's annihilation up close. Moments before the news briefing was due to start, a second post appeared on Twitter saying Selene's brother had been awarded lucrative construction contracts in Seborga, without going through any tendering process. Amara and the other journalists had seen it, but the PM and press secretary were too busy preparing to field the questions they knew would soon be raining down on them from the gathered media. They had been told that the PM would make a statement. After this, a microphone would be passed around so that questions were dealt with one at a time. No time limit had been placed on the briefing and so they could all wait their turns without missing out.

As the hour approached, every available press badge had been allocated according to the traditional media pecking order of their respective audiences' size. The room was packed with faces familiar to the prime minister, and all were smiling, waving and nodding to him as he entered. They were all hoping that he would favour them by singling them out to ask their question. Andrea knew that any one of them would bury him with the power of their pen given the slightest chance.

With his head slightly bowed, he took a deep breath and began somberly, "I have made a big mistake," Raising his head so that he faced directly into the lenses of the cameras, he went on, "I failed to trust you, the Italian voters, to judge me solely by my actions and not listen to gossip and hearsay on the Internet. However, you should know that I had committed myself to support Seborga before I fell in love with the English journalist Selene Morton, and I will tell you why. Seborga represents what's left of the Italy we all love, but which most of us have lost. I saw this tiny rural principality as the antitheses of Milan's pollution, the traffic jams of Turin, the fast food of Rome, the pickpockets of Florence and unemptied bins in Naples. It's the Italy we all remember from our childhood and that tourists come to experience. The air is clean, the streets are safe, people look after their neighbours and the food is both seasonal and local. There are still hundreds of places like Seborga all over Italy, but we are losing them fast. They're being killed off by globalisation, where price and profit are valued more than quality and sustainability."

Andrea paused to take a drink of water. He could see from the expressions on the faces of the journalists that whilst they were eager to get to what they saw as the dirt that had been thrown at him, they were not expecting this line of defence. They were also aware that the PM was not addressing his speech at them, but rather directly at the viewers online and on television.

"Seborga is a microcosm of all that used to be right, but which is now going very wrong with Italy, and the rest of the world. Here was a community that was still clinging to much of what was good. They have resisted change and so far, have succeeded. I saw an opportunity to not only preserve what remained, but to see if we could build a new type of more sustainable community. One that is fit for the twenty-first century. Those initiatives I have put in place in Seborga which prove successful can be rolled out in other small communities, as part of a rejuvenated Italian way of life."

Pausing again for a drink of water, Andrea took stock of his audience's mood, and thought that once again they looked more intrigued by his story than they were frustrated at his avoidance of the reason that they thought they were here.

"In an effort to turn the tide towards a carbon-neutral society we have given Seborga a unique tax system, to incentive the private sector to invest, experiment and innovate. Using innovative technologies and techniques, we intend to reinvigorate farming and create organic produce. Italy has eight thousand kilometres of coastline but dwindling fish stocks. Seaweed could be used to produce fertiliser, fuel and food. We can turn our fishermen into seaweed farmers and allow our fish stocks to recover. Two different private companies will be running trials of solar-powered car re-charging in Seborga for a fleet of pooled vehicles. Tax-free shopping for produce with plastic-free packaging is being trialled, which will save the authorities the increasing costs of collecting and disposing of waste."

The relatively inexperienced politician realised that he was beginning to find a voice that was resonating with a younger audience, such as most of the journalists in the room, but knew he also needed to eventually address the question of a potential conflict of interest.

"Most of the money being already invested in Seborga came from the EU, more from the private sector, and very little from the Italian taxpayer. We have spreadsheets to hand out containing all the figures. Any public funds have been channelled through the Slow Food Movement, a registered charity, independent of myself and the government. Not a single euro of that money was paid to, or through, the Morton family or Princess Alessandra. What is more, when I obtained the latest figures, I was astonished to learn that the man who devised the plans, raised the money and is putting them into action has not, so far, been paid a Euro in salary. Ben Morton, Selene's father, has so far worked for nothing to help his community."

There was a murmuring, apparently of disbelief at this revelation, but as the press were being promised the detailed accounts, they held off baying for blood.

"If you'll excuse the pun, the jewel in the crown of Seborga will be the Albergo Diffuso luxury accommodation, which will see many ancient Rustica houses restored without a euro of public funding. The only obstacle to this project getting underway was the lack of a commercial building large enough to house the hotel rooms' reception and services. Selene was approached and agreed to exchange her one hundred and fifty square metre property in the village for a much smaller, but already restored, cottage outside the village. That exchange is recorded in public records any of you can check with a like-for-like valuation. No money changed hands and Selene made no financial gain. She was merely facilitating one of the key projects."

More murmuring and headshaking suggested that the press would indeed be checking this fact, but they also sensed that this front page story was evaporating before their eyes.

"However, returning to my big mistake, what I now recognise I should have done is to have told you about Selene as soon as we got together. Instead, and also because of a potential conflict of interest with her job as a journalist, like yourselves, I decided not to go public with our relationship. However, because of the exposure of our private lives on the Internet today, she has now lost the job she loved. But for me, that is good news because it removes that obstacle to our being together permanently. Although there is so much that I want to do for Italy, I have decided today that if the price I must pay to have the woman I love, is my job, then I will give that up."

The until-now quiet audience now began shouting, "You are resigning for this woman, Prime Minister?"

Andrea shook head in a deliberately exaggerated way, "I am saying that if the Italian voters do not accept that I have acted honestly, and I am forced to choose between this job and the woman I love, I will step down for her. Furthermore, as I have been accused and tried on social media, the public can also use that method to tell me what their verdict is. Unless there is an overwhelming expression of public confidence on social media by noon tomorrow, I will stand aside as prime minister."

"What about the big contract awarded to Selene Morton's brother's construction company?" shouted one TV journalist. The prime minister's press secretary stepped forward to show him the Twitter post containing this latest accusation.

Smiling at what he saw as the sheer ridiculousness of this apparent revelation, Andrea responded, "That story had no basis in fact. Selene's brother is a young man employed by a private company as a builder's labourer, at fifteen euros an hour. He does not have a construction company. Last time I saw him he had a hammer, a shovel and a wheelbarrow, plus lots of sweat on his brow. Go to Seborga and check for yourselves. That is a made-up story."

Amara was trying to make herself small and inconspicuous at the back of the room. For the first time, she was aware that Andrea and others would be starting to wonder who was behind this deliberate campaign of misinformation. If it were ever to be linked back to her, it would be the end of her career in politics and any hope of becoming Italy's first female prime minister.

As she was moving discretely towards the door, one of the members of the press spotted the Minister for Culture standing behind them in the crowd. A microphone was thrust at her, "Minister, the email that I have just this minute received suggests that you are not backing the PM's support for Seborga. It says that you opposed moving the Sacro Cantina there and suggested that EU funds could have been better spent on other projects. Can we take it that you believe the PM should now resign over his alleged deception?"

A look of horror followed the realisation that her own press release had now been sent to the media by her new assistant.

16. GENOESE RAVIOLI

Walking down Clapham High Street, Selene was struck by the difference in the pace of life between the UK and Italy. Everyone here looked gripped by a sense of urgency to get where they were going. There was no strolling, meandering, or window shopping. Few people stopped to chat, or even exchanged a hello. More coffees were being sold in takeaway cups than were being leisurely sipped in cafes.

When she reached Clapham Common station, Selene asked herself, where had the newsstand gone? How long had it been missing, without her noticing? Every Italian station still had a kiosk selling newspapers, magazines and lottery tickets, but Londoners had gone almost entirely digital. Then she realised that she hardly ever bought a paper copy of the newspaper she wrote for. The newsstand in Clapham was now a pizza slice takeaway, which was perhaps an irony, Selene mused.

Selene had been summoned by text to her London office by her editor. She attended with a heavy heart, knowing full well what was coming. Selene even imagined the phrases her somewhat acerbic boss would use to end her short-lived career as a journalist on a national newspaper. It turned out that she had not entirely foreseen what the editor had in mind for her.

Looking genuinely pleased as she entered the glass-walled office, she was greeted with a broad smile, "Congratulations. You seem to have hit the jackpot and scored the real dolce vita."

Thrown by her surprise warm welcome, Selene forced a smile and thanked her but with less sincerity than she had intended. Outside she could see all her workmates-or were they already former colleagues - pausing to watch the show. She imagined what slaves facing the gladiators in the Colosseum much have felt like, waiting for the thumbs-up, or down.

"You'll have to work your notice, but you already knew that. But that's not too high a price to pay to start sharing a limo, and much else no doubt, with the most handsome politician since JFK. Lucky you."

Selene struggled to understand her boss's position on the revelation that she had been conducting a covert affair with the Italian Prime Minister. She was focussing on the loss of the job she had struggled for years to get. Unbeknownst to her, the seasoned journalist-turned-senior-manager saw it as a business opportunity.

"Selene, darling. You're not a bad writer, but let's face it, the world if full of wannabe Kate Adies and Katharine Grahams. I can replace you tomorrow with an even more eager, younger model and for probably 10k less salary per year. Serendipity has placed you in the right place twice–no, actually, now three times–in just five years, and we have both benefited hugely from that. However, this part of your life is over."

Waving Selene to a chair which she flopped into looking very confused, the editor opened the glass door and called for drinks to be brought in.

"The news business that I have known all my life, and that you thought you were joining, is now over. We're the last dinosaurs left on planet 'News'. Our chairman has openly admitted that this company will never buy another newspaper printing press. In other words, when the current one stops printing in however many years from now, that will be the end of ink on paper news. The business of news has changed. You are fortunate to be getting out now, ahead of the final demise. Too few people today value the truth enough to pay for it. They have settled for sensationalism that they can have for free. Or, more accurately, for what they believe to be free. In fact, they are paying by sacrificing their privacy."

Selene instinctively wanted to argue the moral case for quality news media to keep government, business and criminals under scrutiny. Still, deep down she knew her boss was right and that she was wasting her time.

"You and I need to have our last hurrah and think to our futures. Myself, to retirement at my cottage on the Northumberland coast, and you to your hunky politician in Rome. But before we do that, we have one last scoop to negotiate, and the serialisation of your book to agree upon."

"Book. What book?" asked an astonished Selene. A tray containing prosecco and two glasses arrived and the editor held her finger to lips until the bearer had placed it on her desk and closed the door.

"The book, or maybe books, you will start writing about the crazy goings-on in Seborga. I can visualise the Netflix series now–it will be like a mash-up of EastEnders, The Crown and Inspector Montalbano. Even I'd watch it and I hate TV," added the editor, laughing at her own joke.

The vision of a new life and writing career that was being painted for her did not sound altogether unappealing, and Selene wondered why she had not thought of it herself.

"I've written a number on this piece of paper that I think I can get you from this newspaper for the final exclusive story, plus the rights to serialise the book. If it is acceptable to you, I will go upstairs and see the CEO now. I should be able to get you a verbal agreement right there and then. Then you can get back to your desk and start writing your last ever story for this newspaper. If I can get the nod from 'God' upstairs, I'll get the lawyers to draw up the paperwork. You can sign it later, and we open another bottle of this fizz and all go home happy."

Selene opened the folded paper, nodded without hesitation and then finished her drink in absolute shock while the editor left the room. She sat in a something of a trance until a knock on the glass partition stirred her from her thoughts. A colleague was waving her out of the office and pointing to her computer screen, around which several other reporters were already gathered. Showing was the live TV feed from Rome, where her lover, Andrea, was holding his briefing.

She joined them as all her colleagues watched TV. Soon tears began to roll down Selene's cheeks as the man who she loved publicly offered to give up everything for her. Even some of her hard-nosed reporter colleagues were looking teary as they digested the significance of the commitment they were witnessing. It would later transpire that similar scenes were being played out in front of TV screens in kitchens, cafes, bars and workplaces all over Italy. Andrea's speech struck a nerve with everyone who'd ever been in love.

Even Italian men were moved by Andrea's evident passion for the English reporter. Some news agency had found a year-old photo of Selene in their archives, which was widely used to accompany the stories now circulating. It had been taken on the night that Andrea had first met Selene in Seborga, when she had been wearing the clinging, backless dress that she borrowed from a designer in Monaco. This image alone convinced most Italian males that their prime minister had made the right decision.

The significance of Andrea's impromptu speech was also being analysed with great interest for reasons other than the revelations about his personal life. This was the first time they had heard concrete plans to address some of the environmental concerns he had previously only alluded to. Many younger voters had become disillusioned by politicians paying little more than lip-service to growing worries about climate change, pollution, and the effects of globalisation. Without planning to, his words had galvanised all kinds of groups from across the political spectrum into a concerted and very vocal force.

These were also the same young, tech-savvy groups who almost exclusively used social media to air their grievances and champion their causes. Andrea now became one such cause-and they took to Twitter, Instagram and other online media to support him. By morning it would be clear that Andrea would not only be keeping his job, but that he had also probably garnered even more support for his policies and his party from the opposition. He would have the mandate to act boldly and even more decisively.

In Seborga, with all the orange blossom now in bloom, and the hired-in bees busy fertilising them, Vincenzo had been keeping an eye on the weather forecast. While political storm clouds had been gathering in Rome, very real and potentially more dangerous ones were gathering over the French Alps. For the second time in recent months, the jet stream had slipped down towards northern Scotland, deflecting an Atlantic weather front in over the Bay of Biscay, ultimately heading for Italy. Unfortunately, this was the remains of a tropical storm that had already caused devastation on the east coast of America and still had plenty of pent-up rain looking for an outlet.

Ben and Alessandra watched Andrea on TV at the Osteria, along with Vincenzo who was waiting for his order of Genoese ravioli. The generously filled veal and pork mince parcels were one of his favourites. Of the three, only Vincenzo seemed impervious to the emotions of the moment. Alessandra had a growing concern that she could guess the source of some of some of the wilder accusations in the media but could not speak of this to anyone. Typically, Vincenzo avoided discussing the events on TV by completely changing the subject.

"I have been watching those builders from Ventimiglia who are working on the other projects in the village. On Fridays, they finish work early as you would expect, at around 3 pm. But instead of heading back down the road to the coast, they drive their truck inland towards Negi. About twenty minutes later, they drive back and then head for the coast. They are up to something," Vincenzo declared with absolute certainty. "First thing in the morning, Ben, I think you and I should go and take a look."

There was only one exit from the road to Negi within ten minutes of driving time, and it did not take Vincenzo long to find where the builder's truck had been going. Bright white chunks of plaster, shards of metal and plastic fragments indicated where they had stopped along the Passo del Bandito. The route had been carved into the hillside, leaving a steep side of the left and an unguarded drop to the right. Ben and Vincenzo left the Ape and looked over the edge of the road into the forest below.

"Bastardi," Ben exclaimed, leaving Vincenzo looking slightly shocked at his uncharacteristic bad language.

"As I suspected," Vincenzo said with resignation. An area of previously pristine forest about thirty metres wide and a truck's width was covered in an avalanche of paint cans, empty silicon tubes, packaging, offcuts of plastic pipe, insulation sheets and plasterboard. There was even an old PVC window frame complete with glass.

"They should be taking all this waste to the reclamation site at San Remo. But that is an hour round trip for them, and they have to pay by weight to leave it there."

Ben was lost for further words at this act of wanton irresponsibility but was also determined to shame those responsible. He took plenty of photographs on his mobile phone.

"On Monday, we will go and confront them with this evidence."

"Not so hasty, Ben. If they deny it, we have no real proof it was them. They will stop doing this, but we won't get this cleaned up. Wait until next Friday and I will come and catch them in the act."

Men playing scopa
at bar-restaurant Da U Triu in Sasso,
with aperitivo in the foreground.
Drawing by Linda McCluskey

17. PICAGGE VERDI

Tom managed to get through the days after his encounter with Cristiano and Marius in the piazza by avoiding working alongside him and not mentioning the event when they did meet. He was sure that it must have been evident to both Marius and Vincenzo that something was wrong. Although it had occupied his thoughts, Tom remained unsure about his feelings on the situation. He had thought he'd found a great friend in Marius but now had no idea what to say to him. He had even considered speaking to Alessandra about it. His stepmother had become something of a confidant: a maternal figure that he could talk to who he felt did not judge him. However, as she was also Cristiano's mother, Tom decided it was too complicated.

Alessandra was facing her own dilemma. She was almost sure that the information that had caused Selene to lose her job, and Andrea to almost give up his, had come from Tom's recent conversation with the attractive young journalist in her own restaurant. She knew that no harm would have been intended but still felt sure that he should come clean about his indiscretion to his father and sister. However, she also felt certain that he would be disinclined, having started to gain a little credibility in their eyes. She did not want to fall out with him by being the one to suggest a full confession that he was unlike to agree to.

Ben was already enjoying an aperitivo in the Osteria when Tom arrived for his dinner. By the time he took a seat at his father's table, Alessandra had set another cold beer down before him. As the days had turned into weeks, there had been a gradual thawing of relations between them. Most observers would describe the current relationship as normal for father and adult son. They still held widely differing views on many things but had learned to stay clear of these topics. Ben had also decided only to offer specific advice when specifically asked for it, which was virtually never. Conversations that revolved around food, beer, sport, cars and work gave them enough to talk about, and the latter normally dominated.

Tom was pleased with both the new practical skills he was learning from Vincenzo and the physical fitness that the work had brought him. He'd turned a couple of kilos of fat into muscle and, with his growing golden tan, was attracting some attention from the girls at the beach. He complained to his father about Vincenzo pushing him hard, but Ben could tell his grudging respect for the Italian was growing stronger with each day.

Ben had laughed, perhaps a bit too enthusiastically, at Tom's story of Vincenzo standing on the edge of a terrace, below which he had just rebuilt the retaining wall. Vincenzo knew Tom had not listened to his instructions about filling all the small gaps with stone wedges to make it solid. In his haste to keep up with Marius's work-rate, he had cut corners. With Vincenzo's weight on it, a one-metre section of the wall he had just spent two hours building collapsed into a heap of rocks with the merest pressure from his boot. He pointed to the bucket of smaller stone wedges and said, "Meno velocita, piu forza," (less speed, more strength). Tom had been furious, but also embarrassed at what he knew was his folly.

Alessandra appeared with two dishes of the night's main dish, which was picagge verdi (green noodles with sausage). It was the type of substantial pasta dish that Tom loved. The young man's mood brightened with his dinner's arrival and he enjoyed having some conversation to distract his thoughts from what he should say to Marius.

After placing the steaming bowls on the table, Alessandra warned them that she had baked a walnut cake with honey and ricotta for dessert and that they should, "Leave some appetite for dolce."

Ben had been watching clouds appearing over the mountains in the distance. This water-soaked mist poured like liquid over the ridge and down the slopes, beginning to cloak the valleys like a grey curtain. A breeze got up and started to ruffle the Seborgan flags on the houses around them. The first big spot of rain fell into the dog water bowl left outside the Osteria for customers' pets. It was a drop so large, and struck with such force, as to almost empty the bowl of its original contents. Slowly but surely other drops fell around it, bouncing off the stone slabs of the piazza. In less than a minute the sky had gone black and rain fell in sheets, soaking everything it touched in seconds.

Although they sat under the canopy, Ben and Tom were getting splashed by rain bouncing off planters and tables that were not undercover. They had to move their dishes to another table further inside where they could be dry. Every paved surface was now under a couple of centimetres of water. The gutters on the houses around were overflowing, adding to the deluge. The Alpini troops who had been operating patrols were running back to their temporary barracks on the other side of the piazza, apparently not wishing to spoil their immaculate uniforms or polished weapons.

"These storms do not usually last long," Ben said. "In ten or fifteen minutes, it will probably all be over."

Tom looked outside and sceptically at his father. "You think so?"

Twenty minutes later, the intensity of the rain had not diminished. If anything, it had got worse. Waves of wind drove the rain even harder down the valley. This was a storm of biblical proportions, Ben realised. He witnessed plants and their terracotta pots washed out of a side street by a torrent of fast-flowing water. These were the plants which most residents used to decorate their doorsteps, too heavy to be moved by any storm they had seen before. Then a waste bin came tumbling down, followed by an advertising banner that had been torn off the side of the road. Hearing the noise of the wind and rain, Alessandra came outside to see for herself.

"I've never seen water washing things down the streets like this before. I wonder if the Cookery School is Ok. Parts of the building still only had a temporary roof." She looked at her watch, "Renata could still be working in there, maybe Cristiano too."

Seeing that Alessandra was concerned, Tom volunteered to go and check on them. Tom's t-shirt was soaked through to his skin and sticking to his body within two steps outside. His blonde locks were washed into his eyes and he had to sweep his fringe back to see where he was going. As he made his way down the narrow streets towards the lower part of the village, the water flowing down was getting deeper and faster. It was like no storm he had ever experienced.

Turning into Piazza Monastero, he was shocked to see that the Cookery School, a few steps down from street level, now sat in what looked like a moat of water. The level was approaching half a metre up the new plate glass doors. On closer inspection, he saw that inside the water was even higher. Suddenly, Renata was at the door up past her waist in water. She had a look of terror on her face as she pulled at the handle to try and open it. Tom realised that with the water inside so much higher than that outside, the weight and pressure held the door firmly shut. He pushed at it with his shoulder but without causing any movement at all.

Looking around for something to break the door with, Tom saw a large terracotta plant pot. Waving to Renata to stand back, he threw the pot with all the force he could muster at the door. It shattered into pieces, making no impression on the plate glass. Then he remembered that he and the others had been working just around the corner on the reception for the Albergo

Diffuso. He ran the thirty metres as fast as he could, returning a minute later with his sledgehammer.

Renata was now at the door again, banging on it with both fists in desperation. The water had risen past her waist, and she was beginning to panic. Tom could just hear her calling out for help. He pointed to the hammer he was holding and waved her to stand well out of the way. Standing on the steps leading down to the door gave him a good swing at a point around the door handle. The blow struck where he had planned it to and the whole door shattered into a million pieces, allowing a tsunami of water to surge out into the piazza.

The water flowing out of the building joined with the rain still washing down from the streets all around. The swollen flow searched out the lowest-lying outlet to relieve its pressure. A set of steep stone steps, barely wide enough for one person, dropped some ten metres before turning through ninety degrees and exiting on the road below. It was no longer possible to see the steps as this was now a full-blown waterfall spewing tons of water and detritus onto the street far below, making the main access to the village impassable.

In her rush to get out of the building before the water levels equalised, Renata was knocked off her feet by the force of the flow. She was washed, floundering out of the doorway and banged her head on the stone steps, losing consciousness for a moment. Tom dropped the sledgehammer and scooped up the diminutive chef in his arms, wading across the piazza with her towards higher ground. By now people from nearby houses had realised something was going on and were coming out onto the streets. Placing Renata gently on the floor, her back resting against the wall, she quickly started to regain consciousness.

"Was anyone else in there with you?" Tom asked. "Where is Cristiano?" he urged.

Renata looked very dazed and scared but began to remember, saying, "All of a sudden water burst through the temporary wall between the kitchen and the dining room. It was even coming up under the floors. Cristiano was in the restaurant next door earlier, writing menus."

Neighbours were bringing towels and blankets to wrap the injured chef in. Tom went looking for Cristiano, trying to remember the building's layout from his only visit. The restaurant was in the old monastery's ruins. They had built around remaining stonework and extended it to create the Cookery School. It had a separate entrance with yet another plate glass door, on the same level Renata had been working at. It was also over a metre deep in water and furniture was floating on the surface. There were no lights inside, but Tom realised that the water might have blown all the fuses. There was no sign of any movement inside, but he decided it was better to be safe than sorry and take a look.

Then Tom remembered that he'd dropped the sledgehammer somewhere outside. He waded back to where he had picked up Renata and started reaching down to see if he could feel the hammer. He could just touch the ground without submerging his head and found the hammer on the third attempt. Water was still issuing from the building as though its strongest source was, mysteriously, somewhere inside the former monastery.

There were now several villagers standing in the streets leading down to the small piazza. One of them had sent their neighbour to the Osteria to fetch Ben and Alessandra. Seeing the commotion, the Alpini had finally stirred from the dry of their barracks to check on the Holy relic. With more confidence, Tom swung the three-kilo hammer at the second glass door. Once again it turned to glass beads in an instant and another wave of water swept out. After chairs, tablecloths, and other restaurant fittings rushed by into the street, the flow slowed slightly across the piazza.

Thankfully upright and bobbing along in the torrent which now flowed more steadily out of the building came an emerald, green glass bowl. Acting on some unknown instinct, Tom threw himself on it, as if it was a rugby ball exiting a scrum. Clutching the bowl to his chest but now off his feet, the water carried him away. Managing to free one hand, Tom turned himself onto his back. He struggled to keep his head above water while simultaneously holding onto the object. He managed to gain his bearings just in time to see that he was being swept across the piazza towards the steps. From there he knew there was a huge drop into the road far below.

His choices seemed clear: let go of the bowl and claw his way out of the main steam or be swept over a drop that would likely kill him. Instead, he chose an option which came to him in that instant. Using his spare arm, he managed to turn himself around in the flow so that he was feet first. As he reached the buildings between which the steps exited the piazza, he spread his legs wide and managed to get one foot on either side of the gap, stopping him almost dead. He took the shock and then the strain from the water flow behind on his now strong legs without too much trouble. However, he was now a human dam in the stream with pressure building on his shoulders and water pouring over his head into his eyes and ears. He had no plan for how to extract himself from there and the flow of water showed no sign of abating.

It seemed like minutes but was probably only a few seconds later when he felt something touch his waist, and heard a voice he vaguely recognised. "Are you wearing a good leather belt?"

"Yes," he managed to shout above the roar of water rushing around his ears.

Tom felt the hand grasp the belt and it became tighter around his waist. "I've got a good hold of you. When I say, I'm going to pull you towards me out of the main flow of water. Don't struggle or try to grab at anything, or I might lose you. Just stay limp. I have a rope around my waist; those behind me can use it to haul us both out."

The rescue took place precisely as the voice had said it would. Tom was dragged backwards, still clutching the green glass bowl tightly to his chest. When he was upright again, he saw that it was a sodden Marius who had stopped him from being washed over the edge. And who else but Vincenzo who had pulled them both back to safety using a rope. Ben came over, gently prised the Holy Grail from his grasp and handed it to Alessandra, who passed it to the Alpini. He hugged his son to his chest and said, "You were amazing. Just amazing. I'm so glad you are Ok."

Then Tom remembered he had not found Alessandra's son in the building and blurted out, "I looked, but there was no sign of Cristiano anywhere."

"He's fine, Tom. He'd left work to go home as soon as it started raining. Renata will also be OK; thanks to you, I hear."

Tom seemed to be in a kind of a trance. Everything had happened so fast, and all his reactions had been automatic. It was almost as though there was another force driving him, he would think later when he was alone. Walking back to the Osteria with his father's hand around his shoulder, Tom gradually regained all his senses. He became aware of all the people standing around in the rain, which was still falling, if not quite so heavily as it had done earlier. Some were clapping gently, and others were calling, "Bravo."

18. TAGLIOLINI CON TALEGGIO & TARTUFO

As soon as it was light, Vincenzo was in the Cookery School trying to understand why so much more of the water seemed to have been coming from either inside there or the connected Monastery. Inside the buildings, nearly all the floodwaters had drained away, leaving only a sodden mass of table linen and menus under piles of furniture and pans. He made his way to the cave opening at the rear of the monastery where the Grail had been on display. Inside the subterranean room, the plinth on which the Grail had rested was still fastened to the floor surrounded by rubble and large stone blocks.

One of the room's stone walls had collapsed, the falling blocks apparently just missing the Grail itself. The fall had exposed a void on the other side. It was too dark to see far inside, but from the collecting of debris it appeared that this had been the source of much of the water. Vincenzo surmised that an underground drain must have become overwhelmed with the volume of water and sought out new outlets.

The rain running off every roof and paved surface in the village had been channelled into one place. The walled-up section of the cave must have been a weak spot, and when the force was sufficient it had simply burst open. This explained why the pressure of water was greater inside the building than outside, forcing the doors plate glass shut.

Determined to discover why so much water had ended in the village itself, and why it had not flowed around and away down the mountains as it normally did, Vincenzo began to trace the flood's path backwards. Passing back through the piazza he bumped in Ben, also up early and similarly looking for answers.

"How is. . .," they both started to say, almost in unison. Ben deferred and said, "You first."

"How is Tom?" Vincenzo wanted to know.

"He's absolutely fine and having a late sleep. What about Renata – any ill effects from that knock on the head?"

"She's a tough one. It would take more than that to stop her going to work. But if your son had not acted quickly to release her from that goldfish bowl filling up with water, who knows?"

The two men shared a look that appeared to suggest that they were equally astonished by the turn of events that had seen Tom become the hero of the hour. Together they walked towards the road exiting the village in the direction of Negi, following the trail of rubbish left by the floodwater. They passed the new hotel and spa with its newly tarmacked car park and started walking along the Negi road. The outer edges of the temporary river were clearly defined by a line of flotsam from the forest. Leaves, sticks, pine needles, cones, acorns and chestnut husks all washed out of the land above the village. After a little while, the organic materials became scattered with white specks, which on closer inspection Vincenzo declared to be shards of plastic.

A few hundred metres before they reached the Passo del Bandito, they found more evidence of man-made material tracking back up the hill into the trees. Both men had begun to guess the source of this waste. Vincenzo dropped down from the tarmac road into the culvert running alongside the hill. It was nearly full to the brim with discarded rubbish. Then he crossed the road and dropped down on the opposite side where the land fell away steeply. He walked crouched, as though searching for something, and then suddenly announced, "Si. Bloccato. The storm drain is completely blocked."

Ben joined the big Italian who was bent down and shining a torch into the concrete pipe, which was easily big enough for a man to fit though. All they could see in the distance was compressed plastic sheeting forming a seal in the other end of the black hole. Back on the other side of the road, Vincenzo used a branch to lever some of the leaves and branches from the entrance to the storm drain. He soon uncovered more building waste, including a lot of the lightweight foam insulation they had seen dumped earlier. Finally, in the concrete pit designed to feed water into the storm drain and under the road, was the uPVC window frame and more plastic sheeting. Together, they formed a perfect, almost watertight, dam.

"I hope that construction company has good insurance cover because we will be suing them," Ben threatened.

Standing back up on the road they could now both envisage the scenario as it had unfolded the previous night. The extraordinary storm had poured hundreds of gallons of water on the mountain. This had washed everything unsecured down the hillsides. The first barrier for the torrent was the roads criss-crossing its progress towards the river in the bottom of the valley. These tarmac strips had the potential to become rivers themselves unless they were relieved by man-made culverts and storm drains. This system had coped with all previous storms, but last night had been different.

"Si. I hope that lazy building foreman has a tough skin because he's going to get a visit from me early on Monday," Vincenzo added.

The blocking of the biggest storm drains on one of the steepest hillsides was the first broken link in the fateful chain of events. This event created a build-up of water that flowed along the conveniently- tarmacked road, the path of least resistance towards the village. On the outskirts, a previously permeable earth play area had been concreted over for new car parking, speeding the water's progress into the village. With water flowing both over, and it appeared under, the stone paved piazza, the twelfth century ancient drainage systems were simply overwhelmed by twenty-first century extreme weather.

Tom arrived at the Osteria around 10 am to find it empty except for Alessandra, who was making phone calls to people on a handwritten list in front of her. She stopped to make them both a coffee and get Tom some of her freshly baked focaccia, made with cinnamon-sugar.

"I'm calling insurers, contractors and suppliers. How are you feeling after your heroics last night?"

Tom thought for a minute and then answered, "A bit dazed, if I'm honest."

Alessandra gave him a puzzled look and asked him to explain. The young man confessed that he felt confused by what had happened and was struggling to rationalise his feelings.

"The only way I can explain it is that it genuinely felt like that was someone else out there, last night: not me. I instinctively knew that I had to help that woman get out of that flooded building but have no idea why I risked my life to save that glass bowl."

Tom explained that he had no time whatsoever for religion and thought those that did have a faith were either fools or fanatics. As far as he was concerned, the Holy Grail was a great plot device for Steven Spielberg and Monty Python but was otherwise completely mythical. He thought the idea that this glass bowl was used by Jesus Christ at a dinner in Galilee over two thousand years ago was the biggest con trick he had ever heard of.

"And yet, armed with that point of view, you can't explain why you dove into a foaming torrent to save it, and then clung to it like your life depended on it? Which, in fact, it almost did."

Tom could see the contradiction that he was asking Alessandra to accept but he also understood that this was what was confusing him so much. He had never acted so completely out of character or felt that he was not totally in control of his own actions before that day. For a young man used to being certain about everything, and one hundred percent sure that he was correct in all his beliefs, these unexplainable phenomena were deeply unsettling.

Alessandra said, "I have found that certainty about anything diminishes with the passing of years, until you reach that point where few things are unequivocal. Also, a certain amount of mystery means that hope is not entirely constrained by what we can prove," finding herself unintentionally sermonizing.

Changing the subject, Alessandra asked if he had heard from Selene or seen the news about Andrea, but he had not. She summarised the events of the previous evening in Rome, including the allegations that Selene and he had both benefited financially from public money through their father's connections.

As she spoke, Tom realised that this information could only have come from one source: the pretty journalist he had chatted to right there in the Osteria. To underline the significance of what she was telling him, Alessandra added, "These allegations and revelations from the same source about Selene's relationship with Andrea cost your sister her job and nearly forced the resignation of the prime minister."

Allowing this news to sink in, Alessandra went to get Tom another coffee. She knew that one small Italian cup was never enough to satisfy his northern European caffeine habit and so made him a large café Americano. When she returned, she added, "Those hurt by these allegations will doubtless be conducting a witch hunt for those responsible. While you are the hero of the hour and therefore likely to be judged more sympathetically, even by Selene, this might be a good to time to unburden yourself of anything you feel the need to."

This suggestion left Tom in no doubt that Alessandra knew perfectly well that the information had come from him, but also suggested that she had not yet told his father or sister. Leaving Tom to contemplate his dilemma, Alessandra collected her papers and went back into her kitchen. Tom was sure that, if pushed, that journalist would not hesitate to name him as her source of her information. He also remembered that, in trying to impress her, he had greatly exaggerated his personal role in the reconstruction of Seborga. He recalled that he had strongly suggested that it was his own construction company doing the work.

A little later, as Ben and Vincenzo re-entered the village, they could see something going on outside the Osteria. When they got closer, they could see Tom sat at a table almost surrounded by people. Other groups of villagers were milling around, chatting in the piazza. As they approached it became clear that the villagers had come to thank the young Englishman for the bravery and selflessness that many of them had witnessed first-hand. He had saved not only a life, but also possibly the most cherished relic of Christianity. Vincenzo pushed past his neighbours and grabbed Tom's hand, shaking it vigorously. He said only, "Grazie," but with more conviction than Ben had heard put into any previous thank you, before leaving and heading home to check on Renata.

Ben went out back to ask his wife for a coffee and slice of focaccia before taking a seat next to his son. Recognising that this was now a family discussion, the villagers evaporated into groups with their neighbours to continue their post-flood analysis.

Tom looked confused. "I have no idea what any of them were saying to me. At first they looked angry but then they started shaking my hand and patting me on the back. They do seem to be angry at someone or something else." The young man had got this impression from them.

Ben realised that his son was unsettled by all this attention, even more so than he had been about the events of the night before. It was as if he would like to pretend that none of these things had taken place: to just go back to how things were before the flood. Maybe having found some solidity and natural rhythm in his life, Tom resented what he saw as this being shaken up, Ben speculated.

Now it was Ben's turn to be puzzled. Tom had accused him of not paying him much attention for all the years and now he was the centre of Ben's, and everyone else's, focus. Added to that, his son was from the generation who, as far as Ben was concerned, seemed to live their lives under a social media lens. He assumed he would love being hailed the hero and having his photograph in the paper; yet it seemed not.

The better Ben got to know the relative stranger in front of him, the less he reminded him of the teenager he had left behind with his sister and Ben's ex-wife more than a decade earlier. He had seemed more self-assured at thirteen than he had been when he'd arrived in Seborga at age twenty-five. Although, his self-confidence had grown rapidly since he had started working with Vincenzo. The tough Italian treated him like an equal and that meant he expected him to do everything that he could at that age. He made no concession for Tom being the pampered product of an English, middle-class school system. Tom had also learned to expect no favours if he wanted to earn respect, and he did want that very much.

"Have you spoken to Marius to thank him? And, to apologise for judging him?" Ben asked.

"No, not yet. I will go and find him and do that when I leave here. But first, there is something I need to confess to you." Tom told his father about the young female journalist coming to the Osteria and asking questions, his answers to which might not have all been entirely accurate, he admitted.

Tom messaged Marius saying that he wanted to meet, and he responded straight away to say he and Cristiano had plans today but that Tom was welcome to join them. On the one hand, Tom thought the prospect of apologising to both men at once was just too daunting. However, he also realised that this would get both necessary, unpalatable discussions out of the way in one go. When he asked where he should meet them, Marius messaged him to say that they would call and collect him from the Osteria, but to dress for a walk in the forest.

Tom had spent the intervening hours thinking about what he was going to say to Marius, but the words did not come easy to him. By the time they were due to arrive, the regretful Englishman was no closer to an answer. As it turned out, any planned speech he had devised would have been useless because Marius and Cristiano turned the corner into the piazza accompanied by three girls and another young man. Tom guessed that the strangers, in their late teens, were probably newly arrived students from the Slow Food university.

"A foraging lesson," Cristiano offered by way of explanation for the group outing. The young chef offered his hand to shake, and this time Tom took it and shook it warmly.

Marius did the same and added, "No need for more words."

Tom could not have been more surprised and relieved. Although it had been disconcerting to realise that while he had been sitting in moral judgement on strangers, they had been universally magnanimous toward him. He had arrived here, the outsider, with all his prejudices, preconceptions and bad attitudes. Despite this, since the day he had arrived everyone had treated him with kindness and tolerance. He was, to say the least, contrite and more than slightly ashamed.

Tom was introduced to the students, who all spoke English to a greater or lesser extent and were keen to practice it. The cheerful and vocal party headed off on the road out of town. They took a track heading off east, marked with a hiking sign pointing to Perinaldo. Tom discovered that Marius had grown up a in rural Romania, in an agricultural community that was not so different from the one he now found himself in. His parents had taught him how to reap nature's harvest to supplement what they could grow. The chef and the MSc graduate in agriculture made for a formidable team spotting free food in the hills.

"The first lesson about foraging," Cristiano began, "is that the dish begins with the ingredients. It is the converse of deciding what you want to cook, and then going shopping for what is needed. If you apply conventional thinking, chances are that you will not find everything you want in nature's larder. That could be because of the weather, time of day, the season or just bad luck in finding it. Taking what you find on any day as the starting point, you start to build your dish. If you are lucky and your dog digs up a truffle, and you have some cheese at home, then there's your pasta dish—Tagliolini with Taleggio and Tartufo."

This was a lesson Tom's father had learned early on his relationship with Alessandra. Regional Italian menus are determined by location and season and not the whim of the chef, or indeed, the customer. This is also why Italian food is so varied depending on where you eat it and when. What is available in the cool mountains of the far north, the warm, damp rice fields of the west, and the dry heat of the south, is vastly different. It is a cuisine designed by nature and merely embellished by man.

The spell cast by the region of Liguria, and of Seborga in particular, was beginning to work its magic on Tom. At his lowest ebb during the recent financial mess of his own making, he had begun to realise just how vulnerable he had become. Prior to this, his only battles had been on the rugby field where there were clear rules, and a referee was there to enforce them. Afterwards everyone shook hands like gentlemen and went to the bar for a drink together. The world was a less forgiving place in adulthood, he had learned the hard way.

Faced with no income, no home and no one left he could turn to for help, his childhood shield of invulnerability quickly evaporated. These were foes he could not tackle just with muscle and bravado. If you fall out of the mainstream in a modern westernised society, it is a very long way down. Safety nets are few and wolves are waiting for the weak and unwary. For Tom, finally realising that he still needed people like his estranged father to bail him out was a wakeup call to the realities of what being a man really meant.

Tom had also begun to understand why life was gentler here in Seborga. Most people were part of an extended family support network, who were also in easy reach. As it was most often desperate people who committed petty crime and violence, there was little real need for this to be found here. Even the poorest farmer was a property owner who could provide shelter, eat reasonably well, drink their own wine and look after their families, including their elderly relatives. Foraging for them was not a fashionable hobby. It was part of a cycle of life that had gone on for as long as anyone could remember. The Englishman could not help but think that being penniless in Liguria was not quite as terrifying a prospect as being down on your luck in London.

Marius pointed to a plant growing in the rocks which had leaves shaped like lilies and floral stems like tiny fox gloves, "Ombilicus Rupestris, also known as navelwort, or even, Venus Belly Button. It can be used in a salad or to add flavour to an omelette."

The students bent down to get a closer look and take photographs on their mobile phones. It was Cristiano's turn to spot the next potential ingredient, "Rumex Acetosa, or Common Sorrel, which makes a delicious soup with some potato and onion. It's also good in a salad giving a lemony, acidic zing to otherwise bland leaves."

A few hours passed with the discovery and collection of several edible plants, many of which also had wide ranging medicinal properties. They learned that Malva Sylvestris, better known as mallow, could be used to make a pasta sauce but could also heal a cut wound or treat eczema. Cristiano pointed out, "If you've ever had marshmallows, then that distinct flavour comes from the root of the mallow."

Both Tom and the students were impressed with the pair's knowledge of the countryside larder all around them. They invited Tom to the Cookery School that evening to try some of what they would cook with their haul from the forest, and he agreed without hesitation.

19. TORTA DE CARCIOFI

Following the PM's impromptu press conference and adlib speech, his press secretary was now in awe of his boss. All normal rules of engagement with the media had been thrown out of the window. Nothing had been discussed, analysed or shared with government colleagues beforehand. He had begun by admitting his own errors of judgement, had offered his resignation without anyone calling for it, and had revealed a long-term, risk-laden strategy to his enemies. Any one of these tactics could be fatal for a leader. However, so heartfelt had been his appeal, so sincere his candidness and so breathtakingly bold his plans, that he had rendered the usually baying press pack almost questionless.

Although the initial public reaction online was only slightly more positive than negative, that was only for the first few hours of social media activity. Early online chatter had been taken up with discussion and digestion of all the issues raised. These included topics such as: did he really deceive the public by keeping his relationship with a foreign journalist a secret? Was his intervention in Seborga self-serving or part of a bold plan for a greener, more sustainable Italy? Had he demonstrated poor judgement? Should he resign as a consequence of any of these things?

As no further allegations appeared and most of those previously made were debunked after fact checks, the tide in the PM's favour turned into a tsunami. By the time the late evening TV news was broadcast, the Italian public had made up their collective minds, and the verdict of the jury of public opinion was not guilty.

The consensus was that Andrea was judged to be incredibly brave to have put his love for Selene before his position of power and personal ambition. So convincing had been his argument, that voters also believed his justification for the Seborga projects. What was more, they admired his vision for a sustainable Italy based on traditional values. According to the press secretary, if he had delivered this speech before the election, his party would have gained an even bigger majority. It was clear that the voters had almost unanimously declined Andrea's offer to resign from his post as PM.

Seeing the unbridled enthusiasm of public opinion, even the doubters and schemers amongst his party were queuing up to align themselves with his stance and his newly revealed policies. All except Amara, that was. Her leaked press release had seen her hounded relentlessly by the media all evening, as the only apparent voice of dissent. She had decided to go to ground until the dust settled and was holed up in an obscure hotel drinking her way through the contents of the minibar.

When he finally got some time to himself, Andrea called Selene in London. They eagerly shared their respective good news, although the PM's story had already been broadcast live online for all to see. Selene's sudden career change from journalist to author had been even more rapid than Andrea's recent rise to power. It was undoubtedly as unexpected, she revealed. Although they agreed that it was all too soon to start making plans, they both knew that things had turned out far better than either could have dared to hope.

"Getting our relationship out in the open feels like a huge weight has been lifted off my shoulders," Andrea sighed.

"All the women in our office were in tears watching you speak, myself included," Selene told him. However, the journalist in her could not help asking, "Have you given any thought to who was behind those initial Instagram photo posts?"

"Yes. It has the feeling of an orchestrated attempt to unseat me, and I have a good idea who would like to sit in the PM's chair. For now, I am going to let them stew in the discomfort of the unravelling of their plan."

"But how did they know all that detail about my house in Seborga? And that my brother Tom was working in the village as a builder? Someone has gone to a great deal of trouble to make enquiries on the ground," Selene concluded.

As they chatted, over the TV in the London newsroom came a breaking news story from Reuters about events taking place in Seborga. Mobile phone footage showed a drenched young man with blonde hair wading out of a flooded building carrying an unconscious woman wearing chef's whites.

"Turn on the TV news," Selene urged Andrea. Minutes later, the same young man was pictured swinging a sledgehammer to break a large plate glass door before scooping the famous Sacro Cantina from a torrent of water pouring out of the building, nearly drowning in the process. The floodwater swept him away, with him still clutching firmly onto the priceless relic. Only another dramatic rescue by others saved the young man from being plunged over a ledge to his near-certain death.

"That's Tom!" Selene exclaimed in shock.

"Are you sure? It's dark and the images are blurred by rain on the camera lens."

"It's Tom. I'd recognise that mop of fair hair anywhere. I'll have to hang-up, Andrea. I need to call Dad. I'll call you back when I know he's Ok."

Andrea continued watching and learned for himself that Tom was no longer in any danger. He was pictured walking away from the scene with Ben's arm around his broad shoulders. The PM instinctively knew he needed to get to Seborga by morning. He sent out messages to his staff to make the arrangements. He also messaged Selene to suggest that she meet him there if she could. Gatwick's early flight would get her there by just after nine in the morning.

Being driven overnight from Rome allowed Andrea to gain a few hours of much-needed sleep. He'd arranged with Cecily to shower and breakfast on their boat. From there he would carry on to Nice Airport in time for Selene's flight arriving from London. As the pair drove up the mountain towards Seborga, Andrea outlined his plan to use the publicity from the flood in Seborga to justify his new green strategy and underline his plans.

"Now that we know no one was harmed, the timing could not have been better," he said, looking pleased with himself.

"It is almost like there was an unseen hand at work here," Selene quipped about the legendary effects of the Holy Grail.

"I will take help wherever I can get it," Andrea said, laughing.

The previous night's news had every Italian citizen and many other Europeans glued to their chosen media for further revelations. By cleverly tying his story to the near destruction of the Holy Grail, the newly empowered prime minister was now set to increase that audience to include the more than one billion Catholics in the rest of the world.

Selene explained that she had spoken to her younger brother the previous night and established that he was fine. Physically, at least, as she was sensing that he was not comfortable with how he was already being portrayed in the media and was dreading what seemed likely to follow. Tom explained that he had already endured a brief period of notoriety after posting an unintentionally misogynistic comment online whilst drunk one night.

He had not been prepared for the barrage of abuse that came back at him. He became on overnight pariah, with even his rugby mates avoiding him. Finally, he had cancelled all his social media accounts and since then had led a mostly offline existence. He had found out the hard way that he did not have the self-confidence to be in the limelight, in any capacity.

Andrea listened to what Selene had to say with some sympathy. They both knew that some people would not like what you wrote or said if you operated in the public arena. And some of those who vehemently disagree would cross the line of what is considered reasonable debate, and turn very nasty, abusive, and even threatening.

"You need a thick skin, and it is not for everyone," Andrea agreed.

Selene told him, "Tom does not want to speak to the press. Indeed, he would rather not be mentioned in the media at all, but I fear that particular boat has already sailed."

Andrea thought for a while. "The truth is usually the best default position. Let's tell them that, while he is happy that the lady was not badly hurt and the Grail not damaged, he does not want any publicity and has left the area. Vincenzo or Ben will have to find him somewhere to stay away from the village while things cool down."

"OK. But Tom will have to get all his hair cropped off and buy a baseball cap because he stands out like a sore thumb around here," Selene added, thinking aloud.

Having been briefed overnight by his press secretary, there was a good turnout of journalists and film crews to witness Andrea arrive in Seborga, now very publicly hand-in-hand with Selene. Selene was wearing a cashmere suit by an Italian designer, rather than her usual British label of choice. She looked every inch the perfect politician's partner. The couple went first to the barracks of the Alpini. Andrea wanted to check on the Grail in its temporary resting place and inspect the damage inside the monastery. The prime minister refrained from comment, saying that he would announce his thoughts when he had assessed the whole situation.

Alessandra and Ben joined them in the main piazza for a public display of unity to underline that they had nothing to hide following the previous night's allegations. Together the four walked side-by-side out of the village towards the Passo del Bandito, trailing a gang of media and a few curious villagers behind them. Ben showed them where the floodwater had descended from the mountain, and where its progress had been blocked by discarded plastic. Despite his fine blue wool suit and shiny black shoes, Andrea dropped down into the ditch and started pulling out bits of uPVC, a plastic sheet big enough to wrap a van in, and finally, one of the ubiquitous plastic drinks' bottles.

Using the cola bottle with its red cap as a baton, he began conducting his address to the media, "Look what we are doing to our countryside and our planet. Last night we nearly lost the most precious holy relic in the world. Not to the forces of nature, but because of our irresponsibility. We have overheated the planet by burning carbon, causing these extreme weather events. Not content with that, we have concreted over much of our land and forced our rivers through manmade gaps. Then, to make doubly sure disaster will befall us, we throw away millions of tons of non-biodegradable plastics to block the gaps the rainwater is trying to get through. And the tons of plastic that do get through wash into our seas, choking our wildlife and poisoning our fish." The PM was now pointing his plastic cola bottle out to sea while the camera panned around him to get the full perspective.

"This has to stop. And there is nowhere better than Seborga to start the revolution. From where we are standing, you can see the full cycle of this environmental insanity. Every discarded object, litre of pesticide, and bottle of chemical toiletry that we despoil this land with will eventually end up out there in the Mediterranean. In the same sea where our children play and the fish that we eat swim. Those of us who don't live in places like Seborga have lost sight of that connection between human actions and their consequences for the planet. But by prioritising price and convenience, we have passed on the cost to our environment and the inconvenience to future generations who will have to clean it up. We must take back that responsibility."

Andrea paused, holding his bottle pointed out to sea to allow notetaking and filming.

"This is not only environmental madness; it is economic suicide. We're all paying for these plastic products to be made using what's left of the world's oil, only to throw them away. My government must then use your taxpayers' cash to collect what we can of the plastic and dump it in landfill for future generations to deal with. As I cautioned last night, I can't say for sure that all our new initiatives here in Seborga will work, but we must start somewhere. And, for those that are not completely successful, we must find better alternatives. So, we should support Seborga's efforts to become a low carbon, plastic-free, sustainable economy, and learn from the trials that will be carried out here."

There was an outcry when the journalists learned that they were not going to get a photo opportunity with the PM, his new girlfriend and her heroic brother. Tom was now being tagged 'The Angel of Seborga,' presumably because the Holy Grail's saviour had almost white hair and was angelic in appearance. However disappointed, the media had no choice but to accept that Tom would not be making an appearance. For many, his reluctance to be recognised made his story even more intriguing. They would read all manner of things into his reticence. Still, there was more than enough material to keep them in headline-making copy for several days, so they departed reasonably content.

Andrea and Selene returned to the Osteria where Alessandra had made torta de carciofi (artichoke pie) with local black tomato salad for lunch. Ben had returned from the hairdresser in Bordighera where Tom had his hair cropped close to his scalp, a style he decided he quite liked. He had found his long, fair locks uncomfortable when he was working in the heat and dust. This military cut would be much more comfortable and he agreed with his father that it did make him look quite different, even without the baseball cap they had chosen from a newsstand by the railway station.

Whilst at the station, they both could see that all the newspapers for sale carried blurred photographs of the flood in Seborga. Meanwhile, Vincenzo had arranged for Tom to use a small holiday home in the hills above the village. It belonged to a family from Turin for whom he looked after the property and its gardens. It was Tom's for as long as he needed it, Vincenzo told Ben, dismissing his question about the cost with a wave of his hand.

"The family won't be back here until August."

20. PORCINI

When Andrea and Selene finally departed the village, Ben decided that he needed a walk in the country on his own to clear his head. The land smelled different after the rain. The sky was clear. The air felt fresher than usual, but the odour of damp organic matter and vegetation was strong. The sun was heating the ground and causing steam to rise from the valley.

As he approached the groves where the orange trees had been planted just a few years ago, he could see that there was something not right. The ground below the branches was covered in a carpet of the white petals of orange blossom. Ben realised that these fat, surfboard-shaped petals must have been beaten from their flower stems by the previous night's pounding rain.

Despite the bright sunshine, a dark cloud of despair descended upon Ben on learning that the village's precious blood orange crop appeared to be ruined. How many more disasters could be heaped upon them; could the Grail be cursed, he wondered? He called Vincenzo on his mobile phone to ask if he had seen this latest victim of the storm, and he confirmed that he had. The experienced farmer was, however, not so pessimistic that the entire crop would be lost.

"Many of the flowers will already have been pollinated and should be fine. The flowers and their petals could have already done their job. We might see a reduced crop, but not a total disaster. In a few weeks, we will know how many fruits are likely to come. I'm more worried that some of our terrace stonework at the vineyard might have been washed away. Want to come with me to check?"

Ben had agreed and waited for Vincenzo arriving in his Ape to give him a lift for the short ride to the slopes where his vines were growing. The Ape suddenly drew to a halt, the door was flung open and the sharp-eyed Italian strode a few yards into the forest while removing his penknife from his pocket. Stooping down he cut off three large porcini mushrooms, the first of which was bigger than his splayed hand. Returning to the Ape, Ben had also opened his door and stepped out so as not to be choked by the fumes from the idling old two-stroke engine.

"Lunch?" Ben suggested.

"Si. Gratuita (free)."

As they continued, along the roadside on both sides were piles of leaves and debris, all washed down from the hills by the previous night's storm. Earlier passers-by had cleared many blockages from the single-track road, sometimes only after cutting them up with a chainsaw. Some of the resulting logs were neatly stacked by the roadside, suggesting that someone was coming back to collect them for firewood. Piles of sawdust on the tarmac were evidence of this recycling.

"Only the olive and oak wood are worth saving," Vincenzo said, explaining that the pinewood was open-grained and burnt too quickly but the others grew slower, had greater density and so lasted longer.

When they reached the foot of the hill from where the vine terraces stepped up and clung to the hillside above them, they could see that most of it was intact. Only one small section of stone wall right at the top had slipped down onto the terrace below.

"The first section that Tom built on his own," Vincenzo offered to Ben as an explanation.

"In the light of recent events, I think today we can forgive him that small shortcoming," Ben replied in resignation.

"The many metres of wall that he built later have held firm, which is good," the Italian said, trying to reassure his friend.

Ben told Vincenzo the other thing that he had noticed in the orange groves earlier as they walked. When incentivised by EU grants, many of the farmers had agreed to try changing from olive to orange production, but it had meant clearing the terraces of olive trees ready for planting. Ben had watched in horror and uncertainty as they took chainsaws to their precious olive trees, many well over a hundred years old. As certain as he was that blood oranges offered better economic prospects for the farmers, he could not help fearing the consequences if he had got it wrong. As felled olive trunks began piling up on the ends of the terraces to be recycled into firewood, Ben departed the groves, unable to watch the slaughter any longer.

This morning he had seen that all the stumps left in the ground after the felling were now sprouting vigorous new branches from their sides. Some of these were already a metre high and carried their parent plants' distinctive silver-greens. Ben has always assumed that the trees' felling was the end of the line for them, but here before his eyes, they appeared to be regrowing. Was that anticipated, he wondered? If it was, no one had said so at the time.

"Of course, we knew they would grow back after a few years. You didn't believe we would cut down perfectly good olive trees if there was no way of reviving them? That would be madness. And no one said anything because those EU bureaucrats would have paid us less compensation if they knew the trees could eventually be restored back to production. They are our insurance in case your blood orange experiment doesn't work out."

Ben was unsure whether to be relieved that some of the pressure for his plan to succeed had been removed from him or insulted that he had been kept in the dark that olives trees were apparently almost indestructible. Vincenzo went on to tell him that even wildfires would not completely destroy most forest trees. Given time, olive trees were eventually able to restore themselves. Ben told Vincenzo he would stay awhile in the vineyard and walk back to Seborga later.

In the five years since arriving in rural Italy, Ben felt as though he had learned more of value than in the previous five decades of his life. This micro-nation had all the elements of a larger community, but in miniature. Here, the cycle of production, consumption and waste disposal was transparent. It was not hidden behind a complex food chain and utility infrastructure system. It was all on view for anyone to see and, eventually, to understand, as he had.

His ongoing education in understanding the natural world's workings had caused him to rethink much of what he had previously believed was important. His epiphany had come when he understood the connection between his own small, everyday actions and the environment. This had changed many of his habits for good. He had not bought a disposable plastic razor or shaving foam in five years.

He discovered that, in a largely off-grid community, everything that went down his shower, sink and toilet drain ended up on the land around him. From there it passed into the rivers flowing through the land and finally out into the ocean. Suddenly the purchases of shampoo, soap and toilet cleaner took on a new importance. He would not want to eat food or drink wine grown in the chemical residue of the products he used to buy and throw down the sink. Olives were surely the perfect example of sustainability. They grew without the addition of anything but natural fertiliser, and their fruits could be eaten, drunk and used as soap before ending up back in the soil where they came from with no harm done.

Andrea's speech the previous night and the public's reaction to it proved to him that attitudes were changing. Also, that the village's strategy to create a sustainable economy based on biodiversity and organic methods was the right one. The resulting produce would be increasingly sought after and of higher value than their mass-producing competitors. Ben knew that it was all very commendable being ‘green’ and sustainable, but farmers still had bills to pay and children to bring up. Their business model also had to make commercial sense. It was his task to see that it did.

21. RAVIORE

In an unexpected response to the near tragedy in Seborga, more visitors than usual arrived in the village on what otherwise would have been a quiet weekday. Alessandra busied herself, making pasta to take her mind off things and to have something to serve the influx of customers. Cristiano had dropped off some foraged greens that he had collected but now couldn't use because the Cookery School was out of action. Alessandra used them to make a batch of Raviore, a half-moon shaped dumpling to be filled with the wild herbs.

While she was working, Cecily called Alessandra's mobile.

"While you wait for everything to dry out and for the insurance assessors to do their work, why don't we take a short trip?"

Cecily suggested to Alessandra at the end of their somewhat depressing update on the situation following the flood.

"It's a lovely idea, Cecily, and a break from all this would be welcome, but there's just too much to do here."

Her friend reiterated that there would be little that could be done at the Cookery School until the insurance gave the go ahead. That was very unlikely to happen in the next few days. Cecily also admitted that she had an ulterior motive in offering to take Ben and Alessandra sailing. An issue had arisen that she and Roman would welcome their advice on.

"I'm thinking of an overnight sail to Corsica. There's a wonderful fish restaurant in Saint-Florent that does the most incredible Azziminu (fish soup). Two, or maybe three days max. The last time we made this trip we had dolphins visit us on both the outbound and return journeys," Cecily added for extra appeal.

Alessandra had gone quiet, suggesting to her friend that she was now thinking about her offer. Cecily knew that Ben would go in an instant; it was always Alessandra who did not like to be too far away from the comfort of her kitchen.

"Two days, you say?"

The savvy businesswoman knew it was best to have some scope for negotiation, "Two. Three at most, if the wind is not with us. Pack a weekend bag and be at the dock at six tomorrow night. Bring sweaters. It can be cool out in the open sea in the evening. We'll have supper and then set sail. Fresh croissants in Corsica by morning."

Ben was delighted when Alessandra told him the news. He was only too ready to leave behind all his family, agricultural and construction worries for a few days. Sailing was a new passion for him, and the idea of visiting the not-so-well-known French Island in the Mediterranean was appealing.

"With its French heritage and unique geographical location, there must be some interesting and slightly different food and wine on Corsica," he speculated.

Alessandra had already done a little surfing of the Internet and learned that the cuisine of Corsica had a little more in common with that of Italy than the south of France. There was little sign of the North African ingredients found on the Côte d'Azur. Pasta, gnocchi and polenta were commonly used as the base of dishes.

"I'm sure Cecily will see to it that we taste the best there is," his wife laughed, now feeling a bit brighter about her decision to go, having done a little food research of her own.

Ben's mobile phone vibrated to tell him he had a message. It was from Vincenzo, asking him to come outside the house. In the street, the big man's tanned head was protruding above the windscreen of the Crazy Dutchman's old Kübelwagen. The almost fifty year old, open-top VW-based Jeep was ticking over quietly with a distinctive air-cooled Beetle engine note. Vincenzo had rescued it from its premature gave and revived it.

Every time Ben, and indeed most people saw it, it made them smile. The strange, bright orange, corrugated-panelled, vehicle, had been bequeathed to Selene, along with its late owner's other property in Seborga. It had not run for nearly two years and had been under a tarpaulin outside the back of his shop. Two summers of dust would need washing off to reveal the full glory of its faded satsuma shade.

"Selene asked me if I could get it going so the Tom could use it. Now that he is living up in the hills, he will need some transport. It only needed some new spark plugs and the brakes freeing-off. Want to come with me to surprise him?"

"I can't wait to see his face," Ben said, smiling broadly and stepping into the cab next to Vincenzo.

Tom could hardly get over the shock at his sister's unexpected generosity, especially surprising in the light of his latest folly. Ben told him that he and Alessandra were going sailing for a couple of days. The young man was still too ecstatic about his transport to pay much attention and said, "Enjoy." Tom was thinking about turning up at the beach on Saturday mornings in his quirky retro convertible.

"When you call your sister to thank her, tell her we are sailing to Corsica tomorrow but will be back in a couple of days."

Tom really wanted to hug both men, so grateful was he for what they had done for him in recent weeks, but his false pride still prevented him doing so. His circumstances had turned from having no male figure that he could look up to, to having two quite different role models. They had in common an inner strength that he was yet to acquire, but at least he now knew what it looked like. He was also aware that he had been given another chance at life and was determined to get it right this time.

Discovering that his friend Marius was homosexual, and that Cristiano was his partner, had been a catalyst for change in

Tom's thinking. The events on the night of the flood had made him re-evaluate all the stereotypes he had acquired over the years. Tom was finally learning to judge people by their actions, and not by their words or the labels that society hung on them. Alessandra's and Selene's recent kindness, even in the face of his rudeness and stupidity, were more examples of how wrong he had been about people. He even began to question whether he had been wrong about his mother and his stepfather. Had they been so awful to him, he now wondered?

22. RAVIOLI DI CARCIOFI

"We are far from the first Italians to set our sails for Corsica," Roman said to Alessandra, cryptically.

"Or the first Brits," Ben said, looking over at Cecily, having done some basic Google research into their destination island of over three hundred thousand fiercely independent people.

Alessandra responded, "Yes, colonialists seem to like collecting islands. Originally Italian, before you British took it then traded it to the French, but then Mussolini briefly reclaimed it, only later to be forced to hand it over to the Nazis. Finally, the Moroccans took it back on behalf of the Allies before it was eventually gifted back to France."

"No wonder some say that their food and people have something of an identity crisis," Ben joked.

There was a good breeze pushing the big old wooden yacht south away from the coast and out into open sea. The sun was sinking down into the hills behind the glimmering lights along the coastline. They were now too far out to distinguish between Monaco, Nice or Cannes, which had merged into one long, narrow strip of light. Only the landing lights and vapor trail of jet planes gave away Nice's Côte d'Azur Airport's location.

Ben loved this part of these trips, feeling the excitement build as the coastline faded from view. Sailing was the closest thing to a genuine adventure that Ben had experienced. When he first stepped onto the boat deck, he left his comfort zone behind on the quay. Once away from the shore, he quickly realised that there was only a veneer of wood between him and the incredible power of the ocean. It was simultaneously exhilarating and frightening, and that combination always gave him an adrenaline rush. It also instilled in him the value of a team, where each individual relied upon those around him, in this case for their very survival. The skipper instantly earned respect and became everyone's best friend.

Only a mile or so from the coast, Cecily and her guests had enjoyed a digestivo on the deck watching the sun go down after a supper of some early season ravioli di carciofi al pofumo di timo (artichoke ravioli with thyme). Claude, the skipper, suddenly barked orders to the two crew on deck. Both went below and one returned with a powerful searchlight connected to the power circuit. He pointed the beam out into the sea to the east where other lights could be seen above a line of white water. The other crew member could be heard speaking loudly and deliberately, very clearly into the radio microphone, first in English and then in French. No reply seemed to be forthcoming over the speaker, so he repeated his message.

The distant rising and falling note of an engine could now be heard, its low pitch drone getting slightly louder with each passing minute. Roman went to speak to Claude, who was at the helm. He explained that this boat was travelling at high speed according to the radar, and due to cross their path in just a few minutes.

"Nautical etiquette says that they should change course because we are under sail and they have engines powering them, but you never know these days. There are so many rich idiots around here with huge, high-powered boats but little or no experience, or nautical qualifications. They navigate as they drive on the roads, without care or respect for anyone but themselves. Or they could easily be on drink or drugs, or both. I can't take the chance they will see us at the last minute. Even if they do, they could still panic and turn the wrong way into us."

The crew member came up from below and confirmed there was no answer to his messages on the emergency channel, speculating whether the approaching boat even had their radio turned on, as was required by international law.

Claude waited for a moment to see if there was any response to their flashing spotlight or radio message and then barked more orders, "I need everyone on deck to get ready to come-about and then drop all sails. There is what could be a big boat approaching at extremely high speed and I don't think he knows we are here in his path."

Having just got all the sails up and beginning to make good time in the fresh wind, Cecily knew that this was a real inconvenience that could cost them as much as an hour on their journey. She also knew better than to question the skipper's decision. Everyone, including Roman and Ben, got to the ropes they were assigned and readied themselves. Alessandra and Cecily were poised to coil spare rope as it became free from the cleats. In what seemed like a seamless movement, the skipper started the diesel engine, gave the command to drop the sails and then spun the wheel hard to port, so it was facing into the wind.

The big boat slowly turned ninety degrees, pitching quite considerably while everyone scrabbled about roughly folding the now collapsed sails and gathering rope tails. The boat quickly returned to a level once the sail was down. The diesel engine now pushed the yacht slowly forward in an easterly direction, directly toward the approaching motorboat. Ben looked concerned at this choice of course and turned to Roman and Cecily to ask them to explain what seemed like a counter-intuitive decision.

Cecily told them that Claude had no way of knowing exactly what path the approaching boat would take, and that the diesel engine was too slow to steer completely away from danger. The best strategy was to make the boat as thin a target as possible.

Ben could see the logic in this but asked, "Why motor toward him, when we could steer away?"

Cecily explained, "In terms of the time to contact, it will make little difference, but we can be more manoeuvrable if we are steering toward them. Also, in the worst case, the bow is higher and thinner so more likely to deflect the worst of a collision than the stern. Finally, if they miss us but pass by awfully close, we want the prow to cut through the huge bow wave that will be created. The stern would be swamped."

All of this made perfect sense when explained, Ben realised, but did little to remove the sense of foreboding he was now feeling. He sought out Alessandra and gave her hand a reassuring squeeze.

"Everyone put on their life jackets, and crew prepare to abandon ship if we need to," was the skipper's next commend.

The crew, who were already wearing their life jackets, untied the small inflatable boat and loaded it with two packs of emergency kit, fastening them down with Velcro straps. Then they all waited, as it began to look increasingly like Claude's suspicion had been correct. The droning engine was now much louder and the earlier peaks and troughs in volume had flattened to a more constant note. They could now see the boat's shape quite clearly as it ploughed through the swell, its lights rising and falling slightly with each white-capped wave it cut through.

"I'd say that boat is about fifty metres, Skipper, and doing as much as twenty-five knots," the crewman at the bow shouted back. "But it looks as though it is under a manual helm, as it's not keeping a completely straight line. I think we are slightly on its starboard side at the moment and so should be Ok. Maybe steer another couple of degrees to port and then straighten up."

Hearing this was the worst possible news to Claude. A boat steered by autopilot was at least on a predictable trajectory. It would keep its course no matter what, and they could at least try to manoeuvre out of its way. A boat being steered by hand, possibly by someone not in full control, could do anything. Even a slight inadvertent movement of the helm could change the boat's position by tens of metres by the time it reached them.

The skipper did as was suggested and then throttled back the engine to move steadily forwards. The black hull now appeared bigger, and the noise was louder. They could also hear another faint sound. It was a booming bassline of rap music. It sounded as if a party was in full swing on that boat while it ploughed through some of the busiest waterways for small pleasure and fishing boats anywhere in the world.

"Ben and Roman, please get as much video and as many photographs as you can when it passes but keep one hand with a firm grip on something, because all hell is going to break loose in a minute. We need to trace and report this lunatic to the coastguard." Now, talking only to the two men nearest to him, Claude added, "The best thing that can happen now is that they don't see us and just blast by. If someone spots our lights at the last minute and the helm turns even slightly, we're in trouble. That thing is the weight of two trucks and it's doing thirty miles per hour towards our fragile wooden barrel."

The crewman with the spotlight was now able to illuminate the black hull with the beam but could not yet make out a name on it. All those onboard looked relieved to see that the boat was about to pass on their starboard side at about twenty metres' distance, which only left its bow wave to deal with. The combination of noise coming from its engines, loud rap music, and rushing water drowned out a crew member's reassuring voice on the yacht.

Claude had one hand on the throttle and the other on the top of the helm. As the big black boat drew parallel, he thrust the throttle forwards and span the wheel to starboard toward the passing boat.

"Hold very tight," he bellowed at the top of his voice.

Within seconds the wake wave hit them, washing over their bow and lifting the whole boat a couple of metres higher. A small wall of water rushed down the teak decks as the yacht bucked like a wild horse. The diesel engine pitch raised as the propeller was lifted from the water by the rocking motion of the boat and the prop was allowed to spin briefly without the water's resistance. The skipper throttled back the engine and allowed the yacht to settle into the calmer water inside the V-shape the wake had left behind. They watched the brightly lit powerboat gradually getting smaller as it continued on its journey, unaware of the fear it had caused.

The water in the wake appeared phosphorescent, having been churned and oxygenated by the huge dual propellers of the big boat. It was suddenly incredibly quiet, with only the diesel's gentle burble on tick over and the gentle lapping of waves on the hull.

They all looked at each other, but only one of the French crew felt the need to say anything, "C'était proche."

"Far too close," Claude agreed. "Anyone see the name?"

"Zeno, registered in the Bahamas," the crewman on the stern shouted back before going below to check it on the Internet. "It is a brand-new boat. Built for the Ukrainian rapper, Zeno V, and launched in Genoa very recently. Its twin turbo-charged engines burn two hundred and fifty litres of fuel per hour at full throttle."

"That's roughly a thousand litres of fuel from Genoa to here," calculated Claude.

Alessandra shook her head and sighed, "Tons of plastic, annually burning fuel equivalent of the entire population of our principality. It's a one-man ecological disaster."

"While we can sail from here to Corsica and back on nothing but wind power. Or could have, if we hadn't had to run our engine for five minutes to avoid that idiot," Cecily observed.

"OK. Let's get the sails back up and get underway," Claude ordered.

The terrace at Bordighera Alta is perfect for enjoying a glass of wine watching the sun, going down on the Mediterranean.

Drawing by Linda McCluskey

23. AZZIMINU

Despite the delay caused by the previous night's events, as they were eating breakfast the next morning, the mountainous outline of Corsica slowly crept onto the horizon. Claude went below to check his charts and make a course to take them along the western side of the island's northern peninsula into the Gulf de Saint Florent.

Ben and Alessandra had found it difficult to get to sleep, now both acutely aware of potential perils of sailing at night on the open ocean. There were also strange noises on a boat, particularly an old wooden one. Creaks and groans from the timbers and the sloshing of water in the bilges took on sinister new possibilities. They had both been glad to be greeted on deck by daylight and the sight of dry land.

Most sea traffic from mainland Europe took the route to the east of the island, where the main port of Bastia was to be found. Much of the coastal waters around Corsica are protected by strict marine conservation laws, preventing boats anchoring in many places, so Claude had phoned ahead to book a place in the small harbour at Saint-Florent.

However, along the coastline, there was one stunning cove close to Punta Di Saeta where boats were allowed to drop anchor on the sandy bottom without any danger of damaging the seabed. It was possible to swim in the crystal-clear waters and explore caves eroded into the rocky coastline by centuries of storms. This was to be their pre-lunch destination before sailing the last few miles into port.

The old fishing town on Saint-Florent had, like many other similar places, lost most of its fishing boat fleet. The few that remained served only the local restaurants, whose customers were mainly visiting pleasure boat owners, and who were incapable of, or disinclined to, catch their own fish. The dish they all came for was the famous Corsicanve Azziminu. Although this French island may have retained several dishes from its Italian history, this unique fish stew contained ingredients which may have had their origins in Spain. Star anise and aniseed accompany the saffron, fennel, thyme and tomatoes in this feisty interpretation. The fish can be almost anything but almost always includes lots of shellfish.

Ben had learned that the Saint-Florent-Agriates region's red wines are world-renowned, with grenache being the most widely planted grape, and those grown around nearby Patrimonio seen as the best of breed. Less than twenty per cent of the wines produced in this small region are white. The only grape variety for white wine within the Patrimonio appellation is Malvoisie de Corse. It was this that Cecily recommended as the perfect accompaniment to their lunch.

Food and wine organised, Cecily began to explain the dilemma that she and Roman had been wrestling with. The one on which they wanted the opinion of their good friends. Roman's youngest daughter, Patsy, had been in touch to tell her father about a worrying development. No sooner had her elder sister, Caroline, got back to New York after their recent visit, she had informed Patsy that she planned to mortgage her half of the farm to release cash. Ross, her American broker husband, had previously tried to sell off part of the land to a developer. This plan had come up against local Sicilian opposition of a nature that he had not bargained for. Roman had left the orange farm in trust to the sisters and Patsy had since moved there to run it, hoping her American musician boyfriend would follow her home where they could start a new life together.

Roman and Cecily had been told that there was a property scheme that Caroline's husband was desperate to invest in, but he needed another quarter of a million dollars cash to make his stake up to that of his partners. The young couple had borrowed and cashed in everything they could but were still short and were running out of time. Roman was horrified at the idea of the land he'd inherited from his father being mortgaged to some mercenary American lender. He knew that if Ross's scheme failed or he could not keep up the repayments, the bank would try and foreclose on the farm. Roman neither liked nor trusted his son-in-law, thought he was a poor businessman and a thoroughly untrustworthy individual.

Cecily had met Roman when she first went to buy the blood oranges grown on his farm for her cosmetic products. She still took every orange grown on the farm under a supply contract that suited both parties very well.

"This is where things get tricky for me. I have cash sitting there in the bank earning virtually no interest. Investing in a trusted supplier would normally be sensible vertical integration for me. I have no wish to see an essential supply chain interrupted by introducing a potentially aggressive and disinterested third party lender. I would normally say, let me buy out one half and thereby safeguard my supply. However, these are Roman's daughters, and this situation is not the outcome he'd envisaged for his legacy. Nor is it an intervention in his family affairs that either of us is especially comfortable with."

Ben looked at Alessandra and screwed up his face, feigning pain. He could see his friend's dilemma. Like them, but for different reasons, he was uncomfortable crossing the boundary from friendship into personal family matters. To be sure she understood exactly what they were being asked their opinion on, Alessandra tried to summarise; "Caroline is determined to borrow two hundred and fifty thousand dollars and can use her share of the land as collateral. There's nothing anyone can do to stop her. But that action potentially puts Patsy's share, Roman's legacy, and your supply chain at risk. You have the money, and your intervention could mitigate that risk, but that would leave you as an effective partner, a situation you would rather not be in because of the potential pitfalls."

"That's the crux of it," Cecily agreed. "Reinvesting in this way is also quite tax advantageous for me, but that's another matter," she added.

Ben looked thoughtful, but his worries were less about the validity of his conclusion than whether he should voice it all. His English sensibilities were inclined to avoid expressing any opinion of private money or family matters. Finally, he offered, "Caroline is a grown woman entering into, what is, after all, a business decision with her eyes wide open. We should also remember that she might also be right. For all we know, her husband could be a property genius. He might treble their money with his plans and set them both up for life. The emotional connection to the land shared by Roman and Patsy is not something Caroline feels so deeply. She sees it merely as an asset to leverage as she sees fit."

Roman nodded whilst simultaneously grimacing, believing his friend had also summarised the unfortunate situation with uncanny clarity.

Ben looked directly at Cecily and offered, "So, as your motives cannot be misconstrued, why don't you offer to facilitate Caroline's immediate wish by buying her half of the land? But importantly, also offer her the option to repurchase it within–say–two years, for the same price plus bank rate interest and any transaction costs. That way if her husband's project succeeds, and she feels some remorse about giving up her father's land, she can reclaim it without anyone having lost out. This would mean that Caroline has got what she wanted but Patsy's, and your, position, are safeguarded in the event of their deal in America going wrong."

Aware of both daughters' previously tricky relationship with their father's lover, Alessandra cautioned, "But only if Patsy is completely comfortable with you as her silent partner, of course."

"Better Cecily than a New York banker," observed Roman, horrified by that thought.

Cecily smiled at the simple logic of Ben's suggestion, placing the onus on Caroline to undo the arrangement if their gamble paid off, but at the same time reasonably sure that a buy-back seemed unlikely to happen, whatever the outcome.

"Thanks, you two. Sound advice. I know we were asking the right people. We'll sleep on your suggestion before deciding. Patsy's coming to visit next week to talk to her father and to see where we plan to build our house."

By the time they had unravelled the problem of Roman's farm and talked through potential solutions, the enormous steel kettle dish of spicy fish stew had been and gone in a shower of crumbs from the fresh crispy bread, all washed down with the earthy white local wine. They agreed to forgo a dolce and go straight to coffee, saving their appetite for dinner at another eaterie in the small fishing town.

They had also arranged an appointment with the architect of a house, similar in design to the plan they had for theirs. It had been designed for some friends of Cecily's who lived part of the year here on Corsica. The owners were not there right now. They had arranged for the architect, who had a set of keys, to go with the couples on the visit. That way, he could also answer any technical questions that they might have.

They had booked a local taxi to take them a couple of kilometres to the hillside where the now completed house was situated, set amongst the wine groves. The architect's green Land Rover was parked by the side of the road, exactly where he'd said it would be. When he saw them approaching, the young man waved his arm from the open window for the taxi to follow him off onto a dirt road, which then began climbing up the hillside. After just a few minutes he stopped and got out, leaving the door open and the engine running. The four of them also got out of the airconditioned taxi into the mid-afternoon heat and a settling cloud of dust made by their own vehicles.

"There it is," said the young Corsican.

They all scanned the hillside looking for signs of a building, but there was nothing obvious to be seen.

"Where?" Roman asked impatiently.

"Right there, three hundred metres away in the centre of that hillside, a little higher than our elevation."

They all concentrated on the area where the architect was pointing. Ben was the first to pick out some faint vertical straight lines amongst the vineyard terraces' otherwise irregular surfaces. The hillside's undulating contours were scored through with two-metre-high stone walls retaining the soil in which the vines grew. A thirty metre section of terrace appeared like it had been fenced with planks of wood.

"They could be scaffolding boards," Ben suggested, as they were all equal width and length but slightly different shades of brown, which made them blend well into the stone terrace walls around them.

"Louvre shutters," the architect said, pulling out his mobile phone and selecting an app. He pressed a few links, and all the louvres began to turn simultaneously, revealing the wall of glass windows they had been shielding. "When the house is occupied in the summer, they can be programmed to track the sun, keeping the direct rays out. In the winter they can all be folded back to let in the light and heat."

Ben and Alessandra now understood what Cecily and Roman had been trying to explain about their plans for their proposed new house. This building sat so sympathetically in the landscape that it was almost invisible until any visitor got up close to it. Only from above could you see the straight lines of the structure.

"It's a stealth house," Ben joked. "Perfect if you like privacy and don't want any callers."

The architect elaborated, "Much of the house is underground. It's been dug into the hillside behind, which helps keep the temperature even all year round. It requires virtually no heating, and little cooling."

The visitors drove the remaining few hundred metres to a parking place above the house where they could then see the layout of those parts above ground level. The house still looked relatively modest in size, the pool reaching the terrace's very edge on the ocean side. Its designer was explaining that a barely submerged oxidised steel rim gave the impression of an infinity pool, without the need for an exposed glass wall on the other side. From below, they had seen for themselves that this rusted steel could not be seen protruding from the traditional stone wall terracing.

While the others went inside to look around, Ben checked out the vines growing all around the house. He noted that the planting on the narrow terrace in front of the house and behind the pool was also of vines, further helping the man-made structure blend into its environment.

Ben stooped to pick up a handful of the soil, noting how similar in colour and texture it appeared to that on his land in Seborga. Their taxi driver would later confirm that it was chalk and clay with high limestone levels, remarkably similar to that of western Liguria and its neighbouring region of Provence. Increasingly Ben realised that some of the most sought-after wines were grown on soil not so different from that of his vineyard in Seborga.

On the journey back down the hill after their tour of the house, Ben quizzed the driver, using Cecily as his interpreter.

He answered, "Oui. Patrimonio wines sell for good money in Corsica, some are even exported to mainland France and America," the local bragged with some pride. However, he also admitted that he never drank it, preferring a cheaper local variety from the south of the island that even Cecily could not repeat the name of.

Ben recalled that those on the menu at lunch earlier were all over forty euros a bottle, and some as much as one hundred euros, compared to imported French wine which was as little as ten euros for a carafe. The Patrimonio was bringing a big premium on the prices that were obtained for Rossese, also a local rustic wine with similar provenance. Ben's marketing mind was puzzled as to where perceived added value premium was in this obscure Corsican wine and who was willing to pay it. Was it better-off locals, visitors, or both, he wondered?

Claude briefed Cecily on the weather forecast for the coming days back at the boat, warning that some rough weather was due in between twenty four and thirty six hours. She explained that the winds blowing down from central France's hot plains could create high winds in the Mediterranean. The choices seemed to be leaving today in the clear weather window or risking a rough sail back, or worse, being stuck on Corsica for a few days until the storm passed. With Roman's daughter, Patsy, due to arrive in Menton a couple of days later and no one feeling up to a rough crossing, they universally agreed to leave later that day.

The weather was still beautiful, with little wind. Claude said there was plenty of time for a swim from the beach and pointed out that the sea would almost certainly be flat enough for a relaxing supper onboard once they had got underway. It was the calm before the storm so they should have a pleasant, quiet crossing overnight, and he would ask the chef to go ashore and get the ingredients.

"And a couple of bottles of Patrimonio red," Ben requested. "My treat."

Roman countered, "You already filled up our wine cellar with your wonderful Rossese before we left Menton. These bottles will be my contribution."

Knowing that they were tasting red wines, the chef sought out a butcher to cut thin escallops of local veal to make his own fast version of the Corsican classic, veau aux olives. The same shop supplied him with some charcuterie to start, and some prized Calenzana goats' cheese to follow. The butcher even supplied the Patrimonio wine from his neighbour's vineyard. It would be the perfect end to a short but memorable first visit to Corsica for Ben and Alessandra. They would return, the couple agreed, as they slipped into their bed for a much-needed rest as the boat quietly cut through the swell, heading north.

24. TOAST DI FICHE E RICOTTA

Menton was like a picture postcard in the morning sun. Its painted houses were clambering up the hillside from the harbour in a patchwork of pastel shades between creamy yellow and brown. Dominating everything was the town's enormous church, a plain rectangular slab of primrose embellished only by its unusual belltower. Square at first, the tower becomes round halfway up, as if someone decided it was not grand enough and added a bit as an afterthought.

Ben and Alessandra had breakfast on board the boat in Menton harbour with Roman and Cecily. Alessandra had brought ripe figs from her garden and the chef had sliced these with ricotta cheese on toasted bread before dribbling on some Seborga orange blossom honey. They thanked their friends for the short trip, both saying that it had been a welcome distraction from the challenges of reviving the principality's fortunes.

"There is something about being separated from the land that makes it easier to empty one's head of day-to-day issues and so think more clearly," Ben observed.

Cecily looked at Roman, who seemed to nod his agreement and she announced, "The same for us. Having slept on your suggestion, we have decided to offer Caroline the money she wants for half the farm, with a buy-back clause. We are going to put the idea to Patsy when she arrives tomorrow."

Ben was crossing his fingers behind his back and hoping that going against his instincts in proffering that suggestion did not come back to haunt him. If it all went wrong, and any of their relationships were damaged, he would not forgive himself.

"I am also much more relaxed about things when we are sailing," Alessandra agreed, changing from the subject which she could see was making her husband uncomfortable. "Unfortunately, as soon as I am back on dry land my issues all come flooding back, apparently never having been too far away. I have been asked if I can suggest something special to mark the official launch of the Club's Albergo Diffuso. They tell me that they plan to invite some of their most prominent members. Then there is Vincenzo and Renata's wedding."

Alessandra said that she was worried that neither Vincenzo nor Renata had much money to do anything very extravagant for their wedding. It was too costly for most of Renata's family to fly over there from New York, and she was only able to pay for tickets for her mother and father.

"And yet, they are two of my favourite people in all the world, and they have both waited so long to find each other. I want to make this a special day for them."

As they sipped their coffee and ate croissants, Roman suddenly stopped mid-chew, swallowed the pastry and offered, "Why don't we make it two weddings, one feast, and an opening party?"

Now they all stopped eating and swallowed coffee while digesting what Roman had said.

The Sicilian continued, "There are two churches in Seborga. Am I not right? There is the tiny old Templar church of St Bernardo and the later, larger San Martino. Like Vincenzo and Renata, Cecily and I have few friends or family we would want to invite, but I would love to make a festival for all the villagers. It would also provide a spectacle for the guests of the Club's Albergo Diffuso who could join in the party. The village is used to catering for hundreds of people during the summer festivals. What's the difference?"

"Two Italian weddings in a beautiful old village. No matter how well-off the Club members are, who would not want to be part of that party?" Alessandra acknowledged.

Cecily had only just begun to think about making wedding plans and had never envisaged anything other than a small, private affair for a dozen people, perhaps in a nice restaurant. Roman's proposition was far more ambitious than anything she had anticipated. However, an image of how such a day might look began to take shape in her mind, and it was not altogether unappealing.

"There's only one priest," Alessandra pointed out.

"He can bring in a colleague from Bordighera, or we could stagger the timing so one can preside over both," Ben put forward.

"Vincenzo is still a proud man. He would not be comfortable if he were not contributing equally," was the next obstacle spotted by Alessandra.

Roman thought for a while before saying, "I have now worked with Vincenzo in the orange groves. We understand each other. He's a farmer like me. He can provide good produce: some pigs, vegetables, olives, zucchini and so on. Cecily and I can pay for everything else. No one needs to know any numbers to compare the cost."

Suddenly very enthusiastic about Roman's wedding festival suggestion, Alessandra offered, "I could see if the Club will provide some good live music as their contribution."

The four of them talked over the remaining challenges and between them came up with solutions for every practical, emotional and ecclesiastical obstacle they could think of. They concluded that the idea seemed to provide everyone with what they wanted, whilst allowing no loss of face or denting of pride. They agreed to put it to Vincenzo and Renata-although not necessarily in that order, Alessandra contrived.

"If you are planning to show Patsy the land where you will be building your house, why don't you bring her to the Osteria for dinner? She can see the village, compare our orange groves and meet some of your new neighbours," Alessandra suggested.

"And meet the princess who is to be our head of state," Cecily added, grinning broadly.

"I doubt she will be very excited about meeting a has-been chef and ageing royal relic," Alessandra countered modestly.

"On the contrary." Roman joined in. "Having spent most of her life in American private schools, royalty and Michelin Starred chefs are top of the pecking order as far she and her friends are concerned. When will she ever meet a woman who can not only claim both those titles but who is also beautiful and successful in her own business? You will be her role model, I am sure," added the smiling Sicilian.

"That is just too much responsibility, Roman. Nevertheless, I am looking forward to meeting your daughter. Cecily tells me that she's stunning. I'll invite Tom, so she has someone her age to talk to."

After their guests had departed to return to Seborga, Cecily told Roman that she was driving over to Monaco for a few hours and would be back late afternoon. When she left in the Bentley, there was a bottle of Ben's unlabelled Rossese in her straw shoulder bag. She had read that a restaurant and wine club on the Monaco harbourside held an artisan wine event, and small growers from all over the south of France had entered produce into a tasting. These were predominantly white and Rosé wines, but there were some Grenache and Syrah blends which guests could blind taste and rate. Ribbons would be handed out to the taster's top three in each category and there was some vintage champagne for the winners.

Cecily entered Ben's unbranded wine, describing its origin as "northeast of Menton" which, although that suggested it was in France, was geographically accurate. Both she and Roman believed Ben was producing some excellent wine but wanted an independent view to confirm her instincts. She believed that this blind tasting would be attended by those who appreciated artisan wines. She did not consider wine snobs who stuck rigidly to the classic regions and producers to be her ideal audience. She had arranged to meet a couple of girlfriends for lunch while she awaited the event's outcome.

In Seborga, Tom, Marius and Vincenzo's structural work on the Albergo Diffuso properties was coming to an end. Teams of specialist contractors were now beginning to install plumbing and electrical infrastructure. With an opening deadline fast approaching, several different firms were awarded contacts and worked in parallel on the various buildings. Vincenzo's role continued as an overall site foreman, but Marius would soon be returning to the vineyards. After several months of enjoyable labour, work for Tom was running out.

The prospect of returning to London now filled Tom with dread. Like his father, he had grown to love this strange but beautiful place. Perhaps more importantly, he had found work that he enjoyed doing and was good at. Construction was physically and mentally rewarding. There was nothing better for Tom than standing back to admire some stonework he had completed. Vincenzo had taught him how to instinctively select the right shaped stone for each place in the wall. His speed had increased to almost that of a professional. He also understood structural woodwork and the basics of how a building was held together. The self-belief that he could perhaps one day build his own house was possibly the greatest achievement of his life so far, he decided.

As well as practical skills, the young Englishman's self-respect had returned. He knew that Vincenzo now valued him as a hard worker, and maybe even as a person. That meant a great deal to Tom. He had also noted that his father had begun to mention him and his achievements to people with a new sense of pride in his voice. He had decided that Alessandra was the kindest person, and latterly that her son was one of the strongest characters, he had ever met.

Tom was impressed by the tactful way Cristiano handled his gay relationship in this conservative society, which still had some way to go to accept such things readily. While he avoided any unnecessary public display that might offend older residents' sensibilities, he behaved with total honesty if confronted with direct questions about it. This matter-of-fact approach had disarmed the few people Tom had seen who had been stupid enough to make an issue of his sexuality, himself included. He suspected most of the villagers knew of Cristiano's living arrangements but simply chose not to mention it.

For the first time since school rugby, Tom felt like he belonged to something bigger than himself. He hesitated to admit it openly to anyone, but he felt his new family offered him more than his old one ever had. Also, he'd gone from living in a place where few people knew their neighbours, to having almost everyone in Seborga calling him by his first name. Indeed, since his actions during the flood, the easy-to-spot, blonde-haired Englishman had become something of a celebrity in the area.

Alessandra had asked Cristiano to prepare one of his now perfected Cappon Magro terrines to begin the lunch with Patsy, Cecily and Roman. She thought the light salad and fish dish would be a safe choice for a young woman who was possibly over-conscious of her diet. It was also a spectacular visual feast when all its contrasting colours were displayed on a long white serving dish. Two beautiful large, fresh sea bass, baked Ligurian style with olives and tomatoes, would be the main dish. There would also be sliced oven potatoes on the side, another shared platter that those with bigger appetites, like Tom and Roman, could eat heartily while others could do so sparingly.

Ben and Tom were already seated when Roman's classic Mercedes swung into the piazza with him sitting behind the huge, cream, Bakelite steering wheel.

"Cool," exclaimed Tom, who had never before seen the Sicilian's nineteen-fifties model Ponton.

“Stylish, isn’t it,” agreed Ben.

“Wow. She looks very cool as well,” added Tom, nodding in the direction of the young woman who was sitting forwards in the centre of the back seat, with her hand draped over her father’s shoulder and her head swivelling around to take in the view. Patsy’s hair was so thick and straight with a lustrous quality Cecily said she had never seen the equal of, even amongst all the professional models she had used in her cosmetics business. As she panned around the village, her hair swished back and forth and yet fell back exactly into place when she was at rest. Ben declared her to be, “Striking,” but this seemed like an understatement to Tom with her deep tan and black sunglasses.

Alessandra walked forward into the piazza to greet them, exchanging hugs first with her friends and then Patsy, who looked decidedly uncertain of how she should behave. Despite her father’s reassurances about the informality of the occasion, the young woman seemed ill-at-ease. Sensing some discomfort, Alessandra held onto the young woman’s hand and guided her to the waiting table where she was introduced to Ben and Tom. She had removed her sunglasses, which Ben noticed was a sign of common courtesy that few people seemed to practice these days. One of his pet hates was strangers who believed it was acceptable to hide behind sunglasses indoors, or worse still, under baseball caps, especially when introduced to someone for the first time.

Ben asked Tom to open the prosecco and pour them all a drink. Ben then proposed a toast, “To our new neighbours and their beautiful daughter.”

“And new business partner,” added Cecily, while passing Ben a knowing look.

Tom looked confused, unaware of the background to this impromptu announcement, but Alessandra and Cecily both noticed that he seemed more interested in the younger partner’s appearance. As the delicious courses passed by accompanied by friendly banter and talk of blood oranges, the merits or otherwise of Michelin Stars and even a little Seborgan history, it appeared that any remaining discomfort Patsy might have felt had drained entirely away.

By the time it came to dolce, Cecily and Alessandra, Ben and Roman, and Tom and Patsy held their own side conversations. Patsy's trials of learning to run a fruit farm, even with trusted staff left behind by her father, held Tom enthralled. He asked her to describe the setting of the land and the buildings. He declared it sounded "beautiful" with more volume and enthusiasm than he had intended, causing the others to all look around.

"The farm in Sicily," he offered, by way of explanation for his unintended outburst. Cecily looked at Alessandra, each knowing what the other was thinking.

When coffee was served, Ben told them that he had an announcement of his own. For a moment, he looked earnest.

"I am proud to say that my son Tom has reached the goal that we agreed on several months ago. He took on a big challenge to learn some entirely new skills, in a strange country, and save a substantial sum of money. He has exceeded our, and I suspect his own, expectations." Looking directly at his son, Ben added, "I am really proud, and I confess not a little surprised, by what you have achieved. Vincenzo has saved all the bonus money from meeting the construction deadlines. Your share is enough for you to take a break and have a holiday. Selene says you can use the Kübelwagen if you want to drive somewhere. You could go and explore Italy or France for a month or two, depending on how long you can make your money last."

They all raised their glasses and toasted, "Tom," while the subject of their good wishes looked extremely embarrassed by being put on the spot in this way. However, he was also very grateful that his father had pointedly not mentioned in front of the others the reason for his challenge to earn and save. Having his previous misdemeanours listed in front of Patsy would have been too much for the young man to endure. It also made him realise how foolish he had been back then. Had his father and Alessandra not helped him to change his ways, he knew that his prospects would almost certainly look a lot different at this moment.

By way of encouragement to explore, Roman said, "I drove up here from Sicily in that old Merc, following the coast all the way. Only took five days. I never got over sixty kilometres per hour."

"We're always short of fruit pickers if you're passing our way," Patsy chipped in.

Tom's head was now swimming with emotions and ideas. The sudden realisation that he was liberated of his obligations was both empowering and scary. Never before had he been in a situation where he had money in his pocket, a car, and easy access to places to go with it. However, after effectively setting him free, his father offered a final word of caution.

"In case you're labouring under the false impression that the Kübelwagen can run on fresh air, I have a little secret to share with you. Vincenzo has been regularly topping up your fuel tank from a spare can he keeps for the chainsaw," Ben laughed, "but I did not tell you that."

They all laughed aloud, except Tom, who looked a little embarrassed that he had not already guessed that something was not quite right with the mileage he appeared to be getting from the old jeep. He was once again deeply touched by yet another act of kindness from his supposed tough-guy boss. Tom was a little sad not to be going back to work on the construction site. Once he'd got used to it, he liked the physical work. He also like the camaraderie with his workmates. He was going to miss all of that, he realised.

25. TORTA PASQUALINA

In the days after the flood, in typical Seborga fashion, without any formal organisation or delegation of tasks, the villagers had set about clearing and cleaning the streets. Without waiting for local government help, they shovelled, swept and carried away several truckloads of material washed down off the hills behind the village. Wet rugs that had been stretched across some of the streets looked almost dry after only a day in the resurgent sun. Everyone capable was lending a hand, and those who were not watched on from their doorsteps, offering both encouragement and refreshment.

The clean-up and mostly superficial repairs resulting from the flood in Seborga had been completed in record time. Progress was given impetus by regular requests to the contractors for progress reports from the PM. Viola had from her doorstep scrutinised the operation. At each stage, as a new contractor arrived to begin work, the old lady raised her eyebrows and shook her head, before turning and disappearing back into the darkness of her house. Although she never said as much, Alessandra knew that was her way of saying 'you were warned' about bringing the Holy Grail back to Seborga.

There had been a notable increase in the number of visitors to the village. Not just all the contractors, but the publicity surrounding the flood and the daring rescue of the Grail had brought a steady flow of tourists. Some villagers were beginning to complain about parking problems and long waits to get their coffee from the cafes. However, every B&B room was full, and the tills were ringing at the shops and restaurants. Local produce was flying off the shelves as visitors wanted to take home something connected to the 'home' of the Holy Grail.

Never one to miss a marketing opportunity, Cecily had negotiated concession space in the largest souvenir shop. She arranged for this to be stocked with her blood orange beauty products. These expensive creams and lotions were displayed, along with smart marketing material explaining how the oranges packed with antioxidants were being grown all around Seborga. The first delivery had almost sold out within a week and a special delivery had been sent to restock the shelves.

Tom had set off on his road trip just as more people had started visiting. He had been supplied with a borrowed sleeping bag, rucksack and a cool box containing some beers, plus several days' supply of baked goods from Alessandra and Renata's kitchens, including a large Torta Pasqualina. Vincenzo had given him his two thousand euro bonus and discretely filled up the Kübelwagen with fuel again. He had also assembled a collection of essential tools which he had wrapped neatly in oily rags, fitted into a toolbox and packed in beside the spare wheel, just in case.

Some of the newly arriving visitors were asking at the Osteria if they could meet the 'Angel of Seborga' so it was as well that Tom was no longer around, Alessandra decided. Ben had received a message from Tom to say he had called briefly at Portofino but quickly left again when he found that a coffee cost seven euros and a beer twelve. He was last heard of heading for the Adriatic coast via Parma, where he had the offer of a room from the family of one of the girls enrolled at the Cookery School.

The fruits in Ben's vineyards were ripening nicely, and with all the other projects completed or remarkably close to being, the Englishman had a chance to concentrate on his new passion. He had also been researching the crowd-farming concept mentioned by the Slow Food guys, reading case studies and emailing some of those who had used the new online funding platforms. With the harvest approaching and the opportunity for some great photographs to back up his pitch, Ben decided the time was right to 'dabble his toe in the water' of online investment funding.

There had been no commercial winemaking in Seborga for as long as anyone could remember. However, many farmers with suitable land had grown enough grapes to make wine for themselves and their extended families. The nearest commercial winery was in Dolceaqua, and getting grapes there would require an hour-long journey in specialist transport. Ben wanted to process his own grapes on site and hoped to offer this service to his neighbours. He planned to encourage others in the village to grow more grapes and contribute them to a Seborga wine cooperative.

The former university lecturer in marketing believed that with changing customers tastes and priorities, there was now a fantastic opportunity to obtain premium prices for produce grown in Seborga. The principality had received global publicity in recent years because of its connections to the Knights Templar and the Holy Grail. A greatly raised public awareness of Seborga, combined with the legend surrounding the previously claimed 'health-benefits' of the wine from Ben's vineyard would form the basis of a marketing plan. There was a centuries-old tale told in the bars around the area about Lorenzo's healing wine. It was said that the old man's vines were irrigated by a spring that had miraculously appeared when the Holy Grail was removed from the cave in which it had been hidden. Crippled from birth, Lorenzo had been healed when he started drinking the wine as a teenager. There were other tales of cured snake bites, severe arthritis treated and even barren villagers made fertile again by Lorenzo's 'Holy Grail wine.' This was the very same vineyard that Ben had recently acquired and restored to health with the help of Vincenzo and Marius. The legend of Lorenzo's 'miraculous' wine would provide the basis of a marketing plan. Ben's would be the only commercially available wine made and bottled entirely by hand in Seborga, with all the positive associations that accompanied that provenance.

Ben's would be the only commercially available wine made and bottled entirely by hand in Seborga, with all the positive associations that accompanied that provenance.

Ben had learned that creating a basic winery was not too complicated nor was the equipment prohibitively expensive. Nevertheless, the seventy thousand euro cost was beyond his modest means. He knew that Cecily would invest without hesitating, but he was adamant that he would not mix business and pleasure with his good friends. Andrea had found out that agricultural grants could be obtained from the public sector, but these had to be matched with at least equal private funds.

Crowdfunding seemed like a possible answer, but Ben had narrowed it down to a hybrid version ideal for artisan growers, which was part auction of a share in future production. Those who bought into the concept would be looking for something more than just a financial investment. For the producer, this model was designed to raise maximum funds without equity ownership complication.

Investors would later be invited to come to Seborga to pick, produce and bottle their wine, followed by a harvest festival BBQ. The arrangement would last for five years, with an option to renew. Those who could not or did not want to make the trip would pay for the shipping of their wine but could still feel that they had been part of the process.

Ben believed that the type of investor would be people like him, who were interested in artisan wine growing but recognised that they would never be able to do anything on their own. This way, they could feel that they had part of a project and would later enjoy wine that they could genuinely call their own, having had a hand in its creation. Ben imagined that investors would probably serve their wine to friends at special celebrations or dinner parties and enthral guests with the harvest stories.

If his innovative marketing could achieve somewhere approaching twenty euros per bottle, Ben calculated that he only needed about fifteen small investors to raise the investment he needed. Potentially, if he reached his target figure, for giving up a little over ten percent of his estimated production output, he could do it. At his worst-case scenario of ten euros per bottle, he would be giving up twenty percent of his production for five years, and even that did not seem too high a price.

Before the crowdfunding offering, Selene instigated a highly targeted PR campaign on behalf of her father using the Slow Food Organisation channels. Marius had a friend with a drone camera who had taken aerial footage of the vineyard in which viewers could see the relationship between the land, the mountains and the sea. They had even been able to capture an evening when the mist rolled up from the sea below and enveloped the vines in the damp, salty air. Footage of Seborga was also included, along with images of the Holy Grail and Knights Templar iconography for context. When he felt ready, Ben set the minimum reserve bid at ten euros per bottle, clicked 'start campaign' and closed his laptop lid with his fingers crossed.

26. PINTXOS GILDA

Alessandra was in her Seborga Osteria patiently folding pasta into parcels around a spoonful of filling. She had prepared the traditional Preboggion stuffing by incorporating a dozen different wild herbs, which she had blanched in boiling water before adding a mix of local Prescinseua and Parmesan cheese, plus some breadcrumbs.

She had made only about half of the pasta parcels that she would need for an expected busy service when her phone rang. A vaguely recognisable voice from her distant past announced, slowly and very cautiously, "It's Matteo. Do you remember me?"

All of the blood suddenly drained from Alessandra's head. She became slightly dizzy, found a seat in the deserted Osteria and slumped onto it.

"Is that you, Alessandra? Are you still there?"

"Hello. Yes," was all Alessandra could think of to say.

"I'm sorry if I have shocked you. It's been a very long time," replied the still heavily-Basque-accented voice that strangely now sounded so familiar.

Alessandra had been at her uncle's New York restaurant for nearly two years when Matteo joined the team as a kitchen porter. He arrived as she had, an economic and social refugee, seeking employment, a future without boundaries and a taste for a culture not strangled by tradition. From the Bilbao area of northern Spain, the handsome Basque had grown up in a society even more matriarchal, structured and backwards looking than her own. The pair of young Europeans not only shared a similar background, but were both fiercely determined to become chefs at the highest level their talents would allow.

Both about the same age and working in a kitchen staffed mainly by more mature Puerto Ricans or Mexicans, Alessandra and Matteo were naturally drawn together. During service, the Italian head chef and his two Milanese assistants spoke in their native tongue, as did the Latinos. Matteo translated the bits of kitchen Spanish she had not already learned, and she did the same for the Italian. The pair conversed with each other in English, as both were keen to improve themselves in that language.

Matteo had also arrived armed with food preparation and presentation skills from childhood years working in a family pintxos bar. Alessandra was amazed at how the Spaniard could make something so visually appealing out of a few leftover ingredients from menu dishes. She was familiar with the rustic Italian version–bruschetta–which placed little emphasis on appearance: it was only about flavour and low cost.

In Spanish bars, Pintxos are marketed in an entirely different way. Basque drinkers are tempted to buy their Pintxos snacks for a few euros each from the beautifully displayed treats lined up behind glass counters. In Italy, bruschetta is most often served as a free of charge appetiser with an aperitivo in the early evening.

"Peen-toh" enunciated Matteo in his rough Basque accent.

"Pinto," tried Alessandra, not altogether convincingly.

Matteo laughed at her attempt, showing his immaculate white teeth contrasted against his almost black skin. Alessandra thought he had the colouring of a Gypsy, darker even than the other Latinos in the kitchen.

Working unsocial hours and living with her uncle's family in a strange city, Alessandra had no social life outside of the restaurant. She had got into the habit of staying back after service to practice her dishes and then eat the results. Keen to improve, Matteo asked if he could join her on some of these evenings, and they ended up sharing recipes and techniques. After a couple of weeks, they agreed to each cook the other a course from their home region one night. They drank a fine bottle of chilled Albarino with their respective dishes that Matteo had brought in with him. He'd also brought some Patxaran, sloe-based liqueur, for an after-dinner digestivo.

With his ink-black curly hair tied back in his whites, and his dark face unshaven, Matteo had all the makings of a future TV chef, the young Italian woman decided. After two years in New York starved of contact with anyone her age and heady with alcohol, it had been Alessandra who'd made the first move. She suddenly kissed him full on the lips with all the enthusiasm she could muster. The young man needed no further invitation, and within less than a minute, they were making love against the white tiled wall of the kitchen.

For Alessandra's part, the turn of events may have been unforeseen, but they were not in any way unwelcome. She thought Matteo extremely handsome, plus he seemed kind and honest. Also, she was beginning to think that she must be the only nineteen-year-old virgin in New York. If she later had any doubts, they were only about how she would deal with things when they went back to work the next morning. Matteo was technically her junior in the rigidly hierarchical pecking order of a kitchen. She knew that she would need to keep their liaison secret or cause problems.

Alessandra need not have worried about being in the kitchen with Matteo. When she arrived at work the next morning, her uncle was waiting for her in his office. The kitchen porters had found the Spanish liquor and wine bottle carelessly left on top of the garbage bin and informed their strict Italian boss. He had put two and two together, confronting Matteo when he turned up for work, early, as usual, the next morning. The young man immediately admitted his guilt. He was dismissed on the spot, told to collect his things and leave immediately.

Having collected her thoughts after the shock of hearing Matteo's voice on the phone after all, these years, Alessandra finally managed to say, "What a surprise. What have you been up to?"

Matteo filled in the events of the intervening three decades with a synopsis of his career, beginning with an unexpected and swift departure from New York. He told her that following his dismissal, a relative had sent him an offer of a job in Los Angeles and forty-eight hours later, he was working there. From there, he'd worked in San Francisco and eventually moved to London, from where he was calling now.

"But you could have called me then and explained," Alessandra said, suddenly feeling bafflingly emotional about what was effectively one date almost a lifetime ago.

"I can't repeat what your uncle said he would do to me if I called the restaurant or his house. I had no other way of contacting you. There were no mobile phones back then, remember. That Italian chef also warned me that he would have me blacklisted as a troublemaker in every New York kitchen. When I got the offer to go to LA, there seemed no choice but to go."

Alessandra said nothing; her silence conveyed her renewed sense of betrayal and sadness.

"To be honest, Alessandra, afterwards I thought that you were not only above my pay grade but also out of my league. You were so beautiful and talented and seemed to me so worldly. I could not believe what happened that night. I thought it was just the drink that made you kiss me and was not sure you would want to speak to me again, even if I had called."

Matteo was now sorry he had said what he just had. It had not been his intention to bring up the past in this way but now found himself surprised by Alessandra's reaction. From afar, he had watched her career with interest, picking up every snippet of kitchen gossip or industry media news that mentioned her name. He was astonished when the story emerged a few years later that she was a princess of an obscure principality in Italy. This had convinced him that what had happened was a one off that would never be repeated. He'd moved on with his life but still kept an eye on her career as she scaled the ladder to the top.

Alessandra realised that her over-emotional reaction was ridiculous and the result of the shock of suddenly hearing Matteo's voice, like a ghost from her past. She composed herself and replied, "It's very nice to hear from you, Matteo, but I assume that you have not suddenly decided to make a call you should have made thirty years ago," while trying not to sound any more bitter than her choice of words made inevitable.

"No. You are right. That was not my intention. I too earned a Michelin Star eight years ago and have since gained another."

"Two-star chef. Congratulations. But again, I can assume that you had plenty of people in London to pat you on the back without ringing a former one-star like me in Italy."

"I'm ringing because the guy from the Michelin guide, who I am now quite friendly with, mentioned your name out of the blue recently. He is naturally very guarded when talking about other chefs or restaurants but in passing asked if I knew you or if I had heard anything about you since you'd departed New York. I told him that I was proud to have worked under you very briefly, thought that you were incredibly talented, and that you were working again in your native Seborga. He nodded as if he already knew that."

"And did your friend from Michelin say why he was asking?"

"Alas, he did not. However, I believe that he must have had a good reason to bring up your name after all these years. I would not be too surprised if you get a visit to Seborga, which is why I am calling. I wanted to give you a heads-up so that you're not caught unprepared."

"Well, thank you Matteo, but I don't think Seborga is quite ready for tiny portions of pretentious food dressed up with flowers foraged from a Norwegian fiord and flown halfway around the world because they're just the right shade of blue.

That kind of cooking might still have a market in Copenhagen, San Francisco or London, but never took off in Italy and never will."

"You're angry, Alessandra. I get it, and frankly, I'm flattered. This call was a mistake. I am sorry. I wish you all the luck in the world, with whatever you do. Goodbye."

She sat in the chair for some time still holding the now silent phone to her ear, trying to work out her feelings. She was jealous; she concluded quickly. That could have been her in London with two stars. No, she changed her mind. She was angry. That loser ex-husband, who she had later clung to after Matteo left, had flushed their successful life down the pan with his drug habit. Finally, she felt ashamed. Ashamed that she had spoken to Matteo as she had, and now also sad that she had forgotten all the good things that had happened to her. It had been kind of him to call her, she acknowledged. She had no right to have spoken to him like that.

Her youthful encounter with the handsome Spaniard had been blissful while it lasted, and it had undoubtedly ended memorably in the kitchen that night: really without fault on either side, she now realised. She should have celebrated Matteo's success, rather than being churlish, and must have sounded mean-spirited and bitter. After all, she had made her own choice to return to Seborga to look after her father. The old prince had then seen her happily remarried and surrounded by his family when he later died. It was pointless and frustrating, wondering what might have been. Alessandra resolved to find the number for Matteo and call him back to apologise. She would do it this afternoon, when she had pulled herself together, she decided.

But the phone call had also stirred other old feelings. Although Alessandra had always tried to shy away from the spotlight and concentrate on her cooking, she admitted to herself that she had enjoyed her moments of fame. The glowing reviews and the flattering magazine features had made her proud. Mainly as these accolades were for achievements before anyone knew of her royal title. She never did find out who tipped off the press about her being a princess but always suspected it had been her then-husband and business partner. If it were him, trying to boost their restaurant's takings even further, his ploy had worked. The customers all wanted to be cooked for by, or even meet, the 'princess in the kitchen.'

There were times–not so many these days–when Alessandra missed New York. Matteo's call reminded her of her youth in the most exciting city in the world. A place that could not have been more different than the one she had grown up in. She could source almost any ingredient from anywhere on the planet, at any time of the year. Back then, she thought this was the most liberating thing for a young chef. What became known as 'nouvelle cuisine' was born back then out of the emerging globalisation of ingredients and cooking styles.

A new generation of chefs had now realised that they, and their children, might be the ones paying for their predecessors' excesses. The final irony for Alessandra was that now she had these young chefs coming to Seborga to learn about cooking, precisely because here they had always practised local, unpackaged and seasonal sourcing. Both her life and what she considered good practice had gone full circle.

27. AGNELLO AL PESTO DI FAVA

A handful of sun-weathered locals sat on two adjoining benches in the shade of a big old Ficus tree. There was much pointing and shaking their heads as they watched three young men erect state of the art solar panels. A week ago, a different team had arrived and built what looked like a wooden frame, like those used for growing vines, above six existing parking places on the edge of the village. When they had finished, a sign was erected announcing that this was an experimental project jointly funded by the European Union, FIAT and ENEF Energy.

Today, this team was installing two-metre by one metre black panels on top of the wooden frame already in place. These panels were facing south and would have sun for more than twelve hours each day. This design would provide electrical power from the sun and shade for the cars, reducing their need for fuel-consuming air-conditioning. Two days after the solar panel fitting, a car transporter navigated all the tight hairpin bends to reach the villages and unloaded six brand new Fiat electric cars. These cars had been custom painted in the azure blue of Seborga's flag. The truck driver parked the cars under the solar panels, plugged them into the new charging sockets and then dropped the electronic master keys with Alessandra at the Osteria.

She came out with Ben to admire their latest experiment, but by then the five older men were already running appreciative fingers over the cars' new paintwork and trying to peer into the cabins through the tinted glass.

"Bella, Principessa ma dureranno a lungo," said the boldest of the old farmers, expressing his prediction that they would be damaged or stolen before too long by people from the city.

Just then one of the men pressed a little too hard on the door to test the steel's thickness. An electronic voice emanated from somewhere inside the car, "Stop. Security alert. Possible intruder."

The old man let go of the metal as though he had received an electric shock, but was merely startled by the talking car. All his friends also backed away, looking disturbed by the idea that this car seemed alive with a mind and temper of its own.

Alessandra explained that only those residents who had registered with an account could book a slot to use the cars. The vehicles had satellite trackers, all-round CCTV and a remote disable mode programmed into their systems. A mobile phone application was needed as a key. The cost of hiring them would be debited based on the individual's insurance group, time used, mileage covered, and the number of people in the car. The number of passengers would be checked by CCTV and confirmed by a sensor under each seat. More occupancy would actually reduce the cost to the hirer. The aim was to promote car sharing.

The same mobile phone app could be used to build up transport credits from separating and recycling household waste into bar-coded bags, choosing plastic-free packaging at the store and refilling drinking water bottles at the central dispenser. This trial model was only designed to recover its operating costs and an element of depreciation. Although the cars had a petrol engine, that was only meant to be for emergency use, and any traditional-fuelled mileage was charged at a premium price.

"Good environmental practice will be rewarded with cheap transport," Alessandra tried to explain, but could see that this concept would take some getting used to amongst the older residents.

It was an experiment of as much interest to Fiat and ENEF as to the Italian Prime Minister and those in running the project in Seborga. They had one year to see how well it worked or to discover what problems arose. They all understand that if it were successful, this was a model capable of being rolled out in similar communities all over Italy. It would take this afternoon in the sun to fully charge the cars and they would be available to use that night when Ben and Alessandra planned to drive to Bordighera to test one. Later the following day, the environmental group planned to meet to inspect the new cars and their solar charging point, before their progress review meeting.

When Ben arrived, the Osteria's kitchen smelled sweetly of rosemary, as Alessandra had been roasting lamb for the lunch they would have after the Environmental Committee meeting.

"What are we having?" Ben asked, rubbing his tummy in a circular motion.

"Oven-roasted lamb chops on broad bean pesto."

"A new twist on pork with white beans?" Ben suggested.

"Si, Signore Ben," replied his wife with a small curtsey, mimicking a stereotype of a servant's manner from an old movie.

Cecily arrived first, keen to exchange news with her friend before anyone else on the committee came, so Ben left them to chat alone. Within fifteen minutes a full turnout of members had arrived; only the prime minister was late, having messaged saying that he would join in later by video link from Rome. Before the meeting, each member had submitted to Ben a short, written summary of their progress on their allocated tasks, and he had sent an abridged version to Andrea.

Ben got things started by reporting that he had accessed an electric car after a brief struggle with the app technology and that he and Alessandra had enjoyed a comfortable, almost silent drive to Bordighera market to get the main ingredient for their lunch today. Less than five euros had been charged to his account for the round trip for two, which he considered good value. Having brought back fresh food in a car without air conditioning, as many people would do, he did have one suggestion–that a cool box or insulated bag could be left in the back of each car.

"I have some empty insulated boxes which the fish and meat delivery guys leave at the Osteria. I could clean and recycle these. They would easily fit in the back."

"Problem solved," said Ben.

The prime minister's face suddenly appeared on the laptop screen at the head of the table. The rest of the meeting passed at an astonishingly fast pace, as the young politician demonstrated his people management skills. He prompted speakers in turn, but then politely cut them off if they strayed off-topic or prevaricated. If he had the information on which to base them, his decisions came without hesitation. If no action was appropriate, Andrea made requests for further research directed to individuals with an exact deadline for reporting back to him. There was no ambiguity and no loose ends. He was generous with praise and sparing with admonishment, while at the same time making any disappointment with progress evident to all.

"Compared to most of the meetings I attend, this is a breath of fresh air," Cecily whispered to Alessandra. "These days, no one wants to make a decision or take responsibility. So, nothing gets done. Andrea's more like an entrepreneur than a politician," she added.

Whispering to her friend, Alessandra said, "Let's hope his willingness to take risks is not his undoing."

The initiatives put forward at the inaugural meeting nearly all seemed to have either been activated or progressed as far as possible. Only finding a practical organic fertiliser for the terraces was proving challenging. The suggestion to harvest seaweed had hit some barriers; ironically, mainly on environmental grounds. Because it had not previously been considered, there was insufficient research into the impact of what cutting large swathes of seaweed from the seabed might be on marine life.

Andrea had at once interrupted the scientist from the Monaco Oceanographic Institute. “That’s something we will not resolve in an acceptable timescale. Here’s what we will do instead. I will personally ask the fisherman’s union at Ventimiglia to keep the seaweed which I know comes up every day in their nets, and which they normally throw back. We will get that delivered to Seborga every day for a week to run a proof of concept study on whatever area those seven loads will fertilise. If that is only a few hundred square metres—so be it. In a year we can see if that has improved the soil. In the meantime, you keep looking for a more sustainable supply source.”

Reflecting after the meeting, Ben thought that they had made remarkable progress on a wide variety of issues in a truly short space of time. The take up of plastic-free packaging at the village food store was growing each week. He felt that this acceptance would accelerate with the school’s initiative and now that villagers could also gain transport credits from using it. Andrea reported that the legislation on environmentally friendly building materials was underway, but would take a while longer. Only the sourcing of a local supply of organic fertiliser was preventing progress on all fronts.

“What about the organic matter filtered out during wine production? Stalks, leaves and skin etc,” Ben offered.

“And the tonnes of stones removed from the olives during oil making. They could surely be crushed or ground down,” Alessandra suggested.

Cecily then joined in with, “Then there’s the skin and pulp left over after removing the juice from the blood oranges.”

“Now we might be onto something, but more test sites are required to measure the benefits,” Andrea quickly concluded. “The Slow Food students could surely run some simple tests.

Also, get them to try one with a mix of the three sources of organic material to see if a blend works even better."

Andrea wrapped up the meeting by congratulating everyone on their achievements and thanking them for their time, before reminding each of what he was expecting them to do next. Before ending the video call, he asked, "What am I missing on the lunch menu today, Princess Alessandra?"

After hearing what she had prepared, Andrea sighed and quoted an old Italian proverb, "At the table, we do not grow old," to which Ben responded with another, "Age, like glasses of wine, should not be counted."

Andrea laughed. "Your grasp of Italian culture is getting better, Ben."

"It's understanding Italian women that I need help with," Ben joked.

"Ah, yes. I have a similar problem with English girls," the Italian sympathised.

Alessandra ended their private joke when she said, "I have a Seborgan proverb for you both: a husband who makes fun of his wife, often goes without lunch."

Bordighera harbour overlooked by the belle epoque Villa Garnier.

Drawing by Linda McCluskey

28. TURLE

Roman and Cecily were due in Seborga for dinner with their friends at 7 pm. Cristiano was asked if he would cover for her in the Osteria that evening so that everyone, including Alessandra, could enjoy a relaxed dinner. Her son's agreement to cook that night also allowed Alessandra to dress up more than she would typically in her restaurant. She told Ben that he was to wear his linen suit. Cristiano had devised a special menu, different from that of the other guests in the Osteria. He had done most of the preparation for those dishes earlier in the day. Aware that Cecily and Roman's wedding was coming up, the young chef viewed tonight's dinner as an audition to cater for that event. Knowing that Cecily could easily afford to bring in caterers from Nice, San Remo or even Monaco, Cristiano was determined that would not happen.

Cecily arrived with Roman, who was carrying what looked like a wooden wine box. She was also carrying a small parcel, but neither handed these over when they arrived, as one would if they had been gifts. Instead, they greeted their friends as normal and placed the two items on the table. Ben poured prosecco, and on hearing the cork pop out of the bottle, Cristiano appeared with a plate of sardine fillets with soft white onions, raisins and pine nuts.

"I have a toast, which I will follow with a small confession," Cecily began. "My toast is congratulations to Ben Morton, the award-winning winegrower."

Alessandra raised her glass and looked to Ben for any hint of an explanation, but he seemed just as perplexed as she was. Everyone having chinked and then taken a drink from the glasses, Cecily explained how she had heard about a wine tasting for small artisan growers held in Monaco. She told them that she had taken one of the several unlabelled bottles of his own Rossese that Ben had brought onto the yacht to enjoy during their trip to Corsica and entered it in the competition.

It was the only Italian wine entered. All the others were French and were from established small wineries whose produce had previously been sold commercially. The event sponsors were looking for exceptional products that had greater commercial potential if they received sufficient investment or marketing support. Cecily now handed over the parcel she had brought to Ben, while Roman placed the wine box alongside it.

"Of the twelve entries, your beautiful Rossese wine won the bronze medal in the blind tasting," Cecily said with obvious glee.

Looking shocked and staying silent, Ben opened the brown paper package to discover a slim leather case. Inside that was a coloured ribbon sporting a large bronze medallion, embossed with a wreath of grapevines and inscribed in French. He looked at it, clearly not knowing quite what to say.

Alessandra stepped in to help him out by hugging Cecily, saying, "You little genius. What a great idea. Trust you to be so proactive."

"I'm only a genius because my hunch paid off. I am not sure what I would have done if the judges had declared Ben's wine undrinkable rubbish."

"Yes, that would have made us both look like fools," Ben finally joined in.

"Well, perhaps not you, Ben, because I don't think I would have had the heart to own up and tell you. I would just have kept my foolishness to myself," Cecily said, laughing.

Ben now opened the wine box to reveal an excellent bottle of vintage champagne which was the other prize.

"We took the liberty of keeping that chilled, in case you wanted to open it tonight," Cecily said, laughing.

"What a wonderful start to the evening," Ben said, still clutching his medal and now glowing with pride. "We have our own bit of good news to share. The deadline of my bid to obtain crowd-farming closes later this evening, but it is already past the minimum level that would give me the funds I need to complete the winery. My marketing message seems to have struck a chord with some people."

Roman and Cecily clapped gently, and they joined in with another toast proposed by Alessandra. "My husband, the winegrower and winemaker."

Roman patted Ben on the shoulder. He expressed his astonishment at how he had convinced people who he had never met, who had not visited Seborga, to pay upfront for a wine they had yet to taste, that they would not receive for another year.

"That's the power of marketing, Roman," was all Ben would say on the matter.

While they were chatting, a taxi pulled up outside the Osteria which, despite the recent tourism boom, was still an unfamiliar sight in Seborga. The lone passenger took some time to extract himself from the rear seat, as though they were not as agile as they might once have been. From his stature, skin tone, manner and dress, all four immediately guessed he was a foreigner, probably northern European and most likely English. He had the bearing of a man born to be significant or one who had made himself important through achievement. Perhaps an ex-military or naval man, Ben wondered.

The tourist trade at the Osteria had increased steadily in recent years. These diners were often pre-booked groups, or at least couples, who had made the trip specifically to eat there after reading or seeing some media coverage. There were few walk-in customers and virtually no single foreigners.

What these new customers all had in common was that they were all devout foodies interested in what they saw as their discovery of the little-explored cuisine of the Ligurian Maritime Alps. They were looking for something different to taste, cook, or talk about at their dinner parties back home. They were good customers who ate heartily, drank good wine and tipped well. They would also often take away local produce and write lengthy positive reviews.

Cristiano greeted the stranger, beginning by speaking in Italian but being quickly interrupted by the man speaking in English. Switching languages mid-sentence, Cristiano confirmed his reservation and showed him to a small table set for two. Clearing the unwanted second place setting, the young chef quickly returned with a single sheet paper menu. Before he could rush back to the kitchen, as had been his intention, the man engaged him in a conversation that was unwelcome during this busy service. Cristiano kept turning his head and looking towards the kitchen door as he backed away from the table, but the man showed no sign of ending his apparent interrogation. In the end, Cristiano became more forceful. He apologised to the man but insisted that he had much work to do.

Turning reluctantly to the short menu, the stranger looked less than pleased, as though unused to anyone not paying him full attention. He glanced at the kitchen door every few moments as if expecting Cristiano returning to apologise and answer his questions. A few tables away, the newly-crowned bronze medal winemaker was too busy revelling in his new status to notice any of this. Cecily was also enjoying the smug feeling of having instigated Ben's award and seeing his delight at it. Roman was chatting to Alessandra about Patsy, telling her that he was still worried about her American boyfriend's commitment. The frustrated musician had moved into the farm with his daughter several weeks ago, but still spent much of his days writing songs, making video recordings and sending them to agents in the States.

"He has yet to pick up a shovel or some secateurs. My impression is that if someone rang him up and offered him a singing job, or even a support tour with a mediocre band, he'd pack his bags and go back," the savvy Sicilian told Alessandra.

"That is no situation for my daughter, or for the farm, to be in. He's a nice enough kid, but he's chasing a dream. There's just no commitment. He's only in Sicily with Patsy because for the moment he has not got a better offer."

"I can't judge someone too harshly for chasing their dream," Roman said. "That's what I did, and I found mine. However, I agree that he's a fool if he walks away from Patsy and the farm. I had little to lose when I left, but she is beautiful and kind."

Wishing to change the subject to something more positive but without thinking about it too much, Alessandra asked, "How is your other daughter getting on? Caroline, isn't it? I assume that they will get over for the wedding." Even as she said it, she realised that this was probably not a safe assumption at all.

Roman pursed his lips in a false smile that looked more like a frown. "You would think that she would be happy, wouldn't you? Despite my advice not to, she has extracted the money she wanted out of the farm and let her idiot husband gamble with it. Instead of thanking Cecily, she now gives us the impression we have somehow conspired to side-line her to form a business partnership with Patsy. As for the wedding: frankly no, I am not sure that she will deem our wedding worth a transatlantic trip, no matter how much that pains me. She has not replied to our invitation."

Alessandra noticed that each time anything arrived at the Englishman's table, he tried instigating another conversation with the member of staff delivering it. She assumed that the man must be lonely. Perhaps a widower, she pondered, eating alone in a foreign country. Then she spotted a notepad on the table into which he kept making entries with a pencil which he withdrew from the spine of the book. A travel journal, she guessed.

When their pasta course arrived, talk moved to the wedding plans. Cecily revealed that they had received the agreement of

Seborga's priest that his colleague from Bordighera would conduct a blessing for Cecily and Roman. It would be at the old Templar church of San Bernado, after their civil ceremony. The timing would be thirty minutes after Renata and Vincenzo's full wedding ceremony at the main church of San Lorenzo, to allow any guests who wanted to attend both.

Alessandra reported that Renata had told her that all her arrangements had been finalised. Her parents had now both received their passports, visas and plane tickets. While the women talked, Ben and Roman had begun eating their pasta with enthusiasm.

"Have you tried this?" Ben directed to his wife. "It's incredibly good."

"What is it?" enquired Cecily.

After tasting a forkful, Alessandra replied, "Turle. Shepherds' purse pasta made with homemade cheese and potato. The typical Cucina Bianca (white food) of this region."

"That sounds so stodgy, and yet it's so light," Cecily commented after tasting a forkful.

Alessandra explained that Toma was a soft cheese made by the mountain shepherds mostly for their own consumption. After the cheese is mixed with fluffy boiled potatoes, a little fresh mint is added to the pasta stuffing. The sauce is just butter and parmesan, with a bit of pasta water.

"Although the filling is not too heavy, it's the pasta that is so good. It's thin and slightly elastic and so does not hide all the flavour packed inside. I think this is Cristiano's suggestion as a pasta dish for the wedding feast. Cheese and potato are universal flavours which few people will not like."

The chef explained that when catering for larger numbers of people, the more of the skilled work that could be done well in advance, the better the final product.

"Only overcooking the pasta could spoil a course like this because all the preparation is done beforehand."

"But if this Toma cheese is so rare because it is only made for the shepherds and their families, how are we to source enough to feed two sets of wedding guests?" Cecily queried.

"That is where Vincenzo comes into his own," Alessandra said, smiling knowingly.

The elderly Englishman had finished his pasta and was making more notes, while keeping a watching eye for any staff member who might be willing to talk to him. Sure enough, when one of the young students came to take away his wiped-clean dish, he appeared to be bombarding her with questions. Alessandra decided that she would speak to the gentleman before he left and try to discover his story.

Cecily agreed that with the various backgrounds of the wedding guests, they would have to plan the menu quite carefully to please everyone. She acknowledged that Vincenzo's family and friends, being all local farmers, would surely be little challenge. However, Renata's parents had been poor Mexican immigrants, whilst her new American friends were chefs and foodies from several countries. Cecily's guests would be a mix of mainly wealthy internationals, including several British business associates. An only child with both his parents now deceased, Roman had only his daughters and their respective partners - if they accepted-plus some old farmer friends from Sicily.

Alessandra pulled a face and summarised the diverse tastes that they would have to satisfy with this menu, "So, there's a couple of Mexicans, some New Yorker caterers, your millionaire, international business associates and Roman's Sicilian Mafia connections. Have I forgotten anyone?" she joked.

"Yes, our VIP guest, the Prime Minister of Italy, oh and an Icelandic vegan, who works for me in Monaco," Cecily said, laughing. "Oh, and I nearly forgot, and the Princess of Seborga, who I hear is very choosy about what she eats. So, no pressure at all."

The two women laughed even louder at the absurdity of the situation they had just described. Hearing them laughing, the elderly Englishman looked over to their table and smiled when he caught their eye.

"At least the only journalist present will be Ben's daughter, and so no one will be writing a critical review of the food," Cecily assured her.

Hearing the mention of 'review' caused Alessandra to freeze. She looked around again towards the single Englishman who was once again writing in his notebook.

"No. It couldn't be!" she exclaimed, now looking horrified.

"Couldn't be what?" asked Cecily, their change in tone having now interrupted Ben and Roman's conversation.

"It's impossible," Alessandra continued, apparently speaking to herself and ignoring Cecily.

"What is so unlikely, darling?" Ben asked his wife, seeing the alarm on her face.

Alessandra collected her thoughts and then replied, "That could not be the inspector from Michelin?"

The other three all looked at each other in turn. Each was searching for any clue as to what their friend was referring to.

"You will have to explain, darling, because none of knows what you are talking about."

Alessandra explained about the phone call that she had received a while ago warning that a Michelin restaurant inspector had been making enquiries about her with a former colleague in London. And, that he thought that might be the prelude to an inspection visit to Seborga with a view to an entry in the guide.

"You didn't say anything about this," Ben said, both puzzled and slightly injured by her apparent secrecy.

Alessandra did not respond but quickly left her chair, threw her napkin onto the table and headed in the direction of the kitchen to speak to her son. Emerging a few moments later, she went to talk to the mysterious Englishman. He saw Alessandra approaching and rose from his chair to greet her.

"Have you enjoyed your dinner?" she asked him, smiling. Explaining, "I am the proprietor, and normally the cook, but tonight I am having a night off to dine with my friends."

"You look like you are having a wonderful time with your elegant friends. I have been very envious of your cheerful company. The owner of the establishment and the head chef, you say?" the man checked, trying to clarify her status and avoid her question.

"Si, Alessandra," she responded, leaving out her royal title to avoid having to explain that.

"And the man on the right is your husband?" he probed.

"Yes, a fellow Englishman, Ben Morton. My son is in the kitchen holding the reins for his mother. My son from my first marriage," Alessandra said instinctively, not knowing why she felt the need to explain this detail.

"A cooking dynasty. I must return when the queen is in her kitchen."

Alessandra now wondered if the word 'dynasty's' choice was deliberate and if this amiable stranger knew more than he was letting on. At this moment Cristiano emerged from the kitchen with the man's dolce. Beads of sweat had soaked into his bandana, and he looked more ill at ease than Cecily had ever seen him. Placing the dish on the Englishman's table, he wiped the edge with a clean cloth that he had draped over his arm.

"I will say goodnight before you leave. Enjoy your pudding."

As she left, Cristiano began explaining the dish in English, now eagerly volunteering the details that the guest had previously had to prise out of him. He described the Fruili Venezia Giulia as, "plum-filled potato dumplings with cinnamon and nutmeg."

Alessandra returned to her table where all three were eagerly awaiting her conclusion at the stranger's identity and any further explanation as to why he was here alone.

"And?" enquired Cecily, impatiently, when Alessandra returned to their table.

"I don't think so. He's just a lonely older guy who likes his food and keeps a journal of his travels. However, he has been asking lots of questions about the place and the staff," she added. "And yet, he won't be drawn into commenting on anything he has been served. He responds to every enquiry with another question."

"It doesn't sound like you are completely certain about him to me," Ben challenged. "You won a star in New York. Did you not meet the inspector from Michelin then and get some idea of what they were like?"

"The first we knew about the award of the star was a letter in the post, followed by a story in the New York Times the next day," Alessandra told them. "These people don't identify themselves when they book and they certainly don't visit the kitchen, where I would have been all night."

"What if he were a Michelin reviewer?" asked Roman. "Do you care about his opinion? You have nothing to prove that you have not already. Why bother about him?"

Alessandra knew that Roman was right to point this out. She had told her friends many times how she felt that this part of her life was behind her. Nevertheless, she found herself confused by her feelings about the evolving events. Seeking a Michelin Star at the Osteria had never even crossed her mind. Would she even want it if it were offered: probably not, she concluded? However, she knew that Cristiano wanted nothing more and had nearly fainted when his mother warned him of her suspicion about the man who had already consumed two of his courses. All the blood drained from his face as he tried to recall how well presented the dishes he had sent out had been.

Ben tried to rationalise the likelihood of this man being who Alessandra feared it might be by making one of his checklists and ticking off imaginary boxes: he was mature, a stranger, dining alone, inquisitive, apparently knowledgeable, and evasive.

"We either need to know the depth of his knowledge or the lengths he will go to not to give himself away. We will invite him to join us for a digestivo. Roman can divert him with Sicilian fishing tales while Cecily quizzes him about his favourite places to eat. Alessandra can ask him if he knows how a panna cotta is made and I will test his wine knowledge."

"Good plan," agreed Cecily, intrigued by the idea of secretly investigating the stranger with a devious interrogation of their suspect.

"What if he's found guilty?" Roman asked.

"Then you and Vincenzo will have to do away with him and dispose of the body before he gets away and writes his review," Ben joked.

The elderly Englishman enthusiastically accepted the invitation to join their table. They were all poured some of Cristiano's experimental blood orange version of their usual limoncello digestivo. The man was easy, agreeable company but with a politician's guile when it came to avoiding direct questions. After an hour of talking to the stranger, it felt like he had extracted more from the four of them than they had collectively learned from him.

Nevertheless, they had established that his name was Alistair, he was a well-travelled connoisseur of food and wine but they had no clue how he had made a living or paid for these indulgences. When he learned that Cecily lived on a yacht, he said he had once owned a Swan-a rare and expensive classic sailing boat, she informed them.

Although he was polite and engaged with everyone around the table, two things were evident; it was clear that Alessandra was the focus of his attentions, and there did seem to be a hidden agenda. He clung to her every word and encouraged her to elaborate on any comment she made on any subject.

Afterwards, Cecily said that she was surprised that he did not continue making notes, as he had been before he joined them.

"It has been an enchanting evening in fine company and a beautiful setting," was the stranger's parting assessment, apparently purposefully avoiding any specific reference to the food he had eaten. He had seemed unconcerned that his taxi had been standing in the piazza for at least twenty minutes with the meter running while they chatted. When it pulled away, all four friends looked at each other to see who would voice their opinion first.

It was Ben who broke the silence, "I am going to say no, I don't think he is from Michelin. Not because I think that he could not do the job well, but because I don't believe he would sit down with a chef-proprietor of a place he was evaluating, as he just did. However, if I am wrong, I would say we have nothing to worry about, because I think he has fallen in love with my wife and will award her three stars."

They all laughed, but Alessandra soon became serious again. "I'm now beginning to think he might just be an inspector."

Cecily agreed, saying, "His knowledge of relatively obscure but highly regarded restaurants around the world is impressive. He'd visited the little-known Petit Max in Hampton Wick in the early nineties when it was still opening as a greasy spoon café during the day, only to be transformed into a first-class rustic French bistro at night. After that, they moved further into London and won a Michelin Star. A coincidence?" she proposed.

Then Alessandra remembered, "And then there was The Cleveland Tontine, my chef-friend Eugene's family's place in Yorkshire. He said that he had also dined there, and Eugene acknowledged they could have easily earned a star if they had wanted it. But Eugene chose not to because they said it would bring what he saw as the wrong type of customer and put off all their regulars."

"He certainly knows his French wines, even if he'd never before tried an Italian Rossese," Ben conceded, before qualifying any inferred shortcoming by acknowledging, "but then again, few people outside of Liguria have."

"And he immediately identified the merest hint of cinnamon in Cristiano's Quaresimali," Alessandra added.

With the jury still out on the English stranger's status, Cristiano burst out of the kitchen and almost ran across the Osteria to their table.

"Was it him? What did he say?" the young man quizzed breathlessly.

His mother answered, "We don't know. On the balance of probability, no. We don't think he would have joined us for a digestivo or been quite so amenable if he was here carrying out such important work."

"Unless that is just his way of looking under the skin of the restaurant. If he wanted to find out just how deep the commitment to quality and authenticity goes, he could not rely on just one meal," Cristiano argued, part of him hoping that the English stranger was from Michelin.

Roman as ever had the more measured view and framed his assessment in terms of advice for the young chef, "Whether he is or is not, if his approval is what you aspire to, the lesson is surely to assume any customer from now on could be the next Michelin inspector."

Cristiano mumbled goodnight and headed back to the kitchen with his head down, looking deflated, confused and concerned by the events of the evening, and with Roman's advice ringing in his ears and now burnt into his consciousness.

29. FARINATA

The day before the double weddings dawned damp and misty after an overnight shower, which everyone hoped was not a precursor to worse weather to come. Now that the morning sun had peeked over the roofs of the surrounding houses, the puddles in the piazza were evaporating and turning to steam. There was a frenzy of activity that would have looked like chaos to the outsider, but to the villagers was just like preparing for another festival: a weekly occurrence during the summer.

Vans were arriving, unloading and departing in a relentless stream, like ants delivering food to their nest. Local men were hanging lights on wires suspended over the piazza and another group were hanging Seborgan flags from any available upright. Despite the chaos, empty boxes, and vehicles, the setting for the wedding feast already looked impressive, Ben thought.

Later that day, when all the overhead work was complete, trestle tables and benches would be set out capable of seating four hundred guests. Amid the small army of people in the piazza, Vincenzo was directing operations; every now and then, his booming voice could be heard, "Si, si, si." and then moments later, "No, no, no."

As he approached to offer his help, Ben could detect some tension and urgency in the voice of the usually calm and measured Vincenzo. Ben was handed a bundle and asked to put up signs that would direct strangers to the village towards various facilities around the piazza. Armed with a stapler and a roll of gaffer tape he set about his task, happy to have avoided lifting anything too heavy or having to climb anything too high.

Ben was also relieved to be out of the house. Their home kitchen had been seconded as a pasta-making factory, while other food preparation was concentrated in the Cookery School. Ben had told Vincenzo that the collective chatter from all the village women while they kneaded dough was deafening. He had added that a choking cloud of double-zero flour was hanging in the air and had coated everything on the ground floor.

Ben was fastening the last sign pointing to the toilets when he heard the distinctive sound of an air-cooled VW engine climbing the last hill up the village. As he looked around, Selene's distinctive yellow Kübelwagen with its soft top down turned the corner. Tom's short hair looked almost white against his nut-brown skin. He spotted Ben and waved. Ben put down his tools and went to greet his son, who he had heard little from in the several weeks that he had been away. He did not know that he would be back for the wedding, so this was a great surprise.

"Why didn't you tell me you were coming?"

"I was afraid that you would line up lots of work for me," Tom answered with his famous disarming grin.

"You were right. As you mention it, I now have the funding to build the winery, so your return to Seborga could be good timing. You don't want too much time off, or you'll get flabby again." However, as he said this, Ben noticed that far from putting on weight, Tom looked even fitter than when he had left.

"I have been working. I travelled extensively throughout Italy as well. Me and this old Kübelwagen have visited three new seas–the Adriatic, Ionian and Tyrrhenian."

Ben quickly made a mental map of possible routes to take in these bodies of water and could see that his son must have traversed the full width and length of Italy.

"Alessandra will be delighted to see you, and your sister arrives later today. Andrea can't get here until morning. He's being driven overnight from Rome so that he can get some sleep on the way. Speaking of which, how tired are you, do you need to rest?"

Tom explained that he had spent the night before on Selene's journalist friend's sofa in Genoa, so he had only had a two-and-a-half hour drive this morning.

"I'm ready to help. I'll park the car and then go and see my site foreman and get instructions. By the way, I saw the solar electric car charging station on my way in. Very impressive. Somehow looks strange in this ancient place but I can't wait to try one."

Ben explained that the solar needed to be topped up with main power but that they were looking into the feasibility of siting some additional panels on the walls of the terraces below the car park.

"Oh, and the Albergo Diffuso has opened to visitors. Wait until you see it. It looks wonderful and is already full of wealthy guests."

The Albergo Diffuso had opened all fifteen of its letting rooms ten days earlier. They first had a dry run, when directors and managers from other locations and their partners were asked to try out and critique the rooms and facilities. Only then had they opened to invited VIP guests. Rightly anticipating being oversubscribed, the Club had chartered a large yacht in Monaco for any overspill. Members could book a few days at each location with shuttle transport laid on between them. It was an option proving really popular, meaning that both were now fully booked.

The recently appointed manager of the Albergo Diffuso was a Mancunian with a passion for motorbikes and live music. Kevin had arrived in Seborga two weeks earlier after using his annual leave to drive overland from London on a GS Adventure bike. He had sent his luggage ahead with a carrier. He had previously run the Club's country club offshoot, set in rural Kent, and so was deemed a safe pair of hands for this new Italian venture.

Tom returned from saying hello to Vincenzo, pulling a trolley loaded with aluminium rube frames and explained to his father that they had been asked to assemble these to form a stage. When it was erected, Vincenzo had told him that some plywood sheets were in the back of his Ape for them to fasten to the frame to make a floor. As they walked, Tom, pulling the trolley behind him, began filling in some of the details of his road trip. Ben brought his son up to date with events in Seborga.

"It's great to be back," Tom said with a genuine enthusiasm which was not lost on Ben.

"It's great to have you back," Ben answered with a sincerity not lost on Tom.

Ben reflected on the difference that just one summer had made to their relationship. After Tom arrived bringing with him so many problems, he was almost ready to give up on him, abandoning any hope of the boy changing his errant ways. What a mistake that would have been, he now realised. How much they both would have missed out on. Ben now felt guilty that he had even contemplated walking away from the then troubled soul.

Word quickly got round that Tom was back, and Alessandra brought two beers and a slice of farinata to welcome him back. Ben was also aware of Vincenzo and Alessandra's role in his son's turn around. This place had entirely changed Tom's mindset in the same way it had his several years earlier.

Existing in a small community somehow made it easier to put things into perspective and more challenging to avoid issues that needed to be dealt with. In the same way that Andrea had pointed out at his recent press conference on the environment, in a micronation, the citizens can't ignore the effects of their actions and must deal with them themselves.

Ben reflected that in modern urban society, it is too easy to distance oneself from difficulties to deal with issues. People can change groups of friends, ignore their neighbours, flush waste down a pipe and hand other rubbish over to a local authority.

Ben now realised that being separated from the consequences of our actions makes humans lazy, both in their dealings with people and the world in which we all live. In threatening to send Tom back to London, he had nearly fallen back into that old trap of putting his problem aside for someone else to deal with.

30. CAVAGNETTI

The old horse belonging to the late Prince Claudio had some younger company in his stable for the night before the weddings. Vincenzo had arranged to borrow an open-topped landau and two colts from a nearby farmer in which Renata would ride to the church. Alessandra had suggested that the horses stay in the stables outside Seborga for the night before. She feared that they might be unnerved by a bumpy horsebox journey just before they were needed to be calm in their coach harnesses.

Alessandra had asked Tom to come and help get the horses ready. She thought dealing with animals would be yet another venture outside of his very narrow comfort zone. Having spent all of his life in cities, he'd had little or no contact with animals. Nervously he had agreed, but mainly because Alessandra had sweetened the request for help with the offer of breakfast afterwards. She had been up early and made some Cavagnetti, a sweet bread shaped in a crown around a boiled egg. Usually an Easter treat, it offered a more substantial and easily portable breakfast for a young man with a healthy appetite.

As they walked down the track through the olive grove leading to the stables, the sun was beginning to make its presence felt behind the hills. It had yet to show itself, but an orange glow could be seen in the otherwise pale blue sky where it was soon to breach the ridge. The mist that crept in off the sea sometimes at night was still lingering in the bottom of the river valley. It hung in pockets over a couple of the low-lying fields. Even as they walked, the first shards of sun crept over the mountain. These rays began to burn off the lingering mist and the air temperature seemed to rise noticeably. The real reason Tom had accepted this chance to be alone with Alessandra was that he wanted to ask her something, but so far, had not summoned up the courage to do so.

"I hear from your father that you've had a fun trip," Alessandra offered to kickstart the conversation.

"It was amazing. The best thing I've ever done." Realising that this opening gave him the opportunity to steer the conversation, he added, "I got as far as Sicily."

"Oh, wow. Speaking of which, Patsy is on her way from Sicily to attend the wedding."

Tom hesitated but then admitted, "I know. She arrived back with me yesterday. I dropped her at Cecily's yacht in Menton."

Alessandra looked astonished. "The pair of you drove from Sicily in that Kübelwagen? That's a long way," she added, inferring that it must have involved at least a couple of overnight stops.

Tom nodded and half-smiled, acknowledging that he understood what Alessandra was suggesting without directly asking.

"I spent a week travelling across Italy to the Adriatic and then another week driving south. For the last month, I have been working on Patsy's farm. I converted an old barn into a holiday letting room that she can also use to encourage fruit pickers in the busy season."

"And did her boyfriend help you with this project?" Alessandra probed, already guessing where this conversation was leading.

"At first he did, but he didn't know what he was doing and I don't think he liked taking direction on construction from me. He saw me as a hired labourer. One day he just stopped coming to help and sat playing his guitar indoors on the terrace. I didn't mind because he wasn't much help anyway. I spent much of my time redoing what he had not done properly."

"You mean just like Vincenzo did for you?" she replied, reminding him that it was not so very long ago that he needed such guidance.

"Point made," Tom conceded. "But it did get increasingly difficult after that. He and Patsy were always arguing, and if she invited me for dinner after work, the atmosphere was always tense. She didn't seem happy with their situation."

Tom told her how he had almost finished the barn and was fitting guttering to the roof when Patsy had begun decorating inside. This arrangement meant that they were working together for some days and chatting a lot.

"We just jelled. I don't know why. We don't have much in common. Anyway, when it came time for me to set off back to be here in time for the wedding, Patsy cooked a thank you supper. We all had a few drinks and then some things were said in anger. I walked away and went to bed; otherwise, I was going to lose it with him. I was certain if I did, that would spoil any chance I might ever have with Patsy.

"The next morning when I'd packed my bag, I was going to slip away unnoticed. However, when I got to the car, Patsy came out with a bag packed. She did not say a word but just got in the passenger seat. Her boyfriend was sleeping off a hangover. We drove off, and nothing was said between us until we reached Palermo."

Alessandra had been listening with a mixture of joy and fear, wondering just how all this was going to work out. Although Tom had matured enormously since he'd arrived, he was in so many ways still a boy with little confidence around women. On the other hand, Patsy seemed to know what she wanted, and with her looks, could get almost anything, Alessandra thought. Although she was numerically younger, she was emotionally his elder in so many ways. As handsome as Tom was, with his foolish, boyish behaviour still fresh in everyone's memory, was he ready for what Patsy was? was the question at the forefront of her mind.

"Why do you think Patsy and her boyfriend rowed, Tom? Because of you, or because he would not do any work on the farm?"

"Because he was lazy," Tom answered without hesitation.

"I can see that indolence is not an attractive feature in a man, but he might argue that he was working in his way, writing his music."

"Patsy didn't see it that way," Tom countered. "At least that is what she told me."

"So, you're clear about what Patsy's looking for in a partner?"

This threw Tom. He had not given a single thought to what it was that Patsy wanted. He had been totally preoccupied with what he wanted and how he could get it. Now that Alessandra had nudged him in that direction, he began to see what she was suggesting: that the woman of his dreams was looking for a man to share her life and the farm with. A husband, in fact.

Working on the farm had been idyllic and admiring Patsy at arm's length, she looked like a dream come true. Taking on the responsibility for both-probably for the rest of his life-was a prospect that had never even entered Tom's head. The thought of that liability looked like it had sent a shiver of fear down his spine. Alessandra could almost see the colour draining out of Tom's face as he came to terms with the reality she had brought to his attention. It now seemed so obvious.

"Through no fault of your own you've found yourself in the middle of an existing relationship, which even if flawed, had endured for some years before you came along. Before you break something from which there could be considerable fall out, you should know what you are doing. My father used to warn me that boys say: 'let's play it by ear,' but men say: 'get dressed I've made plans'."

Tom looked confused and concerned.

“Patsy made her position pretty clear when she got in your car to drive back here with you. I think now this is your time to put up or shut up.”

They had arrived at the stable and Alessandra showed Tom how to make friends with the horses before grooming them. She had brought some small apples, two of which she gave to him to feed to the colts. They worked in silence for the next thirty minutes before Tom suddenly announced, “I think I love her, Alessandra.”

There was a long pause during which Alessandra did not react.

“I’ve never felt anything like this before. I can’t sleep. I feel sick. Even my appetite isn’t what it was.”

“Tom. It can’t be a case of ‘I think.’ It would help if you were certain. If you really know that you love her, then maybe you need to tell her ‘to get dressed because you’ve made plans.’”

31. LOUP DE MER A LA MENTON

Without a hint of wind, the water in the bay on Menton was glass-like. Inside the harbour all the boats were still on their moorings, creating perfect mirrored reflections of themselves in the water. Inside Cecily's lovely old ketch, things were not quite so calm. Roman walked into the cabin where Cecily was sat at her dresser, getting ready, and already feeling nervous.

"You won't believe it. I have just seen a message that arrived during the night to say that Caroline and Ross are now on a flight and on their way to Nice. They have finally responded to the wedding invitation."

His wife-to-be stood slowly and turned around.

"Bella sposa (beautiful bride)," exclaimed Roman, changing the subject at seeing Cecily in her wedding outfit. The long, cream, silk-crepe dress had a softly layered neckline, below which it was pin-tucked to show off her slim waist. The fabric rippled like liquid, just from the slight movement of her head.

"Wow. Looks expensive. . .but worth it," he qualified quickly.

"It was, and I am," she replied. "So, they have managed to fit us into their busy schedule," Cecily said, unable to hide her displeasure at this last-minute acceptance.

Cecily could tell that try as he might not to show it, her husband-to-be also had mixed feelings about this unexpected news. However, her own feeling was clear. As much as she knew how much it meant to Roman to have both his daughters at his wedding, she would have been quite happy not to have heard back from Caroline and Ross.

Roman's eldest daughter had made her feelings towards her soon-to-be stepmother obvious. Even after all these years she had still made no attempt to establish any kind of relationship with Cecily. Their most recent encounter over the farm funds had once again confirmed that peace was unlikely to break out anytime soon. Nevertheless, they had sent the invitation, and Cecily was determined its last-minute acceptance would not spoil her day.

In stark contrast of behaviour, his youngest daughter, Patsy, was going to be their driver and take them to the wedding in Cecily's Bentley. Cecily had picked up both their dresses from her seamstress in San Remo. While she had been out, Roman had seen his youngest daughter arrive at the harbour with Tom in his strange yellow car. He had been expecting to pick Patsy up from Nice airport and guessed that they must have been in touch and that Tom had volunteered to do it. Patsy did not offer any other comment on it and so he had left it at that. The day before their wedding, there were just too many other things to worry about.

Roman's few Sicilian guests stayed in a hotel in Menton, and he had enjoyed a local speciality of loup de mer a la Menton with a remoulade sauce, and a few bottles of wine with them the night before. Ben and Vincenzo had joined them earlier for dinner but had left before the night had ended with the Sicilians smoking cigars, drinking Gappa and fishing in the harbour at midnight. Alessandra and Cecily had both agreed that they were too busy for a pre-marital celebration, but they shared a thirty minute video chat over a glass of prosecco.

Renata had still been in the kitchen preparing food when her newly arrived parents came in. As she was too busy to go and meet them, Ben had agreed to collect them and bring them to Seborga. As Renata rushed to hug her parents, she saw over their shoulder her two younger sisters standing in the doorway waiting their turn. Her stream of tears turned to a flood at the realisation they were going to witness her wedding. As she rushed to hug them both at the same time all she could say was, "How? How? How?"

Renata's mother recounted that someone had called Cecily had phoned, saying that she was your friend and that she had thousands of unused airmiles. She said that they would expire soon if she didn't use them, and she would like to bring Renata's family to the wedding. But it was to be a secret. A wedding present to Renata and Vincenzo.

"A few days later seven business-class tickets arrived for the girls, their husbands and the children, and here we all are," her mother explained.

Tom and Alessandra had prepared the horses as much as they could before the newly inspired young man rushed back to the village, saying that he had an errand to run. When they were ready, she and Vincenzo would come and lead the now shining black horses up to the village at the last minute. As head of the Seborga guard, Vincenzo would typically act as master of ceremonies at any official event. As the groom, today he had another responsibility and so had conscripted Marius as his stand-in.

The piazza looked quite fantastic, Ben thought when he passed through mid-morning on his way to carry out one of the many jobs Alessandra had given him. The sun was shining, and there were already a couple of hundred people milling around admiring the scene. From their dress, Ben could see that these were a mixture of villagers adding last-minute touches to decorations, early arriving wedding guests, and tourists who had stumbled on the event by accident on their way to visit the Holy Grail.

At least twenty people were standing at the railings on the piazza's edge looking out at the view. After recent rain, below the valley was a verdant green, broken only by a scattering of terracotta roofs and the winding road up to Seborga from the coast. At this time of year it was a narrow corridor of outlined by coloured roadside flowers snaking through the landscape. The temperate climate of the south-facing coastline of Liguria was awash with exotic flora. Gardens and public spaces overflowed with bougainvillaea, alliums, geraniums and even orchids.

Above these blooms towered giant palms, Ficus trees and every now and then the extraordinary purple haze of a Jacaranda. It is a local tradition that every year palm leaves from Bordighera are sent to the Vatican as a gift for the Pope to use on Palm Sunday. As the road winds away from the coast toward Seborga, these garlands of colour follow until the altitude changes. Then, native species such as rosemary, lavender, broom, and early in the year, mimosa, become more prevalent.

From the piazza's valley edge, the distant Mediterranean glistened in the sunlight as though it knew this was a special day and it had to put on its best face. No visitor witnessing this scene for the first time could fail to be wowed, Ben thought.

Cristiano was running back and forth between the Cookery School, the Osteria and the charcoal braziers set up at one side of the piazza. Several whole porchetta on spits had been slowly cooking since very early morning and would take several more hours before being perfect. One of the students was there tending the charcoal and basting the skins, but the young chef knew these were too important an ingredient not to keep checking on. With Renata now getting ready for her big day, Cristiano was acting head chef and feeling responsible. Also, at the back of his mind almost constantly since his visit was the man who may or may not have been a Michelin restaurant inspector.

Ben said 'Buongiorno' to Viola as he passed her, sitting on her step wearing the same black smock dress, headscarf and mocking look she always wore, oblivious to the heat of the approaching midday. She acknowledged his greeting but shook her head as if in despair at all the strangers in her village. When one tourist asked if they could take a photograph of her, it all got too much for her. She waved them away with her hand, went inside into the darkness and closed the door.

By one o'clock every man and child in the village was scrubbed clean and wearing their best clothes. Most were dispatched to the piazza while their wives or mothers got ready. The result was that every bar seat and shady bench was overflowing with overdressed, perspiring males. The conversation was dominated by food, with everyone having an opinion on whether Cristiano was cooking the porchetta correctly. Their scepticism ranged from was there enough fennel in the stuffing, to whether the spits were too close the flames. Some even suggested he had used the wrong type of charcoal. When it came to food, every Italian had an opinion, and they were all different in some subtle way.

"It should be hardwood charcoal, but I can smell pine in that smoke," said one gnarled old farmer.

"That smell is that cheap tobacco that you smoke," his friend joked, all the others joining in laughing.

The Commander of the Alpini troops tasked with guarding the Holy Grail at the monastery had decided to inspect his forces two hours before the weddings. The soldiers had therefore been up since dawn polishing their boots and shining their weapons. Vincenzo's half-dozen Seborga guards were also looking their uniformed best. They were already performing crowd control at the piazza, which was filling up with wedding guests. When the time came, their main task was to clear a corridor for the carriage to drive through into the centre of the piazza.

Many of the wedding guests were also using this opportunity to visit the Holy Grail, most for the first time in their lives. For the devout, it was the first emotional experience of what should be a memorable day. As it passed midday, a slight breeze had got up, which had been welcomed by the overdressed villagers and guests who were beginning to overheat. This draft also wafted the smells from the roasting porchetta around the piazza, whetting appetites for those who would later enjoy it but causing consternation amongst the Italian soldiers who could only watch over the feast.

The residents of the Albergo Diffuso and all the other accommodation in the village had been invited to join the wedding feast. Almost every single one had accepted with enthusiasm. In keeping with tradition, the bride and groom would abandon any transport before they arrived at the church and walk through the crowds of guests so that everyone could admire them, cheer and clap. Today the crowd would get double the normal spectacle with two bridal processions.

Before they set off on the drive up to Seborga, Cecily said to Roman, "Have you seen what came into the harbour last night?" He shook his head. "Zeno V, the superyacht that nearly ran right over us on our way to Corsica."

"The rapper?" Roman questioned, screwing up his face in distaste. "On any other day, I would go over there right now to tell what I think of him and his music and his driving."

"Luckily for him, we've got a more pleasant task today. So, just keep calm, darling."

The couple planned to get there before Vincenzo and Renata but park on the village's outskirts and then discretely watch the first bride arrive along with everyone else. Marius had cordoned off a parking space for their Bentley. From there, they would walk to San Martino behind the procession. After their friend's wedding service, they would sneak around the back of the village using the narrow lanes to collect the Bentley and then drive up into the piazza as though they had just arrived. In the meantime, after their wedding, Vincenzo and Renata would have retraced their steps back to San Bernado for the second, much shorter, blessing ceremony of Cecily and Roman.

A couple of weeks earlier, Alessandra had given her late-father's dress uniform to Cecily, who took it to San Remo on her dress fittings. They had it altered to Ben's size using one of his suits to get the measurements. The seamstress had also made some much-needed repairs to the frayed fabric and had it dry cleaned. When it had been returned, Alessandra was crestfallen that Ben point-blank refused to wear the former prince's old uniform.

"I am not a prince. I see it as hugely disrespectful to Claudio, who I loved dearly. It would be like wearing his crown. I'm sorry but I can't do it."

"When you married a princess, you took on a role. Perhaps not an official role, but you have a position to uphold in the village. The citizens all look up to you. You know that."

"Alessandra, I'd do anything for you. You know that. But don't ask me to do this. I really would feel extremely uncomfortable. It's just not me."

She had expected some resistance but was surprised at how strongly he felt about what she saw as a small thing. There also seemed to be more than a hint of hypocrisy in his stance. When it had been suggested that she get a dress uniform made for formal occasions, Ben had enthused about the idea. Nevertheless, she let it go for a week and then tried broaching the subject again the day before the wedding, only to get the same reaction. However, her husband did have what sounded like a more valid reason.

"With Cecily, Renata, the Prime Minister of Italy and the Princess of Seborga, plus whoever the VIPs are staying at the Albergo Diffuso, there are already far too many stars for one show. The last thing today needs is an English peacock strutting around."

Then Ben received a text message from his daughter, Selene, confirming that Andrea had arrived at her house and they were ready to leave.

Pétanque (like boules) played at Bordighera Alta, an example of the French influence on this area.

Drawing by Linda McCluskey

32. PORCHETTA

The shiny, bible-black colts had been harnessed to the landau for fifteen minutes so they could get used to their leather restraints in the shade of some trees. The had been fitted with their embroidered white linen ear covers and looked resplendent, if slightly jittery. When the time came, the driver gave them a short test ride along the tarmac road from Negi to collect Renata.

Alessandra was already sat up on her father's old horse and waiting on a grassed area outside the village where the older men played petanque. The carriage came trotting along the road, but the horses were still acting nervously despite the careful preparation. One occasionally skipped a step causing the other to try to rear in its harness, and the driver had to rein them in, speaking to them reassuringly.

As soon as Alessandra trotted out to meet them, the colts seemed to calm down. Even wearing his own white linen headdress, the gentle old stallion was now a familiar friend in an otherwise strange place to the two young horses. Wearing her black dress uniform with its blue sash and her hair in a thick ponytail, Alessandra looked every inch the princess.

She mouthed to her old friend, Renata, to tell her that she looked beautiful before turning the reins to start their slow walk into the village. Renata had chosen a traditional white wedding dress with a veil. Her father wore a plain dark suit over a white shirt, embellished with Western-style silver collar tips, and the whole ensemble was topped with a wide-brimmed black Stetson-a nod to his Mexican cowboy roots.

A ripple of clapping started at the edge of the piazza amongst those who could hear the unfamiliar but distinctive sound of horses' hooves on the tarmac. The applause then rolled back into the crowd as the wedding party rounded the corner. When all of the four hundred or so people could see the princess sitting up high on her horse, then they began cheering as well as clapping. Alessandra's old horse remained unmoved by the noise and kept up his steady pace.

The colts were spooked again and both reared, restrained only by the straps of the harness. Alessandra quickly spun her horse around to face them, causing the youngsters to settle once again. This undiscipline may have been unwelcome to the landau's occupants but looked spectacular to the audience, who snapped hundred photographs.

The remainder of the procession was smooth as they rode gently up into the piazza and through the crowd until it could go no further. Alessandra slipped down from the saddle while Renata's father stepped out of the landau. Marius was there to take the reins and pat the horses reassuringly. They both helped the bride extract herself and the many layers of her dress from the carriage, and paused for people to take photographs. Renata's two nieces were last-minute bridesmaids and now the wedding party was ready for the walk to the church through the narrow streets of Seborga.

The people of Seborga were on every balcony and doorstep, some even on rooftops to get a better view. It took the best part of fifteen minutes to walk the distance that could normally be walked in a third of that. Everyone wanted a photograph or to offer their best wishes. Charcoal smoke from the braziers combined with the roasting porchetta and baking bread's aroma was getting everyone in a party mood. Weddings had been rare in Seborga in recent times, and two in one day was unheard of.

Meanwhile, Vincenzo waited, looking slightly nervous in contrast to the calm authority he usually exuded when wearing his uniform of Captain of the Seborga Guard. In front of the church, the tiny Piazza San Martino was packed, mainly with the groom's party and the small group of guests who could cram into the little church to witness the service. Roman and Cecily were there keeping well back in the shadows, but clapping wildly along with everyone else.

Ben and Tom were to act as best man and usher, respectively. When Vincenzo had asked him, Tom had said it was his proudest moment since being picked to captain the school team for a county cup match. Ben was typically reticent to accept the honour, feeling he might upset any number of more worthy locals as he saw it. But Vincenzo had been insistent, and Ben found him a difficult man to argue with.

To everyone's relief, especially Vincenzo's, the bride's party finally appeared out of the narrow alley opening into the Piazza San Martino. The party was heralded by the uniformed Marius, who walked ahead firmly parting the bystanders to make a way through for the bride. The priest, who had been standing waiting on the steps of San Martino, his bible in his hand, now turned to lead the guests into the dark, cool interior of the church.

Thirty five minutes later, the unlikely pairing had been made. A seemingly perpetual bachelor, farmer, hunter, soldier and all-round giant Italian tough-guy was joined in matrimony to the diminutive, Mexican, workaholic chef from the New York Bronx. Outside there was much cheering, along with the throwing of rice and confetti before a five minute break for photographs. Meanwhile, Patsy, Cecily and Roman slipped away down a side alley for a short stroll around the village back to the car. Roman walked in the middle with Patsy and Cecily looping their arms through his. Up until then, he had heard no more from Caroline and Ross.

As they reached a bend in the path from where they could see the Bentley parked below, they also saw a black Mercedes stretched limousine struggling to navigate the hairpin bends up to the village. The driver had stopped and was now performing a three-point manoeuvre to turn the six-and-a-half-metre motor around the corner. Cars behind them were hooting horns, and drivers who had now been stuck behind the slow-moving limousine for ten kilometres were gesticulating wildly out of their open windows.

"What kind of idiot would bring something like that to a mountain village like this?" Roman said.

As they continued walking, their path came parallel with the road coming up from the coast just at the point the limo was passing.

"It's Caroline," Patsy shrieked, in what seemed to Cecily like a mixture of pleasure, astonishment and embarrassment.

The rear window was down, and a passenger was making an unmistakable gesture with one finger to the drivers behind. They could now all see that it was Ross, and by his side was Caroline.

"What on earth is she wearing?" Cecily asked, more to herself than anyone else. "Are they going horse racing at Ascot after here?"

The driver of the long black Mercedes rental, now sweating in his uniform and cap from the stressful drive up from Monaco, did as he was directed by his passengers and drove up to the edge of the piazza to disembark them. Opening the rear door and stepping back, the chauffer watched as Caroline ducked down low to ensure she and her huge hat left the car intact. The headpiece had been pinned into place at the hotel and removing it for the journey had just not been an option.

Caroline was wearing a white organza, puff-sleeved dress with a giant bow tied at the waist. With the wide-brimmed hat and ultra-thin heels, all the excess of fabric made her appear top-heavy and unstable. Ross opened his own side door and stepped out, smoothing out the trousers of his pale blue suit. It was a size small, in the current style for a slimmer younger man, but just too tight and ill-fitting on a paunchy thirty-something.

The clapping began again, started by the nearest tourists but with others who would not recognise Cecily and Roman joining in. By their attire, the crowd assumed this was the second planned wedding and that this must be the bride and groom. Marius, who had now returned from San Martino to welcome Cecily and Roman, was the first on the scene. A furious Marius screamed, "Who the fuck are you? You can't park that here."

It was Caroline who responded, "How dare you speak to me like that, you little tin solider."

Without his mentor, Vincenzo, by his side, Marius was feeling the weight of responsibility. So far everything had gone like clockwork. He did not want to have a stranger's wedding party, who must have taken a wrong turn and ended up in a different village, spoil this day. Witnessing the whole scene was the sergeant of the Alpini troops. He was all too conscious that the prime minister was due any second. He began to worry that these unknown, and unwanted, strangers in this huge car might be some terrorist plot. He was moved to action; calling over his four nearest men, orders were barked and their weapons were unshouldered.

The troops quickly surrounded the couple and the car and ordered them back in at gunpoint. The driver had the engine running and it was in gear before Caroline got her hat back under the door frame. The limousine driver was reversing quickly out of the piazza just when Patsy drove around the corner. The Bentley's tyres screeched, as did those of the Mercedes, as they both stopped less than a metre apart. Marius ran toward them, still shouting and swearing at the limousine driver and waving him away: requiring a tight manoeuvre his huge car was incapable of achieving.

Patsy, now trying not to show that she was laughing at her big sister, reversed the Bently a few metres and then drove around the Mercedes and up into the piazza, much to the relief of a now highly stressed Marius. The timing was in fact perfect; Cecily was stepping out of the car just as Vincenzo and Renata entered the piazza from the other side. There was now a cacophony of cheering and clapping as the crowd welcomed both the newlyweds and soon-to-be-married couples. Meanwhile, Patsy had gone back to explain the situation to the Alpini and try to prevent her sister and her husband from being arrested or even shot.

She managed to contain her amusement and resisted asking why the show of ostentation. They hugged briefly, but she could tell Caroline was bristling with a mix of anger and discomfort. Ross only looked shamefaced. Patsy guessed that this would not have been his plan and that he had probably gone along with it to keep Caroline quiet. Although she knew him also to be a braggart, this was just too contrived to have been his idea. As sisters, Patsy knew this was Caroline's attempt to upstage Cecily and show how successful they had been in business.

"Wow. It looks like things are going well in the property development business," was Patsy's way of offering her sister a way out of explaining the gratuitous display of wealth.

"Very well," was her curt response. "You look well," she added, with what sounded somewhat like disappointment.

Cecily had helped choose Patsy's strapless, apricot, tulle mini dress. She had thought it a little frivolous and that it made her look even younger than she was, but it was Cecily's wedding and so she went along with it. It had not occurred to her that it also exaggerated the difference between her and her sister's ages, annoying Caroline even further.

"I think we have a wedding to go to. If you wanted to lose the ridiculous hat, this would be a good time while the car is here. I can help you fix your hair again."

While reluctant to admit that she had badly misjudged things, when Caroline had looked at the attire of the assembled crowd of wedding guests and saw all the trestle tables set up for an open-air wedding party, she knew they were both badly over-dressed. She had assumed that with Cecily's fortune and guests, including a princess and the Prime Minister of Italy, that this would be like the weddings she had seen in glossy magazines taking place in Rome or Milan. The last thing she'd expected was a barbeque in a village full of Italian peasant farmers.

Fewer than twenty guests could squeeze into the old Templar church of San Bernado, but the doors were left wide open so many more could see and hear in from outside. The bare stone walls were punctured only by narrow slit windows. The dark interior had been lit with a hundred candles. It was stark, yet beautiful and timeless, those present agreed. Ben never ceased to be in awe of the fact that ancient knights had once stood on the same stone slabs that he was standing on, probably praying for deliverance from the battles they would face in far-away Palestine.

Alessandra was by her husband's side, wondering if this was the first time in the church's 'near thousand year' history that any woman in her wedding dress had stood watching another bride having her own marriage blessed. A single violinist played quietly in the background. It was the triumph of minimalism that she had come to expect from her friend, and which she was sure Roman would appreciate.

Patsy stood next to Tom, both of them trying not to look like a couple but failing because they kept glancing in each other's direction every few seconds. When Alessandra looked over, she saw a tear run down Patsy's cheek. She suspected that, as glad as she was for her father's newfound happiness, she was also being reminded of the loss of her mother. Whatever it was, the emotion of the occasion was apparent on her beautiful young face.

It was difficult to judge what Caroline's feelings were as her eyes gave away no clues at all. Her husband just looked like he wished that he was somewhere else. His previous experiences of Italy had all been bad ones and he still had nightmares about his last visit to Sicily. On his last visit, he had hoped to conclude a deal to develop some of his wife's land on Sicily for building but had been frightened off by local mobsters. He had only ever spoken to his wife about the events of that day, and even she only knew the half of it. He had concluded that country was populated by mobsters and criminals, just like all the TV movies he had seen. They had terrified him.

Finally, the extravagantly costumed Roman Catholic priest from Bordighera splashed some holy water, the groom kissed the bride, and they were all back out in the sunshine of the piazza. Roman appeared relieved. Cecily looked ecstatic and radiant. There would now be an hour before lunch when everyone could catch up with their guests, have yet more photographs taken, enjoy a glass of prosecco and try some of Renata's canapes.

A former banker from London, Drew had become a trusted advisor to Cecily's on her financial and corporate matters. He and his wife Kate-the best photographer in Monaco-had also become friends and were invited to the wedding. Kate had volunteered to take some informal, candid photographs before and after the ceremony and Cecily had eagerly accepted.

There was a carnival atmosphere in the village: more so even than for any of the numerous festivals held there each year. It was as if a double wedding had brought with it twice the joy, and indeed it had for many of those present who knew both couples and how well suited they were. The villagers were riding a wave of good fortune. The future looked brighter, mainly due to the innovative changes but also because of the new blood which had revitalised the village.

During this lull in the proceedings, Tom had arranged with Patsy to show her the Holy Grail. Most of the guests who wanted to had visited before the ceremonies, so there were only a few passing tourists filing past. As the man who had saved the holy relic from almost certain destruction, Tom had earned considerable respect from the Alpini guards looking after what they all called the Sacro Cantina. He had spoken to them earlier and arranged for the protective cover to be raised when he visited with Patsy.

As they entered the old Templar monastery, the guards closed the doors behind them and prevented anyone else from entering. There was then a short wait while the party of four pilgrims inside completed their visit, crossed themselves, and departed.

Now realising that Tom must have arranged this, Patsy said, "A private audience with the Angel of Seborga," teasing Tom with the nickname given to him by the press after the flood from which he'd rescued the ancient glass bowl.

Two of the four soldiers present put down their weapons, unlocked the lid, and carefully lifted the Perspex cover from the Holy Grail. As they approached the display case, one of the other Alpini dimmed the room's lights so that only the uplighter under the emerald green relic remained illuminated.

Patsy stared at the iridescent object in awe. "It looks almost like it's alive," she said, sounding slightly concerned.

"It does, doesn't it," Tom confirmed. "I think it's just the heat from that lamp below, heating the air and causing it to swirl around."

"You're such a cynic. "she admonished. "This is possibly the most important holy relic in Christendom. Even if you're not a believer, please show some deference."

"It's warm to the touch. Again, I think it's the light bulb," Tom argued. "Put your hand inside and feel it."

Patsy recoiled as though the very idea of touching something so holy and so old frightened her. The bowl was fixed at an angle of about thirty degrees so the visitors could see the hexagonal shape of the rim. The glass was so thick and such a deep green that it was impossible to see much though it.

"Go on, feel inside. It's now fixed on that frame so it can't fall off."

Part of her really wanted to be able to say that she was one of the few people in the world ever to have held the Holy Grail. On the other hand, her early convent school upbringing made her wary of showing any disrespect. After just a moment, the former instinct got the better of her, and she gingerly slid her hand over the rim and touched the glass. She let her fingertips savour the moment before moving them around. Suddenly she froze.

"Tom, there's something in here," Patsy said, looking frightened.

"No, that's simply not possible."

He turned and looked at the guards, who both shook their heads.

"What it is?" Tom asked.

"It's small and metal."

"Then get it out. It's not supposed to be there."

Patsy removed the object, and as she did so, realised what it was. Such was the level of her surprise and with the darkness all around, she became disorientated. Thinking that she might faint, Tom took hold of her and pulled her to him. She just stood there in silence, her face pressed against his shoulder, her fist tightly clenched around the object. The soldiers looked at each other for clues, as this was not the reaction that any of them had expected.

"Are you OK, Patsy?" Tom asked.

There was silence for a little while and then finally she said, "I think I need to sit down. Can they turn the lights back on, please?"

One guard dealt with the lighting while another brought a chair, which was kept ready usually for elderly visitors, who might be overcome at seeing the holy relic. Tom guided Patsy to a seated position and for the first time, she looked into his eyes. Then she looked down at her still-clenched first before opening it wide. Tom, who was already uncertain about his last-minute decision, was now close to panic. It was not going as he had hoped. Patsy looked ill, he thought. He wanted her to speak but also feared what she might say. Words that he had not prepared poured from his lips.

"It's all I could afford. I can take it back. I mean that I could change it." Then the words that Viola had said to him after the flood came back to him. She'd said, 'That Grail is cursed,' adding that it had brought 'nothing but bad luck.'

"I'm sorry, Patsy. You're right. This was a mistake."

Patsy now stood and pulled Tom close, like it was her turn to reassure him.

"Hush. You're talking gibberish," she said. "Give me a minute to catch my breath. I had absolutely no idea this was coming. I need a moment to think. Let's go outside where we can be on our own."

The couple apologised for alarming the guards and thanked them for the trouble they had gone to. Back in the sunshine Patsy finally looked at the tiny ring in her hand, but only briefly-apparently not with the slightest interest what it was made of, what stones it contained or indeed even if it fitted. This nonchalance confirmed Tom's worst fear that she was going to hand it back at any moment. What was he thinking of, he asked himself? He had caught her on the rebound from a row with her long-term boyfriend. She was way out of his league; he had embarrassed her and made a fool of himself, he concluded.

They stood in the alley, each with their head on the other's shoulder, attracting strange looks from passers-by. Finally, Patsy stood up straight. She used the hand without the ring to push Tom back a step.

"I have a proposition in response to your proposal. We have known each other just a couple of months and have met just a few times. We had our first kiss just four nights ago. I don't think anyone would disagree that this all seems somewhat hasty."

Seeing the disconsolate look on Tom's face, she added, "The last few weeks have been surprising and the last few days blissful. If I thought for a moment that the joy that we experienced on our short road trip could last forever, I would say yes in an instant."

Tom face changed to one of hope at hearing this, and Patsy's next few words rescued him from the black hole into which he had felt he was descending.

"Let me keep the ring with which I am overcome with happiness. Let's keep this conversation to ourselves and get on with building our relationship. If we both still feel the same in exactly six months from today, I will get down on my knee and beg you to marry me. Deal?"

33. FOCACCIA

Their faces glowing with barely concealed joy, Tom and Patsy returned to the piazza where the wedding guests were taking their seats for the feast. The tables were laid out in five rows forming a wide arc that covered most of the open area. Three long tables were at the focal point of the semi-circle, with the drop to the valley behind them and the Mediterranean in the far distance. Vincenzo and Renata sat with their guests at the centre table. Cecily and Roman were sitting to one side, with the Albergo Diffuso VIP guest seated with Ben and Alessandra, along with Andrea and Selene on the other side.

Patsy was still clutching the ring tightly in her right palm when the first course arrived, as she had no pockets or bag in which to keep it. Handing it back to Tom for safekeeping would send the wrong signal, she decided. Taking the napkin from the table in front of her, she carefully folded it around the ring, making a neat, flat parcel.

Turning to her father, she handed him the parcel and whispered in his ear, "Keep this very safe in your pocket; there is something precious inside this napkin, but do not open it. I'll explain later."

Roman was distracted. All the guests arriving to take their places congratulated him, shaking his hand and patting him on the back. On his left, Cecily was tugging on his sleeve because she had something to ask him. He nodded to Patsy that he had heard her instruction but had taken little notice, in truth. He took the parcel from her and slipped it inside his jacket pocket before turning back to Cecily, who said she wanted him to pass the prosecco down the table.

As she passed by on her way to her table, Alessandra bent and whispered over the shoulder of the seated Cecily, "Did you see him in the crowd at the church?"

"If you mean Alistair, the mysterious Englishman, yes, I did, and I asked him outright why he was here," Cecily replied, looking pleased with her initiative.

"And? And?" Alessandra said, barely able to contain herself.

Cecily paused, making her friend squirm with expectation before revealing, "He's a retired lecturer turned amateur author, carrying out research for a foodie romance set in Liguria."

"Thank God," Alessandra said, exhaling at the same time, with obvious relief at this news. She then confided in her friend that, whoever Alistair was, she had already decided that another star was the last thing she would want. If it had been offered, she was going to turn it down. However, Alessandra had been dreading telling Cristiano of her decision if it had come to that. This news would still be disappointing for him but nowhere near as bad as the alternative she had feared.

Before she continued to her seat, Alessandra added, "Let's hope he has now left Seborga and that we don't hear from him again."

Ben's Seborga wine had been decanted from the substantial green demijohns into one-litre bottles. Cecily had labels printed explaining their provenance. She had decided against buying French champagne and instead had cases of Roero, Sigillo Ducale sparkling Arneis sent from Piedmonte. Cecily's favourite bakers, San Antonio's in Bordighera, had brought up portable ovens and baked bread all morning leading up to the feast. This meant it was not only as fresh as it was possible for it to be, but it took the pressure off the commercial kitchens in Seborga which were all working at full capacity.

Andrea declared Cristiano's Turle pasta course a triumph, adding it was, "A tribute to the teaching of his mother, Princess of Seborga, and queen of Ligurian pasta." Patting his tummy in satisfaction, the prime minister stood, and tapped his glass with his knife loudly enough to gain the other guests' attention on his table.

"Don't worry. It's not a political speech," the prime minister joked. "Roman, Vincenzo and I discussed the seating arrangements beforehand and agreed that these long benches mean we only get to meet two or three people. So, after each course, we men are going to move three places to our left, so we all make some new friends."

Andrea, who had been at the head of the Albergo Diffuso table, led by example by extracting himself from the bench, and moving past Selene to take a place between a man and woman he had never met. Looking around, the guests at the table could see that something similar was happening on Roman's and Vincenzo's tables. The volume of conversion rose markedly as new introductions were made. The Prime Minister of Italy now found himself sitting opposite his recent friend, Zeno, the Ukrainian rapper, and the two exchanged a knuckle bump and a big smile.

"So, you're a member of this Club in London who have opened Seborga's new Albergo Diffuso?" Andrea proposed, by way of the only likely explanation for the rapper's presence at a wedding in a small Italian village.

"I joined the Club in New York, but then started using the London venue when I was in England and met a lot of cool musicians there." The rapper gestured to the new manager of the hotel on his left, "This crazy guy from Manchester asked me if I wanted to come and try out his new place. I was in the area to meet up with my boat which has been brought here from Genoa, and so here I am. I love it! What a cool place. Have you seen the rooms? They're so chilled. My neighbour, a villager who I have never met, came around this morning with some freshly made focaccia for our breakfast. How cool is that?"

The man to his left offered his hand, "Nice to meet you–Marcus-out of work actor."

Zeno laughed, nearly spitting out his prosecco, "Out of work. Yeh, crazy."

Before the rapper could add anything to his contradiction, the attractive woman to his right proffered her hand. "Charlotte. Wife of Marcus. Also currently unemployed."

The Ukrainian laughed again, "You guys kill me."

Andrea ignored what he could see was a private joke and welcomed them both to Italy and the now semi-autonomous Principality of Seborga. Both his new acquaintances observed that the day so far had been more like being on a film set than attending a wedding, and said that they were really pleased that they had come, adding, "Everyone is so friendly and relaxed. It's been a wonderful spectacle."

"Yeh, no one has asked me to sign anything all morning," Zeno added. "People just say hi, or Buongiorno. They're totally cool. I've even given my bodyguards the day off."

Zeno leaned in toward Andrea and whispered, "Those two are only unemployed because they are resting between Hollywood movies. Don't you recognise them?"

They were interrupted by a beautiful young girl to Zeno's left. Andrea guessed she must be a model. She said, "No one's asked for your autograph because no one here knows who the fuc. . ." then realising the company that she was in, stopped mid-sentence, before continuing, "...you are. There are only a dozen people here under thirty. They all look like they have only heard of one Ice-T and that's the one you drink."

All those in earshot laughed, no one more so than Zeno. The as-yet-unnamed girl continued, "And I must say, it is such a refreshing change for me to be treated as an equal. If fact, better than equal; I have received more compliments from the Italian men here today than in a year anywhere in London. They make me feel great. Anyway, I am Anna, and I am especially pleased to meet you; can I call you Andrea, or is it Mr. Prime Minister?"

Now it was Andrea's turn to laugh, "You can call me anything you like; it can't be any worse than my political opponents' names for me. A pleasure to meet you, Anna. And may I say that you look stunning?"

Holding out her upturned palms in a questioning gesture, "totally charming," Anna replied, "There you are. I rest my case. I'm moving to live in Italy."

At Roman's and Cecily's table, Tom had initially sat across from Patsy but when they all moved seats, he ended up opposite Alessandra. She looked along the table to where Patsy was now chatting to Turi, who was making her laugh; probably with his inappropriate stories, she guessed. Just as she was beginning to think something had taken place between Tom and Patsy, he asked, "Why does Viola say the Sacro Cantina is cursed?"

Alessandra thought for second before answering, "Because it seems as though it has been a curse to her and so she believes it will be to others." Realising that this statement would need some explaining, she continued, "Her two teenage brothers fought with the partisans with my father as their leader. When the Nazis found out their names but couldn't catch them, the soldiers came to Seborga and executed their mother and father in front of the teenage Viola. They left her with absolutely no one to support her, except for the other villagers, who rallied around as best they could.

"The Italian partisans were not a single unified group, but faction-ravaged bands of poorly armed and mostly untrained young men separated by geography and ideology. They were communists, Nazis and even royalist supporters who took up arms to fight either the Italian forces, the Nazis or the Allies; and sometimes each other. Claudio's group fought against the occupying Nazi forces and were instrumental in a largely unopposed liberation of the Riviera towards the end of the Second World War.

"In the final hours before the Allied invasion, the two brothers were killed in action in which my father, Prince Claudio, was also wounded. Because of all the secrecy surrounding their activities, later all that Claudio would tell her was that her brothers died to save the Sacro Cantina from the Nazis so it could bring joy to others. No one understood what he meant, and the prince would not elaborate. It was Viola who cursed the Sacro Cantina."

"So only Viola believes it?"

"Exactly, and given Claudio's deliberate vagueness and what happened to her entire family, she has good reason to be a little crazy. But Claudio was right about one thing. The Sacro Cantina has since brought peace to many troubled souls. Did you know that the cathedral in Genoa where it was on display was shelled early in the war, but the bomb did not explode? They still have the huge, unexploded shell in the cathedral. A miracle, many believe. So, no, I do not believe the Grail is cursed, otherwise we would have never brought it to Seborga."

Although it had been sad to hear about Viola's experience, Tom looked very relieved at hearing the other information and his mood brightened. Alessandra resisted the temptation to ask him if anything had happened between him and Patsy, but she had her suspicions by their appearance.

The porchetta and oven potatoes were universally acclaimed by the English, Mexicans, Italians, and other Europeans. Only a couple of vegetarians and vegans amongst the hotel's guests needed to be provided with an alternative, which Renata had prepared the day before. Ben's wine received many compliments and several guests had asked where they might buy some to take home.

Roman had been the first to finish his main course. In the first change of seat, he had found himself sat next to his son-in-law and after only a few minutes looked uncomfortable to Cecily. Ross suggested to his father-in-law that Cecily might want to think about buying stock in their property company. As soon as he finished his course, Roman put down his cutlery and stood up again, ready to change seats with someone else.

When he sat down again between their friends from Monaco, Drew and Kate, he turned to them and said under his breath,

"Thank the Lord I got away from that idiot. If I hear one more time how much money he stands to make from this property development, I swear I'll call him out as the crook he is. He and his Ivy League college mates are selling what he admits are badly made wooden box houses, at inflated prices, to poor young Americans and giving out dodgy mortgages to buy them so that they are getting ripped off twice. And he thinks that's clever. I can't listen to him gloat any longer."

Kate said, "That's terrible. Is it legal?"

"Barely legal," answered her former-banker husband, who knew a thing or two about mortgages.

Roman looked across to his new wife and saw that his eldest daughter had turned her attention to Cecily. She also looked less than pleased about the line of conversation. He guessed that she was now on the receiving end of Ross and Caroline's success story. Roman then realised that every time they changed places, a new set of guests would be subjected to what was in effect a sales pitch from one of them. It became clear that his daughter and son-in-law's attendance today and their ostentatious display was all part of a ploy to suck in more investors by making people think they were doing well from their dubious scheme.

The very idea of members of his own family blatantly using his wedding to canvas money from their friends was too much for Roman. As his blood pressure rose, an idea came to him. He excused himself by saying he needed the bathroom. Instead, he went over to the table where seated were a mixture of villagers from Seborga and Roman's visiting Sicilian neighbours. There was a whispered conversation between Roman and the tallest and youngest of the group.

The giant Sicilian then also rose to his feet and went with Roman to where Cristiano was carving the last of the porchetta, where another whispered conversation took place. A minute later the long pointed blade of the chef's knife pierced the trestle tabletop directly in front of Ross, pinning his napkin to the timber.

The owner of the hand holding the knife then forced his bulk into the space next to Ross and said, "Per il formaggio," (for the cheese) as if that explained everything to the other guests. Even Ross, a food-savvy New Yorker, knew the Italian for cheese, but was unconvinced that was an explanation for the knife. The preppy American looked deeply concerned.

The Sicilian leaned into him and said something in English that appeared to supply the explanation he sought. Finally, he added out loud, "Capisci? You understand?"

Ross nodded vigorously. The man stood, said, "Gotiti il tuo formaggio, (enjoy your cheese)," before returning to his own table.

The American had to call out his wife's name to attract Caroline's attention, who was now sat several places down the table from him. He gestured with his thumb that they were leaving, and when she questioned this with shrugged shoulders and raised eyebrows, Ross showed his wrist and tapped a very shiny, gold Rolex with apparent urgency. Caroline was still puzzled when her husband came around the table and helped her up out of her seat.

"What's the rush? We haven't even had dessert."

"Plane to catch. Don't want to be late," was his curt response, but it seemed to be targeted at the other guests at the table rather than his wife, to whom he then whispered, "Just come with me, I'll explain later."

When they were stood on their own and out of earshot, a conversation took place between them. It involved a lot of hand gestures and some pointing to the table to which the Sicilian had returned. Caroline apparently then agreed to leave. She spoke very briefly to her father and kissed her sister, but merely waved to Cecily as they walked away. The guests all looked to Roman to see if he would offer an explanation, to which all he would say was, "Apparently, they don't like cheese."

Cecily rose and came around to her husband's side of the table for a better explanation. Roman stood and whispered to her, "Ross has been trying to sell shares in his dodgy scheme to our friends and neighbours, and I've had enough of the pair of them. The guy who just spoke to Ross is my former-neighbour's brother: the one who persuaded Ross to leave Sicily in a hurry last time when he'd been trying to develop my farmland. He has just reminded that fool that the Sicilians can find him anywhere-maybe even New York? Between you and I, he's a pussycat. A gentle giant of a farmer. But he does make a very convincing Mafia enforcer."

Cecily might have appeared concerned by the method, but she was relieved at the outcome and seemed to conclude that the end justified the means.

"Don't let their greed and foolishness spoil our day, darling."

"Cecily, nothing could spoil this day. It's their loss. Hopefully, one day she will see that."

Alessandra had found herself sitting next to guests of the Albergo Diffuso. To her left was a man who looked more than seventy years old, perhaps older, but had a physique of someone forty. He also dressed like a much younger man, in casual but expensive-looking clothes. He seemed somehow familiar. His glamorous and much younger partner introduced herself and seemed pleased to meet Alessandra. He was either rude or thought that he did not need an introduction; both amounted to the same thing in Alessandra's eyes. He shook her hand and smiled, as though any honour was all hers.

Alessandra asked them both what they thought of Seborga, to which she responded in glowing terms, but he made no comment. Opposite her were two more English women who seemed desperate to chat with Alessandra and had a barrage of questions, including what it was like to be a princess. She discovered that Emma did something highly technical in the movie business and Helen was an actress when she could get parts, but a yoga instructor when she couldn't. They both said they thought Seborga would make a fantastic film set.

While the undemonstrative older man was checking phone messages, Alessandra caught Ben looking over at her. She gestured a thumb in the man's direction and then held her palms open as if to ask, 'who is this guy?' Ben laughed and made a gesture like he was playing an air-guitar whilst shaking his white hair as best she could. Alessandra now guessed he was in a rock band but thought it must be an older one that she was unfamiliar with. She was a few years younger than Ben and her career in restaurants had left her little time for hobbies, including popular music. Ben took a pen from his inside pocket, scribbled something on a paper napkin and passed it down the table via Selene.

When unfolded, it read: rock legend who played at Woodstock, Live Aid and Glastonbury. Ask him about Jimi Hendrix, Bob Dylan or Freddie Mercury. He's met them all.

Alessandra decided to keep up the pretence of ignorance a little longer and turned to the ageing rocker, asking, "So, you're a musician. Are you in the band that are playing later?"

The time-worn musician guessed her game and went along with it, answering, "Yeah, I'm with the band."

"Are you going to get up and sing later?"

"Well, I've already played with Prince, as well as for a prince and a princess at Live Aid, but this is my first royal lunch date. So, yes, I'll sing you a song or two."

Overhearing this conversation, Zeno now joined in with, "That's a great idea. I haven't played for any royalty at all."

Alessandra was now intrigued. "You're both in this band? Together?"

"Yep. The crazy rocker and the Ukrainian rapper. We're known as Shrink-Rap," the old musician said, teasing her further.

Alessandra was now unsure who was kidding who and turned to Kevin, the manager of the Albergo Diffuso, looking for clarity.

"It's strange but true. These two met at our Club and just hit it off. It's the strangest, but possibly best supergroup ever formed and for one royal command performance only. A rock 'n' roll legend and rhyme artist extraordinaire."

"Well, we are indeed honoured. Intrigued and honoured," Alessandra said, laughing, the others around her now joining in.

The continuing game of musical chairs had finally allowed Cecily to take the seat opposite Zeno, a moment that she had been relishing. She was surprised when he stood to greet her with what seemed like genuine enthusiasm before complimenting her on her dress and her beauty. The rapper thanked her for allowing him and his girlfriend to join in her wedding celebration. He concluded by wishing the newly married couple a long and happy life together. Although somewhat disarmed by this unexpected charm offensive, Cecily was determined to reprimand Zeno for nearly cutting her yacht in two.

"That is your boat moored near mine in Menton Harbour?" she said in an accusatory tone.

Feeling the mood change to one of confrontation, the rapper appeared to be weighing up the possible consequences before answering, "I'm guessing yours in the classy wooden ketch with teak decks and polished brass fittings moored at the end of the quay?"

Again, this was not the response that Cecily was expecting and yet she pressed on with her reprimand. "Yes, and it's still all in one piece, no thanks to your reckless seamanship."

Zeno looked stunned by this unexpected turn of events. He could see that Cecily was furious about something; however, he had no idea what that was.

"You are saying that my boat nearly ran into yours?"

"Yes, at full speed, at night and out in the open ocean. You could have killed us all and left us in the water."

"And where and when did this take place?" the rapper asked, himself now looking a little angry.

"A few weeks ago, about two miles south of San Remo," she replied.

Zeno stood up once again and made a small bow before saying, "I apologise unreservedly, however, I was not onboard my boat. I was touring in America until a few days ago. A delivery crew brought the boat from Genoa to Antibes where I had found a permanent berth for it. The boatbuilder recommended the captain, but I promise you that they will not be doing any more work for them or anyone else if I have my way."

Cecily now felt foolish for jumping to conclusions and for making her allegation so rudely and publicly. She had fallen into the trap that she often warned others of, 'judging books by their covers'. By allowing a stereotypical image of how she believed a rap star would behave, she fell well short of her own standards. Zeno had been charming and gracious, and she now realised that she had insulted him with her unfounded prejudices. She hoped that not too many people had *overheard* her and now wished the ground would swallow her up.

Seeing her extreme discomfort, Zeno leaned across the table and took her hand before beginning to improvise a rap. Very slowly and quietly he rhymed her name into a lyric which soon had the whole table captivated. Someone further down the table began to beat out a rhythm on the tabletop with their hands and Zeno raised his vocal volume.

By the time it ended with the words, "Cecily so silly that you're quick to judge me. Looks can be deceiving but you seem so lovely. There's motion in the ocean and it ain't the ruff sea. She snubbed me but look now she's gunna love me. Seen it in the stars say they call that astronomy. . ." Zeno's voice was drowned out by the cheering and clapping from the table.

"Zeno, you are a very gracious young man for letting me off the hook like that. I was rude and I apologise. I hope you will forgive me and that we might become friends. Before you leave Menton, you must come on board for drinks or dinner, or both."

"Sure. That'd be cool," Zeno replied, looking to his girlfriend for confirmation only to find her already nodding vigorously because the model knew exactly who Cecily was and all about her famous cosmetics brands.

Cecily thought she should move on while she still had some dignity remaining and squeezed in between Andrea and Roman. She wanted to warn Roman that she had met the rapper whose boat had nearly hit them, in case her husband bumped into him before she had a chance to explain. She didn't want Roman's Sicilian knifeman unleashed again.

"He a sweetheart. It was a hired-in delivery crew in charge of his boat that night off San Remo. Zeno was on tour in the USA and not even onboard. He is now mortified with embarrassment about what I told him and promises to see that those irresponsible idiots are never hired again."

Andrea added, "Yes, Zeno is not at all what you might expect, is he. All that macho posturing when he performs is just an act. He's an intelligent, sensitive guy when you get to know him. Did you know that his boat is designed to be upcycled?"

Roman and Cecily shook their heads in unison, apparently mystified by this concept. "Upcycled?" Cecily questioned.

"That is how I met him. The boat's designers contacted me to explain the idea that, at the end of its useful life, its double-skinned hull can be taken apart and upturned to make insulated portable buildings. They are strong but lightweight and can be easily transported to disaster areas or third world famine-struck places. The upper deck superstructure was demountable as another accommodation unit. All the interior fittings are reusable. It's the first boat of its type. An Italian innovation. That's why I agreed to attend the launch."

Ben arrived, and Cecily stood to let him sit in her place at the table.

"Sit here, Ben. I want to go and chat to Alessandra and Renata."

"Ah, Ben, good, we have a chance to catch up on what's been happening," was Andrea's warm greeting.

Ben told the prime minister about the private investment he had raised through the crowd-farming scheme for the winery, and that his Rossese had won a bronze medal at a tasting in Monaco.

"Congratulations on both. I saw the label on the bottles that we have been drinking from. A richly deserved acknowledgement. It's a delicious wine."

"How are our eco-experiments going? Do we have any obvious winners or losers yet?" Andrea asked Ben.

"People are a little reticent to try the electric cars. I think they feel that there are just too many uncertainties for many older people. They harbour concerns about driving an electric car for the first time, insurance, running out of power and so on. It will take time."

Andrea thought for a while and suggested, "We need an early adopter. A trailblazer from the traditional community. What about Vincenzo? If people see him using them, they will feel it is Ok."

Ben said that he thought this was an excellent idea.

"Alessandra has been trying to be highly visible in buying the plastic-free loose products from the store. That has encouraged a few other villagers to try them, but there has been reluctance from many to giving up the well-advertised big brands."

"After seeing Alessandra's fabulous hair today, they should be queuing up to buy that loose shampoo," Andrea said.

Ben smiled and continued, "The school plastic survey that you visited has helped raise awareness in every home. Children are excellent at pestering parents when they become enthused about a subject."

Ben told the PM that he had spotted one unexpected phenomenon.

"French day-trippers have seen the price saving to be had and are driving over with their bottles to be refilled, staying to have lunch. They seem to have a keener eye for a bargain that our own citizens and are making it a reason for day out."

Andrea seemed sure things would turn around, saying, "The more people see others using it, the sooner they will be converted. We will get there."

Andrea acknowledged that he was aware that several of the other environmental initiatives would take longer to evaluate. However, he thought the early signs were very encouraging. He revealed that he was already beginning to think about a national roll-out of reduced tax on plastic-free packaged goods. In a recent government brainstorming session, his advisors had pointed out that such a policy also offered an advantage to many Italian producers over imported brands.

"In just a few short months, we have made more actual progress here in Seborga than the previous government did in years of just talking about it. You and Alessandra should be proud, Ben."

The handsome young prime minister was riding high on a tide of popularity. The polls suggested that if he held a snap election, he would considerably increase his existing majority, a situation almost unprecedented in a generation of Italian politics. Since the Second World War, Italy had seen sixty-six prime ministers come and go. Andrea had already beaten the average term served by them and showed no signs of losing his job just yet. Feeling full of good food and goodwill, helped by a slight buzz from Ben's Rossese, Andrea leaned back on his chair enjoying a rare moment of relaxation with people who had become his friends.

"So how does it feel to be married again, Roman?" he asked.

"It feels good, Andrea. Maybe you should try it?" he replied, casting a nod in the direction of Selene, who was deep in conversation with Alessandra and the two new brides.

Andrea looked over his shoulder and saw Selene, who looked radiant, and was reminded of his good fortune. Selene had splashed out some of the advance from her book to buy an expensive black silk, plunging neckline dress from a young Italian designer. It was split at each side and held together with straps, and the hem stopped just above the knee. Andrea had helped her choose it, saying, 'it was sexy yet sophisticated.' With her blonde hair and fair skin, it had undoubtedly gained many compliments from the men around the piazza.

"For what it's worth, you have my blessing, Andrea," Ben chipped in.

"Roman, there's nothing that would make me happier than to have Selene as my wife. I have been on the brink of proposing several times during the last year but with this crazy job, the relentless media attention, plus my son to think of. . .there never seems to be a good time."

34. TORTA NUZIALE MILLE-FEUILLE

It was time for the wedding speeches. Tom and Marius were ushering everyone back to their original seats. Despite the minor chaos caused by Andrea's suggestion of seat switching, during the lunch some unfounded prejudices had been debunked, a few stereotypes dismantled, and many new friends made.

The band had quietly slipped onto the stage to check their instruments and tap microphones in preparation for the first dance. The chefs, cooks and their student helpers were taking a much-needed break. They huddled together, smoking, like comrades moulded together by having survived the heat of battle. They discretely pointed out guests who they thought were sporting the best and worst fashions. The soldiers of the Alpini sweltered in the mid-afternoon heat but did not dare relax with their prime minister present.

Selene squeezed back onto the bench next to Andrea, just as Cecily was also taking her seat opposite. One of the bridesmaids brought Cecily's small bouquet over and placed it in front of her. As she did so, the young girl knocked over a glass of prosecco. It fell towards Selene's side of the table but did not break. Most of the liquid stayed on the surface of the table, but a little tipped over the edge onto Selene's lap. She stood quickly to shake off the droplets from her precious new dress.

Instinctively, Roman reached into his pocket for the handkerchief he always kept there and handed the cloth to

Andrea. He patted the front of Selene's dress with it and then mopped up the remaining small patch on the table.

"No harm was done," Selene assured everyone as she sat back down.

Vincenzo was now on his feet about to give his speech. He looked more like a prisoner facing a firing squad, thought Ben. It was short and to the point, as everyone had expected. Fortunately, Roman's oratory skills were more refined, and he had some well-chosen words in praise of his new wife and their relatively new friends. Only Cecily noticed the merest hint of sadness in his words, momentarily speculating as to the likely cause.

Although he had tried to resist because he was tired of making speeches, Andrea had finally agreed to say a few words on behalf of all the guests. When the applause following Roman's speech died down, the prime minister pushed away the plate from which he had been eating wedding cake and got to his feet.

A hush settled as he did so. Andrea used the white cloth that Roman gave him to wipe the crumbs from his lips. As he did so, a small, shiny object fell from the unfolded napkin. As if in slow motion, the white gold band tumbled a couple of times in mid-air before it fell upright into Selene's as yet untouched dessert. There it sat, its single diamond sparkling in the bright sunshine, sending out shards of light like a beacon to those around.

Cecily saw the ring fall, as did Patsy, and Tom, who was sitting by his sister's side. Just as he looked like he was about to say something, Patsy kicked him under the table and his mouth closed again. When Tom looked across at her for an explanation she was gently shaking her head and mouthing 'no.' It was Cecily who spoke, leaving those who could not see in no doubt, spontaneously announcing, "An engagement ring. How fabulously clever."

First Selene, and then Andrea, followed her stare to the ring now sitting glinting in the whipped-cream-topped mille-feuille slice. Roman, who also had no idea where the ring had come from, looked at Andrea, raised his eyes to the heavens, shrugged his shoulders and offered,

"Now seems to be that good time you've been waiting for, hey Andrea?"

THE END

ACKNOWLEDGEMENTS

These three books owe much to the following people:

Steve Chambers, Alex Wilton Regan, Fabio Mazzon, Valerio Dogliotti, Linda Bulloch, Chris Noble, Linda McCluskey, Mike Brough, Mark Dezzani, Alistair Johnson, Danilo and Patrizia Mantegna, Elisa Cassini, Vittorio Cassini, Julie & Geoff Perry, Andrea Sabbion, Louise Pratt, Amber Bulloch, John McArdle, Linda McCluskey, Eugene McCoy, Matthew Rippon, Linda Findlay, Daryl Chadwick, James Butterfield, Diane Kane, Carolyn Emmerson, India Hammond, Melinda Miller, David Penman, Scott Penman, Gillian McNally, Enrica Monzani, Trish Young and Alysia Sutcliffe.

Thank you all so much.~James Vasey

BIOGRAPHY

Photo courtesy: Kaidi-Katariin Knox

A former magazine editor and university lecturer,
James Vasey who is now retired, divides his time
between Northumberland in England and Liguria in Italy.
His accidental discovery of the ancient village of Seborga,
its historical connection to the Knights Templar,
as well as its unique culture and traditional Ligurian cuisine
were the inspiration for his first book, Cooking up a Country.
However, what was planned as a one-off, was quickly followed by
Unlikely Pairing and Recipe For A Nation, all within three years.

Thank you for reading about Ben and Alessandra's adventures in these three books. At the time of writing, discussions are well advanced on the making of a film based on this story.

For updates follow me on:

www.facebook.com/jamesvaseyauthor

To view a video and photographs of Seborga as well as regular news about the culture, food and wine of the region.

Sign-up for our mailing list to receive updates on the story, free tasters of the next instalment and exclusive invitations to related events.

Enter your email at www.jamesvasey.co.uk

PRIVACY: If you provide us with your email address by subscribing to this service, we will only use it to periodically send the type of information described above. We will not share your details with any third party unless you expressly give us permission to do so. You will be able to unsubscribe from this mailing list at any time.

Special thanks Stelios Haji-Ioannou, founder of EasyJet :
At a point in my life when times were hard, the advent of low-cost airlines still made it possible for me to explore Italy. Since that first Easyjet flight, over twenty years ago, barely a year has passed without visiting this beautiful part of the world. These experiences have broadened the horizons of our children and now our grandchildren. It is serendipitous that my discovery of Liguria has also led to my writing three novels set in the area and that one of these has found its way into the hands of Stelios Haji-Ioannou (pictured), the man who made it all possible.